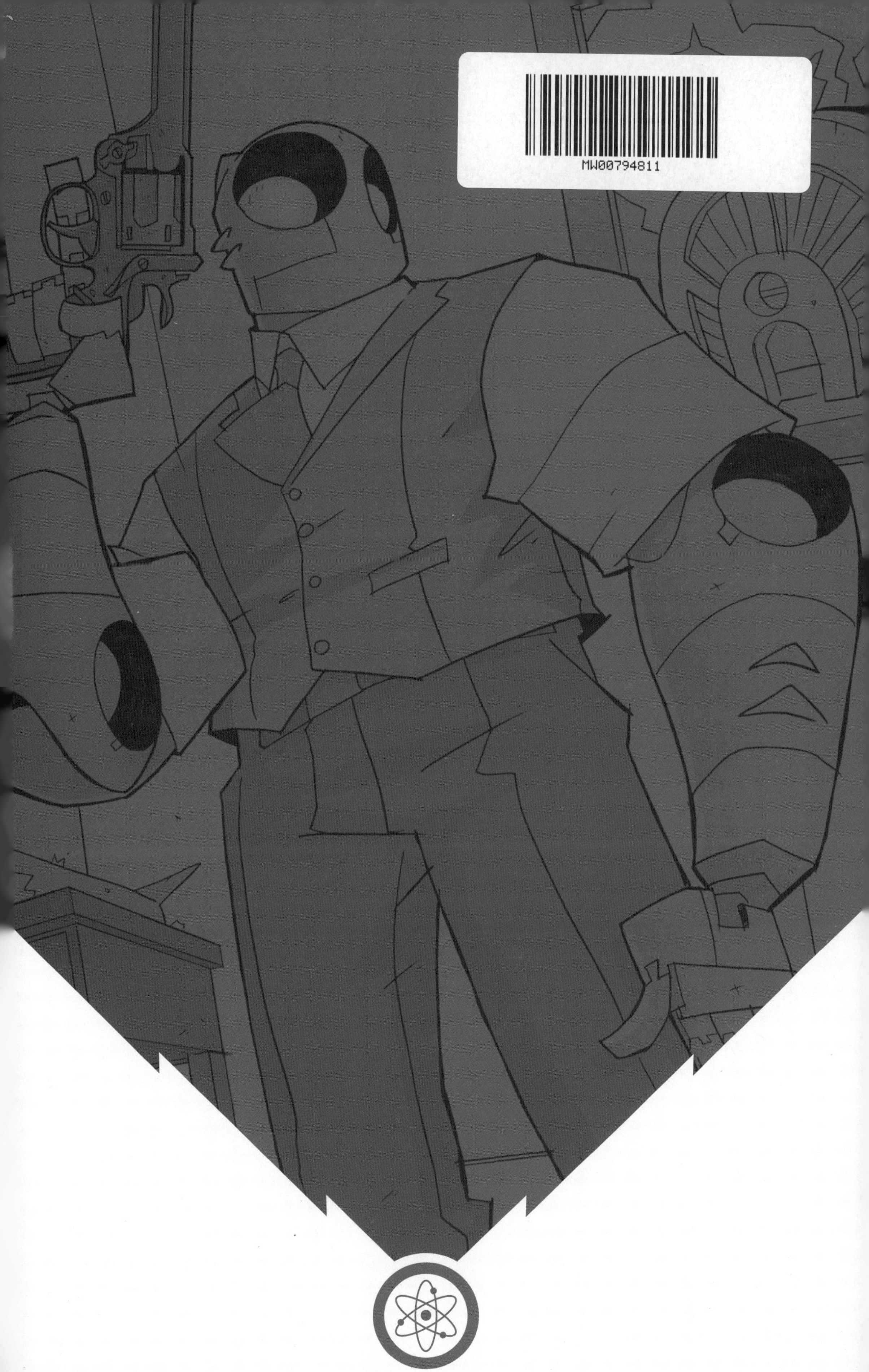

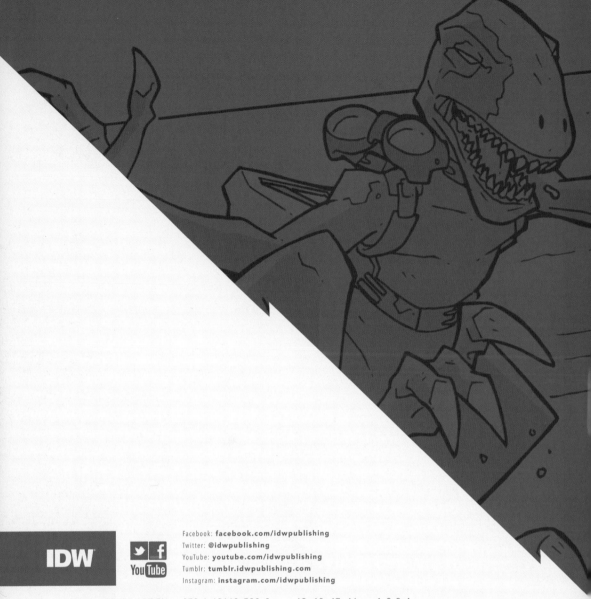

IDW

Facebook: **facebook.com/idwpublishing**
Twitter: **@idwpublishing**
YouTube: **youtube.com/idwpublishing**
Tumblr: **tumblr.idwpublishing.com**
Instagram: **instagram.com/idwpublishing**

YouTube

COVER ART BY
SCOTT WEGENER
AND ANTHONY CLARK

COLLECTION EDITS BY
JUSTIN EISINGER
AND ALONZO SIMON

COLLECTION DESIGN BY
JEFF POWELL

978-1-63140-528-0   19 18 17 16   1 2 3 4

Ted Adams, CEO & Publisher
Greg Goldstein, President & COO
Robbie Robbins, EVP/Sr. Graphic Artist
Chris Ryall, Chief Creative Officer/Editor-in-Chief
Matthew Ruzicka, CPA, Chief Financial Officer
Dirk Wood, VP of Marketing
Lorelei Bunjes, VP of Digital Services
Jeff Webber, VP of Digital and Subsidiary Rights
Jerry Bennington, VP of New Product Development

TESLADYNE LLC

IDW founded by Ted Adams, Alex Garner,
Kris Oprisko, and Robbie Robbins

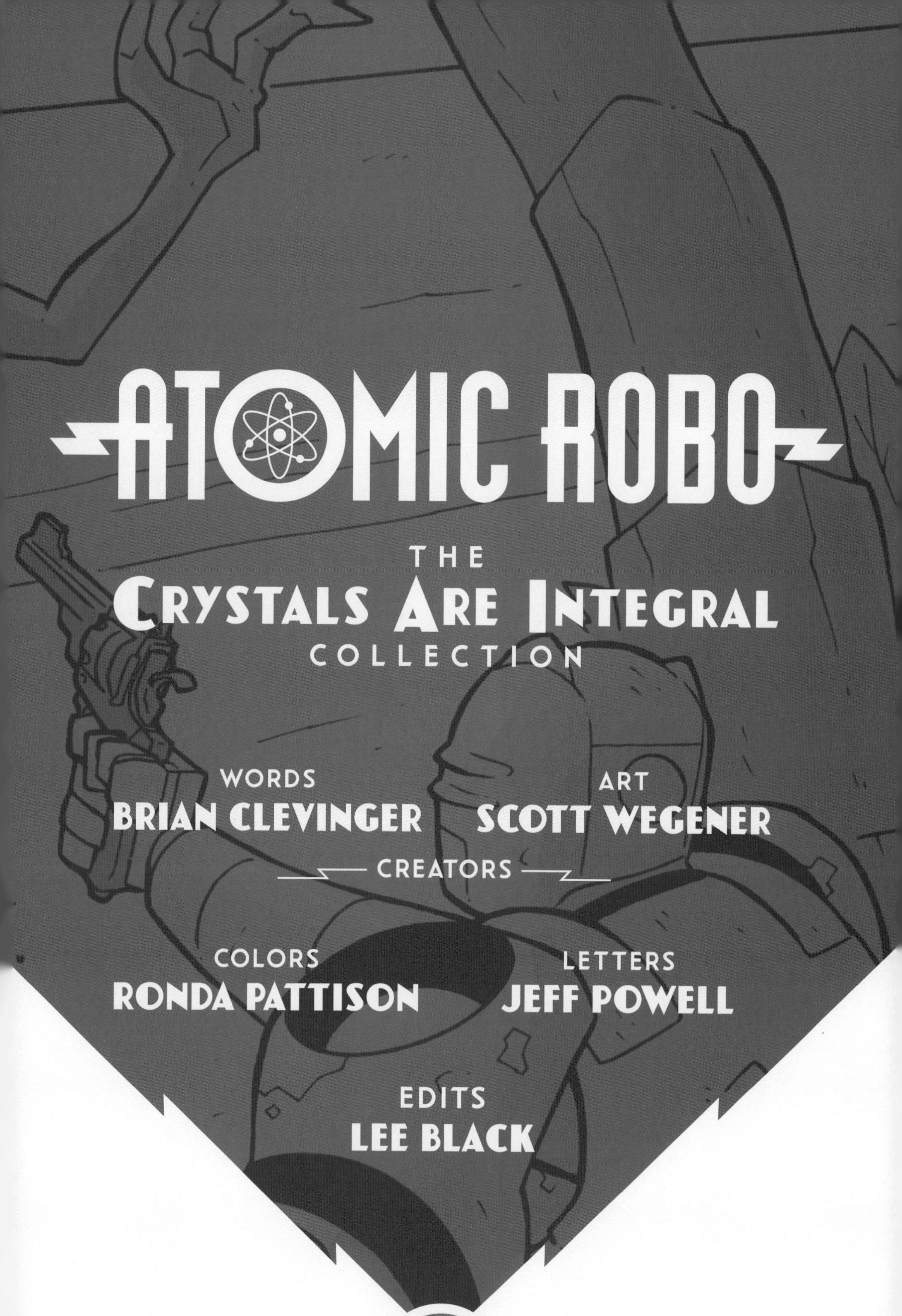

ATOMIC ROBO

THE CRYSTALS ARE INTEGRAL COLLECTION

WORDS
BRIAN CLEVINGER

ART
SCOTT WEGENER

CREATORS

COLORS
RONDA PATTISON

LETTERS
JEFF POWELL

EDITS
LEE BLACK

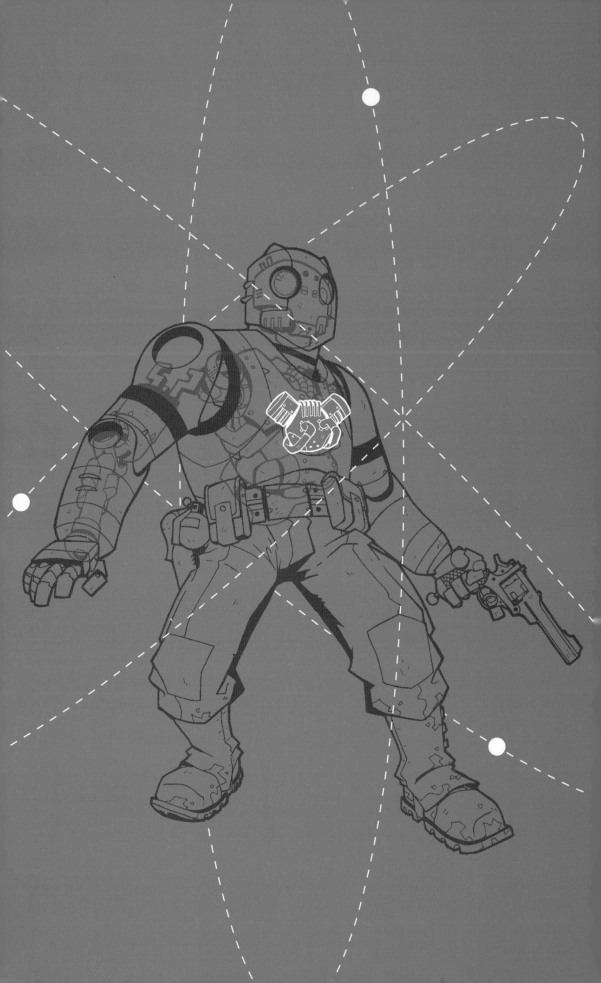

REVENGE OF THE VAMPIRE DIMENSION

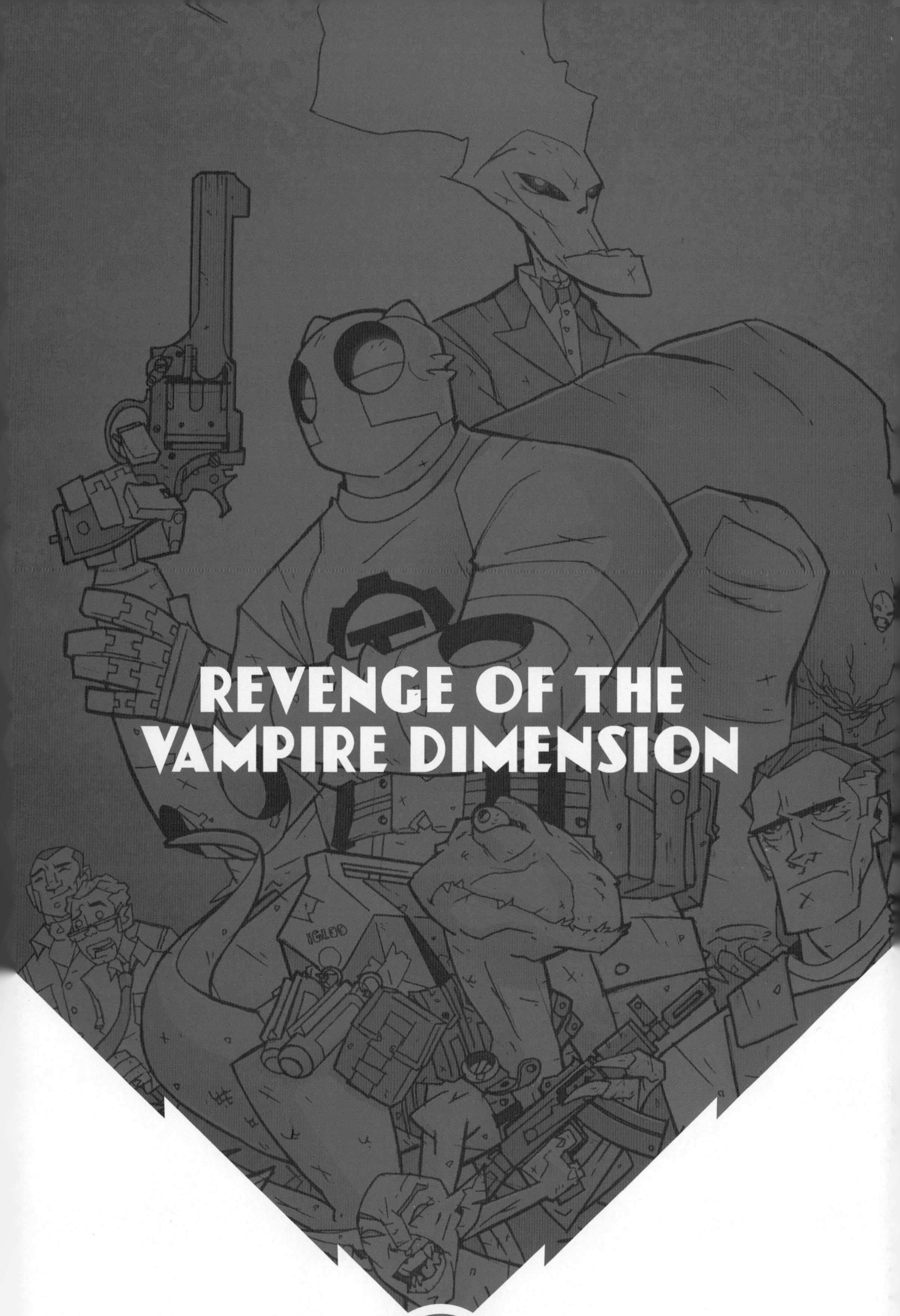

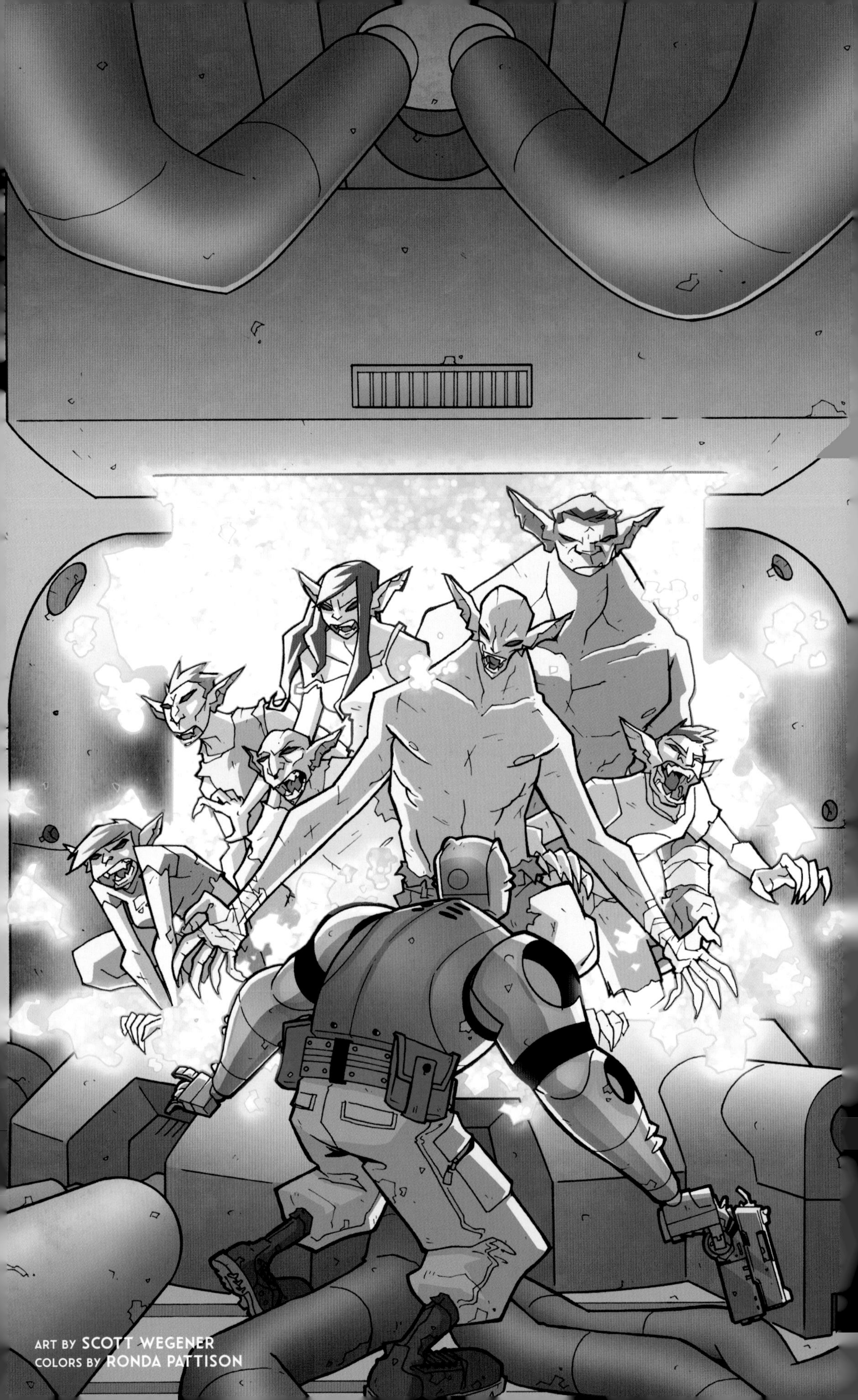
ART BY SCOTT WEGENER
COLORS BY RONDA PATTISON

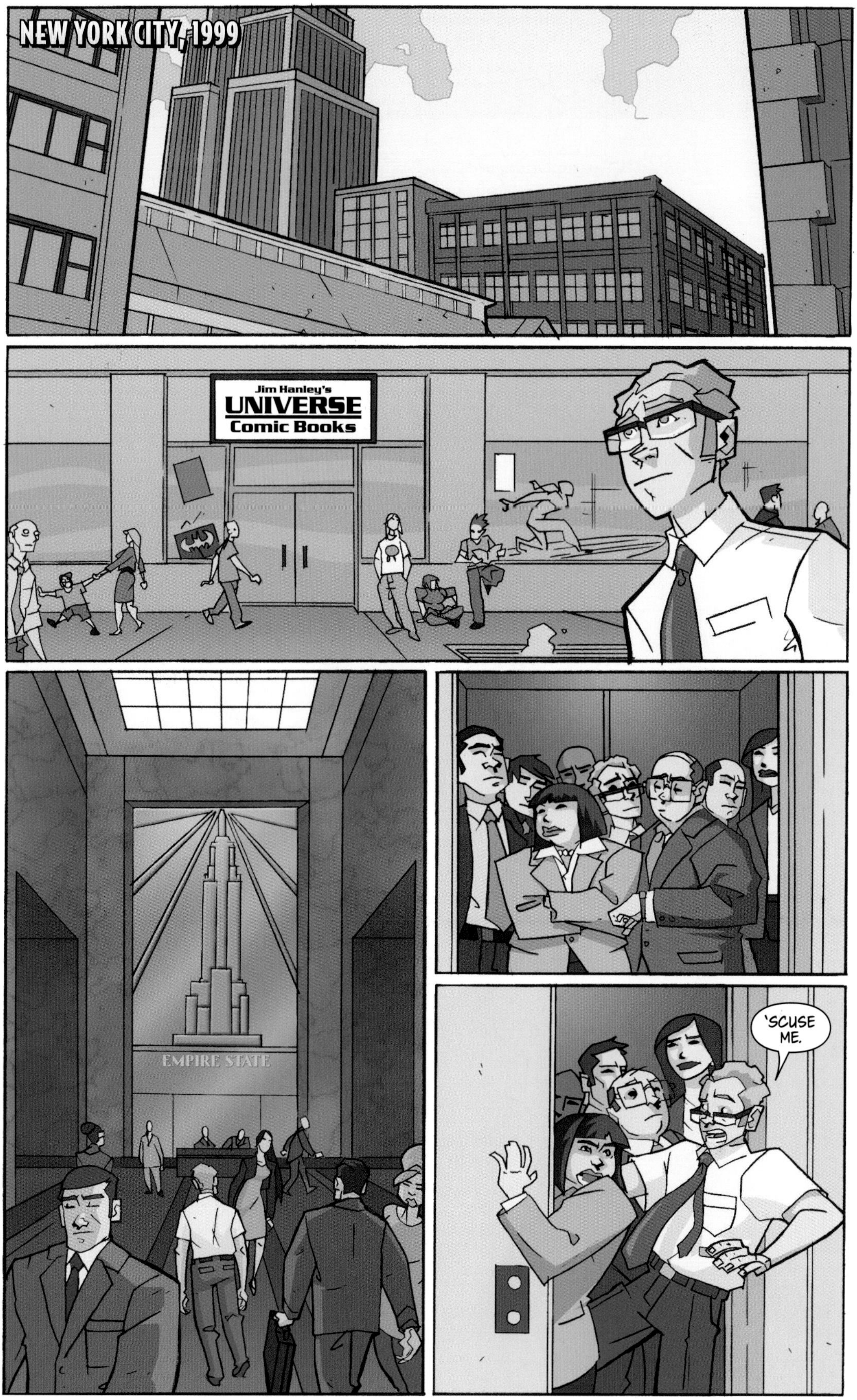
NEW YORK CITY, 1999
Jim Hanley's UNIVERSE Comic Books
EMPIRE STATE
'SCUSE ME.

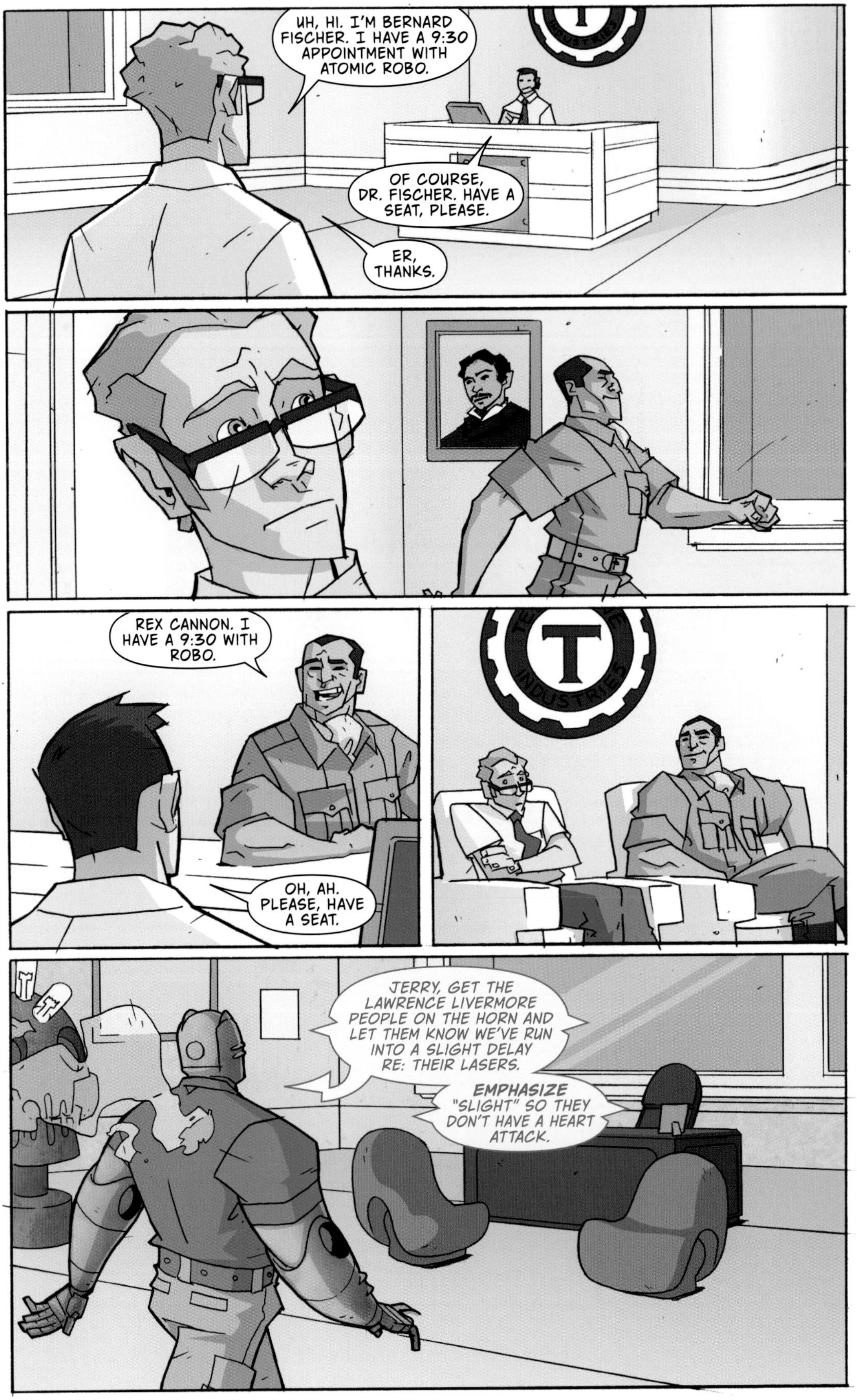
UH, HI. I'M BERNARD FISCHER. I HAVE A 9:30 APPOINTMENT WITH ATOMIC ROBO.
OF COURSE, DR. FISCHER. HAVE A SEAT, PLEASE.
ER, THANKS.
REX CANNON. I HAVE A 9:30 WITH ROBO.
OH, AH. PLEASE, HAVE A SEAT.
JERRY, GET THE LAWRENCE LIVERMORE PEOPLE ON THE HORN AND LET THEM KNOW WE'VE RUN INTO A SLIGHT DELAY RE: THEIR LASERS.
EMPHASIZE "SLIGHT" SO THEY DON'T HAVE A HEART ATTACK.

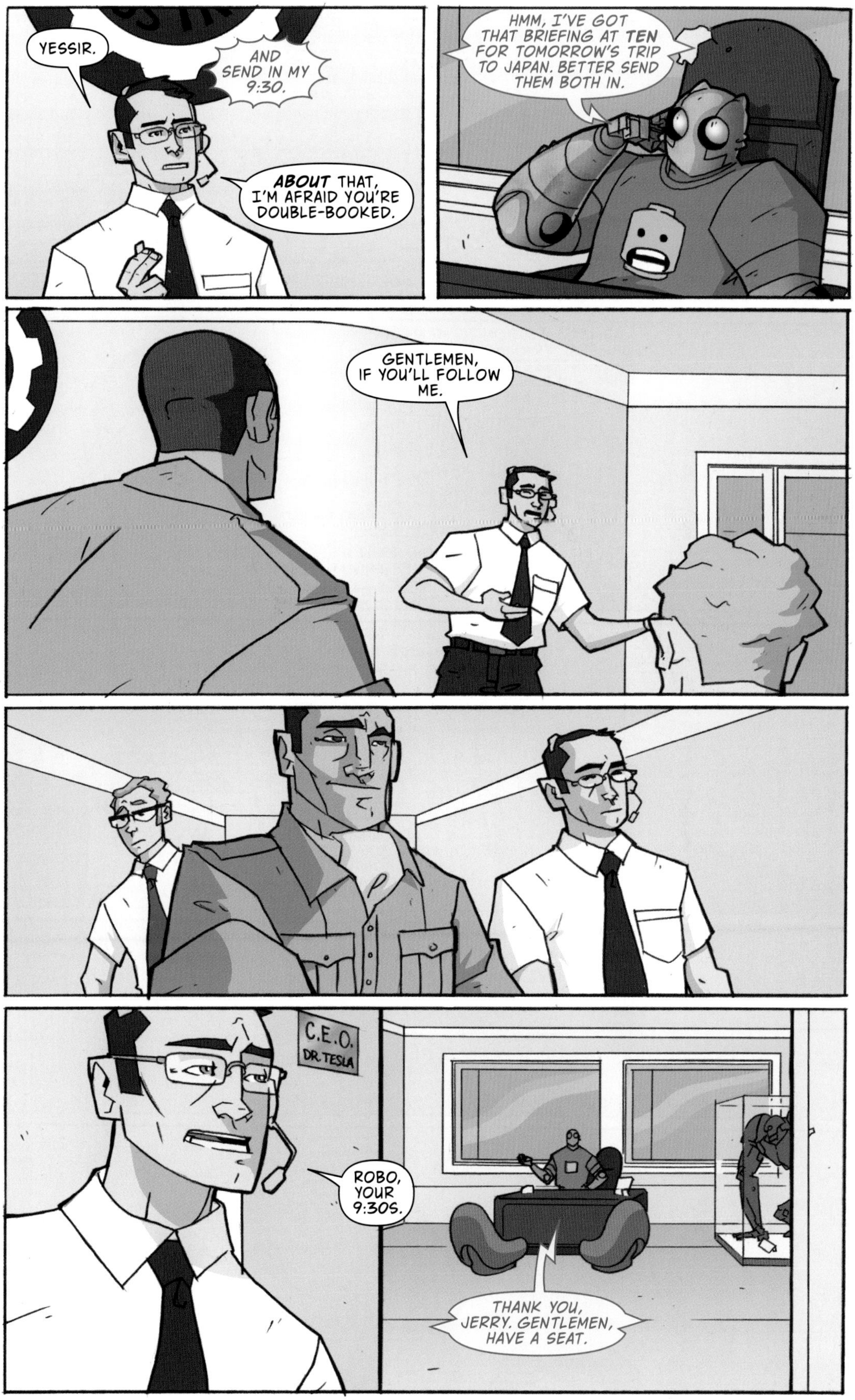
YESSIR.
AND SEND IN MY 9:30.
ABOUT THAT, I'M AFRAID YOU'RE DOUBLE-BOOKED.
HMM, I'VE GOT THAT BRIEFING AT TEN FOR TOMORROW'S TRIP TO JAPAN. BETTER SEND THEM BOTH IN.
GENTLEMEN, IF YOU'LL FOLLOW ME.
C.E.O. DR. TESLA
ROBO, YOUR 9:30S.
THANK YOU, JERRY. GENTLEMEN, HAVE A SEAT.

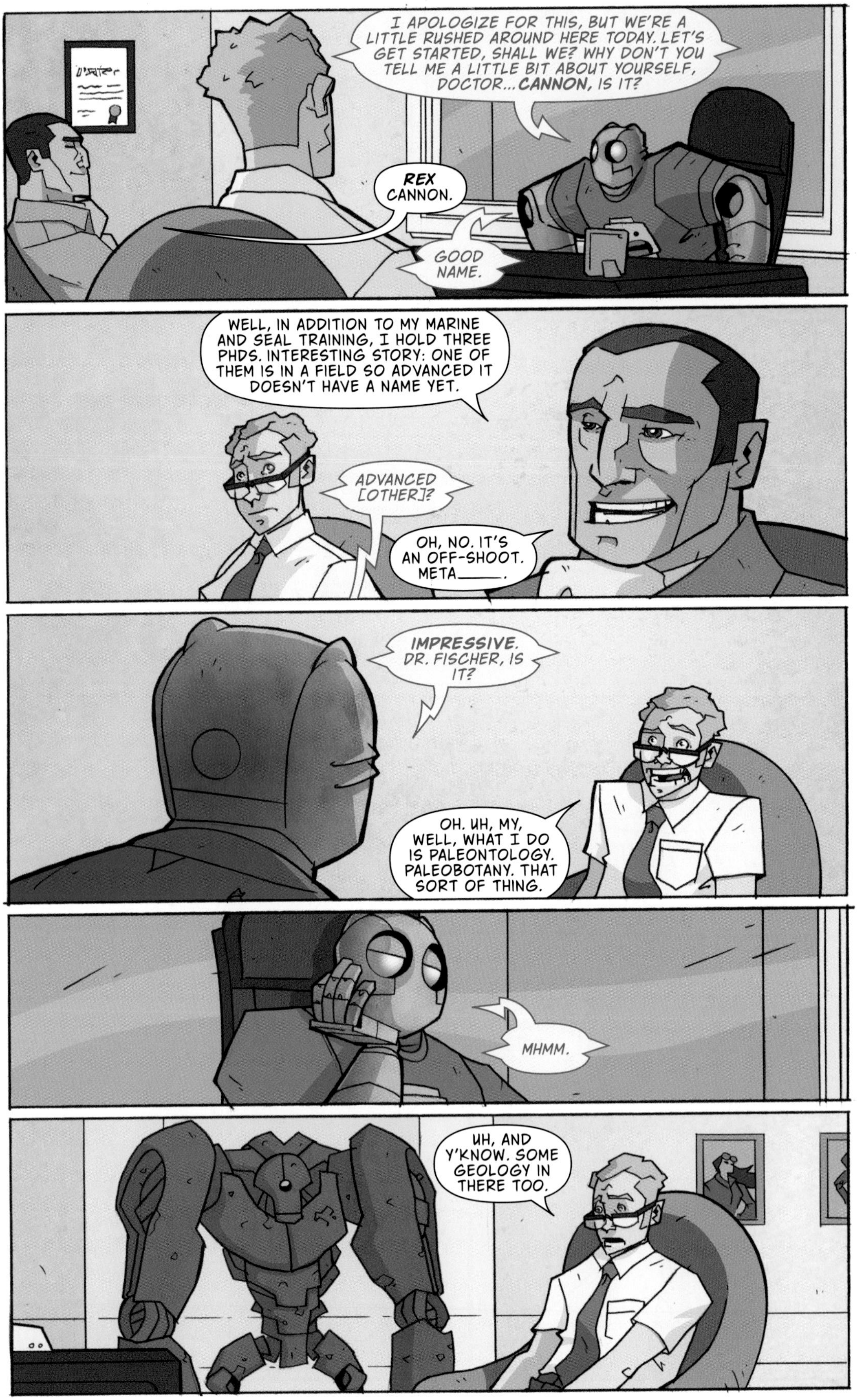
I APOLOGIZE FOR THIS, BUT WE'RE A LITTLE RUSHED AROUND HERE TODAY. LET'S GET STARTED, SHALL WE? WHY DON'T YOU TELL ME A LITTLE BIT ABOUT YOURSELF, DOCTOR... CANNON, IS IT?
REX CANNON.
GOOD NAME.
WELL, IN ADDITION TO MY MARINE AND SEAL TRAINING, I HOLD THREE PHDS. INTERESTING STORY: ONE OF THEM IS IN A FIELD SO ADVANCED IT DOESN'T HAVE A NAME YET.
ADVANCED [OTHER]?
OH, NO. IT'S AN OFF-SHOOT. META_____.
IMPRESSIVE. DR. FISCHER, IS IT?
OH. UH, MY, WELL, WHAT I DO IS PALEONTOLOGY. PALEOBOTANY. THAT SORT OF THING.
MHMM.
UH, AND Y'KNOW. SOME GEOLOGY IN THERE TOO.

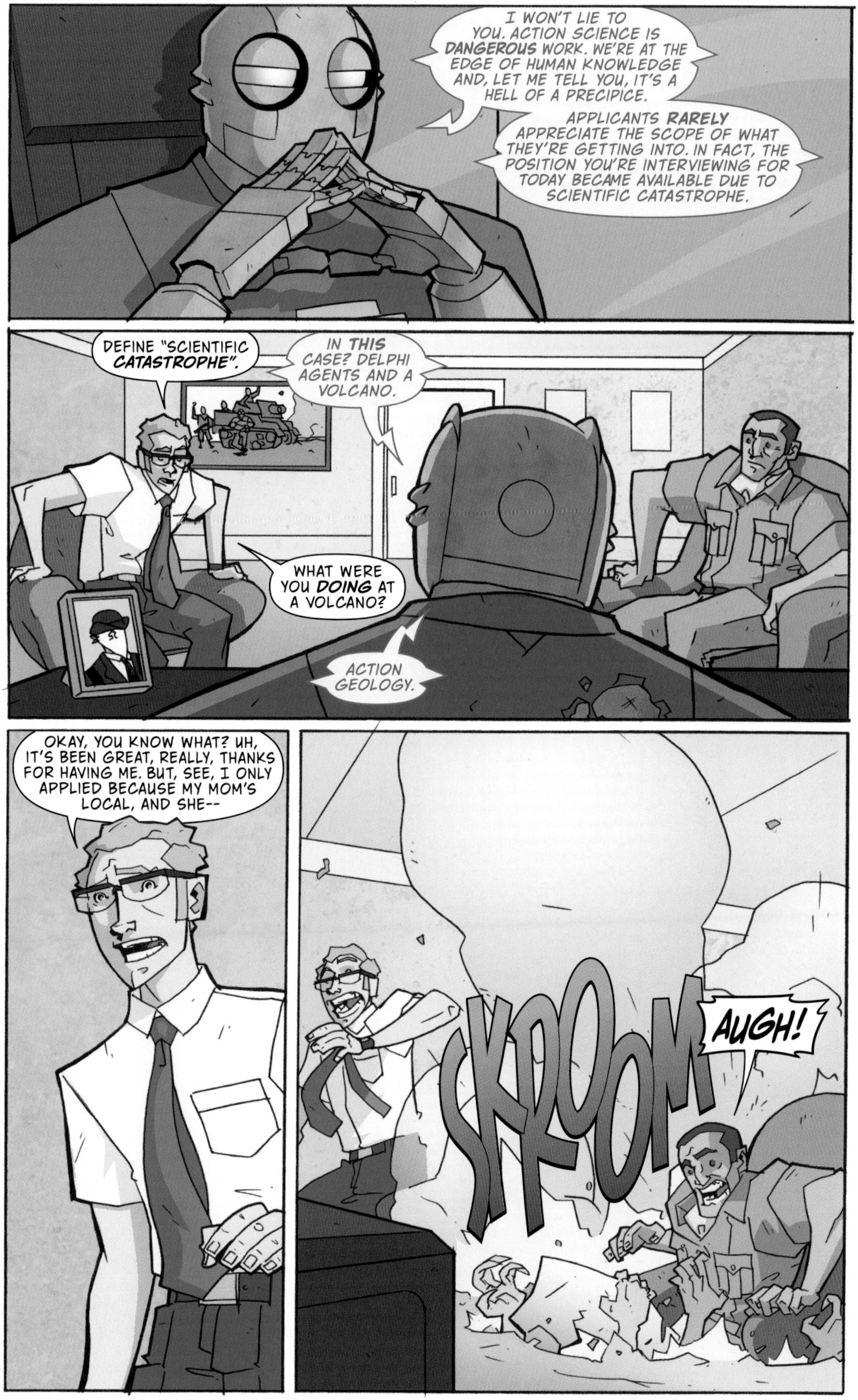
I WON'T LIE TO YOU. ACTION SCIENCE IS DANGEROUS WORK. WE'RE AT THE EDGE OF HUMAN KNOWLEDGE AND, LET ME TELL YOU, IT'S A HELL OF A PRECIPICE.
APPLICANTS RARELY APPRECIATE THE SCOPE OF WHAT THEY'RE GETTING INTO. IN FACT, THE POSITION YOU'RE INTERVIEWING FOR TODAY BECAME AVAILABLE DUE TO SCIENTIFIC CATASTROPHE.
DEFINE "SCIENTIFIC CATASTROPHE".
IN THIS CASE? DELPHI AGENTS AND A VOLCANO.
WHAT WERE YOU DOING AT A VOLCANO?
ACTION GEOLOGY.
OKAY, YOU KNOW WHAT? UH, IT'S BEEN GREAT, REALLY, THANKS FOR HAVING ME. BUT, SEE, I ONLY APPLIED BECAUSE MY MOM'S LOCAL, AND SHE--
SKROOM
AUGH!

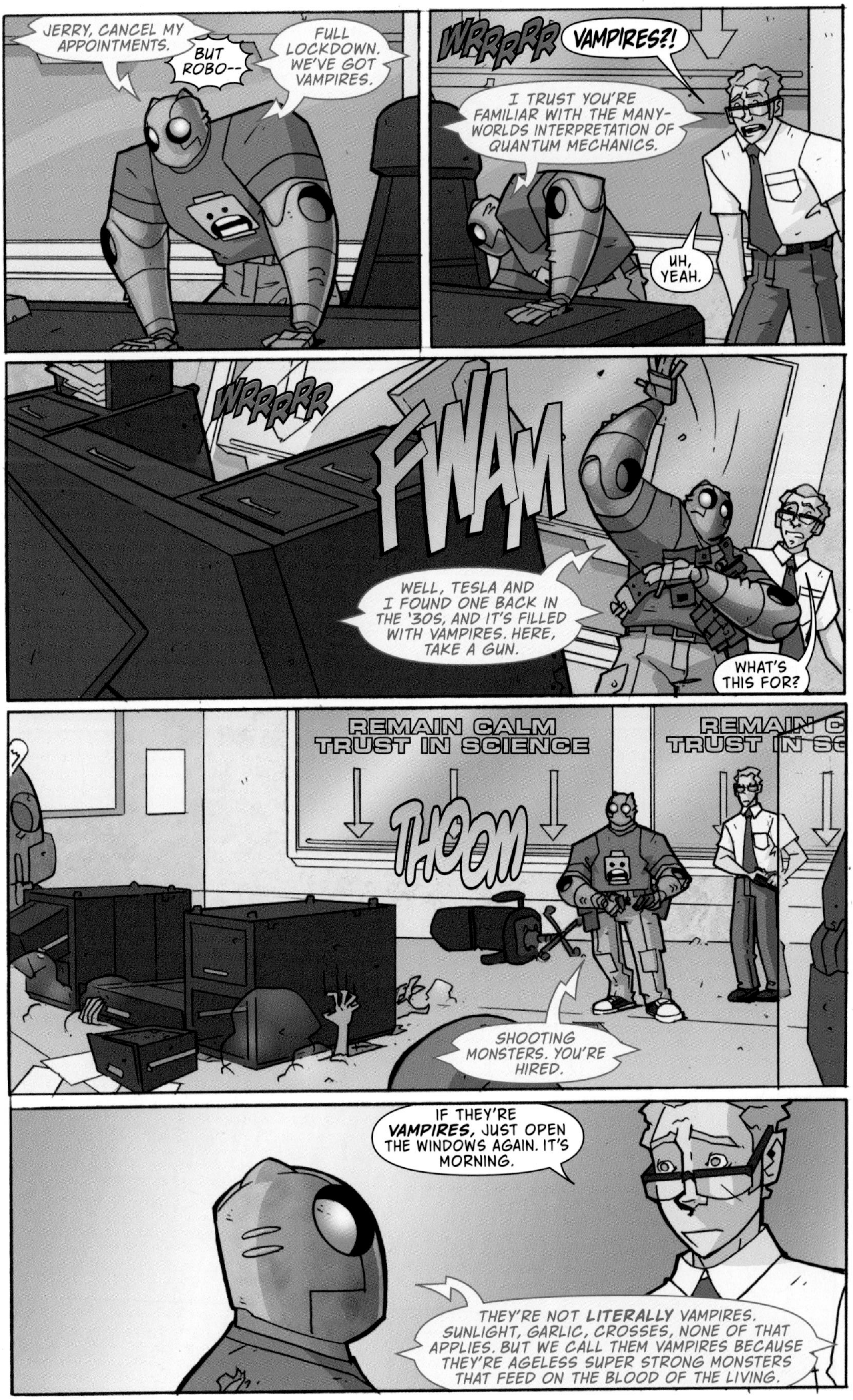
JERRY, CANCEL MY APPOINTMENTS.
BUT ROBO--
FULL LOCKDOWN. WE'VE GOT VAMPIRES.
WRRRRRR
VAMPIRES?!
I TRUST YOU'RE FAMILIAR WITH THE MANY-WORLDS INTERPRETATION OF QUANTUM MECHANICS.
UH, YEAH.
WRRRRR
FWAM
WELL, TESLA AND I FOUND ONE BACK IN THE '30S, AND IT'S FILLED WITH VAMPIRES. HERE, TAKE A GUN.
WHAT'S THIS FOR?
REMAIN CALM TRUST IN SCIENCE
REMAIN C TRUST IN SC
THOOM
SHOOTING MONSTERS. YOU'RE HIRED.
IF THEY'RE VAMPIRES, JUST OPEN THE WINDOWS AGAIN. IT'S MORNING.
THEY'RE NOT LITERALLY VAMPIRES. SUNLIGHT, GARLIC, CROSSES, NONE OF THAT APPLIES. BUT WE CALL THEM VAMPIRES BECAUSE THEY'RE AGELESS SUPER STRONG MONSTERS THAT FEED ON THE BLOOD OF THE LIVING.

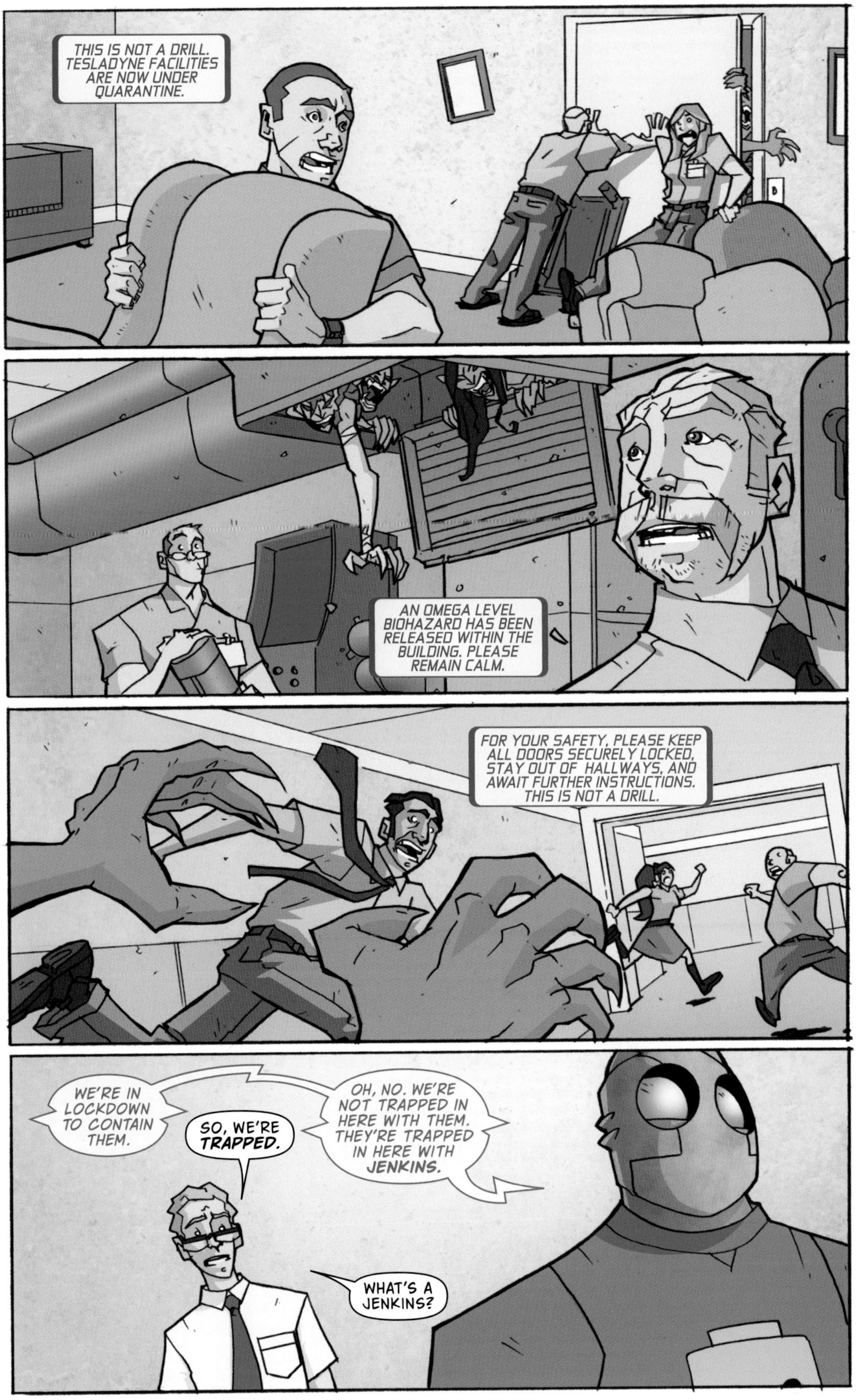
THIS IS NOT A DRILL. TESLADYNE FACILITIES ARE NOW UNDER QUARANTINE.
AN OMEGA LEVEL BIOHAZARD HAS BEEN RELEASED WITHIN THE BUILDING. PLEASE REMAIN CALM.
FOR YOUR SAFETY, PLEASE KEEP ALL DOORS SECURELY LOCKED, STAY OUT OF HALLWAYS, AND AWAIT FURTHER INSTRUCTIONS. THIS IS NOT A DRILL.
WE'RE IN LOCKDOWN TO CONTAIN THEM.
SO, WE'RE TRAPPED.
OH, NO. WE'RE NOT TRAPPED IN HERE WITH THEM. THEY'RE TRAPPED IN HERE WITH JENKINS.
WHAT'S A JENKINS?

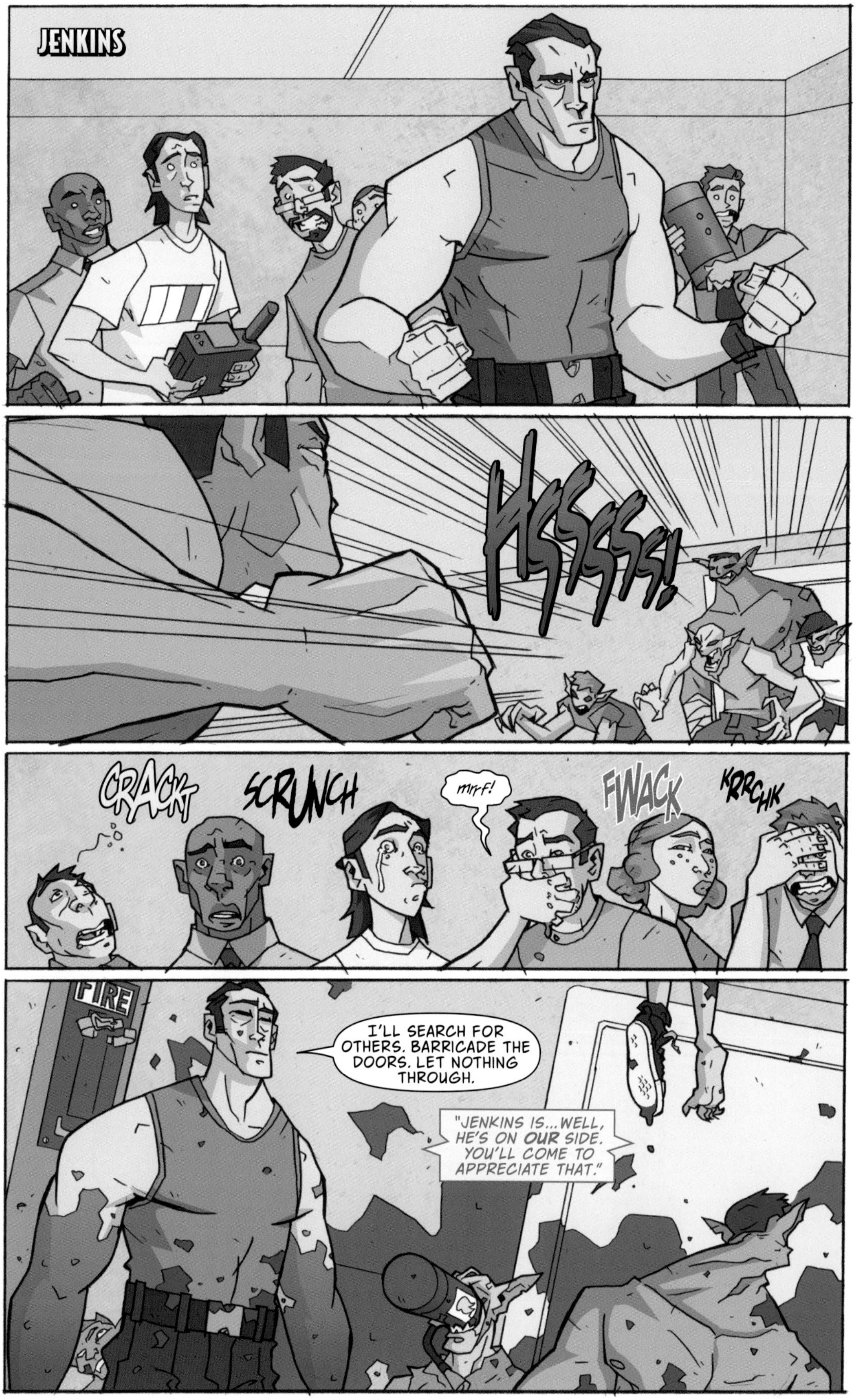
JENKINS
HSSSSSS!
CRACK!
SCRUNCH
mrrf!
FWACK
KRRCHK
FIRE
I'LL SEARCH FOR OTHERS. BARRICADE THE DOORS. LET NOTHING THROUGH.
"JENKINS IS...WELL, HE'S ON OUR SIDE. YOU'LL COME TO APPRECIATE THAT."

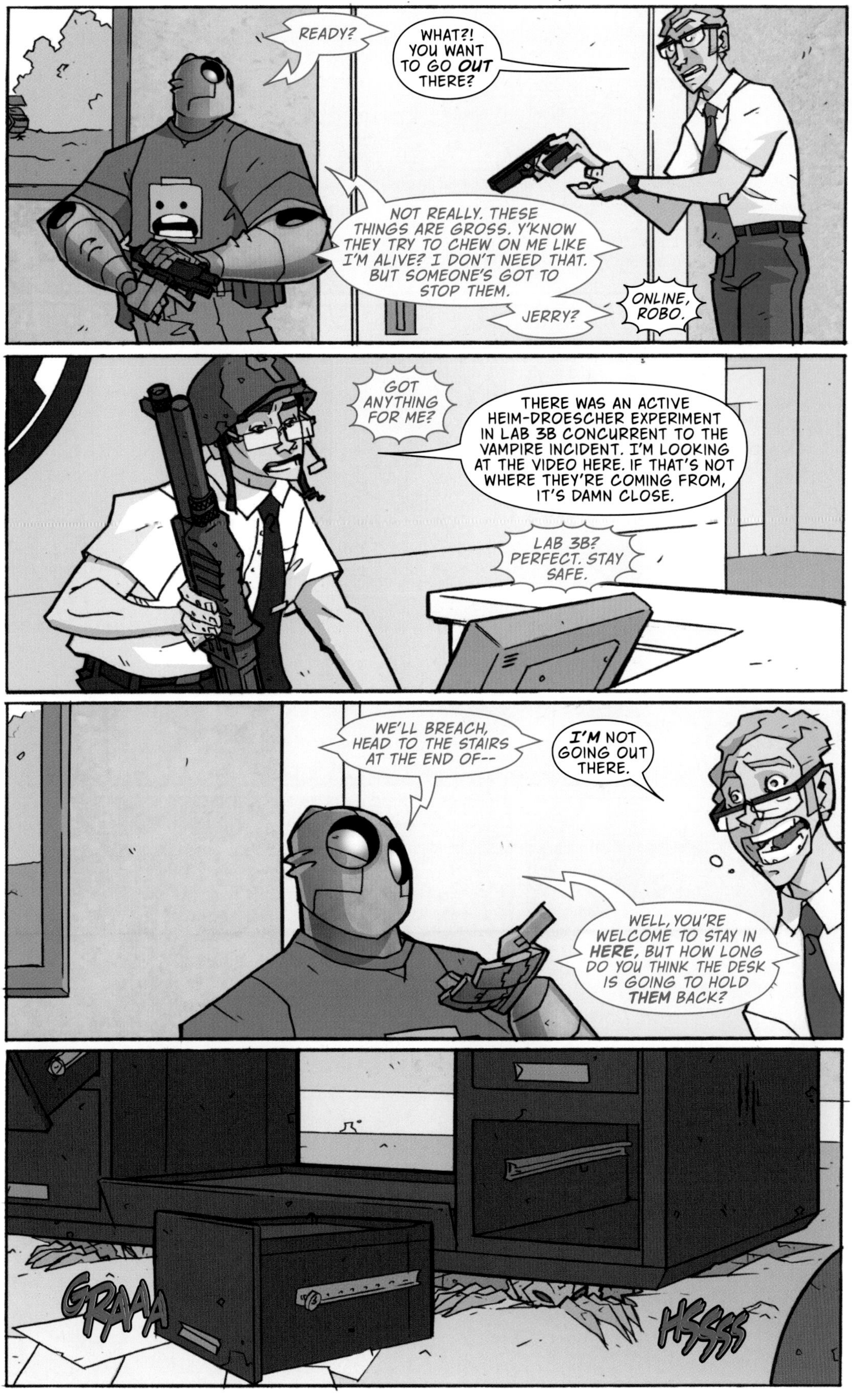
READY?
WHAT?! YOU WANT TO GO OUT THERE?
NOT REALLY. THESE THINGS ARE GROSS. Y'KNOW THEY TRY TO CHEW ON ME LIKE I'M ALIVE? I DON'T NEED THAT. BUT SOMEONE'S GOT TO STOP THEM.
JERRY?
ONLINE, ROBO.
GOT ANYTHING FOR ME?
THERE WAS AN ACTIVE HEIM-DROESCHER EXPERIMENT IN LAB 3B CONCURRENT TO THE VAMPIRE INCIDENT. I'M LOOKING AT THE VIDEO HERE. IF THAT'S NOT WHERE THEY'RE COMING FROM, IT'S DAMN CLOSE.
LAB 3B? PERFECT. STAY SAFE.
WE'LL BREACH, HEAD TO THE STAIRS AT THE END OF--
I'M NOT GOING OUT THERE.
WELL, YOU'RE WELCOME TO STAY IN HERE, BUT HOW LONG DO YOU THINK THE DESK IS GOING TO HOLD THEM BACK?
GRAAA
HSSSS

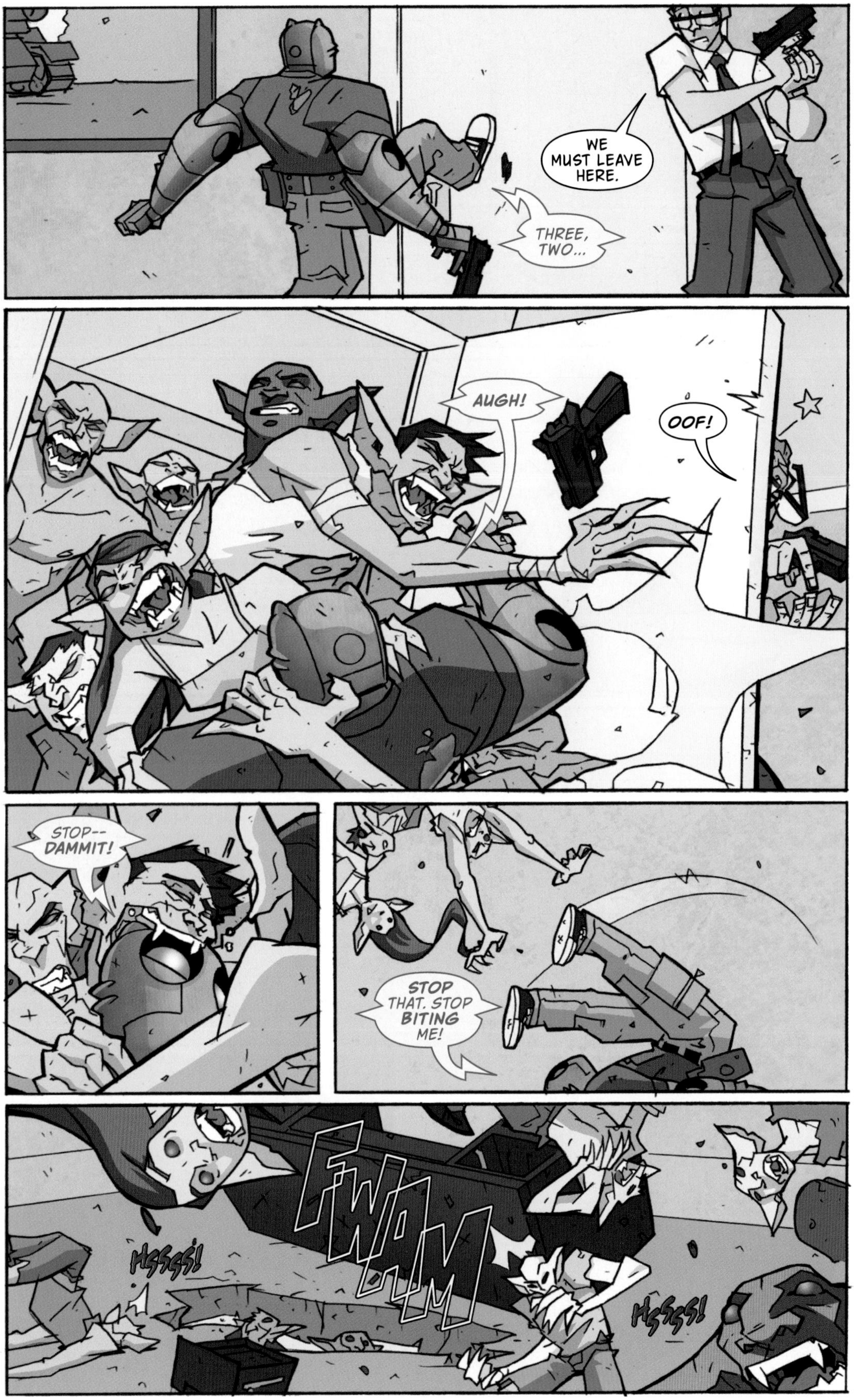
WE MUST LEAVE HERE.
THREE, TWO...
AUGH!
OOF!
STOP-- DAMMIT!
STOP THAT. STOP BITING ME!
FWOOM
HSSSS!
HSSSS!

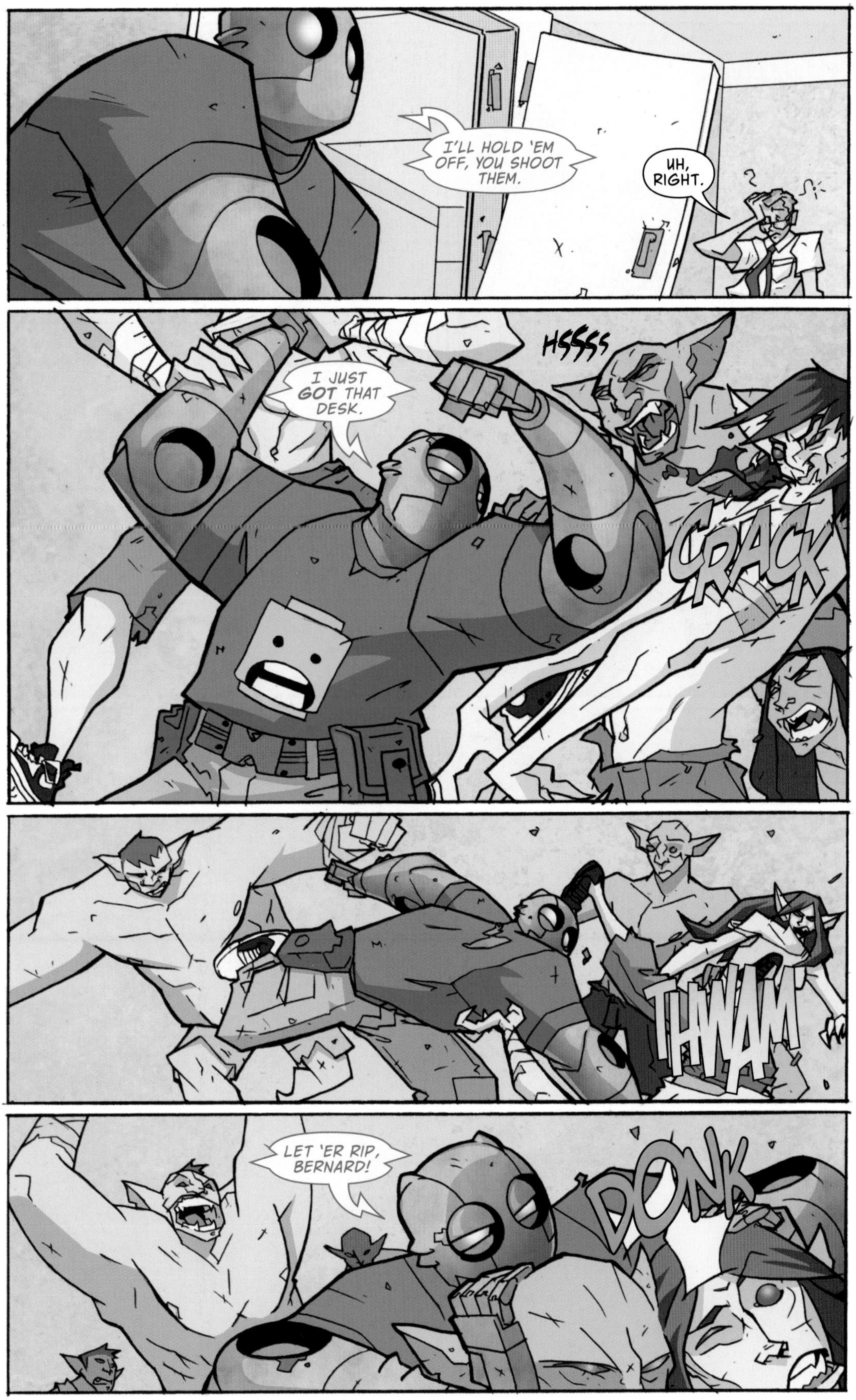
I'LL HOLD 'EM OFF, YOU SHOOT THEM.
UH, RIGHT.
HSSSS
I JUST GOT THAT DESK.
CRACK
THWAM
LET 'ER RIP, BERNARD!
DONK

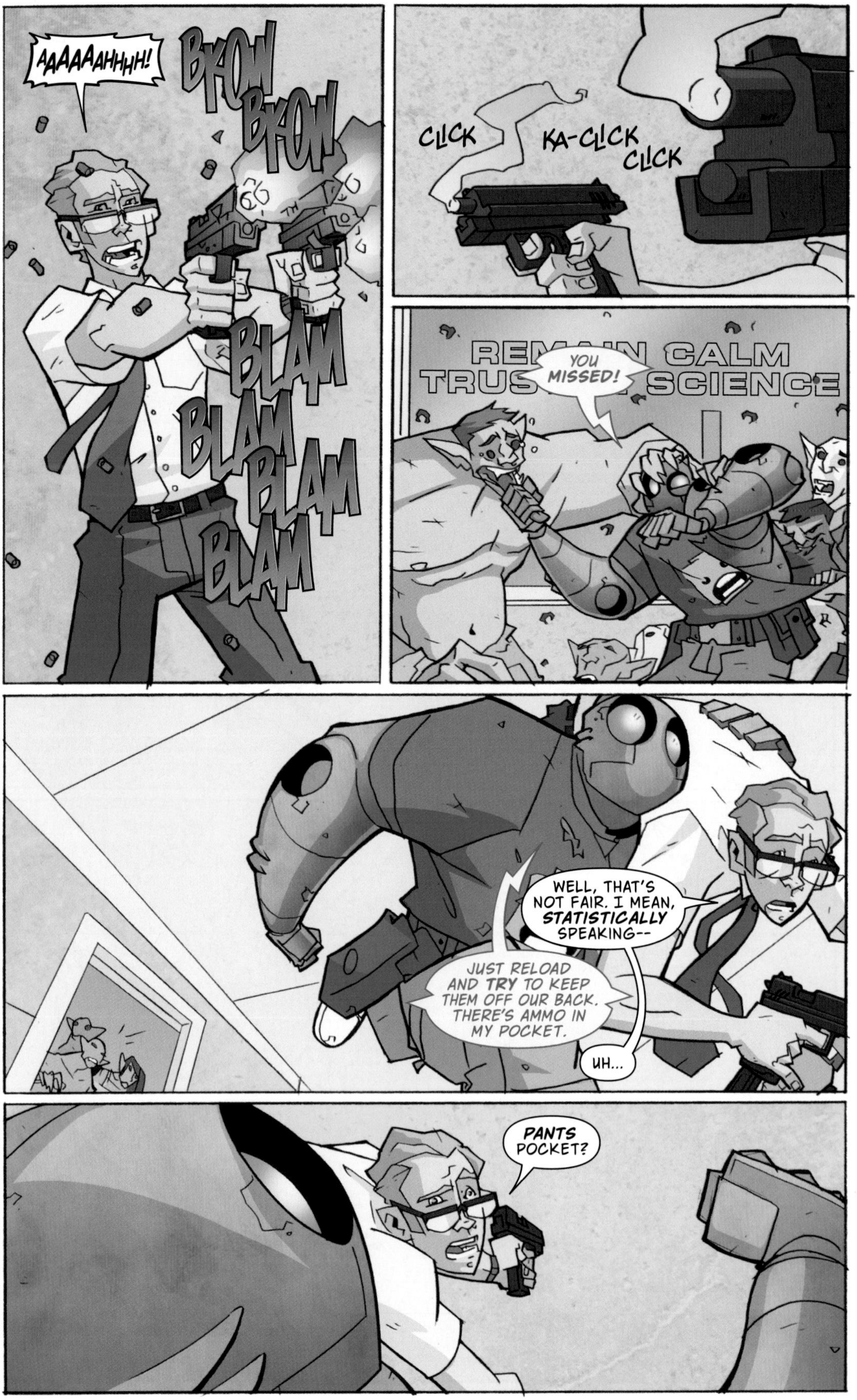
AAAAAAHHHH!
BKOW BKOW
BLAM BLAM BLAM BLAM
CLICK
KA-CLICK CLICK
REMAIN CALM TRUST IN SCIENCE
YOU MISSED!
WELL, THAT'S NOT FAIR. I MEAN, STATISTICALLY SPEAKING--
JUST RELOAD AND TRY TO KEEP THEM OFF OUR BACK. THERE'S AMMO IN MY POCKET.
UH...
PANTS POCKET?

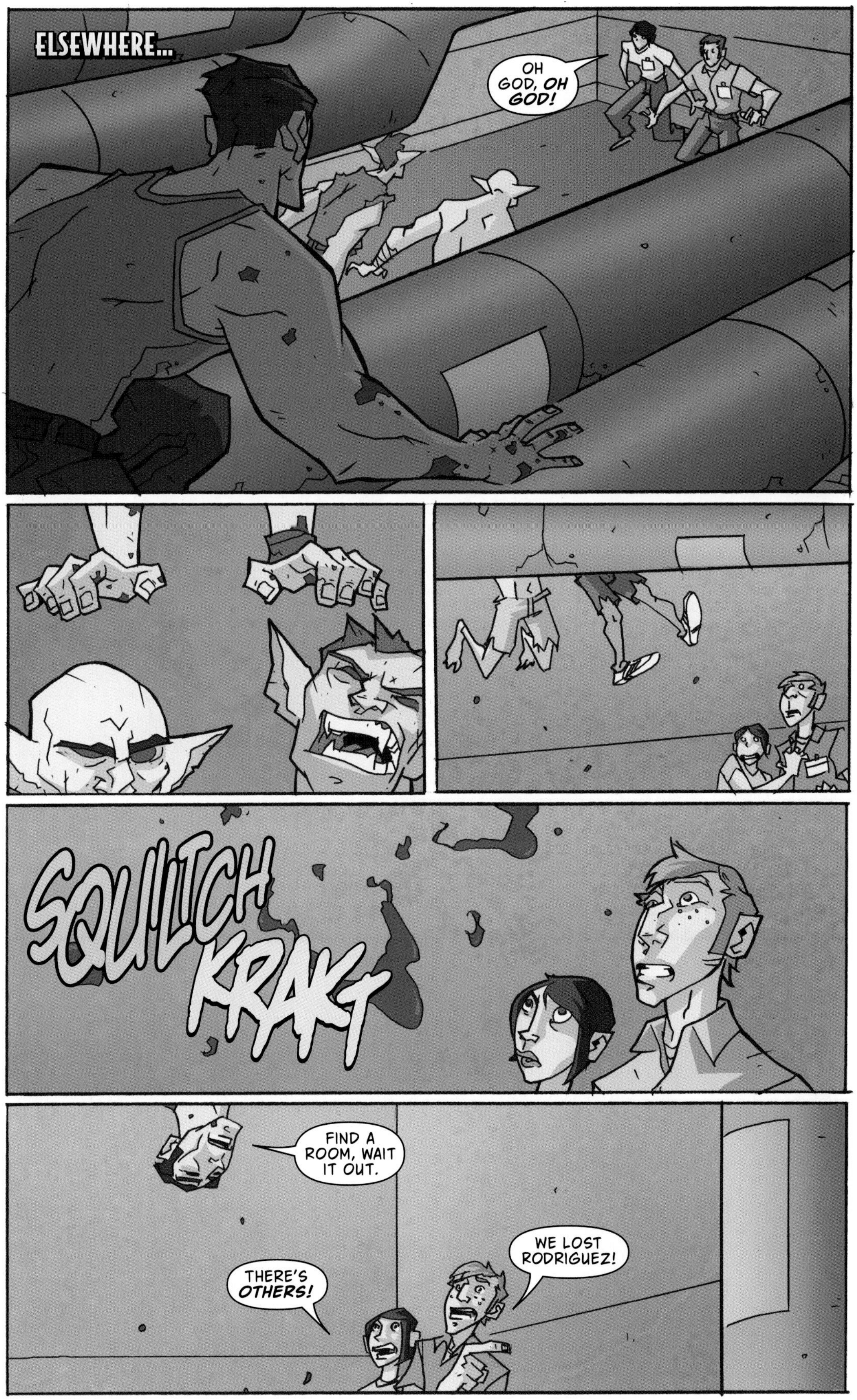
ELSEWHERE...
OH GOD, OH GOD!
SQUILTCH
KRAKT
FIND A ROOM, WAIT IT OUT.
WE LOST RODRIGUEZ!
THERE'S OTHERS!

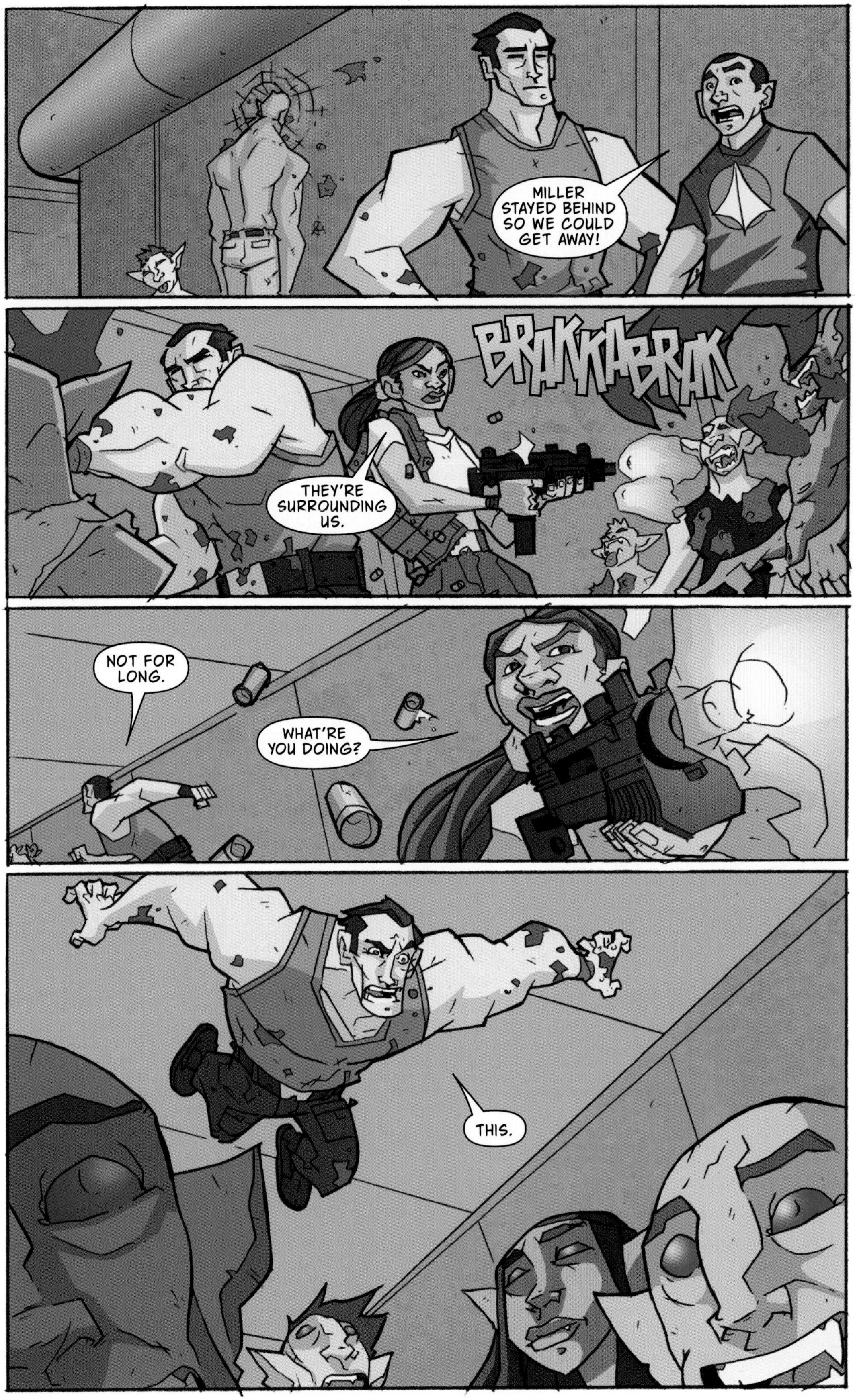
MILLER STAYED BEHIND SO WE COULD GET AWAY!
BRAKKABRAK
THEY'RE SURROUNDING US.
NOT FOR LONG.
WHAT'RE YOU DOING?
THIS.

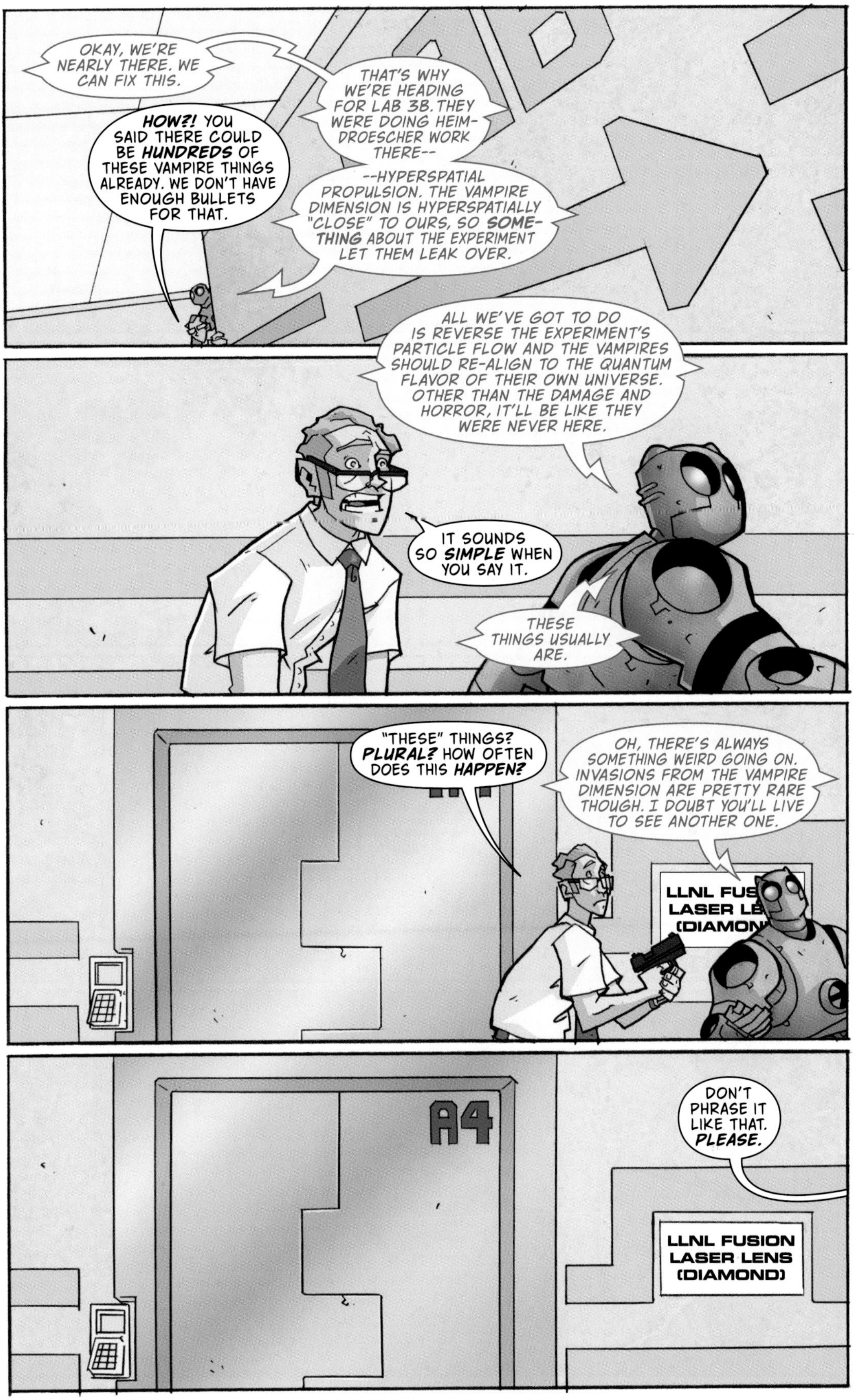
OKAY, WE'RE NEARLY THERE. WE CAN FIX THIS.
THAT'S WHY WE'RE HEADING FOR LAB 3B. THEY WERE DOING HEIM-DROESCHER WORK THERE--
HOW?! YOU SAID THERE COULD BE HUNDREDS OF THESE VAMPIRE THINGS ALREADY. WE DON'T HAVE ENOUGH BULLETS FOR THAT.
--HYPERSPATIAL PROPULSION. THE VAMPIRE DIMENSION IS HYPERSPATIALLY "CLOSE" TO OURS, SO SOME-THING ABOUT THE EXPERIMENT LET THEM LEAK OVER.
ALL WE'VE GOT TO DO IS REVERSE THE EXPERIMENT'S PARTICLE FLOW AND THE VAMPIRES SHOULD RE-ALIGN TO THE QUANTUM FLAVOR OF THEIR OWN UNIVERSE. OTHER THAN THE DAMAGE AND HORROR, IT'LL BE LIKE THEY WERE NEVER HERE.
IT SOUNDS SO SIMPLE WHEN YOU SAY IT.
THESE THINGS USUALLY ARE.
"THESE" THINGS? PLURAL? HOW OFTEN DOES THIS HAPPEN?
OH, THERE'S ALWAYS SOMETHING WEIRD GOING ON. INVASIONS FROM THE VAMPIRE DIMENSION ARE PRETTY RARE THOUGH. I DOUBT YOU'LL LIVE TO SEE ANOTHER ONE.
A4
DON'T PHRASE IT LIKE THAT. PLEASE.
LLNL FUSION LASER LENS (DIAMOND)

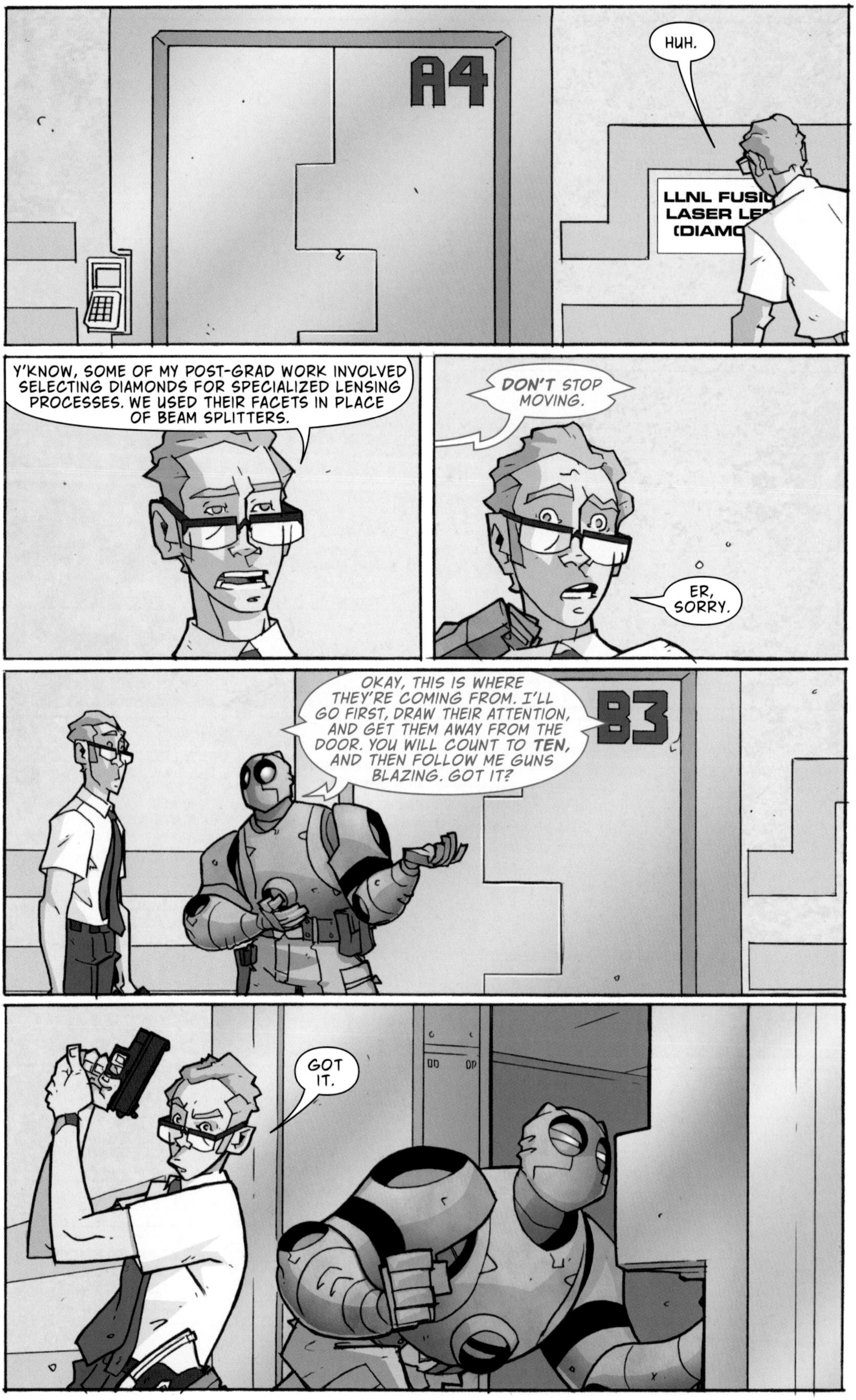
A4
HUH.
Y'KNOW, SOME OF MY POST-GRAD WORK INVOLVED SELECTING DIAMONDS FOR SPECIALIZED LENSING PROCESSES. WE USED THEIR FACETS IN PLACE OF BEAM SPLITTERS.
DON'T STOP MOVING.
ER, SORRY.
OKAY, THIS IS WHERE THEY'RE COMING FROM. I'LL GO FIRST, DRAW THEIR ATTENTION, AND GET THEM AWAY FROM THE DOOR. YOU WILL COUNT TO TEN, AND THEN FOLLOW ME GUNS BLAZING. GOT IT?
B3
GOT IT.

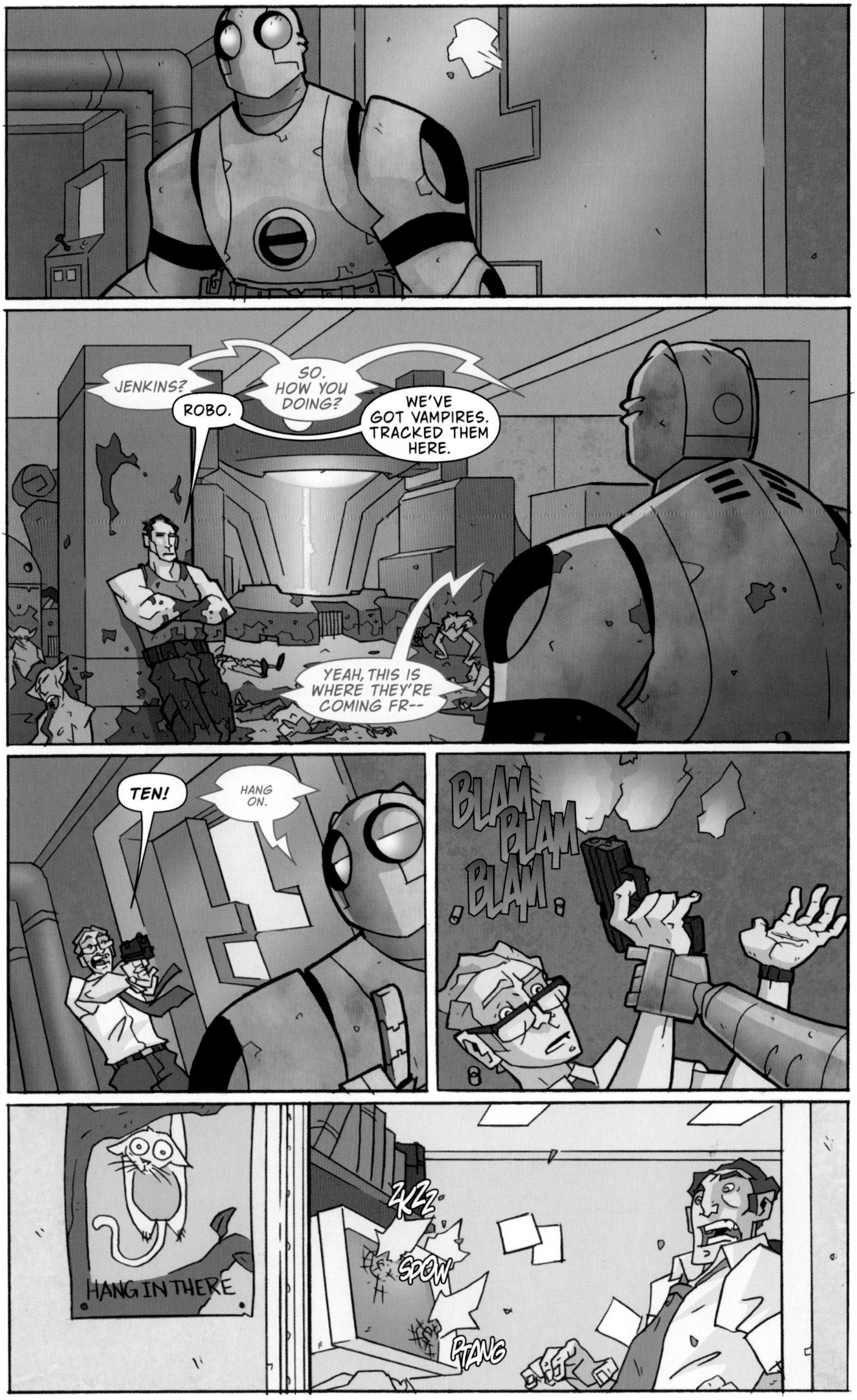
JENKINS?
ROBO.
SO. HOW YOU DOING?
WE'VE GOT VAMPIRES. TRACKED THEM HERE.
YEAH, THIS IS WHERE THEY'RE COMING FR--
TEN!
HANG ON.
BLAM BLAM BLAM
HANG IN THERE
ZKZZ
SPOW
PTANG

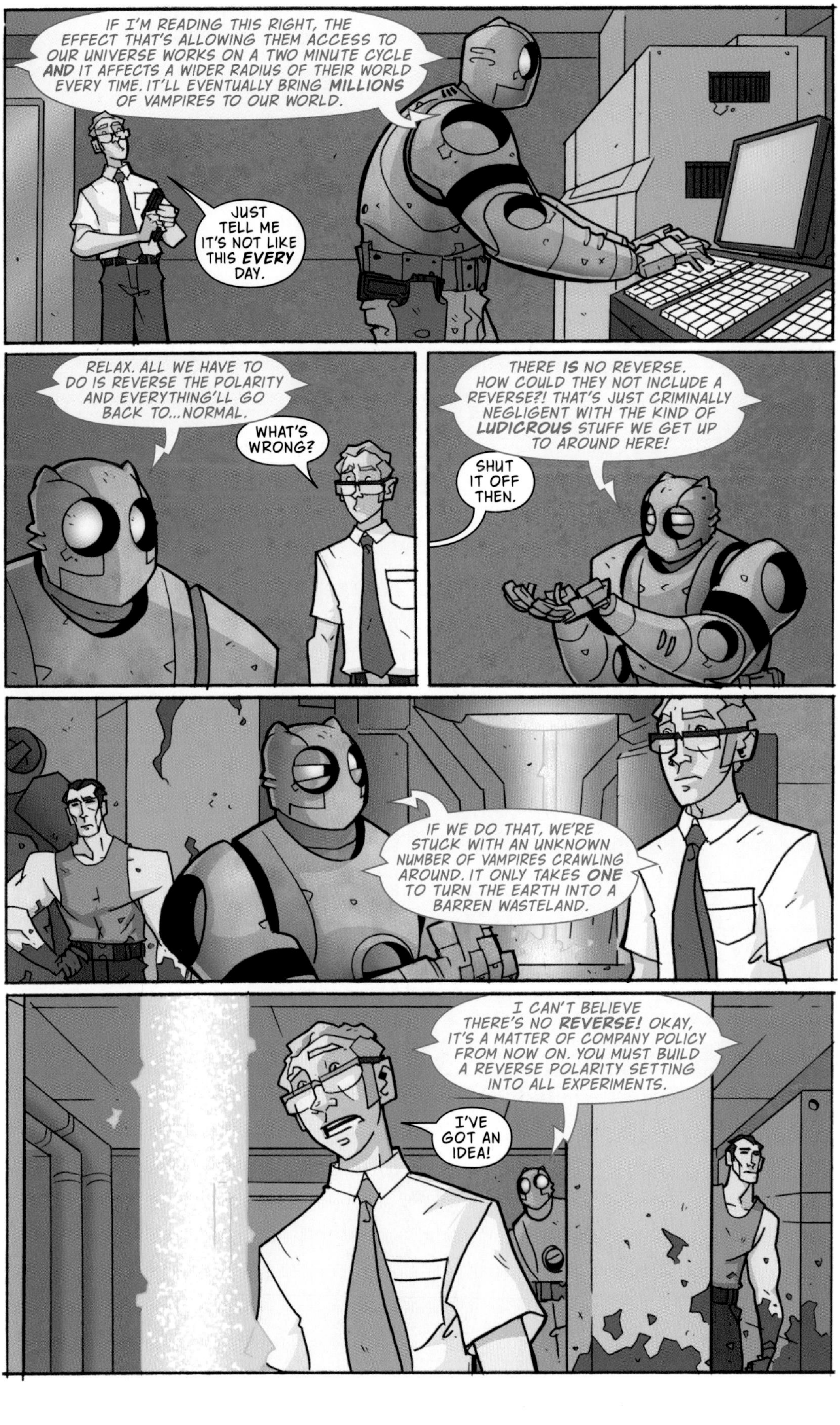
IF I'M READING THIS RIGHT, THE EFFECT THAT'S ALLOWING THEM ACCESS TO OUR UNIVERSE WORKS ON A TWO MINUTE CYCLE AND IT AFFECTS A WIDER RADIUS OF THEIR WORLD EVERY TIME. IT'LL EVENTUALLY BRING MILLIONS OF VAMPIRES TO OUR WORLD.
JUST TELL ME IT'S NOT LIKE THIS EVERY DAY.
RELAX. ALL WE HAVE TO DO IS REVERSE THE POLARITY AND EVERYTHING'LL GO BACK TO...NORMAL.
WHAT'S WRONG?
THERE IS NO REVERSE. HOW COULD THEY NOT INCLUDE A REVERSE?! THAT'S JUST CRIMINALLY NEGLIGENT WITH THE KIND OF LUDICROUS STUFF WE GET UP TO AROUND HERE!
SHUT IT OFF THEN.
IF WE DO THAT, WE'RE STUCK WITH AN UNKNOWN NUMBER OF VAMPIRES CRAWLING AROUND. IT ONLY TAKES ONE TO TURN THE EARTH INTO A BARREN WASTELAND.
I CAN'T BELIEVE THERE'S NO REVERSE! OKAY, IT'S A MATTER OF COMPANY POLICY FROM NOW ON. YOU MUST BUILD A REVERSE POLARITY SETTING INTO ALL EXPERIMENTS.
I'VE GOT AN IDEA!

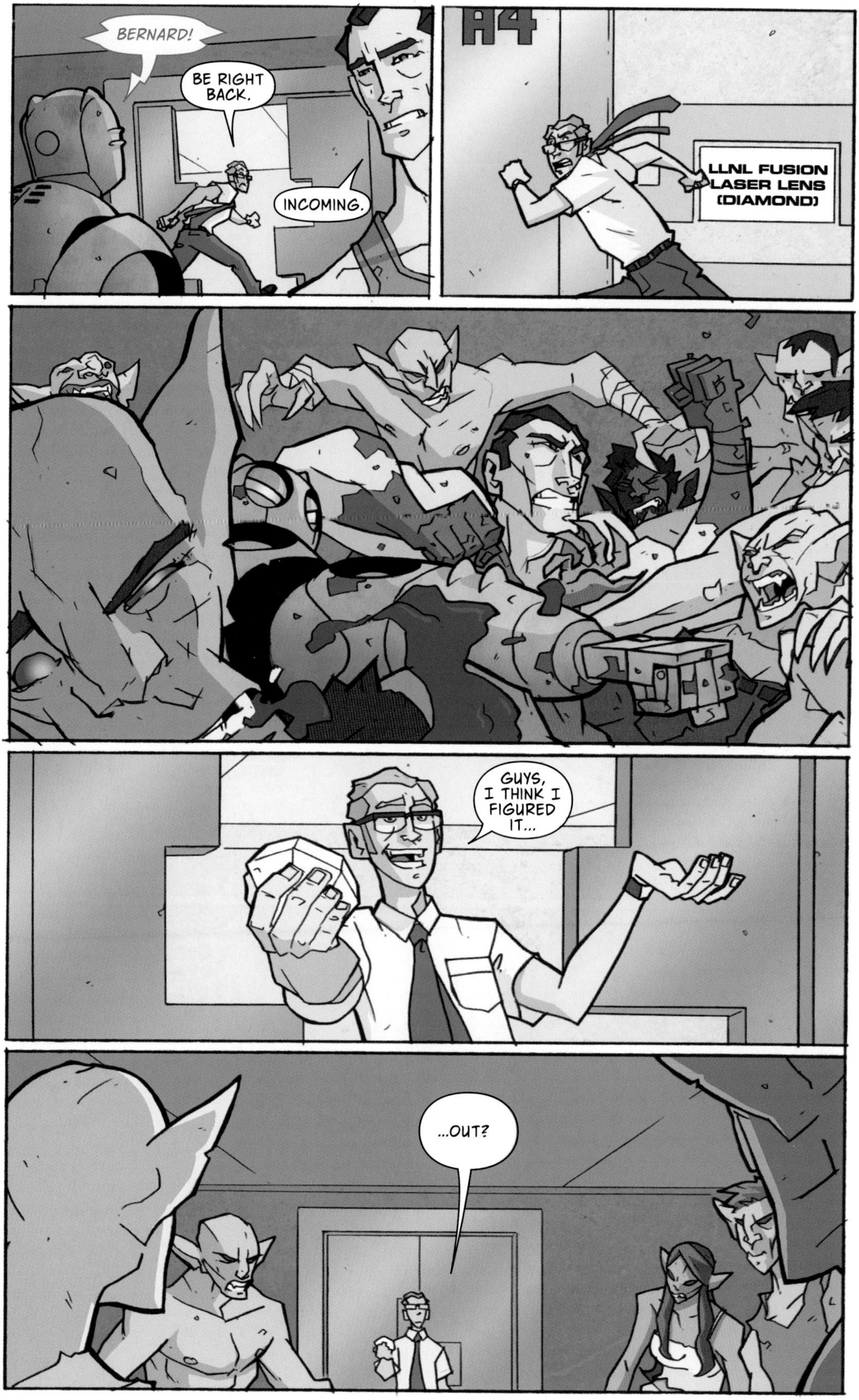
BERNARD!
BE RIGHT BACK.
INCOMING.
A4
LLNL FUSION LASER LENS (DIAMOND)
GUYS, I THINK I FIGURED IT...
...OUT?

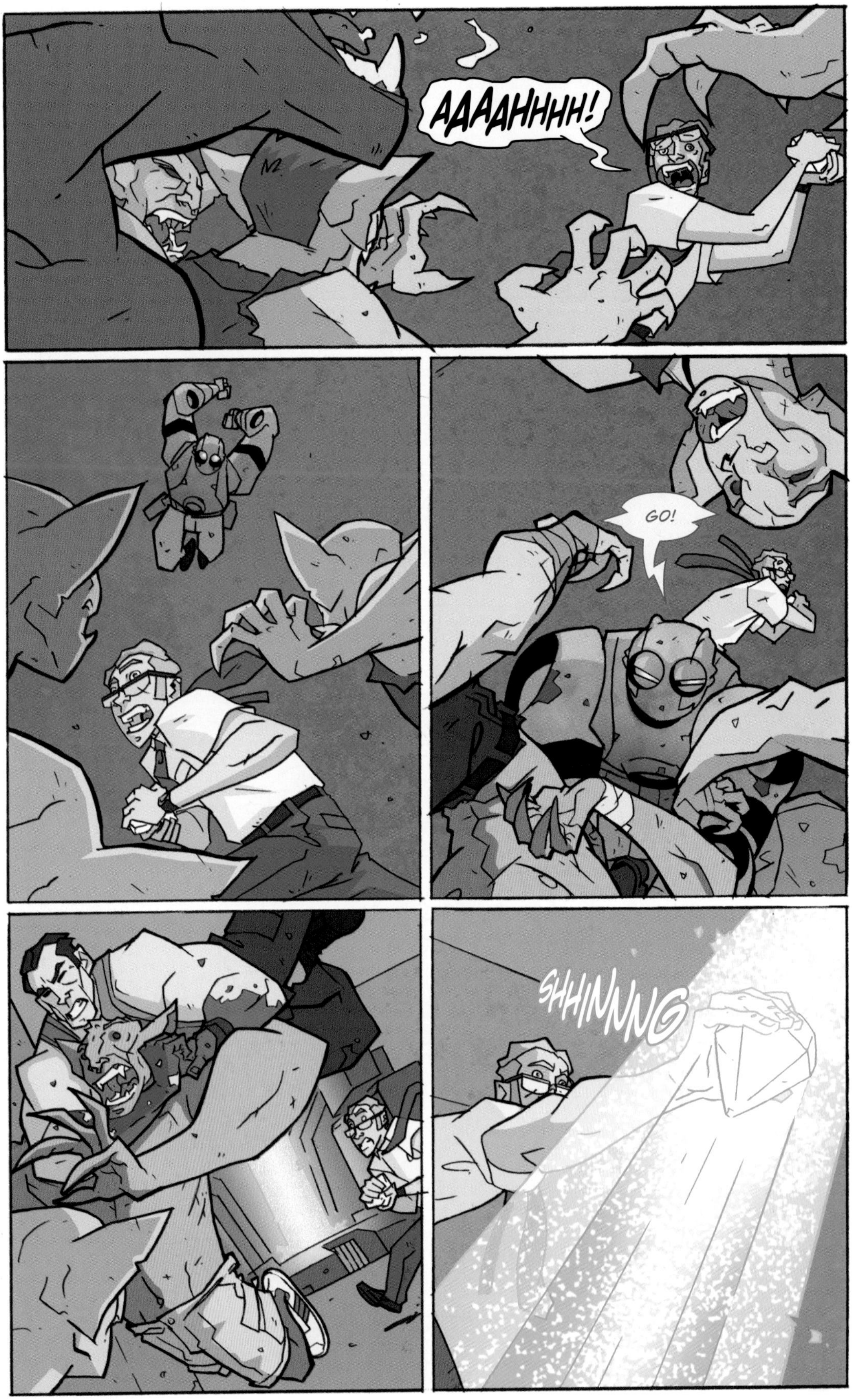
AAAAHHHH!
GO!
SHHINNNG

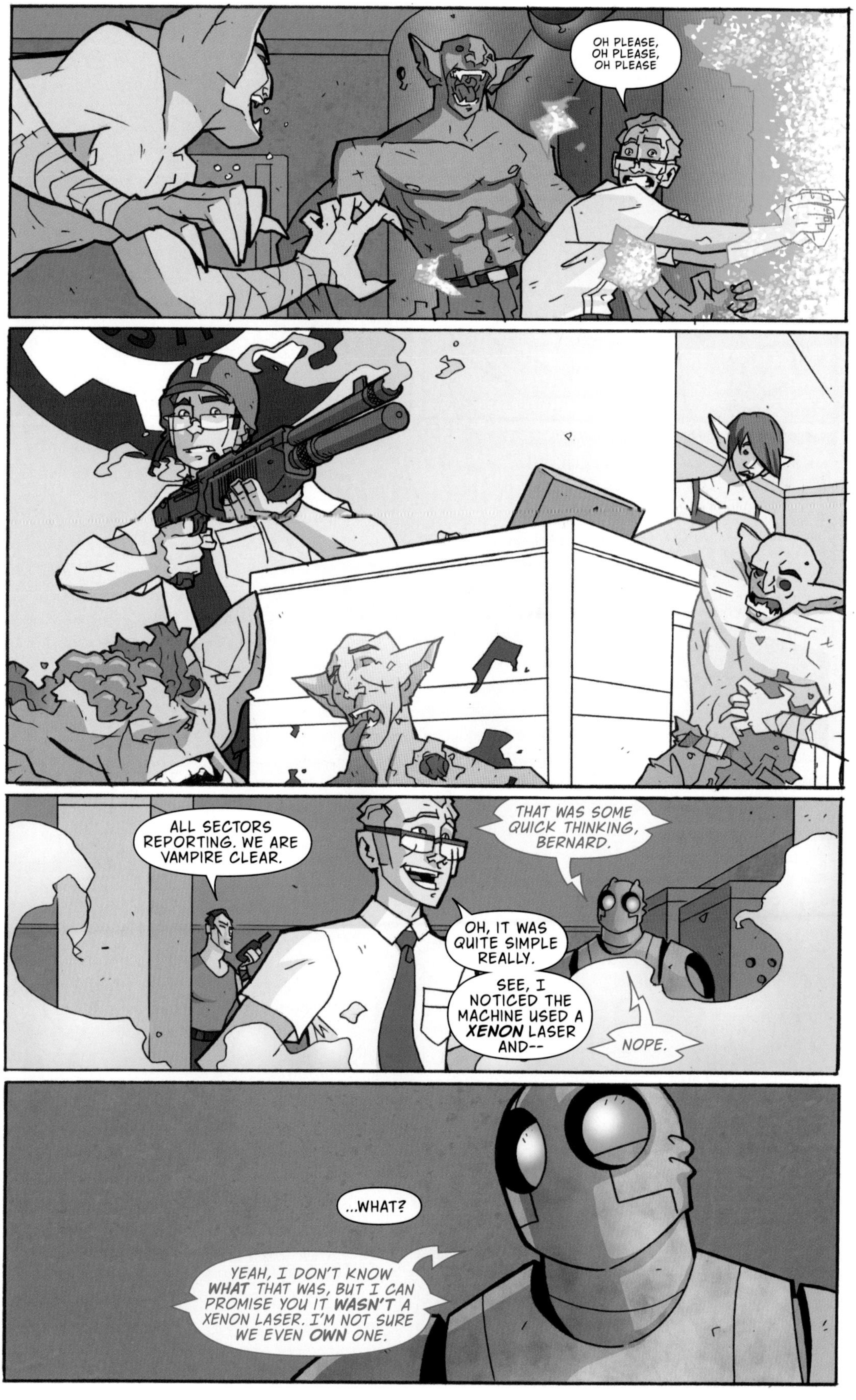

OH PLEASE, OH PLEASE, OH PLEASE
ALL SECTORS REPORTING. WE ARE VAMPIRE CLEAR.
THAT WAS SOME QUICK THINKING, BERNARD.
OH, IT WAS QUITE SIMPLE REALLY.
SEE, I NOTICED THE MACHINE USED A XENON LASER AND--
NOPE.
...WHAT?
YEAH, I DON'T KNOW WHAT THAT WAS, BUT I CAN PROMISE YOU IT WASN'T A XENON LASER. I'M NOT SURE WE EVEN OWN ONE.

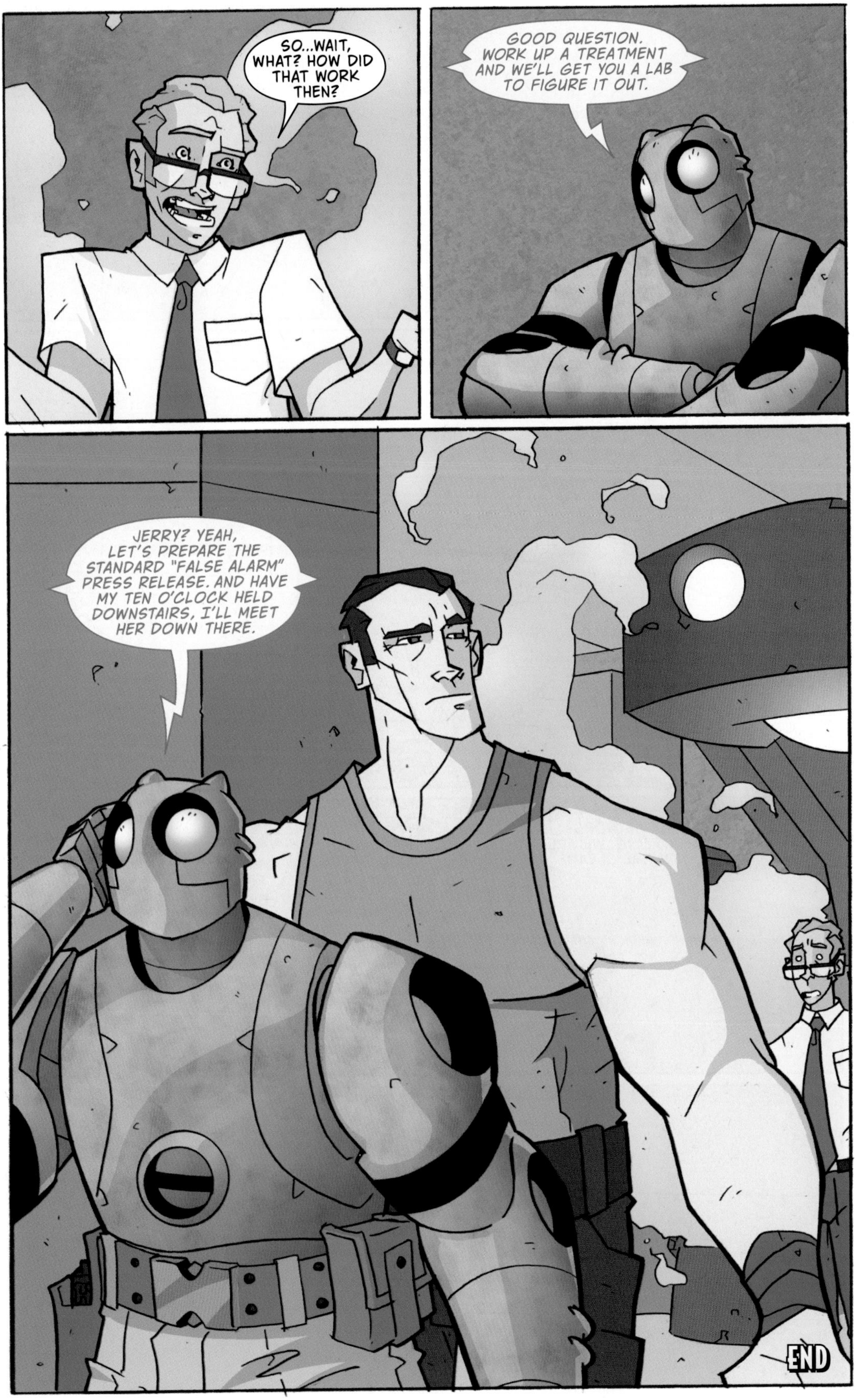
SO...WAIT, WHAT? HOW DID THAT WORK THEN?
GOOD QUESTION. WORK UP A TREATMENT AND WE'LL GET YOU A LAB TO FIGURE IT OUT.
JERRY? YEAH, LET'S PREPARE THE STANDARD "FALSE ALARM" PRESS RELEASE. AND HAVE MY TEN O'CLOCK HELD DOWNSTAIRS, I'LL MEET HER DOWN THERE.
END

ATOMIC ROBO BIG IN JAPAN

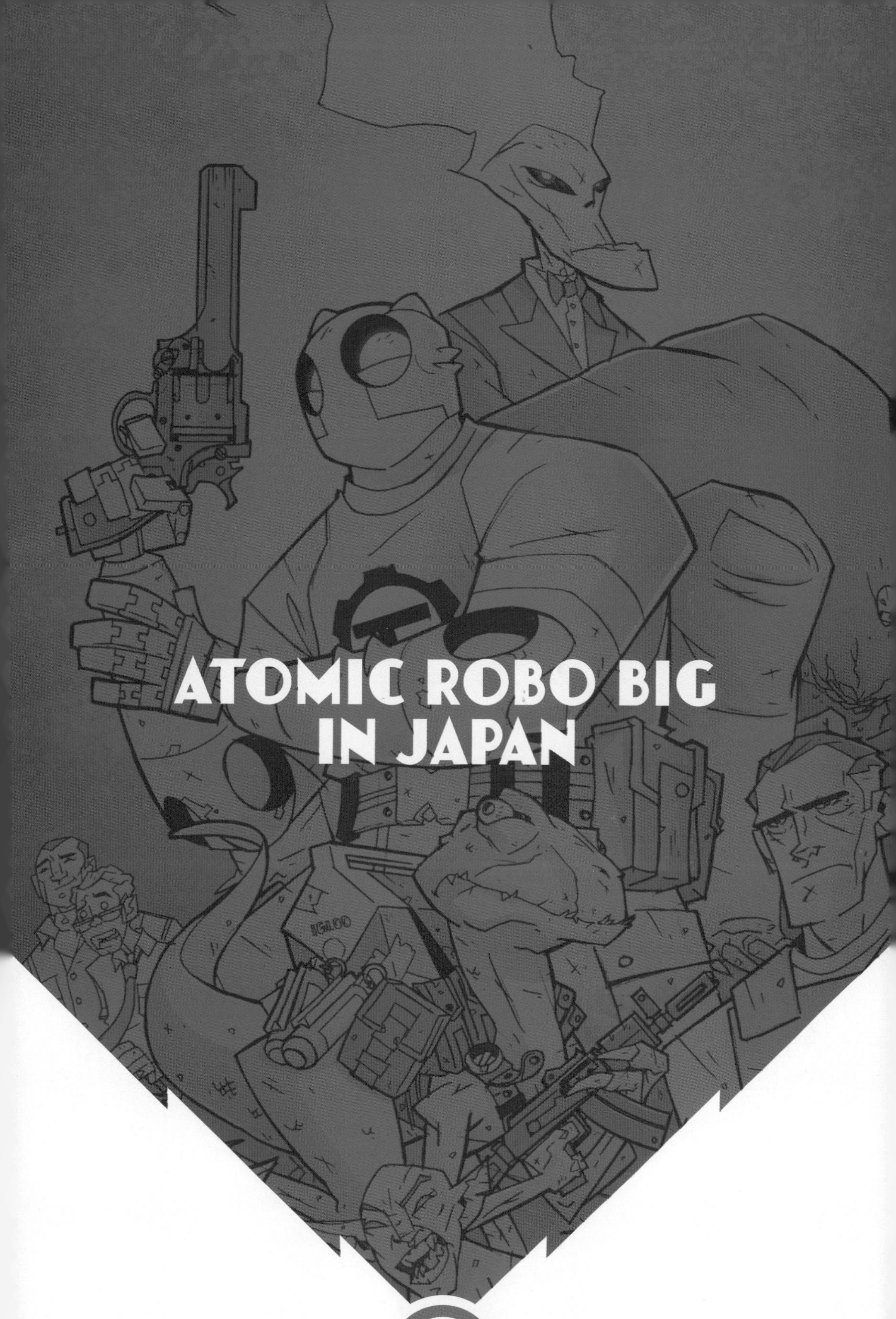

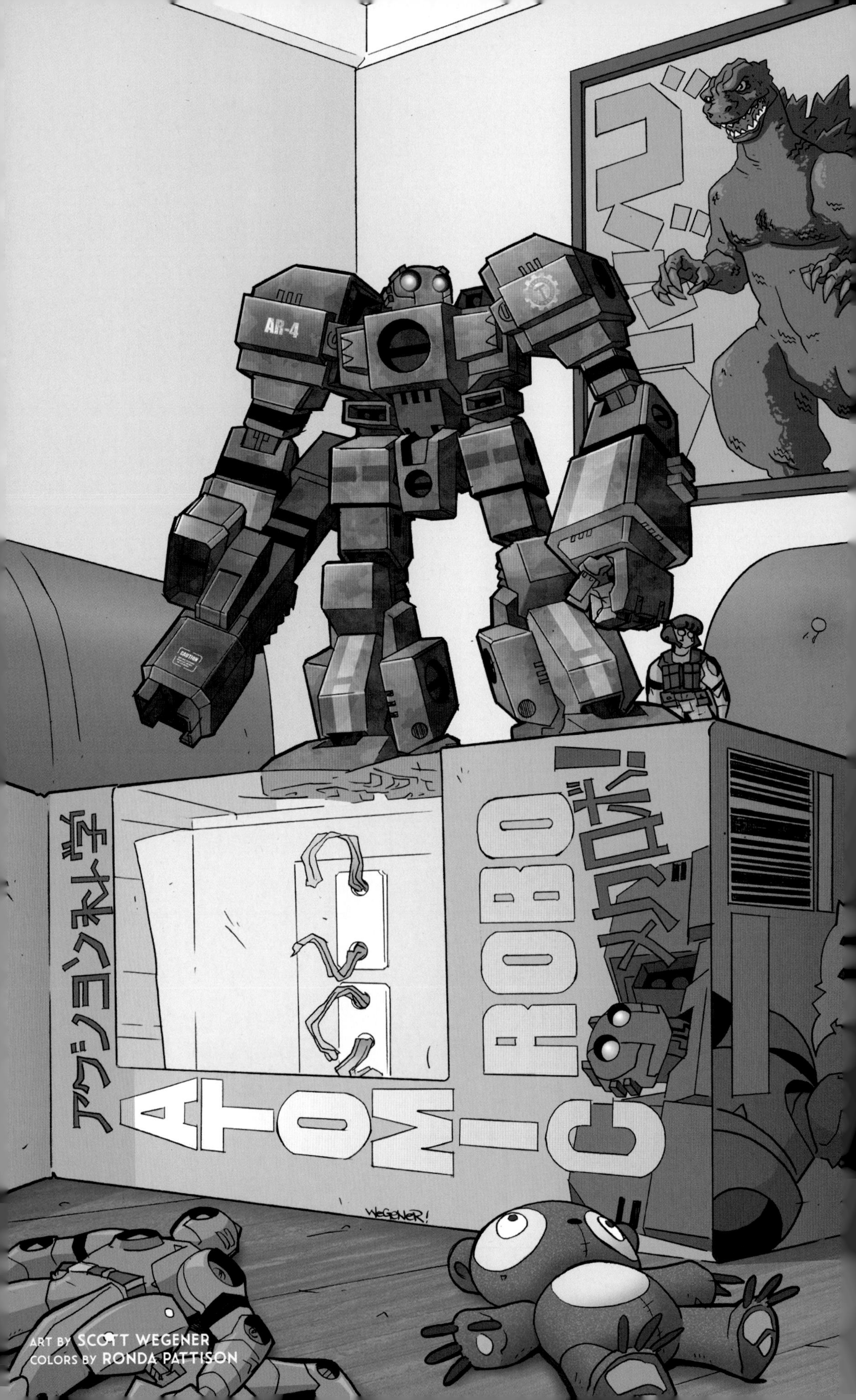
AR-4
ATOMIC ROBO!
WEGENER!
ART BY SCOTT WEGENER
COLORS BY RONDA PATTISON

TOKYO INTERNATIONAL AIRPORT, 1999

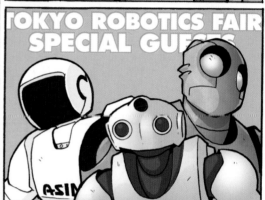

TOKYO ROBOTICS FAIR
SPECIAL GUESTS

BIG SCIENCE INCORPORATED

ATOMIC ROBO! IT HAS BEEN TOO LONG.

IT HAS, DR. YUMENO.

HOW IS JAPAN TREATING YOU?

LIKE ELVIS.

AND YOU DON'T EVEN SING!

BUT I CAN.

OH, ROBO. NO YOU CAN'T.

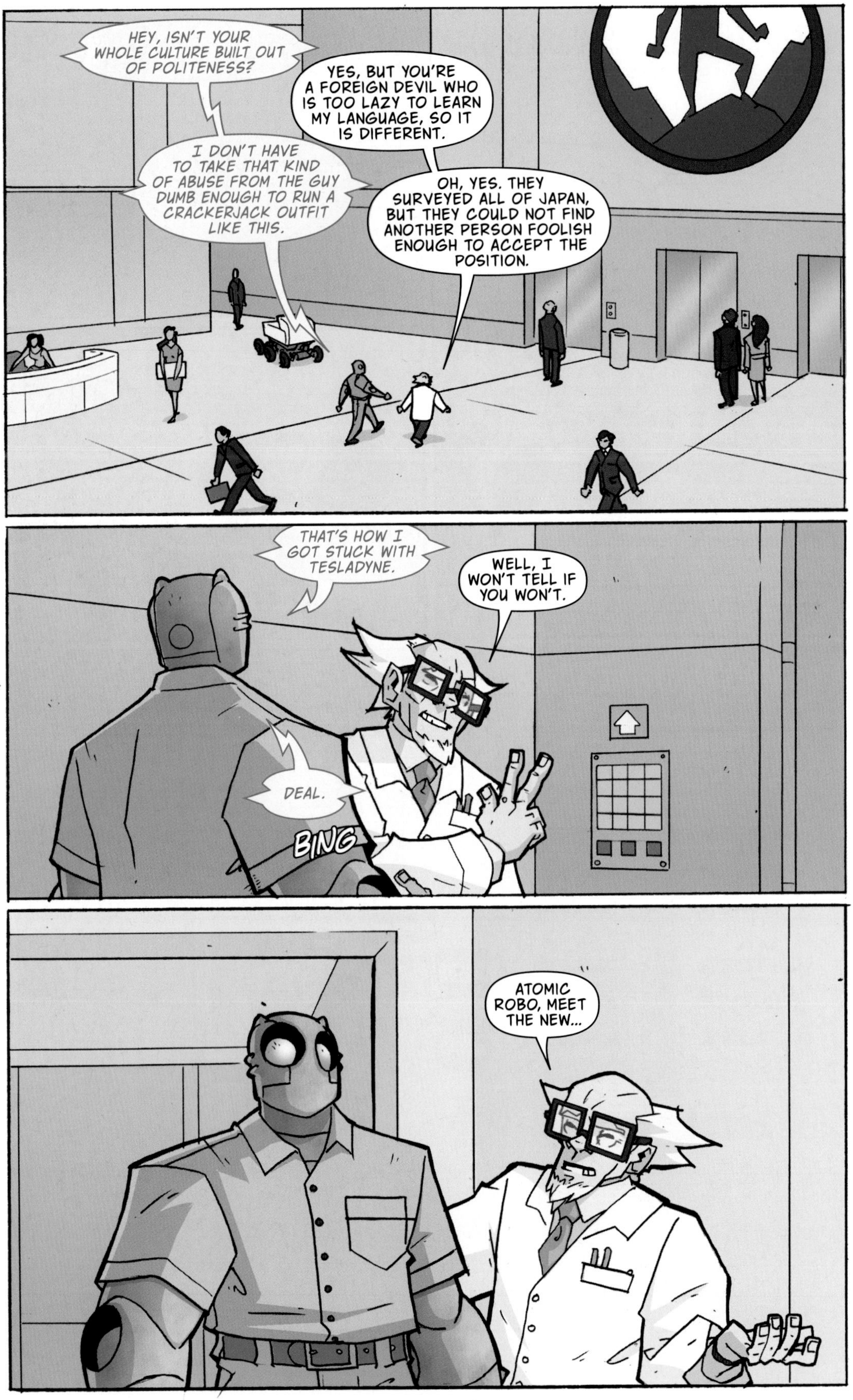
HEY, ISN'T YOUR WHOLE CULTURE BUILT OUT OF POLITENESS?
YES, BUT YOU'RE A FOREIGN DEVIL WHO IS TOO LAZY TO LEARN MY LANGUAGE, SO IT IS DIFFERENT.
I DON'T HAVE TO TAKE THAT KIND OF ABUSE FROM THE GUY DUMB ENOUGH TO RUN A CRACKERJACK OUTFIT LIKE THIS.
OH, YES. THEY SURVEYED ALL OF JAPAN, BUT THEY COULD NOT FIND ANOTHER PERSON FOOLISH ENOUGH TO ACCEPT THE POSITION.
THAT'S HOW I GOT STUCK WITH TESLADYNE.
WELL, I WON'T TELL IF YOU WON'T.
DEAL.
BING
ATOMIC ROBO, MEET THE NEW...

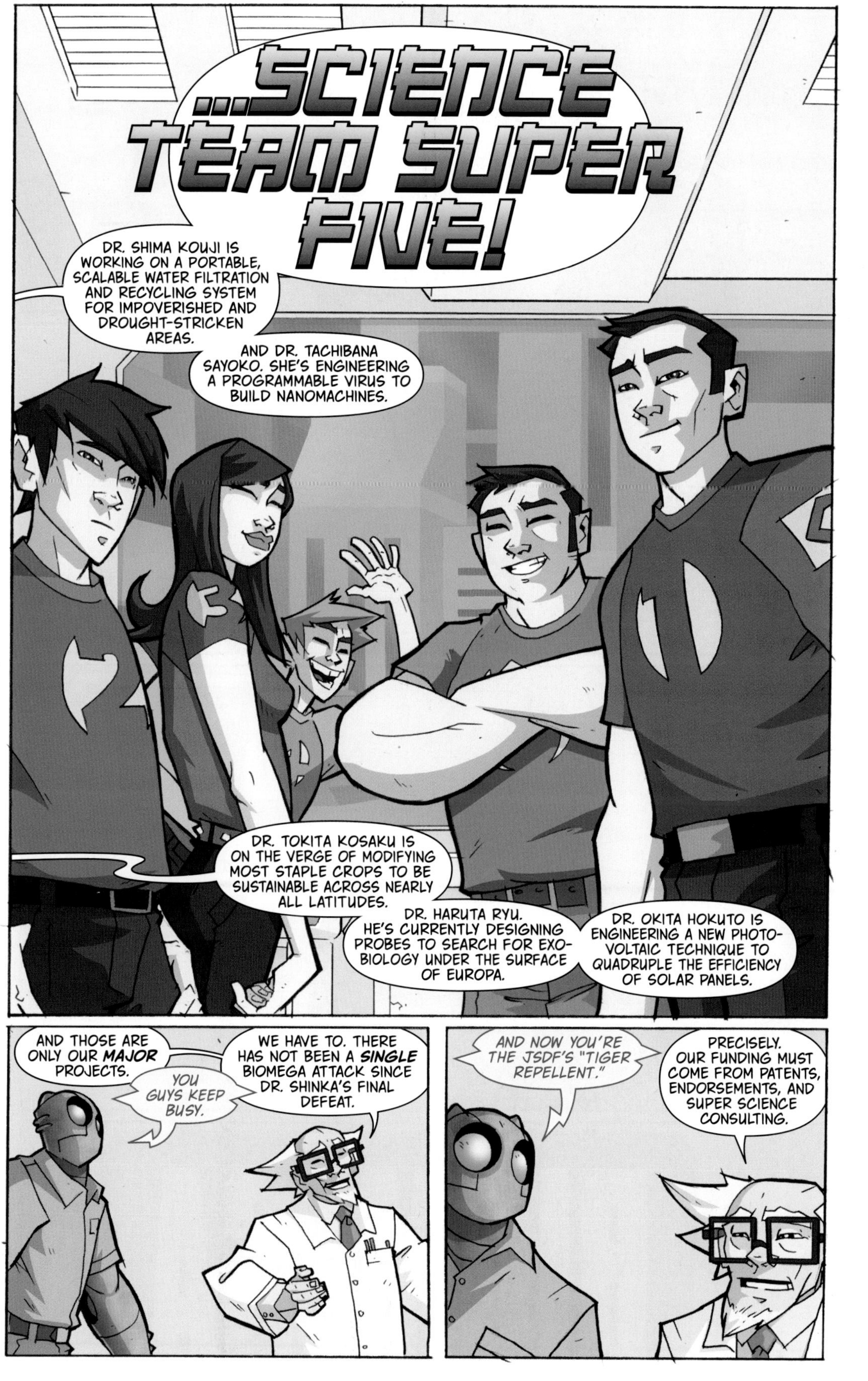
...SCIENCE TEAM SUPER FIVE!
DR. SHIMA KOUJI IS WORKING ON A PORTABLE, SCALABLE WATER FILTRATION AND RECYCLING SYSTEM FOR IMPOVERISHED AND DROUGHT-STRICKEN AREAS.
AND DR. TACHIBANA SAYOKO. SHE'S ENGINEERING A PROGRAMMABLE VIRUS TO BUILD NANOMACHINES.
DR. TOKITA KOSAKU IS ON THE VERGE OF MODIFYING MOST STAPLE CROPS TO BE SUSTAINABLE ACROSS NEARLY ALL LATITUDES.
DR. HARUTA RYU. HE'S CURRENTLY DESIGNING PROBES TO SEARCH FOR EXO-BIOLOGY UNDER THE SURFACE OF EUROPA.
DR. OKITA HOKUTO IS ENGINEERING A NEW PHOTO-VOLTAIC TECHNIQUE TO QUADRUPLE THE EFFICIENCY OF SOLAR PANELS.
AND THOSE ARE ONLY OUR **MAJOR** PROJECTS.
YOU GUYS KEEP BUSY.
WE HAVE TO. THERE HAS NOT BEEN A **SINGLE** BIOMEGA ATTACK SINCE DR. SHINKA'S FINAL DEFEAT.
AND NOW YOU'RE THE JSDF'S "TIGER REPELLENT."
PRECISELY. OUR FUNDING MUST COME FROM PATENTS, ENDORSEMENTS, AND SUPER SCIENCE CONSULTING.

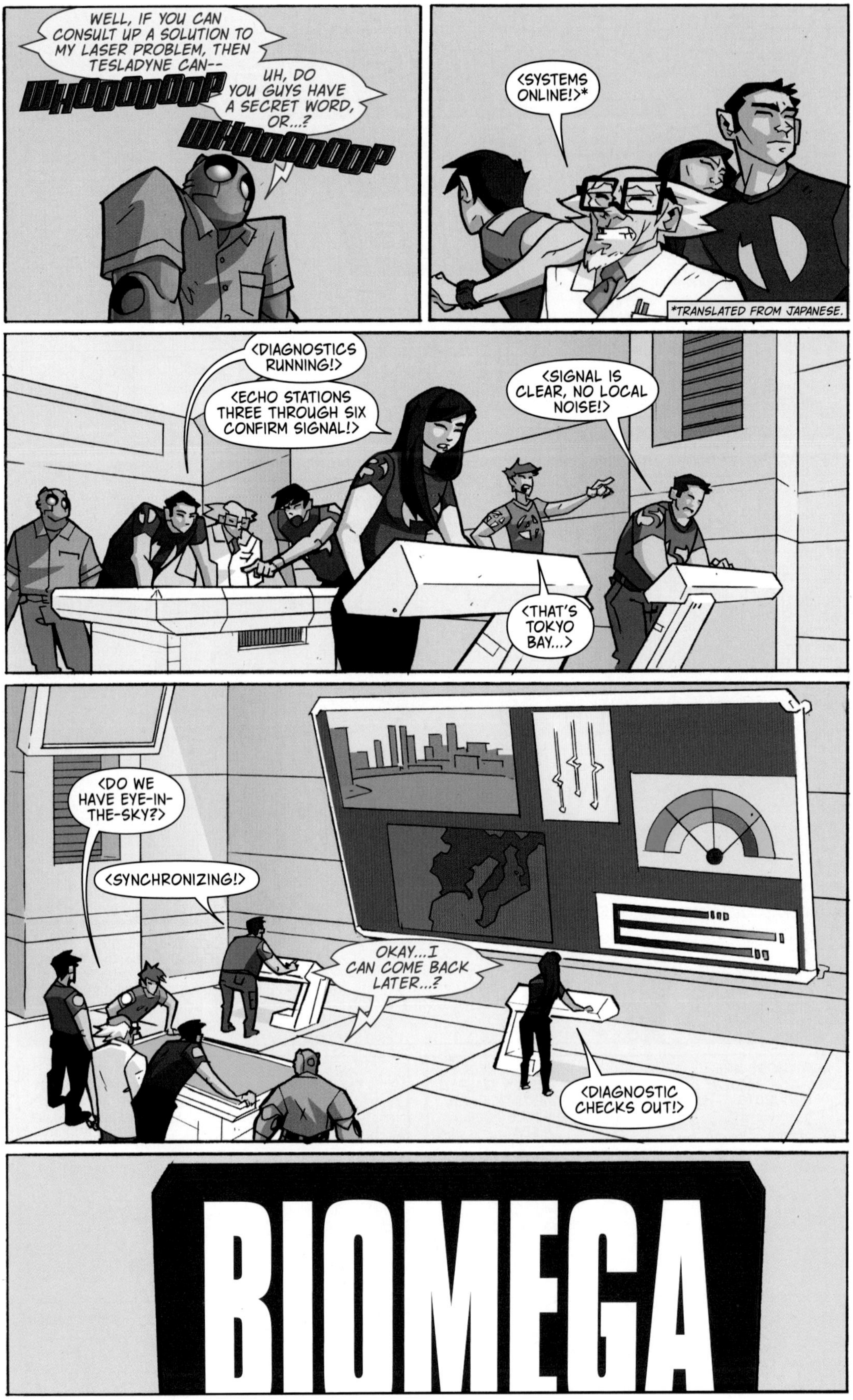
WELL, IF YOU CAN CONSULT UP A SOLUTION TO MY LASER PROBLEM, THEN TESLADYNE CAN--
WHOOOOOOOP
UH, DO YOU GUYS HAVE A SECRET WORD, OR...?
WHOOOOOOOP
<SYSTEMS ONLINE!>*
*TRANSLATED FROM JAPANESE.
<DIAGNOSTICS RUNNING!>
<ECHO STATIONS THREE THROUGH SIX CONFIRM SIGNAL!>
<SIGNAL IS CLEAR, NO LOCAL NOISE!>
<THAT'S TOKYO BAY...>
<DO WE HAVE EYE-IN-THE-SKY?>
<SYNCHRONIZING!>
OKAY...I CAN COME BACK LATER...?
<DIAGNOSTIC CHECKS OUT!>
BIOMEGA

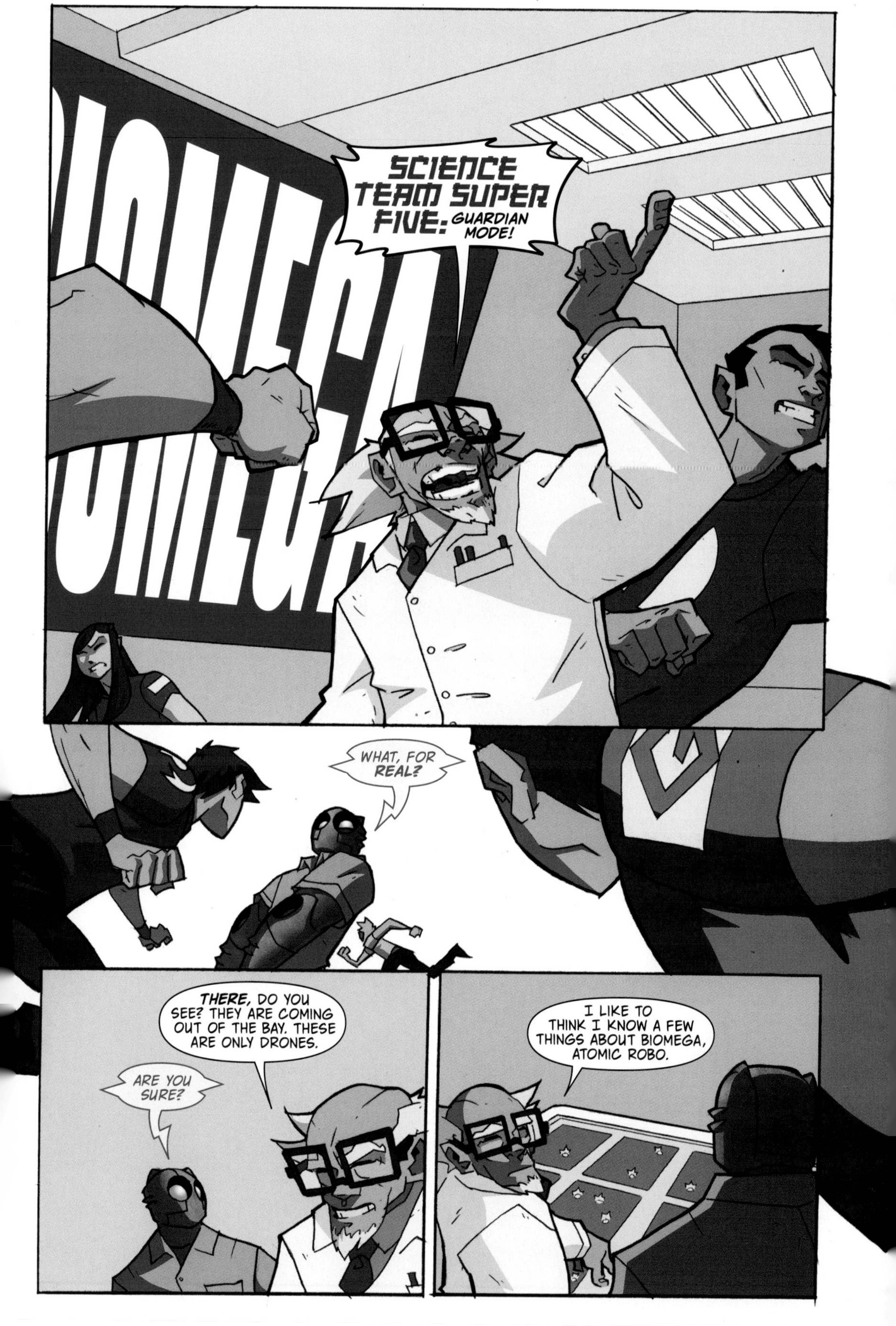
SCIENCE TEAM SUPER FIVE: GUARDIAN MODE!
WHAT, FOR REAL?
THERE, DO YOU SEE? THEY ARE COMING OUT OF THE BAY. THESE ARE ONLY DRONES.
ARE YOU SURE?
I LIKE TO THINK I KNOW A FEW THINGS ABOUT BIOMEGA, ATOMIC ROBO.

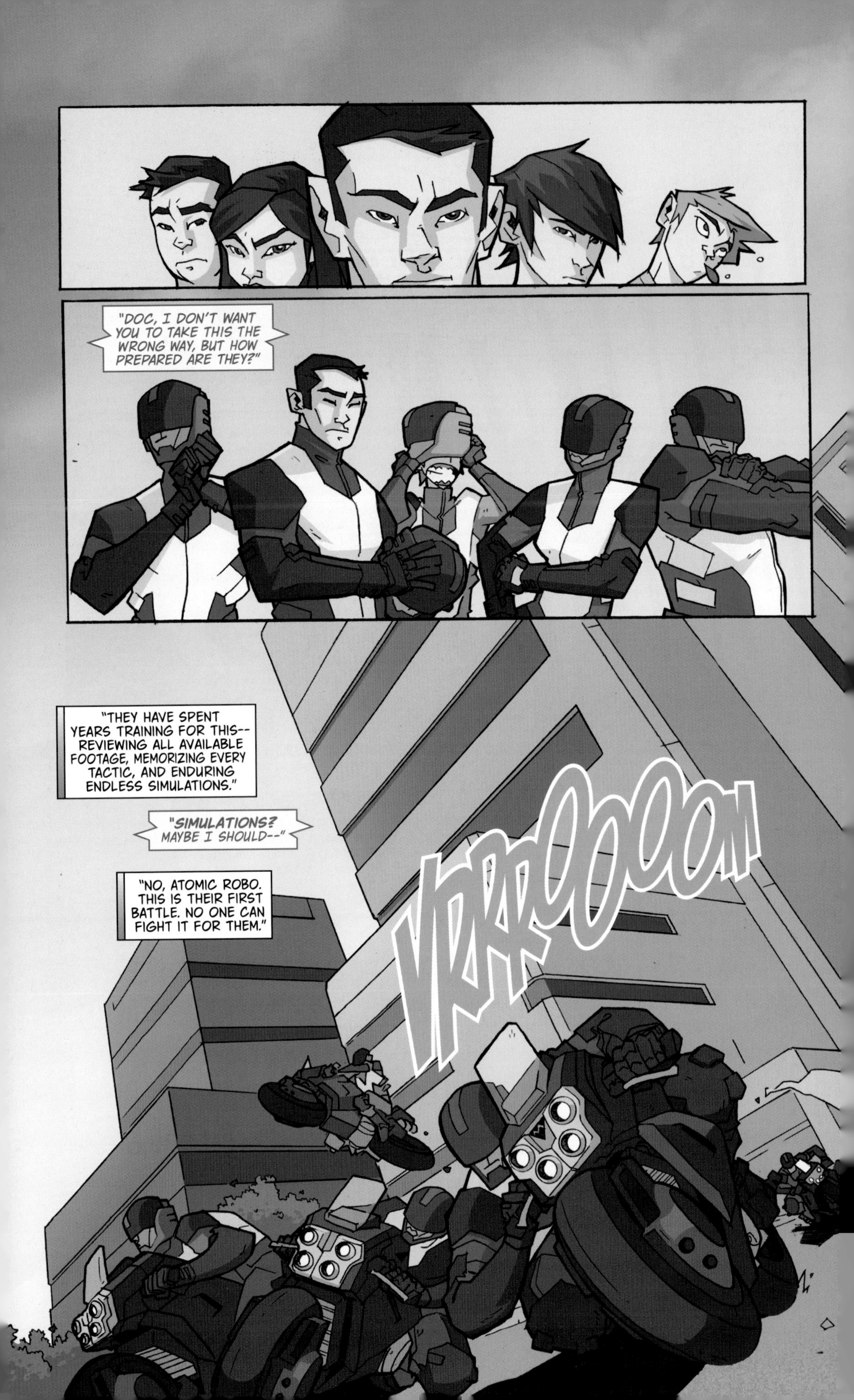
"DOC, I DON'T WANT YOU TO TAKE THIS THE WRONG WAY, BUT HOW PREPARED ARE THEY?"
"THEY HAVE SPENT YEARS TRAINING FOR THIS-- REVIEWING ALL AVAILABLE FOOTAGE, MEMORIZING EVERY TACTIC, AND ENDURING ENDLESS SIMULATIONS."
"SIMULATIONS? MAYBE I SHOULD--"
"NO, ATOMIC ROBO. THIS IS THEIR FIRST BATTLE. NO ONE CAN FIGHT IT FOR THEM."
VRRROOOOOM

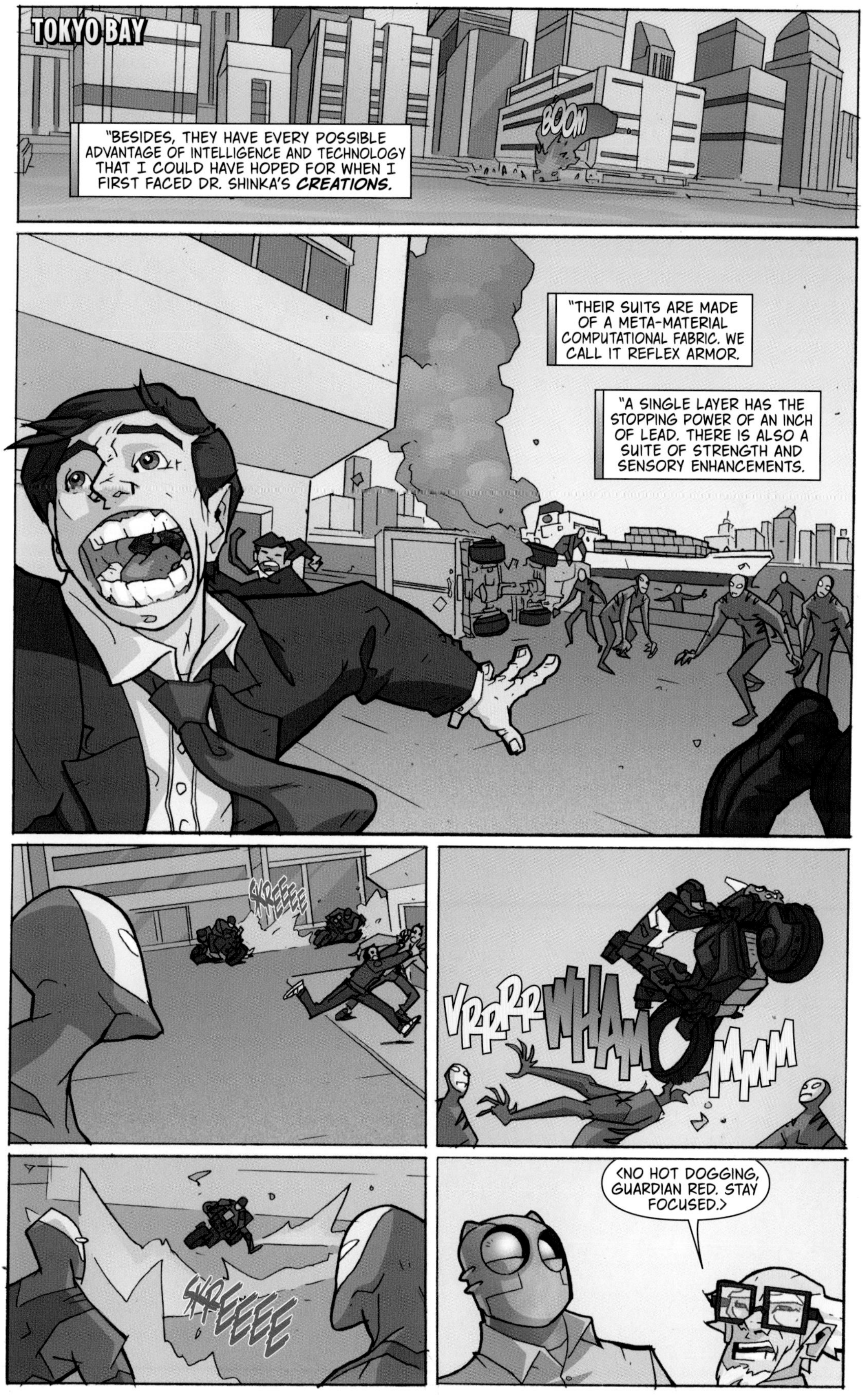
TOKYO BAY
"BESIDES, THEY HAVE EVERY POSSIBLE ADVANTAGE OF INTELLIGENCE AND TECHNOLOGY THAT I COULD HAVE HOPED FOR WHEN I FIRST FACED DR. SHINKA'S CREATIONS.
BOOM
"THEIR SUITS ARE MADE OF A META-MATERIAL COMPUTATIONAL FABRIC. WE CALL IT REFLEX ARMOR.
"A SINGLE LAYER HAS THE STOPPING POWER OF AN INCH OF LEAD. THERE IS ALSO A SUITE OF STRENGTH AND SENSORY ENHANCEMENTS.
SKREEEEE
VRRRR WHAM MMM
SKREEEEE
<NO HOT DOGGING, GUARDIAN RED. STAY FOCUSED.>

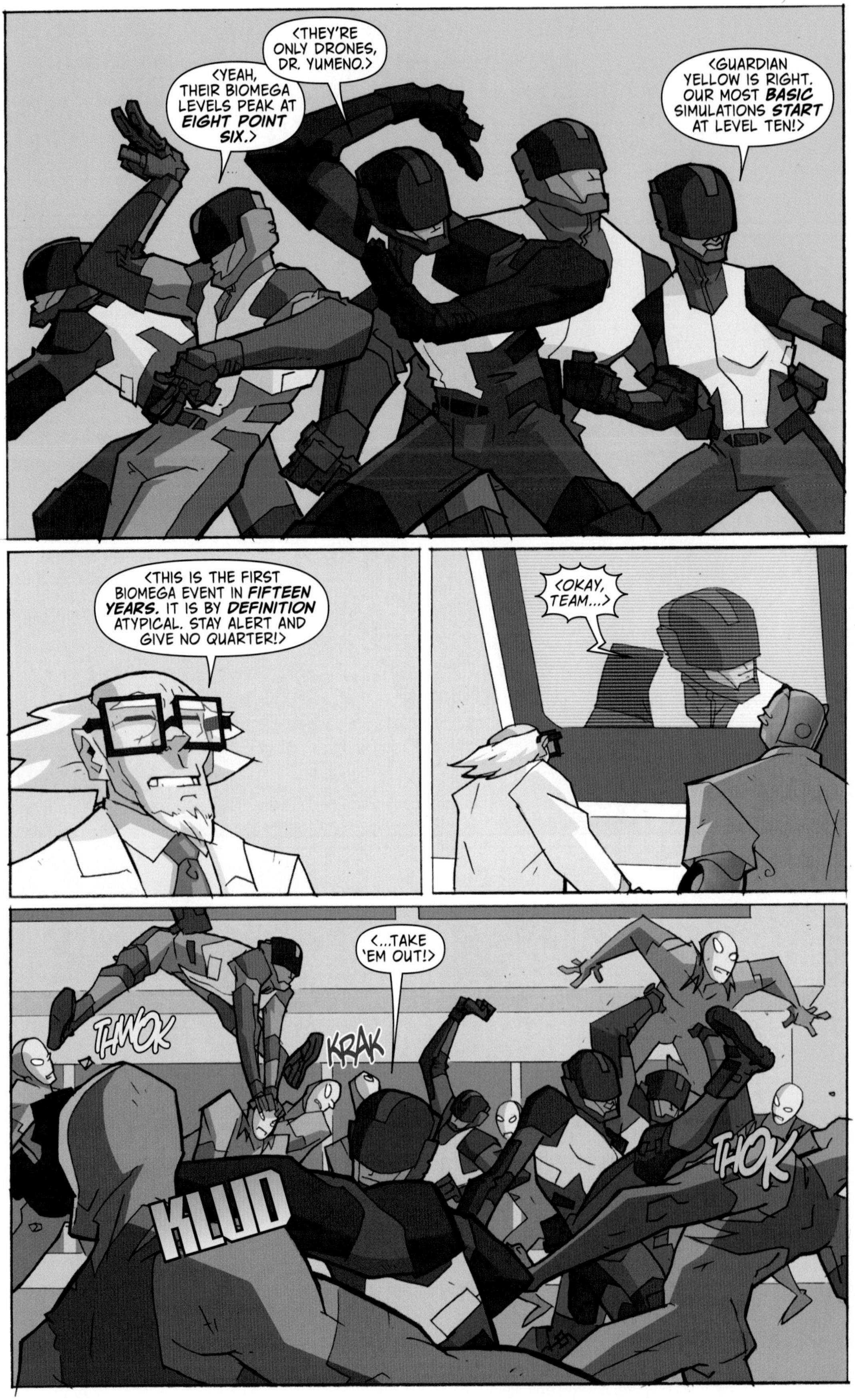
<YEAH, THEIR BIOMEGA LEVELS PEAK AT EIGHT POINT SIX.>
<THEY'RE ONLY DRONES, DR. YUMENO.>
<GUARDIAN YELLOW IS RIGHT. OUR MOST BASIC SIMULATIONS START AT LEVEL TEN!>
<THIS IS THE FIRST BIOMEGA EVENT IN FIFTEEN YEARS. IT IS BY DEFINITION ATYPICAL. STAY ALERT AND GIVE NO QUARTER!>
<OKAY, TEAM...>
<...TAKE 'EM OUT!>
THWOK
KRAK
THOK
KLUD

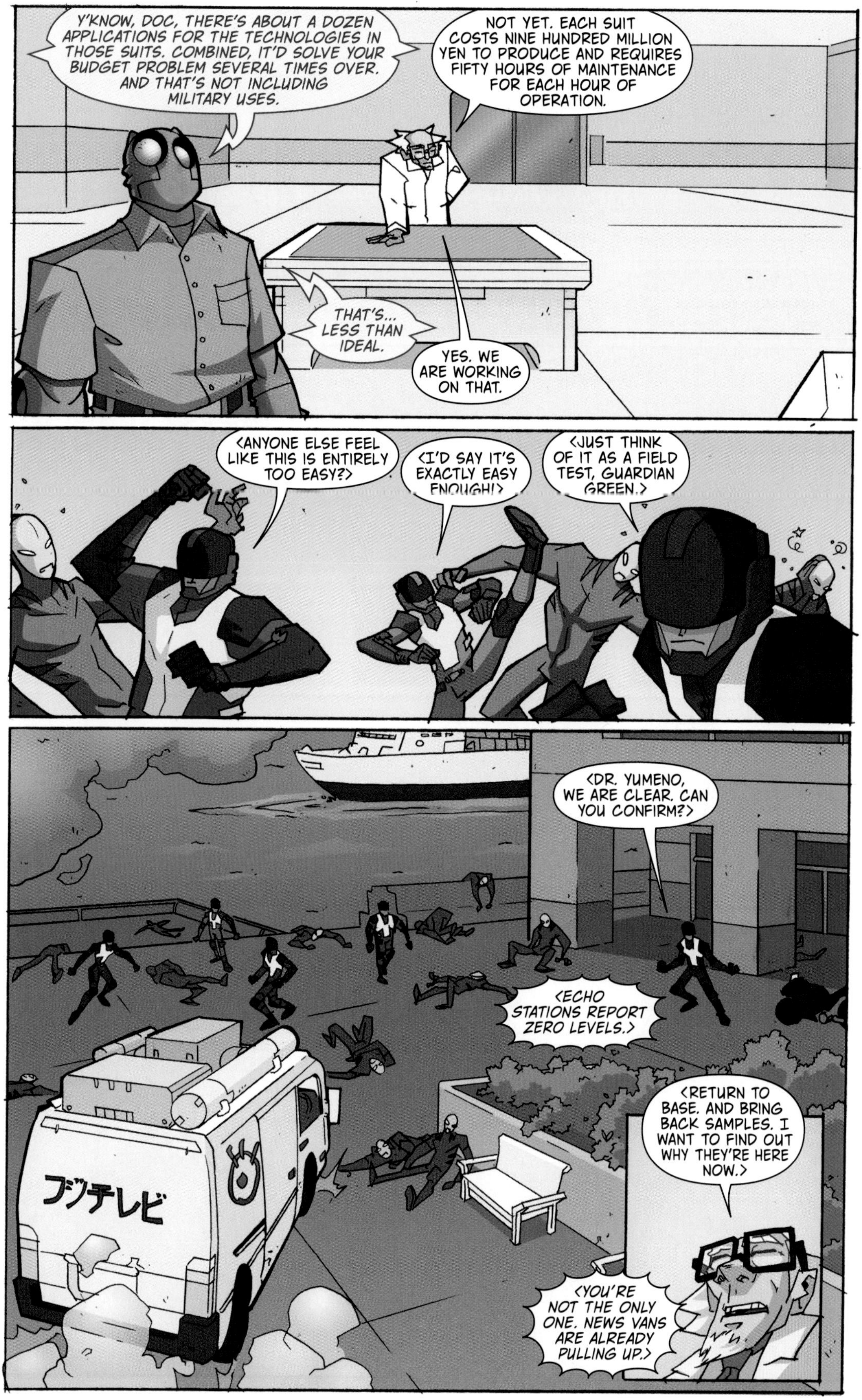
Y'KNOW, DOC, THERE'S ABOUT A DOZEN APPLICATIONS FOR THE TECHNOLOGIES IN THOSE SUITS. COMBINED, IT'D SOLVE YOUR BUDGET PROBLEM SEVERAL TIMES OVER. AND THAT'S NOT INCLUDING MILITARY USES.
NOT YET. EACH SUIT COSTS NINE HUNDRED MILLION YEN TO PRODUCE AND REQUIRES FIFTY HOURS OF MAINTENANCE FOR EACH HOUR OF OPERATION.
THAT'S... LESS THAN IDEAL.
YES. WE ARE WORKING ON THAT.
<ANYONE ELSE FEEL LIKE THIS IS ENTIRELY TOO EASY?>
<I'D SAY IT'S EXACTLY EASY ENOUGH!>
<JUST THINK OF IT AS A FIELD TEST, GUARDIAN GREEN.>
<DR. YUMENO, WE ARE CLEAR. CAN YOU CONFIRM?>
<ECHO STATIONS REPORT ZERO LEVELS.>
<RETURN TO BASE. AND BRING BACK SAMPLES. I WANT TO FIND OUT WHY THEY'RE HERE NOW.>
<YOU'RE NOT THE ONLY ONE. NEWS VANS ARE ALREADY PULLING UP.>
フジテレビ

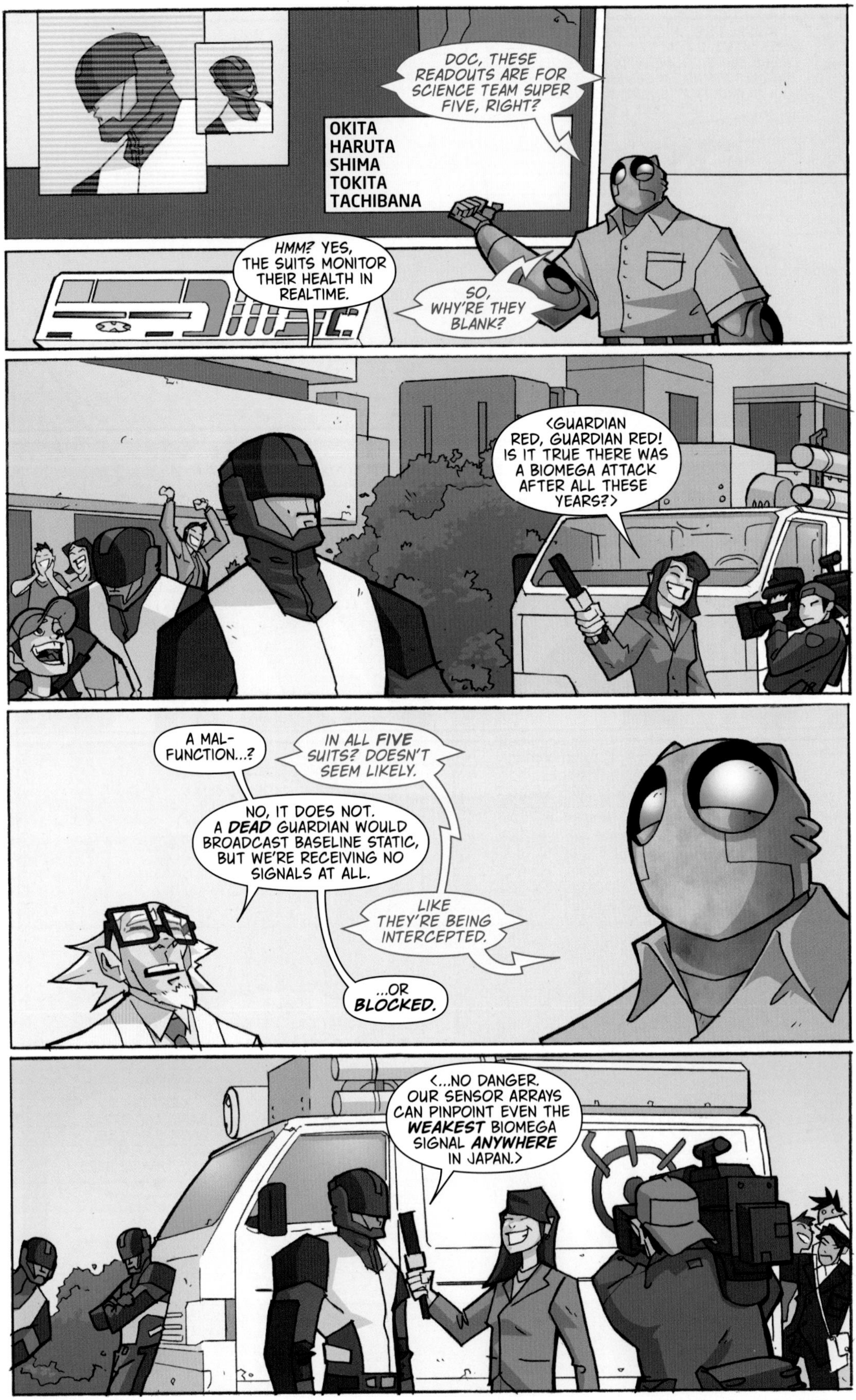

OKITA
HARUTA
SHIMA
TOKITA
TACHIBANA
DOC, THESE READOUTS ARE FOR SCIENCE TEAM SUPER FIVE, RIGHT?
HMM? YES, THE SUITS MONITOR THEIR HEALTH IN REALTIME.
SO, WHY'RE THEY BLANK?
<GUARDIAN RED, GUARDIAN RED! IS IT TRUE THERE WAS A BIOMEGA ATTACK AFTER ALL THESE YEARS?>
A MAL-FUNCTION...?
IN ALL FIVE SUITS? DOESN'T SEEM LIKELY.
NO, IT DOES NOT. A DEAD GUARDIAN WOULD BROADCAST BASELINE STATIC, BUT WE'RE RECEIVING NO SIGNALS AT ALL.
LIKE THEY'RE BEING INTERCEPTED.
...OR BLOCKED.
<...NO DANGER. OUR SENSOR ARRAYS CAN PINPOINT EVEN THE WEAKEST BIOMEGA SIGNAL ANYWHERE IN JAPAN.>

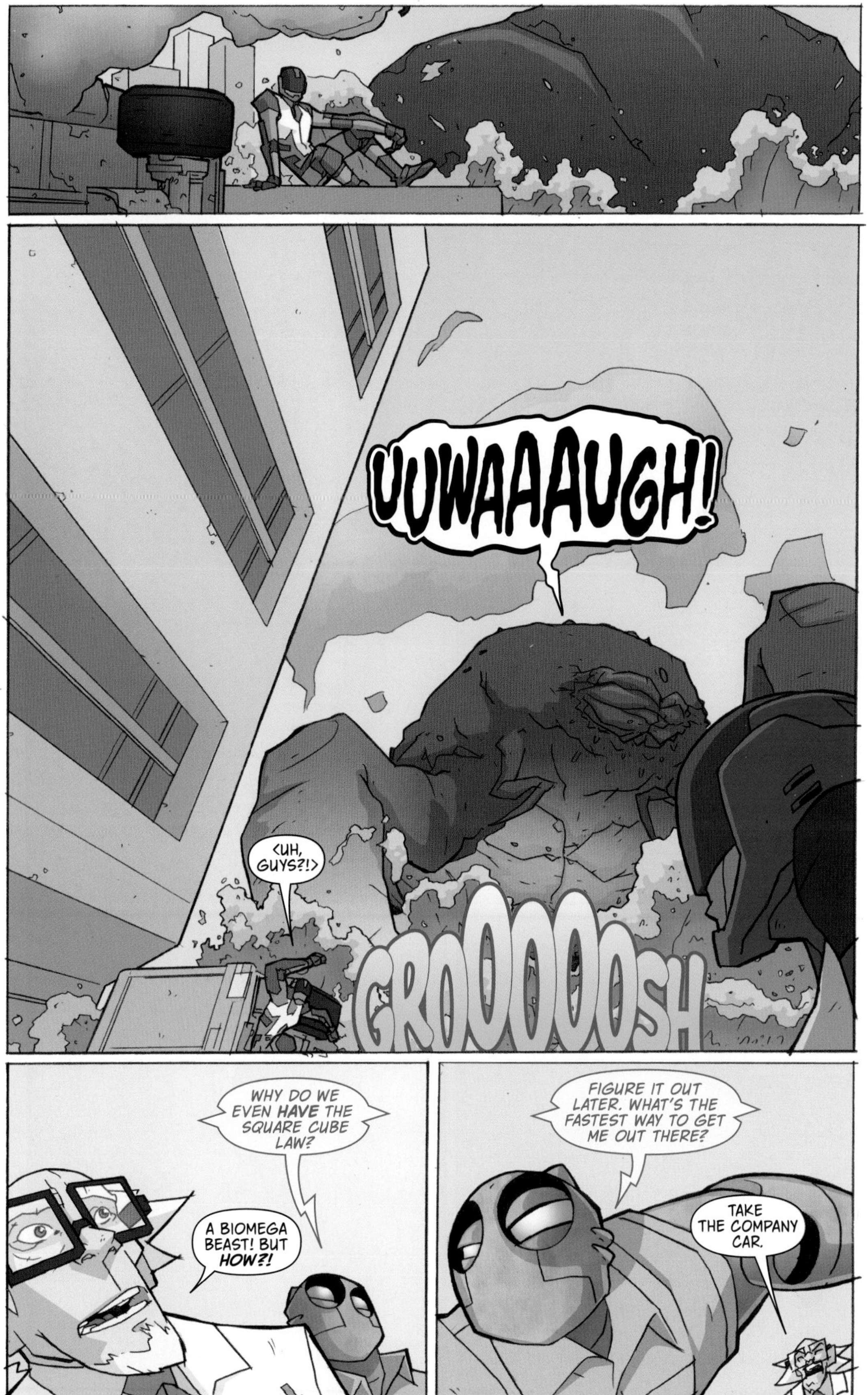

UUWAAAUGH!
<UH, GUYS?!>
GROOOOOSH
A BIOMEGA BEAST! BUT **HOW?!**
WHY DO WE EVEN **HAVE** THE SQUARE CUBE LAW?
FIGURE IT OUT LATER. WHAT'S THE FASTEST WAY TO GET ME OUT THERE?
TAKE THE COMPANY CAR.

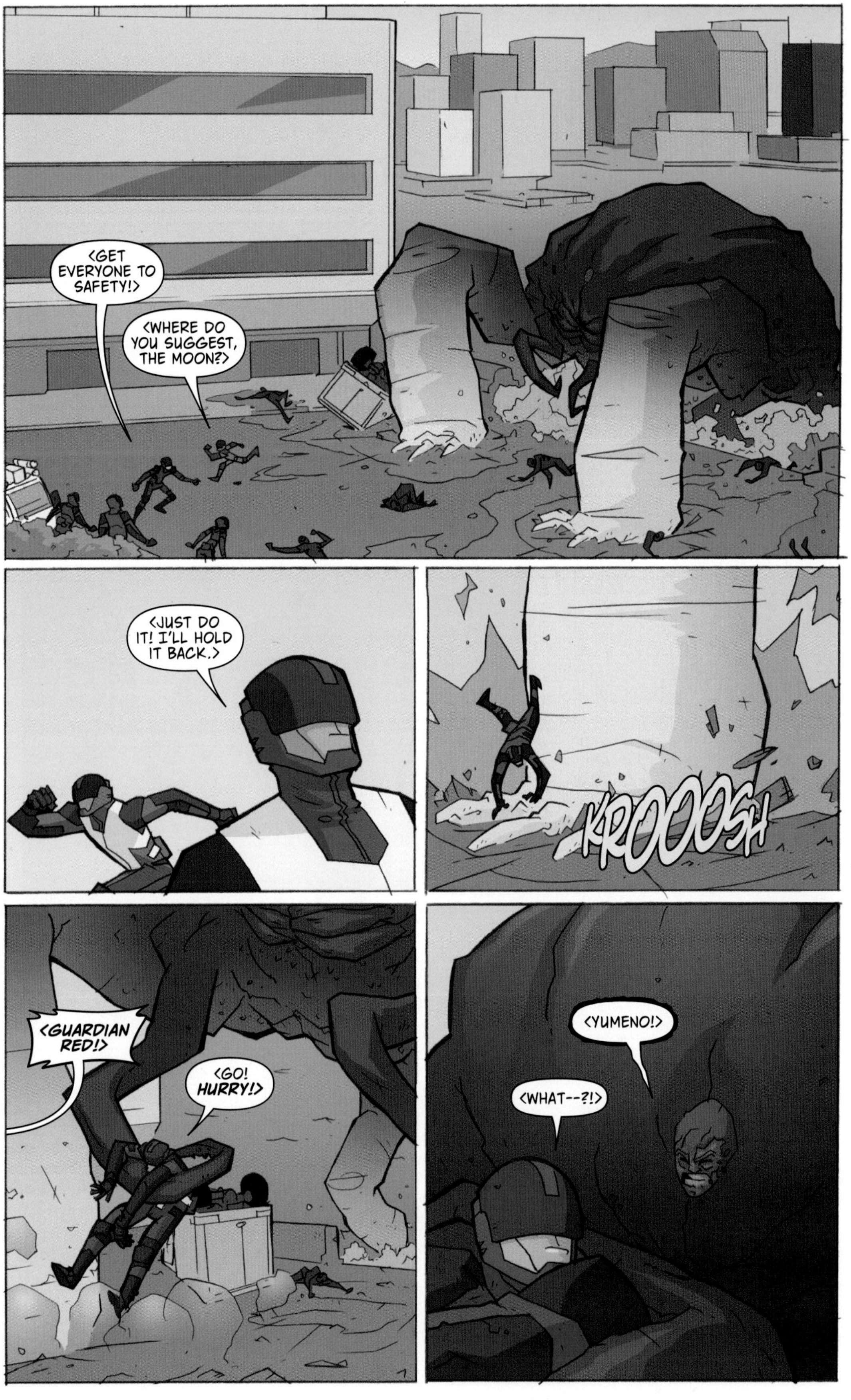
<GET EVERYONE TO SAFETY!>
<WHERE DO YOU SUGGEST, THE MOON?>
<JUST DO IT! I'LL HOLD IT BACK.>
KROOOSH
<GUARDIAN RED!>
<GO! HURRY!>
<YUMENO!>
<WHAT--?!>

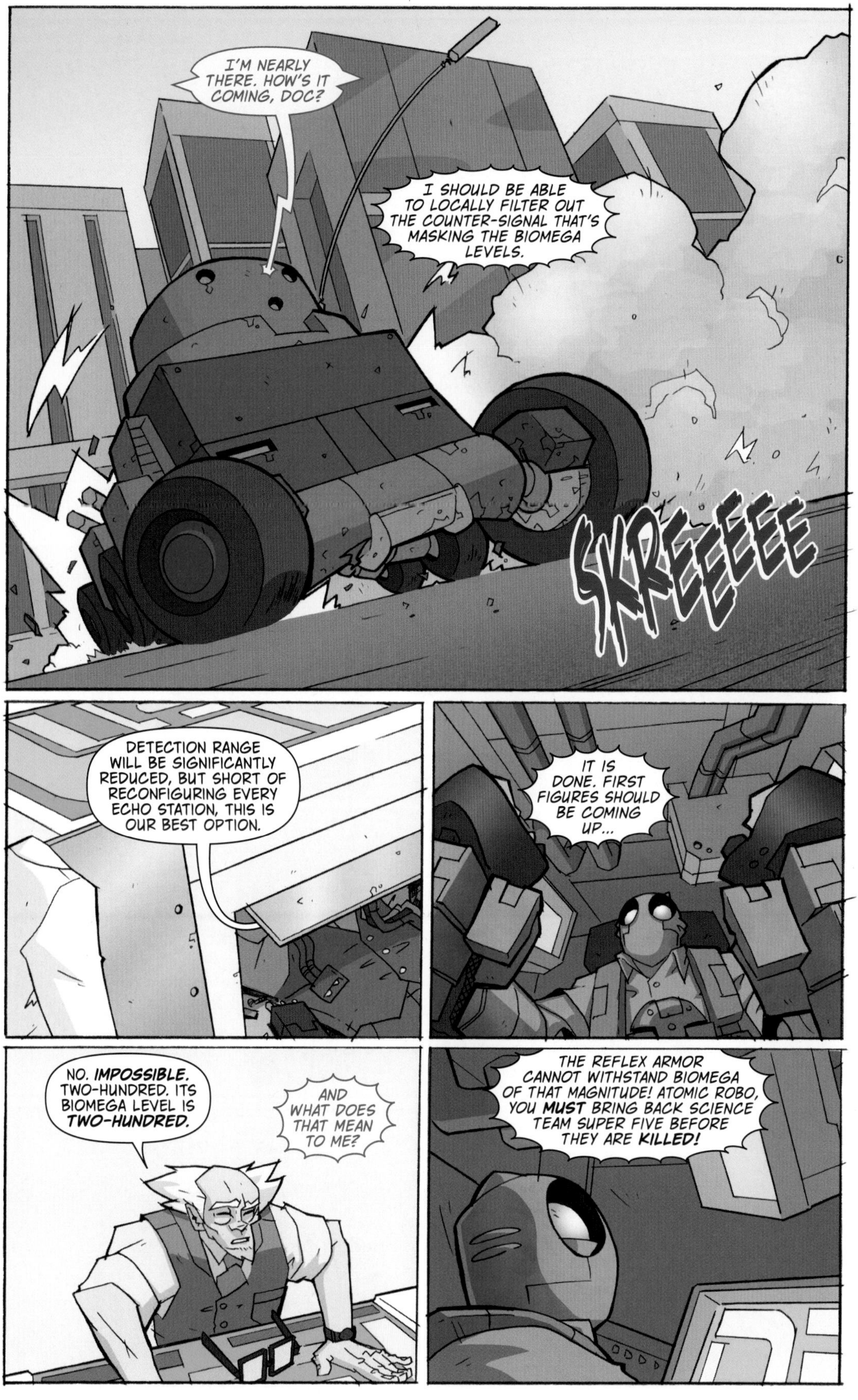
I'M NEARLY THERE. HOW'S IT COMING, DOC?
I SHOULD BE ABLE TO LOCALLY FILTER OUT THE COUNTER-SIGNAL THAT'S MASKING THE BIOMEGA LEVELS.
SKREEEEEE
DETECTION RANGE WILL BE SIGNIFICANTLY REDUCED, BUT SHORT OF RECONFIGURING EVERY ECHO STATION, THIS IS OUR BEST OPTION.
IT IS DONE. FIRST FIGURES SHOULD BE COMING UP...
NO. IMPOSSIBLE. TWO-HUNDRED. ITS BIOMEGA LEVEL IS TWO-HUNDRED.
AND WHAT DOES THAT MEAN TO ME?
THE REFLEX ARMOR CANNOT WITHSTAND BIOMEGA OF THAT MAGNITUDE! ATOMIC ROBO, YOU MUST BRING BACK SCIENCE TEAM SUPER FIVE BEFORE THEY ARE KILLED!

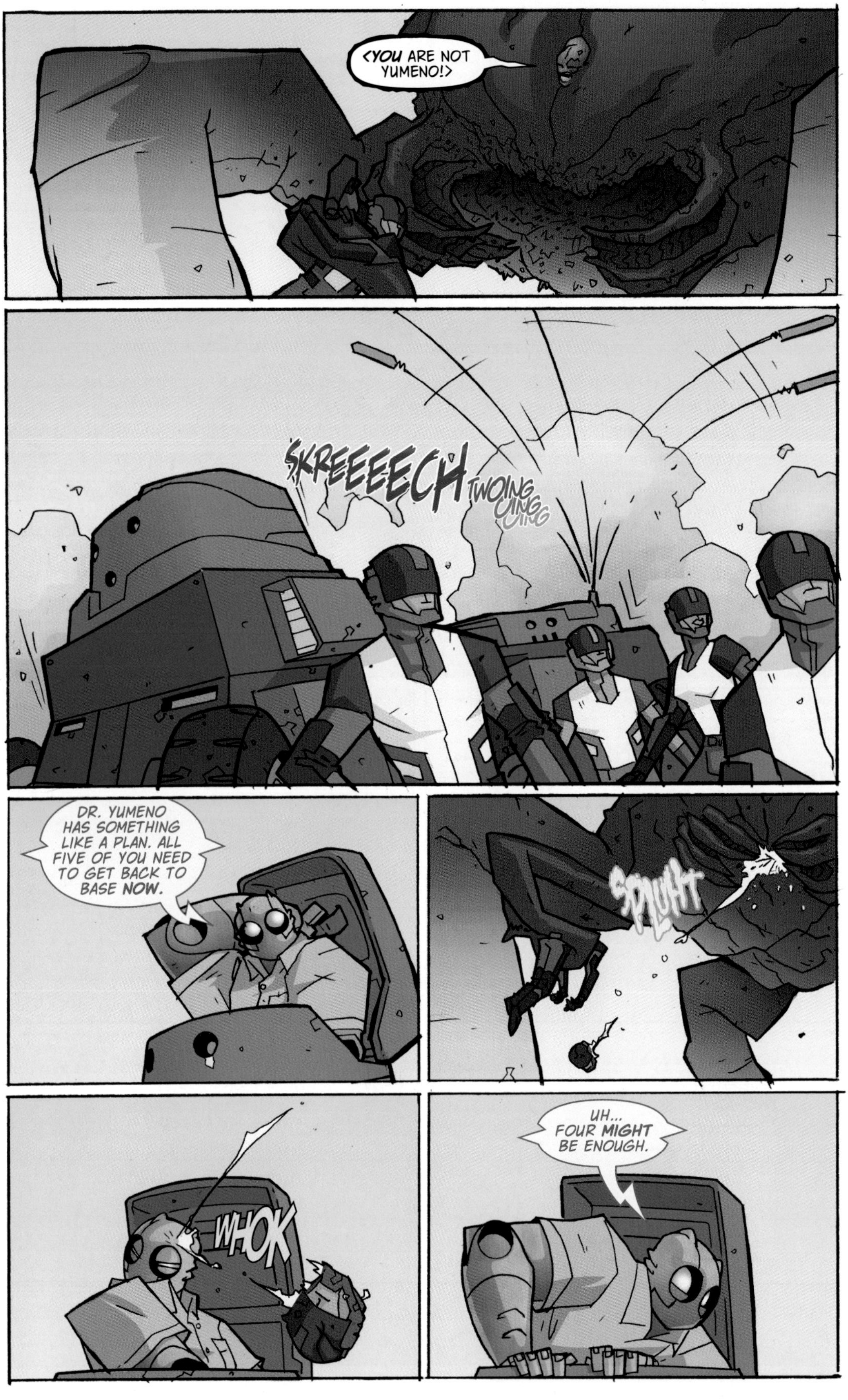

<YOU ARE NOT YUMENO!>
SKREEEEECH
TWOING
DR. YUMENO HAS SOMETHING LIKE A PLAN. ALL FIVE OF YOU NEED TO GET BACK TO BASE NOW.
SPLUHT
WHOK
UH... FOUR MIGHT BE ENOUGH.

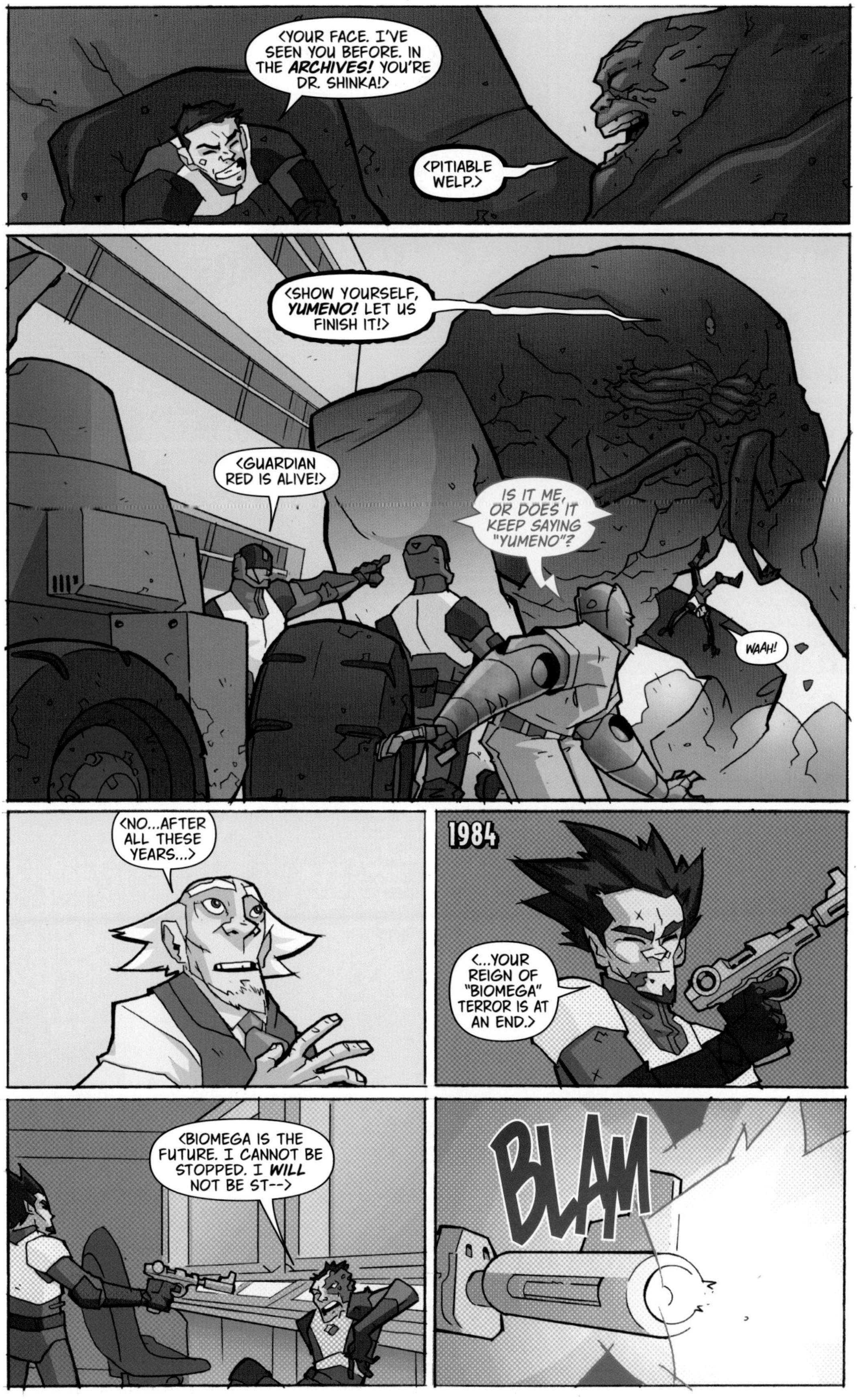
<YOUR FACE. I'VE SEEN YOU BEFORE. IN THE **ARCHIVES!** YOU'RE DR. SHINKA!>
<PITIABLE WELP.>
<SHOW YOURSELF, **YUMENO!** LET US FINISH IT!>
<GUARDIAN RED IS ALIVE!>
IS IT ME, OR DOES IT KEEP SAYING "YUMENO"?
WAAH!
<NO...AFTER ALL THESE YEARS...>
1984
<...YOUR REIGN OF "BIOMEGA" TERROR IS AT AN END.>
<BIOMEGA IS THE FUTURE. I CANNOT BE STOPPED. I **WILL** NOT BE ST-->
BLAM

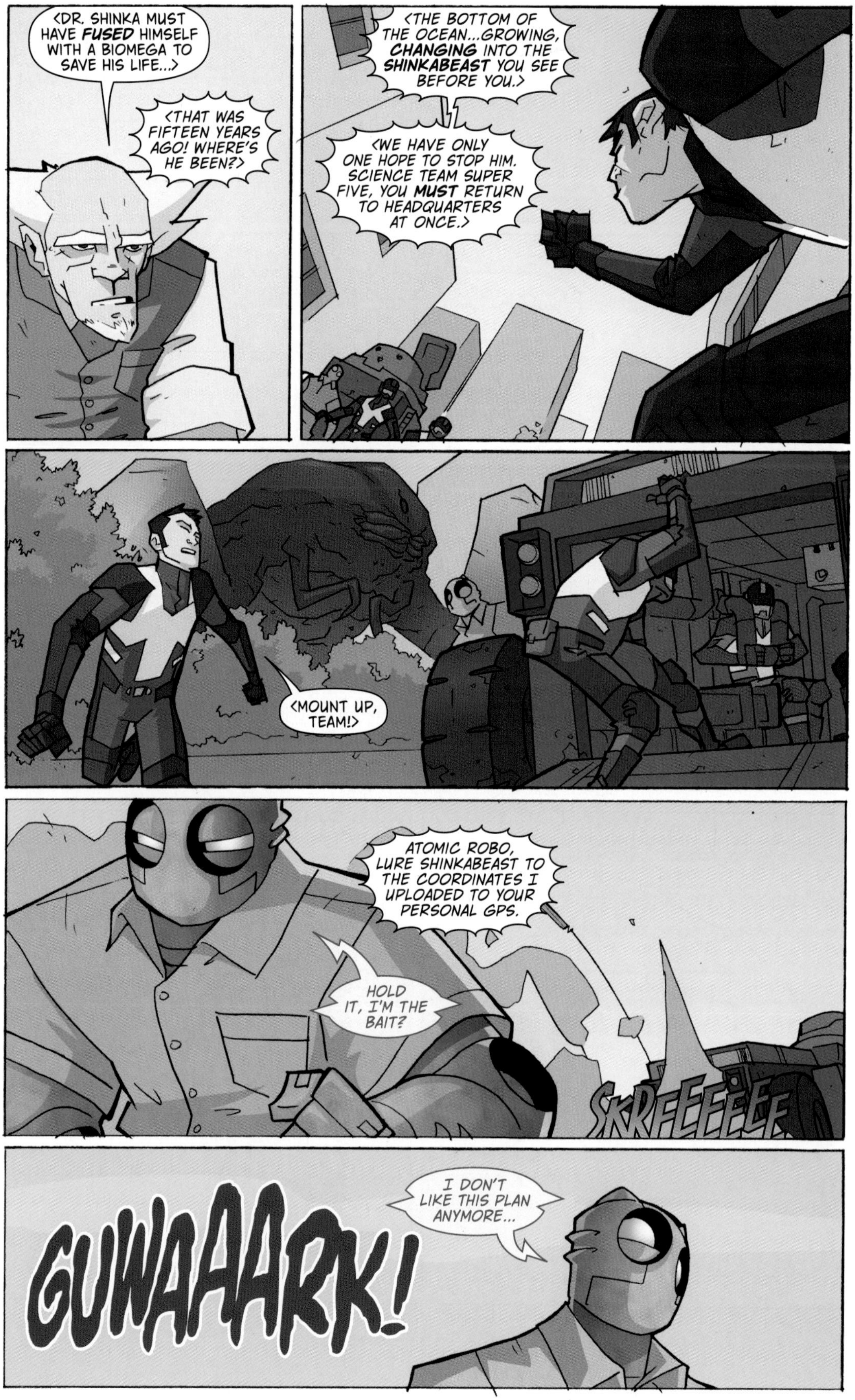
<DR. SHINKA MUST HAVE **FUSED** HIMSELF WITH A BIOMEGA TO SAVE HIS LIFE...>
<THAT WAS FIFTEEN YEARS AGO! WHERE'S HE BEEN?>
<THE BOTTOM OF THE OCEAN...GROWING, **CHANGING** INTO THE **SHINKABEAST** YOU SEE BEFORE YOU.>
<WE HAVE ONLY ONE HOPE TO STOP HIM. SCIENCE TEAM SUPER FIVE, YOU **MUST** RETURN TO HEADQUARTERS AT ONCE.>
<MOUNT UP, TEAM!>
ATOMIC ROBO, LURE SHINKABEAST TO THE COORDINATES I UPLOADED TO YOUR PERSONAL GPS.
HOLD IT, I'M THE BAIT?
SKREEEEEEF
GUWAAARK!
I DON'T LIKE THIS PLAN ANYMORE...

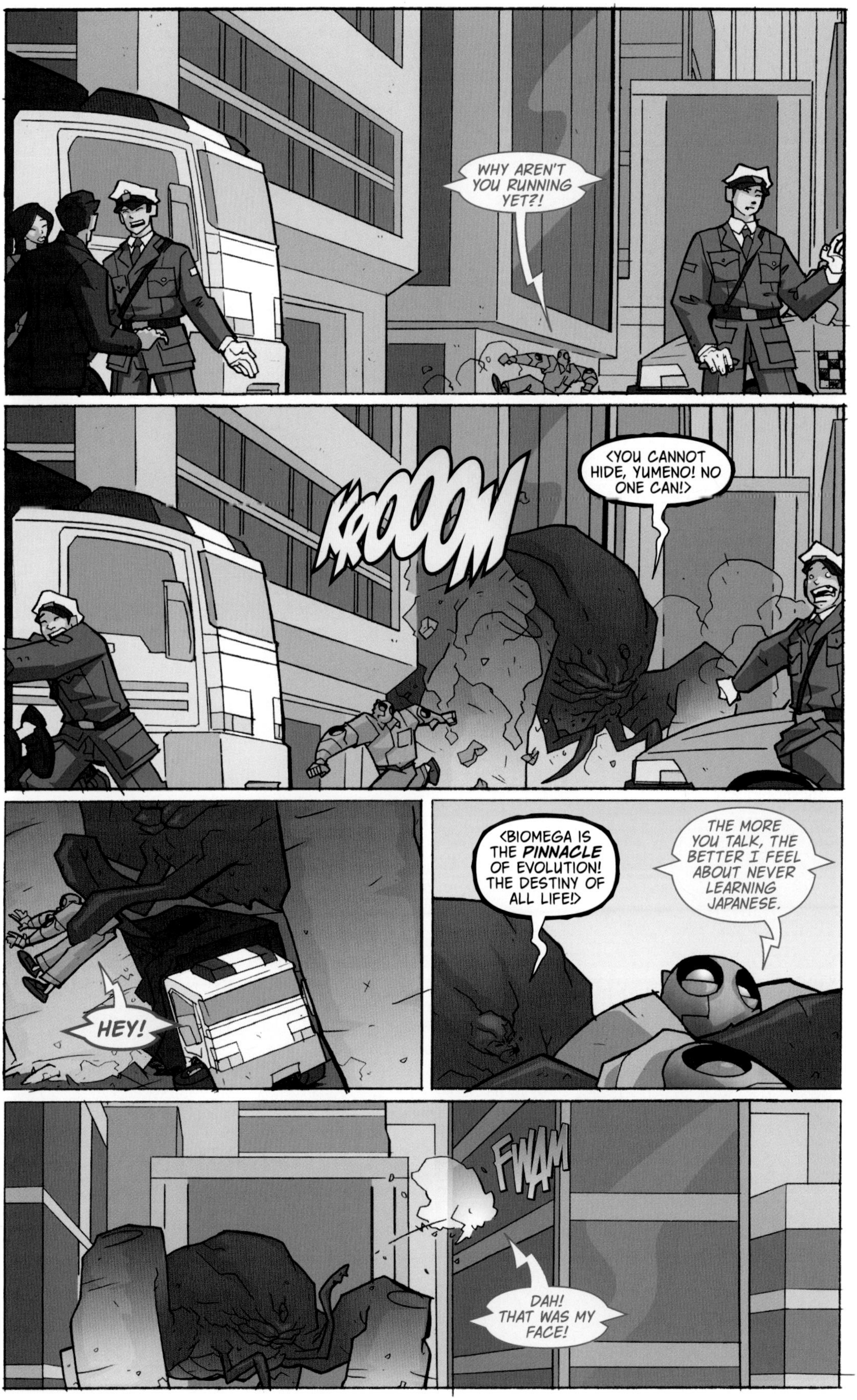
WHY AREN'T YOU RUNNING YET?!
KROOOM
<YOU CANNOT HIDE, YUMENO! NO ONE CAN!>
HEY!
<BIOMEGA IS THE **PINNACLE** OF EVOLUTION! THE DESTINY OF ALL LIFE!>
THE MORE YOU TALK, THE BETTER I FEEL ABOUT NEVER LEARNING JAPANESE.
FWAM
DAH! THAT WAS MY FACE!

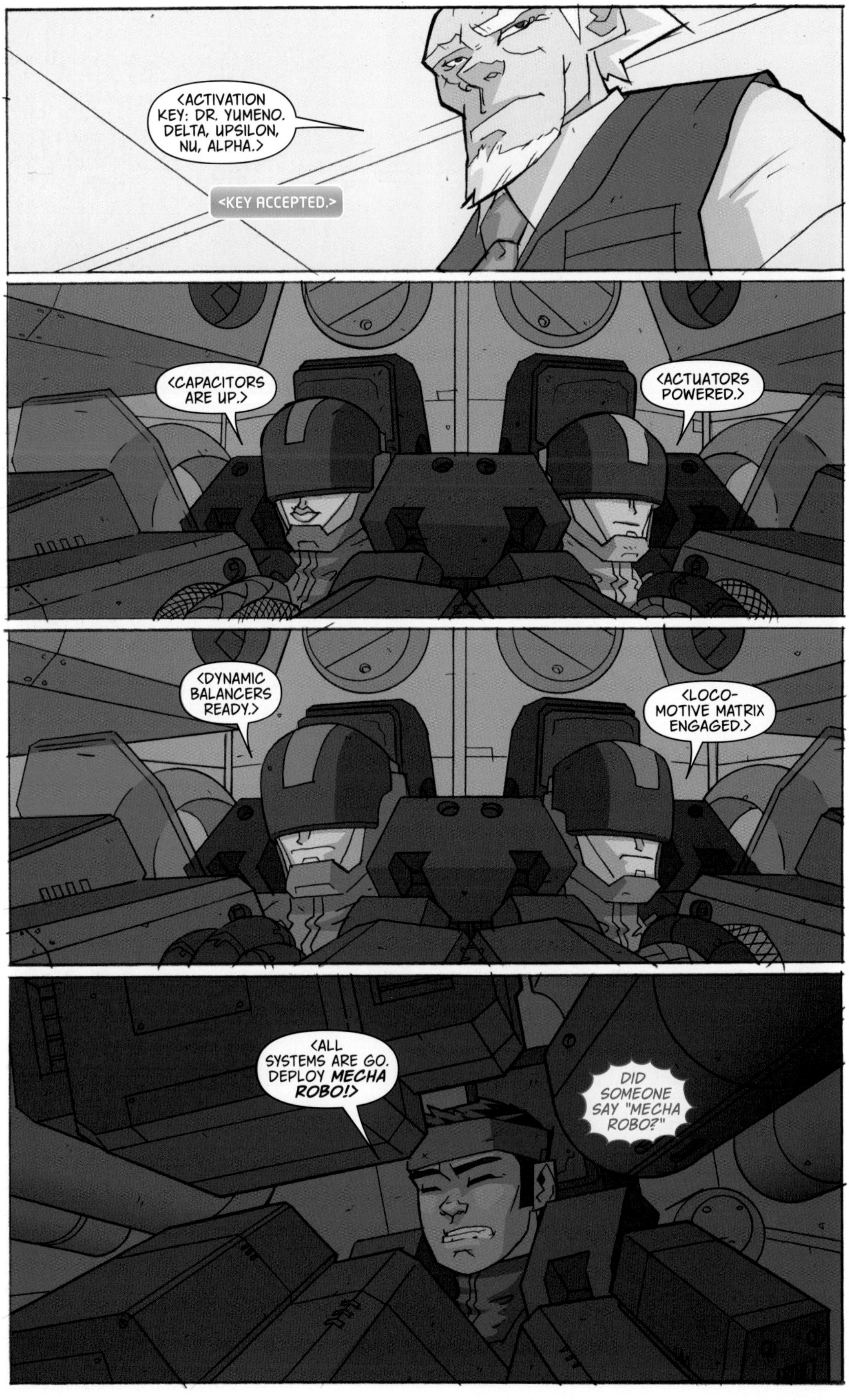
<ACTIVATION KEY: DR. YUMENO. DELTA, UPSILON, NU, ALPHA.>
<KEY ACCEPTED.>
<CAPACITORS ARE UP.>
<ACTUATORS POWERED.>
<DYNAMIC BALANCERS READY.>
<LOCO-MOTIVE MATRIX ENGAGED.>
<ALL SYSTEMS ARE GO. DEPLOY **MECHA ROBO!**>
DID SOMEONE SAY "MECHA ROBO?"

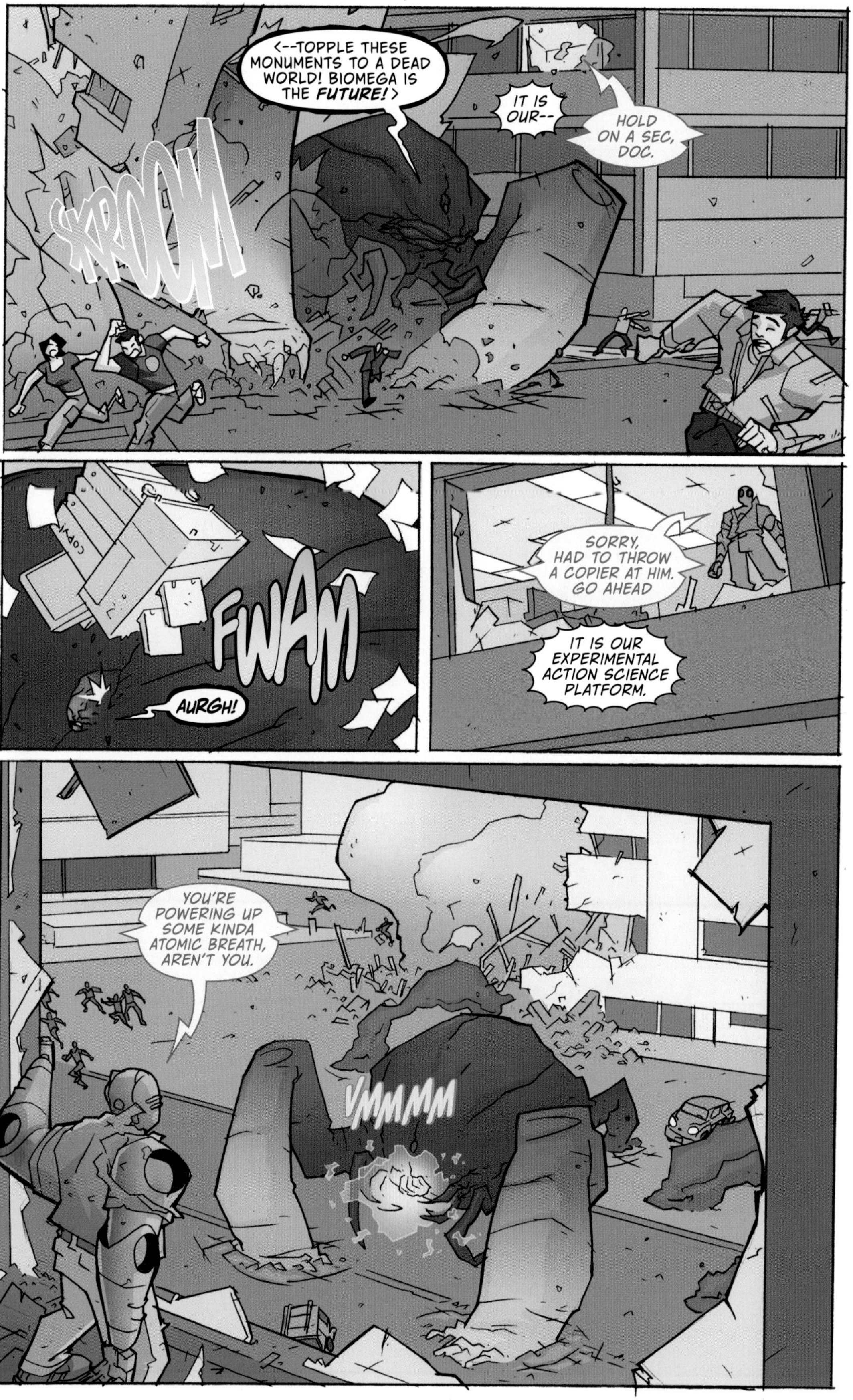
<--TOPPLE THESE MONUMENTS TO A DEAD WORLD! BIOMEGA IS THE *FUTURE!*>
IT IS OUR--
HOLD ON A SEC, DOC.
SKROOM
FWAM
AURGH!
SORRY, HAD TO THROW A COPIER AT HIM. GO AHEAD
IT IS OUR EXPERIMENTAL ACTION SCIENCE PLATFORM.
YOU'RE POWERING UP SOME KINDA ATOMIC BREATH, AREN'T YOU.
VMMMM

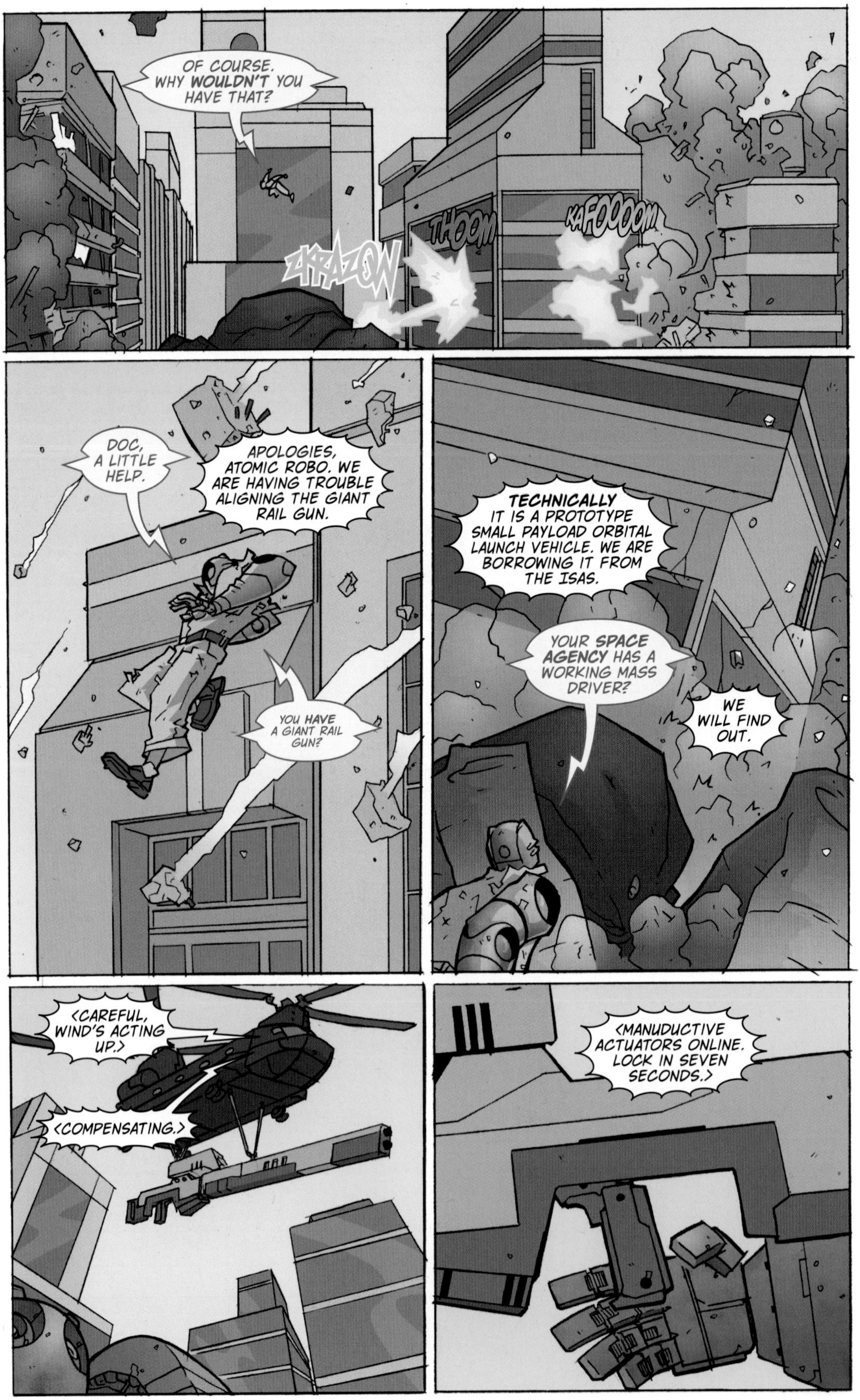
OF COURSE. WHY WOULDN'T YOU HAVE THAT?
ZKRAZOW
THOOM
KAFOOOOM
DOC, A LITTLE HELP.
APOLOGIES, ATOMIC ROBO. WE ARE HAVING TROUBLE ALIGNING THE GIANT RAIL GUN.
YOU HAVE A GIANT RAIL GUN?
TECHNICALLY IT IS A PROTOTYPE SMALL PAYLOAD ORBITAL LAUNCH VEHICLE. WE ARE BORROWING IT FROM THE ISAS.
YOUR SPACE AGENCY HAS A WORKING MASS DRIVER?
WE WILL FIND OUT.
<CAREFUL, WIND'S ACTING UP.>
<COMPENSATING.>
<MANUDUCTIVE ACTUATORS ONLINE. LOCK IN SEVEN SECONDS.>

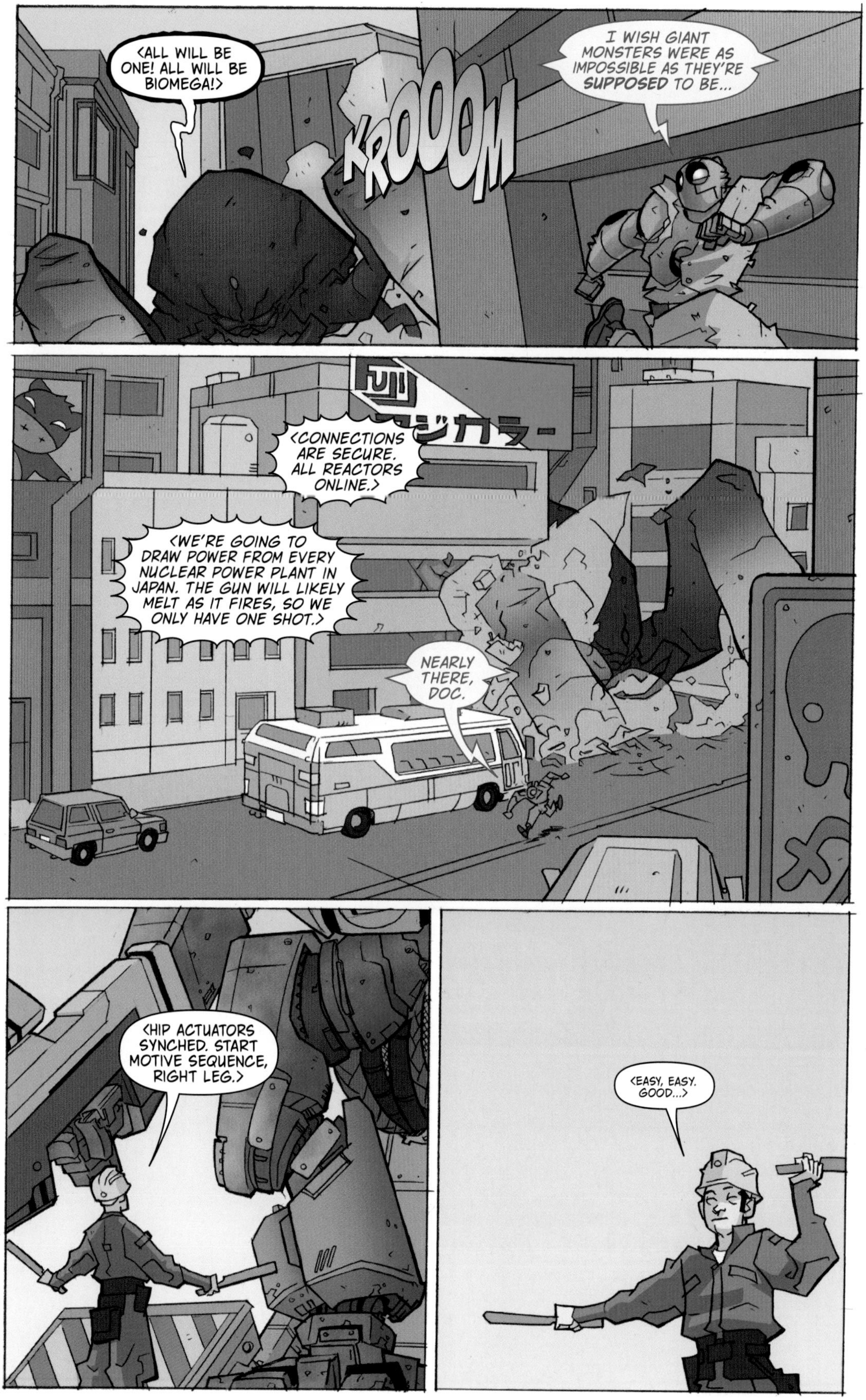

<ALL WILL BE ONE! ALL WILL BE BIOMEGA!>
KROOOM
I WISH GIANT MONSTERS WERE AS IMPOSSIBLE AS THEY'RE SUPPOSED TO BE...
FUJI
<CONNECTIONS ARE SECURE. ALL REACTORS ONLINE.>
<WE'RE GOING TO DRAW POWER FROM EVERY NUCLEAR POWER PLANT IN JAPAN. THE GUN WILL LIKELY MELT AS IT FIRES, SO WE ONLY HAVE ONE SHOT.>
NEARLY THERE, DOC.
<HIP ACTUATORS SYNCHED. START MOTIVE SEQUENCE, RIGHT LEG.>
<EASY, EASY. GOOD...>

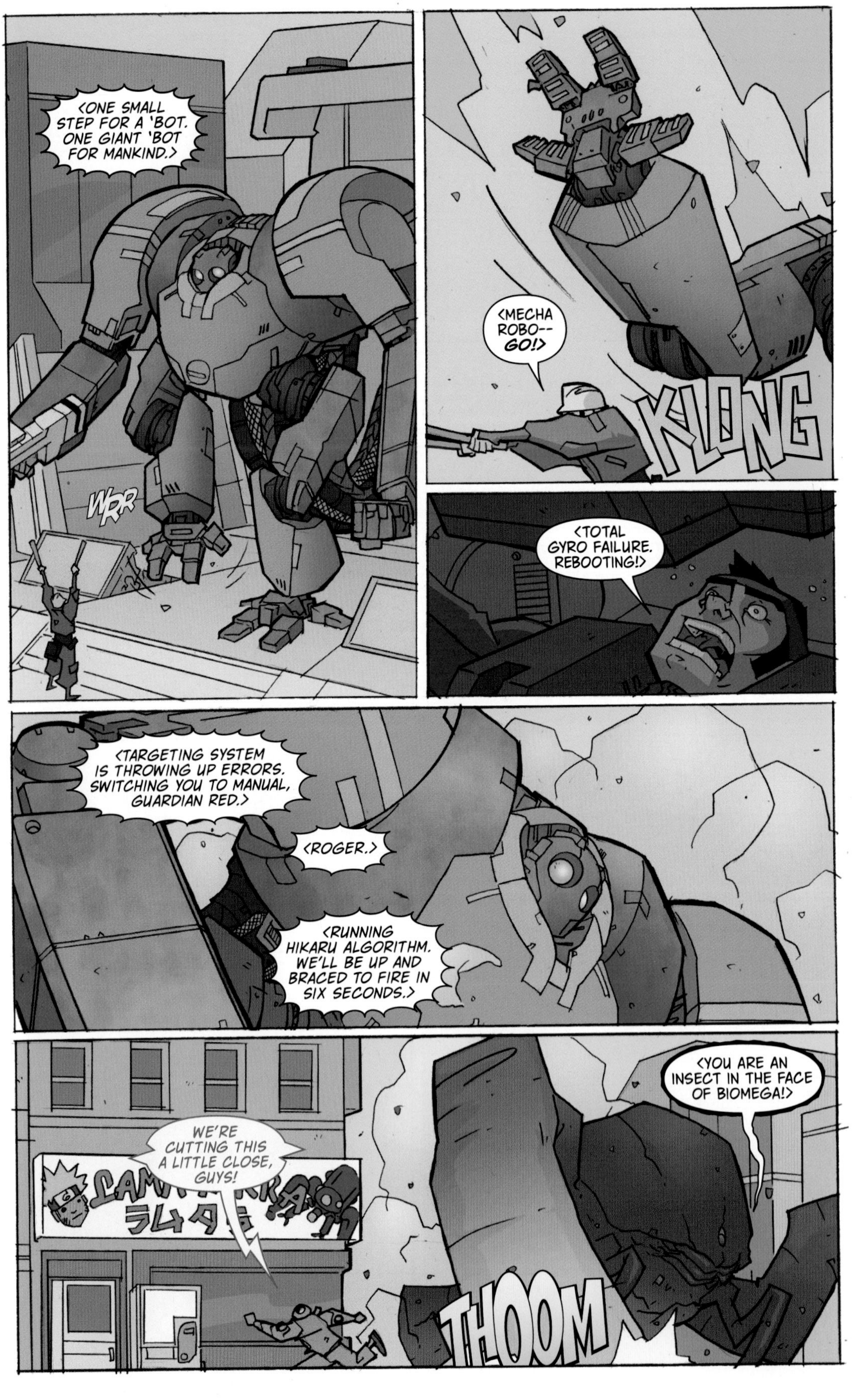

<ONE SMALL STEP FOR A 'BOT. ONE GIANT 'BOT FOR MANKIND.>
WRR
<MECHA ROBO-- GO!>
KLONG
<TOTAL GYRO FAILURE. REBOOTING!>
<TARGETING SYSTEM IS THROWING UP ERRORS. SWITCHING YOU TO MANUAL, GUARDIAN RED.>
<ROGER.>
<RUNNING HIKARU ALGORITHM. WE'LL BE UP AND BRACED TO FIRE IN SIX SECONDS.>
WE'RE CUTTING THIS A LITTLE CLOSE, GUYS!
<YOU ARE AN INSECT IN THE FACE OF BIOMEGA!>
THOOM

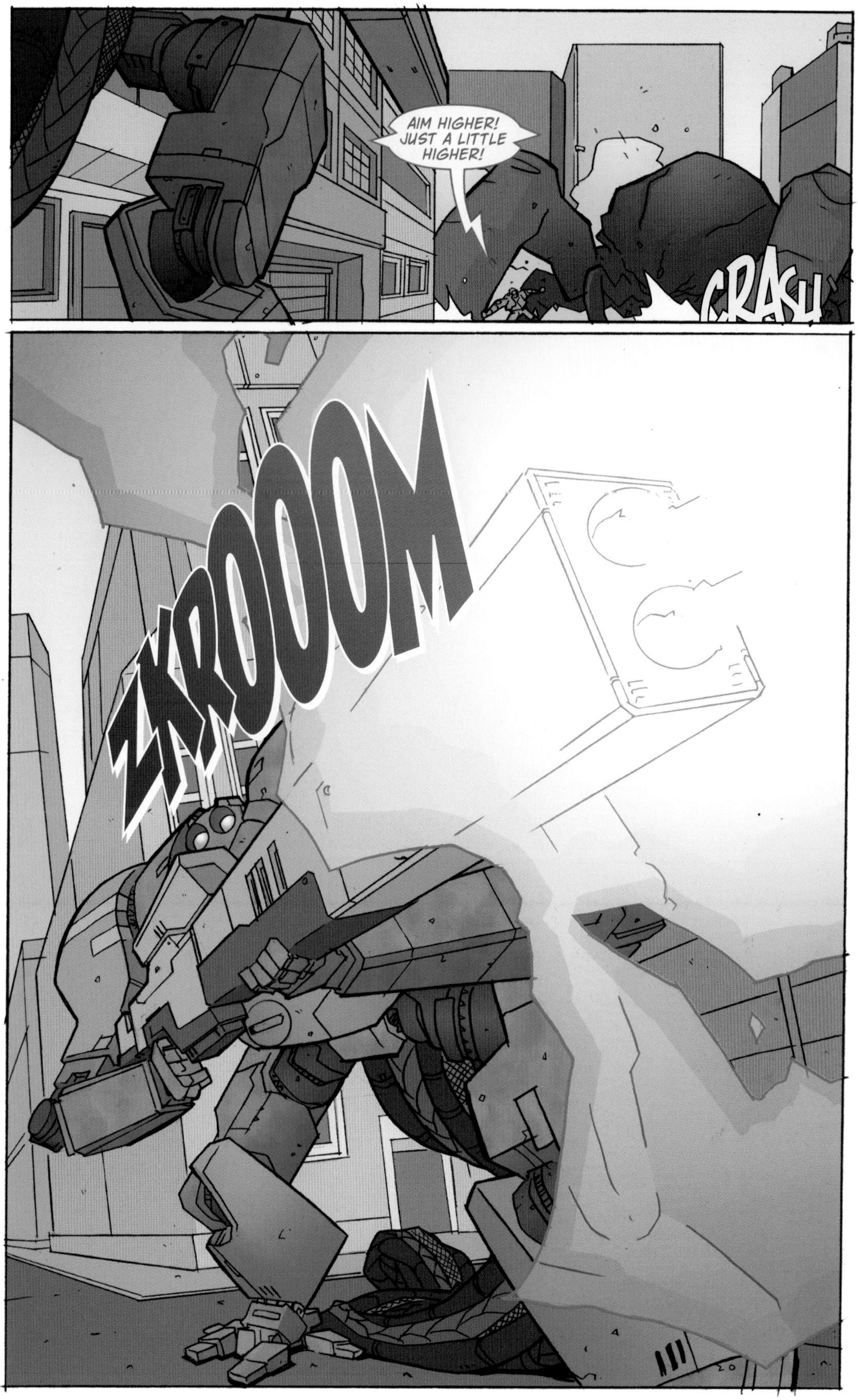
AIM HIGHER! JUST A LITTLE HIGHER!
CRASH
ZKROOOM

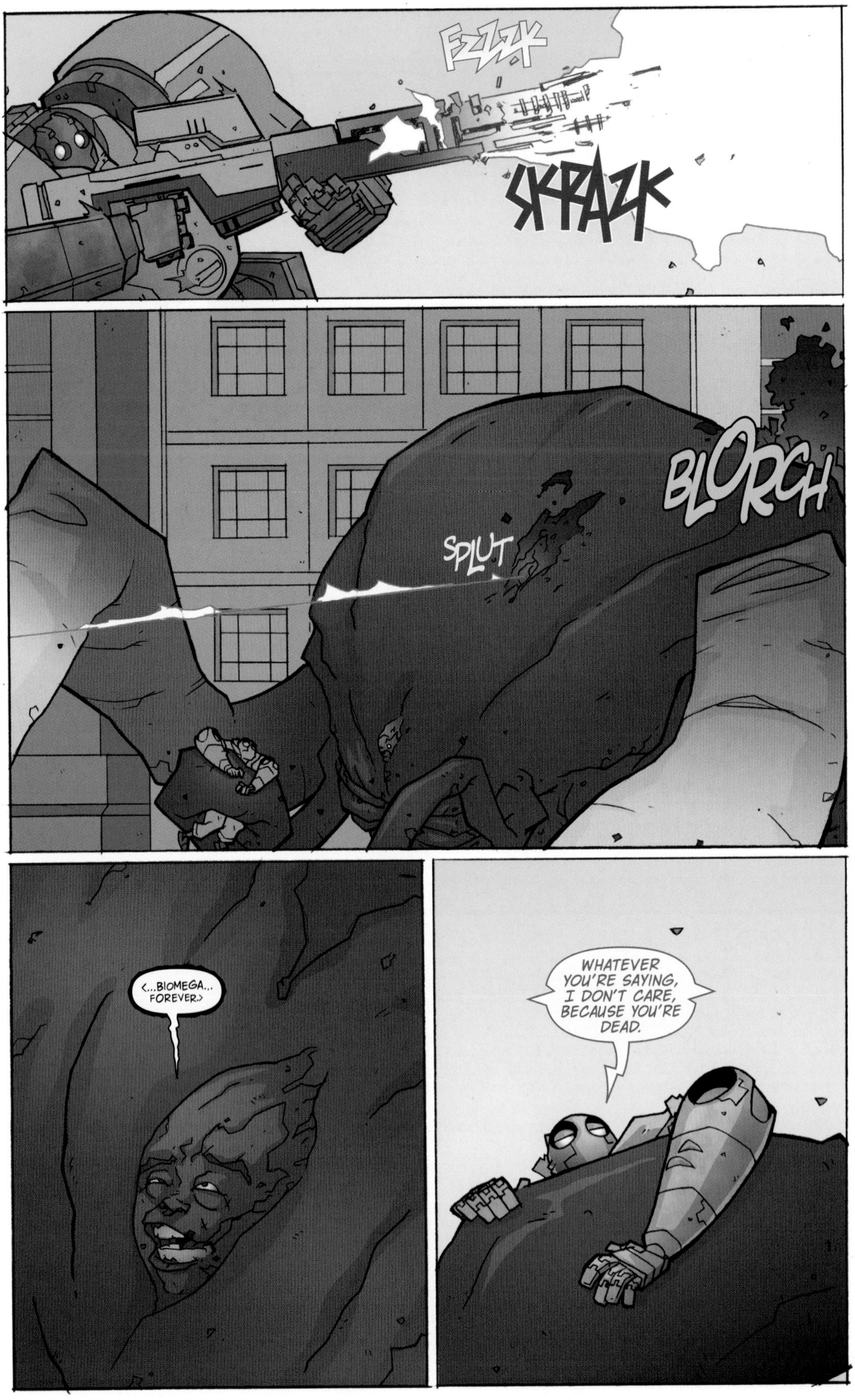
FZZZK
SKRAZK
SPLUT
BLORCH
<...BIOMEGA... FOREVER.>
WHATEVER YOU'RE SAYING, I DON'T CARE, BECAUSE YOU'RE DEAD.

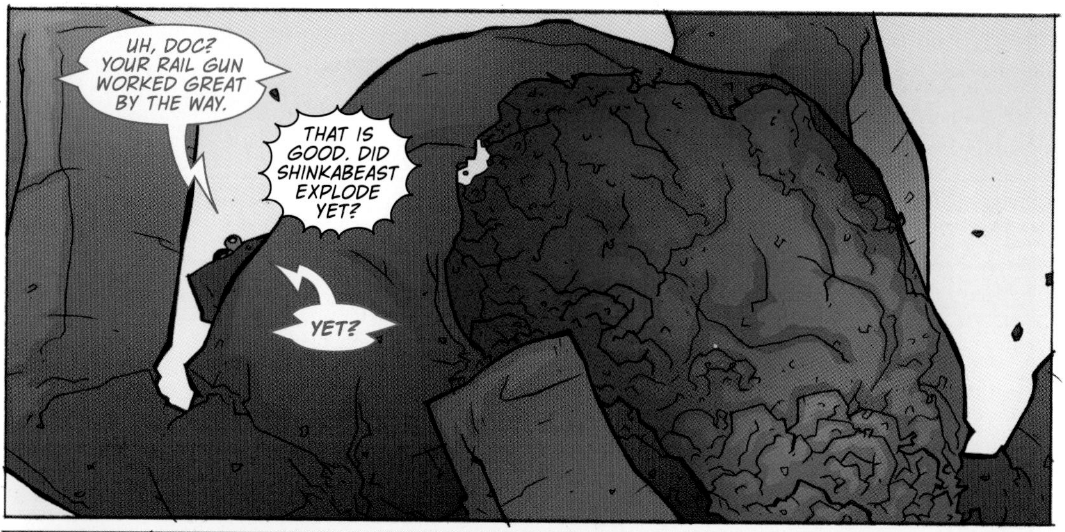
UH, DOC? YOUR RAIL GUN WORKED GREAT BY THE WAY.
THAT IS GOOD. DID SHINKABEAST EXPLODE YET?
YET?

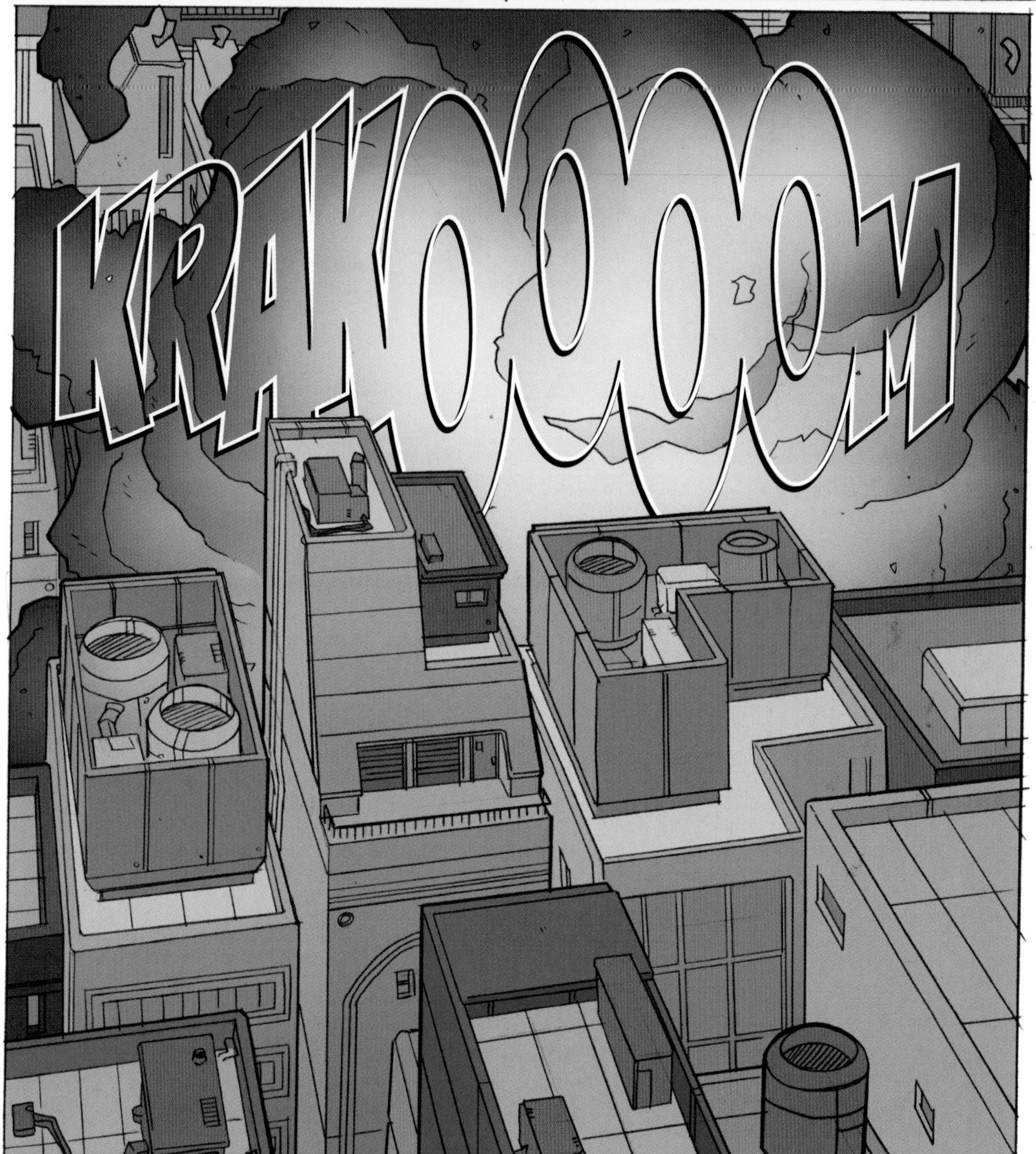
KRAKOOOOM

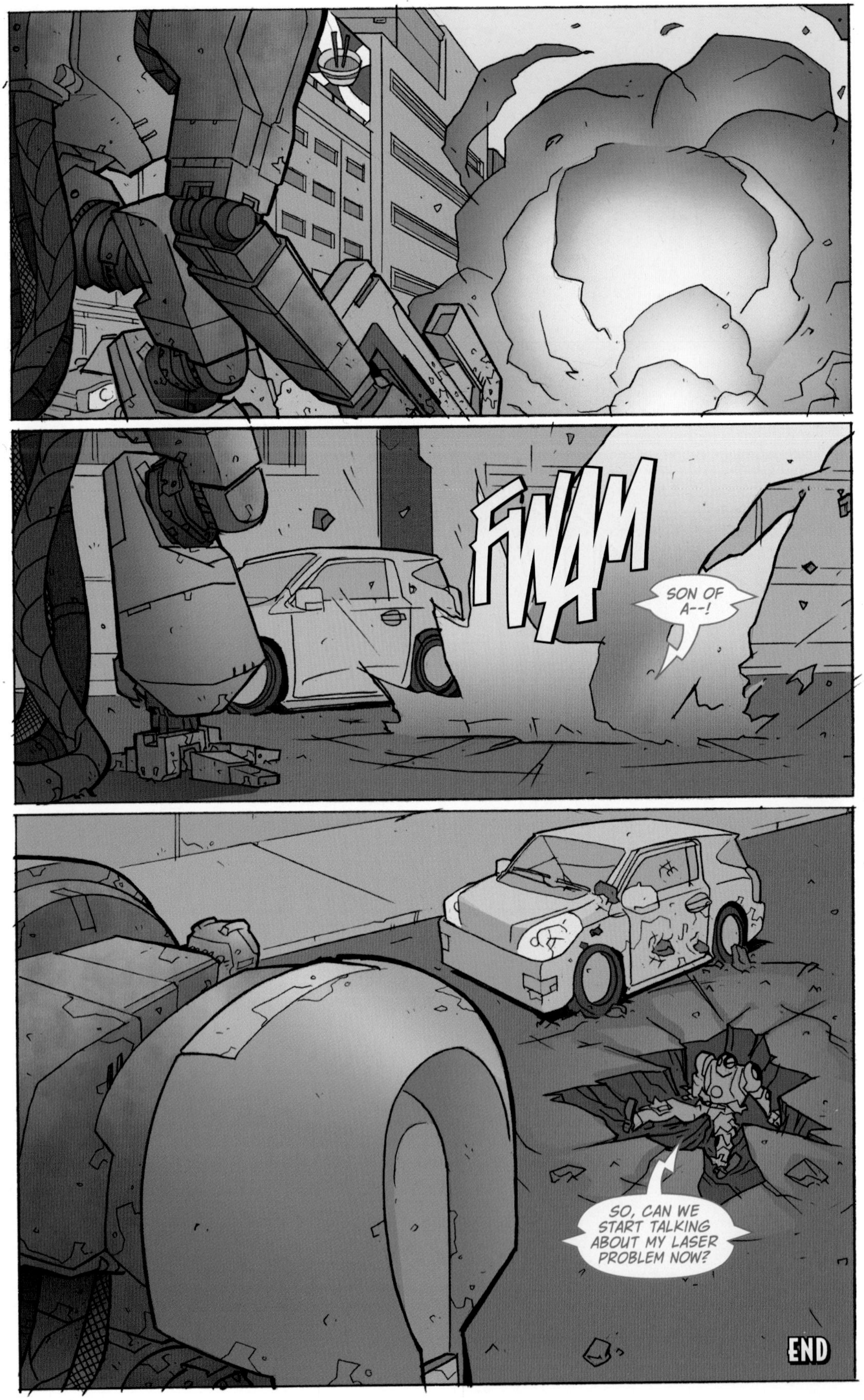
FWAM
SON OF A--!
SO, CAN WE START TALKING ABOUT MY LASER PROBLEM NOW?
END

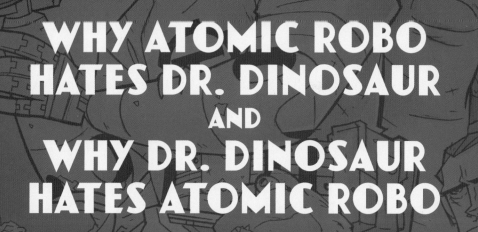

WHY ATOMIC ROBO HATES DR. DINOSAUR
AND
WHY DR. DINOSAUR HATES ATOMIC ROBO

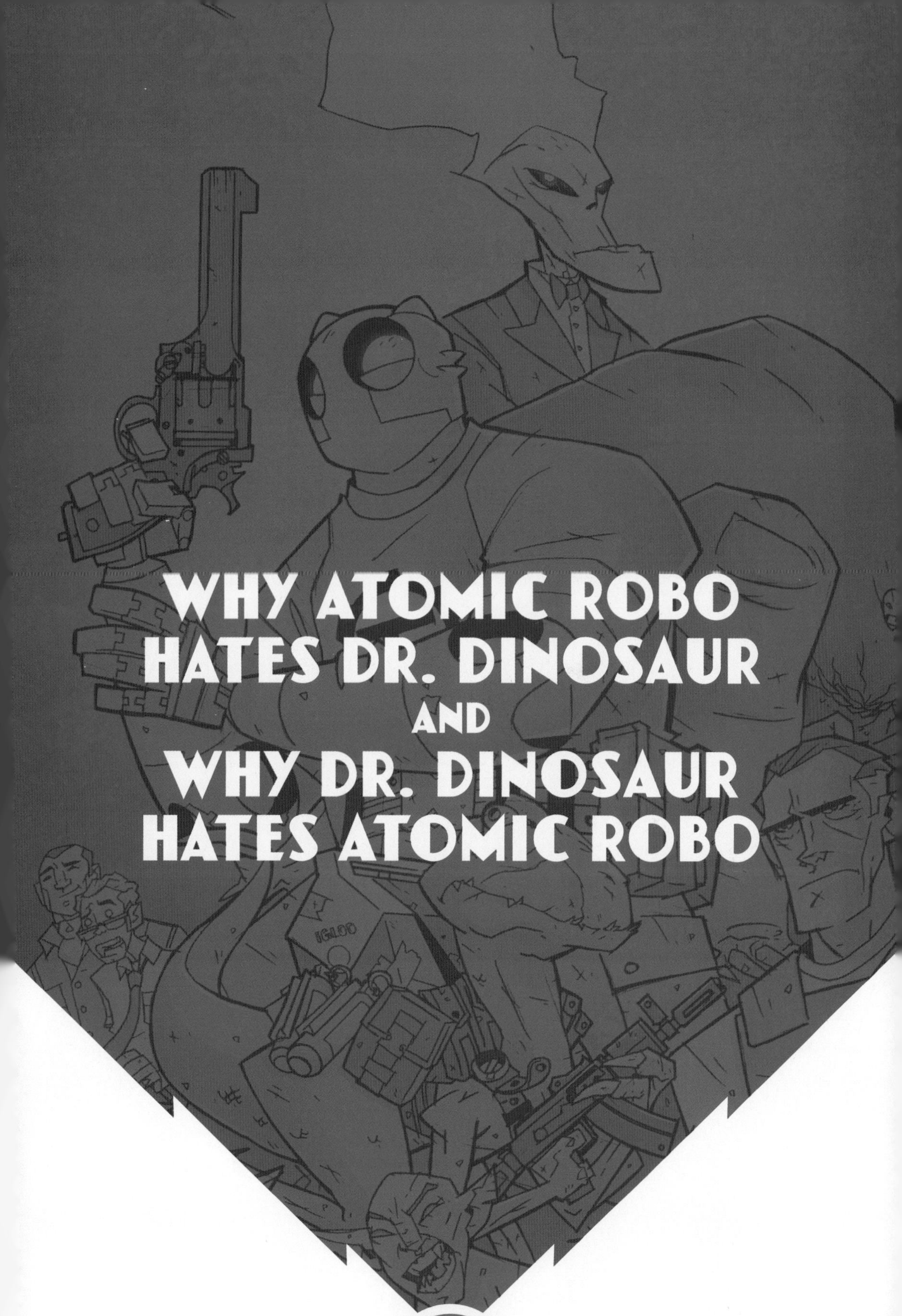

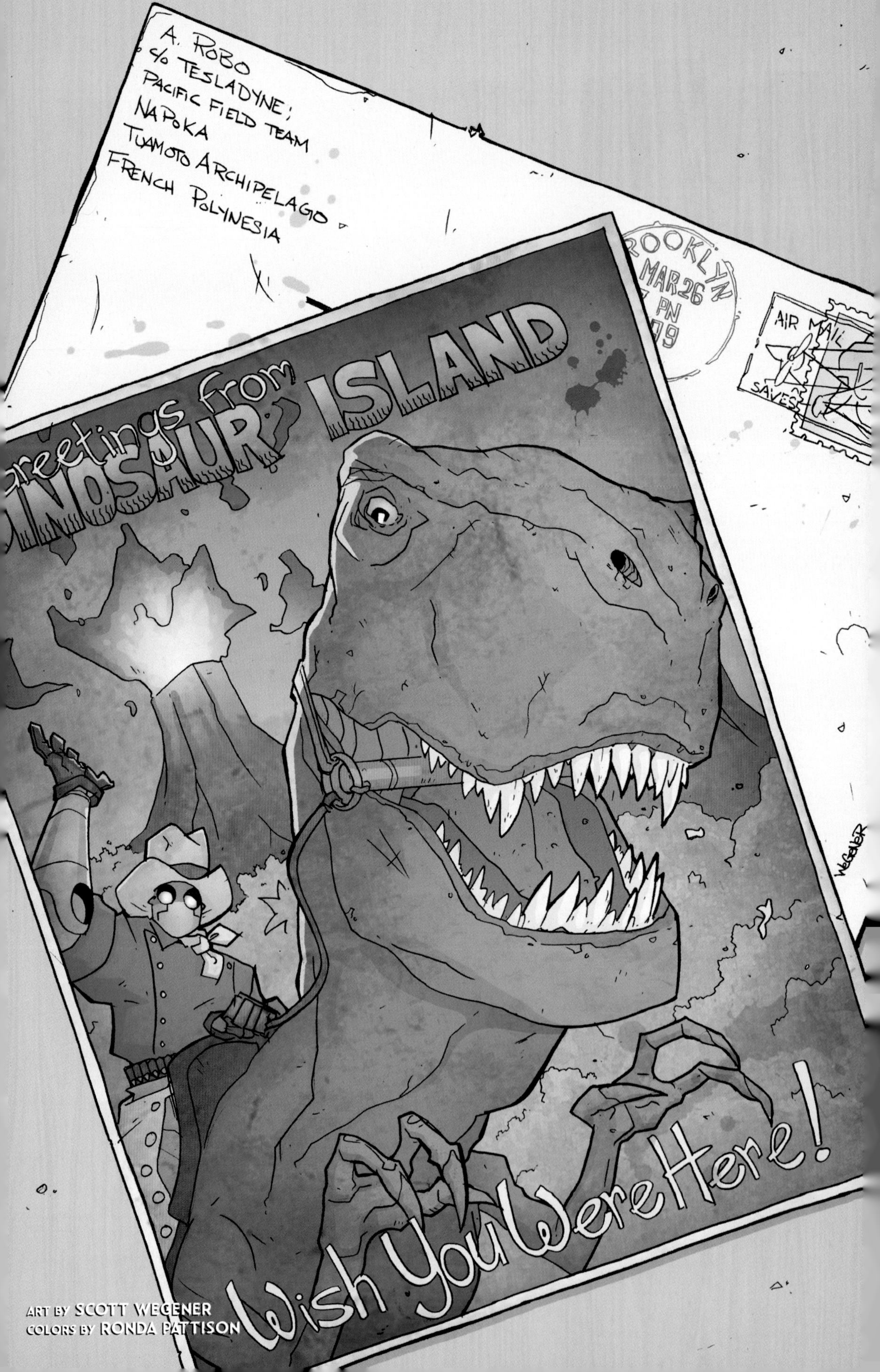
A. ROBO
c/o TESLADYNE;
PACIFIC FIELD TEAM
NAPOKA
TUAMOTO ARCHIPELAGO
FRENCH POLYNESIA
BROOKLYN
MAR 26
PM
AIR MAIL
SAVES
Greetings from
DINOSAUR ISLAND
WEGENER
Wish You Were Here!

ART BY SCOTT WEGENER
COLORS BY RONDA PATTISON

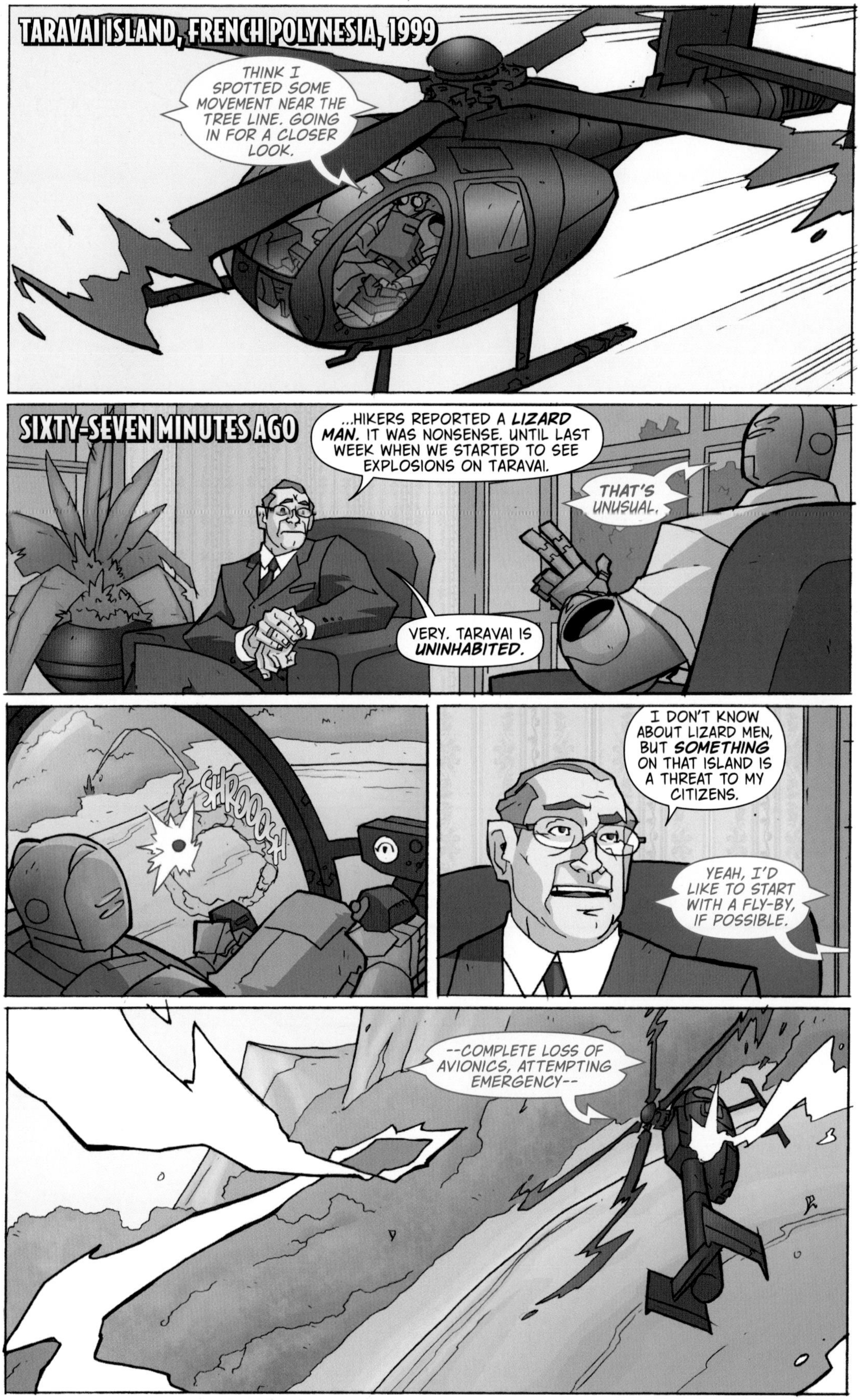
TARAVAI ISLAND, FRENCH POLYNESIA, 1999
THINK I SPOTTED SOME MOVEMENT NEAR THE TREE LINE. GOING IN FOR A CLOSER LOOK.
SIXTY-SEVEN MINUTES AGO
...HIKERS REPORTED A LIZARD MAN. IT WAS NONSENSE. UNTIL LAST WEEK WHEN WE STARTED TO SEE EXPLOSIONS ON TARAVAI.
THAT'S UNUSUAL.
VERY. TARAVAI IS UNINHABITED.
SHROOOOM
I DON'T KNOW ABOUT LIZARD MEN, BUT SOMETHING ON THAT ISLAND IS A THREAT TO MY CITIZENS.
YEAH, I'D LIKE TO START WITH A FLY-BY, IF POSSIBLE.
--COMPLETE LOSS OF AVIONICS, ATTEMPTING EMERGENCY--

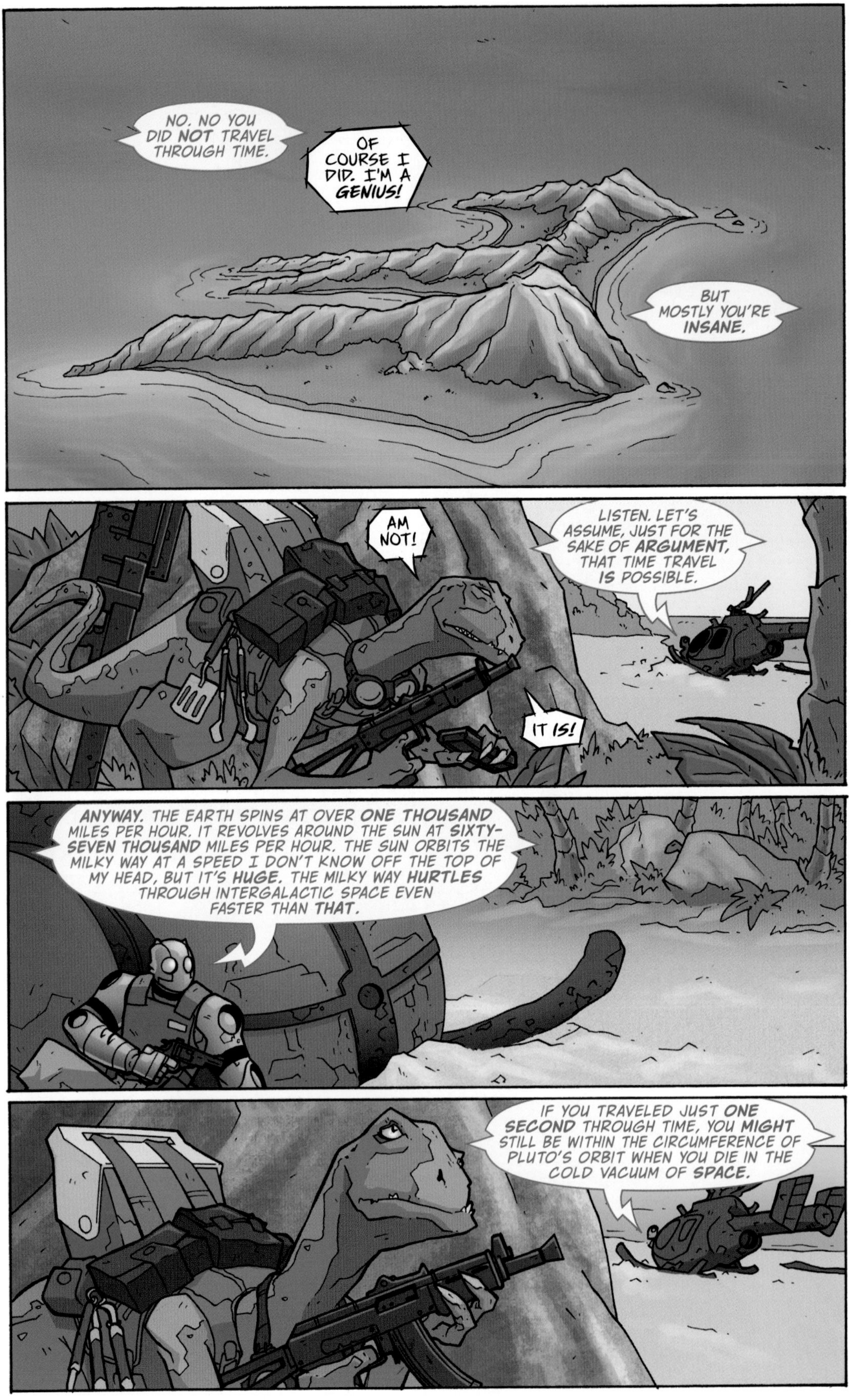
NO. NO YOU DID NOT TRAVEL THROUGH TIME.
OF COURSE I DID. I'M A GENIUS!
BUT MOSTLY YOU'RE INSANE.
AM NOT!
LISTEN. LET'S ASSUME, JUST FOR THE SAKE OF ARGUMENT, THAT TIME TRAVEL IS POSSIBLE.
IT IS!
ANYWAY. THE EARTH SPINS AT OVER ONE THOUSAND MILES PER HOUR. IT REVOLVES AROUND THE SUN AT SIXTY-SEVEN THOUSAND MILES PER HOUR. THE SUN ORBITS THE MILKY WAY AT A SPEED I DON'T KNOW OFF THE TOP OF MY HEAD, BUT IT'S HUGE. THE MILKY WAY HURTLES THROUGH INTERGALACTIC SPACE EVEN FASTER THAN THAT.
IF YOU TRAVELED JUST ONE SECOND THROUGH TIME, YOU MIGHT STILL BE WITHIN THE CIRCUMFERENCE OF PLUTO'S ORBIT WHEN YOU DIE IN THE COLD VACUUM OF SPACE.

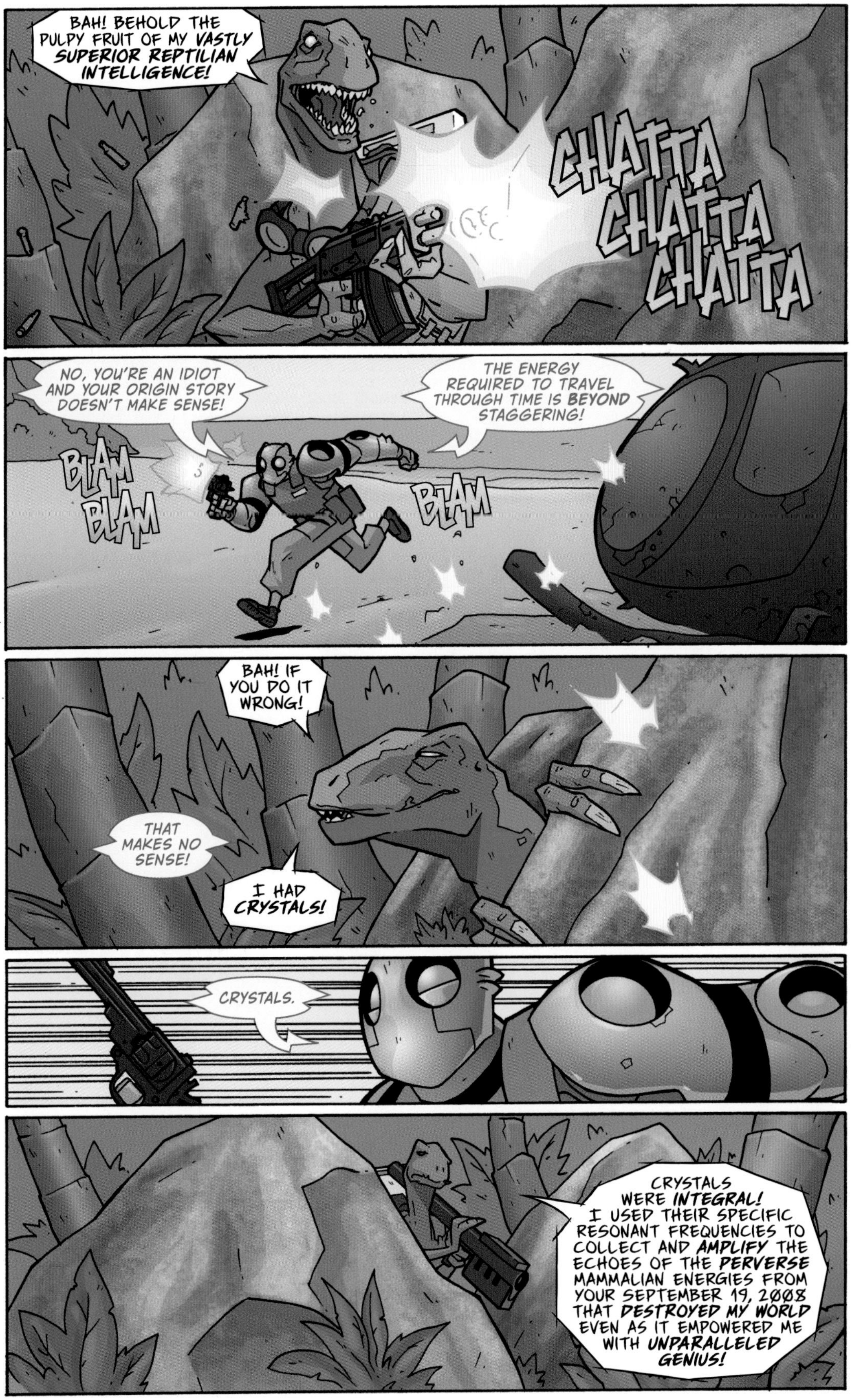

BAH! BEHOLD THE PULPY FRUIT OF MY VASTLY SUPERIOR REPTILIAN INTELLIGENCE!
CHATTA CHATTA CHATTA
NO, YOU'RE AN IDIOT AND YOUR ORIGIN STORY DOESN'T MAKE SENSE!
THE ENERGY REQUIRED TO TRAVEL THROUGH TIME IS BEYOND STAGGERING!
BLAM BLAM
BLAM
BAH! IF YOU DO IT WRONG!
THAT MAKES NO SENSE!
I HAD CRYSTALS!
CRYSTALS.
CRYSTALS WERE INTEGRAL! I USED THEIR SPECIFIC RESONANT FREQUENCIES TO COLLECT AND AMPLIFY THE ECHOES OF THE PERVERSE MAMMALIAN ENERGIES FROM YOUR SEPTEMBER 19, 2008 THAT DESTROYED MY WORLD EVEN AS IT EMPOWERED ME WITH UNPARALLELED GENIUS!

YOU KNOW YOU'RE ABOUT TEN YEARS TOO SOON, RIGHT?
TIME ENOUGH TO ENACT MY BRILLIANT MASTER PLAN! I'M A GENIUS, NOT AN IDIOT!
SO, MAMMAL ENERGIES TRAVELED BACKWARDS THROUGH TIME AND KILLED THE DINOSAURS BUT SOMEHOW MUTATED YOU INTO A SUPER GENIUS, THUS ALLOWING YOU TO FIGURE ALL THIS OUT, AND THEN TO CONSTRUCT A TIME MACHINE OUT OF WHAT I CAN ONLY ASSUME TO BE FRONDS AND ROCKS.
AND CRYSTALS!
SHROOOOOOSH
BOOM
DO YOU HAVE ANY IDEA HOW MANY WAYS THAT'S STUPID?
HERE'S ONE: YOU SPEAK ENGLISH!

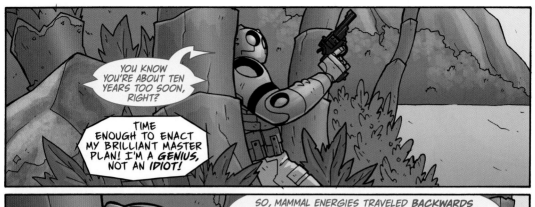

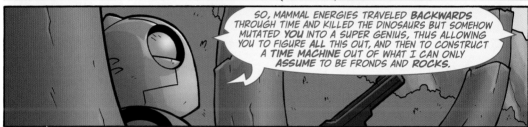

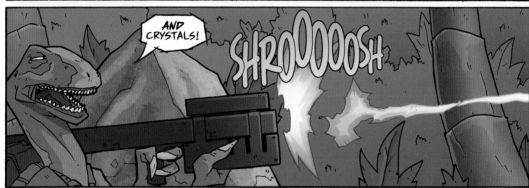

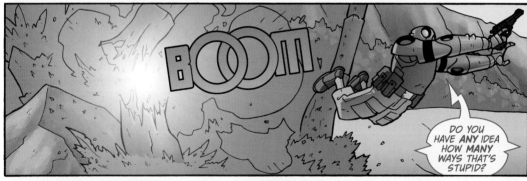

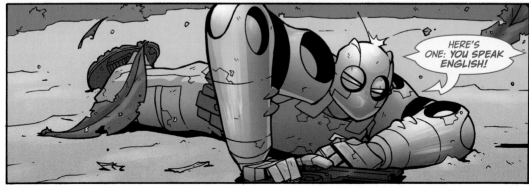

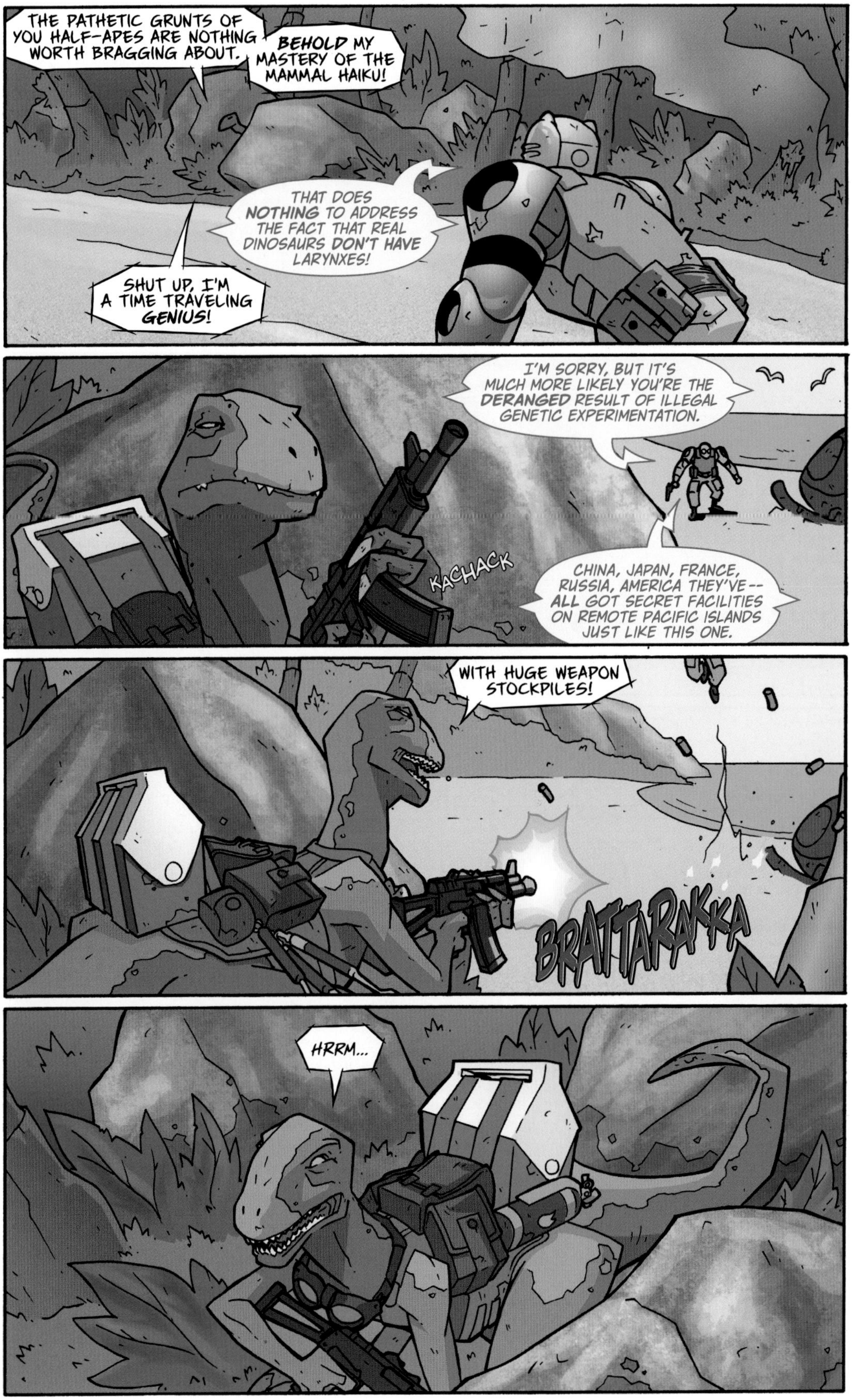
THE PATHETIC GRUNTS OF YOU HALF-APES ARE NOTHING WORTH BRAGGING ABOUT.
BEHOLD MY MASTERY OF THE MAMMAL HAIKU!
THAT DOES NOTHING TO ADDRESS THE FACT THAT REAL DINOSAURS DON'T HAVE LARYNXES!
SHUT UP, I'M A TIME TRAVELING GENIUS!
I'M SORRY, BUT IT'S MUCH MORE LIKELY YOU'RE THE DERANGED RESULT OF ILLEGAL GENETIC EXPERIMENTATION.
KACHACK
CHINA, JAPAN, FRANCE, RUSSIA, AMERICA THEY'VE-- ALL GOT SECRET FACILITIES ON REMOTE PACIFIC ISLANDS JUST LIKE THIS ONE.
WITH HUGE WEAPON STOCKPILES!
BRATTARAKKA
HRRM...

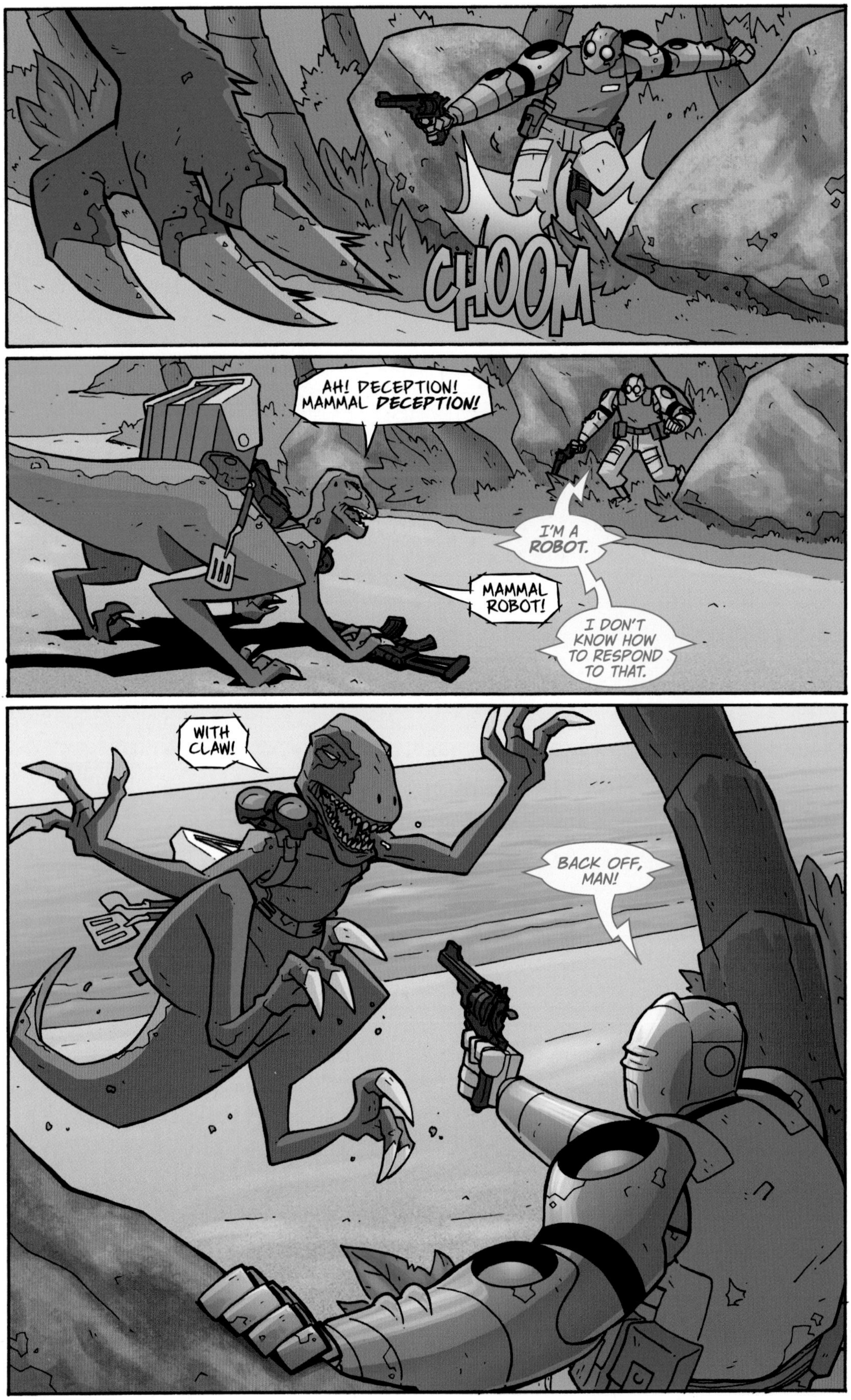
CHOOM
AH! DECEPTION! MAMMAL DECEPTION!
I'M A ROBOT.
MAMMAL ROBOT!
I DON'T KNOW HOW TO RESPOND TO THAT.
WITH CLAW!
BACK OFF, MAN!

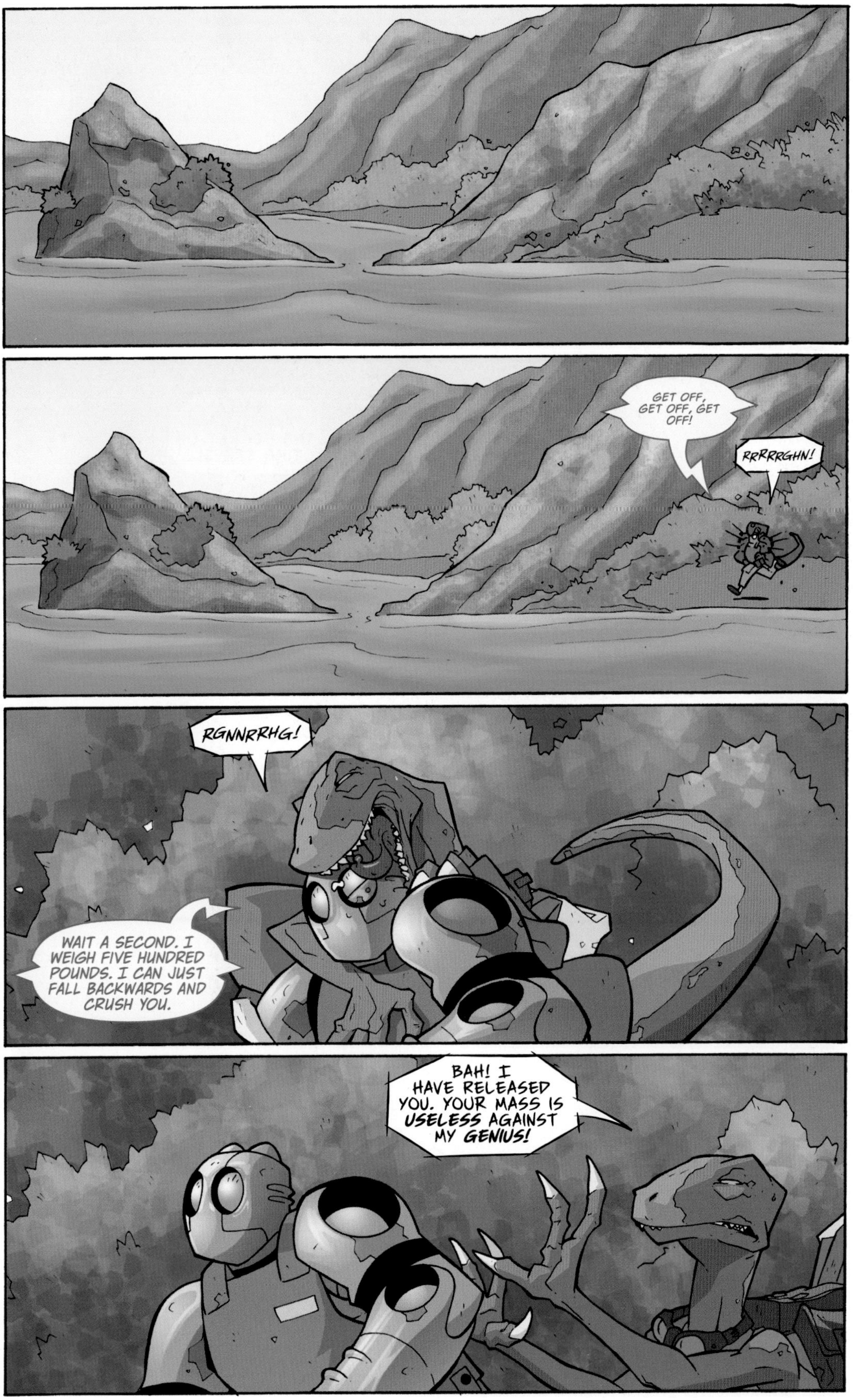
GET OFF, GET OFF, GET OFF!
RRRRRGHN!
RGNNRRHG!
WAIT A SECOND. I WEIGH FIVE HUNDRED POUNDS. I CAN JUST FALL BACKWARDS AND CRUSH YOU.
BAH! I HAVE RELEASED YOU. YOUR MASS IS USELESS AGAINST MY GENIUS!

OKAY, I'LL JUST HAVE TO USE BULLETS THEN.
WAIT! TAKE IT. TAKE THE SECRET OF TIME TRAVEL.
KTUNK
igloo
IF THIS IS FILLED WITH ROCKS, I AM GOING TO KILL YOU.

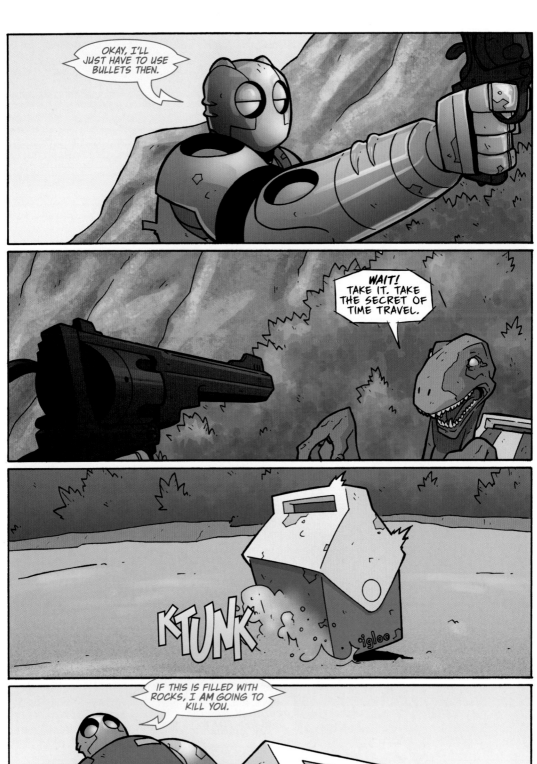

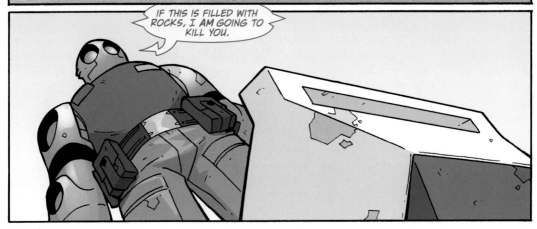

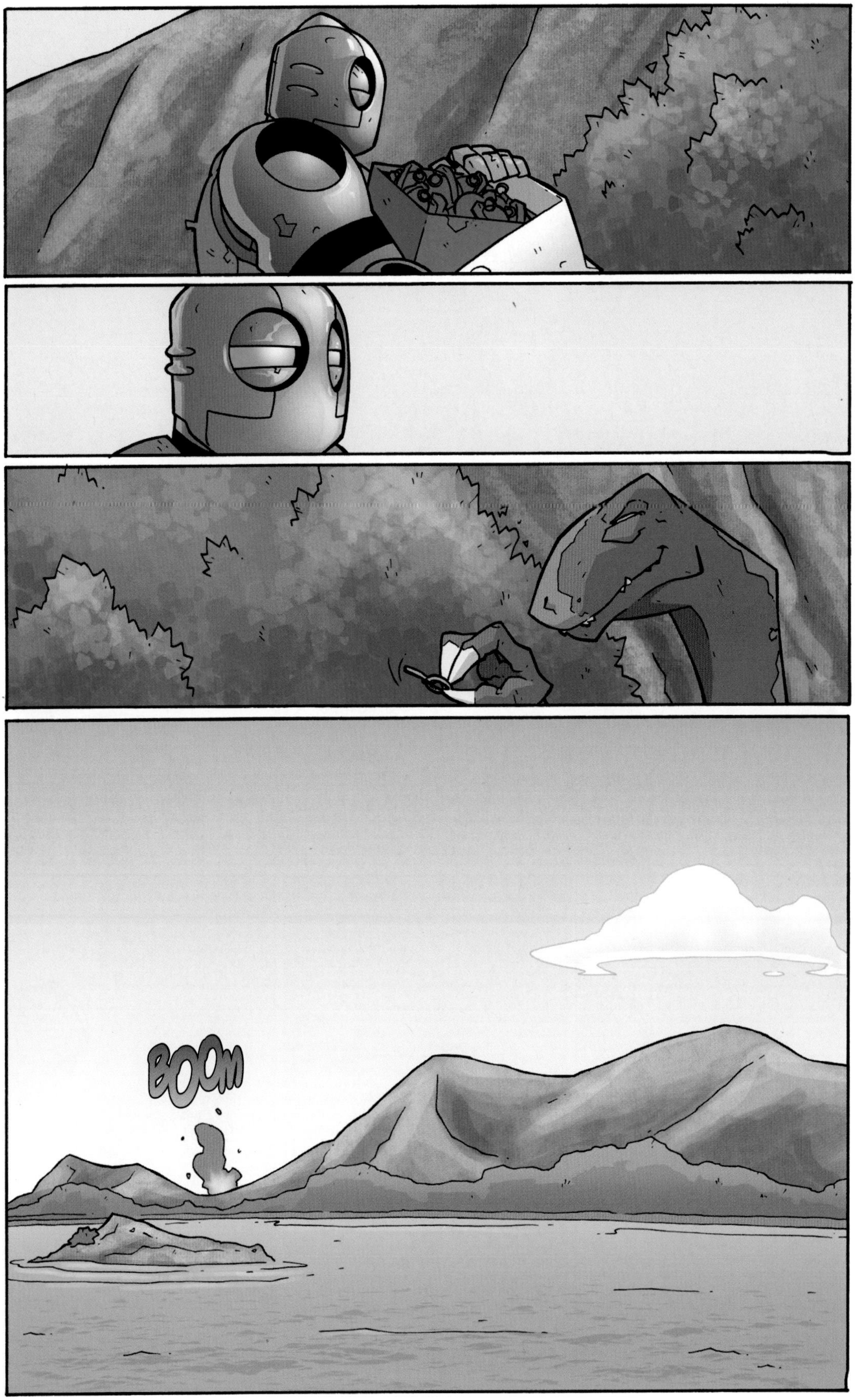
BOOM

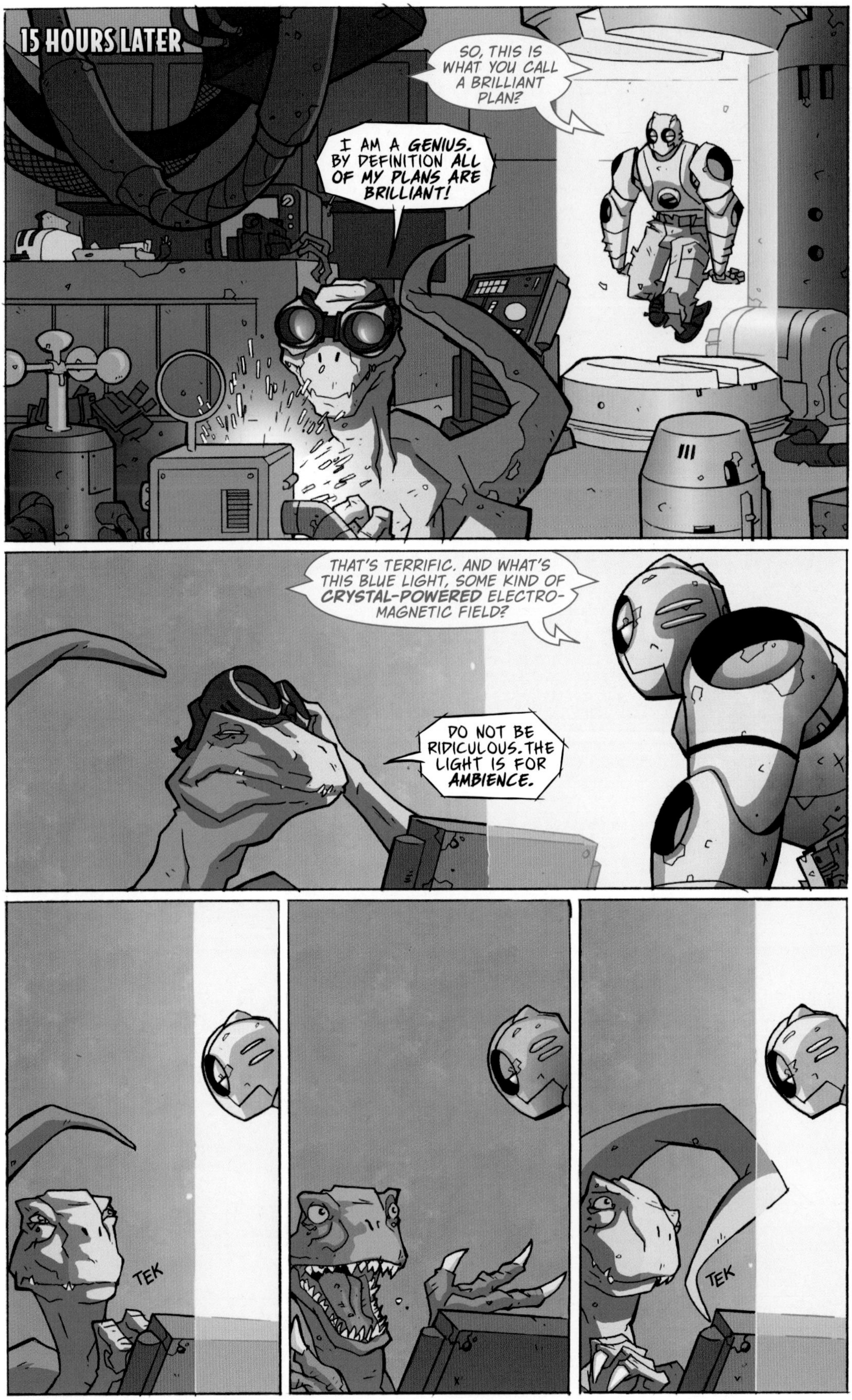
15 HOURS LATER
SO, THIS IS WHAT YOU CALL A BRILLIANT PLAN?
I AM A GENIUS. BY DEFINITION ALL OF MY PLANS ARE BRILLIANT!
THAT'S TERRIFIC. AND WHAT'S THIS BLUE LIGHT, SOME KIND OF CRYSTAL-POWERED ELECTRO-MAGNETIC FIELD?
DO NOT BE RIDICULOUS. THE LIGHT IS FOR AMBIENCE.
TEK
TEK

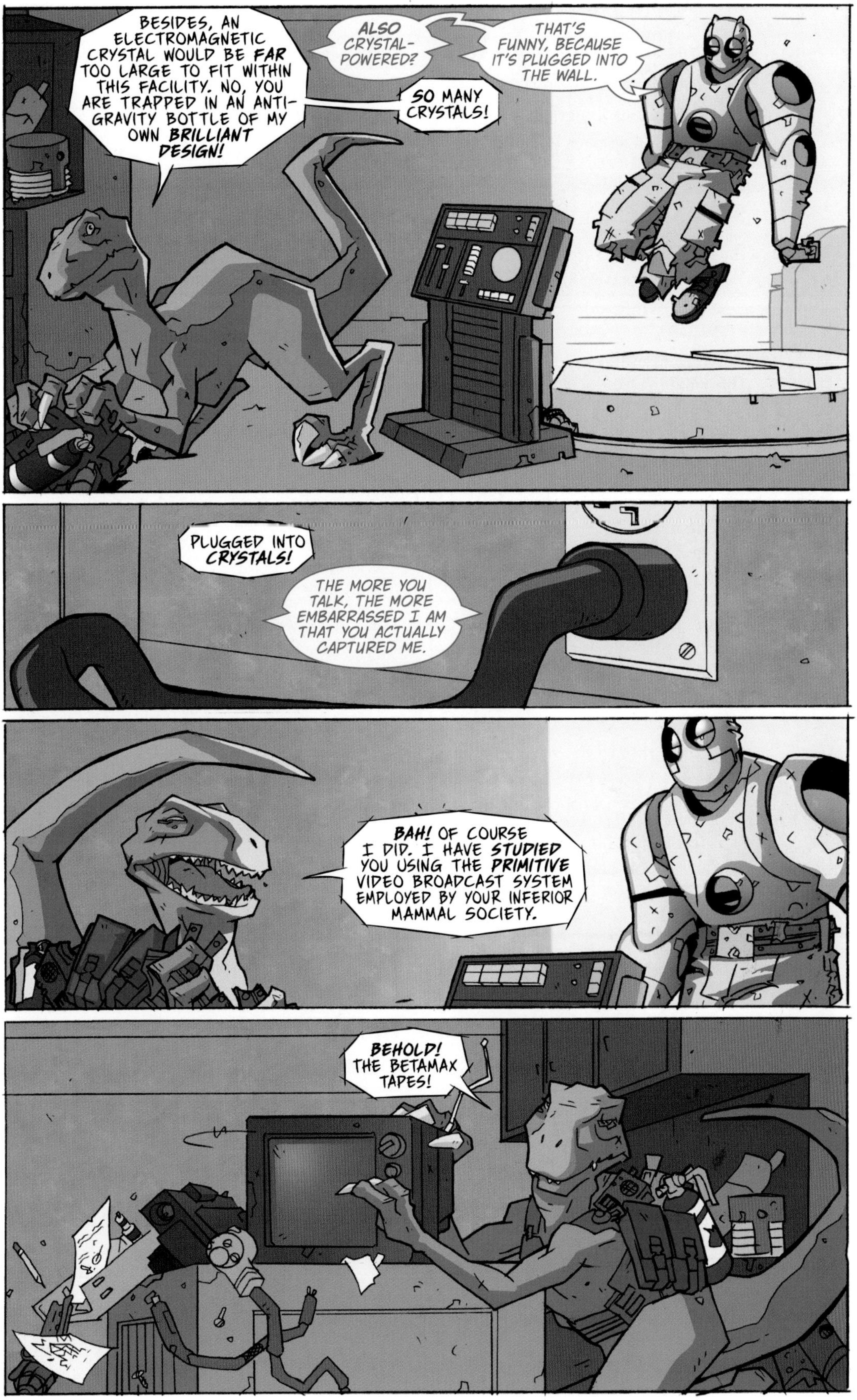
BESIDES, AN ELECTROMAGNETIC CRYSTAL WOULD BE FAR TOO LARGE TO FIT WITHIN THIS FACILITY. NO, YOU ARE TRAPPED IN AN ANTI-GRAVITY BOTTLE OF MY OWN BRILLIANT DESIGN!
ALSO CRYSTAL-POWERED?
THAT'S FUNNY, BECAUSE IT'S PLUGGED INTO THE WALL.
SO MANY CRYSTALS!
PLUGGED INTO CRYSTALS!
THE MORE YOU TALK, THE MORE EMBARRASSED I AM THAT YOU ACTUALLY CAPTURED ME.
BAH! OF COURSE I DID. I HAVE STUDIED YOU USING THE PRIMITIVE VIDEO BROADCAST SYSTEM EMPLOYED BY YOUR INFERIOR MAMMAL SOCIETY.
BEHOLD! THE BETAMAX TAPES!

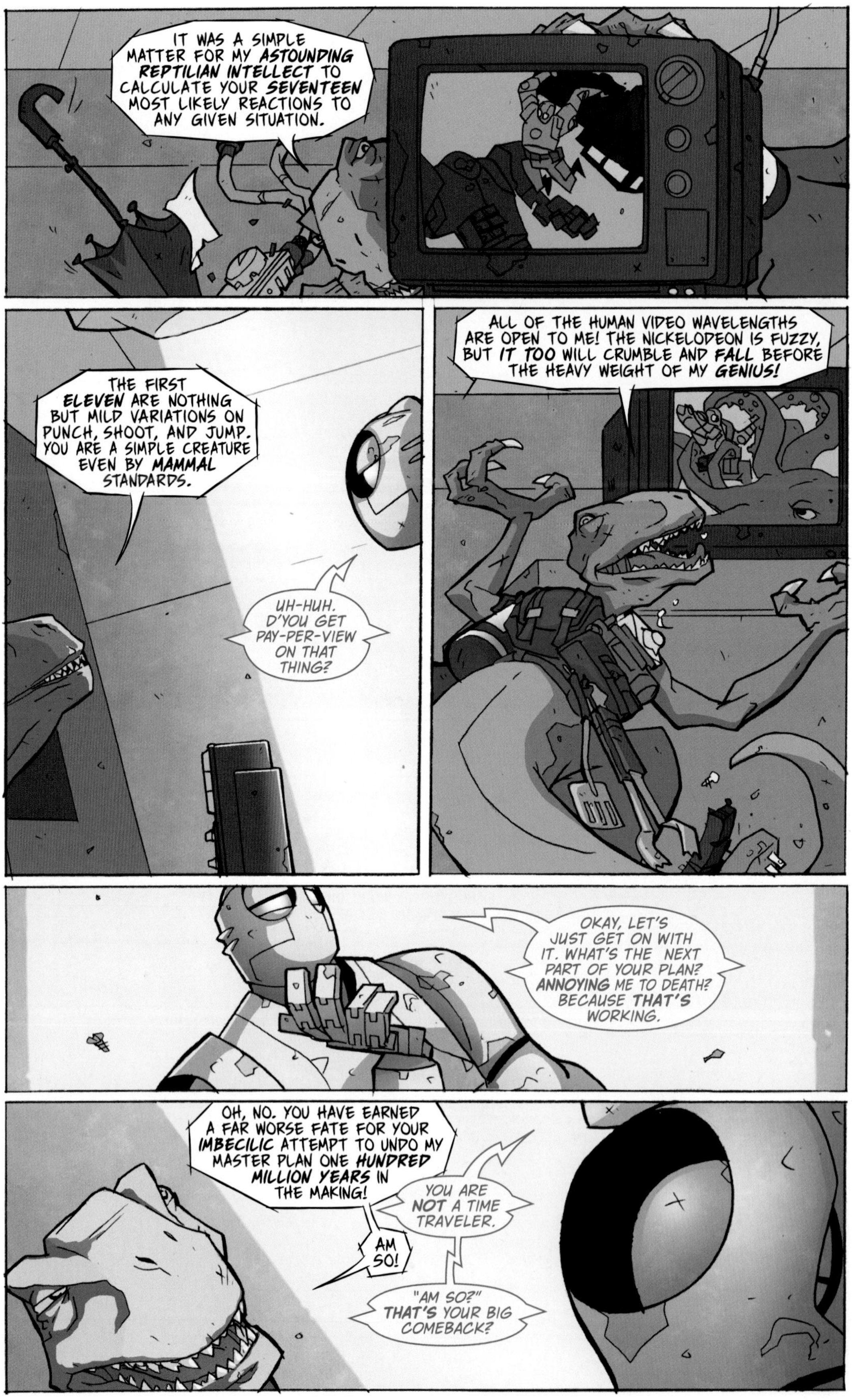
IT WAS A SIMPLE MATTER FOR MY ASTOUNDING REPTILIAN INTELLECT TO CALCULATE YOUR SEVENTEEN MOST LIKELY REACTIONS TO ANY GIVEN SITUATION.
THE FIRST ELEVEN ARE NOTHING BUT MILD VARIATIONS ON PUNCH, SHOOT, AND JUMP. YOU ARE A SIMPLE CREATURE EVEN BY MAMMAL STANDARDS.
UH-HUH. D'YOU GET PAY-PER-VIEW ON THAT THING?
ALL OF THE HUMAN VIDEO WAVELENGTHS ARE OPEN TO ME! THE NICKELODEON IS FUZZY, BUT IT TOO WILL CRUMBLE AND FALL BEFORE THE HEAVY WEIGHT OF MY GENIUS!
OKAY, LET'S JUST GET ON WITH IT. WHAT'S THE NEXT PART OF YOUR PLAN? ANNOYING ME TO DEATH? BECAUSE THAT'S WORKING.
OH, NO. YOU HAVE EARNED A FAR WORSE FATE FOR YOUR IMBECILIC ATTEMPT TO UNDO MY MASTER PLAN ONE HUNDRED MILLION YEARS IN THE MAKING!
YOU ARE NOT A TIME TRAVELER.
AM SO!
"AM SO?" THAT'S YOUR BIG COMEBACK?

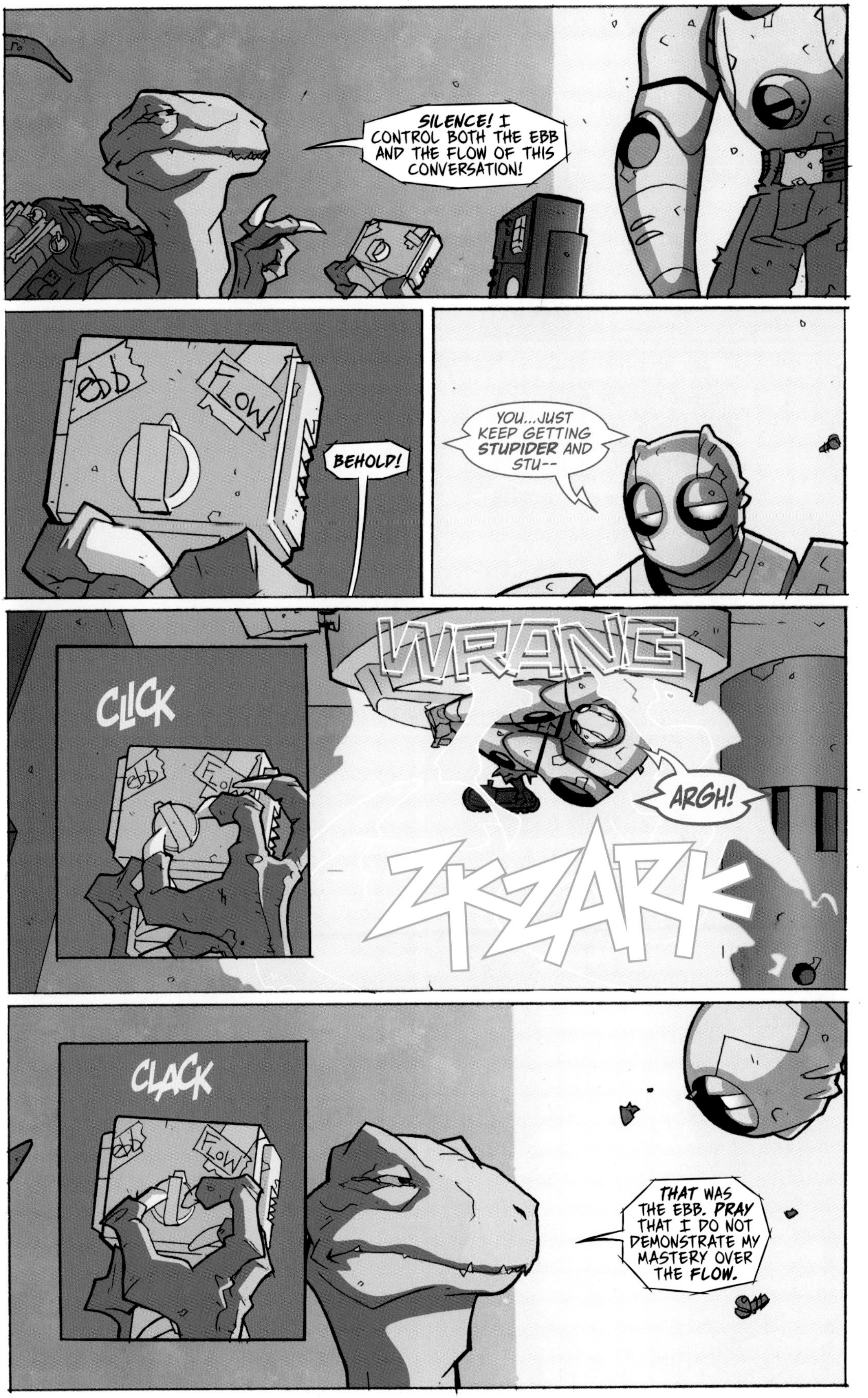
SILENCE! I CONTROL BOTH THE EBB AND THE FLOW OF THIS CONVERSATION!
EBB
FLOW
BEHOLD!
YOU...JUST KEEP GETTING STUPIDER AND STU--
CLICK
WRANG
ARGH!
ZKZARK
CLACK
THAT WAS THE EBB. PRAY THAT I DO NOT DEMONSTRATE MY MASTERY OVER THE FLOW.

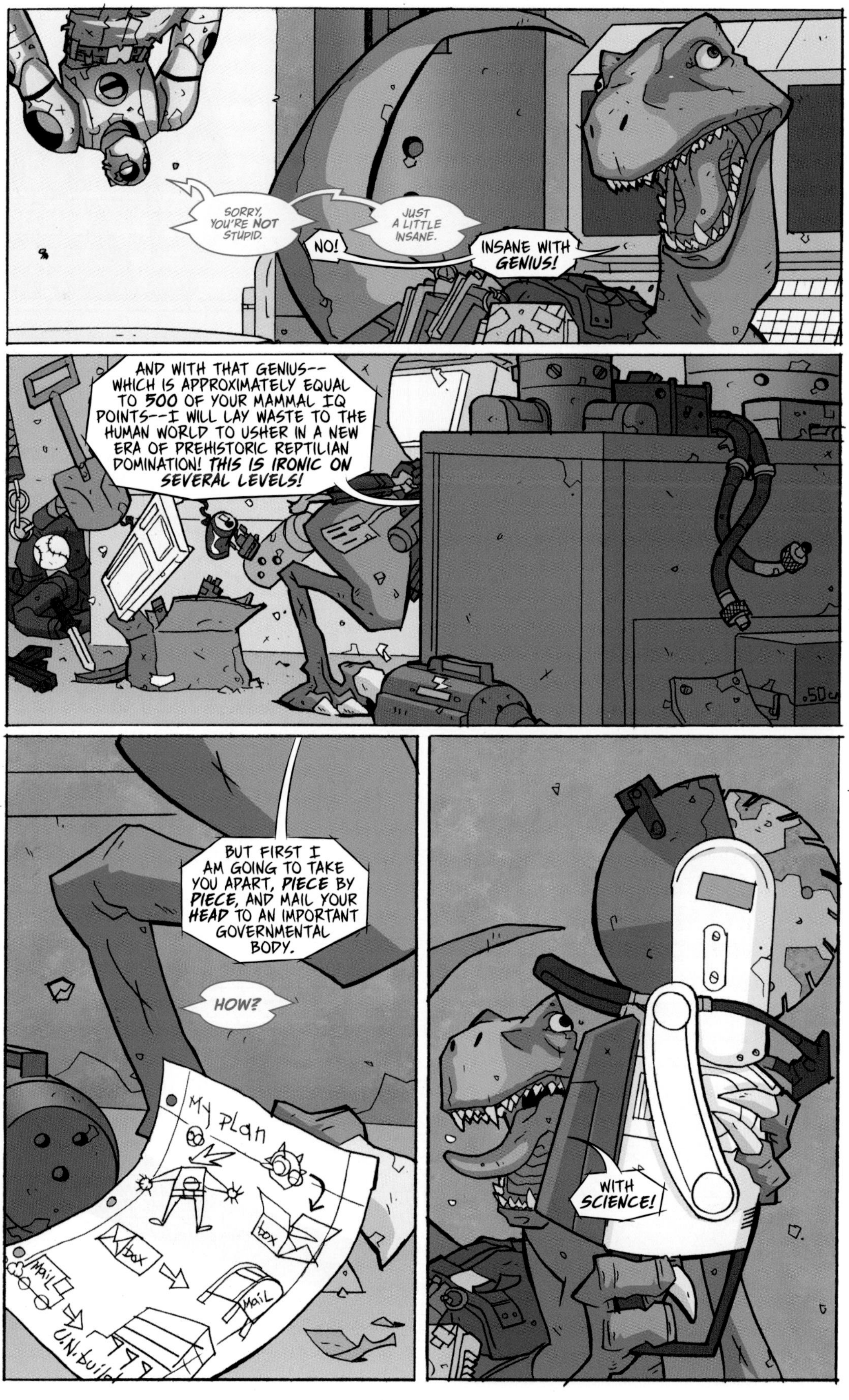
SORRY, YOU'RE NOT STUPID.
JUST A LITTLE INSANE.
NO!
INSANE WITH GENIUS!
AND WITH THAT GENIUS-- WHICH IS APPROXIMATELY EQUAL TO 500 OF YOUR MAMMAL IQ POINTS--I WILL LAY WASTE TO THE HUMAN WORLD TO USHER IN A NEW ERA OF PREHISTORIC REPTILIAN DOMINATION! THIS IS IRONIC ON SEVERAL LEVELS!
BUT FIRST I AM GOING TO TAKE YOU APART, PIECE BY PIECE, AND MAIL YOUR HEAD TO AN IMPORTANT GOVERNMENTAL BODY.
HOW?
My Plan
box
box
Mail
Mail
U.N. build
WITH SCIENCE!

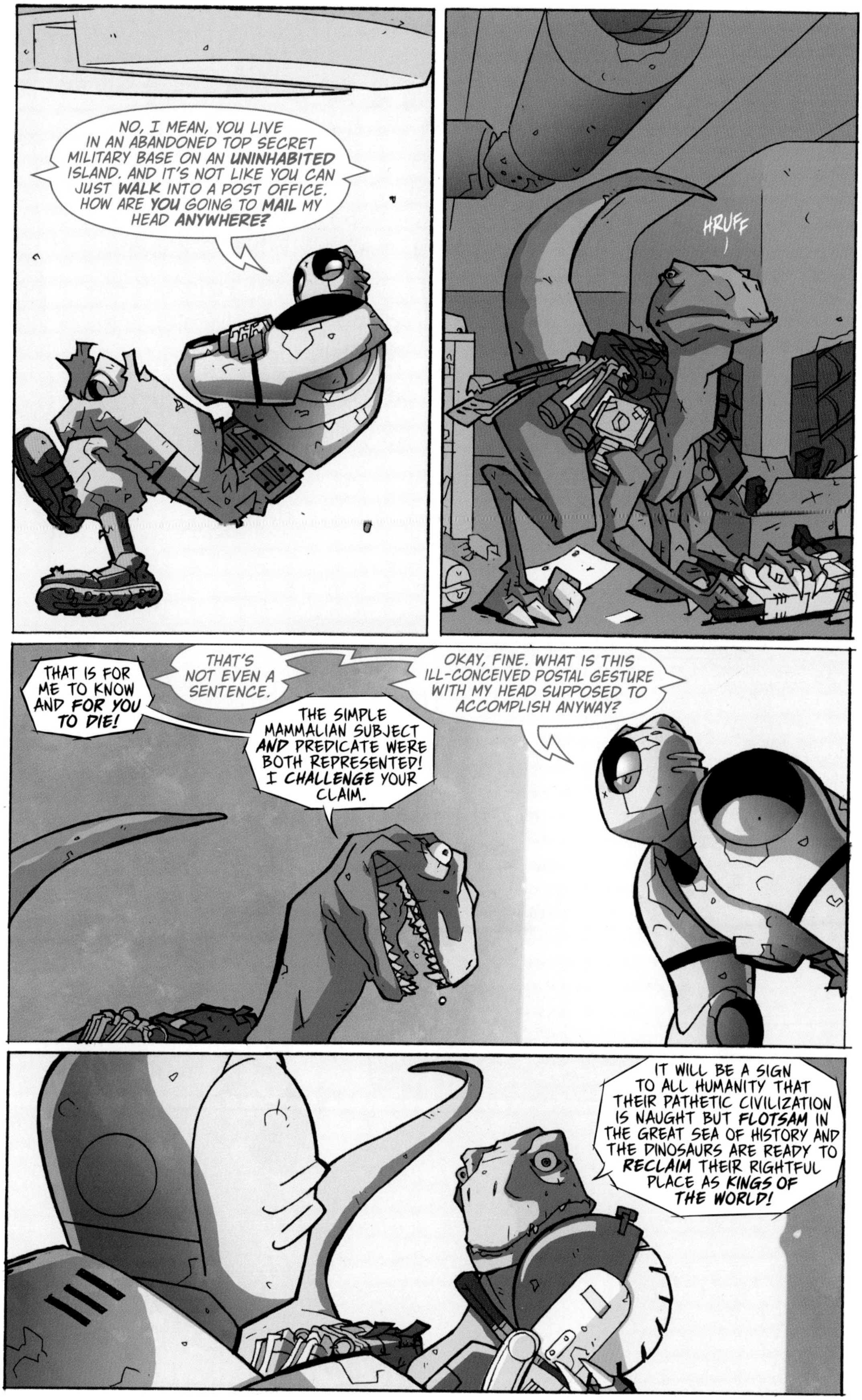
NO, I MEAN, YOU LIVE IN AN ABANDONED TOP SECRET MILITARY BASE ON AN UNINHABITED ISLAND. AND IT'S NOT LIKE YOU CAN JUST WALK INTO A POST OFFICE. HOW ARE YOU GOING TO MAIL MY HEAD ANYWHERE?
HRUFF
THAT IS FOR ME TO KNOW AND FOR YOU TO DIE!
THAT'S NOT EVEN A SENTENCE.
THE SIMPLE MAMMALIAN SUBJECT AND PREDICATE WERE BOTH REPRESENTED! I CHALLENGE YOUR CLAIM.
OKAY, FINE. WHAT IS THIS ILL-CONCEIVED POSTAL GESTURE WITH MY HEAD SUPPOSED TO ACCOMPLISH ANYWAY?
IT WILL BE A SIGN TO ALL HUMANITY THAT THEIR PATHETIC CIVILIZATION IS NAUGHT BUT FLOTSAM IN THE GREAT SEA OF HISTORY AND THE DINOSAURS ARE READY TO RECLAIM THEIR RIGHTFUL PLACE AS KINGS OF THE WORLD!

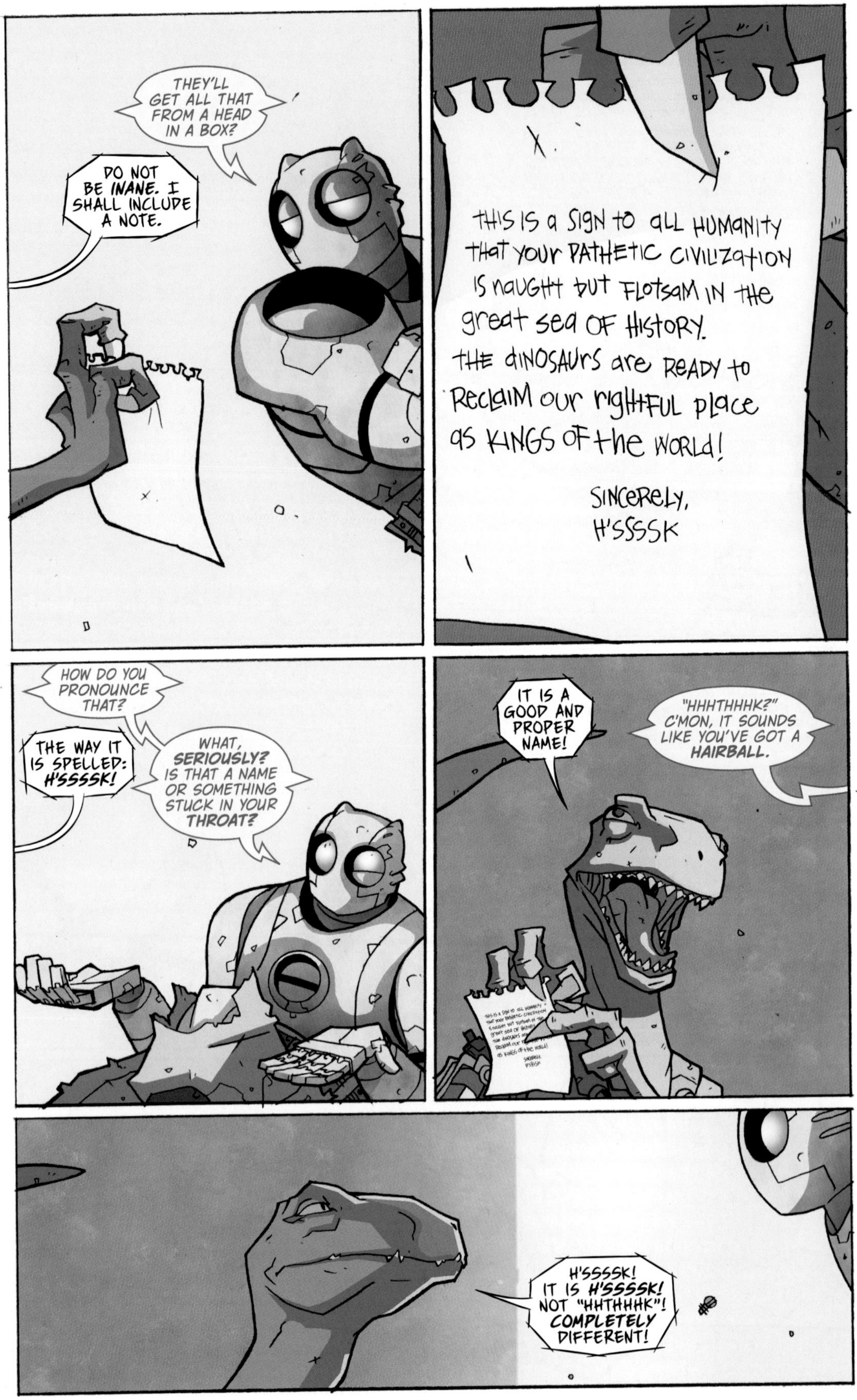

THEY'LL GET ALL THAT FROM A HEAD IN A BOX?
DO NOT BE INANE. I SHALL INCLUDE A NOTE.
THIS IS A SIGN TO ALL HUMANITY THAT YOUR PATHETIC CIVILIZATION IS NAUGHT BUT FLOTSAM IN THE GREAT SEA OF HISTORY.
THE DINOSAURS ARE READY TO RECLAIM OUR RIGHTFUL PLACE AS KINGS OF THE WORLD!
SINCERELY, H'SSSSK
HOW DO YOU PRONOUNCE THAT?
THE WAY IT IS SPELLED: H'SSSSK!
WHAT, SERIOUSLY? IS THAT A NAME OR SOMETHING STUCK IN YOUR THROAT?
IT IS A GOOD AND PROPER NAME!
"HHHTHHHK?" C'MON, IT SOUNDS LIKE YOU'VE GOT A HAIRBALL.
H'SSSSK! IT IS H'SSSSK! NOT "HHTHHHK"! COMPLETELY DIFFERENT!

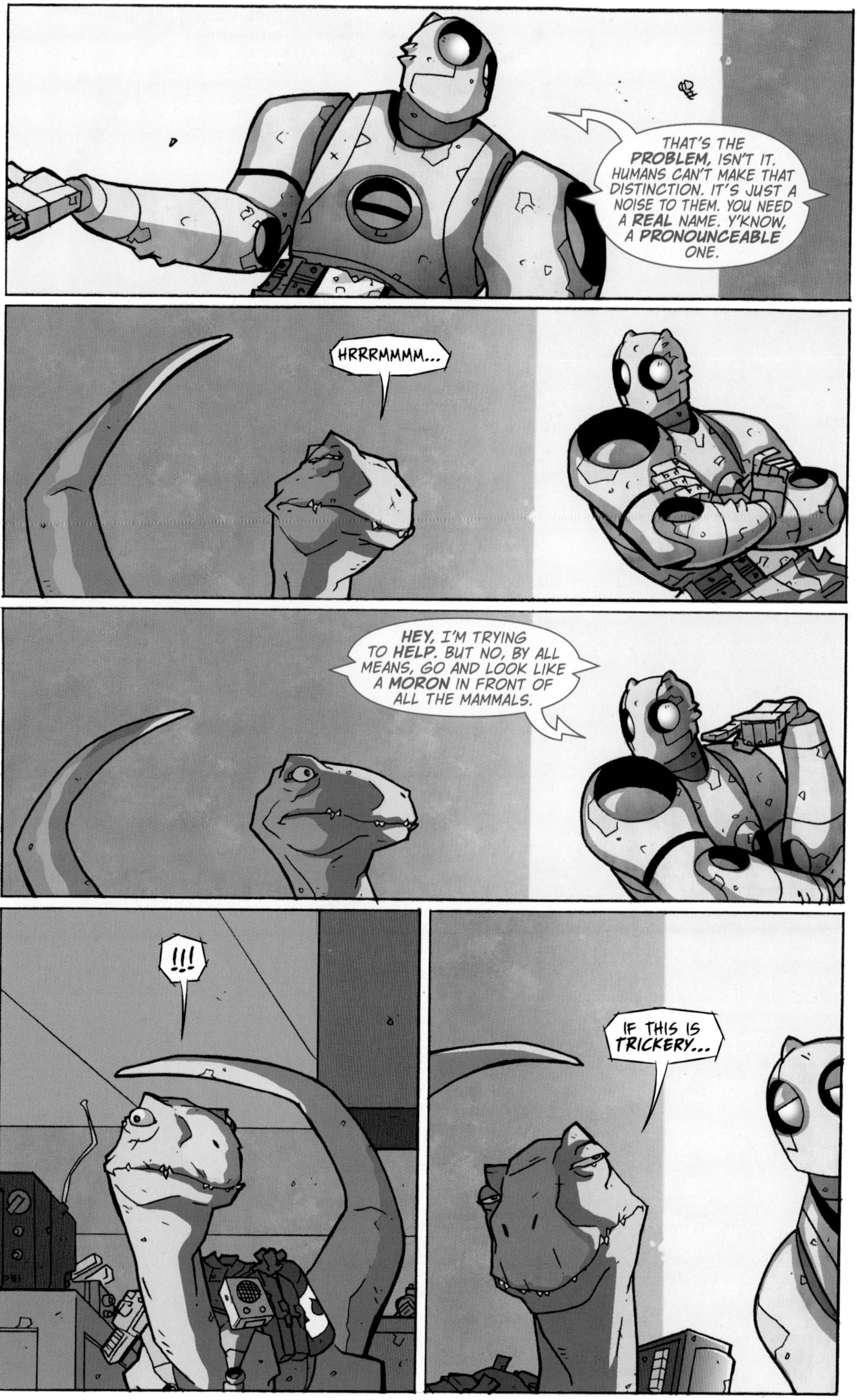
THAT'S THE PROBLEM, ISN'T IT. HUMANS CAN'T MAKE THAT DISTINCTION. IT'S JUST A NOISE TO THEM. YOU NEED A REAL NAME. Y'KNOW, A PRONOUNCEABLE ONE.
HRRRMMMM...
HEY, I'M TRYING TO HELP. BUT NO, BY ALL MEANS, GO AND LOOK LIKE A MORON IN FRONT OF ALL THE MAMMALS.
!!!
IF THIS IS TRICKERY...

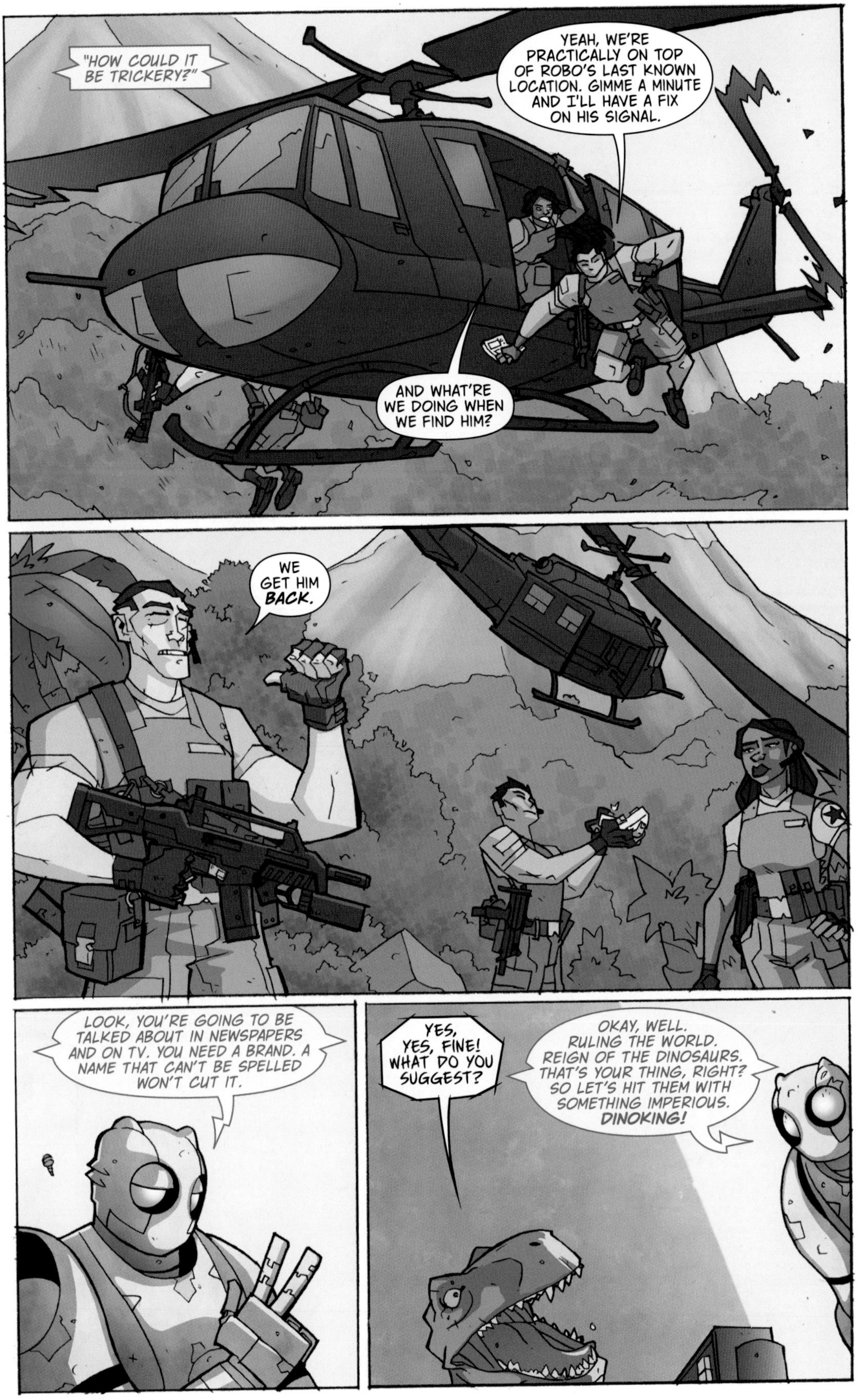
"HOW COULD IT BE TRICKERY?"
YEAH, WE'RE PRACTICALLY ON TOP OF ROBO'S LAST KNOWN LOCATION. GIMME A MINUTE AND I'LL HAVE A FIX ON HIS SIGNAL.
AND WHAT'RE WE DOING WHEN WE FIND HIM?
WE GET HIM **BACK.**
LOOK, YOU'RE GOING TO BE TALKED ABOUT IN NEWSPAPERS AND ON TV. YOU NEED A BRAND. A NAME THAT CAN'T BE SPELLED WON'T CUT IT.
YES, YES, FINE! WHAT DO YOU SUGGEST?
OKAY, WELL. RULING THE WORLD. REIGN OF THE DINOSAURS. THAT'S YOUR THING, RIGHT? SO LET'S HIT THEM WITH SOMETHING IMPERIOUS. **DINOKING!**

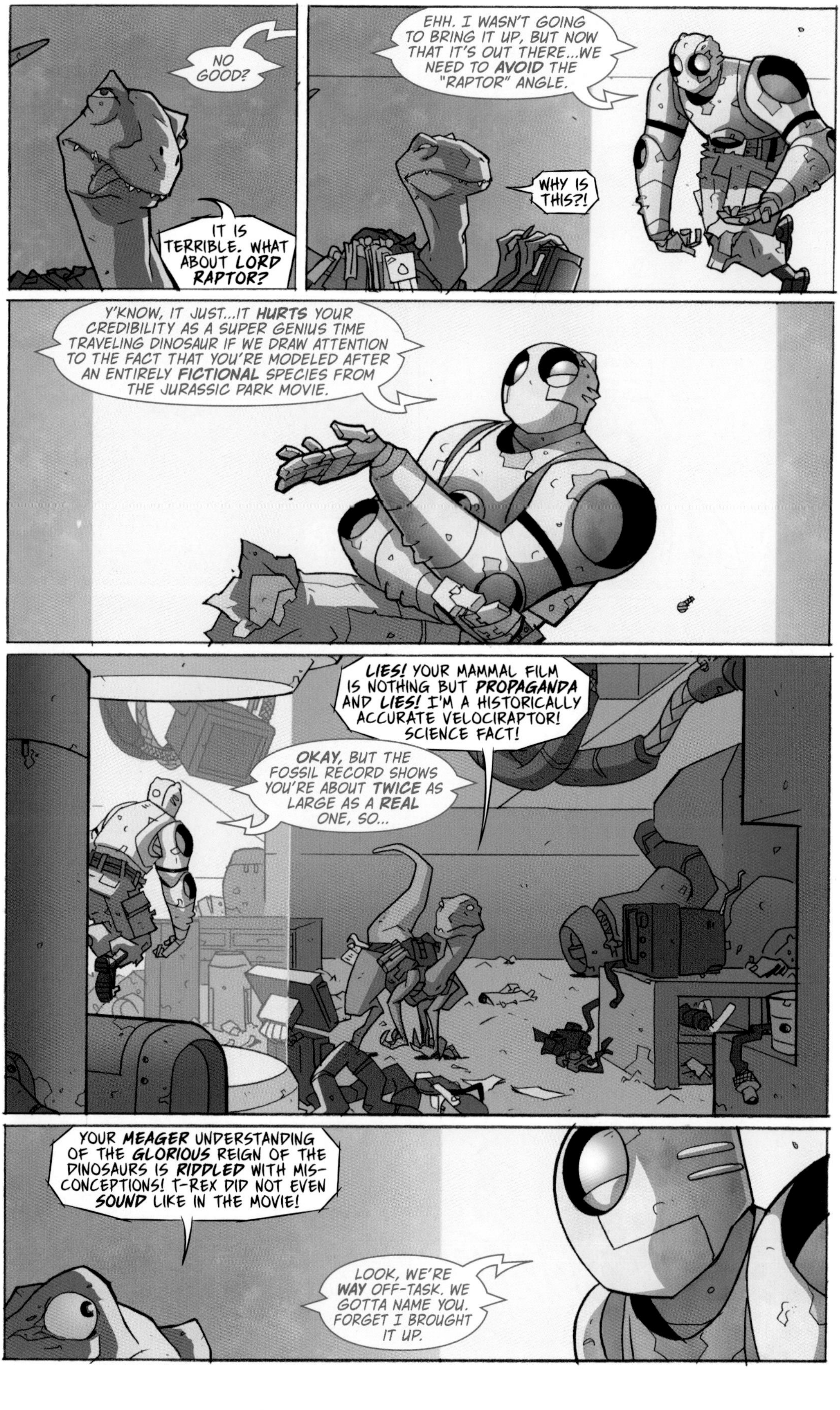
NO GOOD?
IT IS TERRIBLE. WHAT ABOUT LORD RAPTOR?
EHH. I WASN'T GOING TO BRING IT UP, BUT NOW THAT IT'S OUT THERE...WE NEED TO AVOID THE "RAPTOR" ANGLE.
WHY IS THIS?!
Y'KNOW, IT JUST...IT HURTS YOUR CREDIBILITY AS A SUPER GENIUS TIME TRAVELING DINOSAUR IF WE DRAW ATTENTION TO THE FACT THAT YOU'RE MODELED AFTER AN ENTIRELY FICTIONAL SPECIES FROM THE JURASSIC PARK MOVIE.
LIES! YOUR MAMMAL FILM IS NOTHING BUT PROPAGANDA AND LIES! I'M A HISTORICALLY ACCURATE VELOCIRAPTOR! SCIENCE FACT!
OKAY, BUT THE FOSSIL RECORD SHOWS YOU'RE ABOUT TWICE AS LARGE AS A REAL ONE, SO...
YOUR MEAGER UNDERSTANDING OF THE GLORIOUS REIGN OF THE DINOSAURS IS RIDDLED WITH MISCONCEPTIONS! T-REX DID NOT EVEN SOUND LIKE IN THE MOVIE!
LOOK, WE'RE WAY OFF-TASK. WE GOTTA NAME YOU. FORGET I BROUGHT IT UP.

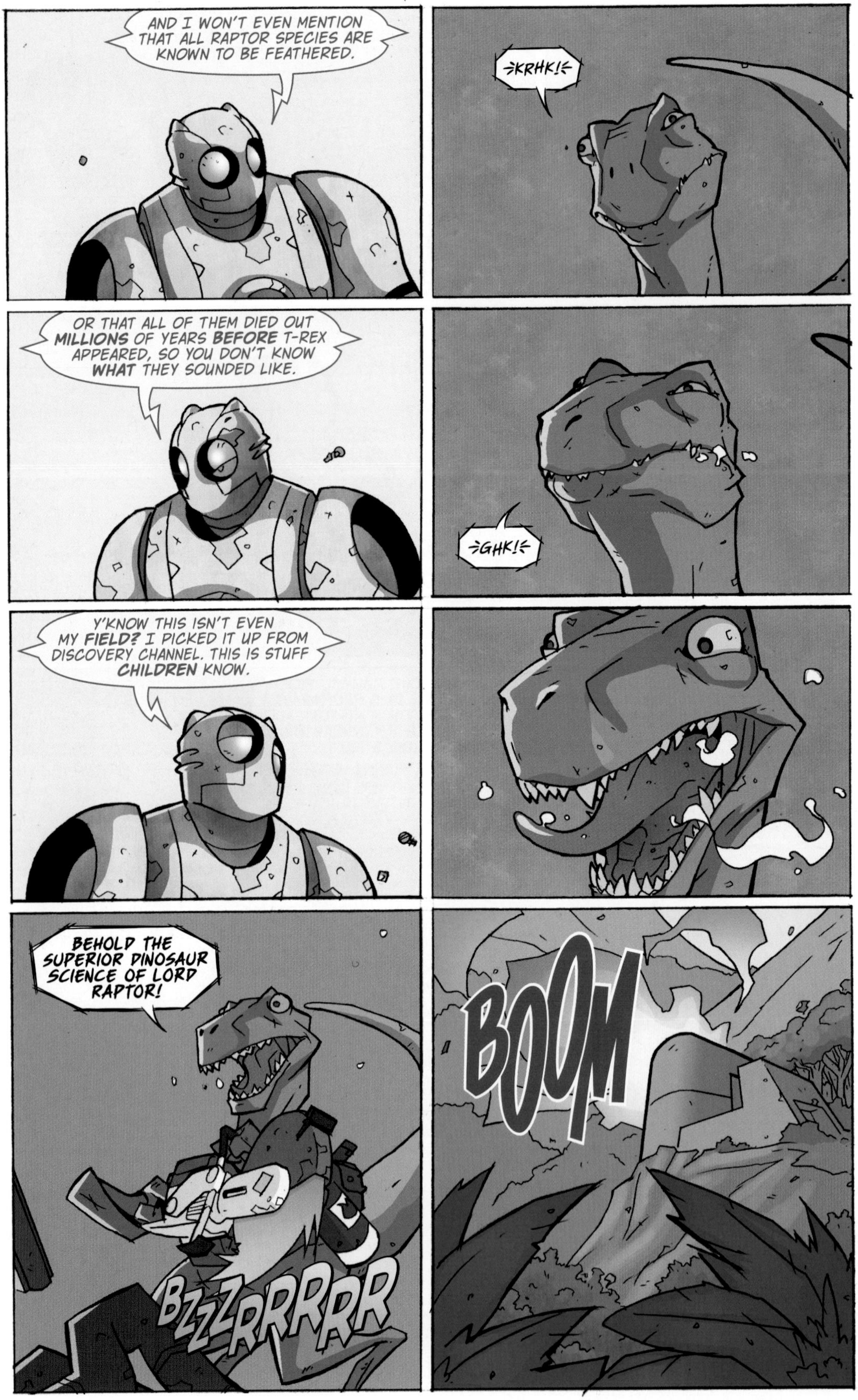
AND I WON'T EVEN MENTION THAT ALL RAPTOR SPECIES ARE KNOWN TO BE FEATHERED.
KRHK!
OR THAT ALL OF THEM DIED OUT MILLIONS OF YEARS BEFORE T-REX APPEARED, SO YOU DON'T KNOW WHAT THEY SOUNDED LIKE.
GHK!
Y'KNOW THIS ISN'T EVEN MY FIELD? I PICKED IT UP FROM DISCOVERY CHANNEL. THIS IS STUFF CHILDREN KNOW.
BEHOLD THE SUPERIOR DINOSAUR SCIENCE OF LORD RAPTOR!
BZZZRRRRRR
BOOM

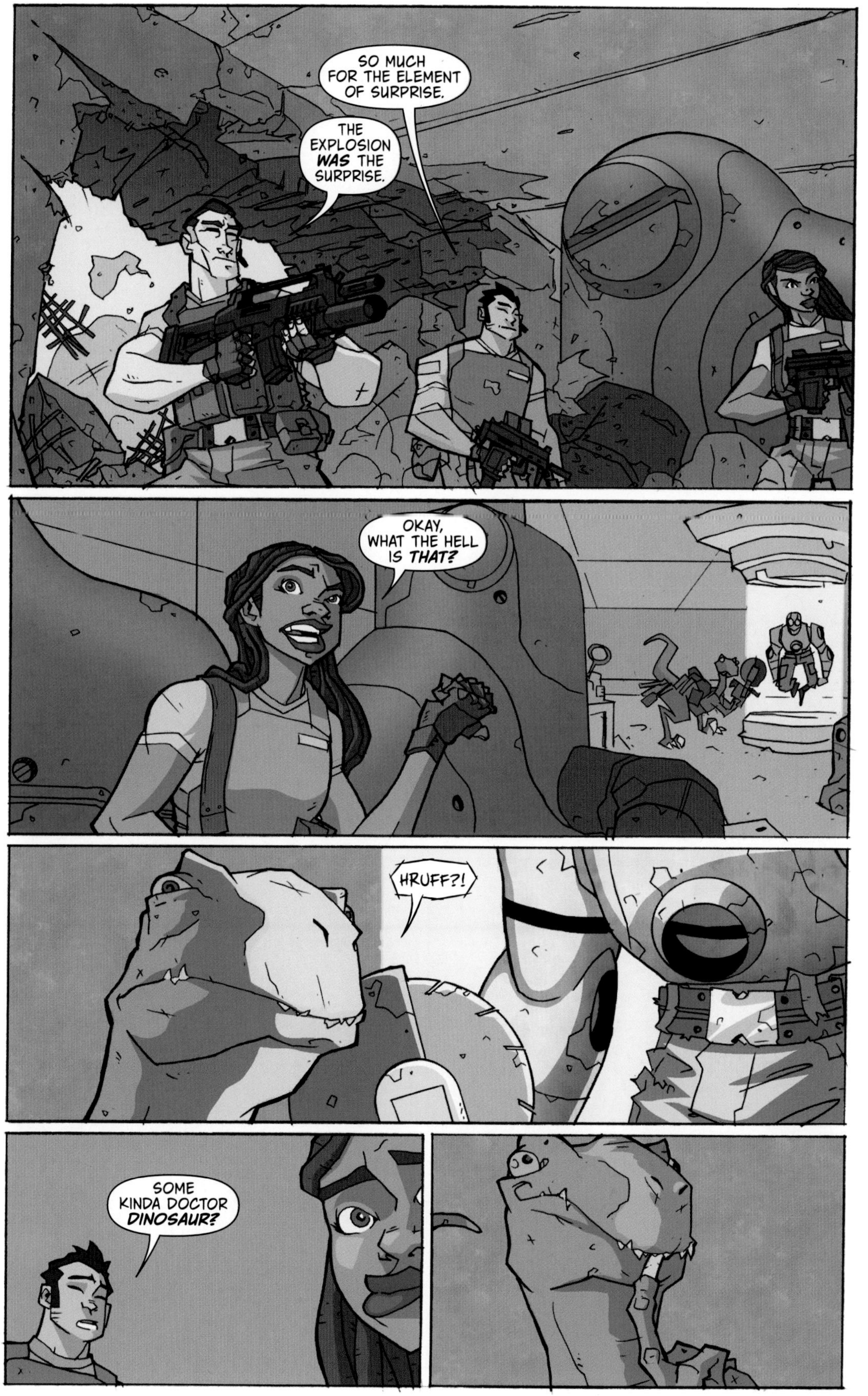
SO MUCH FOR THE ELEMENT OF SURPRISE.
THE EXPLOSION WAS THE SURPRISE.
OKAY, WHAT THE HELL IS THAT?
HRUFF?!
SOME KINDA DOCTOR DINOSAUR?

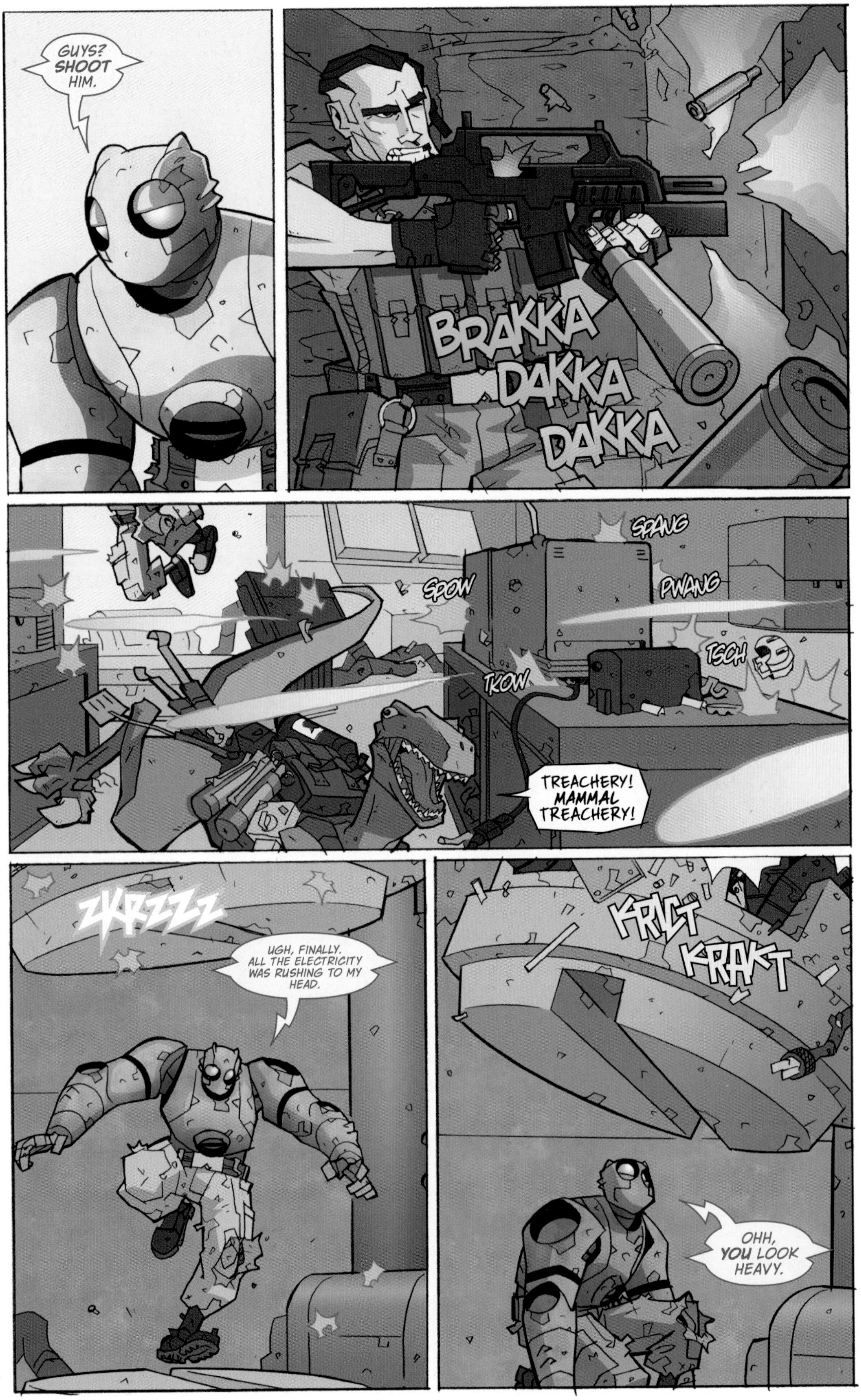
GUYS? SHOOT HIM.
BRAKKA DAKKA DAKKA
SPANG
SPOW
PWANG
TSCH
TKOW
TREACHERY! MAMMAL TREACHERY!
ZKRZZZ
UGH, FINALLY. ALL THE ELECTRICITY WAS RUSHING TO MY HEAD.
KRICT KRAKT
OHH, YOU LOOK HEAVY.

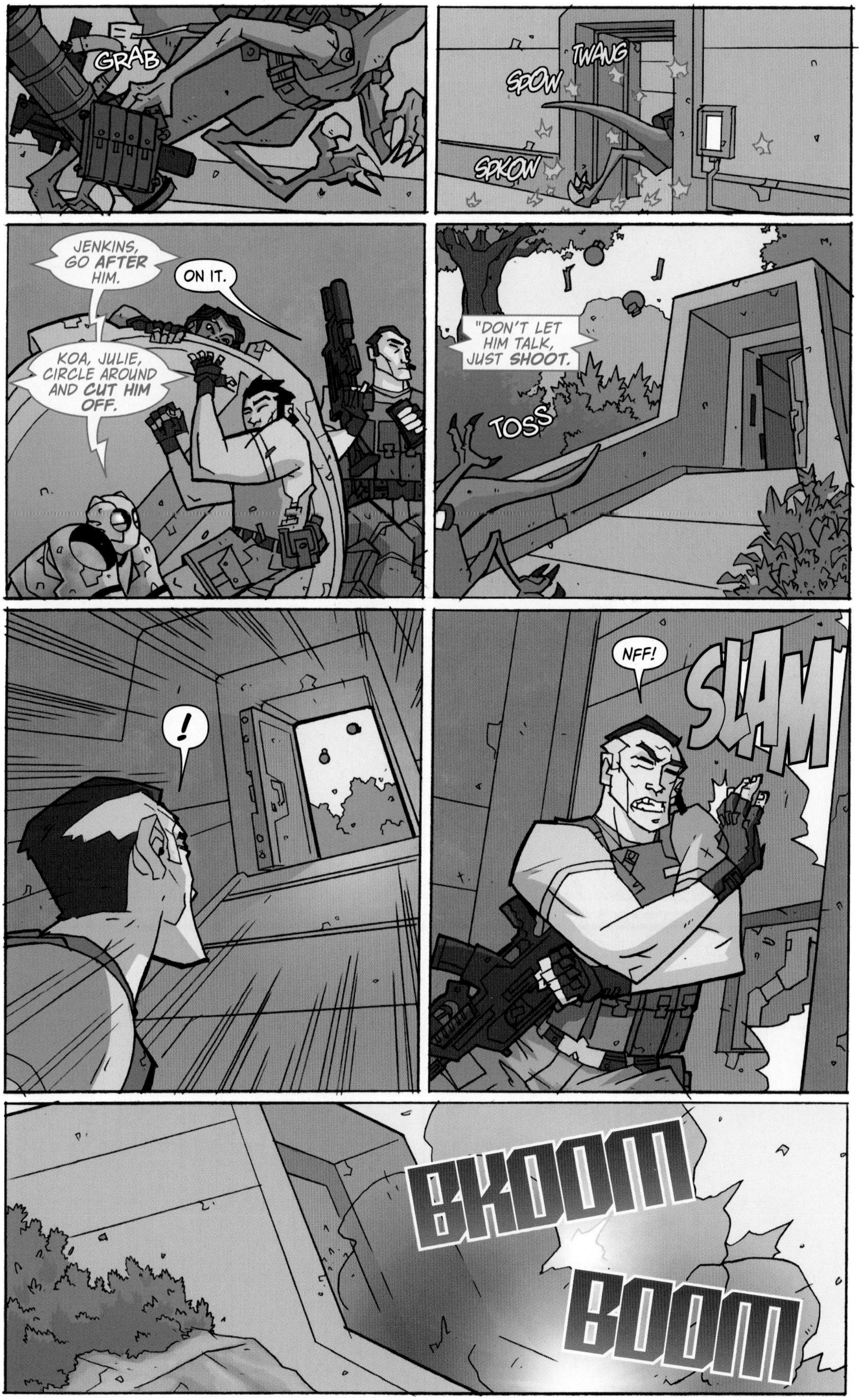
GRAB
TWANG
SPOW
SPKOW
JENKINS, GO AFTER HIM.
ON IT.
KOA, JULIE, CIRCLE AROUND AND CUT HIM OFF.
"DON'T LET HIM TALK, JUST SHOOT.
TOSS
!
NFF!
SLAM
BKOOM
BOOM

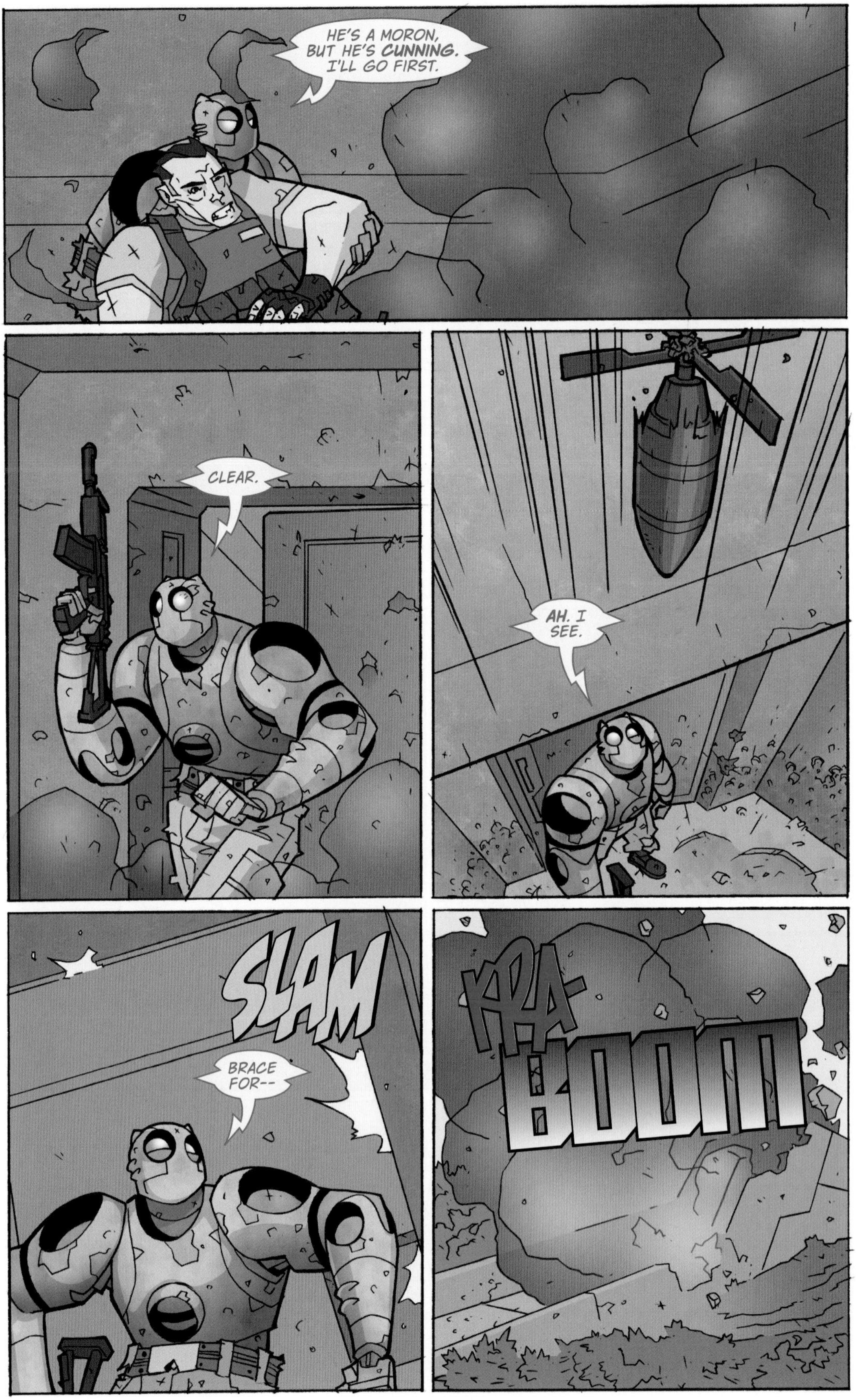
HE'S A MORON, BUT HE'S **CUNNING.** I'LL GO FIRST.
CLEAR.
AH. I SEE.
SLAM
BRACE FOR--
KRA-BOOM

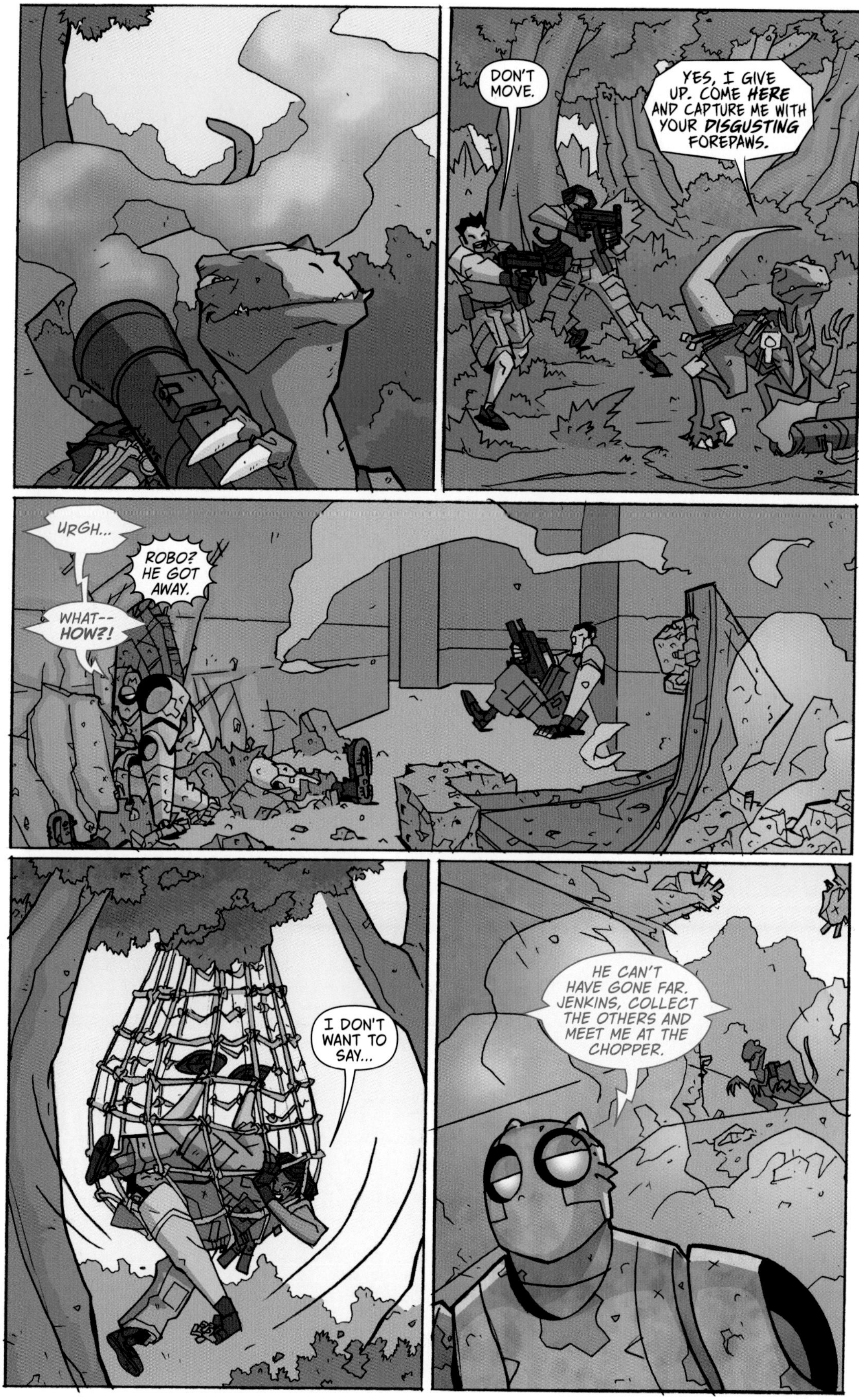
DON'T MOVE.
YES, I GIVE UP. COME HERE AND CAPTURE ME WITH YOUR DISGUSTING FOREPAWS.
URGH...
ROBO? HE GOT AWAY.
WHAT-- HOW?!
I DON'T WANT TO SAY...
HE CAN'T HAVE GONE FAR. JENKINS, COLLECT THE OTHERS AND MEET ME AT THE CHOPPER.

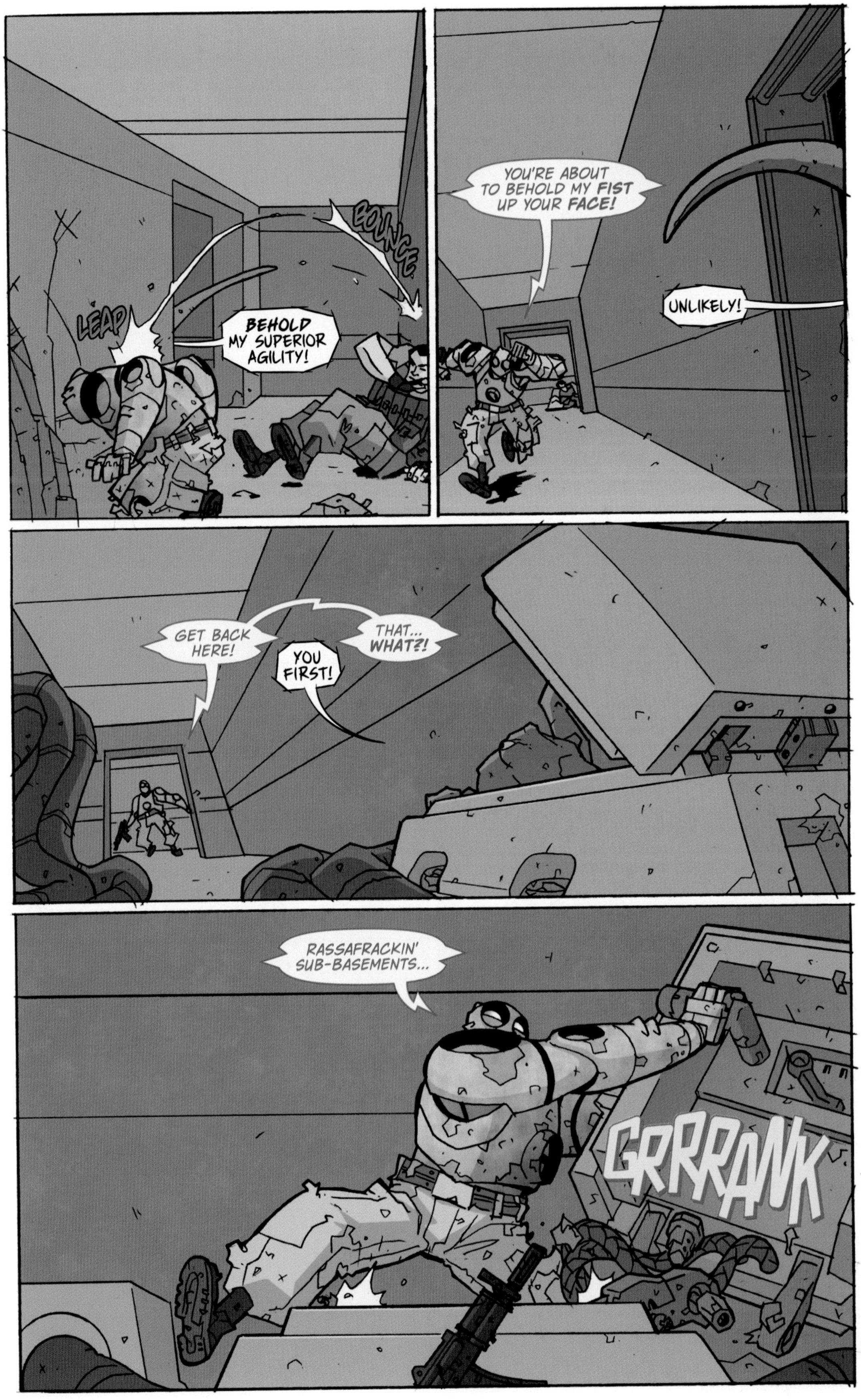
LEAP
BOUNCE
BEHOLD MY SUPERIOR AGILITY!
YOU'RE ABOUT TO BEHOLD MY FIST UP YOUR FACE!
UNLIKELY!
GET BACK HERE!
YOU FIRST!
THAT... WHAT?!
RASSAFRACKIN' SUB-BASEMENTS...
GRRRANK

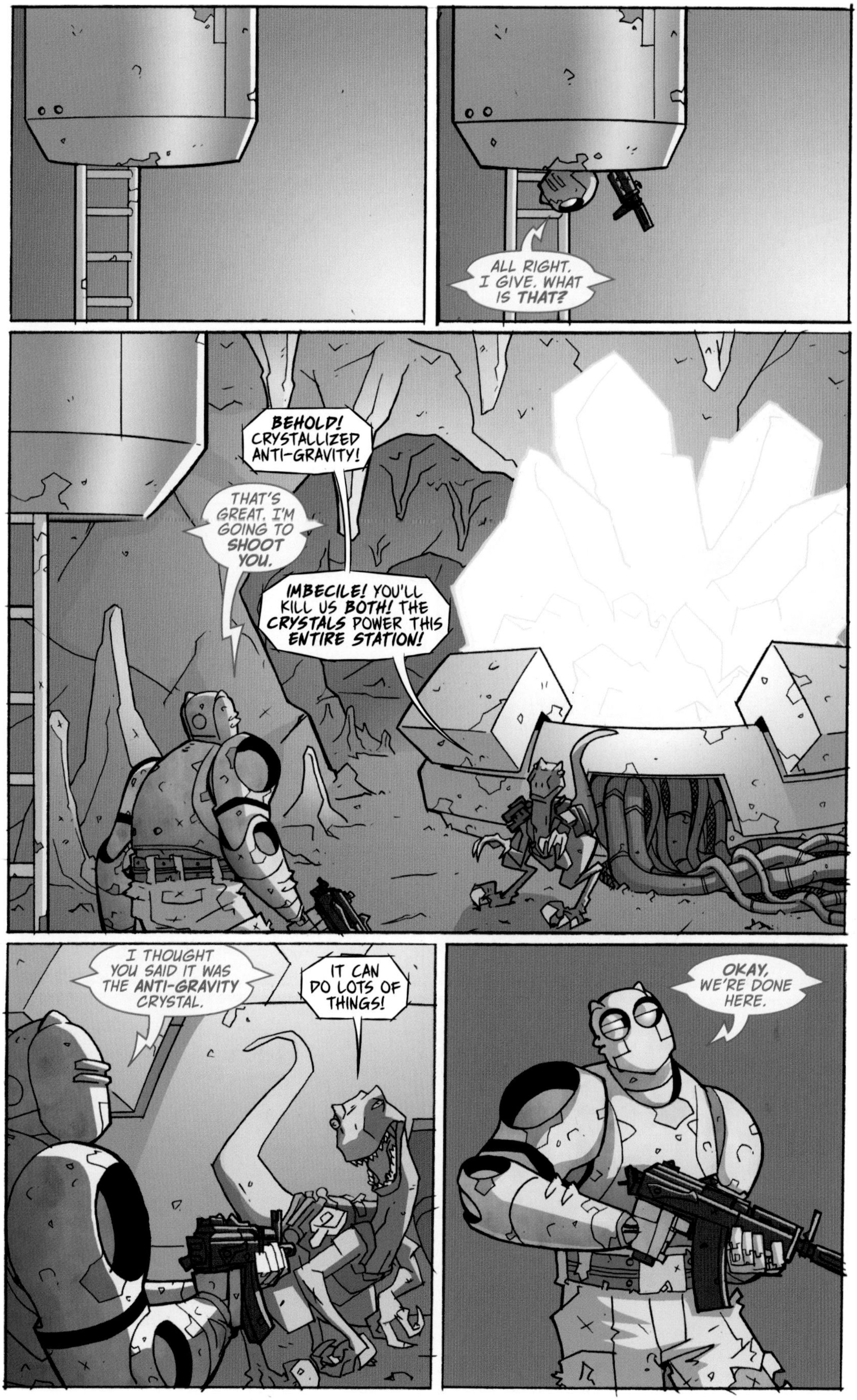
ALL RIGHT. I GIVE. WHAT IS THAT?
BEHOLD! CRYSTALLIZED ANTI-GRAVITY!
THAT'S GREAT. I'M GOING TO SHOOT YOU.
IMBECILE! YOU'LL KILL US BOTH! THE CRYSTALS POWER THIS ENTIRE STATION!
I THOUGHT YOU SAID IT WAS THE ANTI-GRAVITY CRYSTAL.
IT CAN DO LOTS OF THINGS!
OKAY, WE'RE DONE HERE.

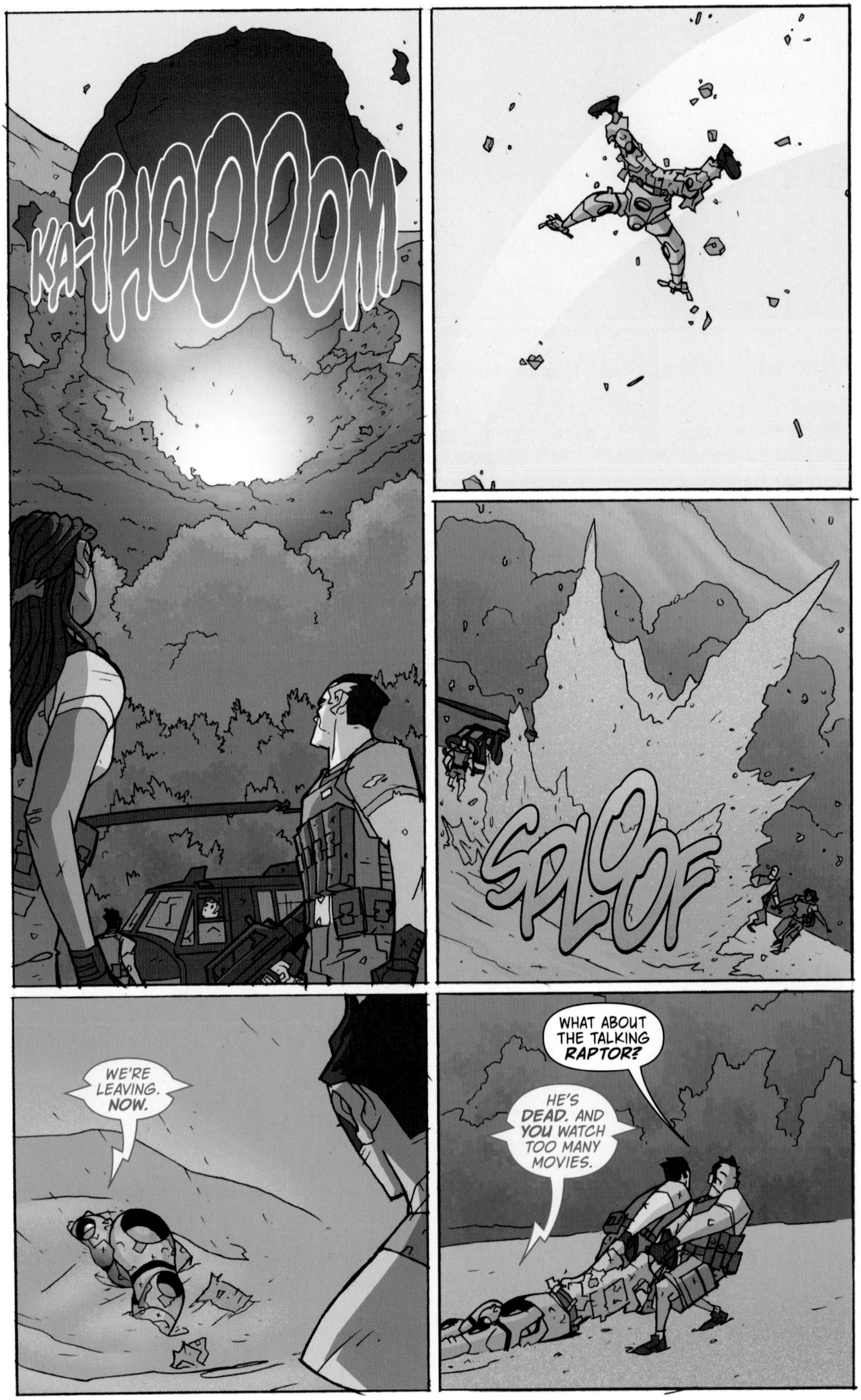
KA-THOOOOM
SPLOOF
WE'RE LEAVING. NOW.
WHAT ABOUT THE TALKING RAPTOR?
HE'S DEAD. AND YOU WATCH TOO MANY MOVIES.

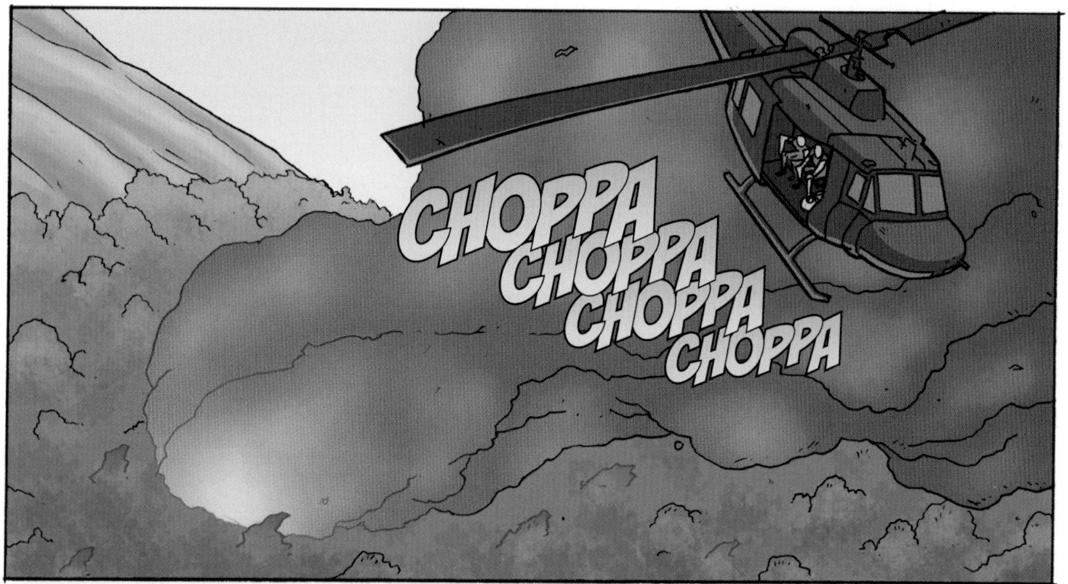
CHOPPA
CHOPPA
CHOPPA
CHOPPA

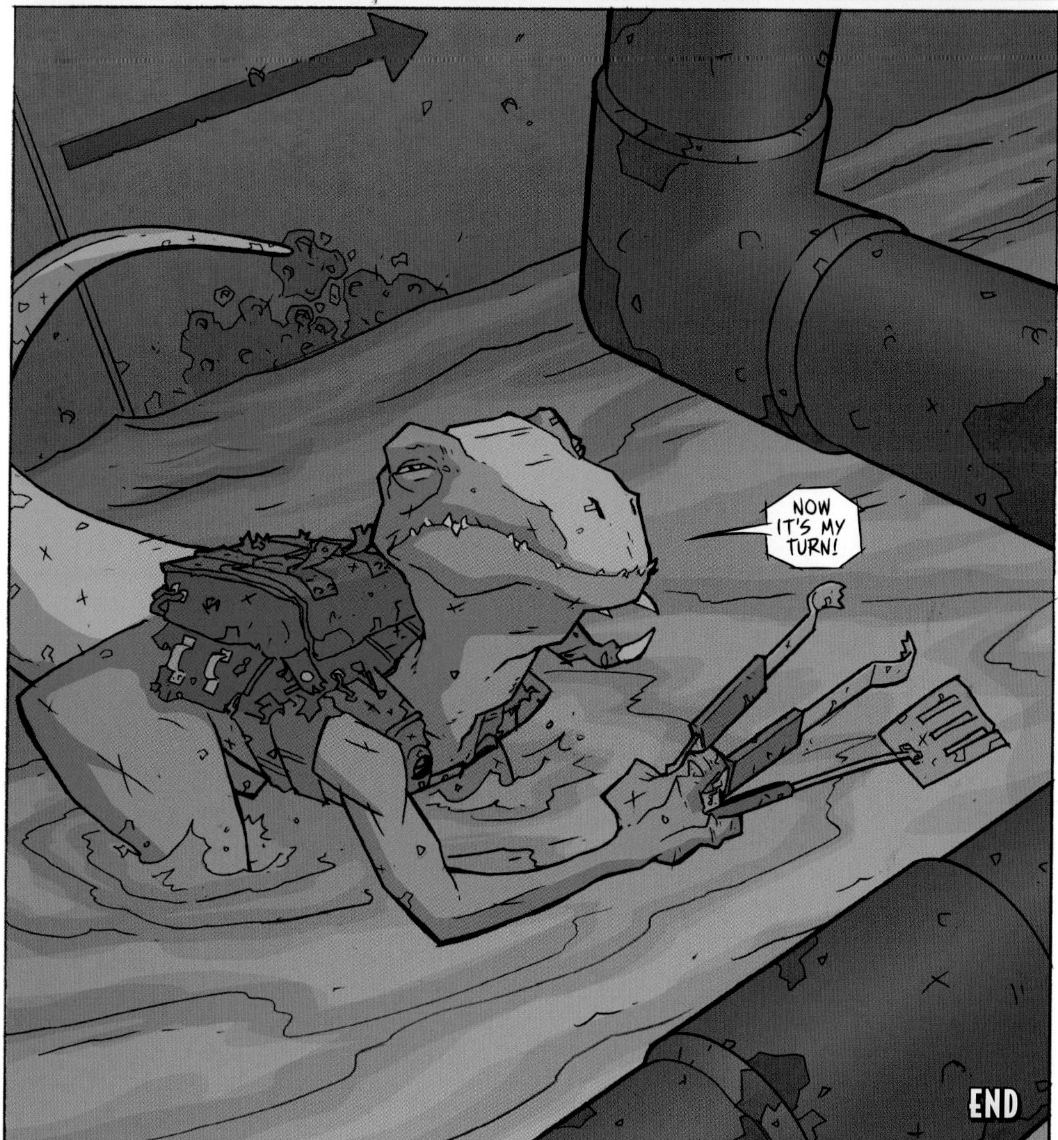
NOW IT'S MY TURN!
END

ATOMIC ROBO FREE COMIC BOOK DAY 2009 COVER

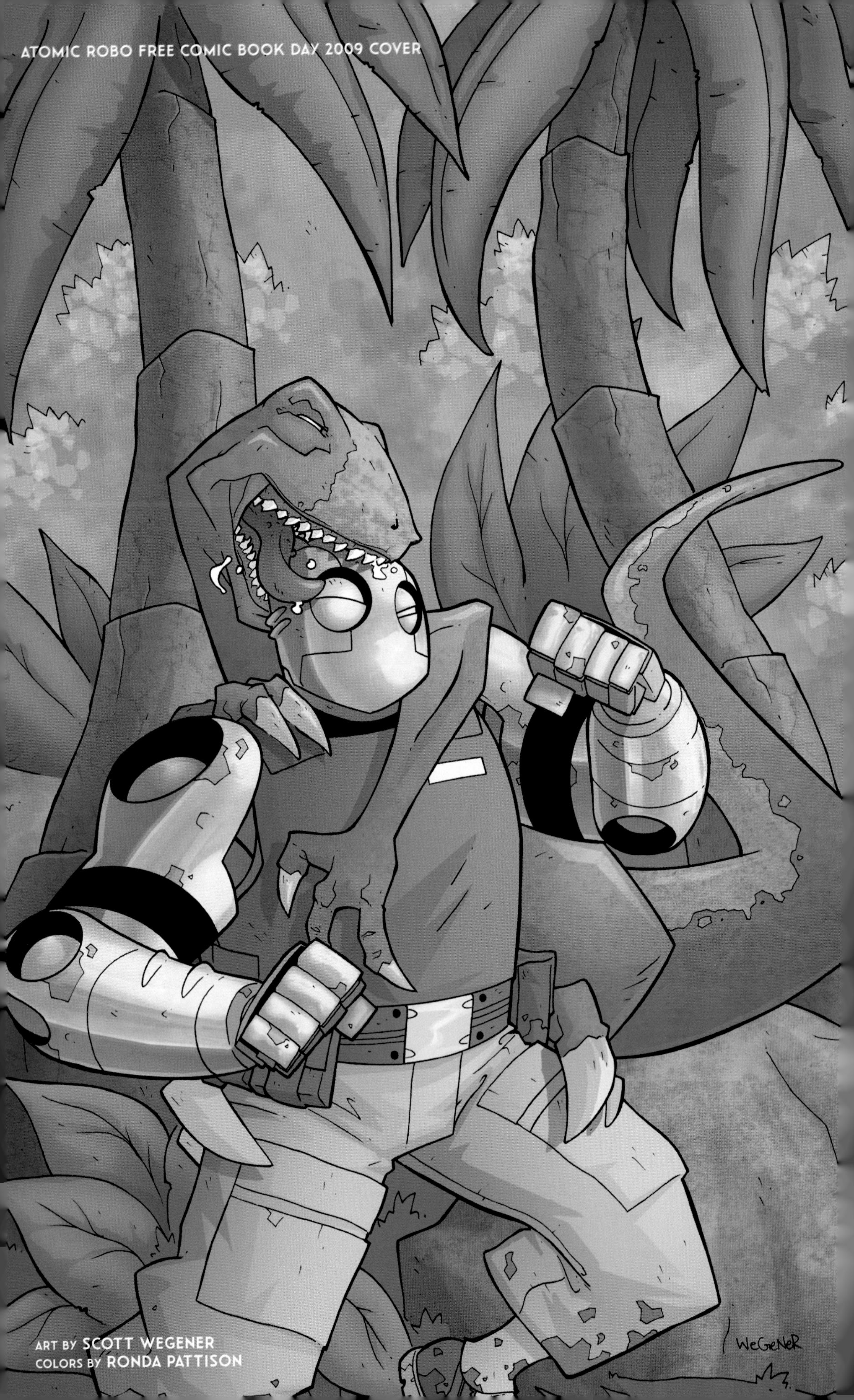
WEGENER

ART BY SCOTT WEGENER
COLORS BY RONDA PATTISON

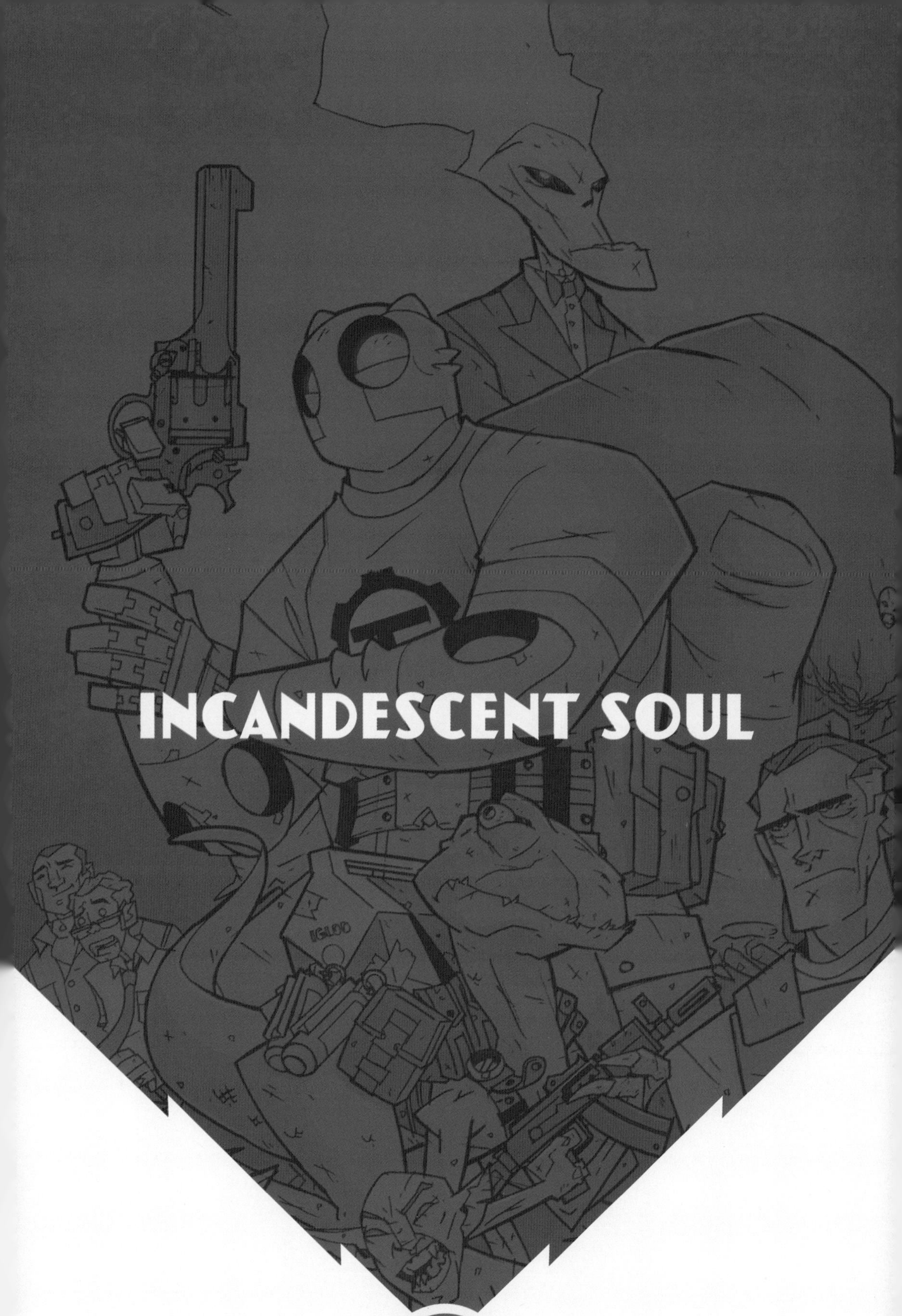
IGLOO

INCANDESCENT SOUL

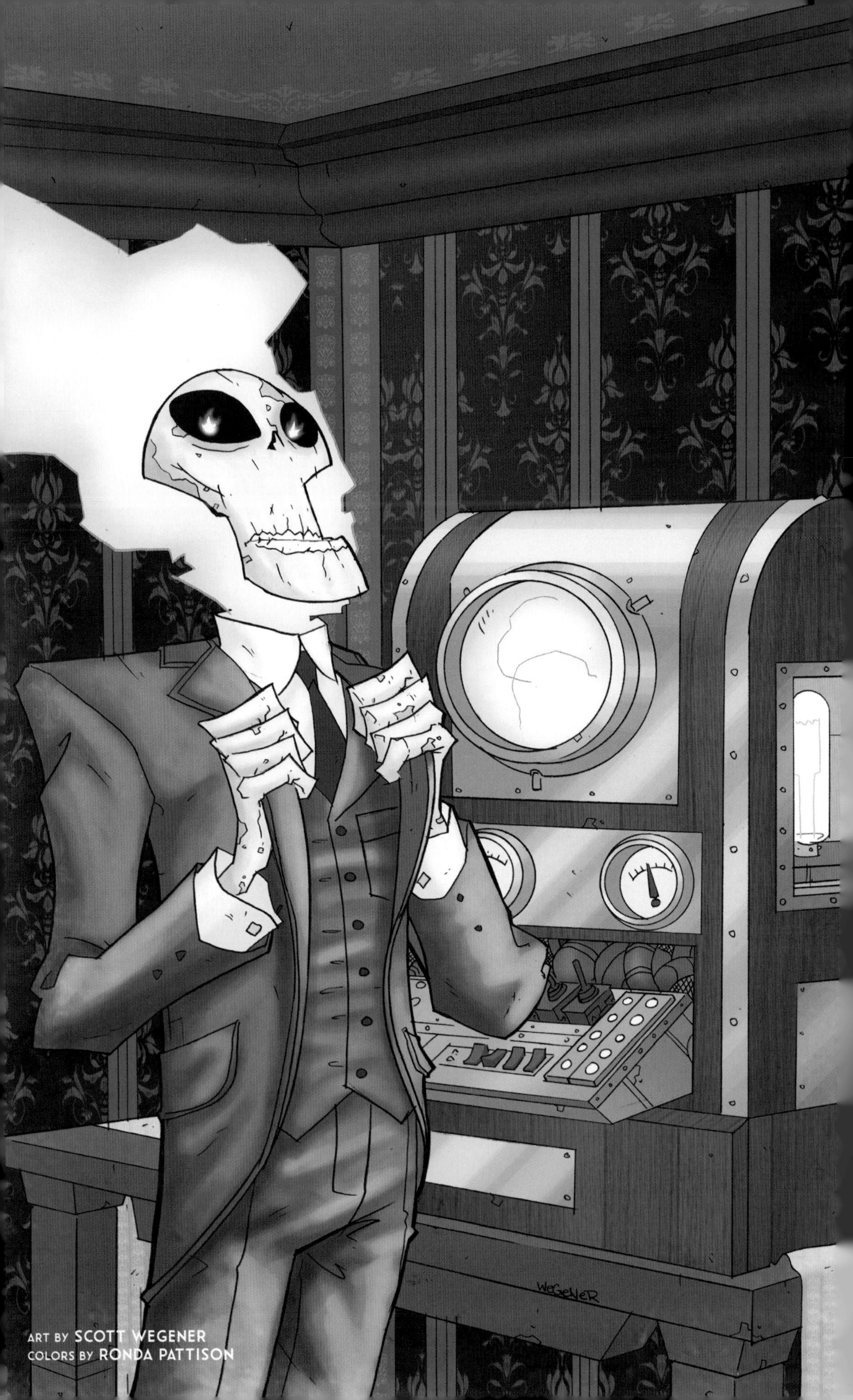
WEGENER

ART BY SCOTT WEGENER
COLORS BY RONDA PATTISON

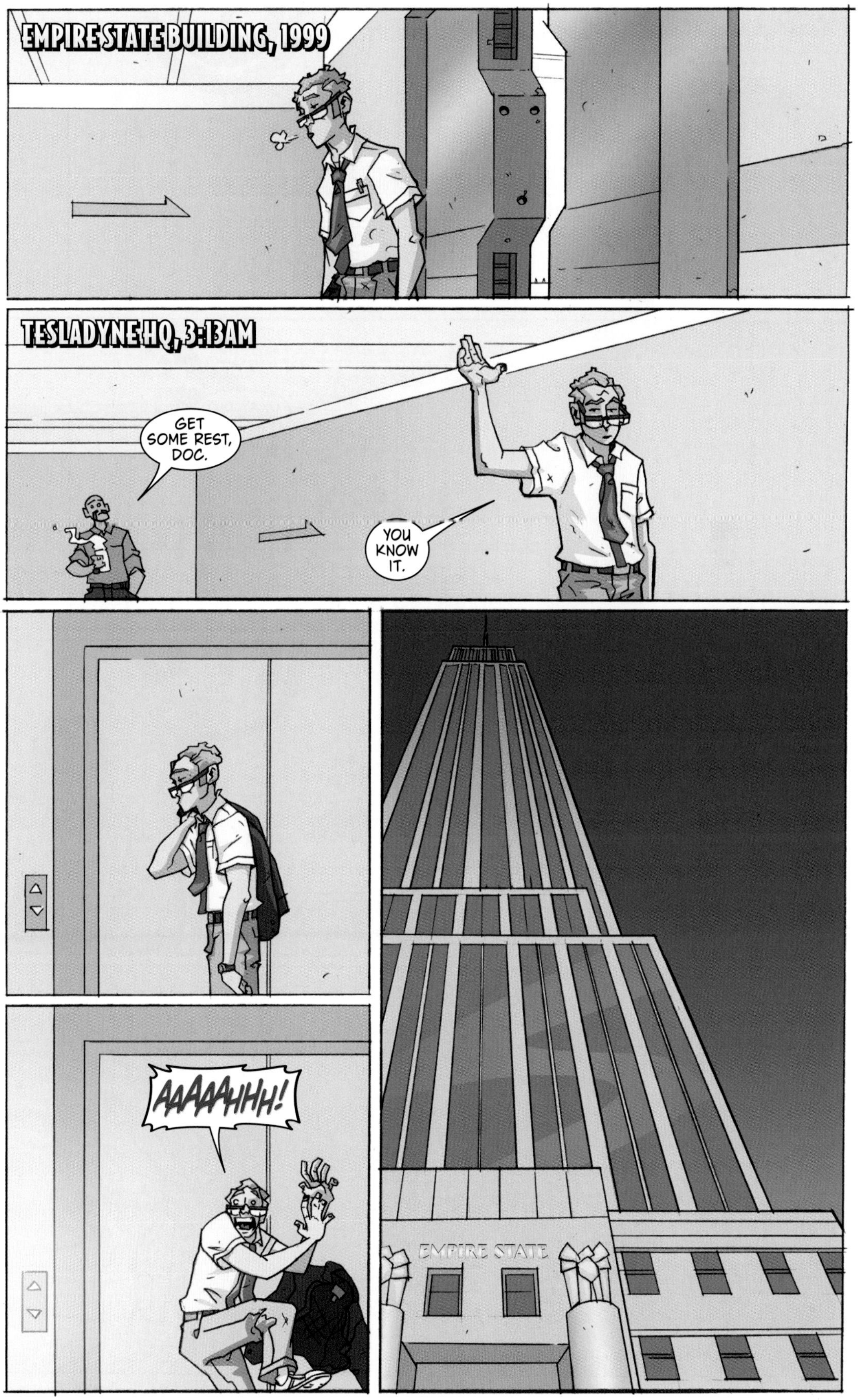
EMPIRE STATE BUILDING, 1999
TESLADYNE HQ, 3:13AM
GET SOME REST, DOC.
YOU KNOW IT.
EMPIRE STATE
AAAAHHH!

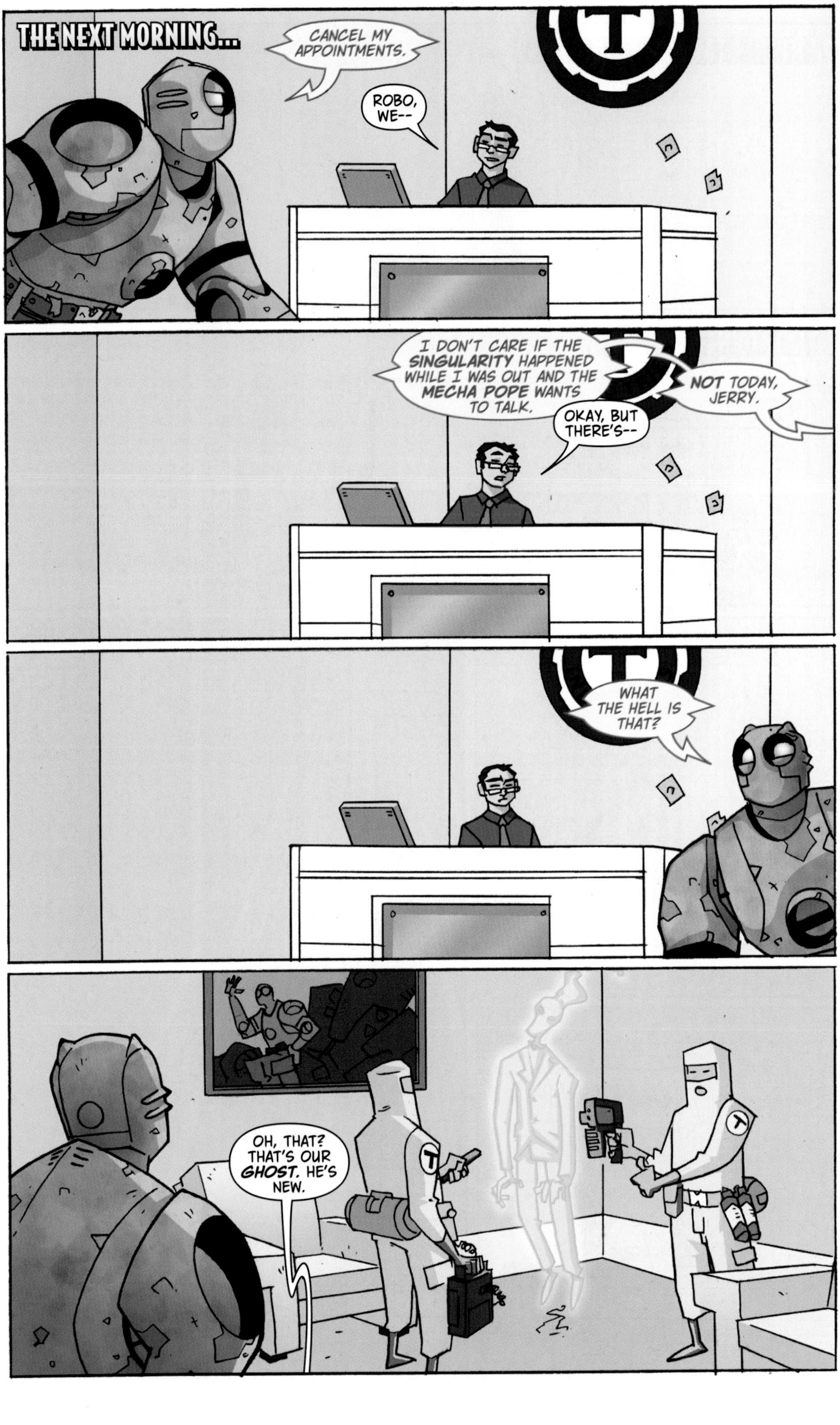
THE NEXT MORNING...
CANCEL MY APPOINTMENTS.
ROBO, WE--
I DON'T CARE IF THE SINGULARITY HAPPENED WHILE I WAS OUT AND THE MECHA POPE WANTS TO TALK.
NOT TODAY, JERRY.
OKAY, BUT THERE'S--
WHAT THE HELL IS THAT?
OH, THAT? THAT'S OUR GHOST. HE'S NEW.

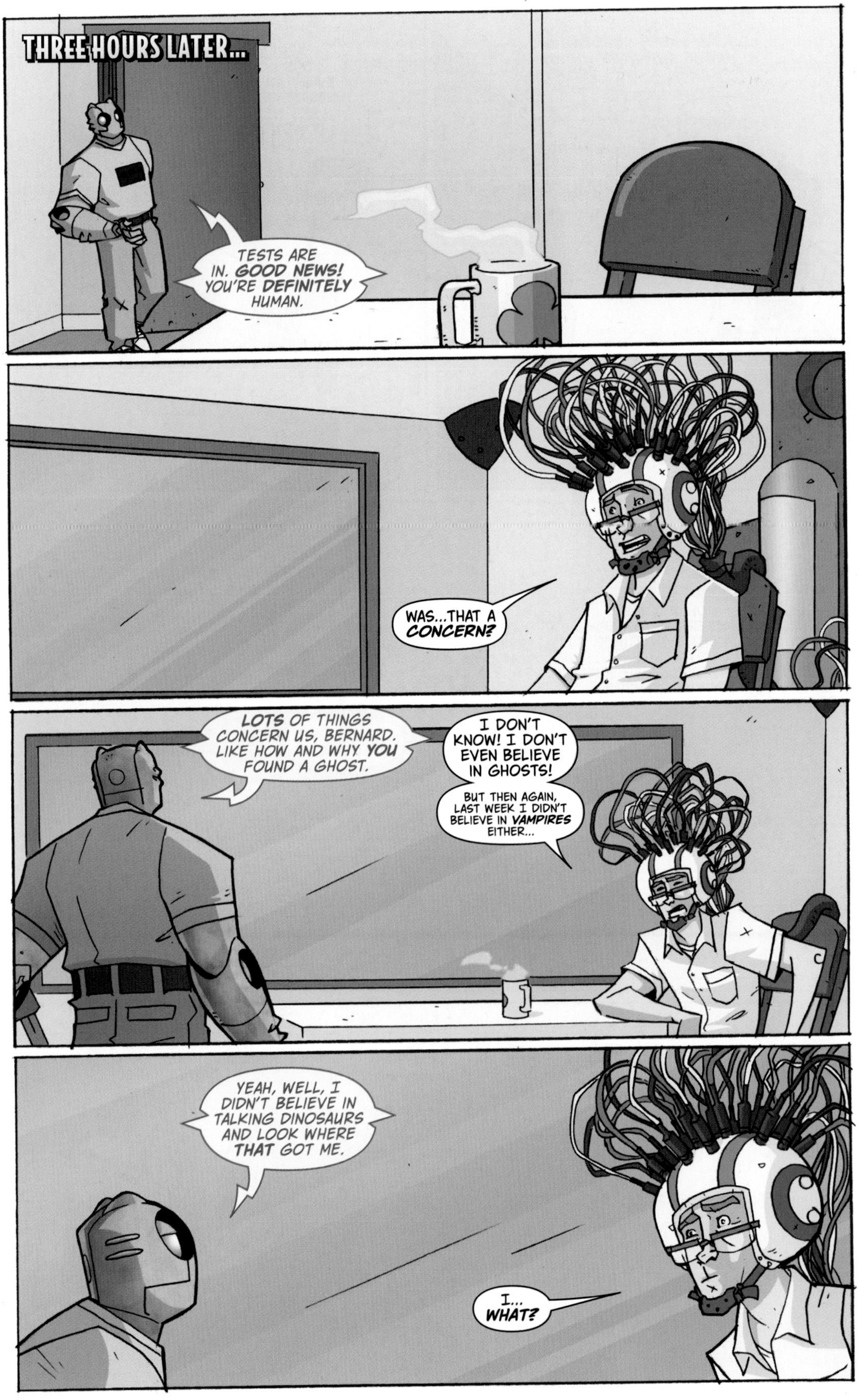
THREE HOURS LATER...
TESTS ARE IN. GOOD NEWS! YOU'RE DEFINITELY HUMAN.
WAS...THAT A CONCERN?
LOTS OF THINGS CONCERN US, BERNARD. LIKE HOW AND WHY YOU FOUND A GHOST.
I DON'T KNOW! I DON'T EVEN BELIEVE IN GHOSTS!
BUT THEN AGAIN, LAST WEEK I DIDN'T BELIEVE IN VAMPIRES EITHER...
YEAH, WELL, I DIDN'T BELIEVE IN TALKING DINOSAURS AND LOOK WHERE THAT GOT ME.
I... WHAT?

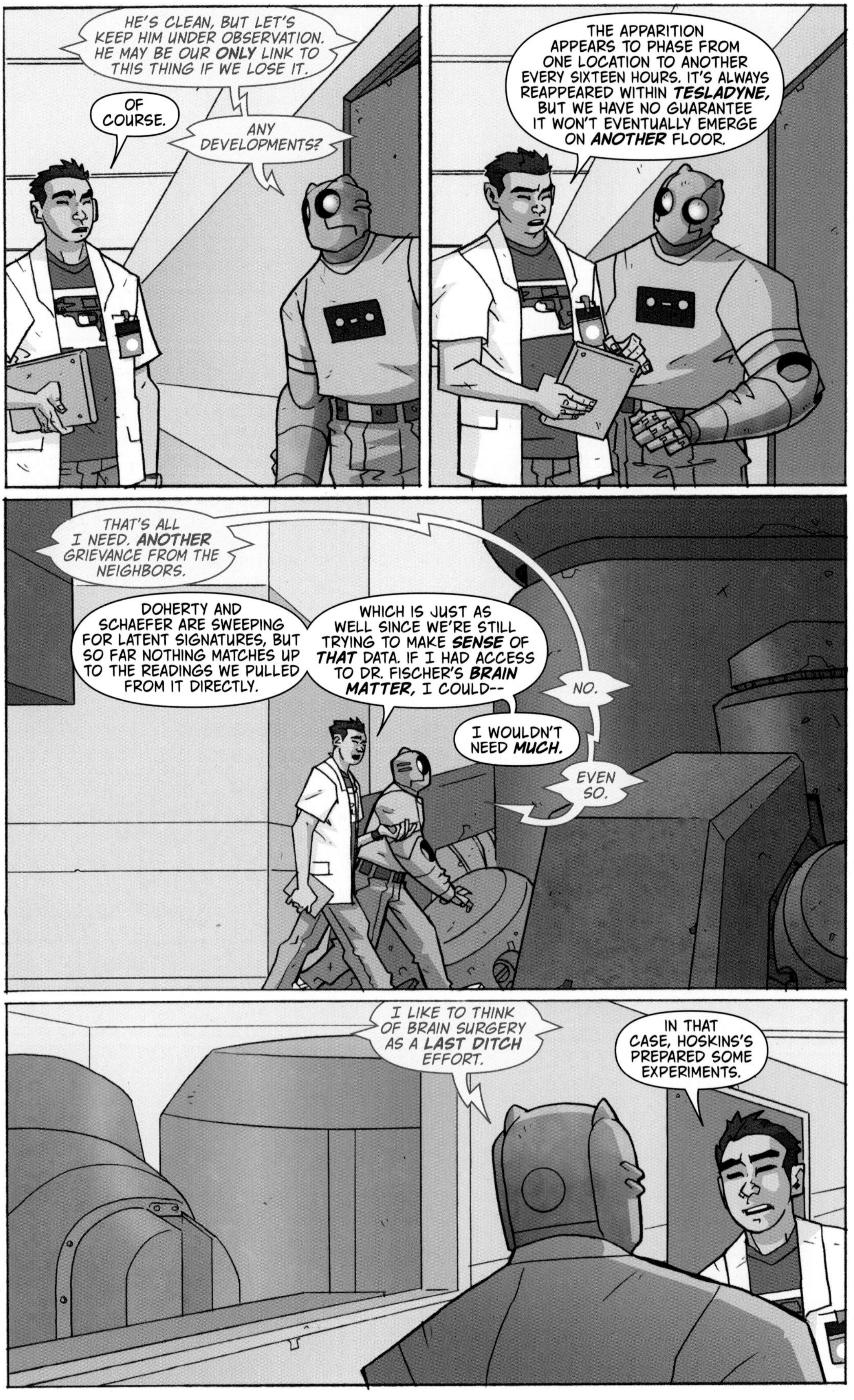
HE'S CLEAN, BUT LET'S KEEP HIM UNDER OBSERVATION. HE MAY BE OUR ONLY LINK TO THIS THING IF WE LOSE IT.
OF COURSE.
ANY DEVELOPMENTS?
THE APPARITION APPEARS TO PHASE FROM ONE LOCATION TO ANOTHER EVERY SIXTEEN HOURS. IT'S ALWAYS REAPPEARED WITHIN TESLADYNE, BUT WE HAVE NO GUARANTEE IT WON'T EVENTUALLY EMERGE ON ANOTHER FLOOR.
THAT'S ALL I NEED. ANOTHER GRIEVANCE FROM THE NEIGHBORS.
DOHERTY AND SCHAEFER ARE SWEEPING FOR LATENT SIGNATURES, BUT SO FAR NOTHING MATCHES UP TO THE READINGS WE PULLED FROM IT DIRECTLY.
WHICH IS JUST AS WELL SINCE WE'RE STILL TRYING TO MAKE SENSE OF THAT DATA. IF I HAD ACCESS TO DR. FISCHER'S BRAIN MATTER, I COULD--
NO.
I WOULDN'T NEED MUCH.
EVEN SO.
I LIKE TO THINK OF BRAIN SURGERY AS A LAST DITCH EFFORT.
IN THAT CASE, HOSKINS'S PREPARED SOME EXPERIMENTS.

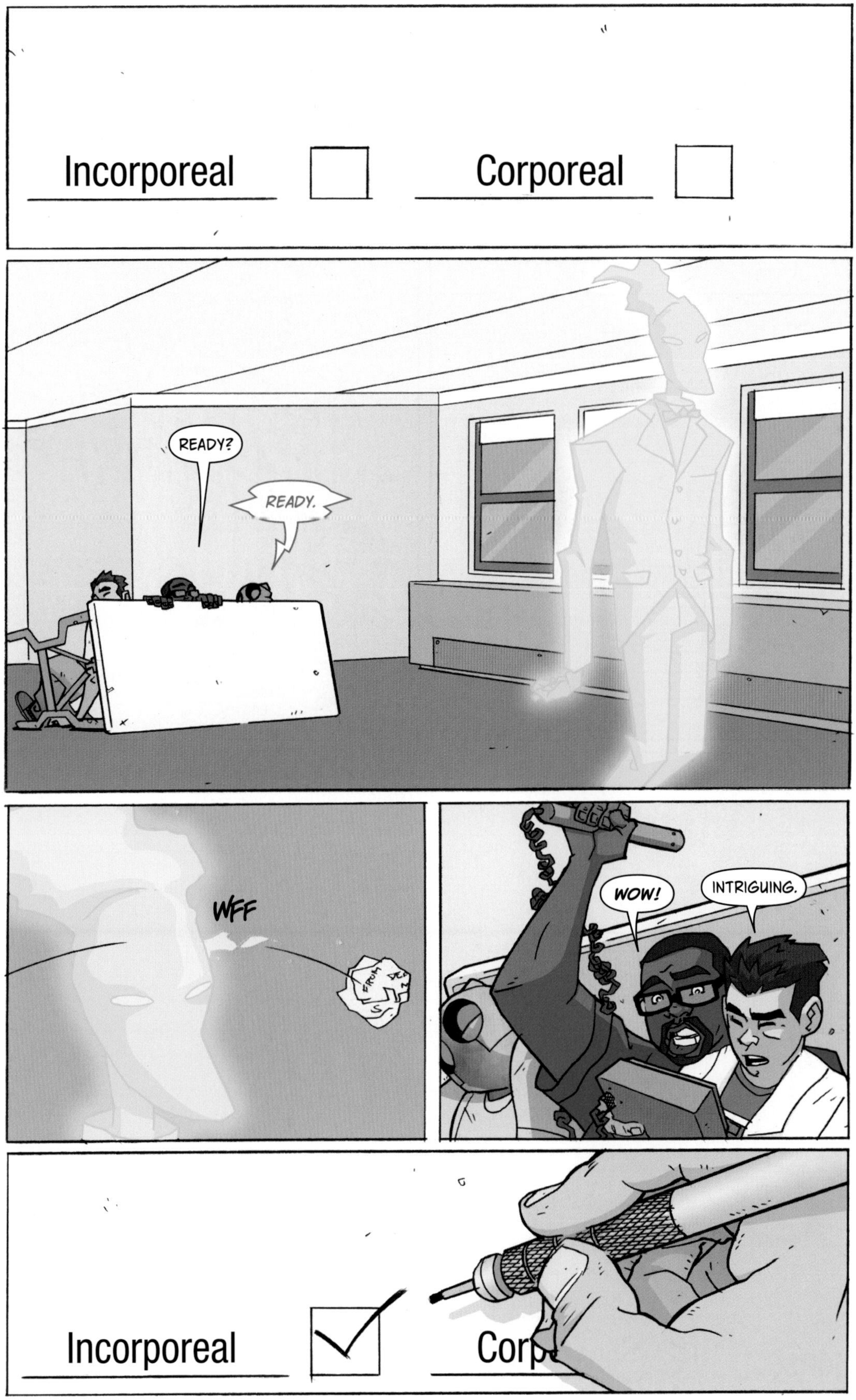

Incorporeal
Corporeal
READY?
READY.
WFF
WOW!
INTRIGUING.
Incorporeal

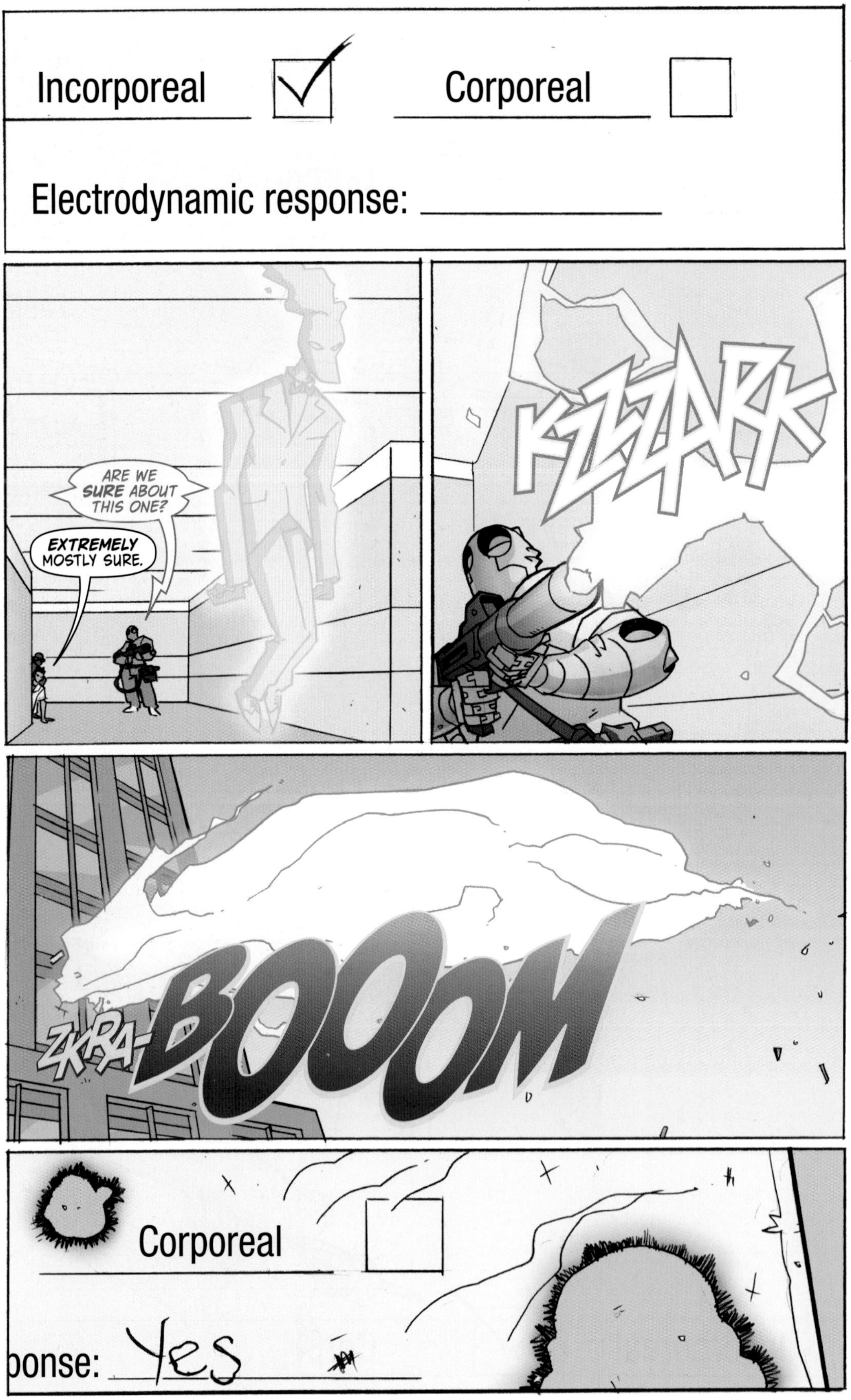

Incorporeal
Corporeal
Electrodynamic response:
ARE WE SURE ABOUT THIS ONE?
EXTREMELY MOSTLY SURE.
KZZZARK
ZKRA-BOOOM
Corporeal
ponse: Yes

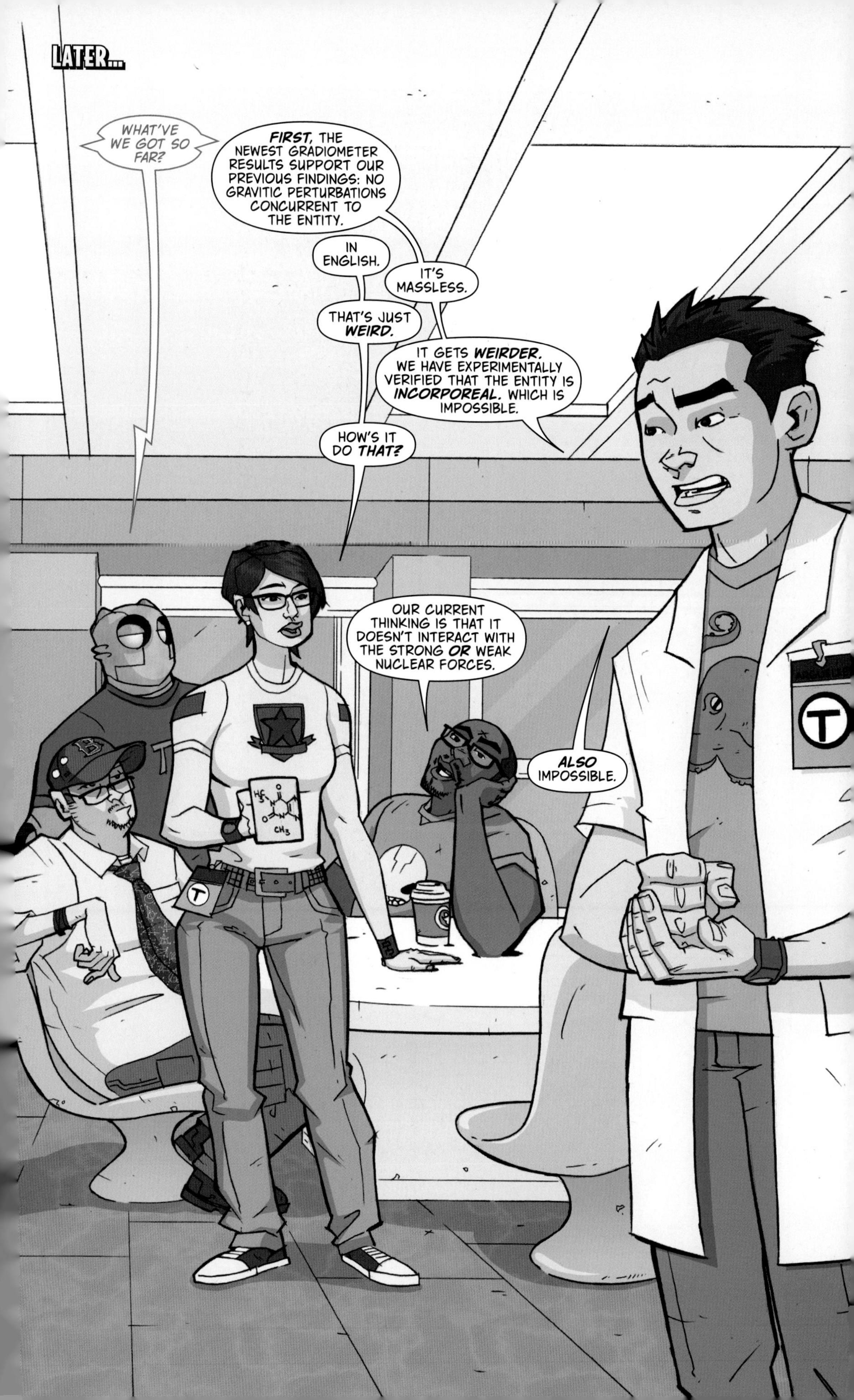
LATER...
WHAT'VE WE GOT SO FAR?
FIRST, THE NEWEST GRADIOMETER RESULTS SUPPORT OUR PREVIOUS FINDINGS: NO GRAVITIC PERTURBATIONS CONCURRENT TO THE ENTITY.
IN ENGLISH.
IT'S MASSLESS.
THAT'S JUST WEIRD.
IT GETS WEIRDER. WE HAVE EXPERIMENTALLY VERIFIED THAT THE ENTITY IS INCORPOREAL. WHICH IS IMPOSSIBLE.
HOW'S IT DO THAT?
OUR CURRENT THINKING IS THAT IT DOESN'T INTERACT WITH THE STRONG OR WEAK NUCLEAR FORCES.
ALSO IMPOSSIBLE.

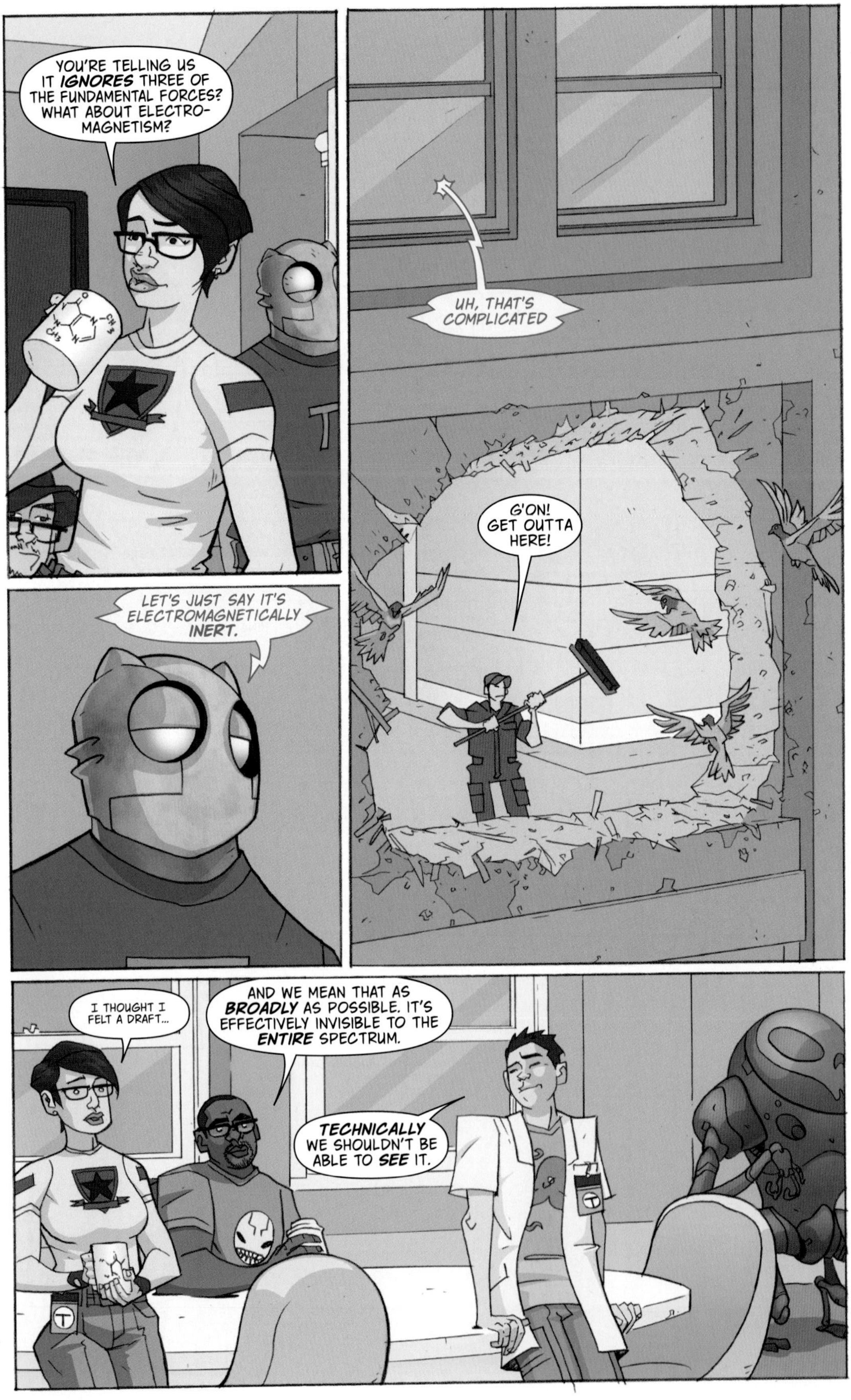
YOU'RE TELLING US IT **IGNORES** THREE OF THE FUNDAMENTAL FORCES? WHAT ABOUT ELECTRO-MAGNETISM?
UH, THAT'S COMPLICATED
G'ON! GET OUTTA HERE!
LET'S JUST SAY IT'S ELECTROMAGNETICALLY **INERT.**
I THOUGHT I FELT A DRAFT...
AND WE MEAN THAT AS **BROADLY** AS POSSIBLE. IT'S EFFECTIVELY INVISIBLE TO THE **ENTIRE** SPECTRUM.
TECHNICALLY WE SHOULDN'T BE ABLE TO **SEE** IT.

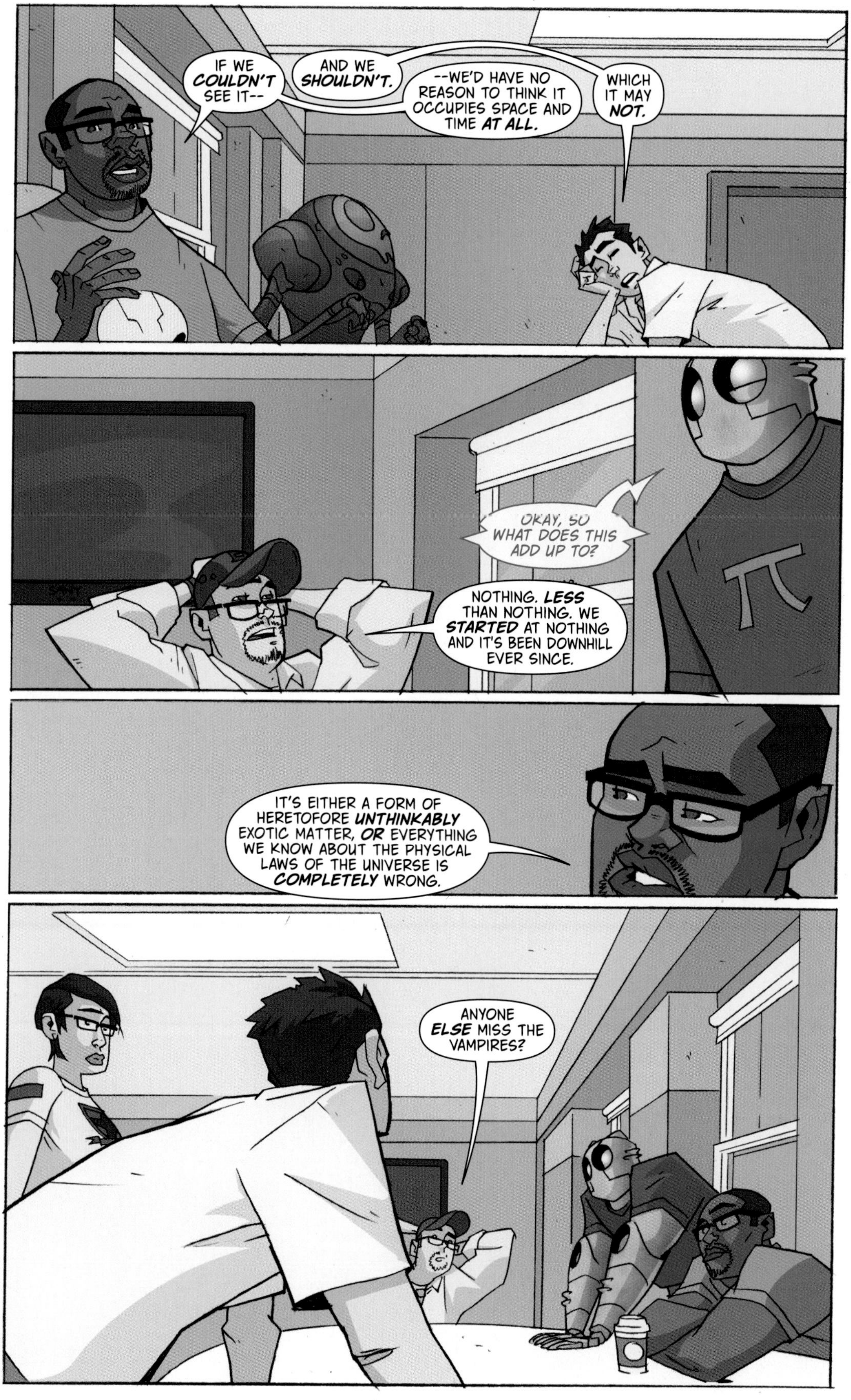

IF WE COULDN'T SEE IT--
AND WE SHOULDN'T.
--WE'D HAVE NO REASON TO THINK IT OCCUPIES SPACE AND TIME AT ALL.
WHICH IT MAY NOT.
OKAY, SO WHAT DOES THIS ADD UP TO?
NOTHING. LESS THAN NOTHING. WE STARTED AT NOTHING AND IT'S BEEN DOWNHILL EVER SINCE.
IT'S EITHER A FORM OF HERETOFORE UNTHINKABLY EXOTIC MATTER, OR EVERYTHING WE KNOW ABOUT THE PHYSICAL LAWS OF THE UNIVERSE IS COMPLETELY WRONG.
ANYONE ELSE MISS THE VAMPIRES?

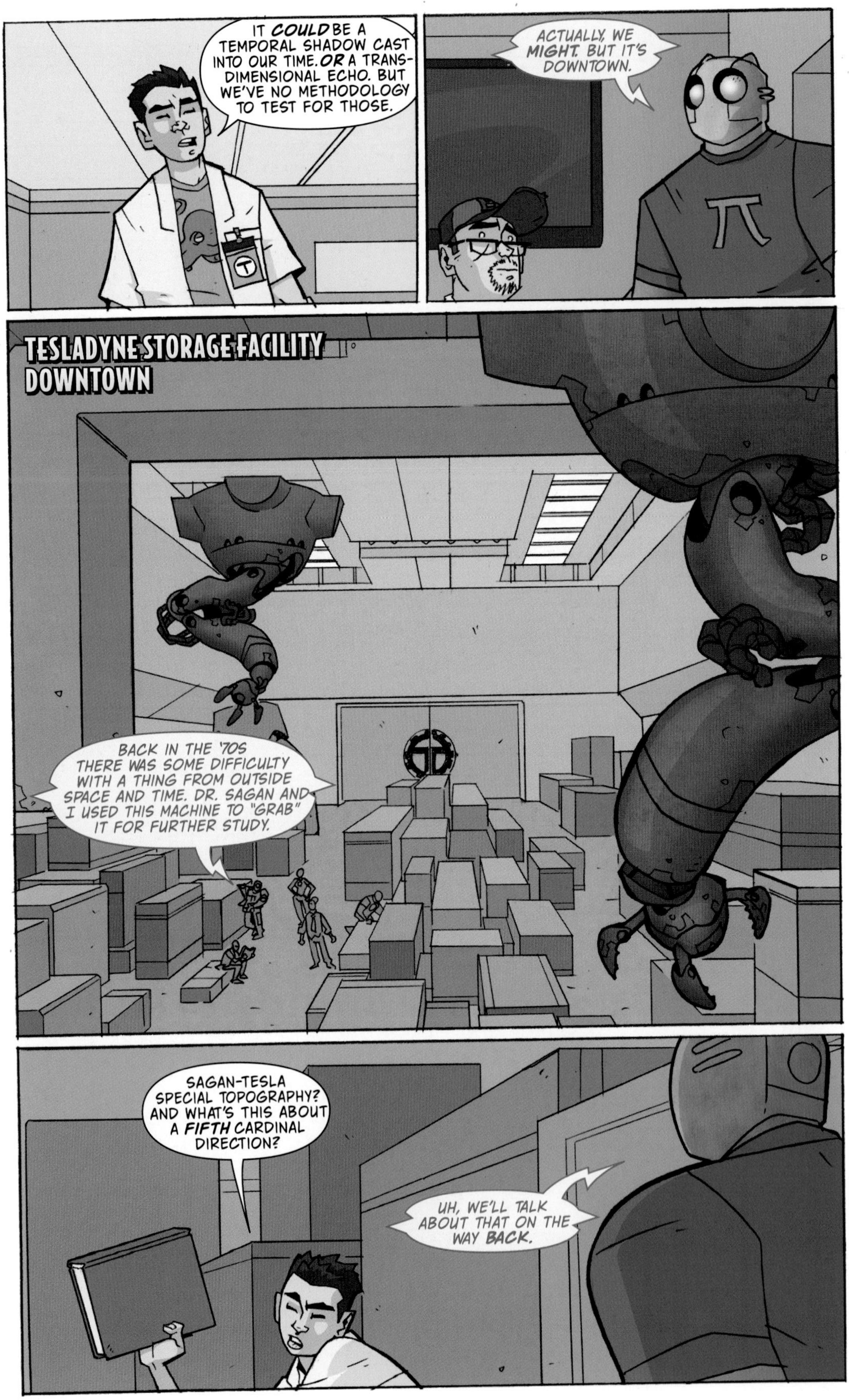
IT COULD BE A TEMPORAL SHADOW CAST INTO OUR TIME. OR A TRANS-DIMENSIONAL ECHO. BUT WE'VE NO METHODOLOGY TO TEST FOR THOSE.
ACTUALLY, WE MIGHT. BUT IT'S DOWNTOWN.
TESLADYNE STORAGE FACILITY
DOWNTOWN
BACK IN THE '70S THERE WAS SOME DIFFICULTY WITH A THING FROM OUTSIDE SPACE AND TIME. DR. SAGAN AND I USED THIS MACHINE TO "GRAB" IT FOR FURTHER STUDY.
SAGAN-TESLA SPECIAL TOPOGRAPHY? AND WHAT'S THIS ABOUT A FIFTH CARDINAL DIRECTION?
UH, WE'LL TALK ABOUT THAT ON THE WAY BACK.

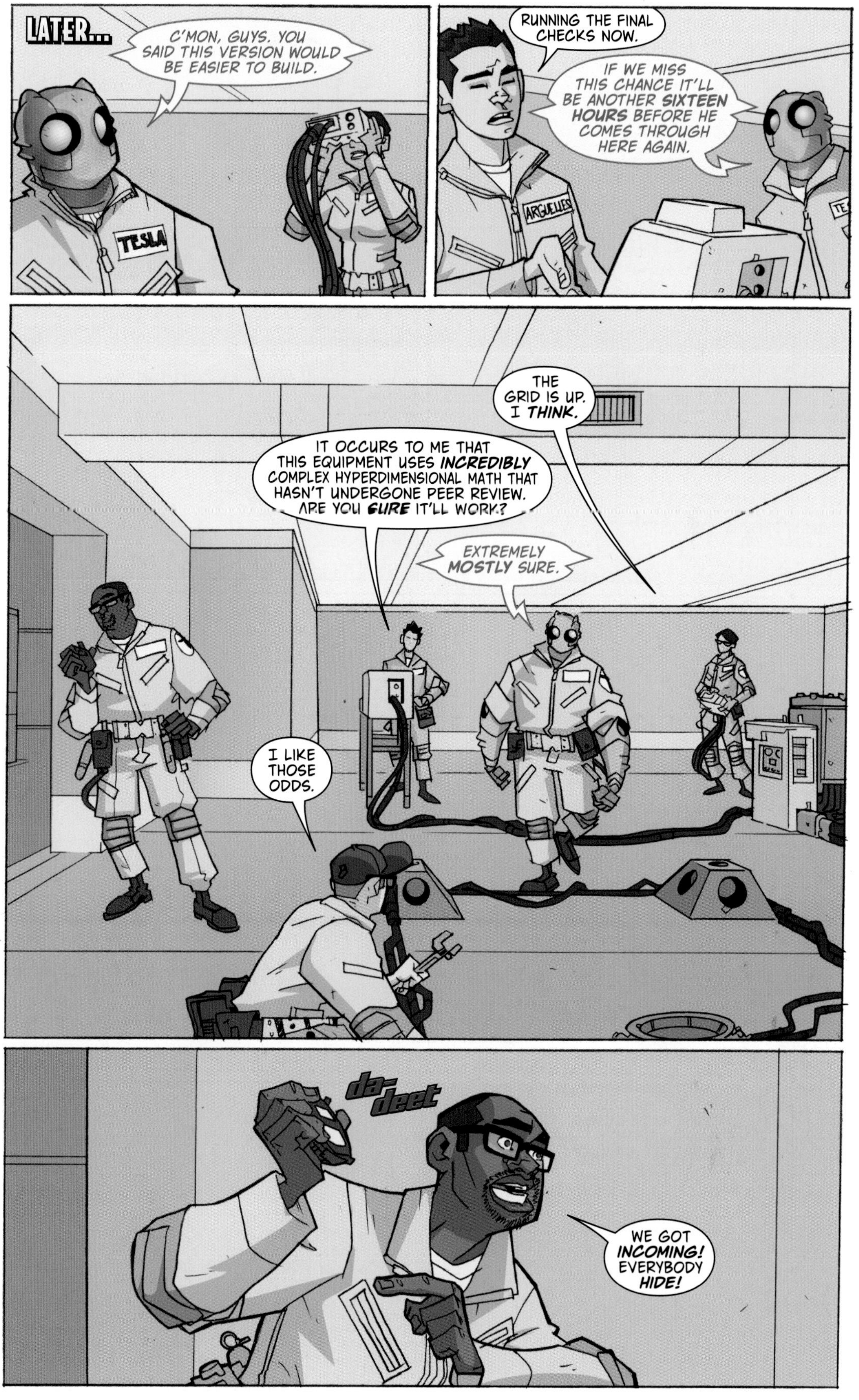
LATER...
C'MON, GUYS. YOU SAID THIS VERSION WOULD BE EASIER TO BUILD.
RUNNING THE FINAL CHECKS NOW.
IF WE MISS THIS CHANCE IT'LL BE ANOTHER SIXTEEN HOURS BEFORE HE COMES THROUGH HERE AGAIN.
TESLA
ARGUELLES
THE GRID IS UP. I THINK.
IT OCCURS TO ME THAT THIS EQUIPMENT USES INCREDIBLY COMPLEX HYPERDIMENSIONAL MATH THAT HASN'T UNDERGONE PEER REVIEW. ARE YOU SURE IT'LL WORK?
EXTREMELY MOSTLY SURE.
I LIKE THOSE ODDS.
da-deet
WE GOT INCOMING! EVERYBODY HIDE!

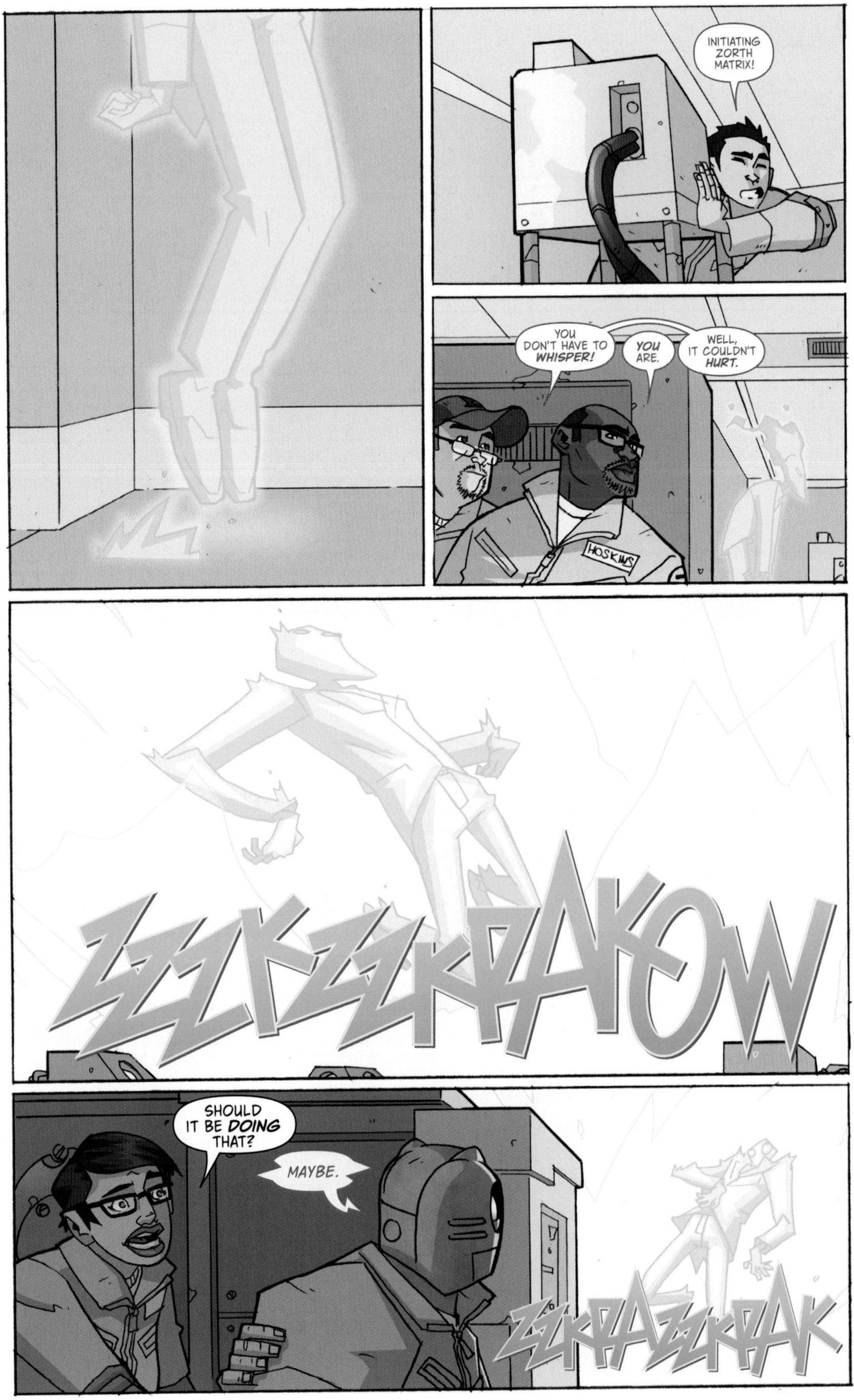
INITIATING ZORTH MATRIX!
YOU DON'T HAVE TO *WHISPER!*
YOU ARE.
WELL, IT COULDN'T *HURT.*
HOSKINS
ZZZKZZZKRAKOW
SHOULD IT BE *DOING* THAT?
MAYBE.
ZZKRAZZZKRAK

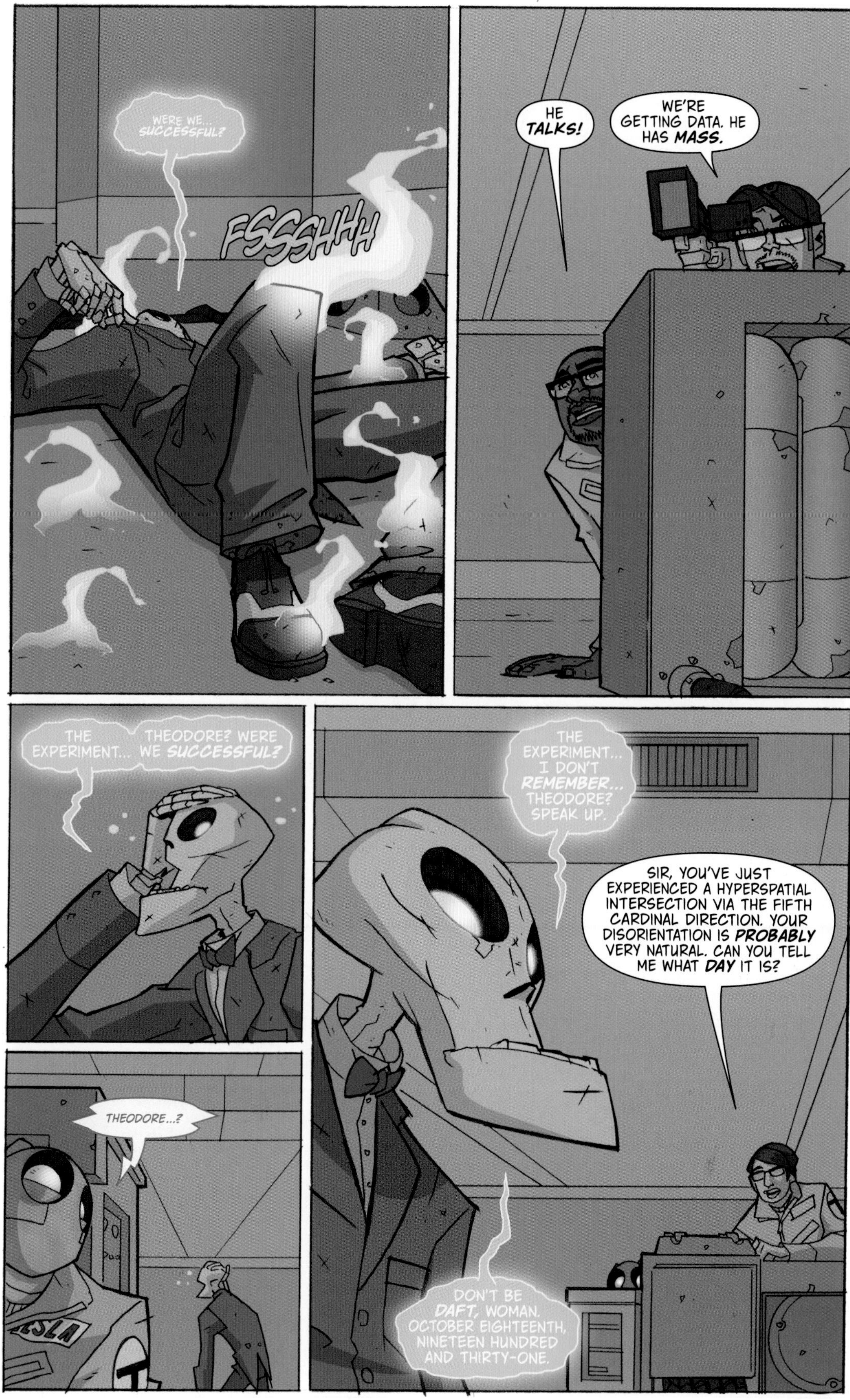
WERE WE... SUCCESSFUL?
FSSSHHH
HE TALKS!
WE'RE GETTING DATA. HE HAS MASS.
THE EXPERIMENT...
THEODORE? WERE WE SUCCESSFUL?
THE EXPERIMENT... I DON'T REMEMBER... THEODORE? SPEAK UP.
SIR, YOU'VE JUST EXPERIENCED A HYPERSPATIAL INTERSECTION VIA THE FIFTH CARDINAL DIRECTION. YOUR DISORIENTATION IS PROBABLY VERY NATURAL. CAN YOU TELL ME WHAT DAY IT IS?
THEODORE...?
DON'T BE DAFT, WOMAN. OCTOBER EIGHTEENTH, NINETEEN HUNDRED AND THIRTY-ONE.

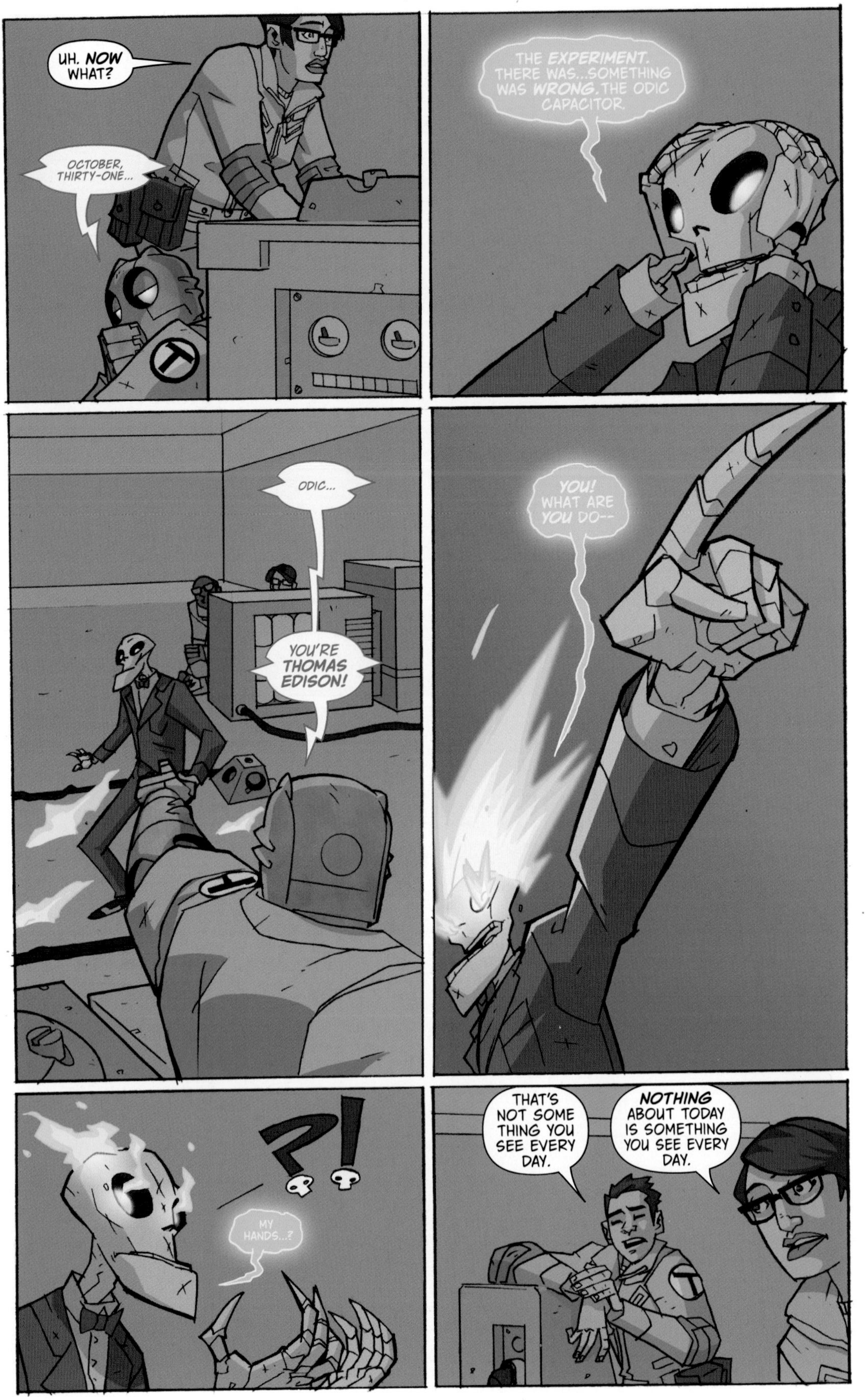
UH. NOW WHAT?
OCTOBER, THIRTY-ONE...
THE EXPERIMENT. THERE WAS...SOMETHING WAS WRONG. THE ODIC CAPACITOR.
ODIC...
YOU'RE THOMAS EDISON!
YOU! WHAT ARE YOU DO--
?!
MY HANDS...?
THAT'S NOT SOME THING YOU SEE EVERY DAY.
NOTHING ABOUT TODAY IS SOMETHING YOU SEE EVERY DAY.

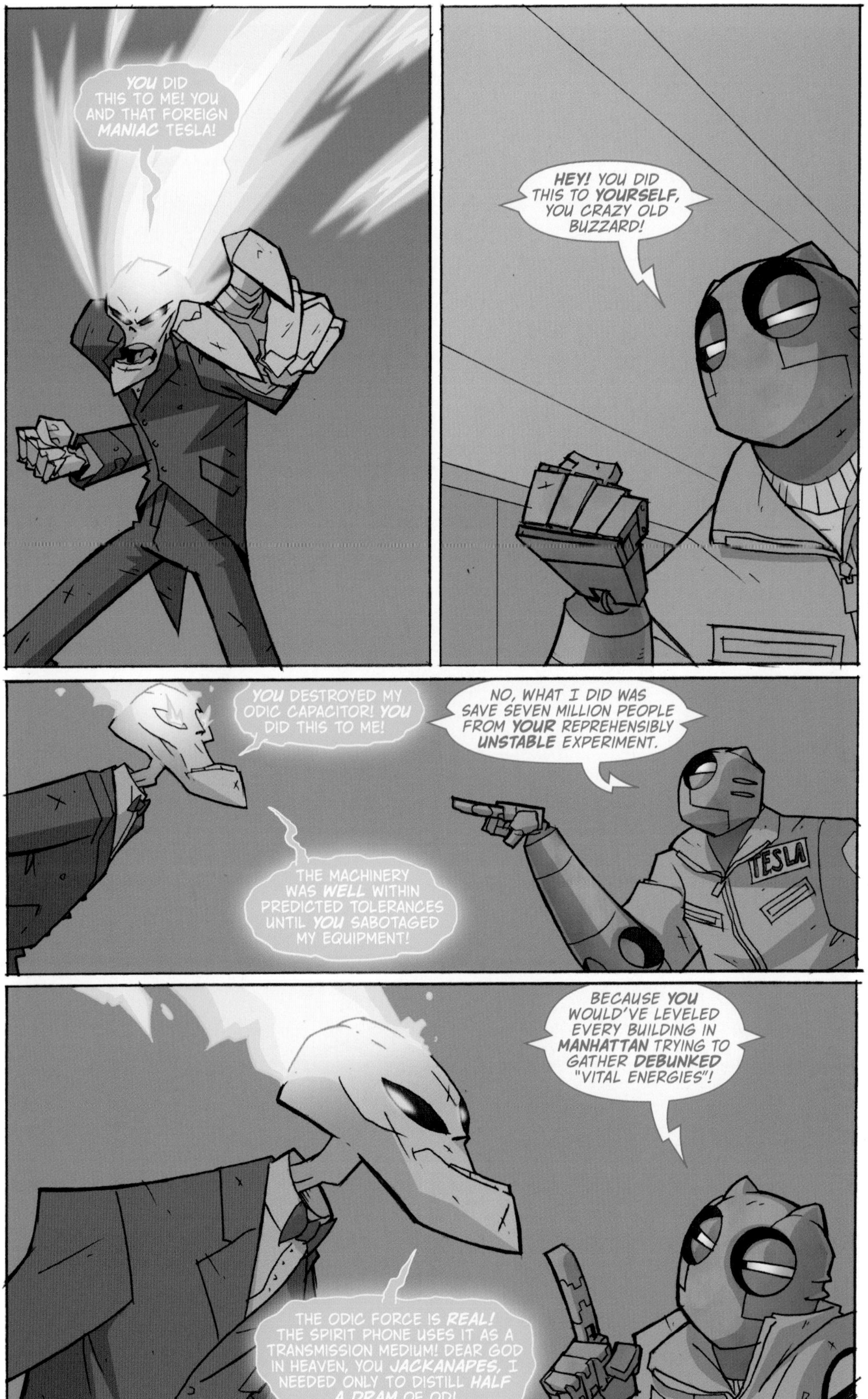
YOU DID THIS TO ME! YOU AND THAT FOREIGN MANIAC TESLA!
HEY! YOU DID THIS TO YOURSELF, YOU CRAZY OLD BUZZARD!
YOU DESTROYED MY ODIC CAPACITOR! YOU DID THIS TO ME!
NO, WHAT I DID WAS SAVE SEVEN MILLION PEOPLE FROM YOUR REPREHENSIBLY UNSTABLE EXPERIMENT.
THE MACHINERY WAS WELL WITHIN PREDICTED TOLERANCES UNTIL YOU SABOTAGED MY EQUIPMENT!
TESLA
BECAUSE YOU WOULD'VE LEVELED EVERY BUILDING IN MANHATTAN TRYING TO GATHER DEBUNKED "VITAL ENERGIES"!
THE ODIC FORCE IS REAL! THE SPIRIT PHONE USES IT AS A TRANSMISSION MEDIUM! DEAR GOD IN HEAVEN, YOU JACKANAPES, I NEEDED ONLY TO DISTILL HALF A DRAM OF OD!

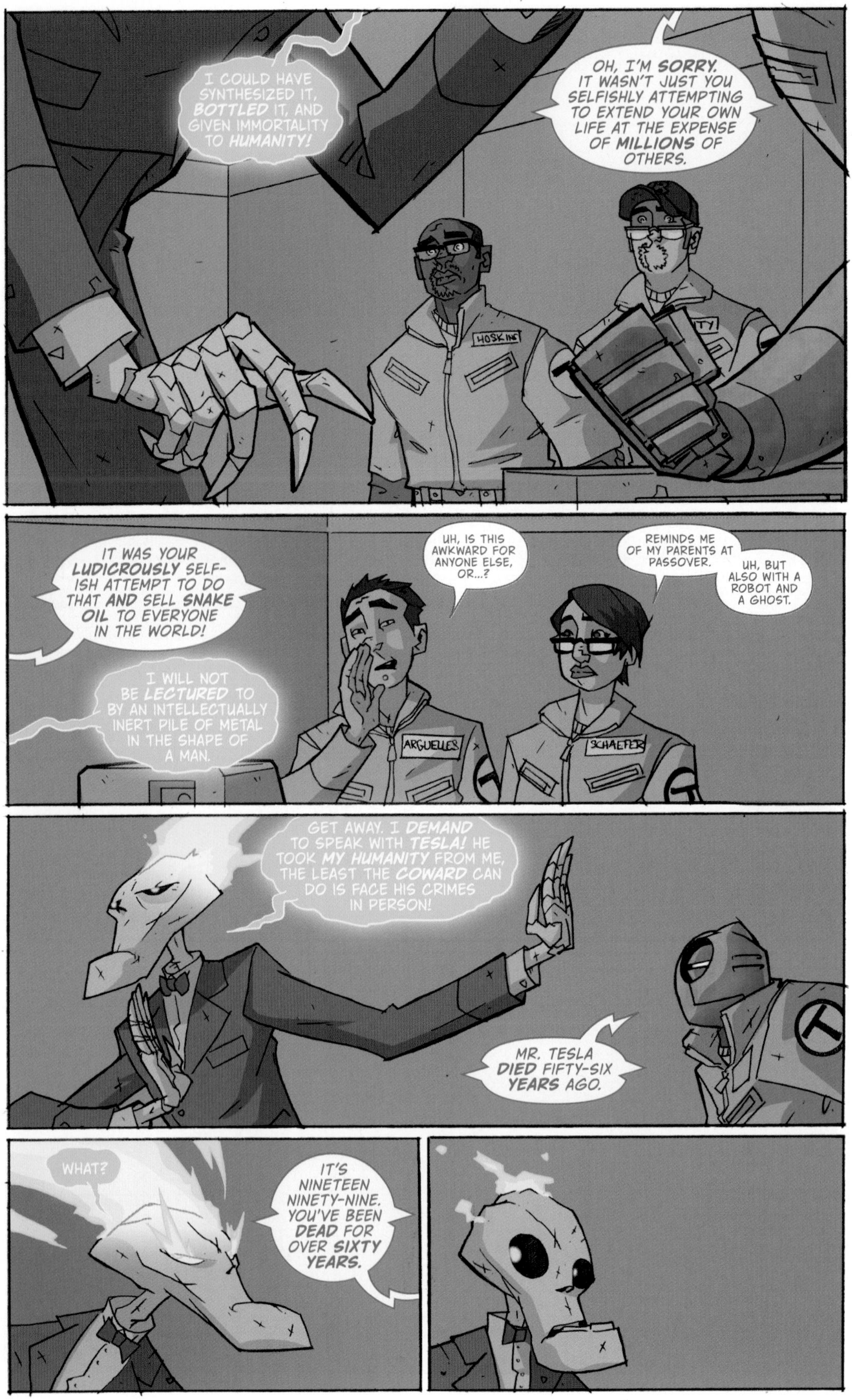
I COULD HAVE SYNTHESIZED IT, BOTTLED IT, AND GIVEN IMMORTALITY TO HUMANITY!
OH, I'M SORRY. IT WASN'T JUST YOU SELFISHLY ATTEMPTING TO EXTEND YOUR OWN LIFE AT THE EXPENSE OF MILLIONS OF OTHERS.
HOSKINS
IT WAS YOUR LUDICROUSLY SELF-ISH ATTEMPT TO DO THAT AND SELL SNAKE OIL TO EVERYONE IN THE WORLD!
I WILL NOT BE LECTURED TO BY AN INTELLECTUALLY INERT PILE OF METAL IN THE SHAPE OF A MAN.
UH, IS THIS AWKWARD FOR ANYONE ELSE, OR...?
REMINDS ME OF MY PARENTS AT PASSOVER.
UH, BUT ALSO WITH A ROBOT AND A GHOST.
ARGUELLES
SCHAEFER
GET AWAY. I DEMAND TO SPEAK WITH TESLA! HE TOOK MY HUMANITY FROM ME, THE LEAST THE COWARD CAN DO IS FACE HIS CRIMES IN PERSON!
MR. TESLA DIED FIFTY-SIX YEARS AGO.
WHAT?
IT'S NINETEEN NINETY-NINE. YOU'VE BEEN DEAD FOR OVER SIXTY YEARS.

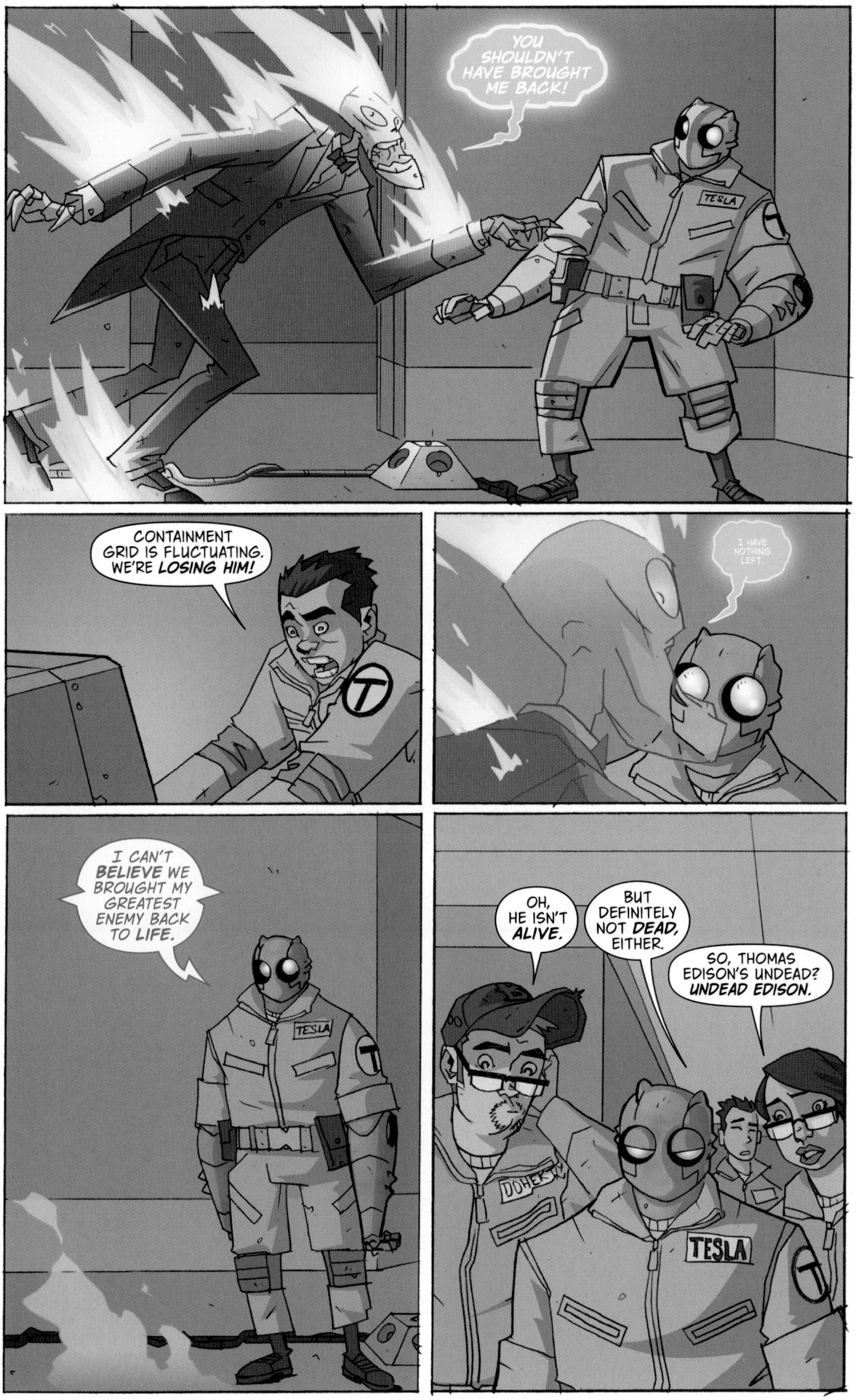
YOU SHOULDN'T HAVE BROUGHT ME BACK!
TESLA
CONTAINMENT GRID IS FLUCTUATING. WE'RE LOSING HIM!
I HAVE NOTHING LEFT.
I CAN'T BELIEVE WE BROUGHT MY GREATEST ENEMY BACK TO LIFE.
TESLA
OH, HE ISN'T ALIVE.
BUT DEFINITELY NOT DEAD, EITHER.
SO, THOMAS EDISON'S UNDEAD? UNDEAD EDISON.
DOHERTY
TESLA

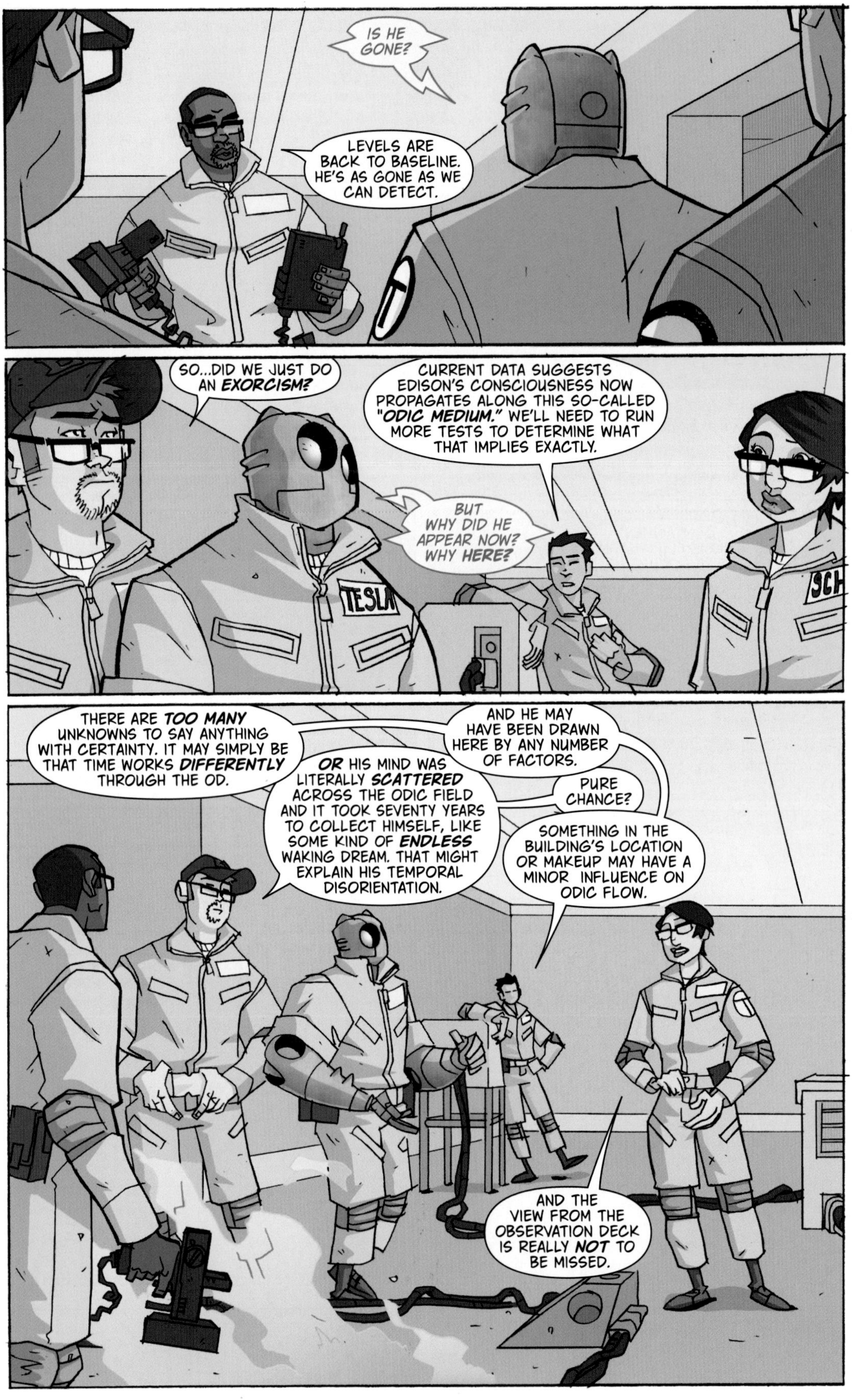
IS HE GONE?
LEVELS ARE BACK TO BASELINE. HE'S AS GONE AS WE CAN DETECT.
SO...DID WE JUST DO AN EXORCISM?
CURRENT DATA SUGGESTS EDISON'S CONSCIOUSNESS NOW PROPAGATES ALONG THIS SO-CALLED "ODIC MEDIUM." WE'LL NEED TO RUN MORE TESTS TO DETERMINE WHAT THAT IMPLIES EXACTLY.
BUT WHY DID HE APPEAR NOW? WHY HERE?
TESLA
SCH
THERE ARE TOO MANY UNKNOWNS TO SAY ANYTHING WITH CERTAINTY. IT MAY SIMPLY BE THAT TIME WORKS DIFFERENTLY THROUGH THE OD.
OR HIS MIND WAS LITERALLY SCATTERED ACROSS THE ODIC FIELD AND IT TOOK SEVENTY YEARS TO COLLECT HIMSELF, LIKE SOME KIND OF ENDLESS WAKING DREAM. THAT MIGHT EXPLAIN HIS TEMPORAL DISORIENTATION.
AND HE MAY HAVE BEEN DRAWN HERE BY ANY NUMBER OF FACTORS.
PURE CHANCE?
SOMETHING IN THE BUILDING'S LOCATION OR MAKEUP MAY HAVE A MINOR INFLUENCE ON ODIC FLOW.
AND THE VIEW FROM THE OBSERVATION DECK IS REALLY NOT TO BE MISSED.

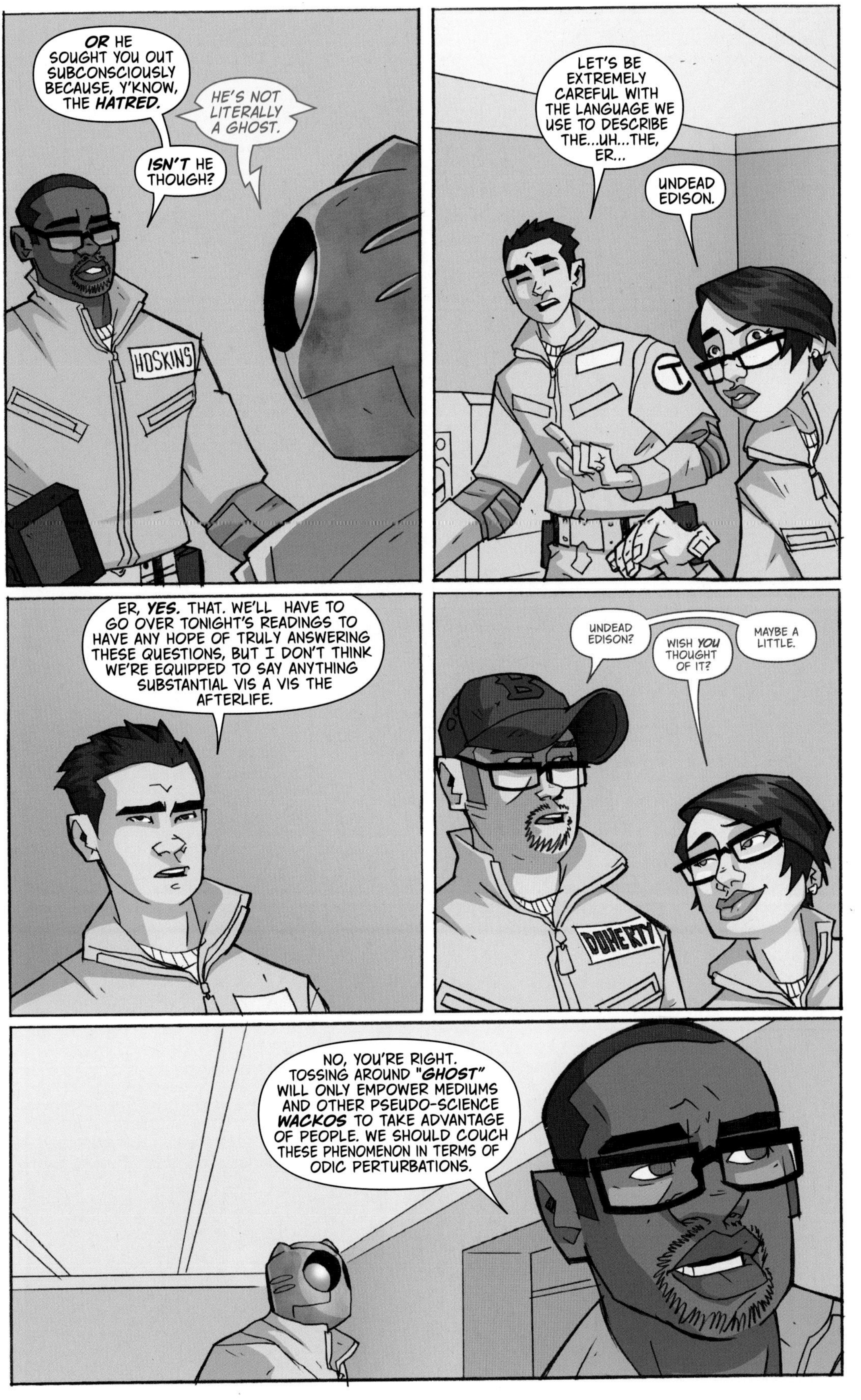
OR HE SOUGHT YOU OUT SUBCONSCIOUSLY BECAUSE, Y'KNOW, THE HATRED.
HE'S NOT LITERALLY A GHOST.
ISN'T HE THOUGH?
HOSKINS
LET'S BE EXTREMELY CAREFUL WITH THE LANGUAGE WE USE TO DESCRIBE THE...UH...THE, ER...
UNDEAD EDISON.
ER, YES. THAT. WE'LL HAVE TO GO OVER TONIGHT'S READINGS TO HAVE ANY HOPE OF TRULY ANSWERING THESE QUESTIONS, BUT I DON'T THINK WE'RE EQUIPPED TO SAY ANYTHING SUBSTANTIAL VIS A VIS THE AFTERLIFE.
UNDEAD EDISON?
WISH YOU THOUGHT OF IT?
MAYBE A LITTLE.
DOHERTY
NO, YOU'RE RIGHT. TOSSING AROUND "GHOST" WILL ONLY EMPOWER MEDIUMS AND OTHER PSEUDO-SCIENCE WACKOS TO TAKE ADVANTAGE OF PEOPLE. WE SHOULD COUCH THESE PHENOMENON IN TERMS OF ODIC PERTURBATIONS.

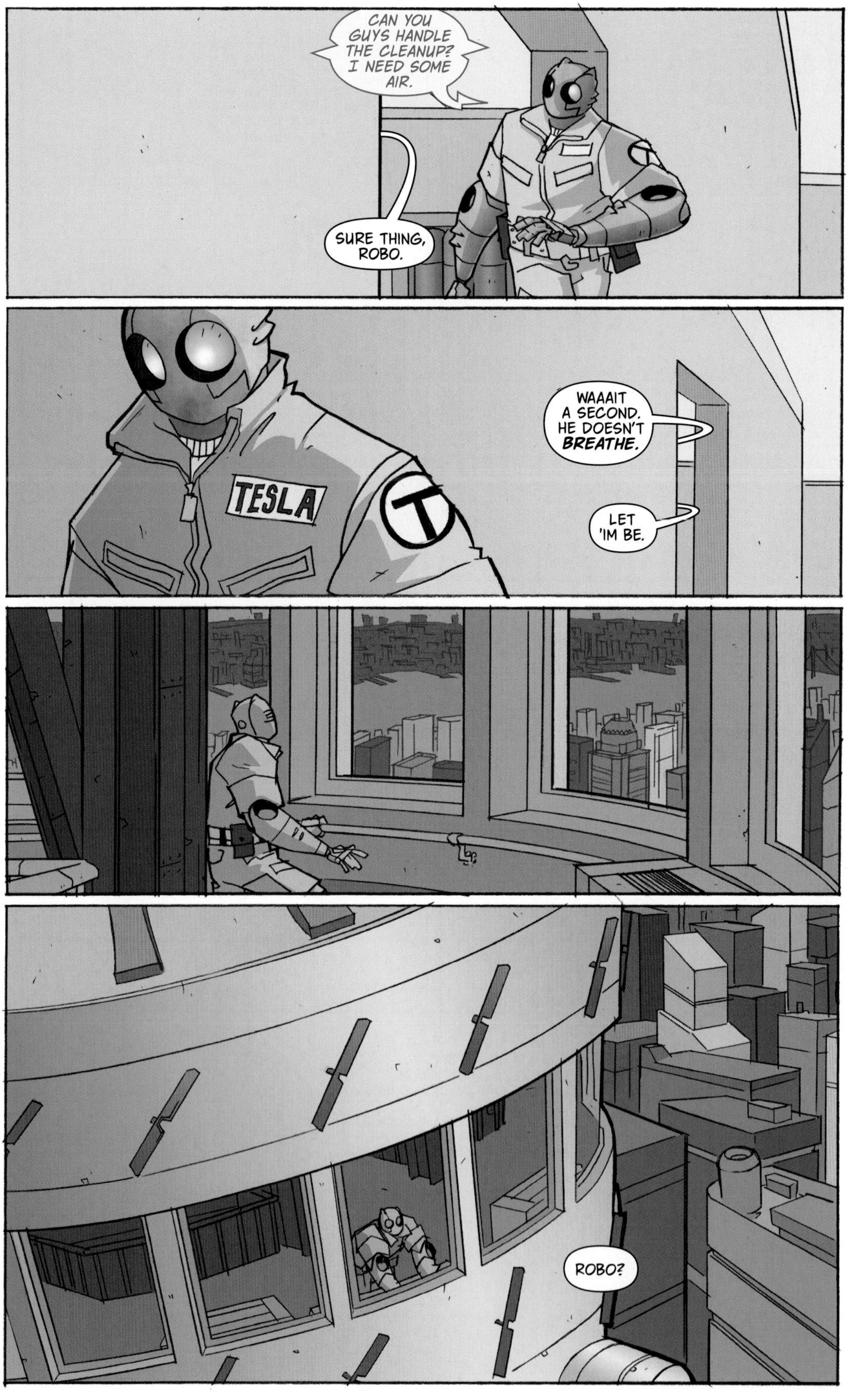
CAN YOU GUYS HANDLE THE CLEANUP? I NEED SOME AIR.
SURE THING, ROBO.
TESLA
WAAAIT A SECOND. HE DOESN'T *BREATHE.*
LET 'IM BE.
ROBO?

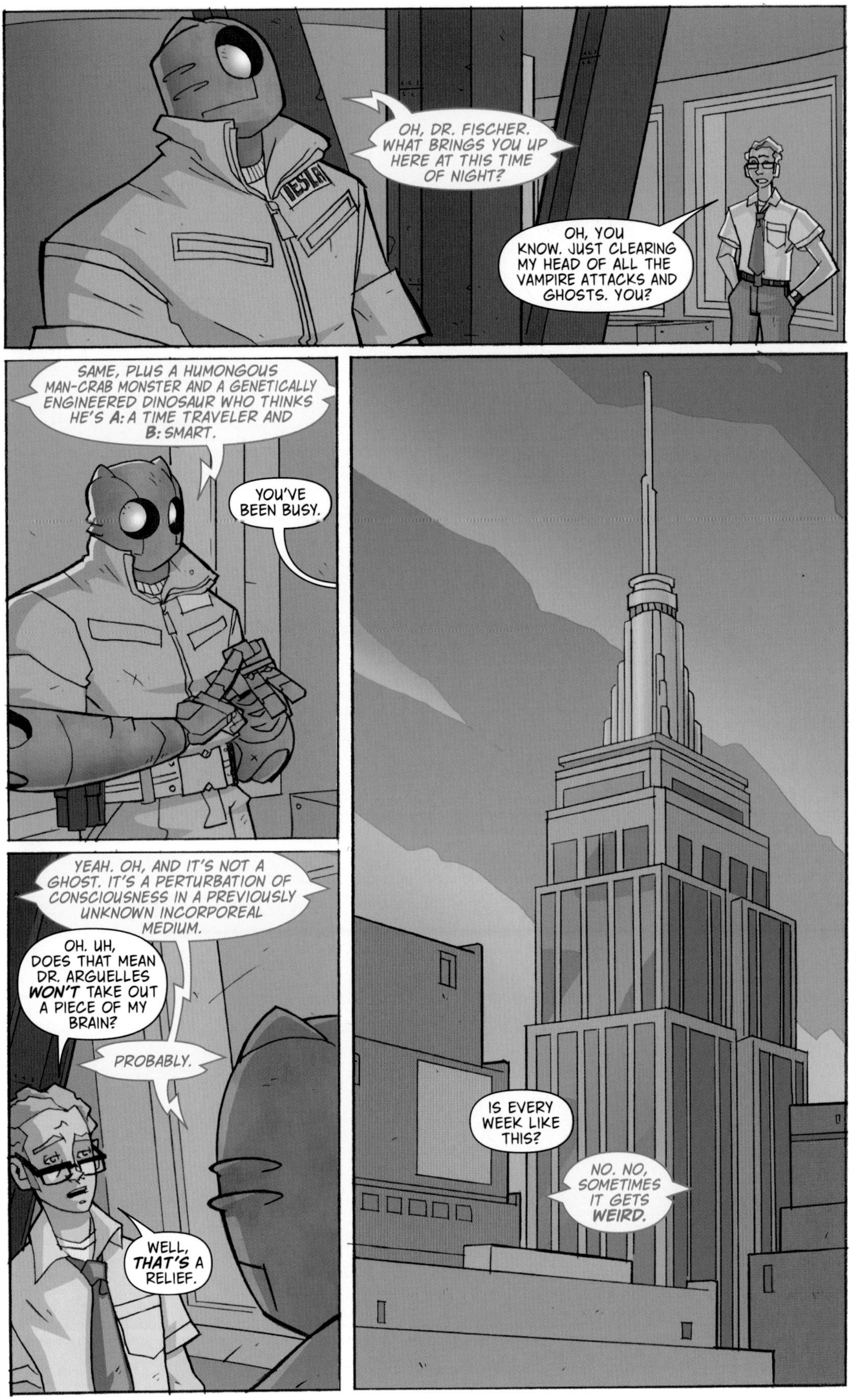

OH, DR. FISCHER. WHAT BRINGS YOU UP HERE AT THIS TIME OF NIGHT?
OH, YOU KNOW. JUST CLEARING MY HEAD OF ALL THE VAMPIRE ATTACKS AND GHOSTS. YOU?
SAME, PLUS A HUMONGOUS MAN-CRAB MONSTER AND A GENETICALLY ENGINEERED DINOSAUR WHO THINKS HE'S A: A TIME TRAVELER AND B: SMART.
YOU'VE BEEN BUSY.
YEAH. OH, AND IT'S NOT A GHOST. IT'S A PERTURBATION OF CONSCIOUSNESS IN A PREVIOUSLY UNKNOWN INCORPOREAL MEDIUM.
OH. UH, DOES THAT MEAN DR. ARGUELLES WON'T TAKE OUT A PIECE OF MY BRAIN?
PROBABLY.
WELL, THAT'S A RELIEF.
IS EVERY WEEK LIKE THIS?
NO. NO, SOMETIMES IT GETS WEIRD.

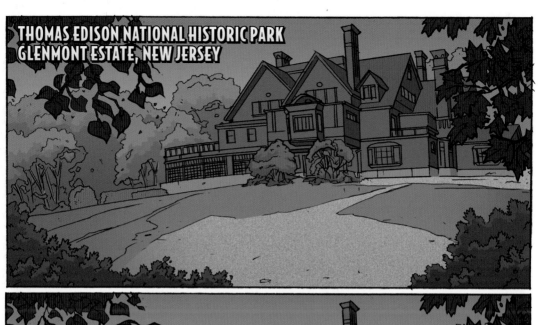

THOMAS EDISON NATIONAL HISTORIC PARK
GLENMONT ESTATE, NEW JERSEY

YOU SHOULDN'T HAVE BROUGHT ME BACK.

END

THE MAN WITH TWO SKULLS

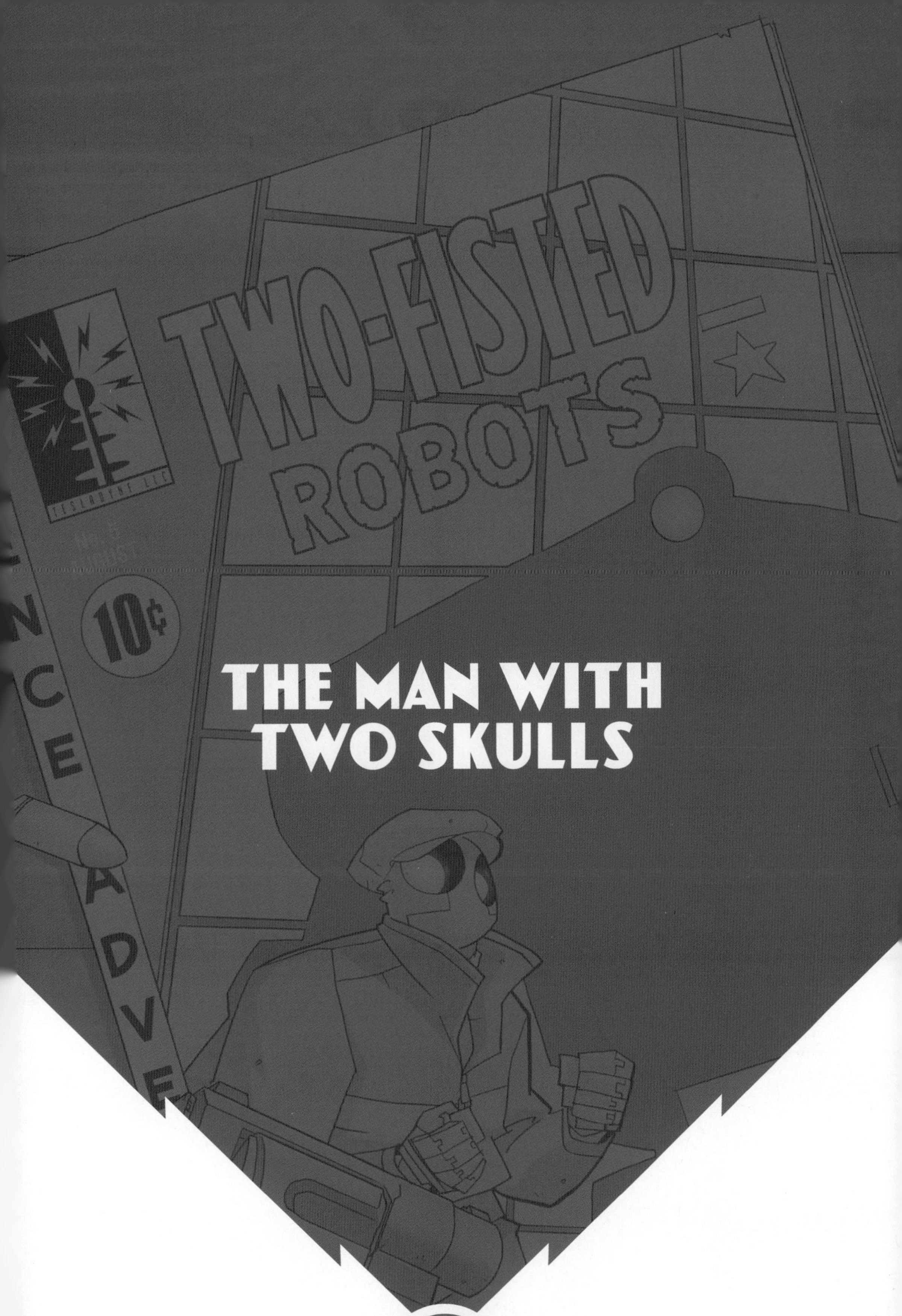
TWO-FISTED
ROBOTS
TESLADYNE LLC
10¢

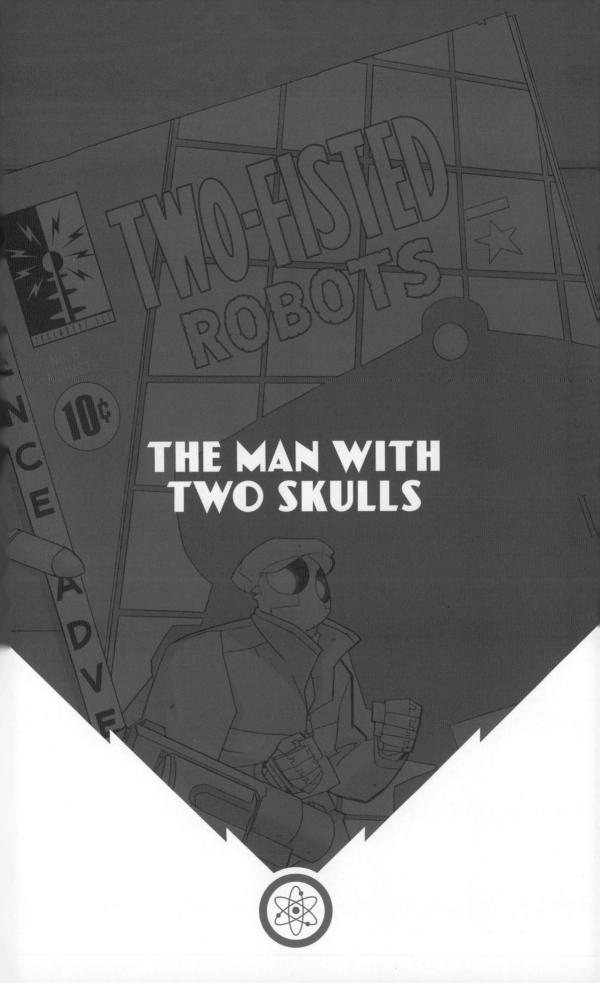

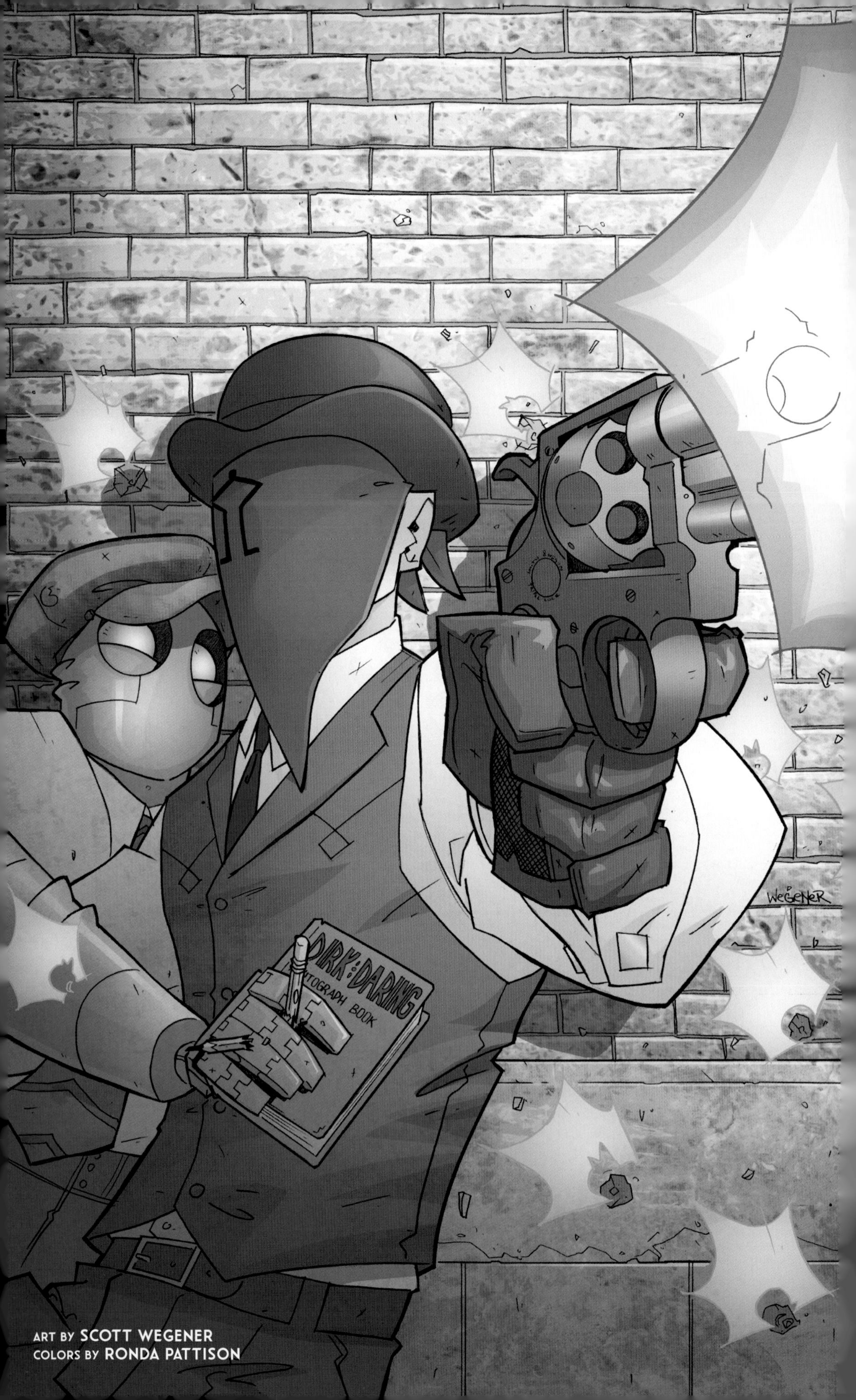
DIRK DARING
WEGENER

ART BY SCOTT WEGENER
COLORS BY RONDA PATTISON

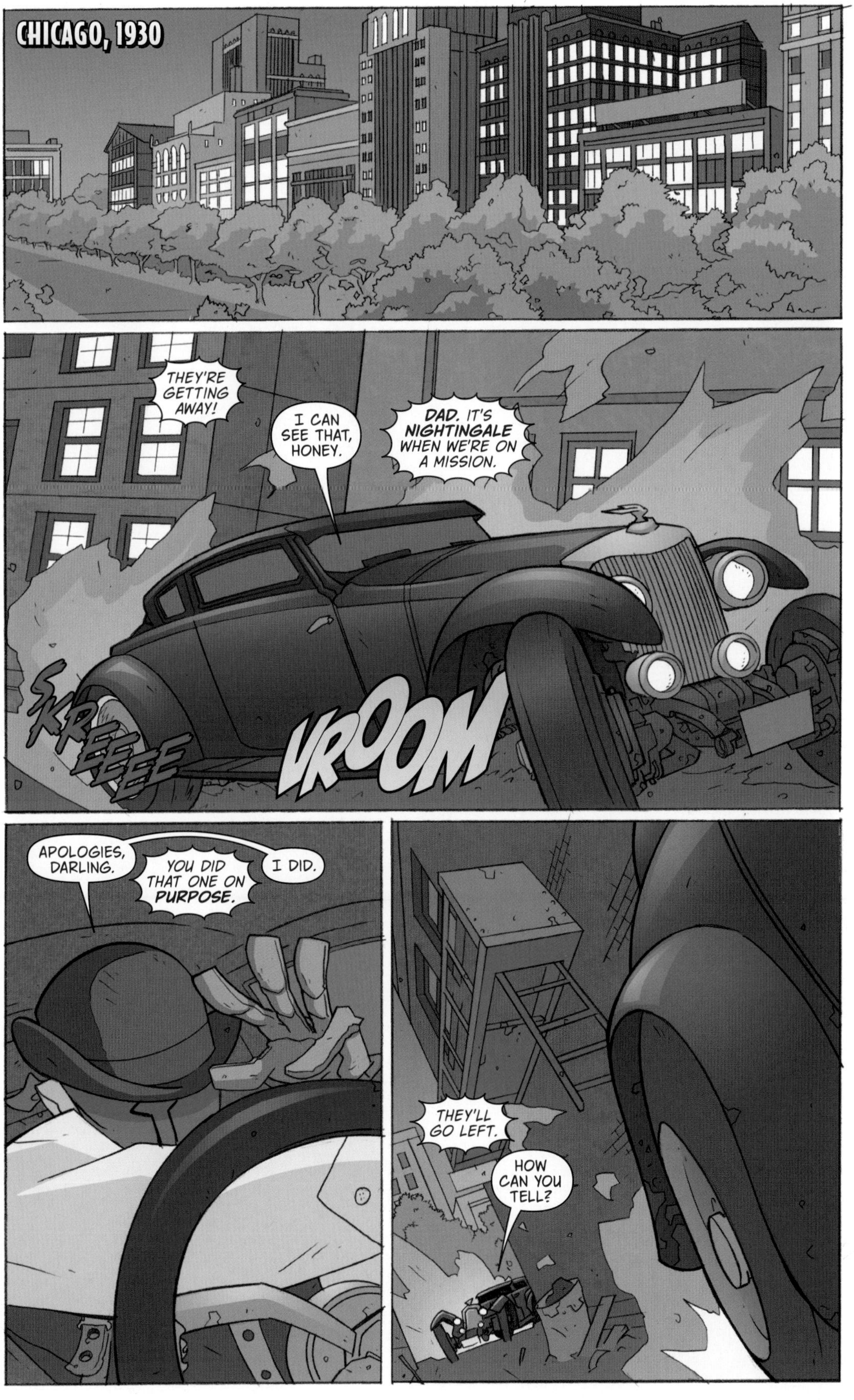
CHICAGO, 1930
THEY'RE GETTING AWAY!
I CAN SEE THAT, HONEY.
DAD. IT'S NIGHTINGALE WHEN WE'RE ON A MISSION.
SKREEEEE
VROOM
APOLOGIES, DARLING.
YOU DID THAT ONE ON PURPOSE.
I DID.
THEY'LL GO LEFT.
HOW CAN YOU TELL?

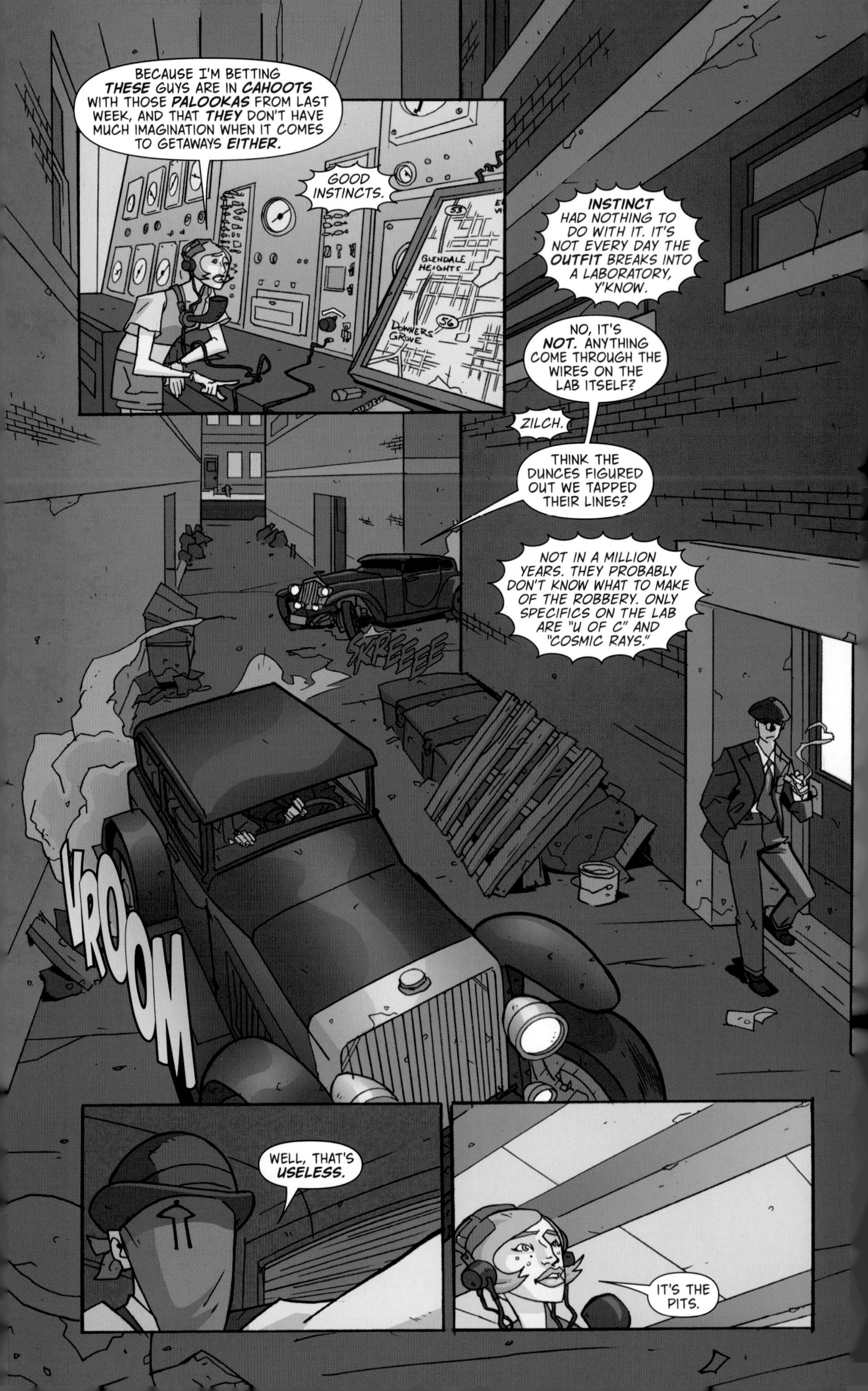
BECAUSE I'M BETTING THESE GUYS ARE IN CAHOOTS WITH THOSE PALOOKAS FROM LAST WEEK, AND THAT THEY DON'T HAVE MUCH IMAGINATION WHEN IT COMES TO GETAWAYS EITHER.
GOOD INSTINCTS.
53
GLENDALE HEIGHTS
56
DOWNERS GROVE
INSTINCT HAD NOTHING TO DO WITH IT. IT'S NOT EVERY DAY THE OUTFIT BREAKS INTO A LABORATORY, Y'KNOW.
NO, IT'S NOT. ANYTHING COME THROUGH THE WIRES ON THE LAB ITSELF?
ZILCH.
THINK THE DUNCES FIGURED OUT WE TAPPED THEIR LINES?
NOT IN A MILLION YEARS. THEY PROBABLY DON'T KNOW WHAT TO MAKE OF THE ROBBERY. ONLY SPECIFICS ON THE LAB ARE "U OF C" AND "COSMIC RAYS."
SKREEEEE
VROOOM
WELL, THAT'S USELESS.
IT'S THE PITS.

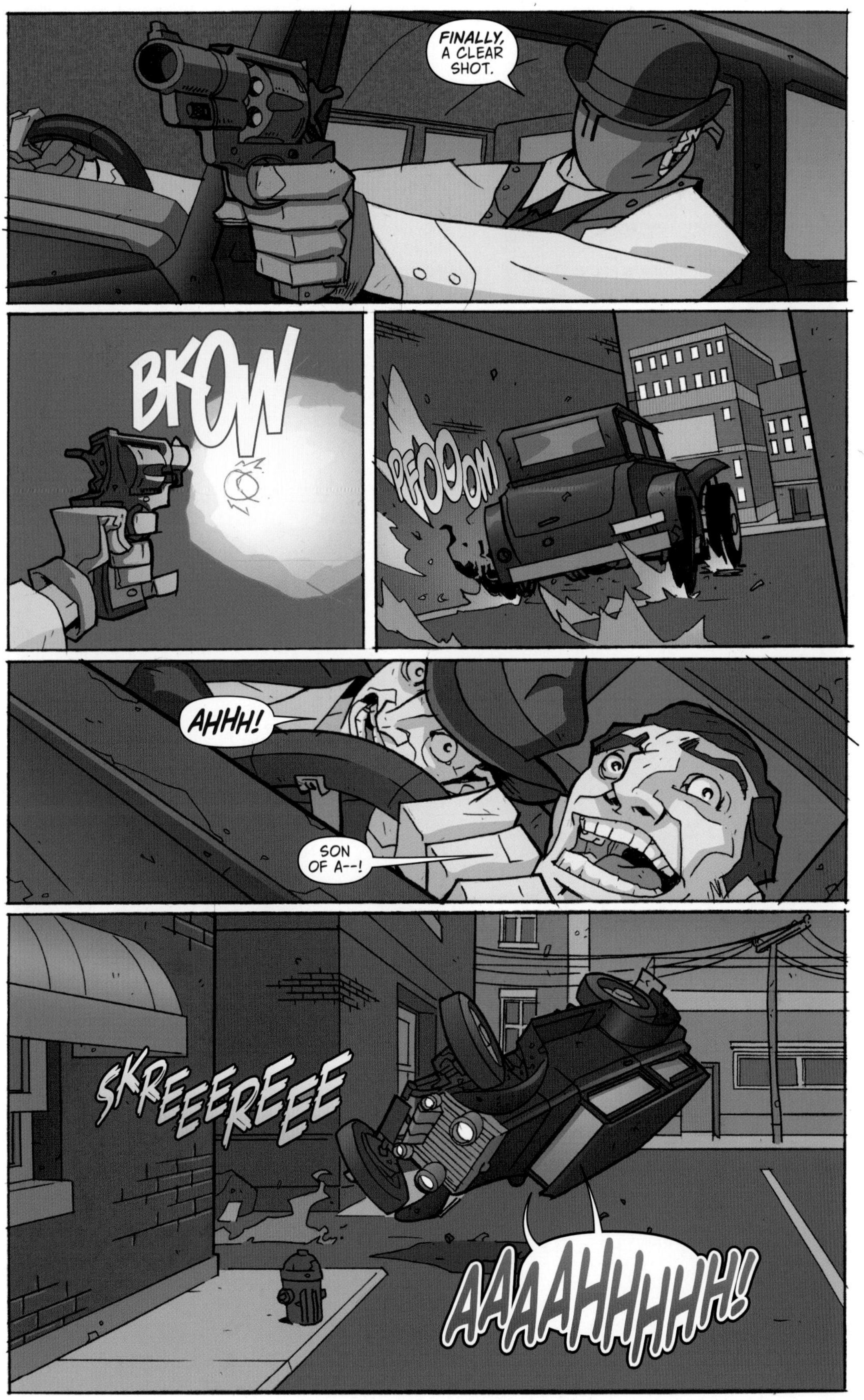
FINALLY, A CLEAR SHOT.
BKOW
PFOOOOM
AHHH!
SON OF A--!
SKREEEREEE
AAAAHHHHH!

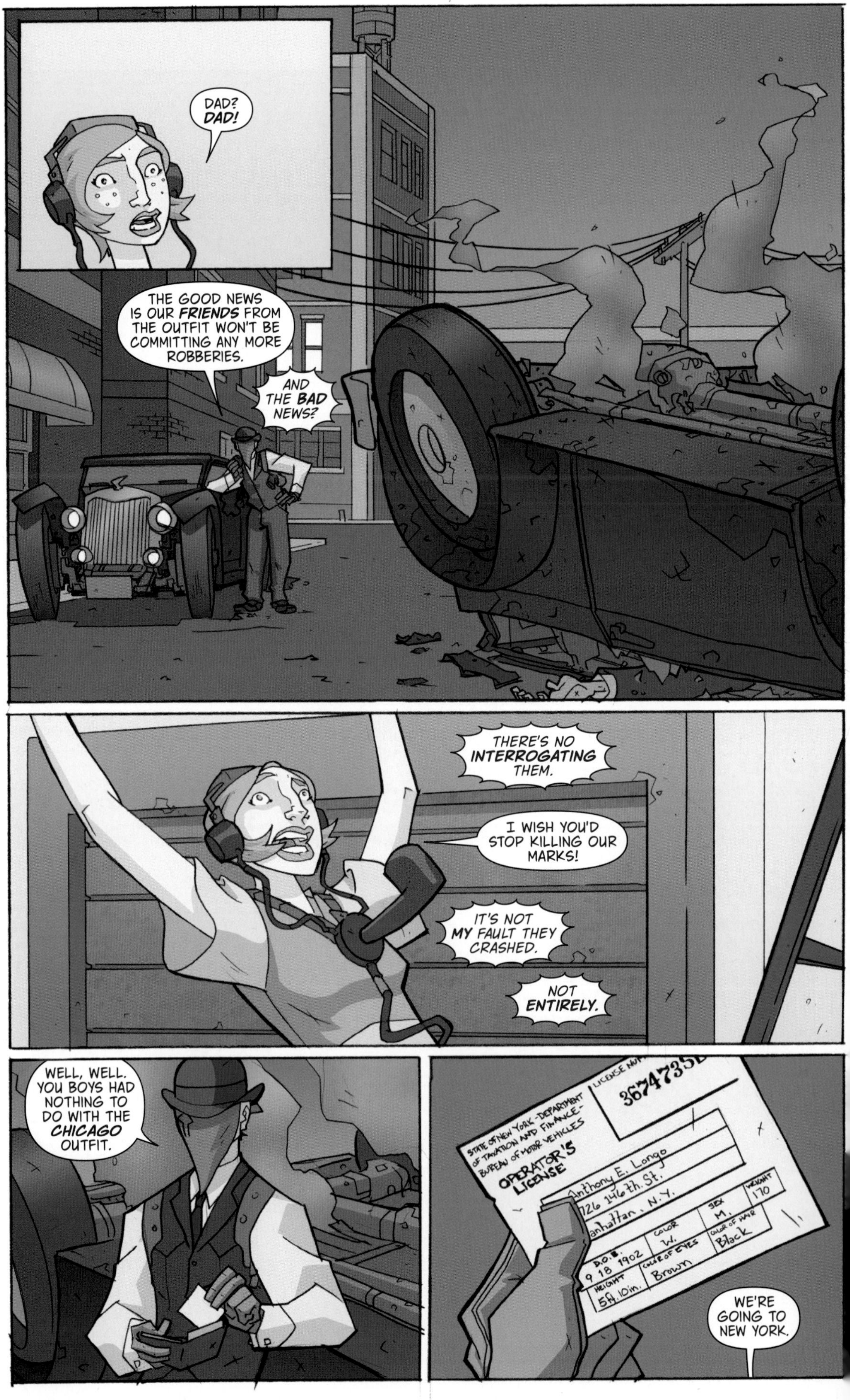
DAD? DAD!
THE GOOD NEWS IS OUR FRIENDS FROM THE OUTFIT WON'T BE COMMITTING ANY MORE ROBBERIES.
AND THE BAD NEWS?
THERE'S NO INTERROGATING THEM.
I WISH YOU'D STOP KILLING OUR MARKS!
IT'S NOT MY FAULT THEY CRASHED.
NOT ENTIRELY.
WELL, WELL. YOU BOYS HAD NOTHING TO DO WITH THE CHICAGO OUTFIT.
STATE OF NEW YORK - DEPARTMENT OF TAXATION AND FINANCE - BUREAU OF MOTOR VEHICLES
OPERATOR'S LICENSE
Anthony E. Longo
SEX M.
WEIGHT 170
COLOR W.
COLOR OF HAIR Black
D.O.B. 9 18 1902
COLOR OF EYES Brown
HEIGHT 5ft. 10in.
WE'RE GOING TO NEW YORK.

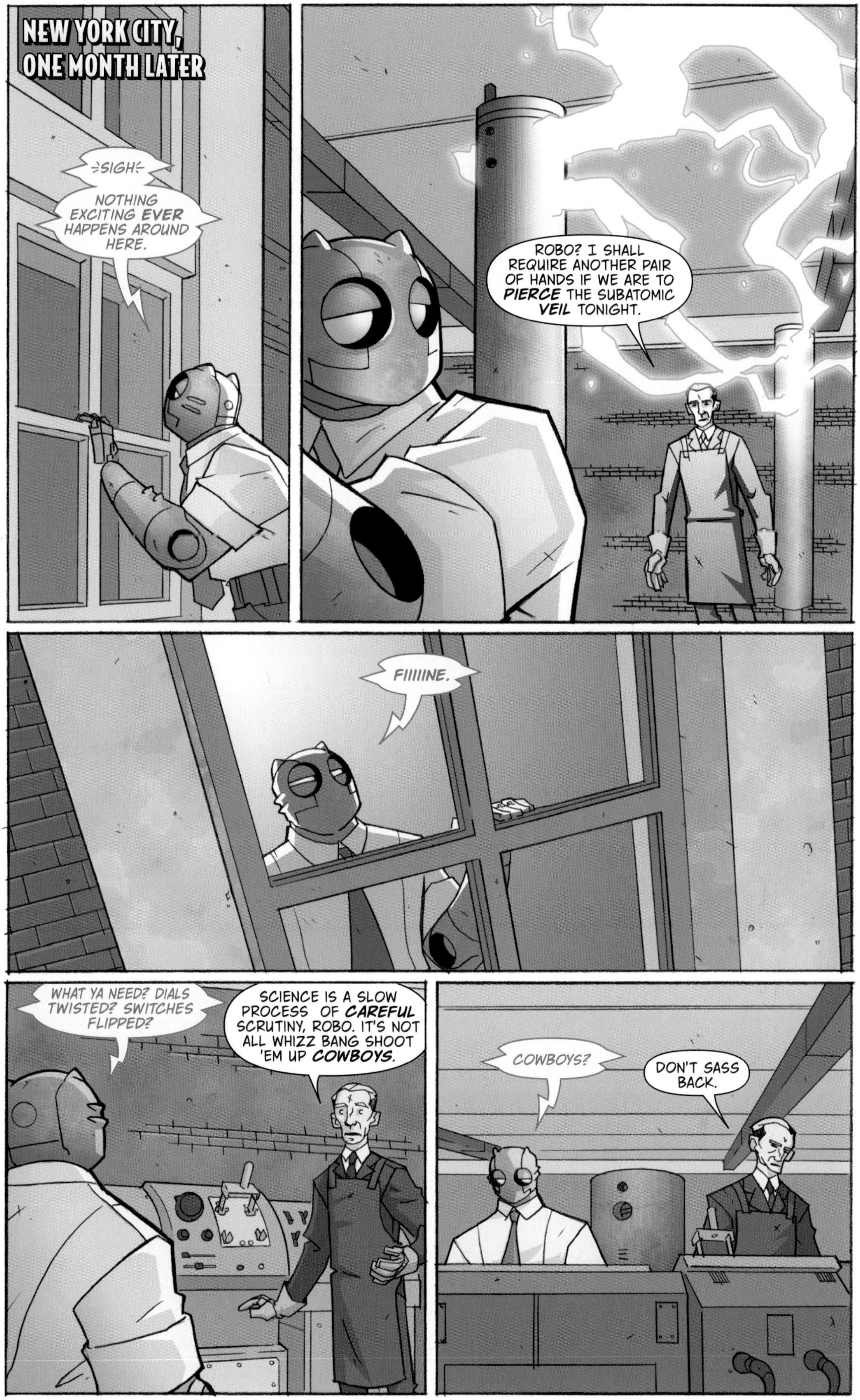
NEW YORK CITY, ONE MONTH LATER
SIGH
NOTHING EXCITING EVER HAPPENS AROUND HERE.
ROBO? I SHALL REQUIRE ANOTHER PAIR OF HANDS IF WE ARE TO PIERCE THE SUBATOMIC VEIL TONIGHT.
FIIIIINE.
WHAT YA NEED? DIALS TWISTED? SWITCHES FLIPPED?
SCIENCE IS A SLOW PROCESS OF CAREFUL SCRUTINY, ROBO. IT'S NOT ALL WHIZZ BANG SHOOT 'EM UP COWBOYS.
COWBOYS?
DON'T SASS BACK.

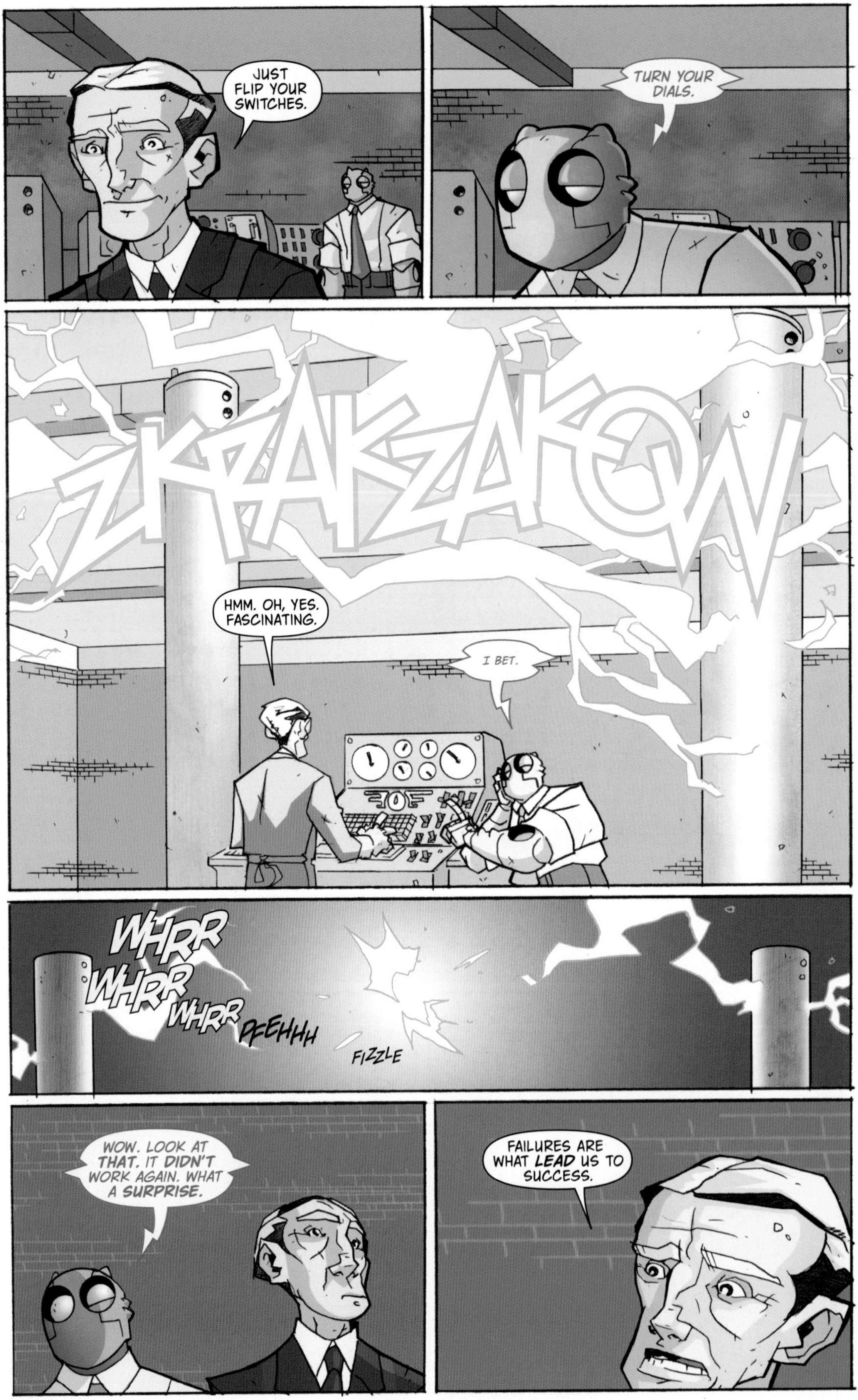
JUST FLIP YOUR SWITCHES.
TURN YOUR DIALS.
ZKRAKZAKOW
HMM. OH, YES. FASCINATING.
I BET.
WHRR
WHRR
WHRR
PFEHHH
FIZZLE
WOW. LOOK AT THAT. IT DIDN'T WORK AGAIN. WHAT A SURPRISE.
FAILURES ARE WHAT LEAD US TO SUCCESS.

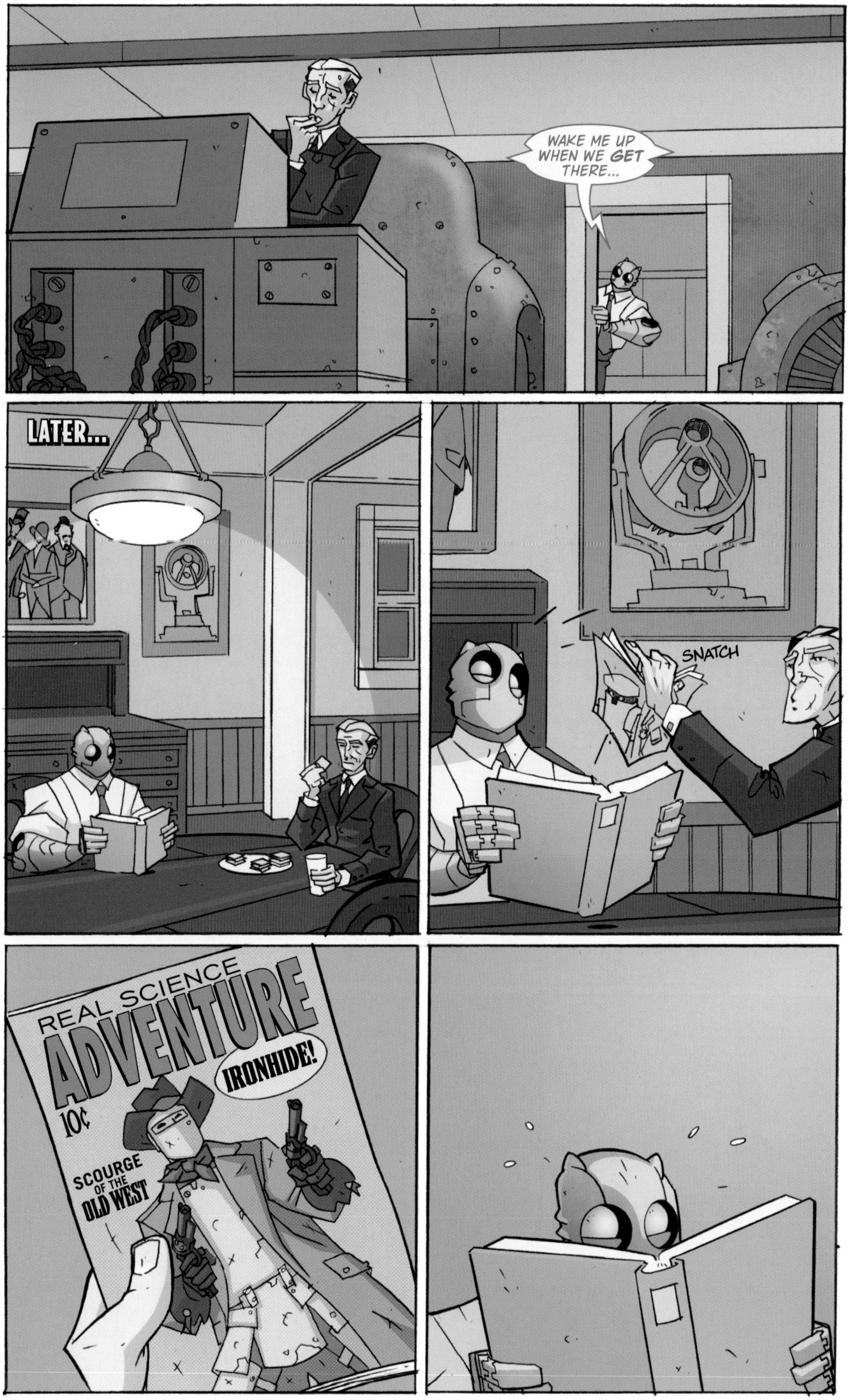
WAKE ME UP WHEN WE GET THERE...
LATER...
SNATCH
REAL SCIENCE
ADVENTURE
IRONHIDE!
10¢
SCOURGE OF THE OLD WEST

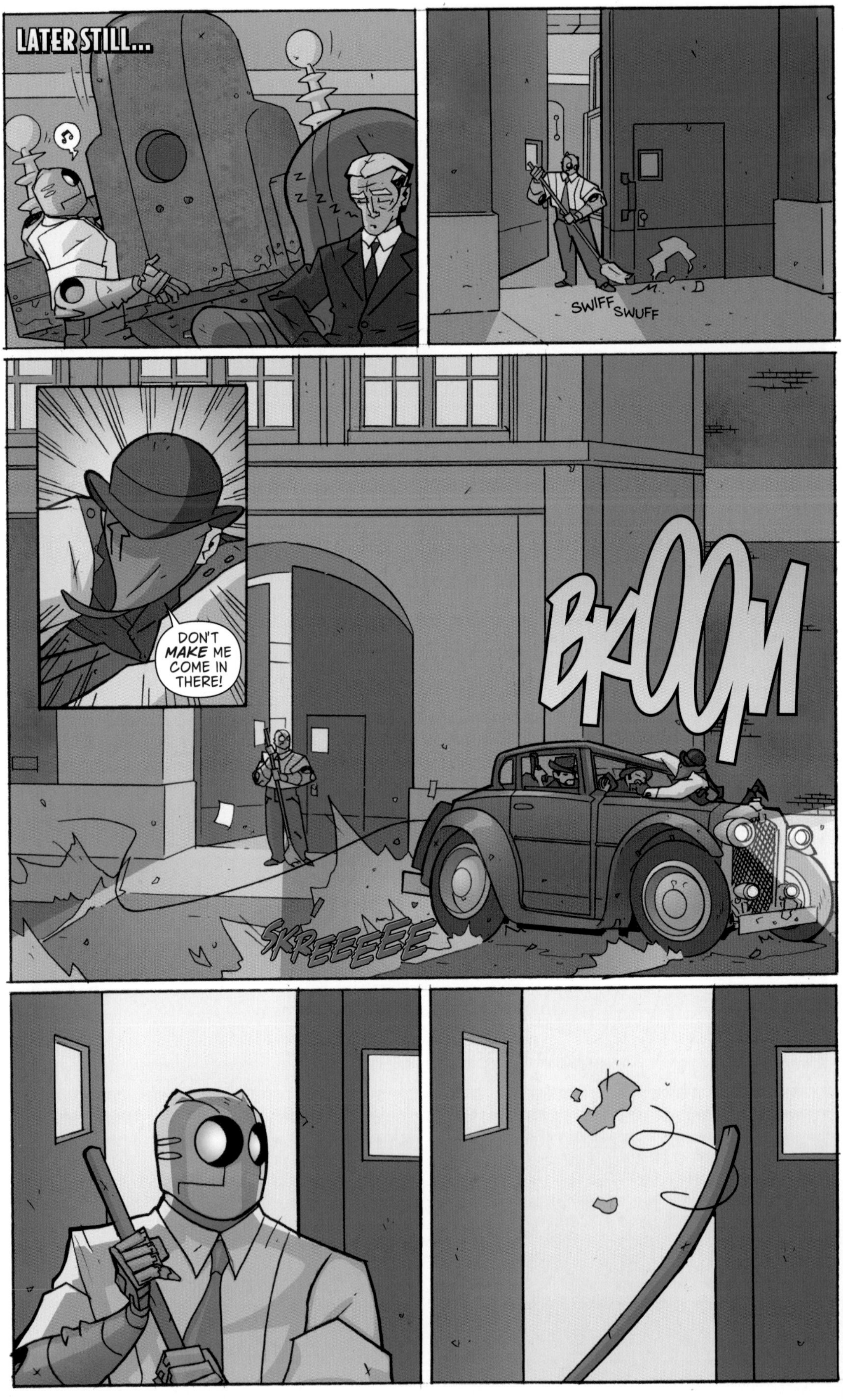
LATER STILL...
SWIFF SWUFF
DON'T MAKE ME COME IN THERE!
BKOOM
SKREEEEEE

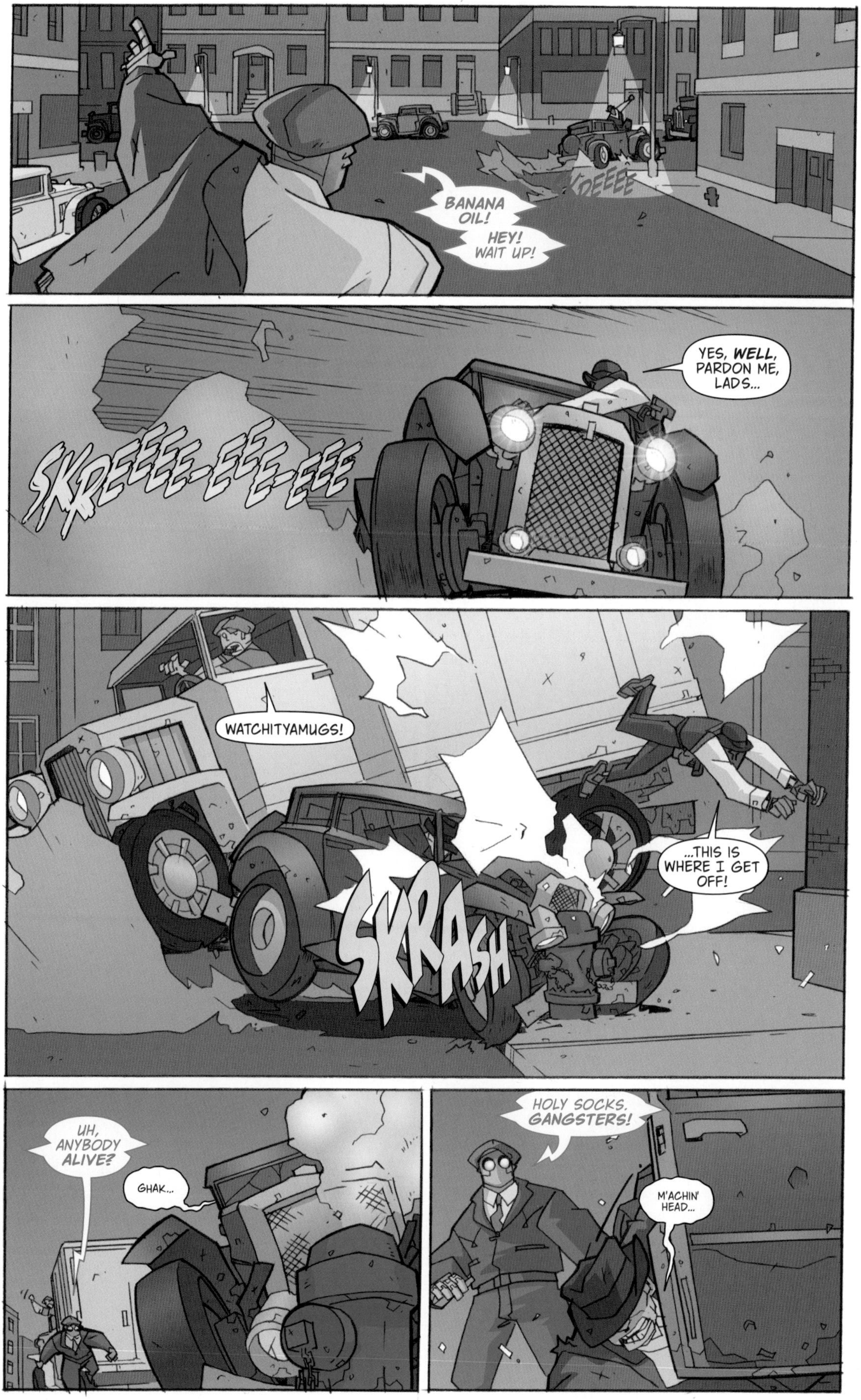

BANANA OIL!
HEY! WAIT UP!
SKREEEE
YES, WELL, PARDON ME, LADS...
SKREEEEE-EEE-E-EEE
WATCHITYAMUGS!
...THIS IS WHERE I GET OFF!
SKRASH
UH, ANYBODY ALIVE?
GHAK...
HOLY SOCKS. GANGSTERS!
M'ACHIN' HEAD...

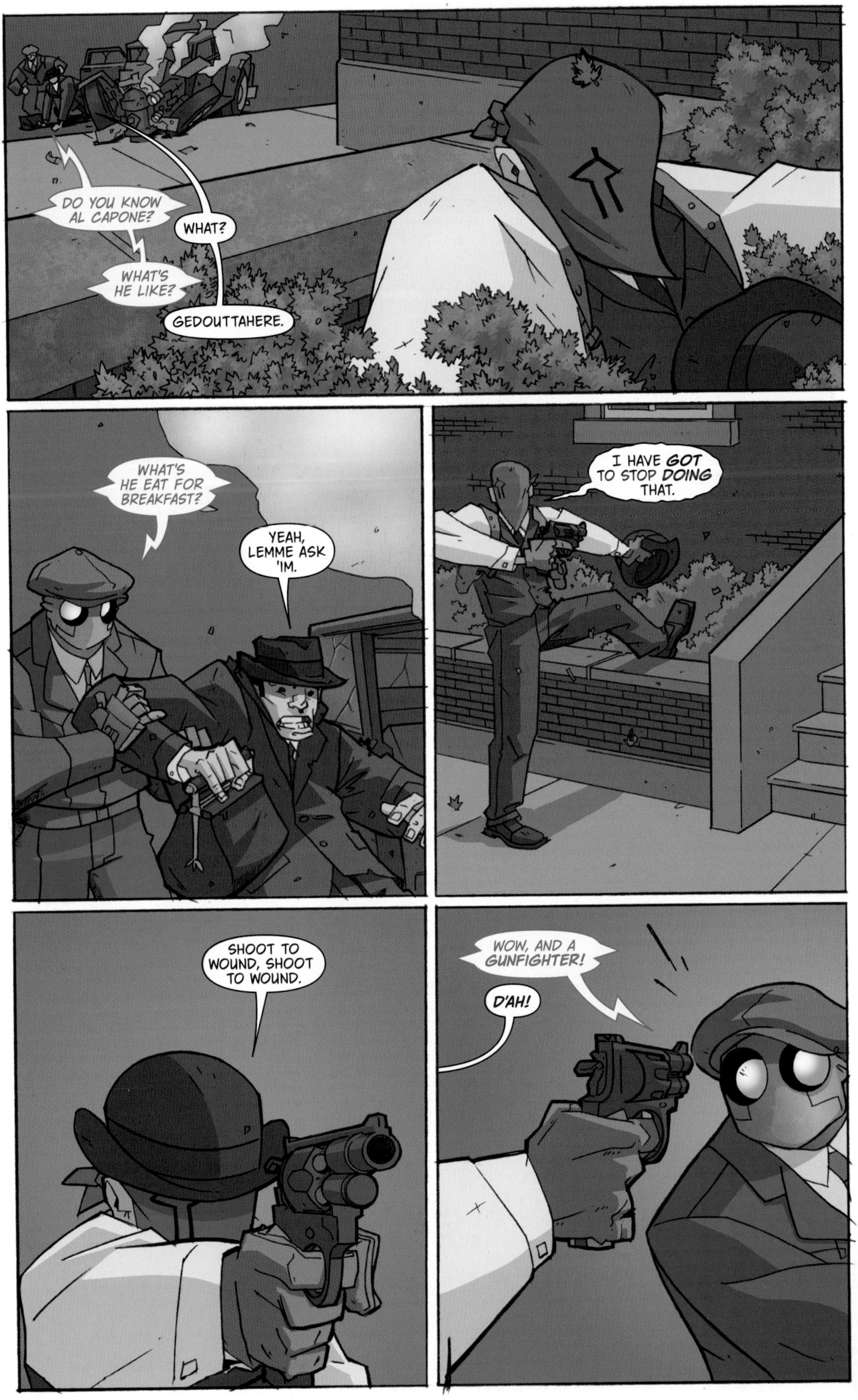
DO YOU KNOW AL CAPONE?
WHAT?
WHAT'S HE LIKE?
GEDOUTTAHERE.
WHAT'S HE EAT FOR BREAKFAST?
YEAH, LEMME ASK 'IM.
I HAVE GOT TO STOP DOING THAT.
SHOOT TO WOUND, SHOOT TO WOUND.
WOW, AND A GUNFIGHTER!
D'AH!

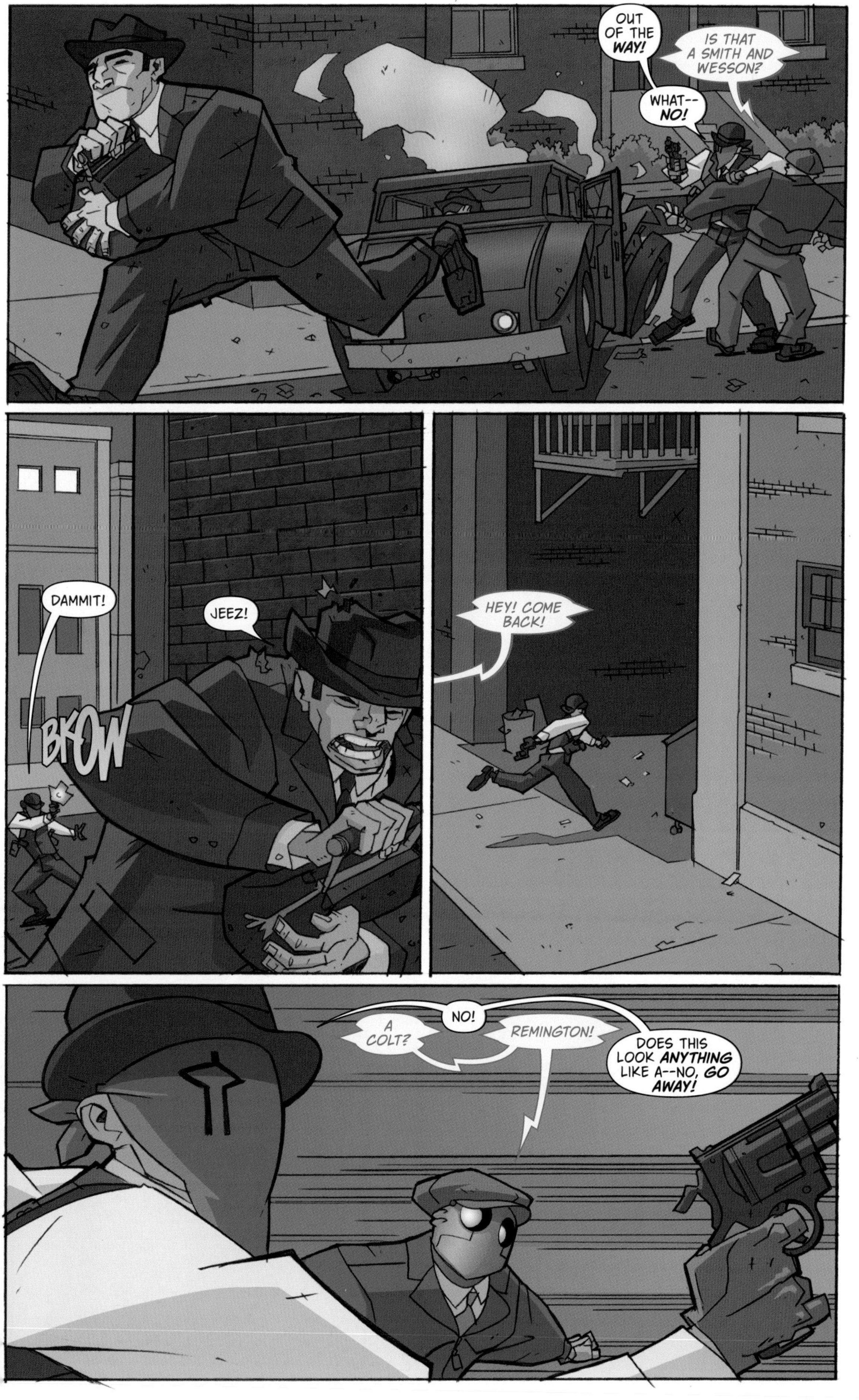
OUT OF THE WAY!
IS THAT A SMITH AND WESSON?
WHAT--NO!
DAMMIT!
BKOW
JEEZ!
HEY! COME BACK!
A COLT?
NO!
REMINGTON!
DOES THIS LOOK ANYTHING LIKE A--NO, GO AWAY!

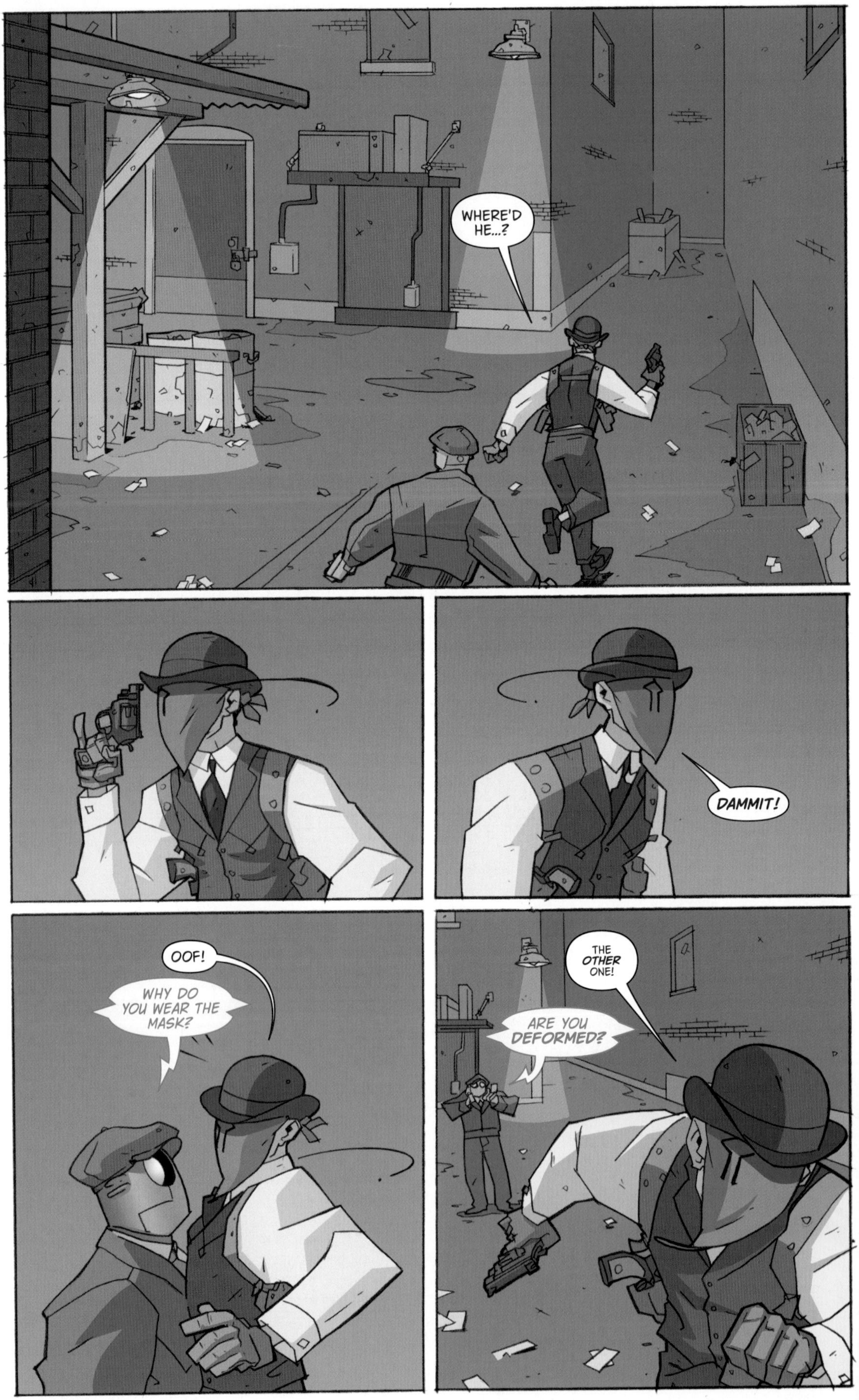
WHERE'D HE...?
DAMMIT!
OOF!
WHY DO YOU WEAR THE MASK?
THE OTHER ONE!
ARE YOU DEFORMED?

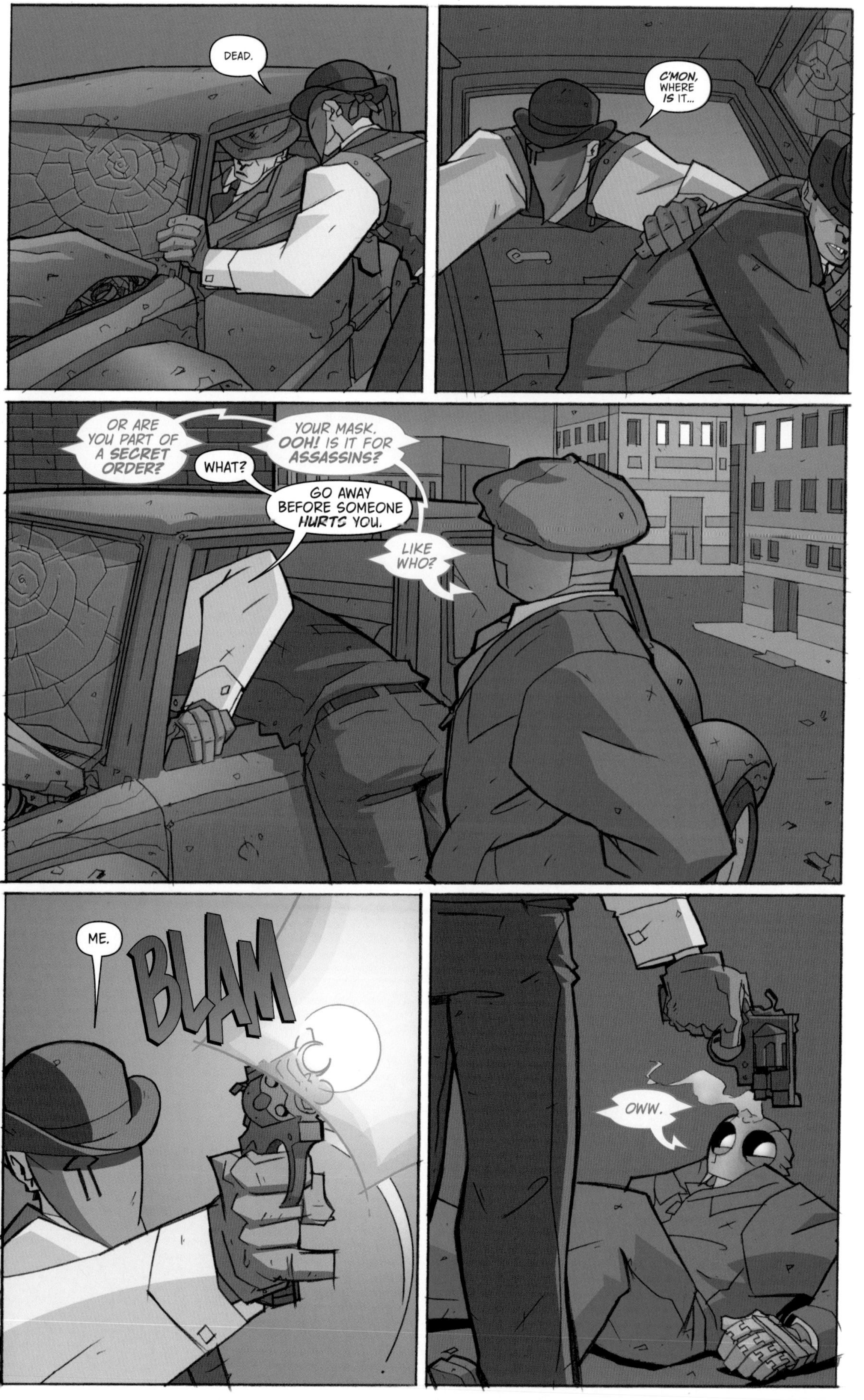
DEAD.
C'MON, WHERE IS IT...
YOUR MASK. OOH! IS IT FOR ASSASSINS?
OR ARE YOU PART OF A SECRET ORDER?
WHAT?
GO AWAY BEFORE SOMEONE HURTS YOU.
LIKE WHO?
ME.
BLAM
OWW.

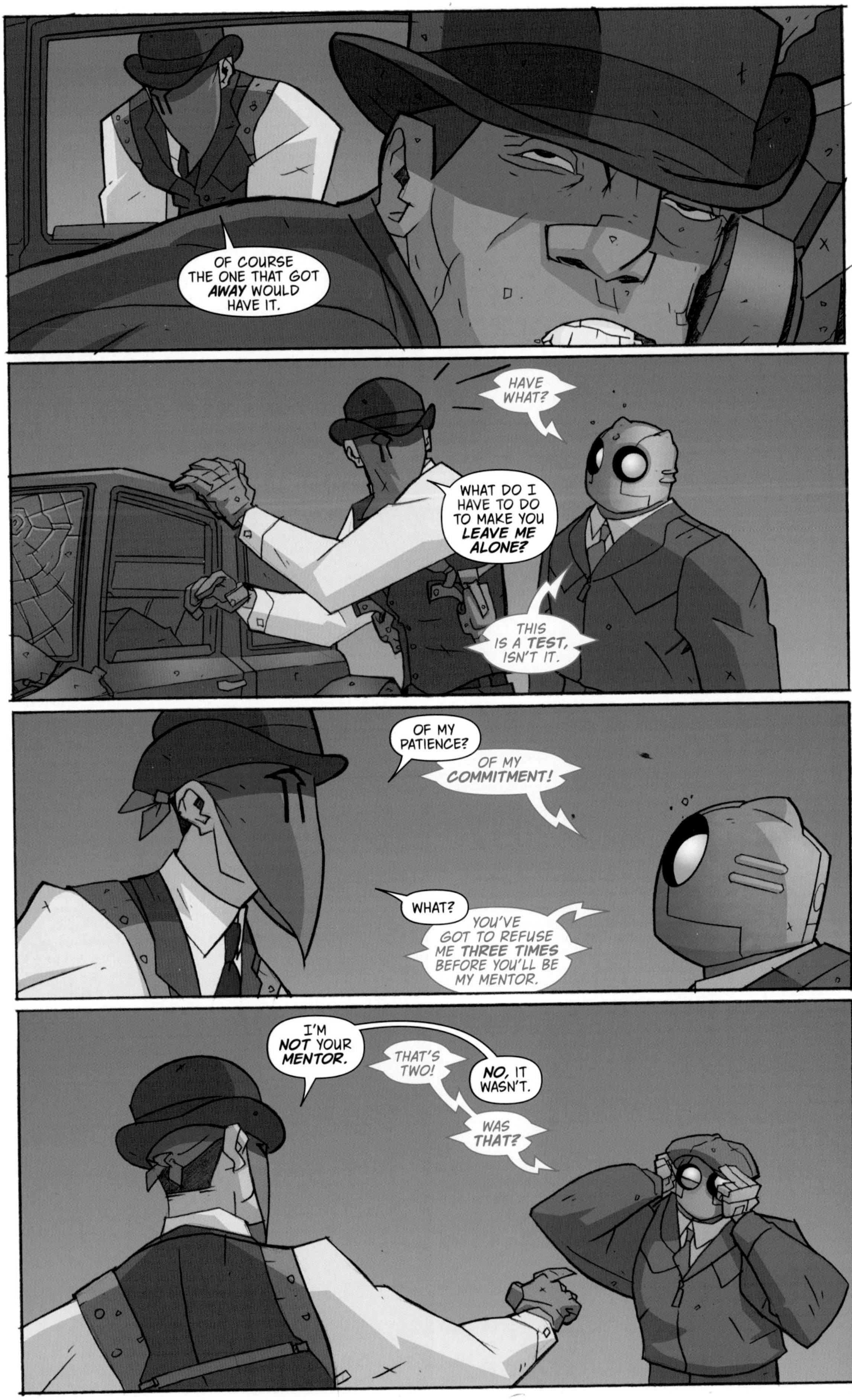
OF COURSE THE ONE THAT GOT AWAY WOULD HAVE IT.
HAVE WHAT?
WHAT DO I HAVE TO DO TO MAKE YOU LEAVE ME ALONE?
THIS IS A TEST, ISN'T IT.
OF MY PATIENCE?
OF MY COMMITMENT!
WHAT?
YOU'VE GOT TO REFUSE ME THREE TIMES BEFORE YOU'LL BE MY MENTOR.
I'M NOT YOUR MENTOR.
THAT'S TWO!
NO, IT WASN'T.
WAS THAT?

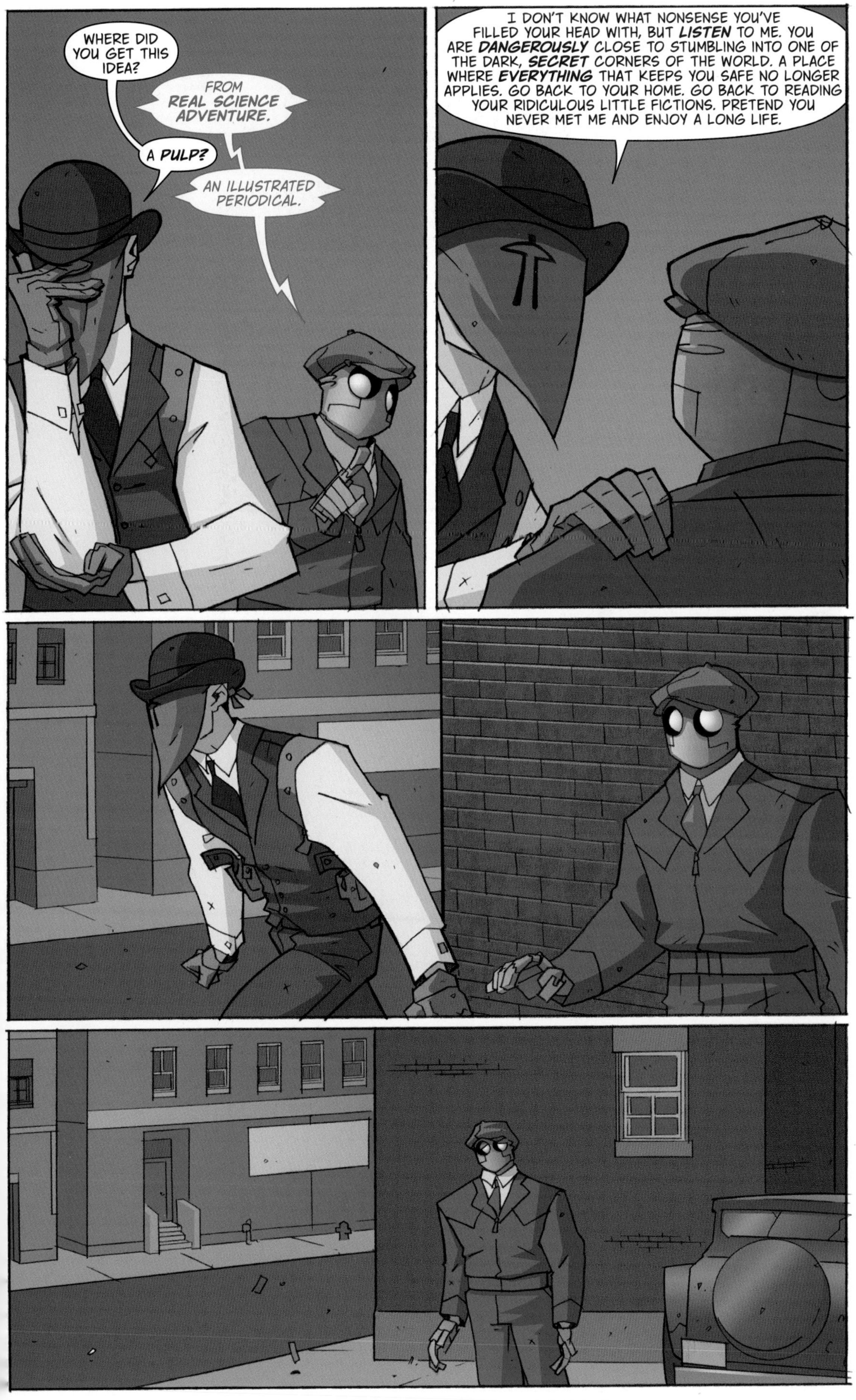
WHERE DID YOU GET THIS IDEA?
FROM REAL SCIENCE ADVENTURE.
A PULP?
AN ILLUSTRATED PERIODICAL.
I DON'T KNOW WHAT NONSENSE YOU'VE FILLED YOUR HEAD WITH, BUT LISTEN TO ME. YOU ARE DANGEROUSLY CLOSE TO STUMBLING INTO ONE OF THE DARK, SECRET CORNERS OF THE WORLD. A PLACE WHERE EVERYTHING THAT KEEPS YOU SAFE NO LONGER APPLIES. GO BACK TO YOUR HOME. GO BACK TO READING YOUR RIDICULOUS LITTLE FICTIONS. PRETEND YOU NEVER MET ME AND ENJOY A LONG LIFE.

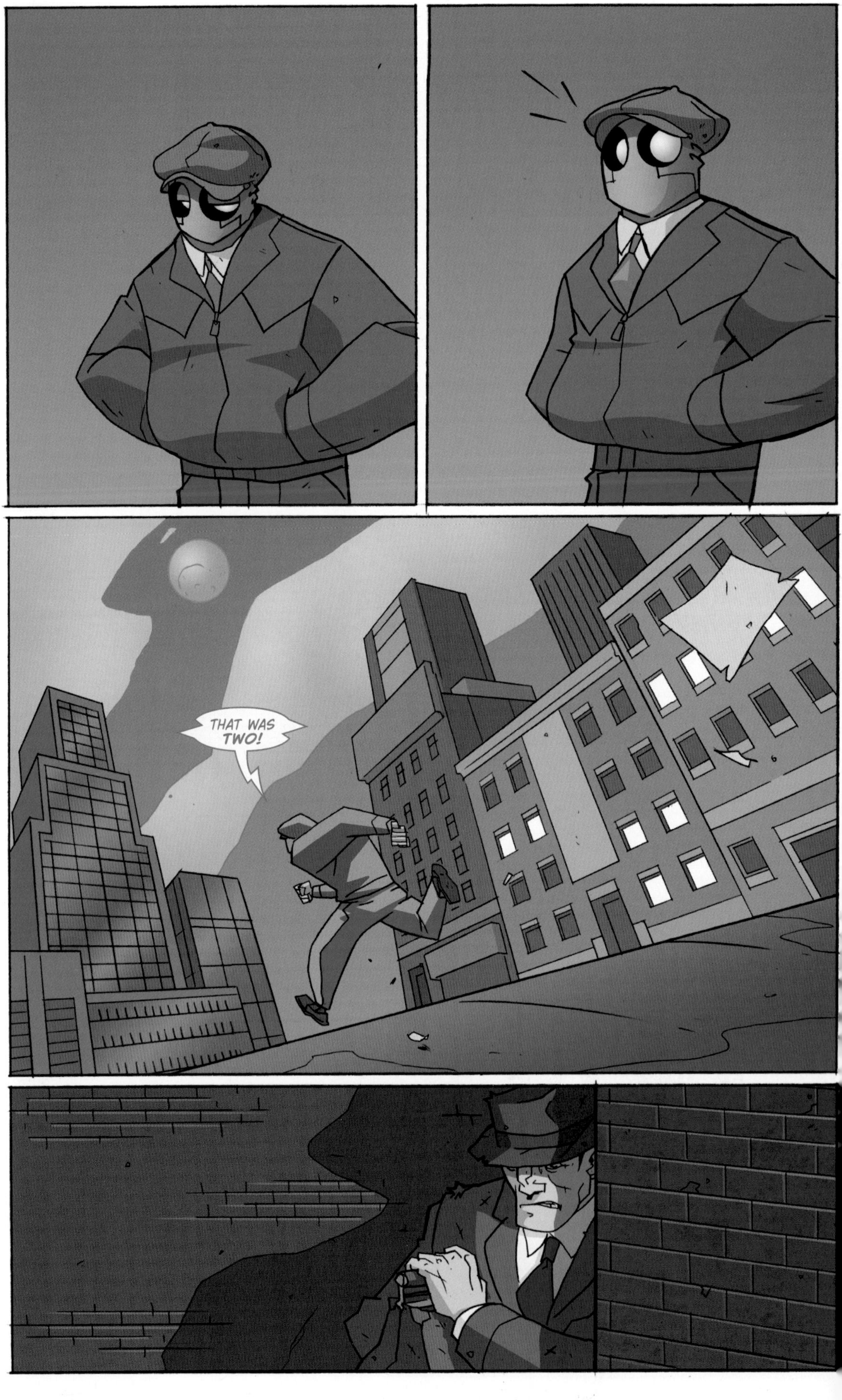
THAT WAS TWO!

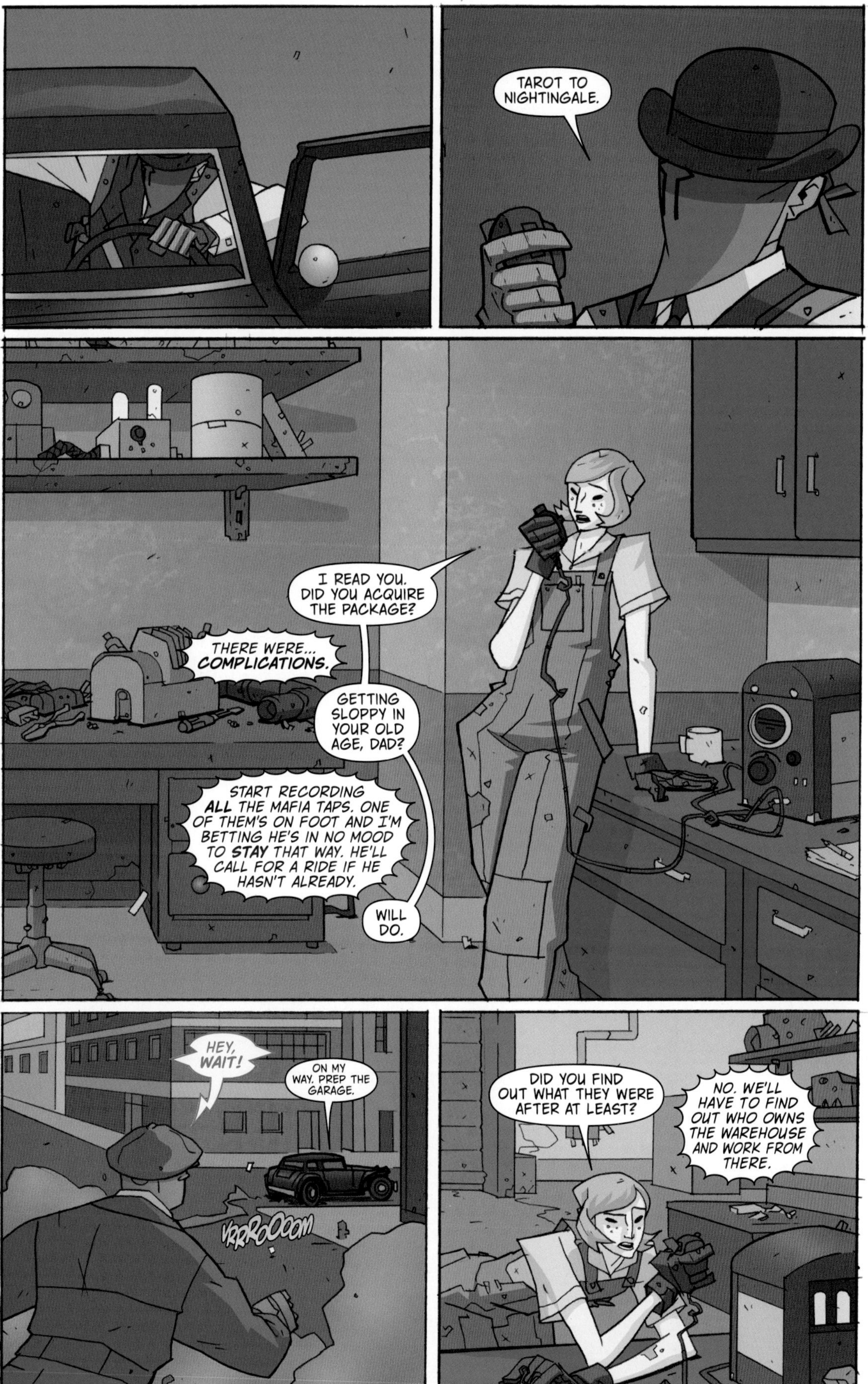
TAROT TO NIGHTINGALE.
I READ YOU. DID YOU ACQUIRE THE PACKAGE?
THERE WERE... **COMPLICATIONS.**
GETTING SLOPPY IN YOUR OLD AGE, DAD?
START RECORDING **ALL** THE MAFIA TAPS. ONE OF THEM'S ON FOOT AND I'M BETTING HE'S IN NO MOOD TO **STAY** THAT WAY. HE'LL CALL FOR A RIDE IF HE HASN'T ALREADY.
WILL DO.
HEY, **WAIT!**
ON MY WAY. PREP THE GARAGE.
VRRROOOOM
DID YOU FIND OUT WHAT THEY WERE AFTER AT LEAST?
NO. WE'LL HAVE TO FIND OUT WHO OWNS THE WAREHOUSE AND WORK FROM THERE.

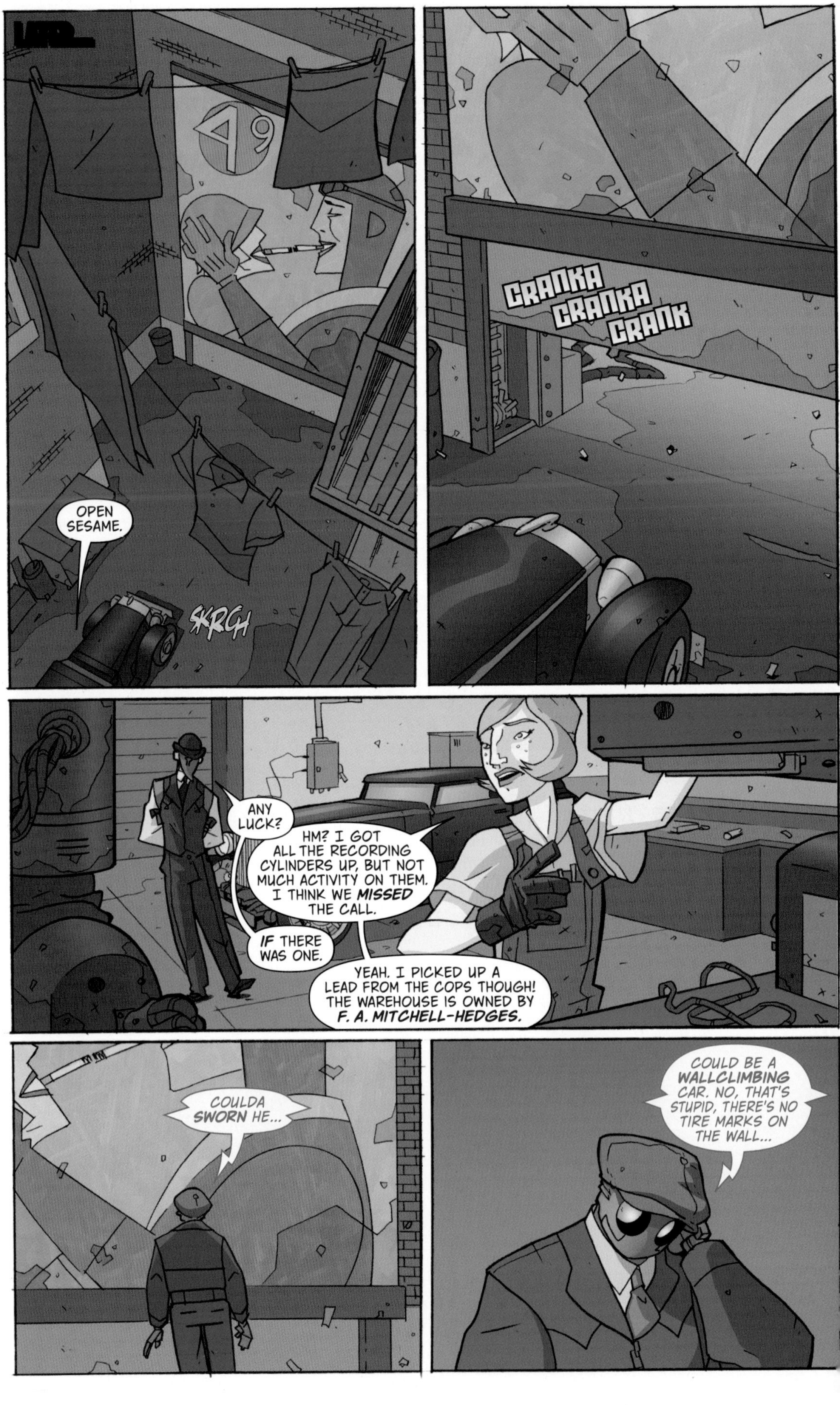
OPEN SESAME.
SKRCH
CRANKA CRANKA CRANK
ANY LUCK?
HM? I GOT ALL THE RECORDING CYLINDERS UP, BUT NOT MUCH ACTIVITY ON THEM. I THINK WE MISSED THE CALL.
IF THERE WAS ONE.
YEAH. I PICKED UP A LEAD FROM THE COPS THOUGH! THE WAREHOUSE IS OWNED BY F. A. MITCHELL-HEDGES.
COULDA SWORN HE...
COULD BE A WALLCLIMBING CAR. NO, THAT'S STUPID, THERE'S NO TIRE MARKS ON THE WALL...

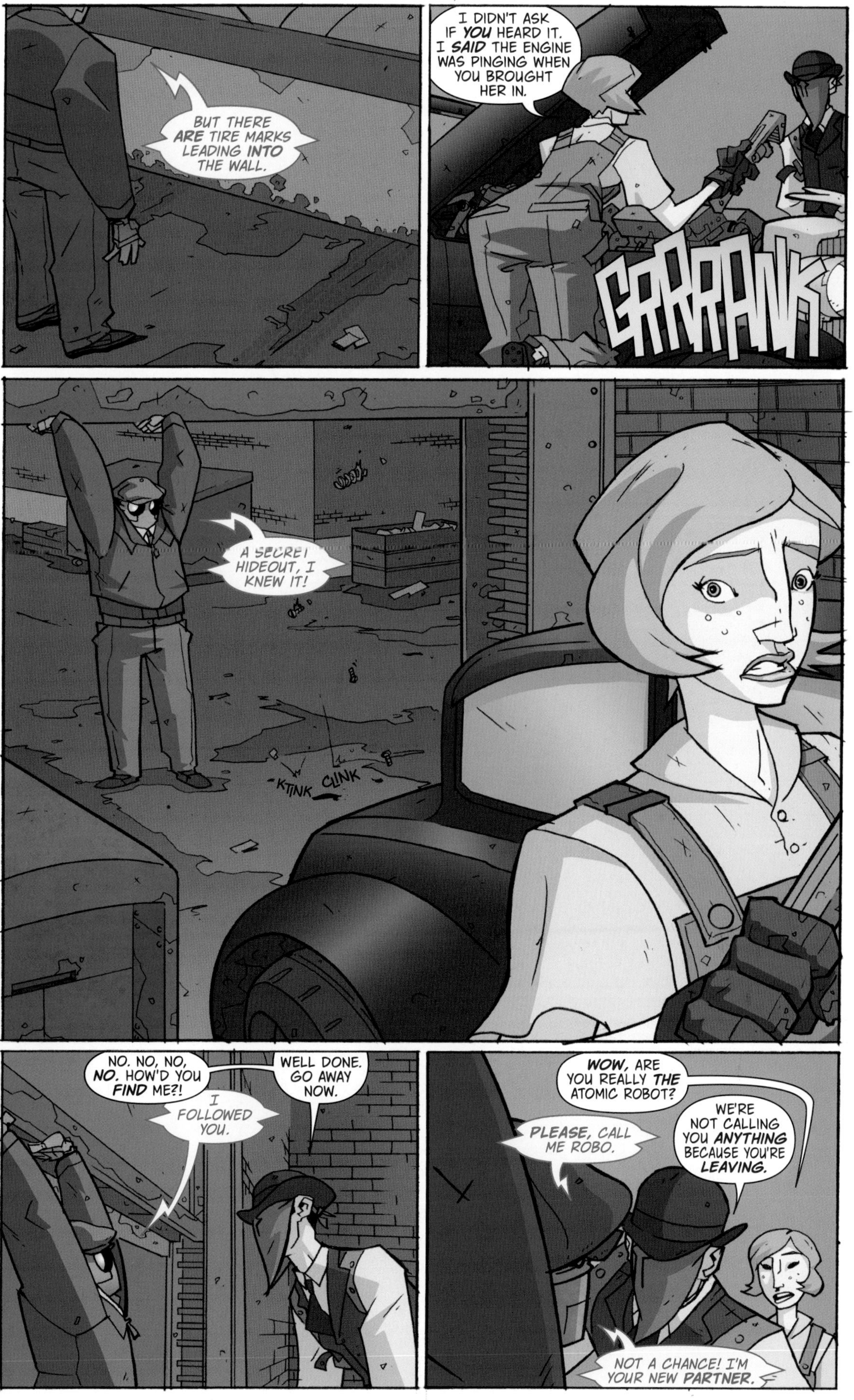

BUT THERE ARE TIRE MARKS LEADING INTO THE WALL.
I DIDN'T ASK IF YOU HEARD IT. I SAID THE ENGINE WAS PINGING WHEN YOU BROUGHT HER IN.
GRRRANK
A SECRET HIDEOUT, I KNEW IT!
KTINK
CLINK
NO. NO, NO, NO. HOW'D YOU FIND ME?!
I FOLLOWED YOU.
WELL DONE. GO AWAY NOW.
WOW, ARE YOU REALLY THE ATOMIC ROBOT?
PLEASE, CALL ME ROBO.
WE'RE NOT CALLING YOU ANYTHING BECAUSE YOU'RE LEAVING.
NOT A CHANCE! I'M YOUR NEW PARTNER.

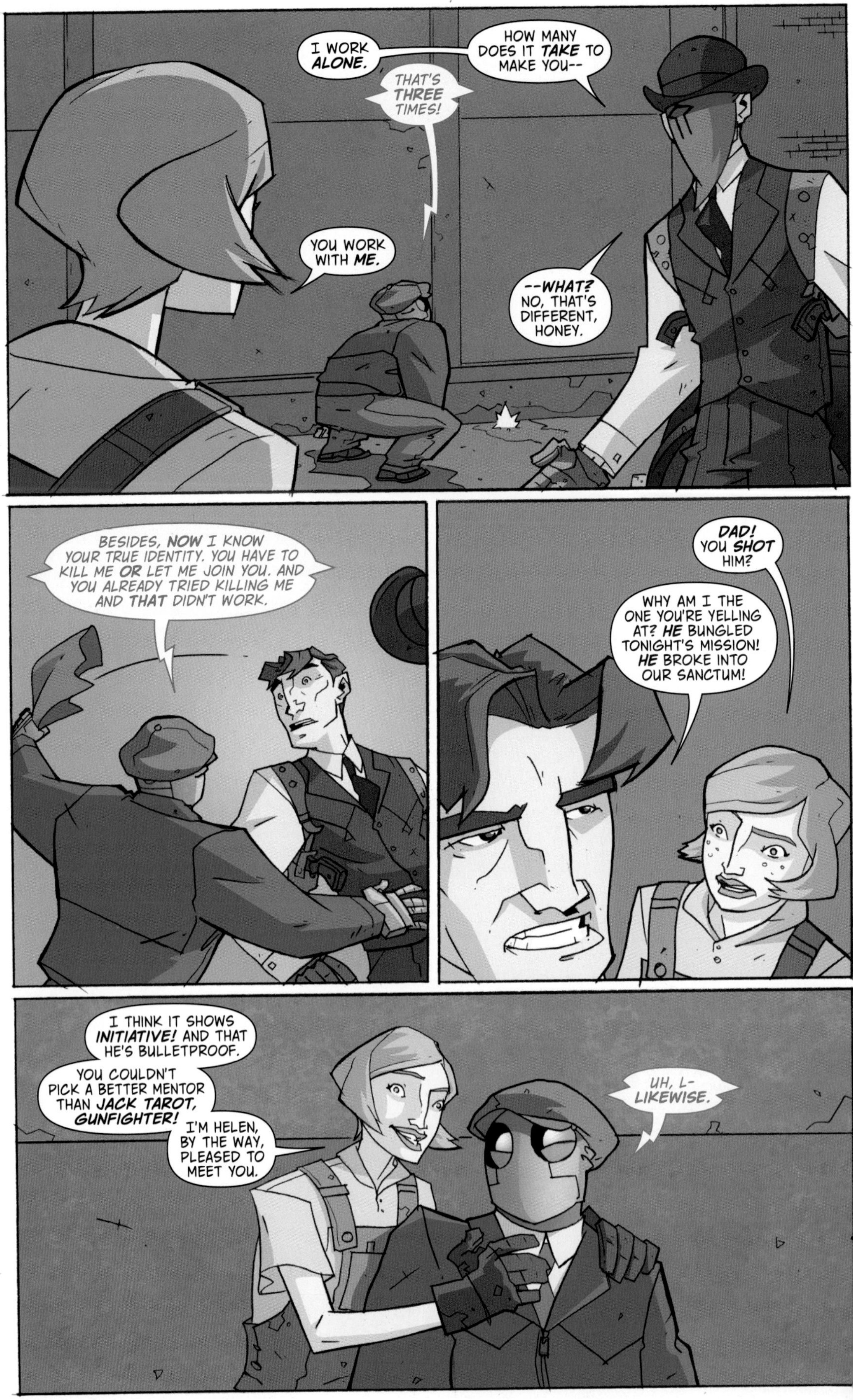
I WORK ALONE.
HOW MANY DOES IT TAKE TO MAKE YOU--
THAT'S THREE TIMES!
YOU WORK WITH ME.
--WHAT? NO, THAT'S DIFFERENT, HONEY.
BESIDES, NOW I KNOW YOUR TRUE IDENTITY. YOU HAVE TO KILL ME OR LET ME JOIN YOU. AND YOU ALREADY TRIED KILLING ME AND THAT DIDN'T WORK.
DAD! YOU SHOT HIM?
WHY AM I THE ONE YOU'RE YELLING AT? HE BUNGLED TONIGHT'S MISSION! HE BROKE INTO OUR SANCTUM!
I THINK IT SHOWS INITIATIVE! AND THAT HE'S BULLETPROOF.
YOU COULDN'T PICK A BETTER MENTOR THAN JACK TAROT, GUNFIGHTER!
I'M HELEN, BY THE WAY, PLEASED TO MEET YOU.
UH, L-LIKEWISE.

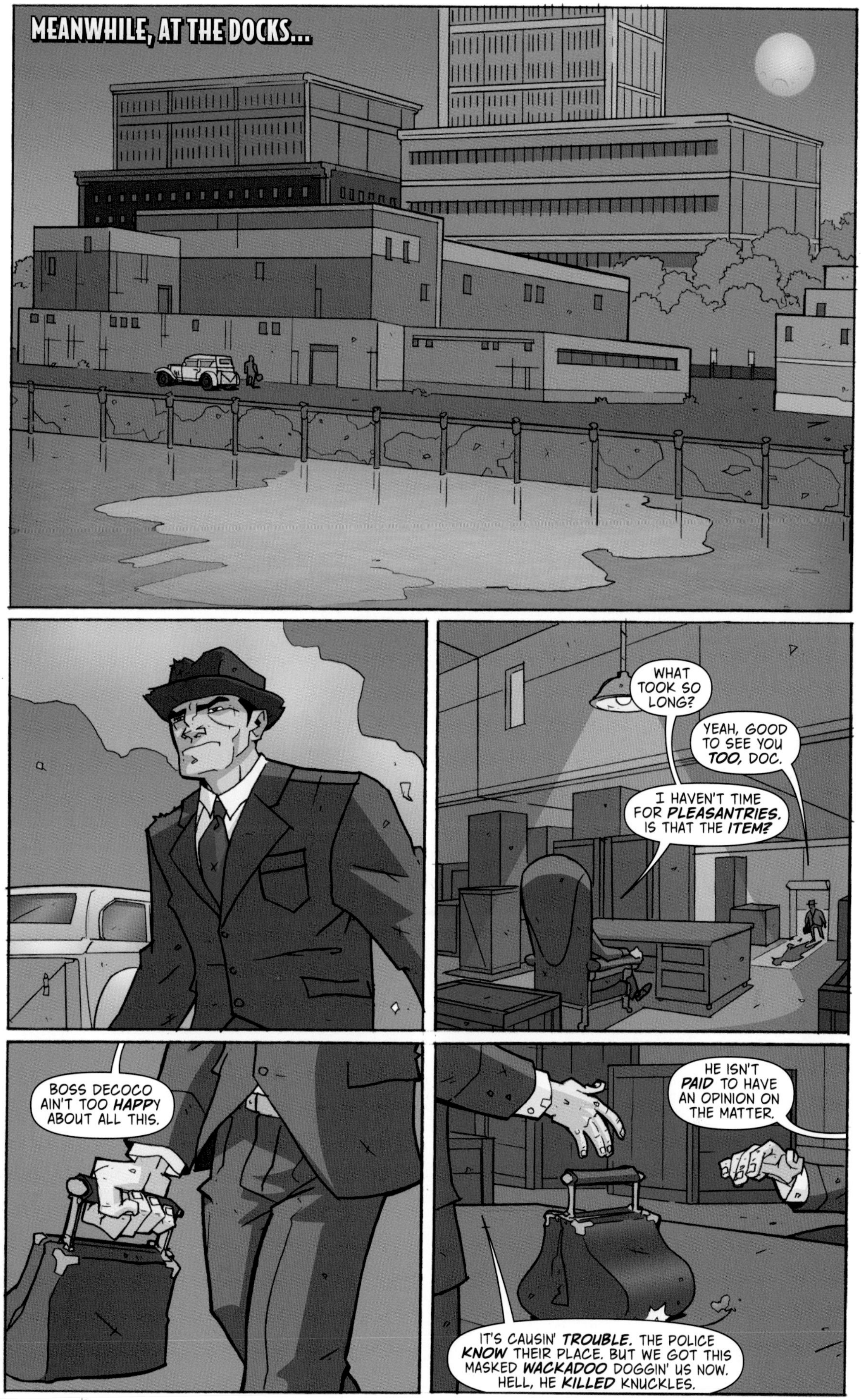
MEANWHILE, AT THE DOCKS...
WHAT TOOK SO LONG?
YEAH, GOOD TO SEE YOU TOO, DOC.
I HAVEN'T TIME FOR PLEASANTRIES. IS THAT THE ITEM?
BOSS DECOCO AIN'T TOO HAPPY ABOUT ALL THIS.
HE ISN'T PAID TO HAVE AN OPINION ON THE MATTER.
IT'S CAUSIN' TROUBLE. THE POLICE KNOW THEIR PLACE. BUT WE GOT THIS MASKED WACKADOO DOGGIN' US NOW. HELL, HE KILLED KNUCKLES.

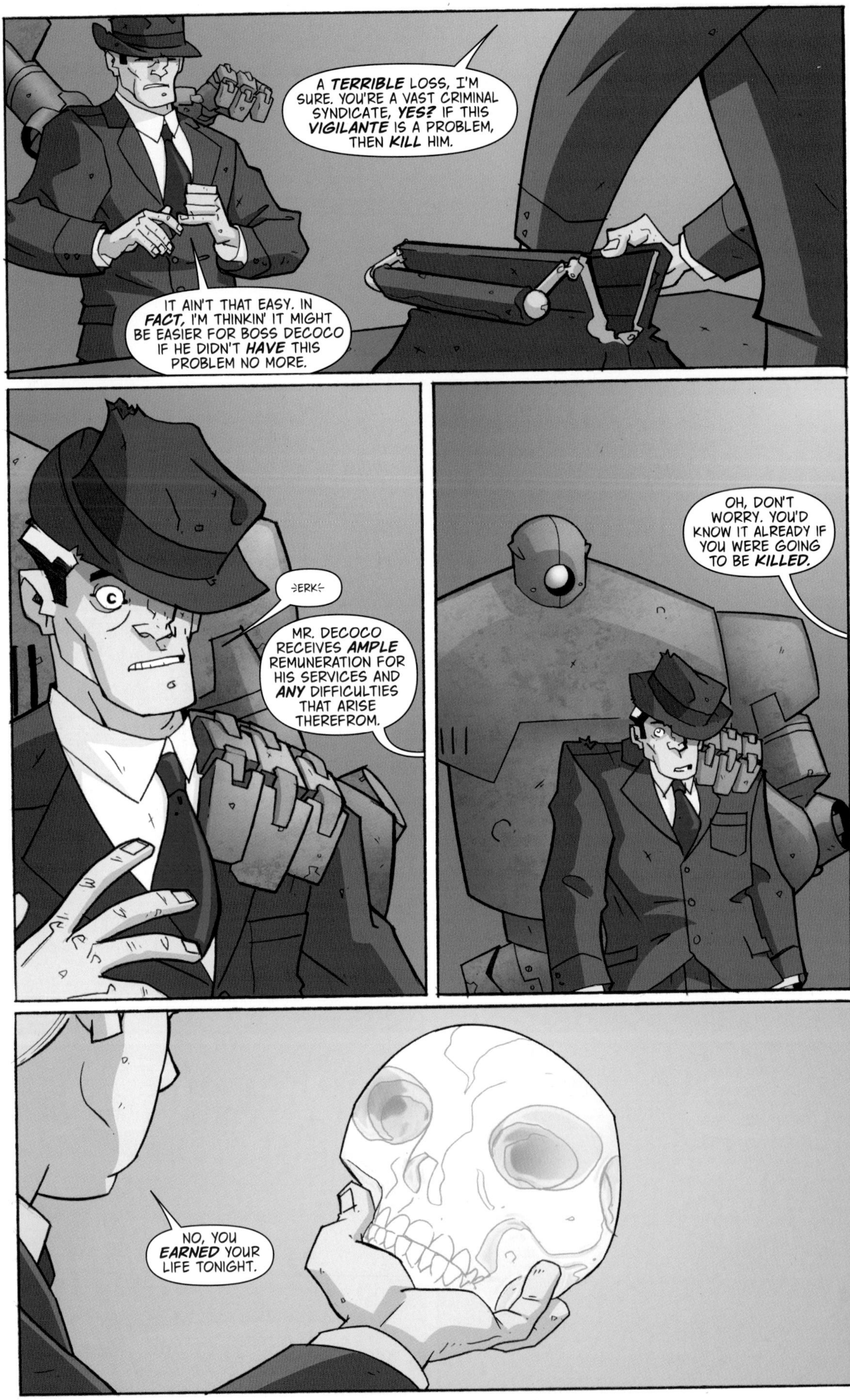
A TERRIBLE LOSS, I'M SURE. YOU'RE A VAST CRIMINAL SYNDICATE, YES? IF THIS VIGILANTE IS A PROBLEM, THEN KILL HIM.
IT AIN'T THAT EASY. IN FACT, I'M THINKIN' IT MIGHT BE EASIER FOR BOSS DECOCO IF HE DIDN'T HAVE THIS PROBLEM NO MORE.
ERK
MR. DECOCO RECEIVES AMPLE REMUNERATION FOR HIS SERVICES AND ANY DIFFICULTIES THAT ARISE THEREFROM.
OH, DON'T WORRY. YOU'D KNOW IT ALREADY IF YOU WERE GOING TO BE KILLED.
NO, YOU EARNED YOUR LIFE TONIGHT.

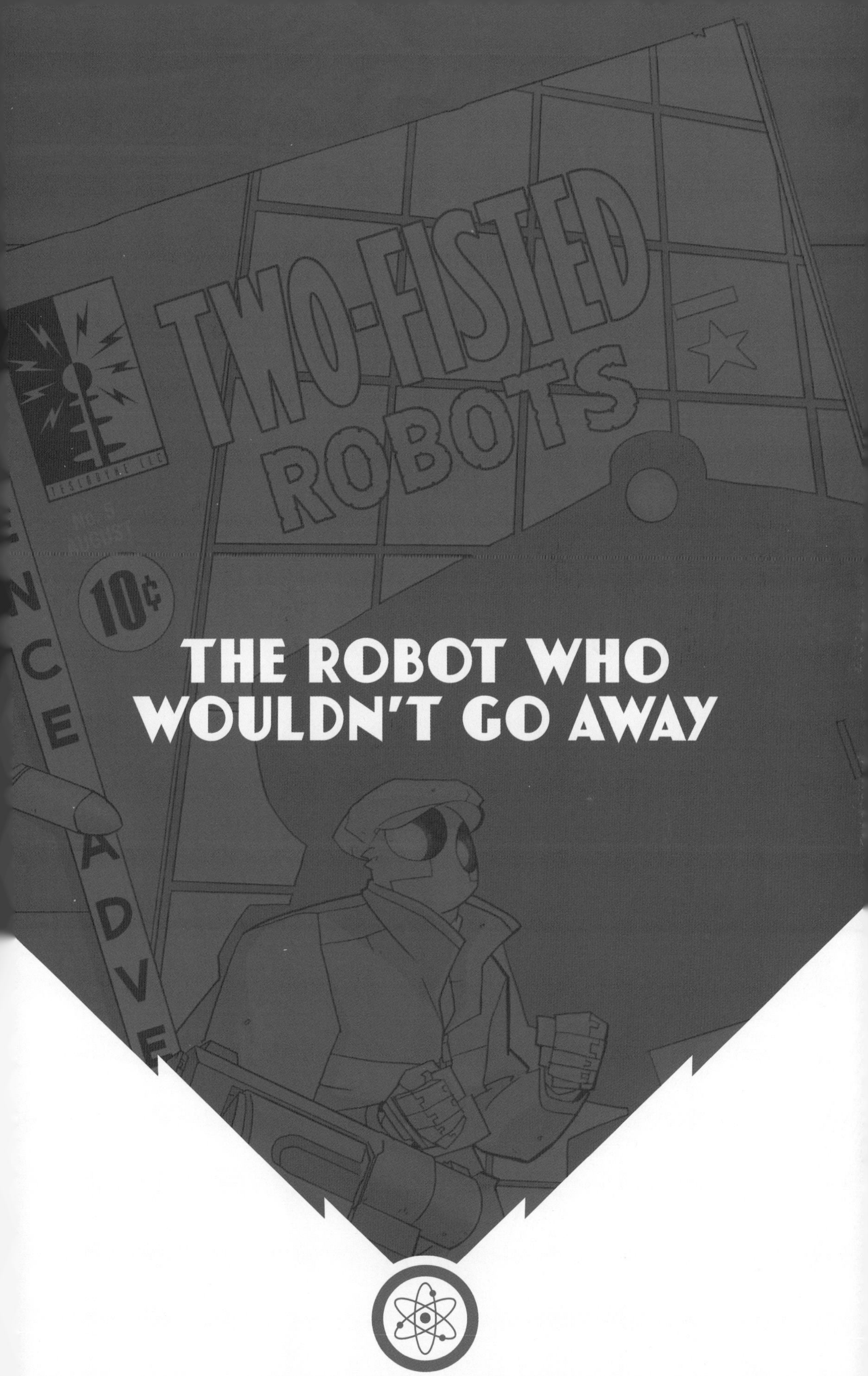
TWO-FISTED
ROBOTS
TESLADYNE LLC
No. 5
AUGUST
10¢

THE ROBOT WHO WOULDN'T GO AWAY

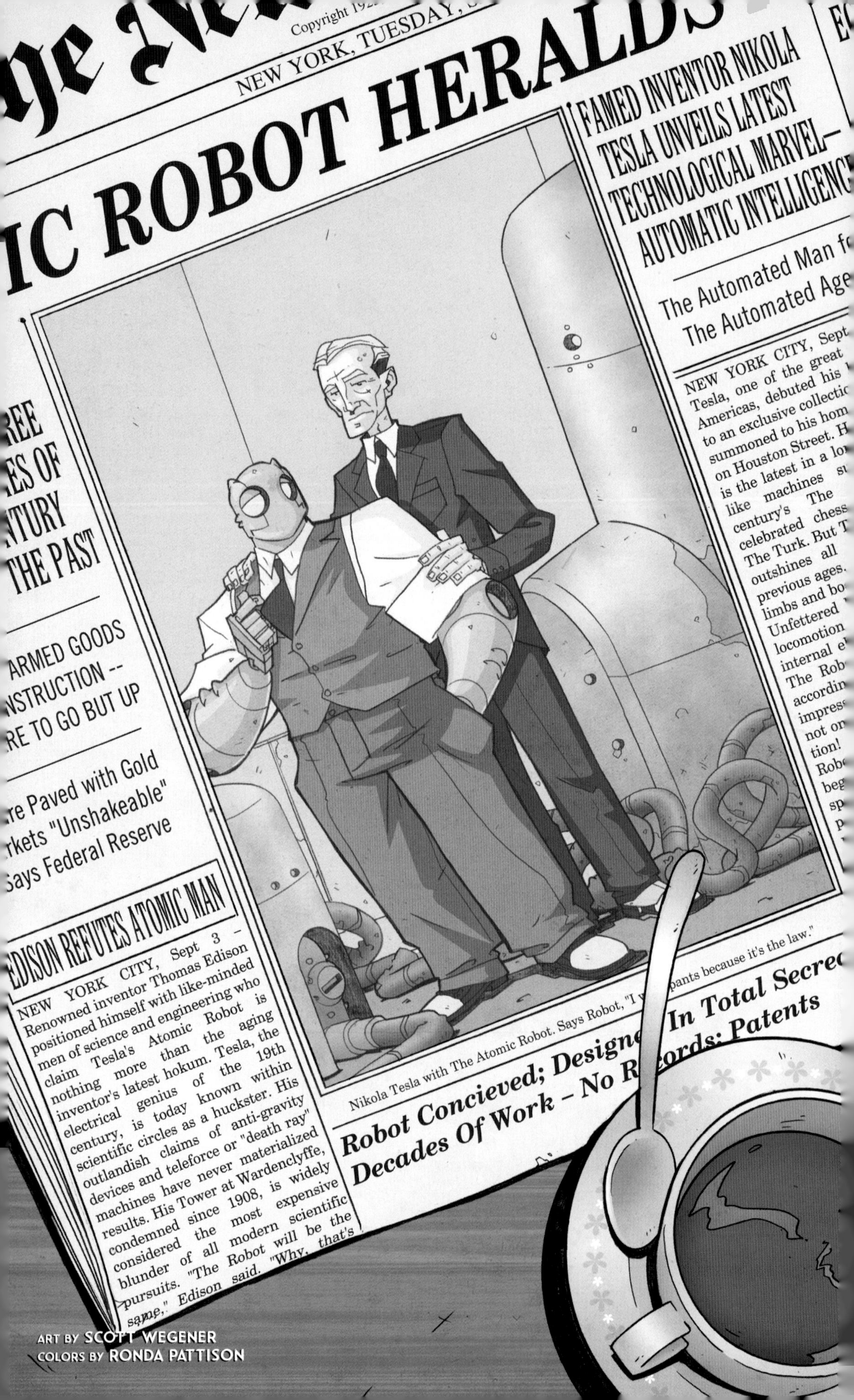
Copyright 192
NEW YORK, TUESDAY,
IC ROBOT HERALDS
FAMED INVENTOR NIKOLA TESLA UNVEILS LATEST TECHNOLOGICAL MARVEL— AUTOMATIC INTELLIGENC
The Automated Man f
The Automated Age
NEW YORK CITY, Sept Tesla, one of the great Americas, debuted his to an exclusive collectic summoned to his hom on Houston Street. H is the latest in a lo like machines century's The celebrated chess The Turk. But T outshines all previous ages. limbs and bo Unfettered locomotion internal e The Rob accordin impress not on tion! Rob beg sp p
REE
ES OF
NTURY
THE PAST
ARMED GOODS
NSTRUCTION --
RE TO GO BUT UP
re Paved with Gold
rkets "Unshakeable"
Says Federal Reserve
EDISON REFUTES ATOMIC MAN
NEW YORK CITY, Sept 3 – Renowned inventor Thomas Edison positioned himself with like-minded men of science and engineering who claim Tesla's Atomic Robot is nothing more than the aging inventor's latest hokum. Tesla, the electrical genius of the 19th century, is today known within scientific circles as a huckster. His outlandish claims of anti-gravity devices and teleforce or "death ray" machines have never materialized results. His Tower at Wardenclyffe, condemned since 1908, is widely considered the most expensive blunder of all modern scientific pursuits. "The Robot will be the same," Edison said. "Why, that's
Nikola Tesla with The Atomic Robot. Says Robot, "I w pants because it's the law."
Robot Concieved; Designe In Total Secre
Decades Of Work – No R cords; Patents
ART BY SCOTT WEGENER
COLORS BY RONDA PATTISON

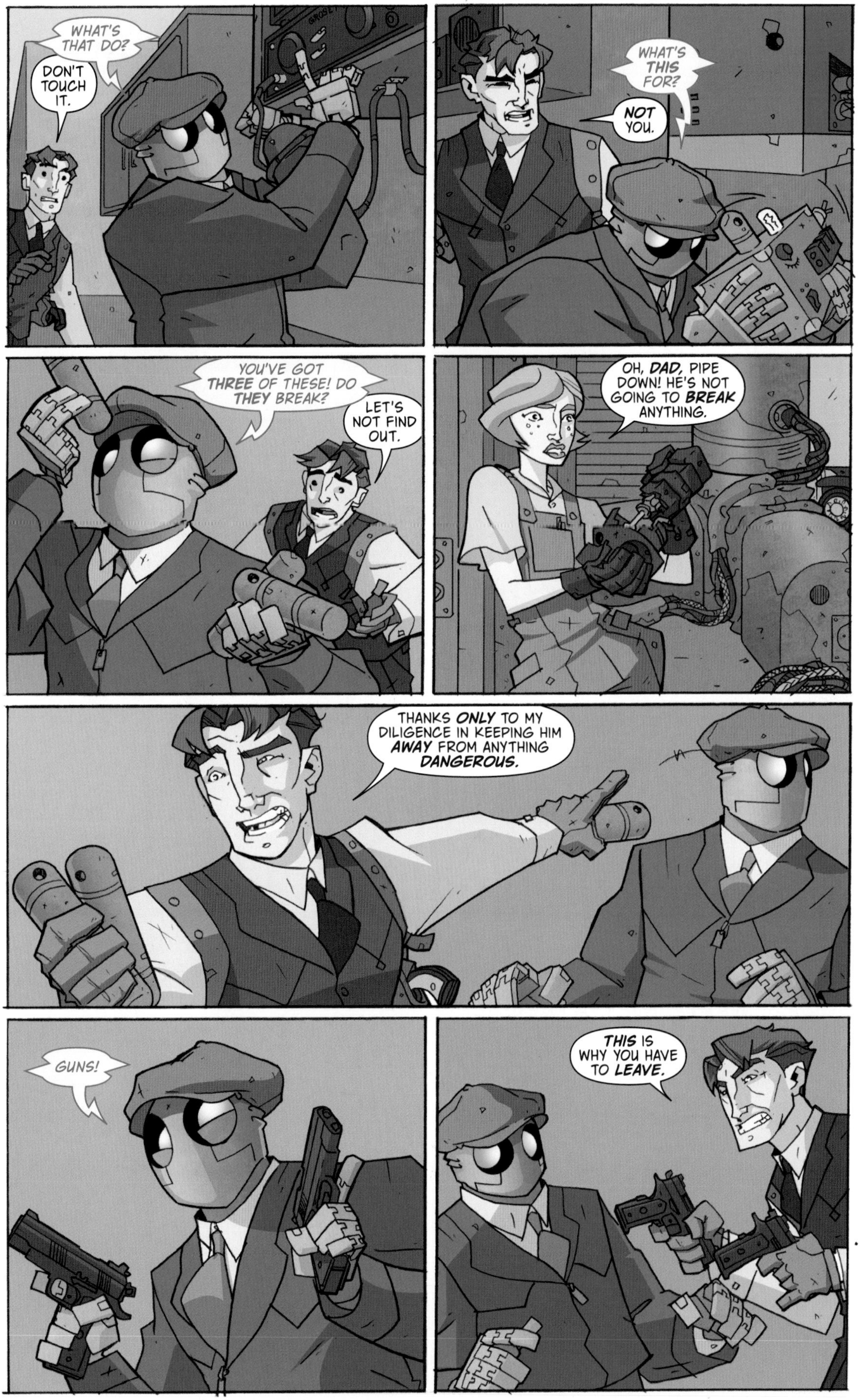
WHAT'S THAT DO?
DON'T TOUCH IT.
WHAT'S THIS FOR?
NOT YOU.
YOU'VE GOT THREE OF THESE! DO THEY BREAK?
LET'S NOT FIND OUT.
OH, DAD, PIPE DOWN! HE'S NOT GOING TO BREAK ANYTHING.
THANKS ONLY TO MY DILIGENCE IN KEEPING HIM AWAY FROM ANYTHING DANGEROUS.
GUNS!
THIS IS WHY YOU HAVE TO LEAVE.

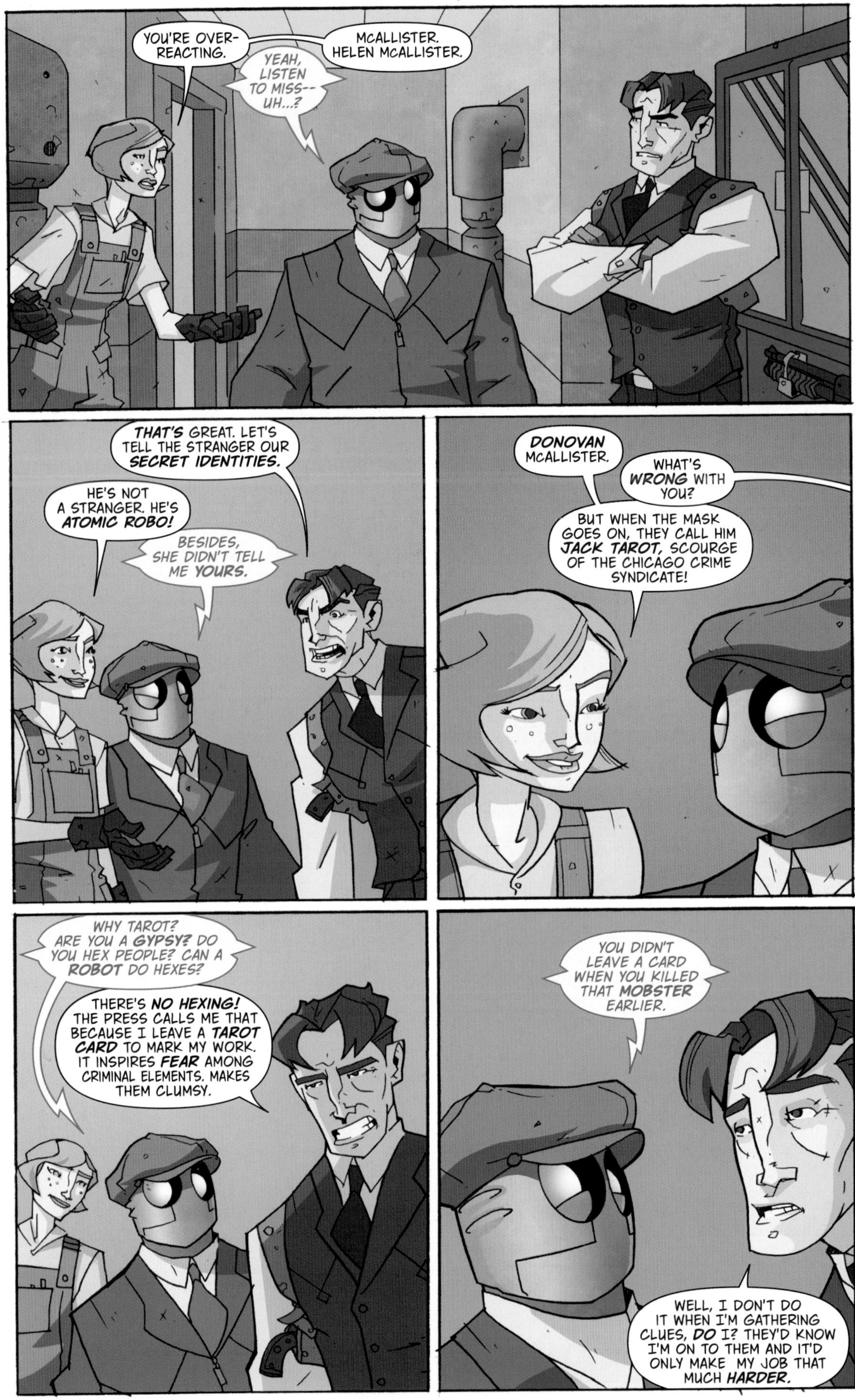
YOU'RE OVER-REACTING.
MCALLISTER. HELEN MCALLISTER.
YEAH, LISTEN TO MISS-- UH...?
THAT'S GREAT. LET'S TELL THE STRANGER OUR SECRET IDENTITIES.
HE'S NOT A STRANGER. HE'S ATOMIC ROBO!
BESIDES, SHE DIDN'T TELL ME YOURS.
DONOVAN MCALLISTER.
WHAT'S WRONG WITH YOU?
BUT WHEN THE MASK GOES ON, THEY CALL HIM JACK TAROT, SCOURGE OF THE CHICAGO CRIME SYNDICATE!
WHY TAROT? ARE YOU A GYPSY? DO YOU HEX PEOPLE? CAN A ROBOT DO HEXES?
THERE'S NO HEXING! THE PRESS CALLS ME THAT BECAUSE I LEAVE A TAROT CARD TO MARK MY WORK. IT INSPIRES FEAR AMONG CRIMINAL ELEMENTS. MAKES THEM CLUMSY.
YOU DIDN'T LEAVE A CARD WHEN YOU KILLED THAT MOBSTER EARLIER.
WELL, I DON'T DO IT WHEN I'M GATHERING CLUES, DO I? THEY'D KNOW I'M ON TO THEM AND IT'D ONLY MAKE MY JOB THAT MUCH HARDER.

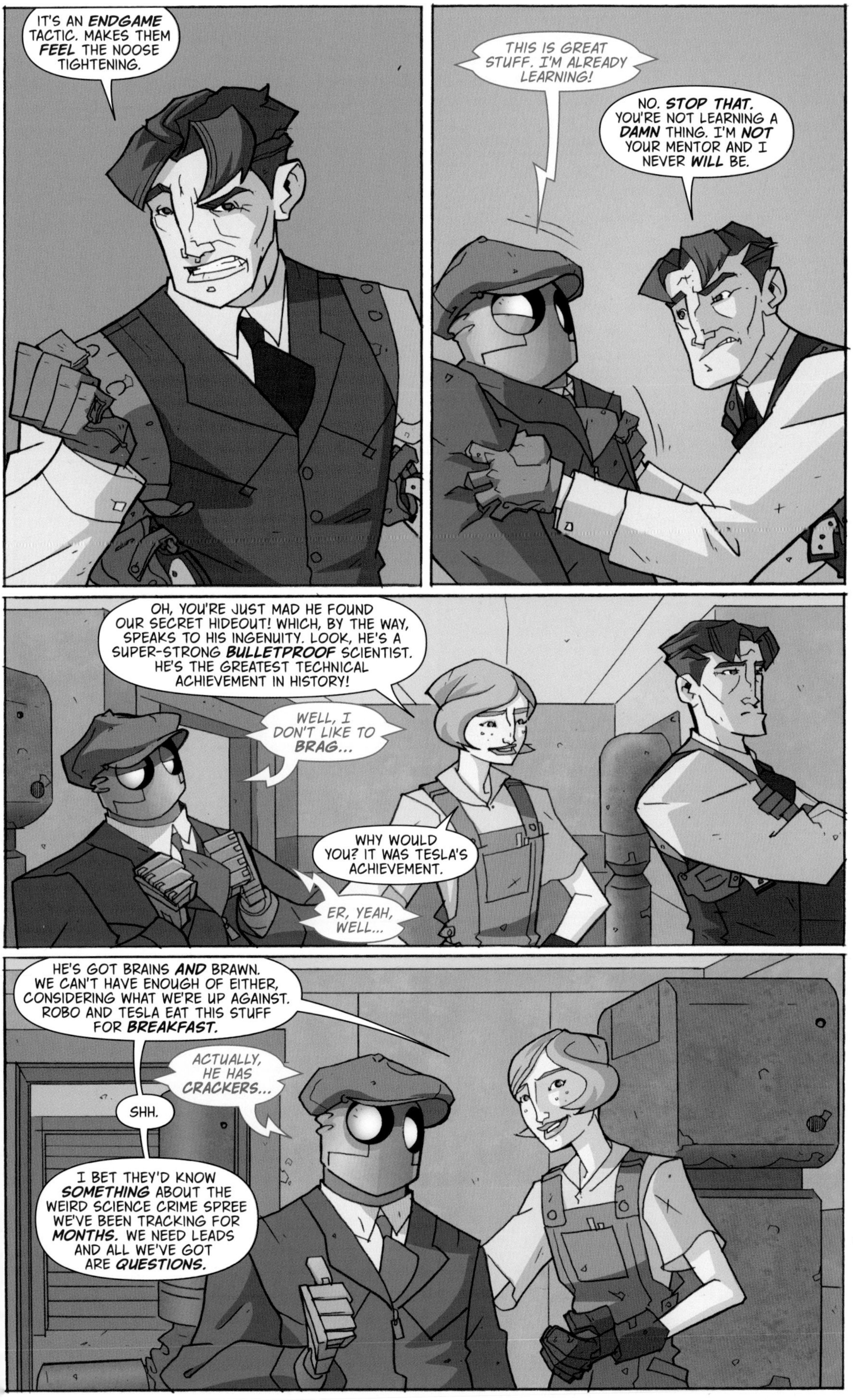

IT'S AN ENDGAME TACTIC. MAKES THEM FEEL THE NOOSE TIGHTENING.
THIS IS GREAT STUFF. I'M ALREADY LEARNING!
NO. STOP THAT. YOU'RE NOT LEARNING A DAMN THING. I'M NOT YOUR MENTOR AND I NEVER WILL BE.
OH, YOU'RE JUST MAD HE FOUND OUR SECRET HIDEOUT! WHICH, BY THE WAY, SPEAKS TO HIS INGENUITY. LOOK, HE'S A SUPER-STRONG BULLETPROOF SCIENTIST. HE'S THE GREATEST TECHNICAL ACHIEVEMENT IN HISTORY!
WELL, I DON'T LIKE TO BRAG...
WHY WOULD YOU? IT WAS TESLA'S ACHIEVEMENT.
ER, YEAH, WELL...
HE'S GOT BRAINS AND BRAWN. WE CAN'T HAVE ENOUGH OF EITHER, CONSIDERING WHAT WE'RE UP AGAINST. ROBO AND TESLA EAT THIS STUFF FOR BREAKFAST.
ACTUALLY, HE HAS CRACKERS...
SHH.
I BET THEY'D KNOW SOMETHING ABOUT THE WEIRD SCIENCE CRIME SPREE WE'VE BEEN TRACKING FOR MONTHS. WE NEED LEADS AND ALL WE'VE GOT ARE QUESTIONS.

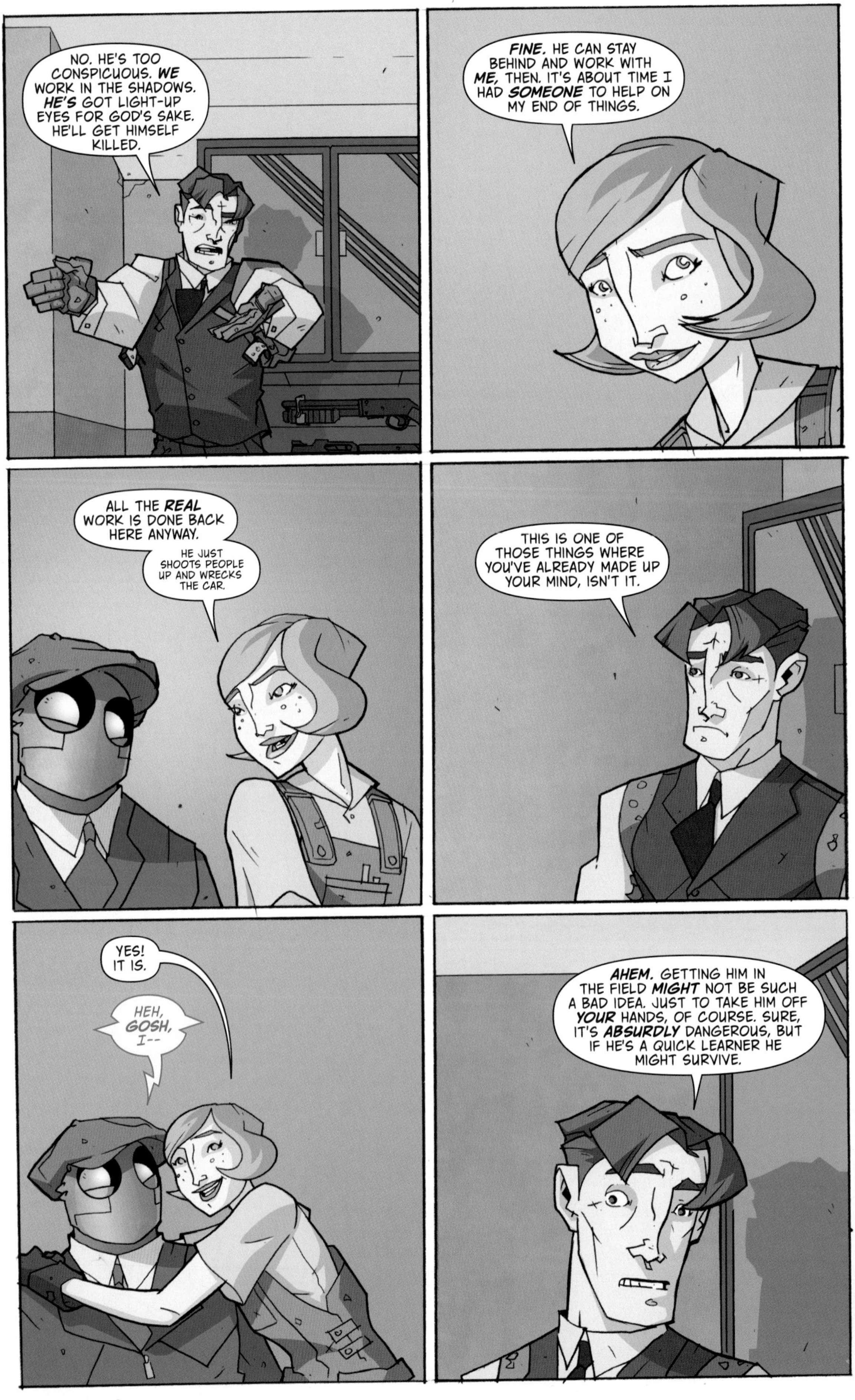
NO. HE'S TOO CONSPICUOUS. WE WORK IN THE SHADOWS. HE'S GOT LIGHT-UP EYES FOR GOD'S SAKE. HE'LL GET HIMSELF KILLED.
FINE. HE CAN STAY BEHIND AND WORK WITH ME, THEN. IT'S ABOUT TIME I HAD SOMEONE TO HELP ON MY END OF THINGS.
ALL THE REAL WORK IS DONE BACK HERE ANYWAY.
HE JUST SHOOTS PEOPLE UP AND WRECKS THE CAR.
THIS IS ONE OF THOSE THINGS WHERE YOU'VE ALREADY MADE UP YOUR MIND, ISN'T IT.
YES! IT IS.
HEH, GOSH, I--
AHEM. GETTING HIM IN THE FIELD MIGHT NOT BE SUCH A BAD IDEA. JUST TO TAKE HIM OFF YOUR HANDS, OF COURSE. SURE, IT'S ABSURDLY DANGEROUS, BUT IF HE'S A QUICK LEARNER HE MIGHT SURVIVE.

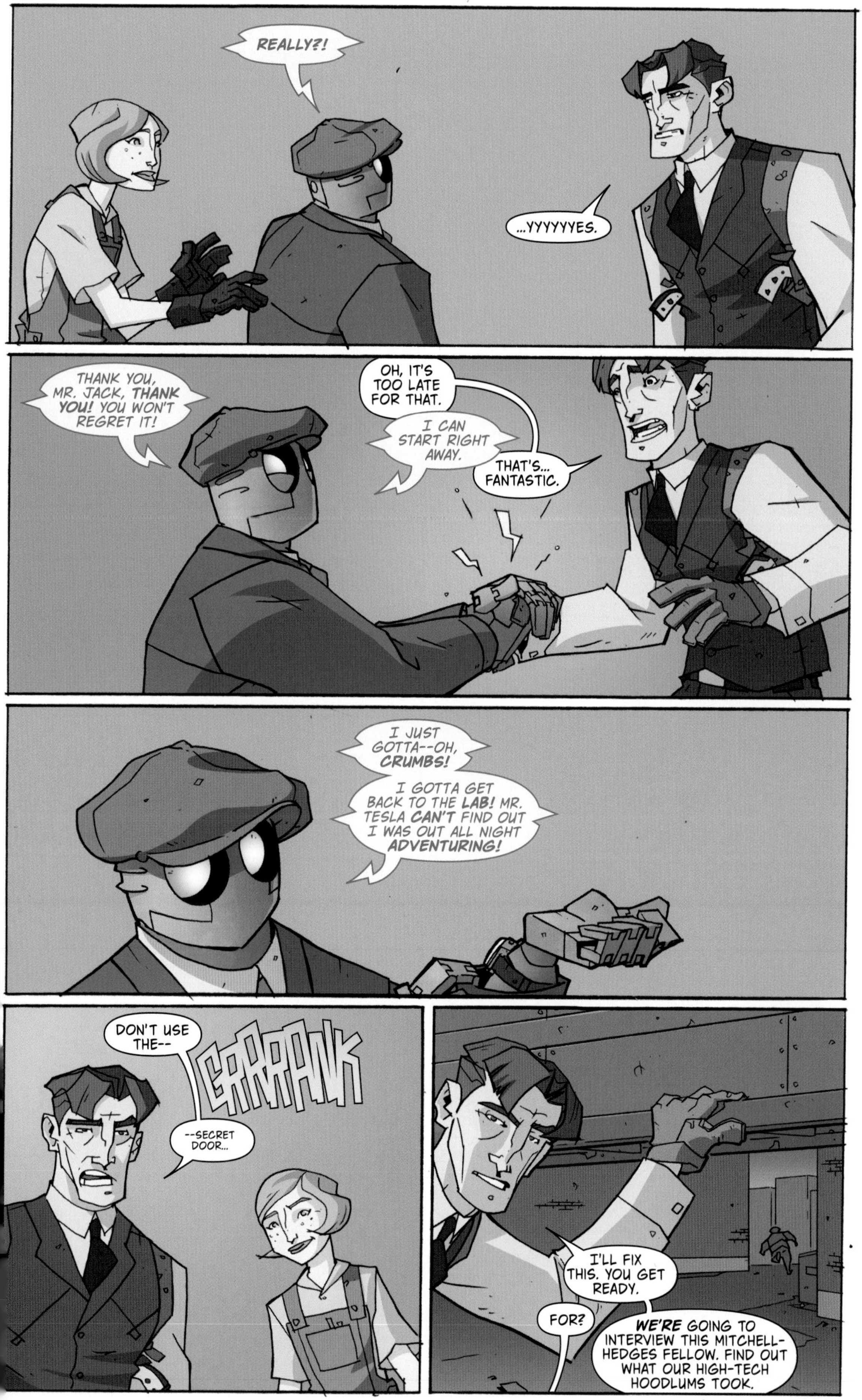
REALLY?!
...YYYYYYES.
THANK YOU, MR. JACK, THANK YOU! YOU WON'T REGRET IT!
OH, IT'S TOO LATE FOR THAT.
I CAN START RIGHT AWAY.
THAT'S... FANTASTIC.
I JUST GOTTA--OH, CRUMBS!
I GOTTA GET BACK TO THE LAB! MR. TESLA CAN'T FIND OUT I WAS OUT ALL NIGHT ADVENTURING!
DON'T USE THE--
GRRRANK
--SECRET DOOR...
I'LL FIX THIS. YOU GET READY.
FOR?
WE'RE GOING TO INTERVIEW THIS MITCHELL-HEDGES FELLOW. FIND OUT WHAT OUR HIGH-TECH HOODLUMS TOOK.

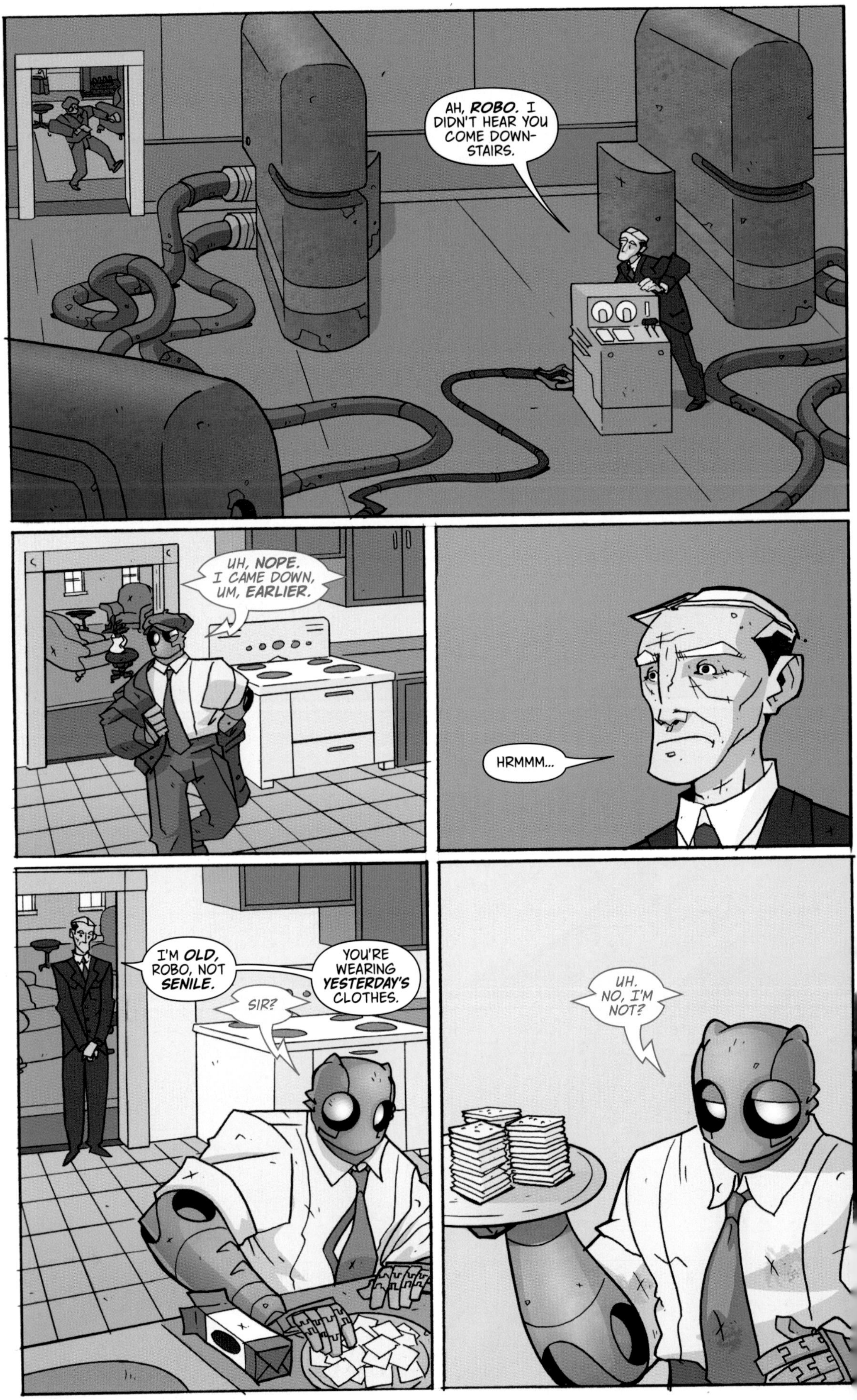
AH, ROBO. I DIDN'T HEAR YOU COME DOWN-STAIRS.
UH, NOPE. I CAME DOWN, UM, EARLIER.
HRMMM...
I'M OLD, ROBO, NOT SENILE.
SIR?
YOU'RE WEARING YESTERDAY'S CLOTHES.
UH. NO, I'M NOT?

YOU'RE A SHAMBLES, ROBO. ANY FOOL COULD SEE WHAT YOU'VE DONE.
ER... I...
YOU SPENT ALL NIGHT CLEANING THE GARAGE TO AVOID YOUR STUDIES.
THAT...OKAY, YES. I DID THAT THING.
A DOCTORATE IS NOT THE END OF YOUR LEARNING.
I KNOW, MR. TESLA.
GO ON, NOW. CHANGE BEFORE BREAKFAST. WE HAVE WORK TO CONDUCT AFTERWARD.
VECTOR ANALYSIS
GIVEN THE RESULTS OF LAST NIGHT'S EXPERIMENT--
Y'MEAN THE FAILURE?
THERE IS NO FAILURE IN SCIENCE, ROBO. ONLY MISSTEPS ON THE PATH TO GREATER UNDERSTANDING.
LET'S SEE WHAT WE CAN DO TO PHYSICS TODAY, HM?

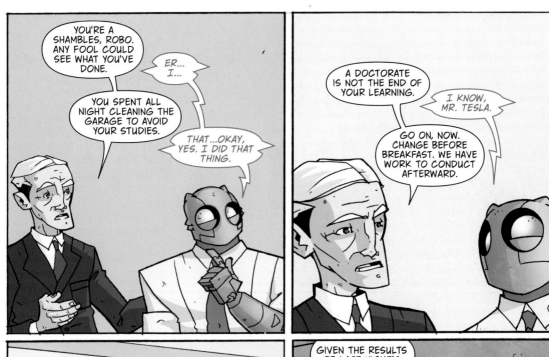

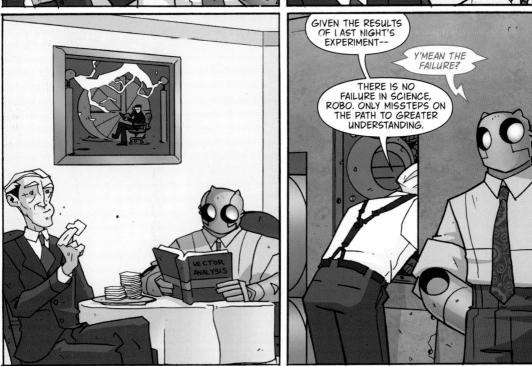

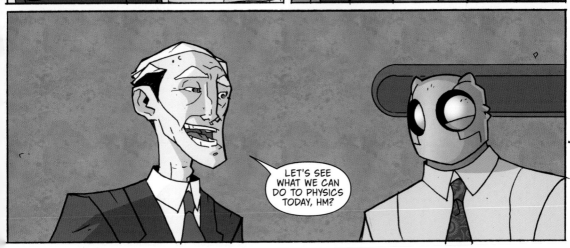

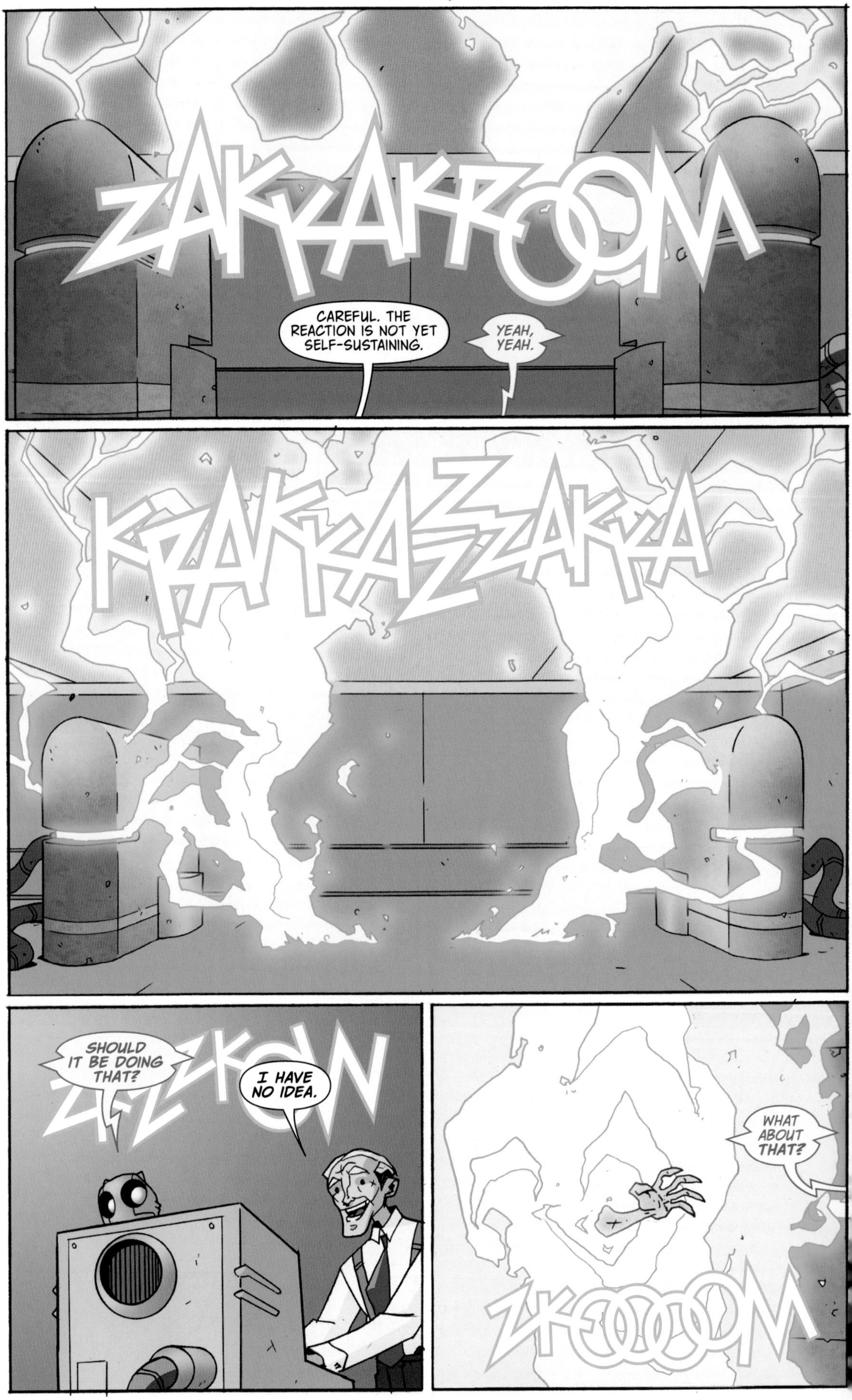

ZAKKAKROOM
CAREFUL. THE REACTION IS NOT YET SELF-SUSTAINING.
YEAH, YEAH.
KRAKKAZZZAKKA
SHOULD IT BE DOING THAT?
ZZZKOW
I HAVE NO IDEA.
WHAT ABOUT THAT?
ZKOOOOOM

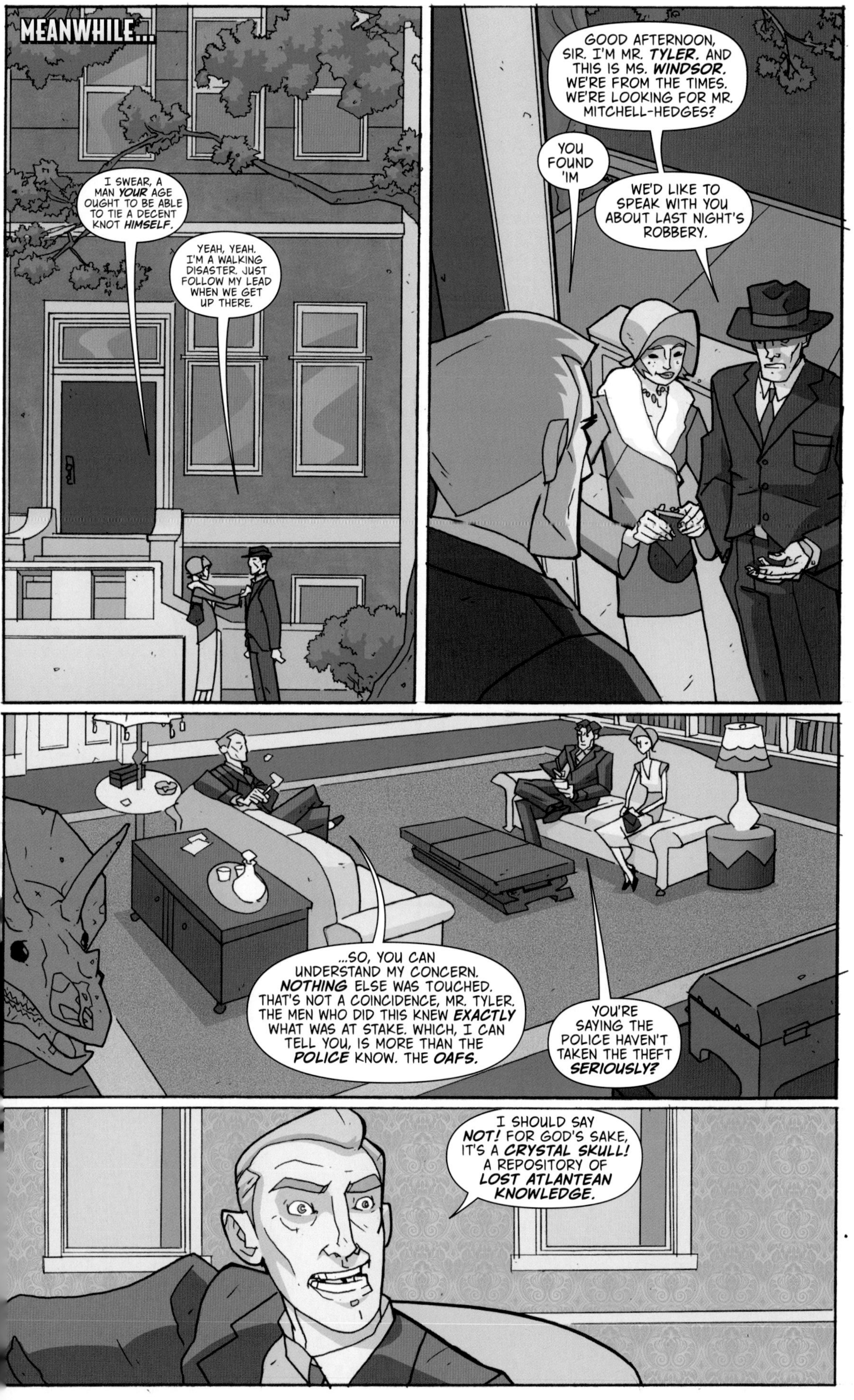
MEANWHILE...
I SWEAR, A MAN YOUR AGE OUGHT TO BE ABLE TO TIE A DECENT KNOT HIMSELF.
YEAH, YEAH. I'M A WALKING DISASTER. JUST FOLLOW MY LEAD WHEN WE GET UP THERE.
GOOD AFTERNOON, SIR. I'M MR. TYLER. AND THIS IS MS. WINDSOR. WE'RE FROM THE TIMES. WE'RE LOOKING FOR MR. MITCHELL-HEDGES?
YOU FOUND 'IM
WE'D LIKE TO SPEAK WITH YOU ABOUT LAST NIGHT'S ROBBERY.
...SO, YOU CAN UNDERSTAND MY CONCERN. NOTHING ELSE WAS TOUCHED. THAT'S NOT A COINCIDENCE, MR. TYLER. THE MEN WHO DID THIS KNEW EXACTLY WHAT WAS AT STAKE. WHICH, I CAN TELL YOU, IS MORE THAN THE POLICE KNOW. THE OAFS.
YOU'RE SAYING THE POLICE HAVEN'T TAKEN THE THEFT SERIOUSLY?
I SHOULD SAY NOT! FOR GOD'S SAKE, IT'S A CRYSTAL SKULL! A REPOSITORY OF LOST ATLANTEAN KNOWLEDGE.

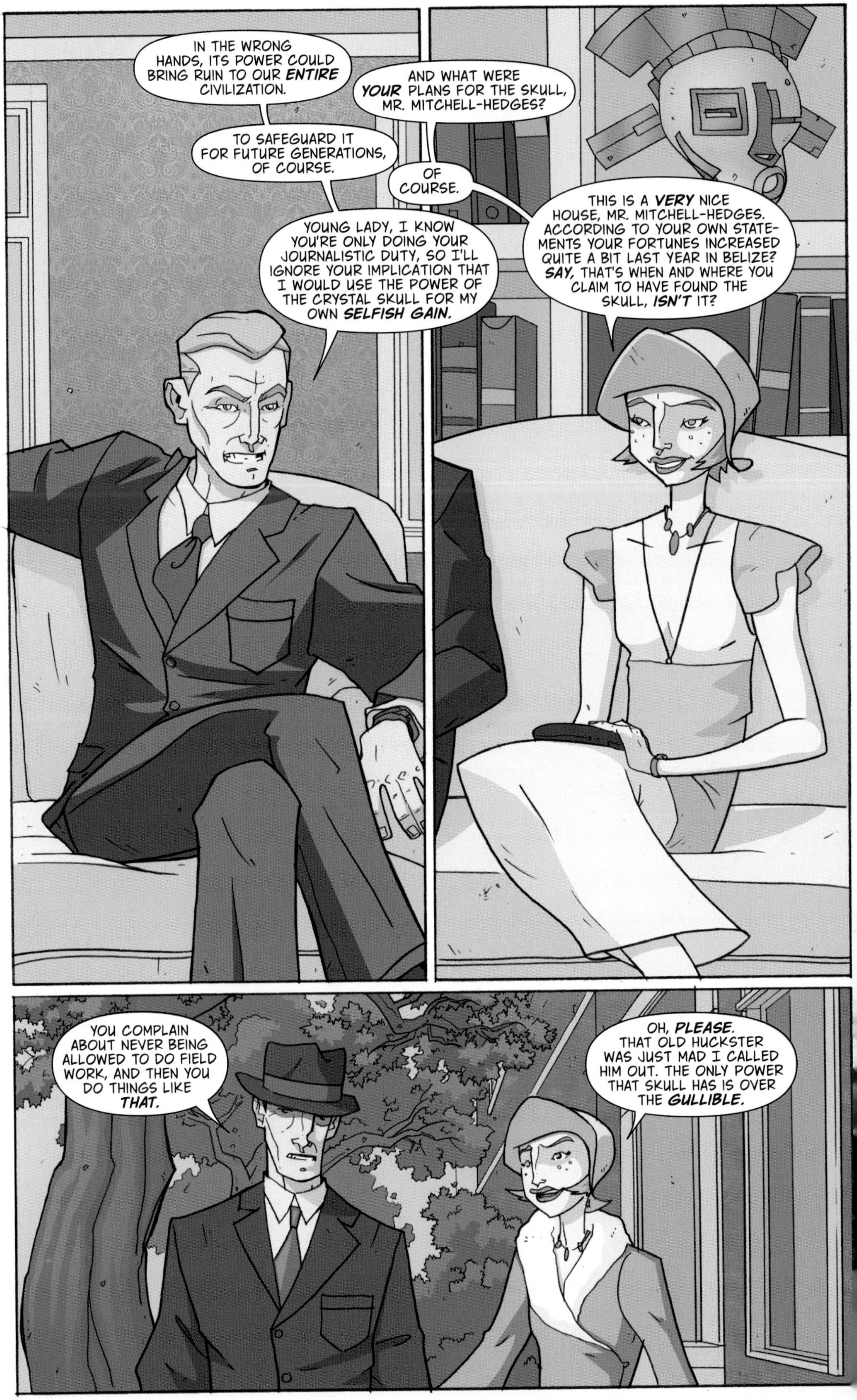
IN THE WRONG HANDS, ITS POWER COULD BRING RUIN TO OUR ENTIRE CIVILIZATION.
AND WHAT WERE YOUR PLANS FOR THE SKULL, MR. MITCHELL-HEDGES?
TO SAFEGUARD IT FOR FUTURE GENERATIONS, OF COURSE.
OF COURSE.
YOUNG LADY, I KNOW YOU'RE ONLY DOING YOUR JOURNALISTIC DUTY, SO I'LL IGNORE YOUR IMPLICATION THAT I WOULD USE THE POWER OF THE CRYSTAL SKULL FOR MY OWN SELFISH GAIN.
THIS IS A VERY NICE HOUSE, MR. MITCHELL-HEDGES. ACCORDING TO YOUR OWN STATEMENTS YOUR FORTUNES INCREASED QUITE A BIT LAST YEAR IN BELIZE? SAY, THAT'S WHEN AND WHERE YOU CLAIM TO HAVE FOUND THE SKULL, ISN'T IT?
YOU COMPLAIN ABOUT NEVER BEING ALLOWED TO DO FIELD WORK, AND THEN YOU DO THINGS LIKE THAT.
OH, PLEASE. THAT OLD HUCKSTER WAS JUST MAD I CALLED HIM OUT. THE ONLY POWER THAT SKULL HAS IS OVER THE GULLIBLE.

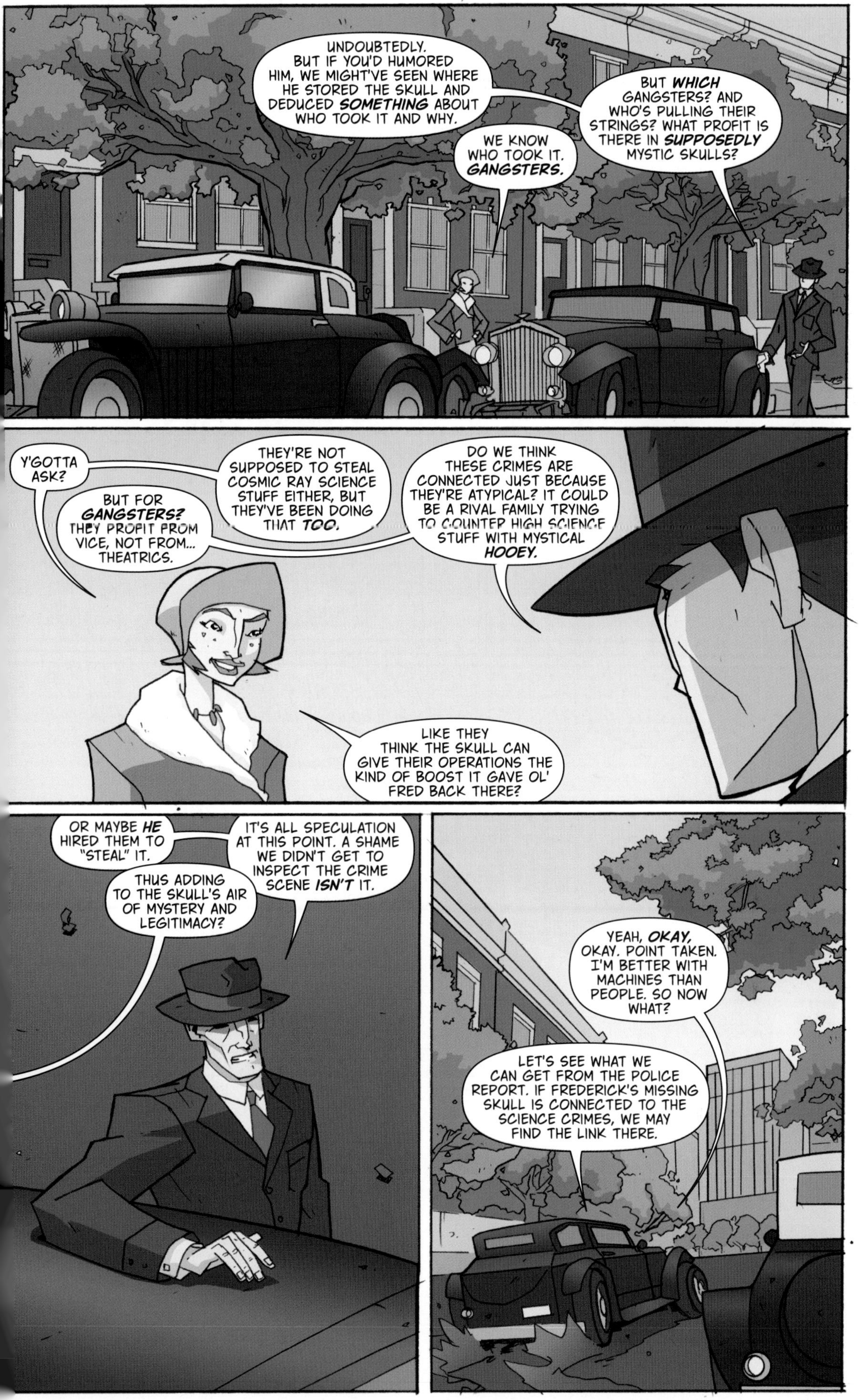
UNDOUBTEDLY. BUT IF YOU'D HUMORED HIM, WE MIGHT'VE SEEN WHERE HE STORED THE SKULL AND DEDUCED SOMETHING ABOUT WHO TOOK IT AND WHY.
WE KNOW WHO TOOK IT. GANGSTERS.
BUT WHICH GANGSTERS? AND WHO'S PULLING THEIR STRINGS? WHAT PROFIT IS THERE IN SUPPOSEDLY MYSTIC SKULLS?
Y'GOTTA ASK?
THEY'RE NOT SUPPOSED TO STEAL COSMIC RAY SCIENCE STUFF EITHER, BUT THEY'VE BEEN DOING THAT TOO.
BUT FOR GANGSTERS? THEY PROFIT FROM VICE, NOT FROM... THEATRICS.
DO WE THINK THESE CRIMES ARE CONNECTED JUST BECAUSE THEY'RE ATYPICAL? IT COULD BE A RIVAL FAMILY TRYING TO COUNTER HIGH SCIENCE STUFF WITH MYSTICAL HOOEY.
LIKE THEY THINK THE SKULL CAN GIVE THEIR OPERATIONS THE KIND OF BOOST IT GAVE OL' FRED BACK THERE?
OR MAYBE HE HIRED THEM TO "STEAL" IT.
THUS ADDING TO THE SKULL'S AIR OF MYSTERY AND LEGITIMACY?
IT'S ALL SPECULATION AT THIS POINT. A SHAME WE DIDN'T GET TO INSPECT THE CRIME SCENE ISN'T IT.
YEAH, OKAY, OKAY. POINT TAKEN. I'M BETTER WITH MACHINES THAN PEOPLE. SO NOW WHAT?
LET'S SEE WHAT WE CAN GET FROM THE POLICE REPORT. IF FREDERICK'S MISSING SKULL IS CONNECTED TO THE SCIENCE CRIMES, WE MAY FIND THE LINK THERE.

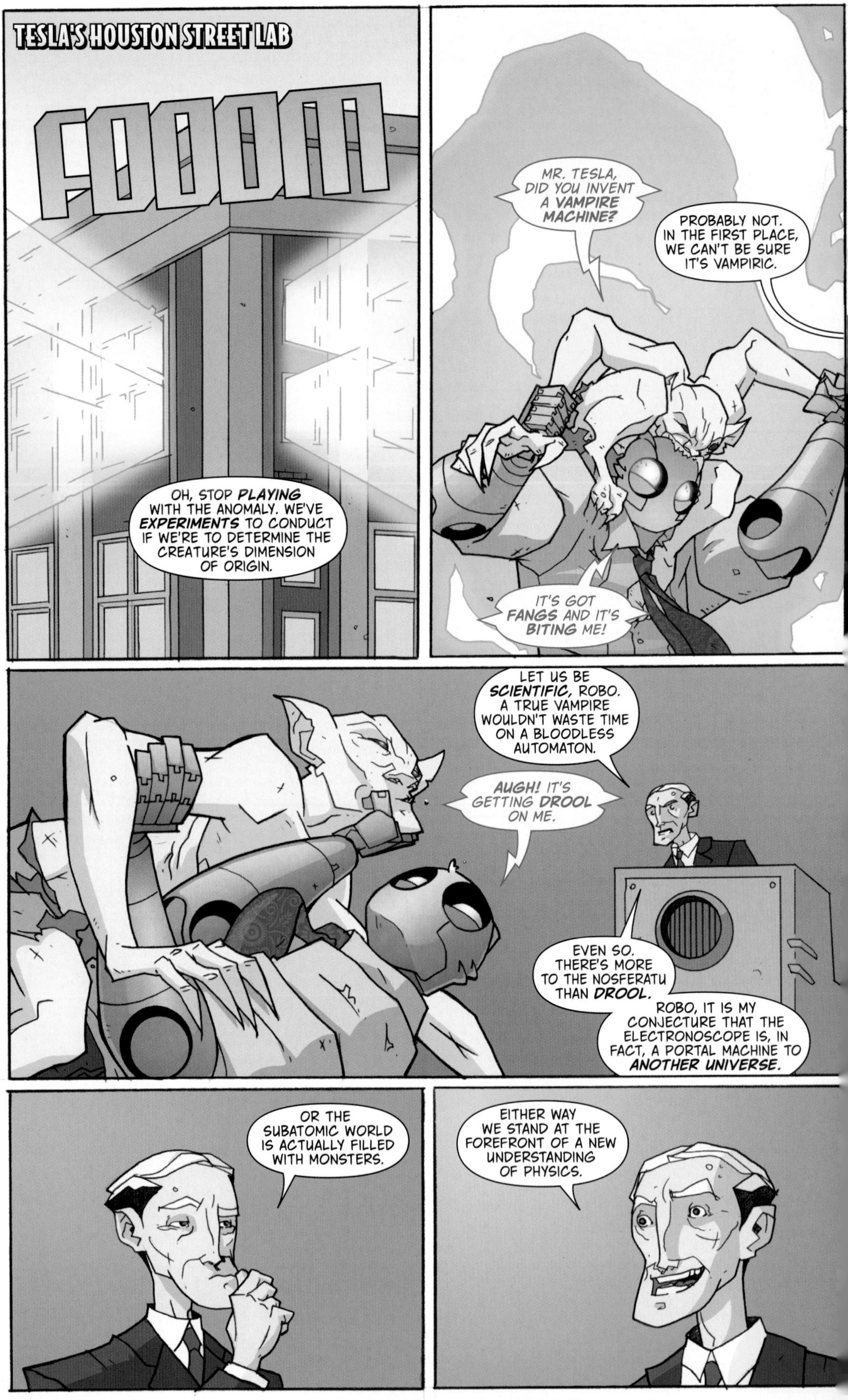
TESLA'S HOUSTON STREET LAB
FOOOM
OH, STOP PLAYING WITH THE ANOMALY. WE'VE EXPERIMENTS TO CONDUCT IF WE'RE TO DETERMINE THE CREATURE'S DIMENSION OF ORIGIN.
MR. TESLA, DID YOU INVENT A VAMPIRE MACHINE?
PROBABLY NOT. IN THE FIRST PLACE, WE CAN'T BE SURE IT'S VAMPIRIC.
IT'S GOT FANGS AND IT'S BITING ME!
LET US BE SCIENTIFIC, ROBO. A TRUE VAMPIRE WOULDN'T WASTE TIME ON A BLOODLESS AUTOMATON.
AUGH! IT'S GETTING DROOL ON ME.
EVEN SO. THERE'S MORE TO THE NOSFERATU THAN DROOL.
ROBO, IT IS MY CONJECTURE THAT THE ELECTRONOSCOPE IS, IN FACT, A PORTAL MACHINE TO ANOTHER UNIVERSE.
OR THE SUBATOMIC WORLD IS ACTUALLY FILLED WITH MONSTERS.
EITHER WAY WE STAND AT THE FOREFRONT OF A NEW UNDERSTANDING OF PHYSICS.

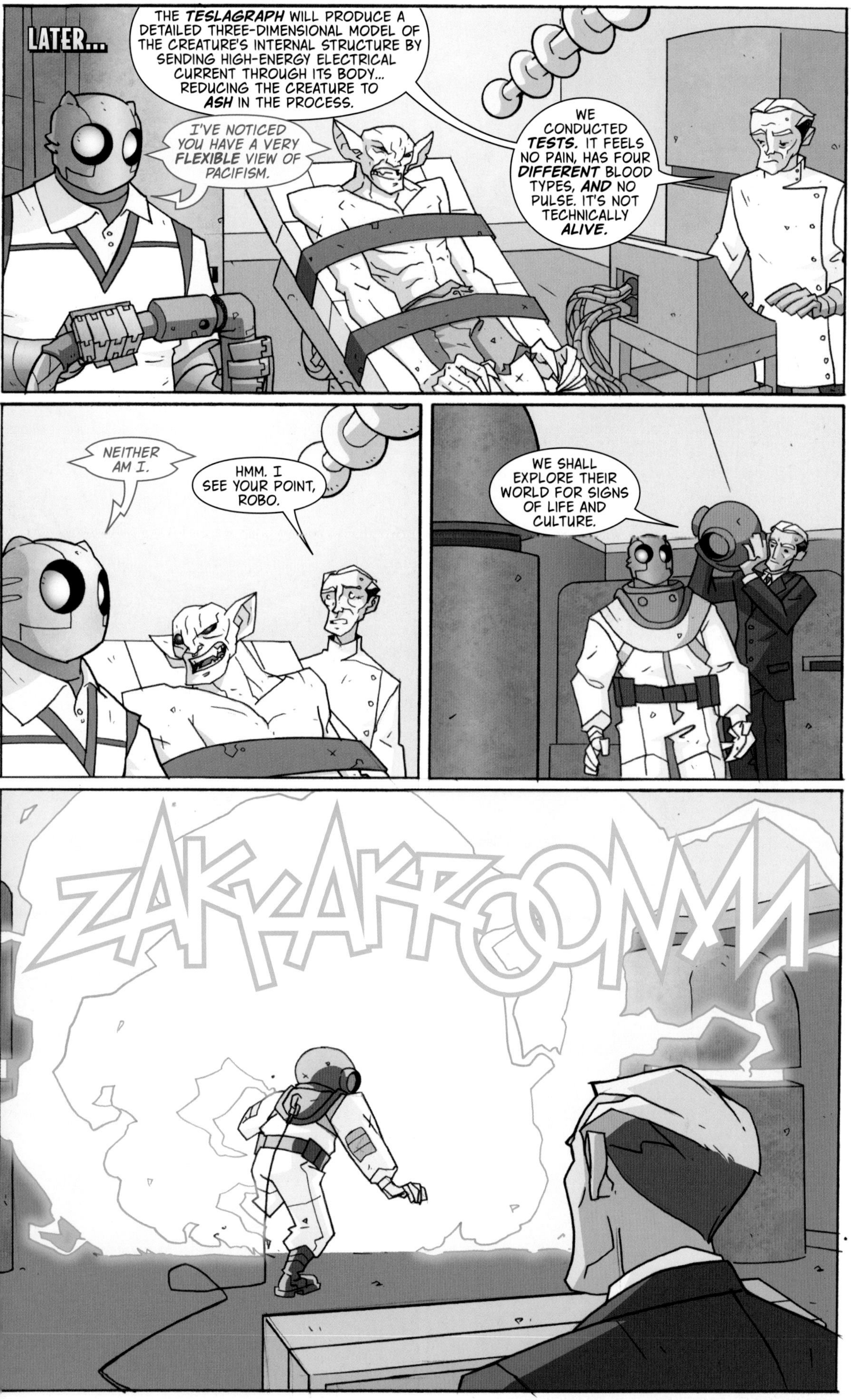
LATER...
THE TESLAGRAPH WILL PRODUCE A DETAILED THREE-DIMENSIONAL MODEL OF THE CREATURE'S INTERNAL STRUCTURE BY SENDING HIGH-ENERGY ELECTRICAL CURRENT THROUGH ITS BODY... REDUCING THE CREATURE TO ASH IN THE PROCESS.
I'VE NOTICED YOU HAVE A VERY FLEXIBLE VIEW OF PACIFISM.
WE CONDUCTED TESTS. IT FEELS NO PAIN, HAS FOUR DIFFERENT BLOOD TYPES, AND NO PULSE. IT'S NOT TECHNICALLY ALIVE.
NEITHER AM I.
HMM. I SEE YOUR POINT, ROBO.
WE SHALL EXPLORE THEIR WORLD FOR SIGNS OF LIFE AND CULTURE.
ZAKAKROOMM

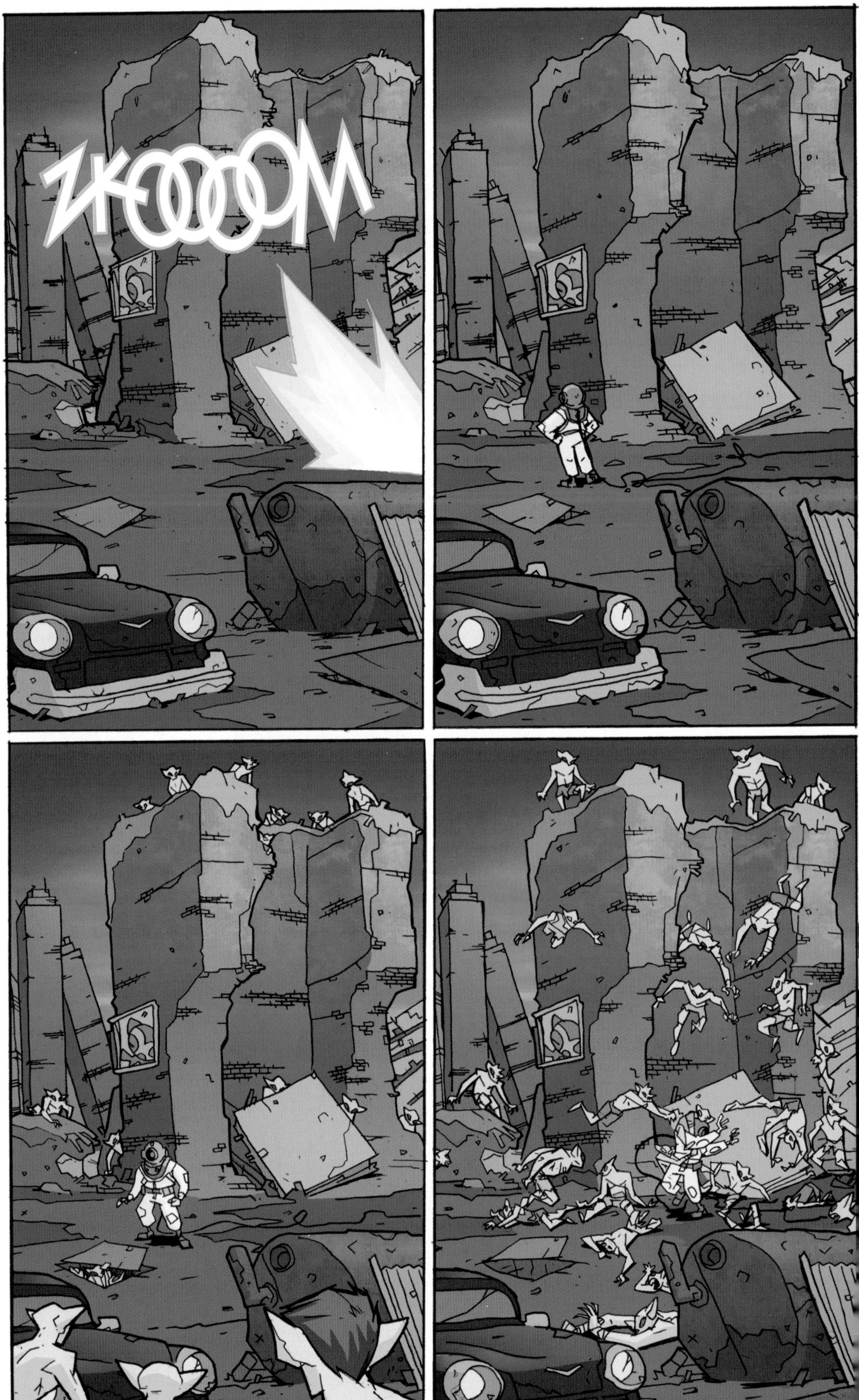
ZKOOOOM

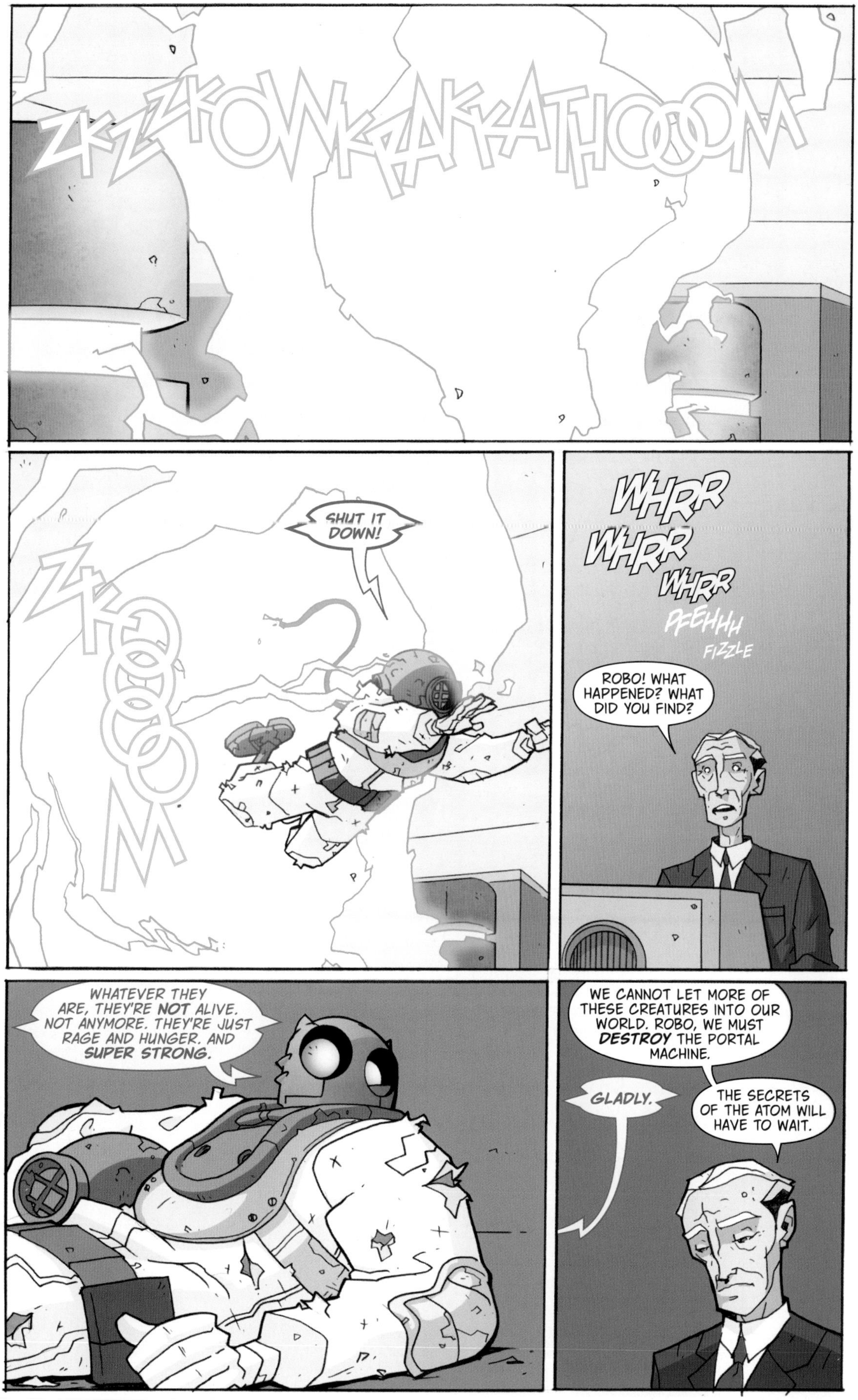
ZKZZKOWKRAKKATHOOOOM
SHUT IT DOWN!
ZKOOOOOM
WHRR
WHRR
WHRR
PFEHHH
FIZZLE
ROBO! WHAT HAPPENED? WHAT DID YOU FIND?
WHATEVER THEY ARE, THEY'RE NOT ALIVE. NOT ANYMORE. THEY'RE JUST RAGE AND HUNGER. AND SUPER STRONG.
WE CANNOT LET MORE OF THESE CREATURES INTO OUR WORLD. ROBO, WE MUST DESTROY THE PORTAL MACHINE.
GLADLY.
THE SECRETS OF THE ATOM WILL HAVE TO WAIT.

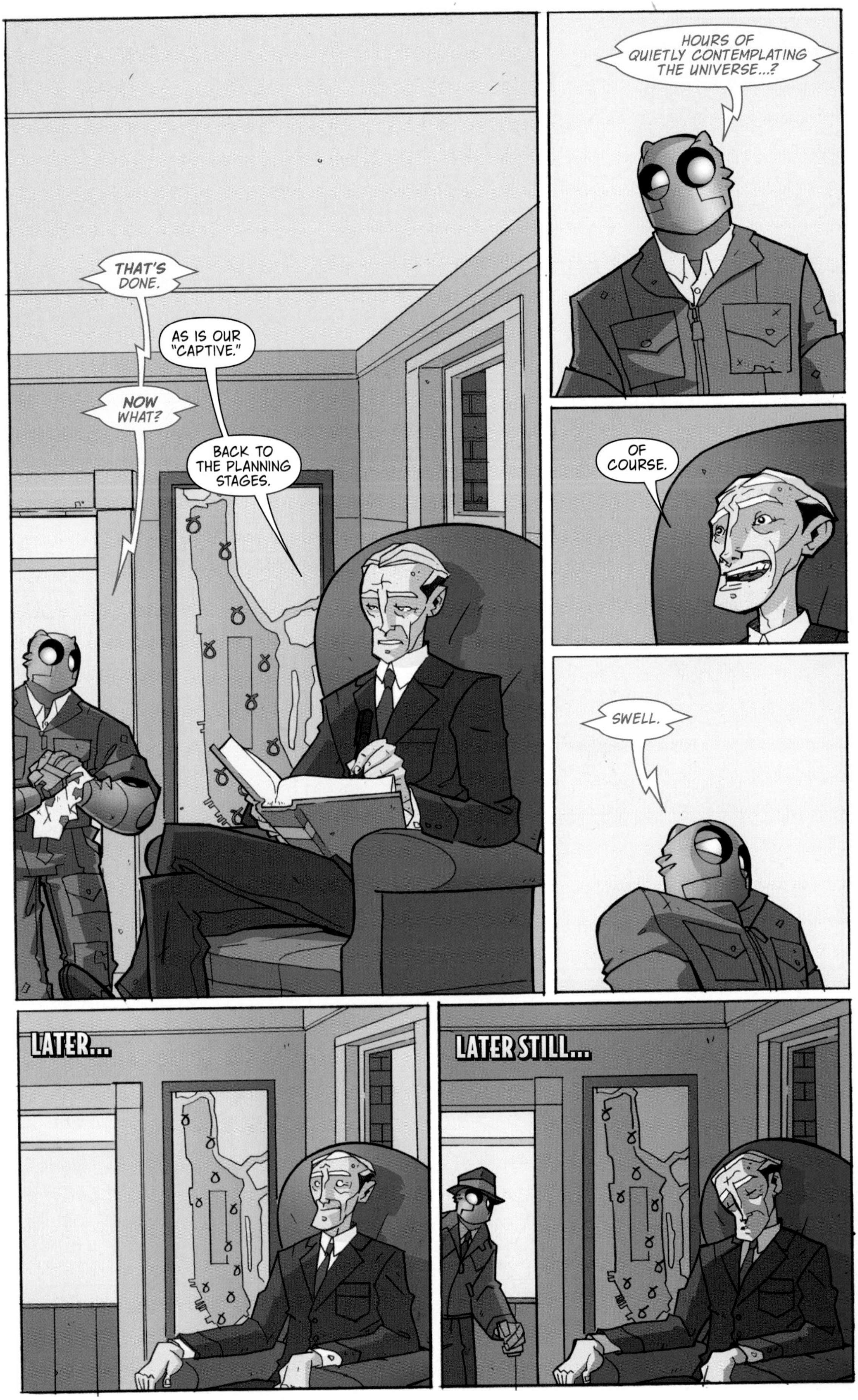
THAT'S DONE.
AS IS OUR "CAPTIVE."
NOW WHAT?
BACK TO THE PLANNING STAGES.
HOURS OF QUIETLY CONTEMPLATING THE UNIVERSE...?
OF COURSE.
SWELL.
LATER...
LATER STILL...

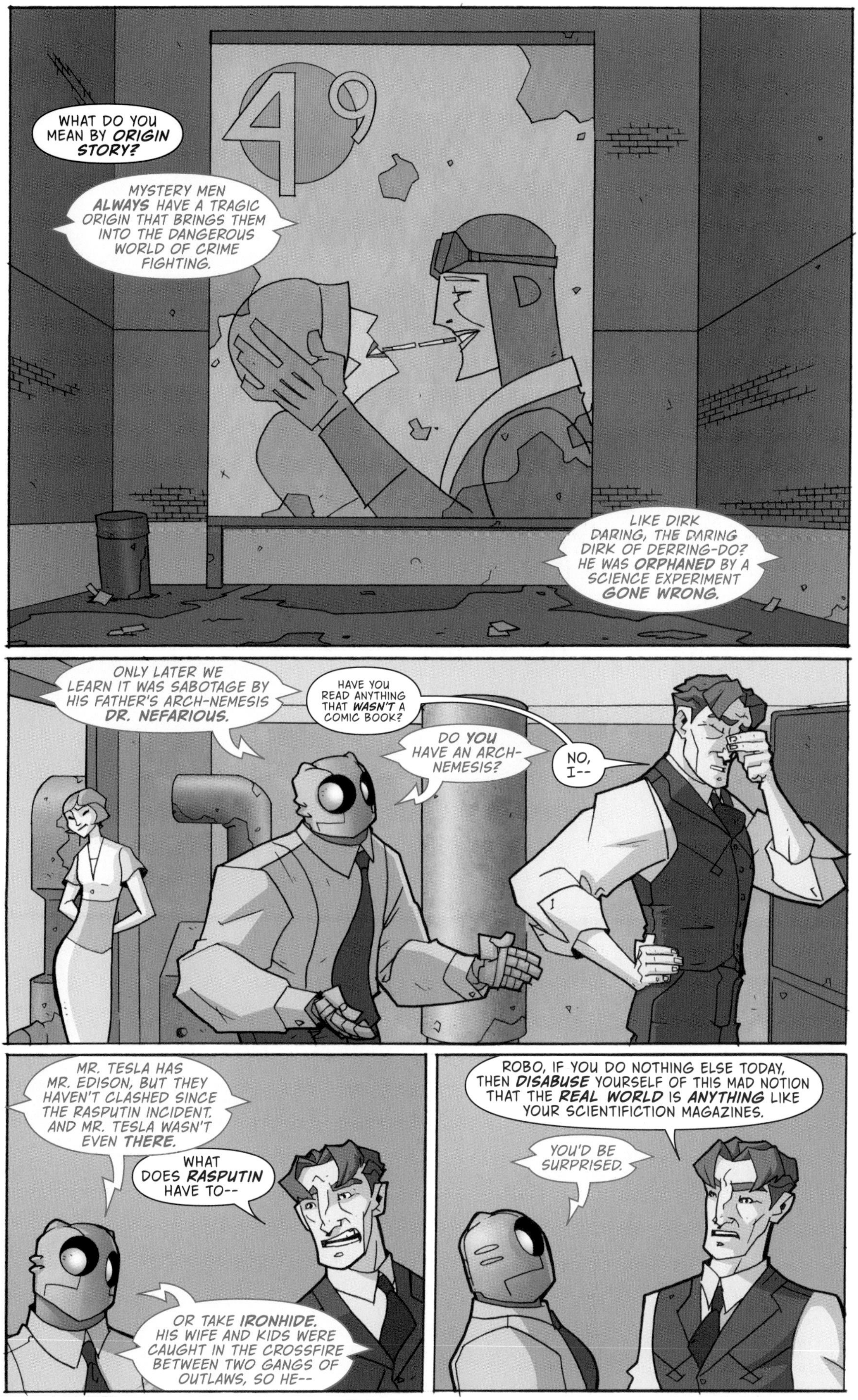
WHAT DO YOU MEAN BY ORIGIN STORY?
MYSTERY MEN ALWAYS HAVE A TRAGIC ORIGIN THAT BRINGS THEM INTO THE DANGEROUS WORLD OF CRIME FIGHTING.
LIKE DIRK DARING, THE DARING DIRK OF DERRING-DO? HE WAS ORPHANED BY A SCIENCE EXPERIMENT GONE WRONG.
ONLY LATER WE LEARN IT WAS SABOTAGE BY HIS FATHER'S ARCH-NEMESIS DR. NEFARIOUS.
HAVE YOU READ ANYTHING THAT WASN'T A COMIC BOOK?
DO YOU HAVE AN ARCH-NEMESIS?
NO, I--
MR. TESLA HAS MR. EDISON, BUT THEY HAVEN'T CLASHED SINCE THE RASPUTIN INCIDENT. AND MR. TESLA WASN'T EVEN THERE.
WHAT DOES RASPUTIN HAVE TO--
OR TAKE IRONHIDE. HIS WIFE AND KIDS WERE CAUGHT IN THE CROSSFIRE BETWEEN TWO GANGS OF OUTLAWS, SO HE--
ROBO, IF YOU DO NOTHING ELSE TODAY, THEN DISABUSE YOURSELF OF THIS MAD NOTION THAT THE REAL WORLD IS ANYTHING LIKE YOUR SCIENTIFICTION MAGAZINES.
YOU'D BE SURPRISED.

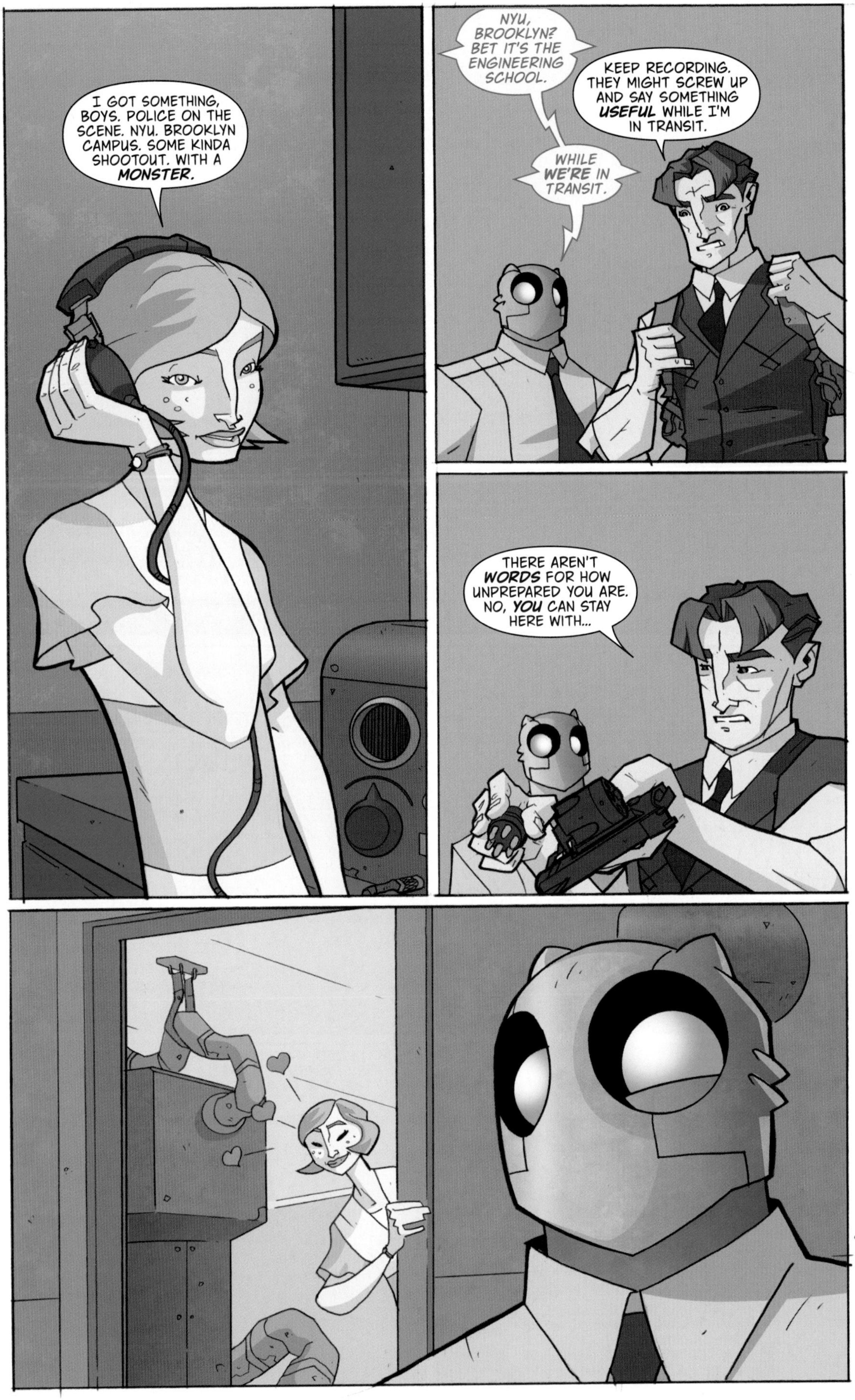
I GOT SOMETHING, BOYS. POLICE ON THE SCENE. NYU. BROOKLYN CAMPUS. SOME KINDA SHOOTOUT. WITH A MONSTER.
NYU, BROOKLYN? BET IT'S THE ENGINEERING SCHOOL.
KEEP RECORDING. THEY MIGHT SCREW UP AND SAY SOMETHING USEFUL WHILE I'M IN TRANSIT.
WHILE WE'RE IN TRANSIT.
THERE AREN'T WORDS FOR HOW UNPREPARED YOU ARE. NO, YOU CAN STAY HERE WITH...

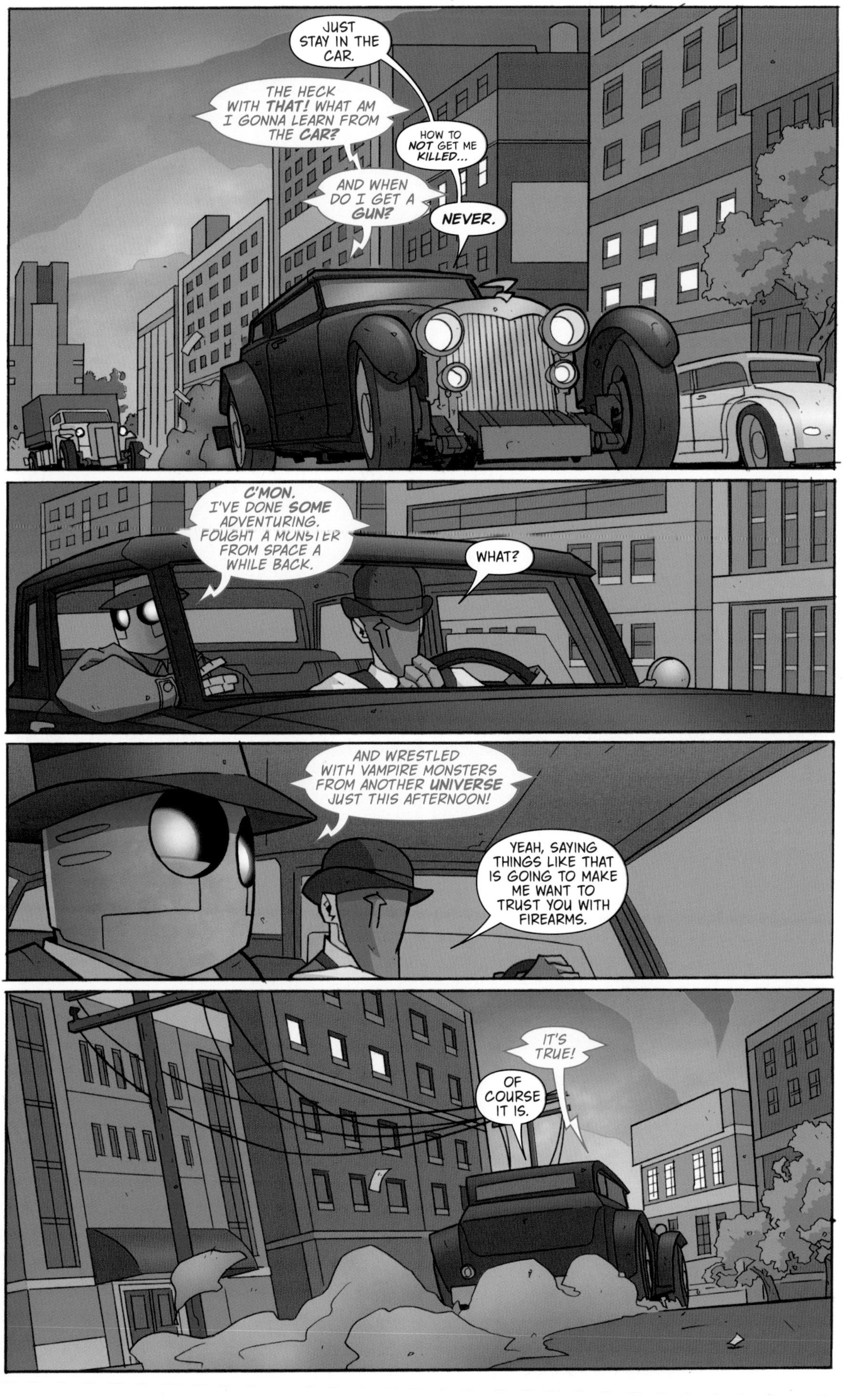
JUST STAY IN THE CAR.
THE HECK WITH THAT! WHAT AM I GONNA LEARN FROM THE CAR?
HOW TO NOT GET ME KILLED...
AND WHEN DO I GET A GUN?
NEVER.
C'MON. I'VE DONE SOME ADVENTURING. FOUGHT A MONSTER FROM SPACE A WHILE BACK.
WHAT?
AND WRESTLED WITH VAMPIRE MONSTERS FROM ANOTHER UNIVERSE JUST THIS AFTERNOON!
YEAH, SAYING THINGS LIKE THAT IS GOING TO MAKE ME WANT TO TRUST YOU WITH FIREARMS.
IT'S TRUE!
OF COURSE IT IS.

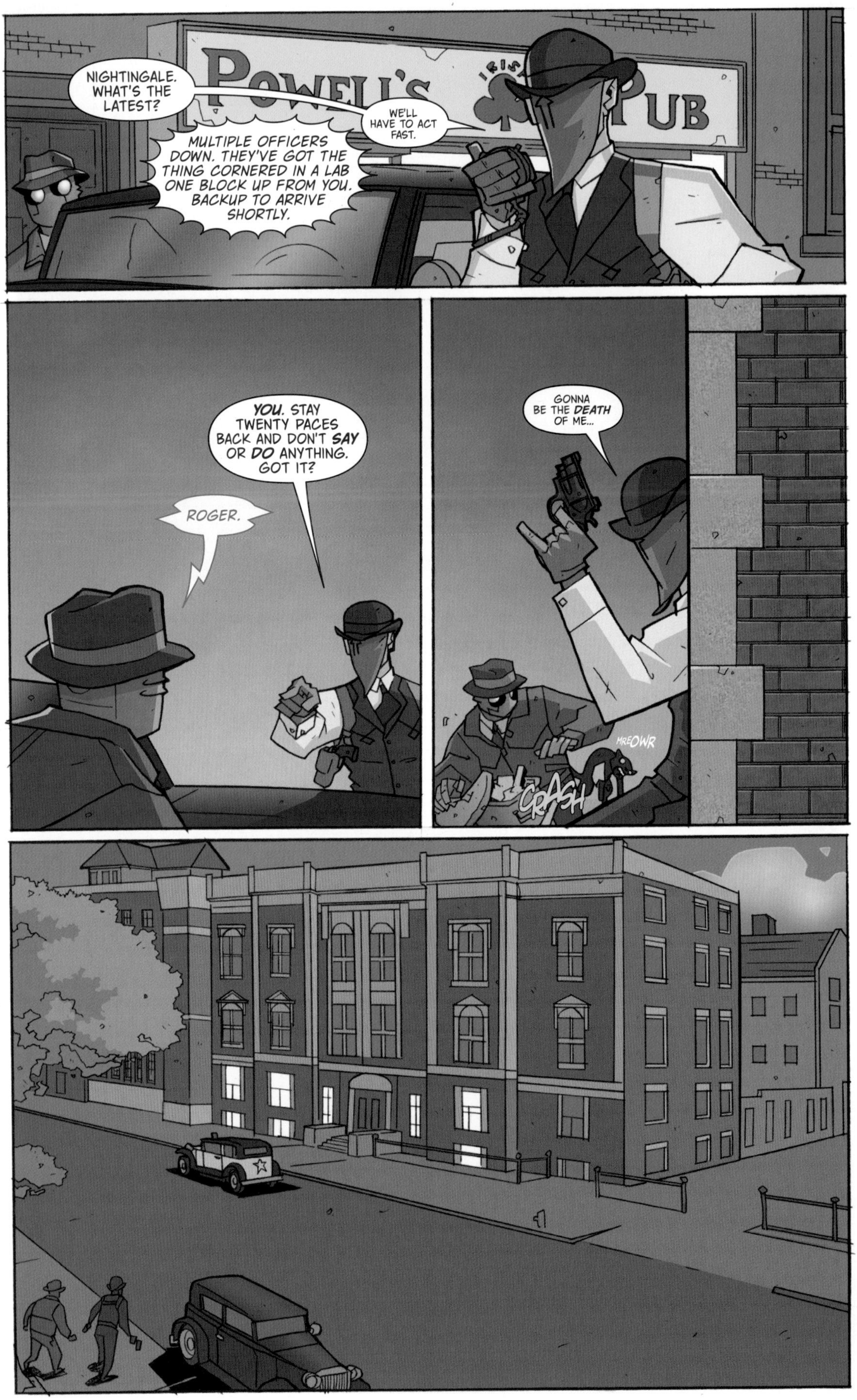
POWELL'S IRISH PUB
NIGHTINGALE. WHAT'S THE LATEST?
WE'LL HAVE TO ACT FAST.
MULTIPLE OFFICERS DOWN. THEY'VE GOT THE THING CORNERED IN A LAB ONE BLOCK UP FROM YOU. BACKUP TO ARRIVE SHORTLY.
YOU. STAY TWENTY PACES BACK AND DON'T SAY OR DO ANYTHING. GOT IT?
ROGER.
GONNA BE THE DEATH OF ME...
MREOWR
CRASH

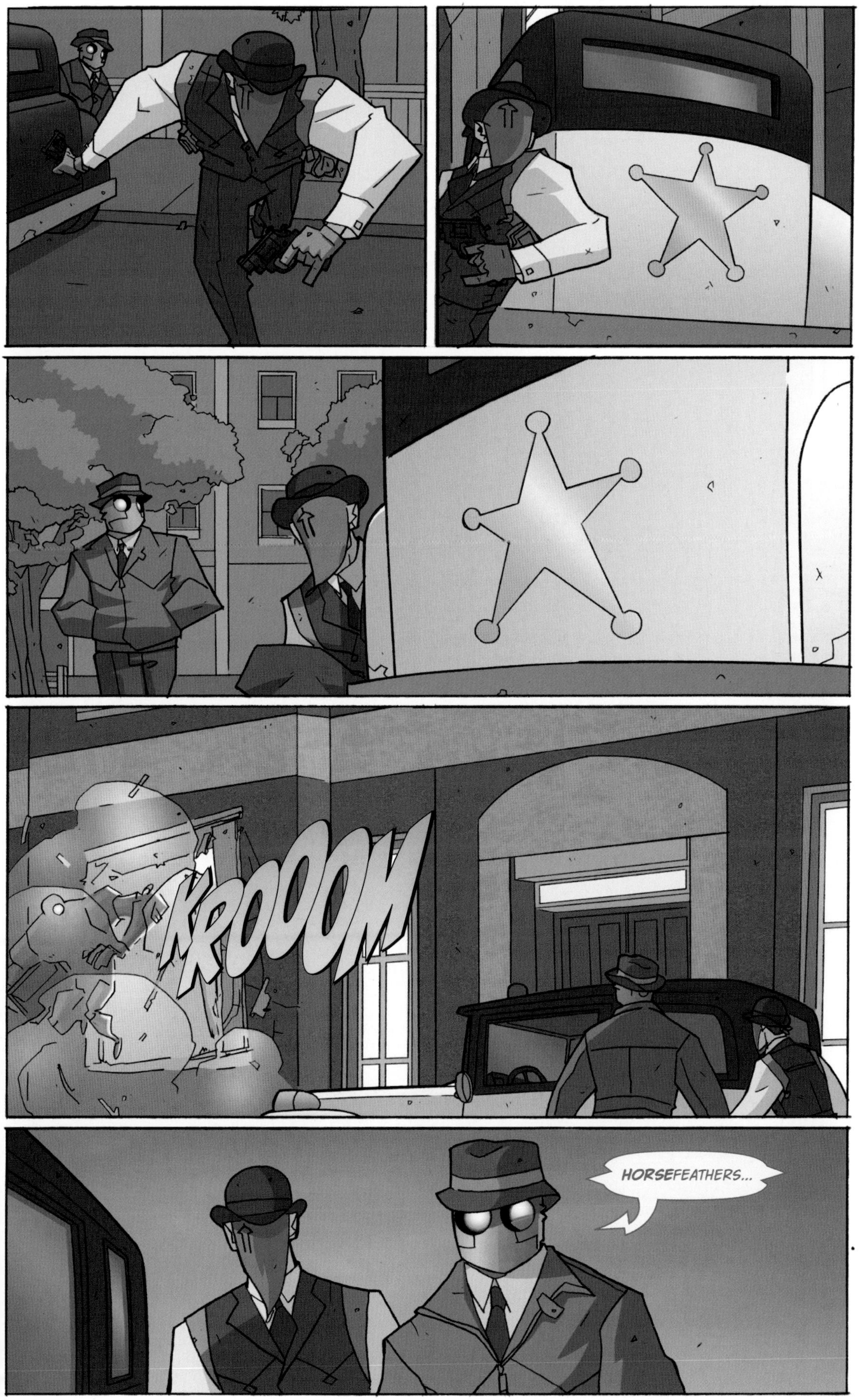
KROOOM
HORSEFEATHERS...

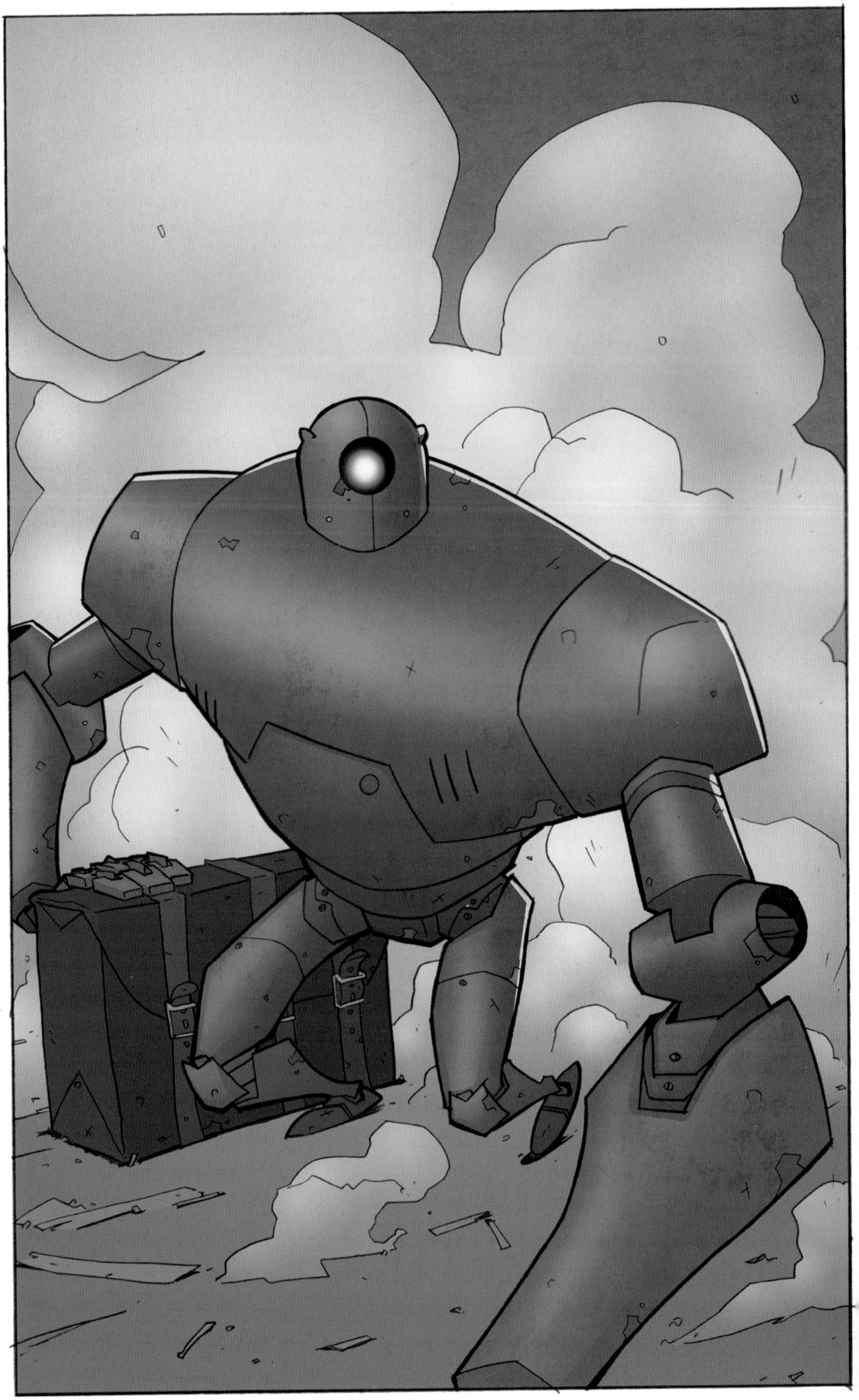

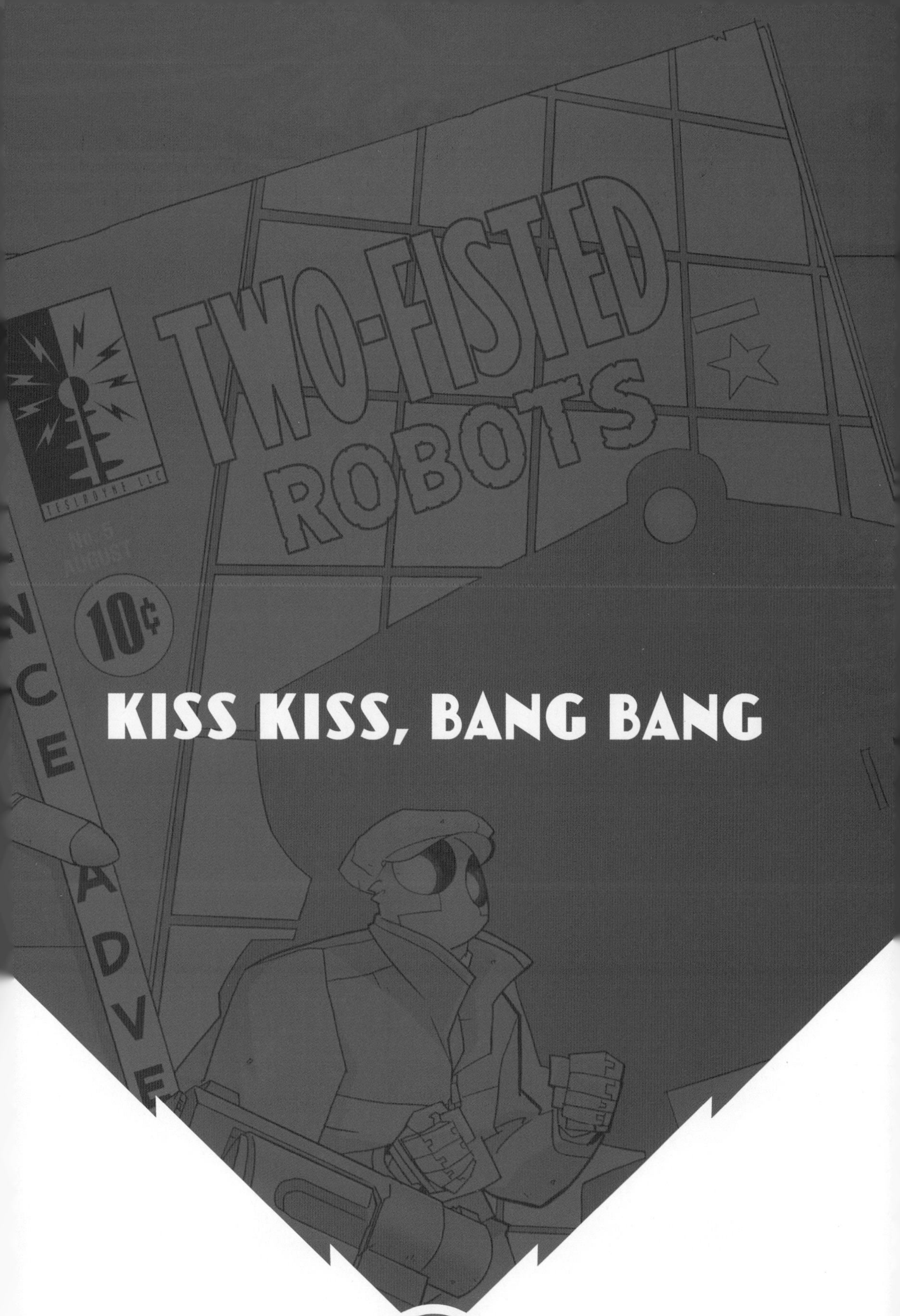
TWO-FISTED ROBOTS
10¢

KISS KISS, BANG BANG

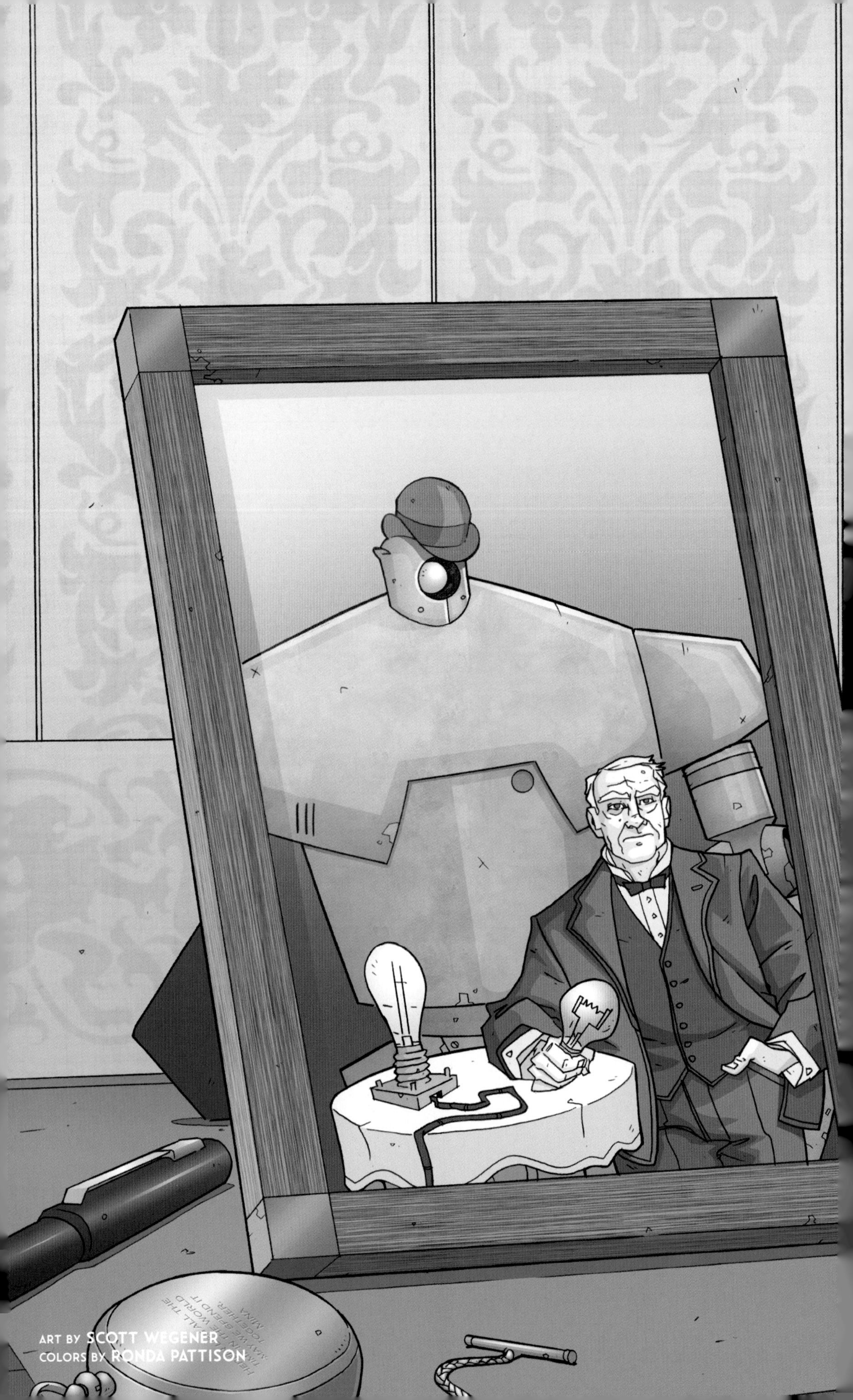
TIME IN THE WORLD
MAY WE SPEND IT
TOGETHER,
MINA
ART BY SCOTT WEGENER
COLORS BY RONDA PATTISON

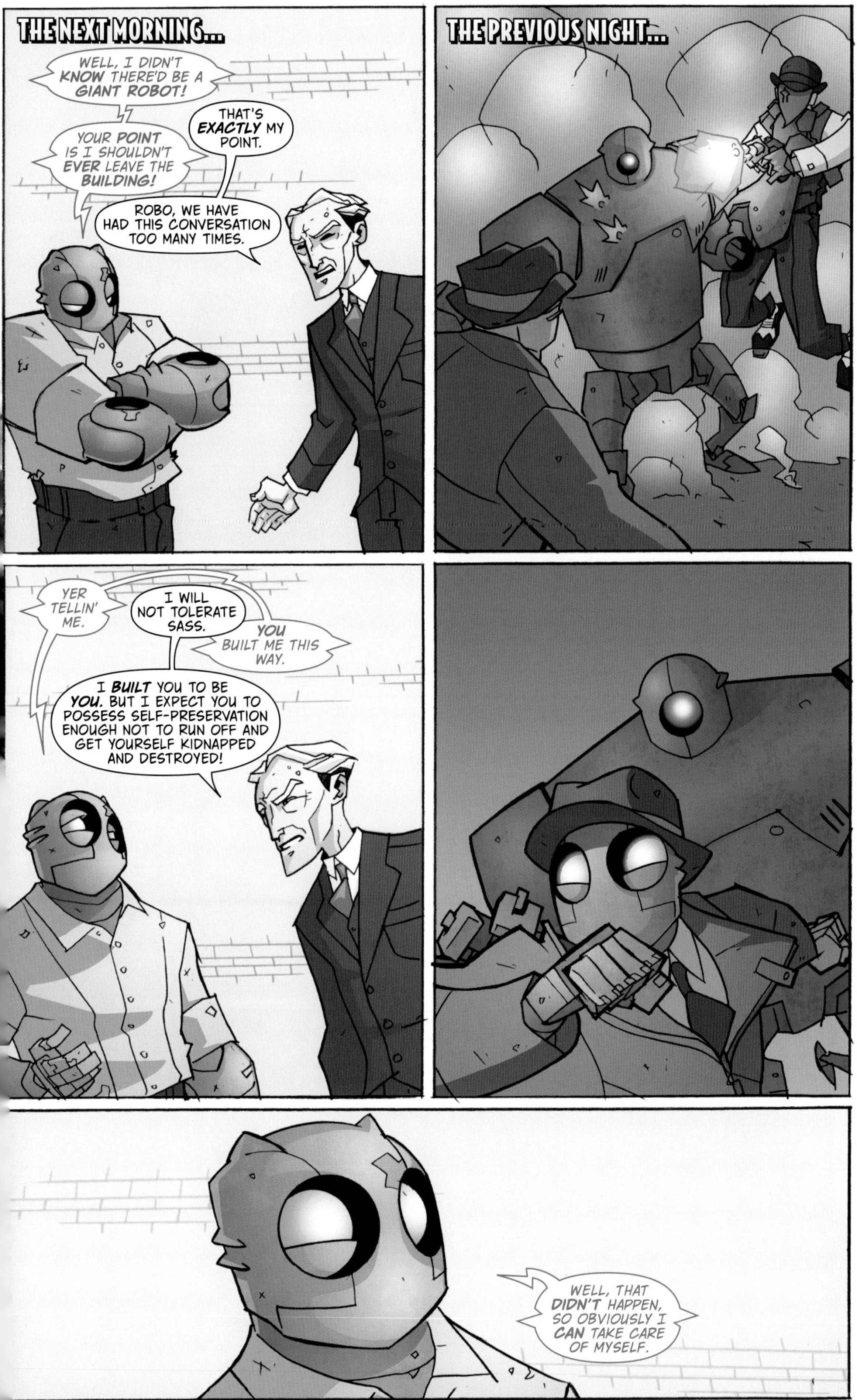
THE NEXT MORNING...
WELL, I DIDN'T KNOW THERE'D BE A GIANT ROBOT!
YOUR POINT IS I SHOULDN'T EVER LEAVE THE BUILDING!
THAT'S EXACTLY MY POINT.
ROBO, WE HAVE HAD THIS CONVERSATION TOO MANY TIMES.
THE PREVIOUS NIGHT...
YER TELLIN' ME.
I WILL NOT TOLERATE SASS.
YOU BUILT ME THIS WAY.
I BUILT YOU TO BE YOU. BUT I EXPECT YOU TO POSSESS SELF-PRESERVATION ENOUGH NOT TO RUN OFF AND GET YOURSELF KIDNAPPED AND DESTROYED!
WELL, THAT DIDN'T HAPPEN, SO OBVIOUSLY I CAN TAKE CARE OF MYSELF.

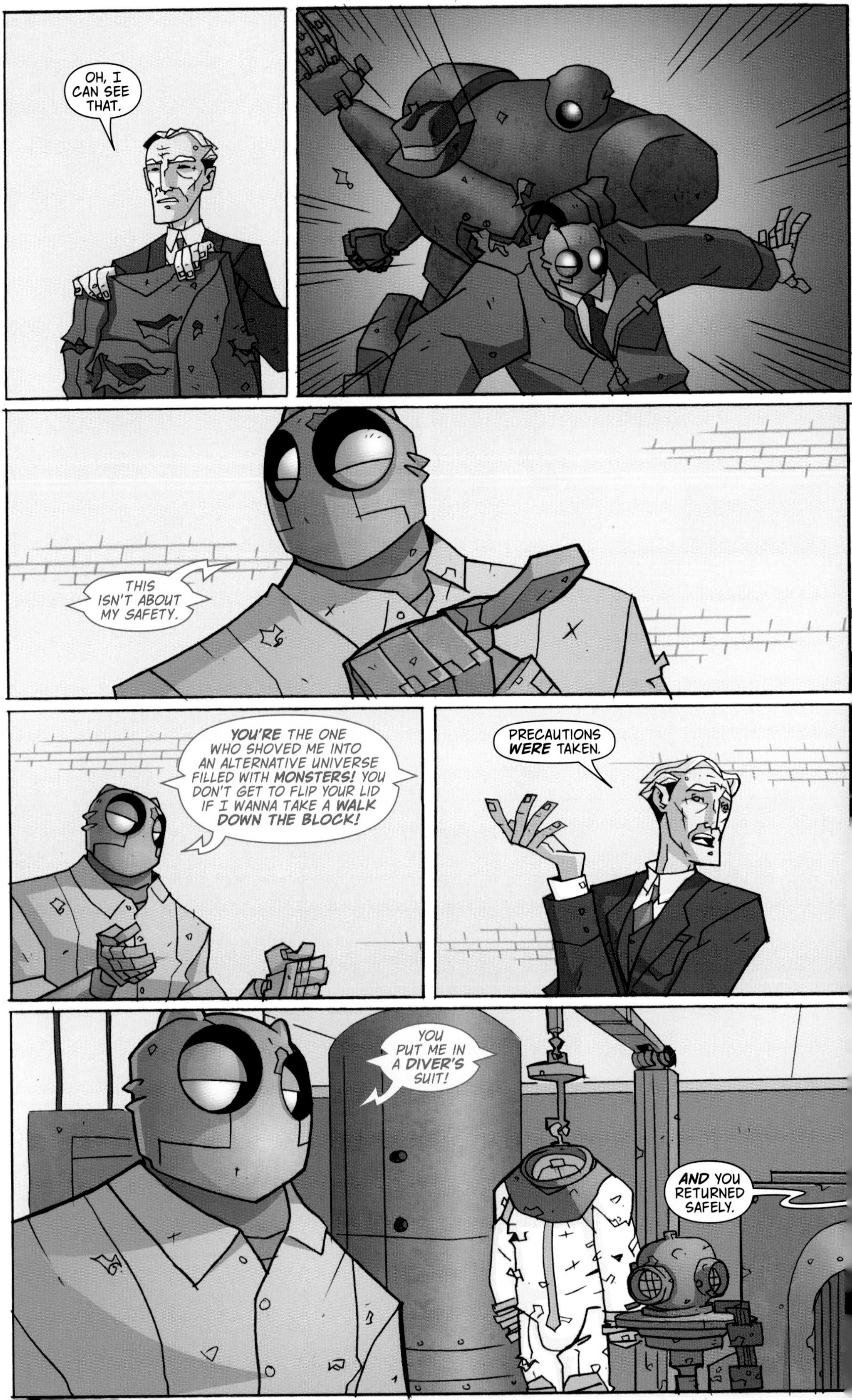
OH, I CAN SEE THAT.
THIS ISN'T ABOUT MY SAFETY.
YOU'RE THE ONE WHO SHOVED ME INTO AN ALTERNATIVE UNIVERSE FILLED WITH MONSTERS! YOU DON'T GET TO FLIP YOUR LID IF I WANNA TAKE A WALK DOWN THE BLOCK!
PRECAUTIONS WERE TAKEN.
YOU PUT ME IN A DIVER'S SUIT!
AND YOU RETURNED SAFELY.

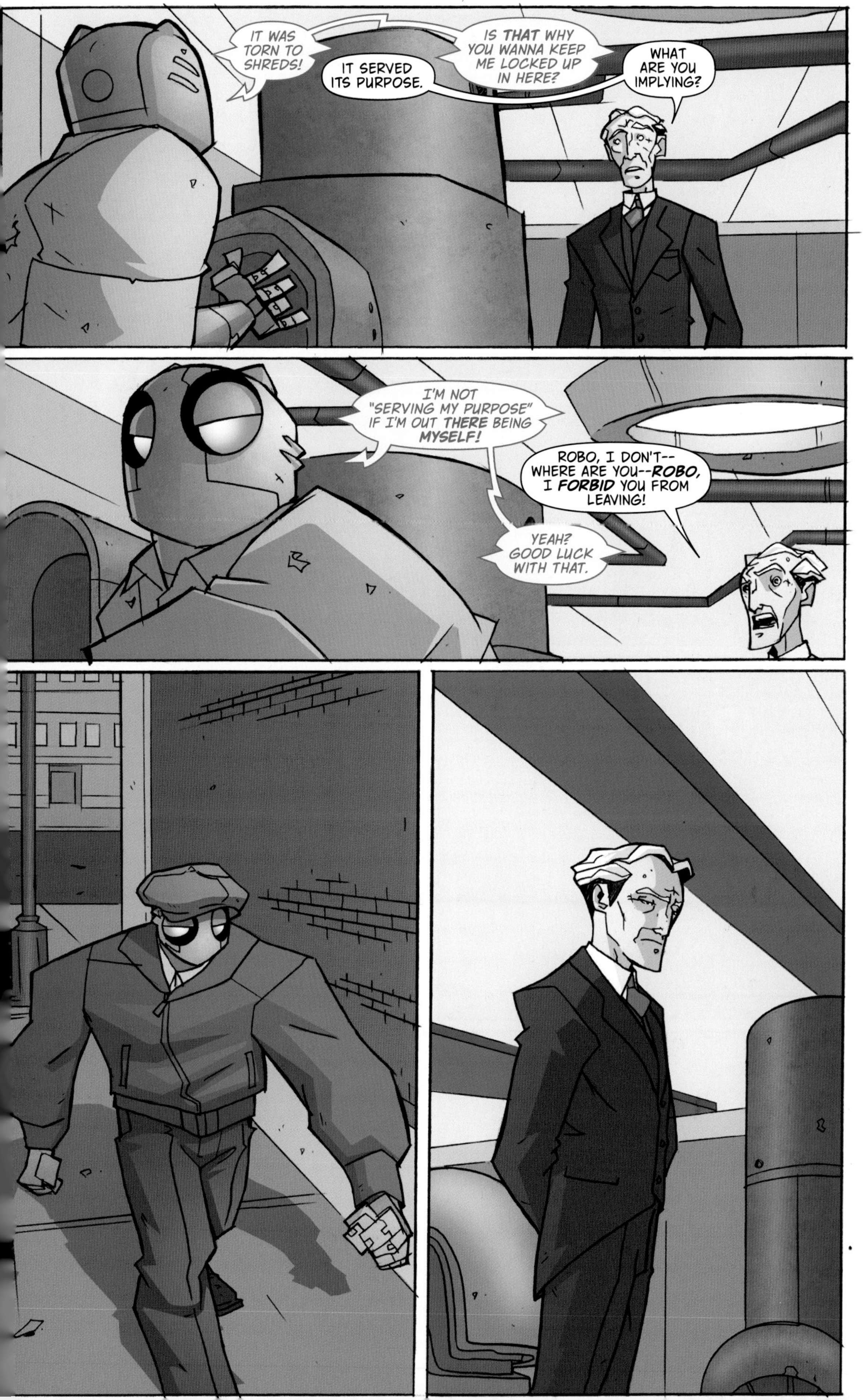
IT WAS TORN TO SHREDS!
IT SERVED ITS PURPOSE.
IS THAT WHY YOU WANNA KEEP ME LOCKED UP IN HERE?
WHAT ARE YOU IMPLYING?
I'M NOT "SERVING MY PURPOSE" IF I'M OUT THERE BEING MYSELF!
ROBO, I DON'T--WHERE ARE YOU--ROBO, I FORBID YOU FROM LEAVING!
YEAH? GOOD LUCK WITH THAT.

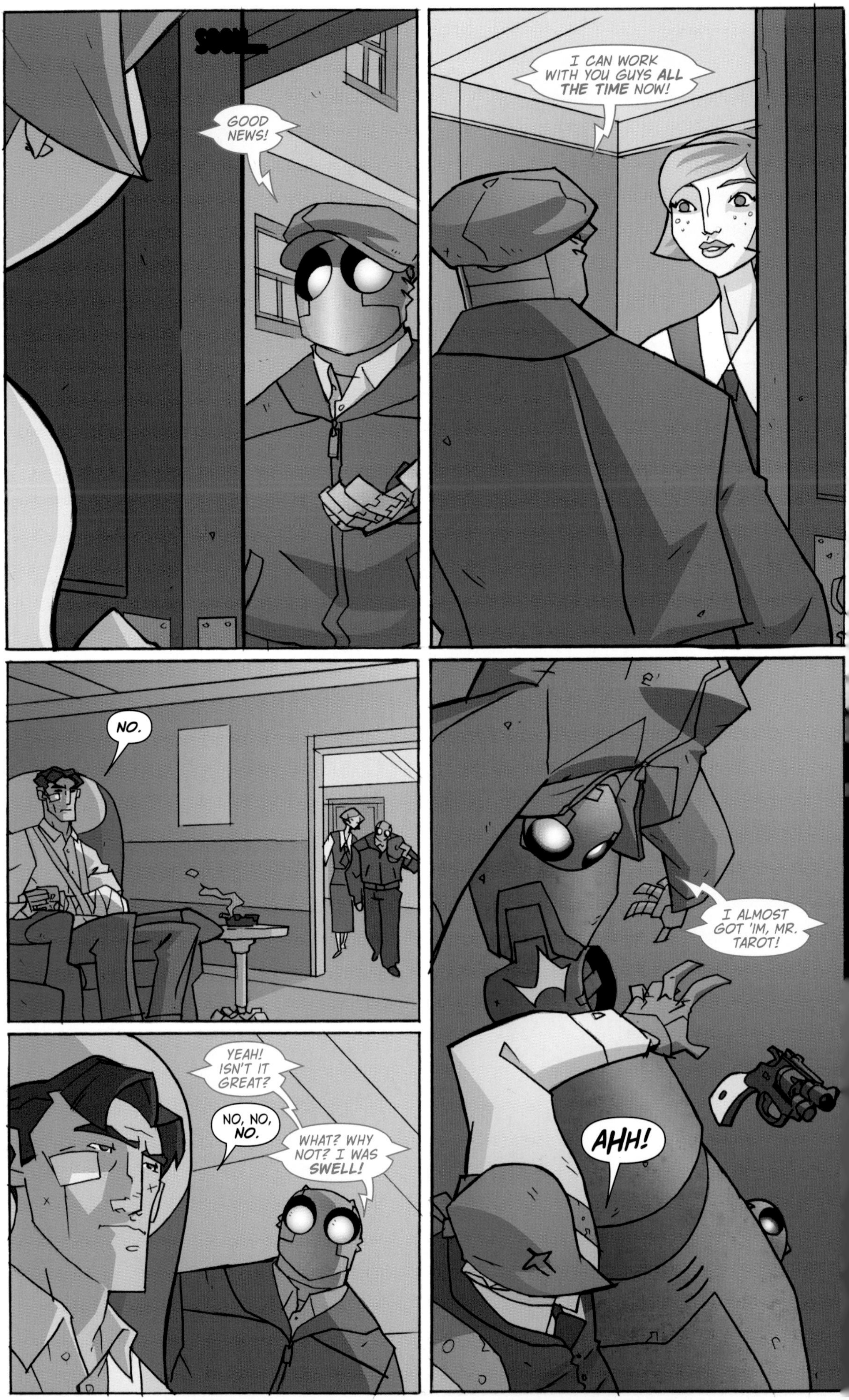
SOON...
GOOD NEWS!
I CAN WORK WITH YOU GUYS ALL THE TIME NOW!
NO.
I ALMOST GOT 'IM, MR. TAROT!
AHH!
YEAH! ISN'T IT GREAT?
NO, NO, NO.
WHAT? WHY NOT? I WAS SWELL!

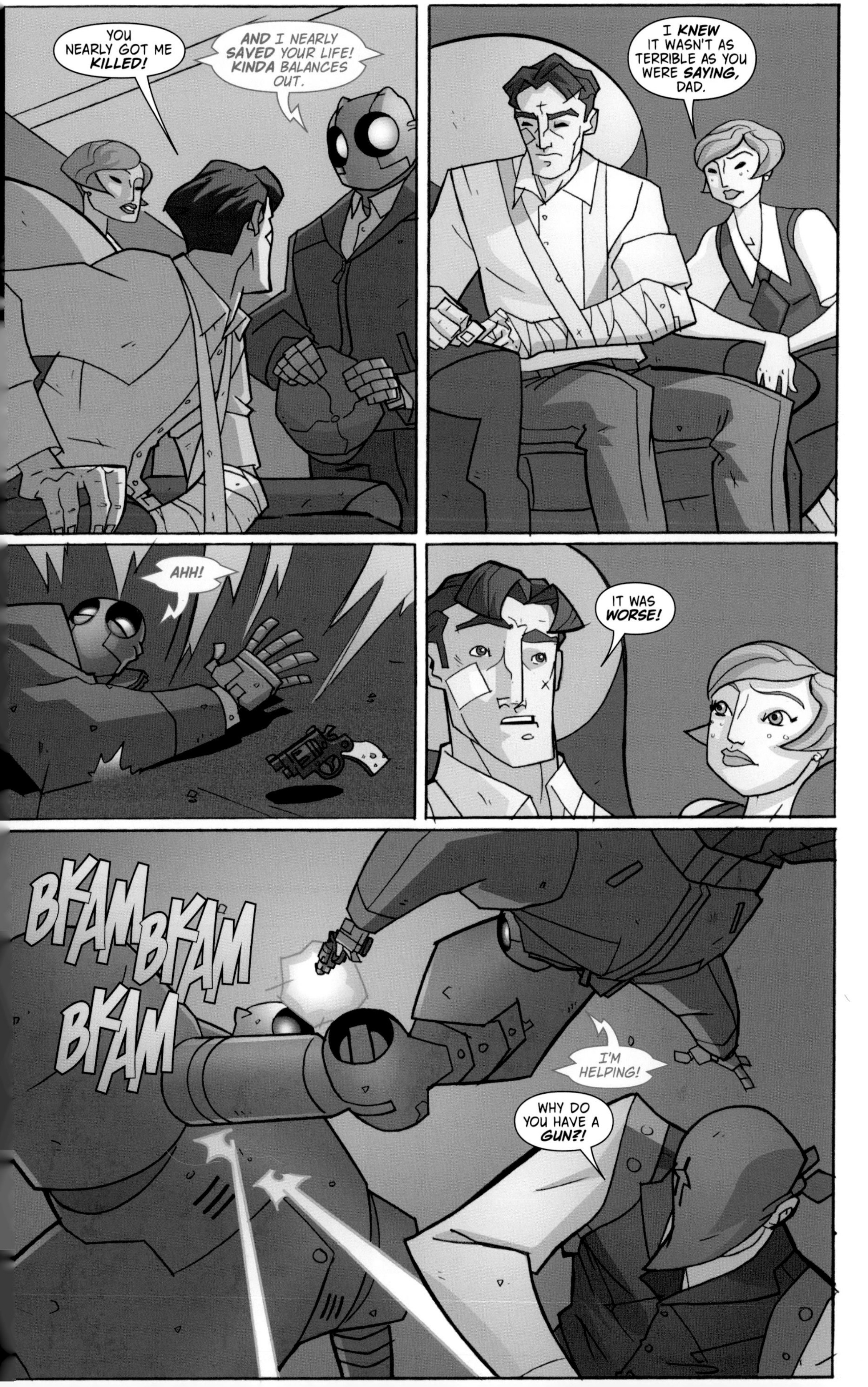
YOU NEARLY GOT ME KILLED!
AND I NEARLY SAVED YOUR LIFE! KINDA BALANCES OUT.
I KNEW IT WASN'T AS TERRIBLE AS YOU WERE SAYING, DAD.
AHH!
IT WAS WORSE!
BKAM BKAM BKAM
I'M HELPING!
WHY DO YOU HAVE A GUN?!

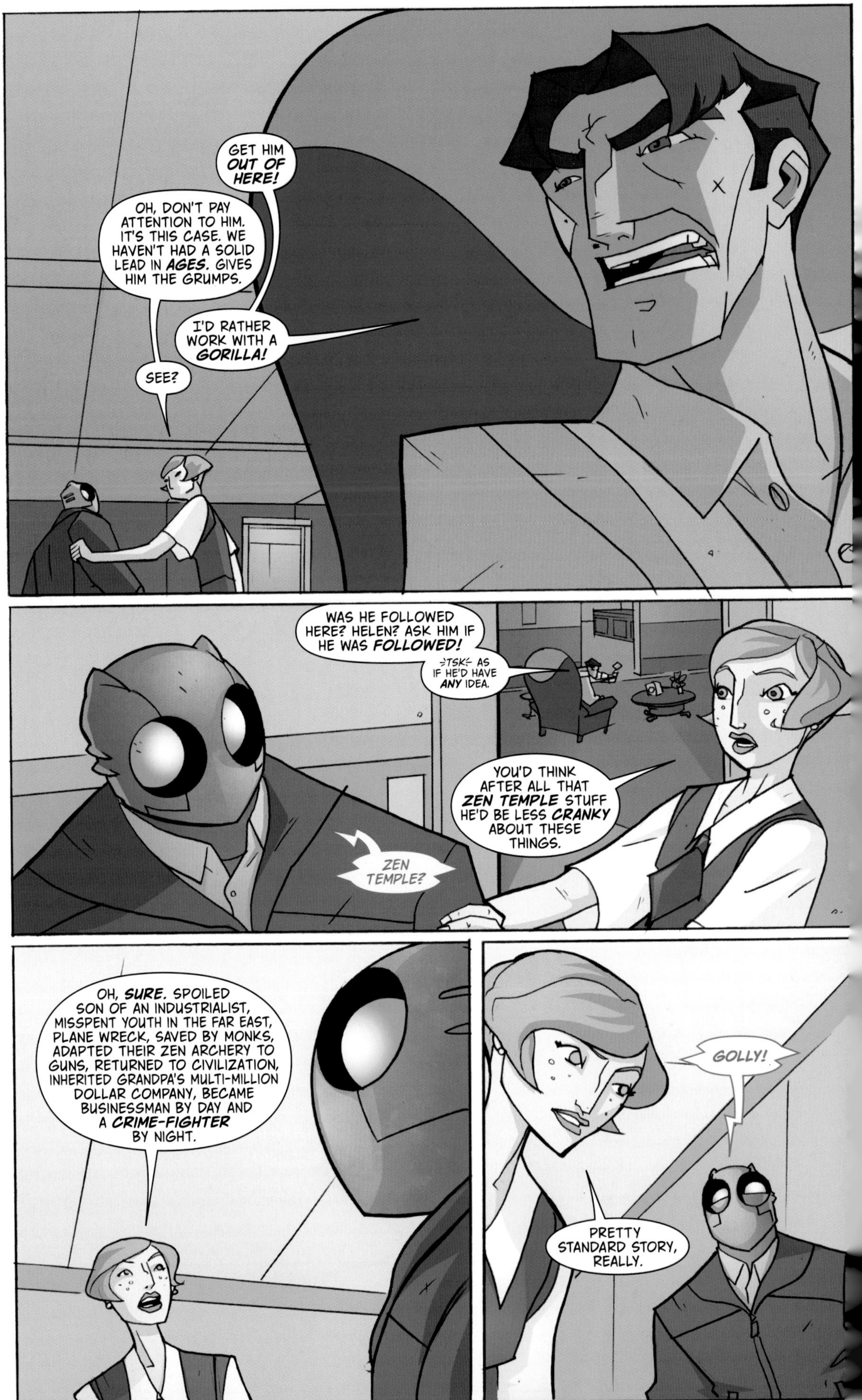
GET HIM OUT OF HERE!
OH, DON'T PAY ATTENTION TO HIM. IT'S THIS CASE. WE HAVEN'T HAD A SOLID LEAD IN AGES. GIVES HIM THE GRUMPS.
I'D RATHER WORK WITH A GORILLA!
SEE?
WAS HE FOLLOWED HERE? HELEN? ASK HIM IF HE WAS FOLLOWED!
TSK AS IF HE'D HAVE ANY IDEA.
YOU'D THINK AFTER ALL THAT ZEN TEMPLE STUFF HE'D BE LESS CRANKY ABOUT THESE THINGS.
ZEN TEMPLE?
OH, SURE. SPOILED SON OF AN INDUSTRIALIST, MISSPENT YOUTH IN THE FAR EAST, PLANE WRECK, SAVED BY MONKS, ADAPTED THEIR ZEN ARCHERY TO GUNS, RETURNED TO CIVILIZATION, INHERITED GRANDPA'S MULTI-MILLION DOLLAR COMPANY, BECAME BUSINESSMAN BY DAY AND A CRIME-FIGHTER BY NIGHT.
GOLLY!
PRETTY STANDARD STORY, REALLY.

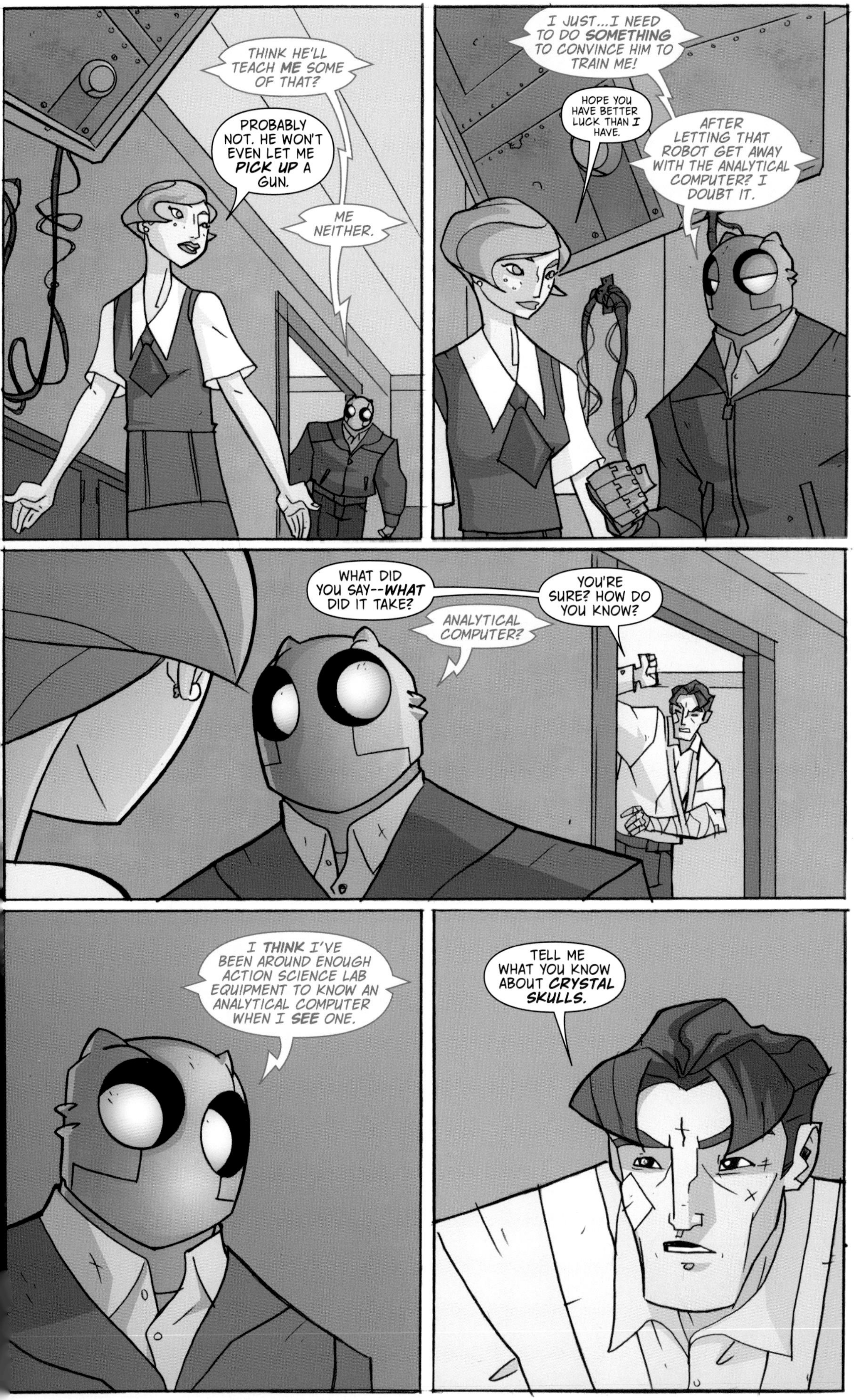
THINK HE'LL TEACH ME SOME OF THAT?
PROBABLY NOT. HE WON'T EVEN LET ME PICK UP A GUN.
ME NEITHER.
I JUST...I NEED TO DO SOMETHING TO CONVINCE HIM TO TRAIN ME!
HOPE YOU HAVE BETTER LUCK THAN I HAVE.
AFTER LETTING THAT ROBOT GET AWAY WITH THE ANALYTICAL COMPUTER? I DOUBT IT.
WHAT DID YOU SAY--WHAT DID IT TAKE?
ANALYTICAL COMPUTER?
YOU'RE SURE? HOW DO YOU KNOW?
I THINK I'VE BEEN AROUND ENOUGH ACTION SCIENCE LAB EQUIPMENT TO KNOW AN ANALYTICAL COMPUTER WHEN I SEE ONE.
TELL ME WHAT YOU KNOW ABOUT CRYSTAL SKULLS.

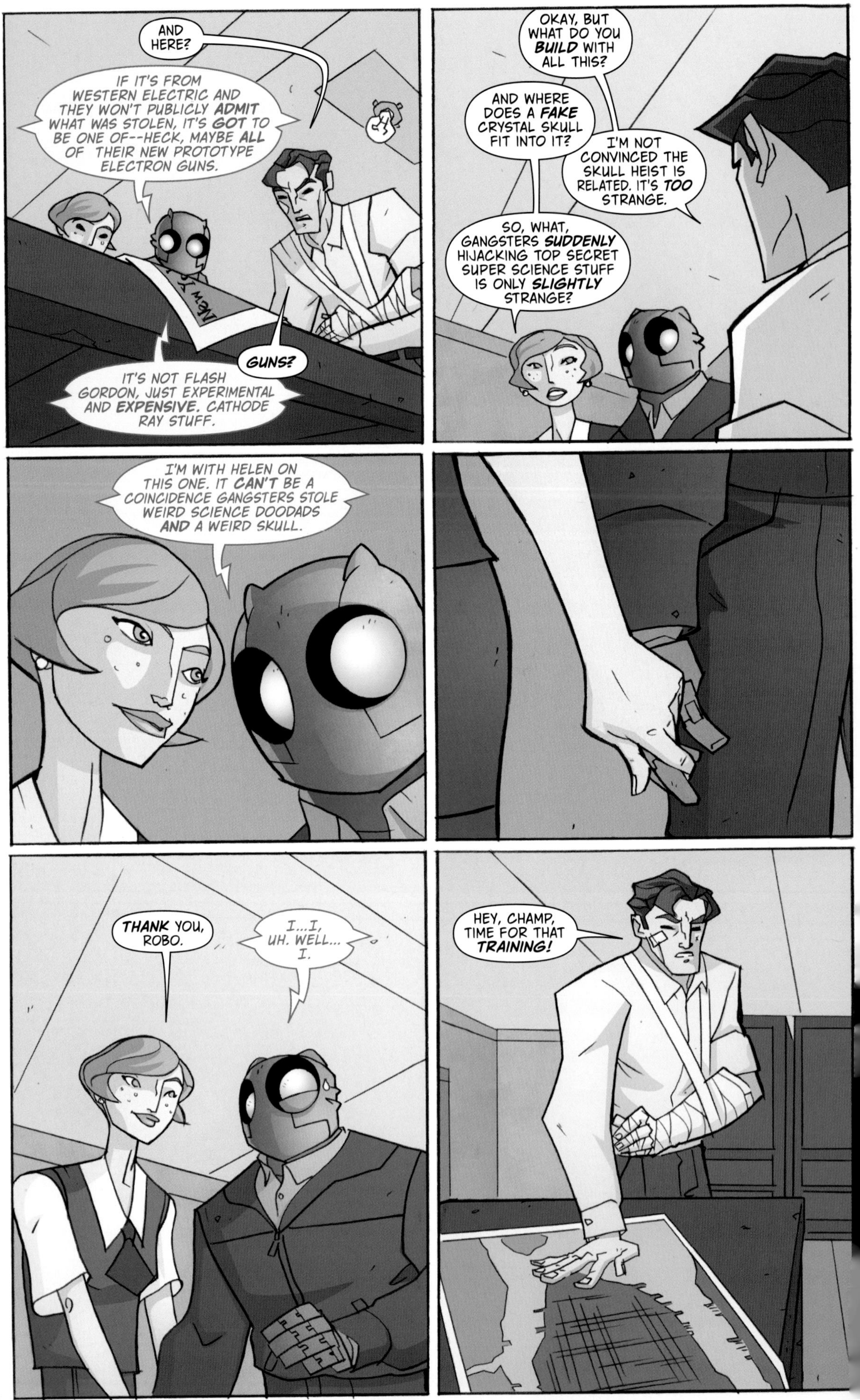
AND HERE?
IF IT'S FROM WESTERN ELECTRIC AND THEY WON'T PUBLICLY ADMIT WHAT WAS STOLEN, IT'S GOT TO BE ONE OF--HECK, MAYBE ALL OF THEIR NEW PROTOTYPE ELECTRON GUNS.
GUNS?
IT'S NOT FLASH GORDON, JUST EXPERIMENTAL AND EXPENSIVE. CATHODE RAY STUFF.
OKAY, BUT WHAT DO YOU BUILD WITH ALL THIS?
AND WHERE DOES A FAKE CRYSTAL SKULL FIT INTO IT?
I'M NOT CONVINCED THE SKULL HEIST IS RELATED. IT'S TOO STRANGE.
SO, WHAT, GANGSTERS SUDDENLY HIJACKING TOP SECRET SUPER SCIENCE STUFF IS ONLY SLIGHTLY STRANGE?
I'M WITH HELEN ON THIS ONE. IT CAN'T BE A COINCIDENCE GANGSTERS STOLE WEIRD SCIENCE DOODADS AND A WEIRD SKULL.
THANK YOU, ROBO.
I...I, UH. WELL... I.
HEY, CHAMP, TIME FOR THAT TRAINING!

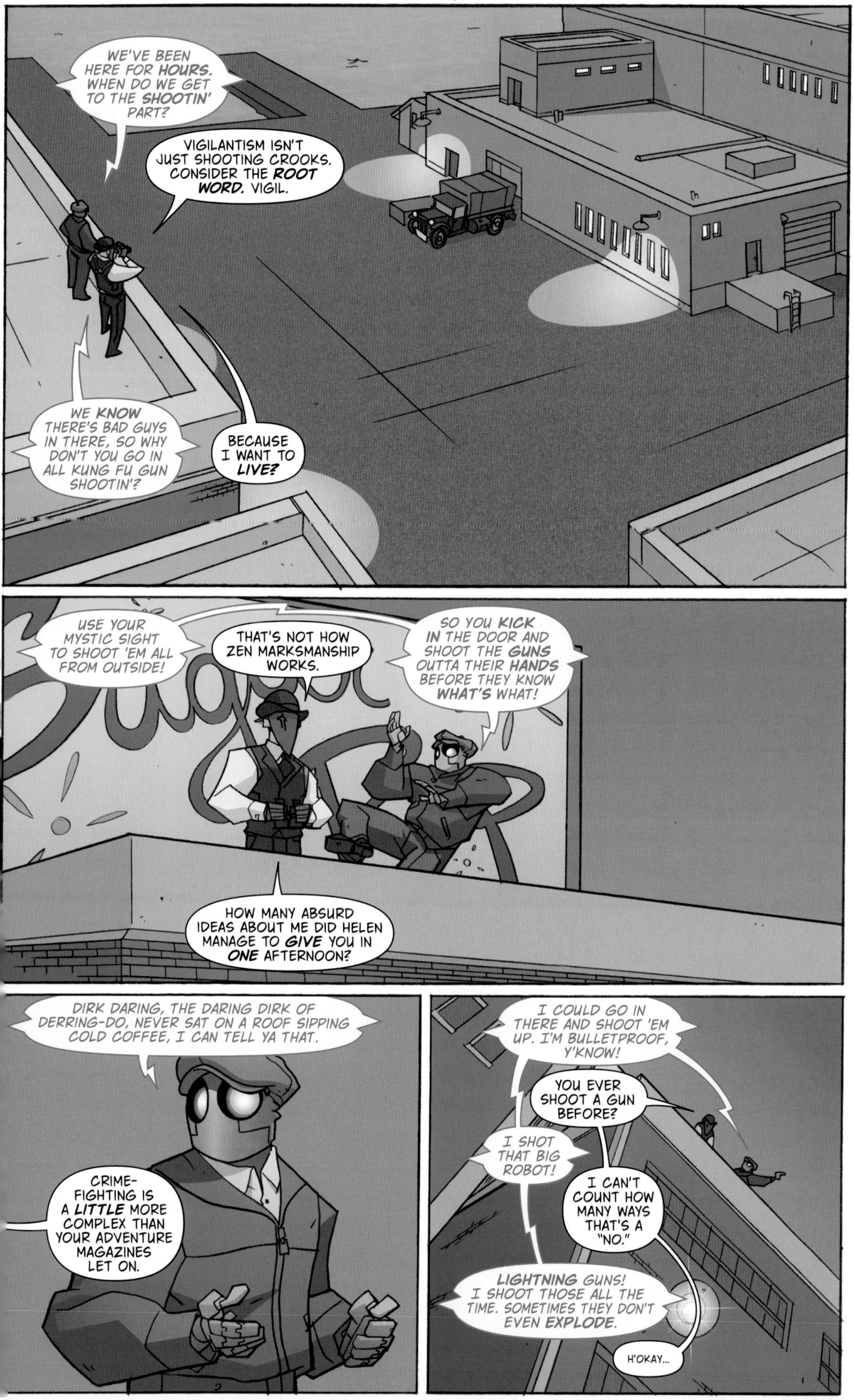
WE'VE BEEN HERE FOR HOURS. WHEN DO WE GET TO THE SHOOTIN' PART?
VIGILANTISM ISN'T JUST SHOOTING CROOKS. CONSIDER THE ROOT WORD. VIGIL.
WE KNOW THERE'S BAD GUYS IN THERE, SO WHY DON'T YOU GO IN ALL KUNG FU GUN SHOOTIN'?
BECAUSE I WANT TO LIVE?
USE YOUR MYSTIC SIGHT TO SHOOT 'EM ALL FROM OUTSIDE!
THAT'S NOT HOW ZEN MARKSMANSHIP WORKS.
SO YOU KICK IN THE DOOR AND SHOOT THE GUNS OUTTA THEIR HANDS BEFORE THEY KNOW WHAT'S WHAT!
HOW MANY ABSURD IDEAS ABOUT ME DID HELEN MANAGE TO GIVE YOU IN ONE AFTERNOON?
DIRK DARING, THE DARING DIRK OF DERRING-DO, NEVER SAT ON A ROOF SIPPING COLD COFFEE, I CAN TELL YA THAT.
CRIME-FIGHTING IS A LITTLE MORE COMPLEX THAN YOUR ADVENTURE MAGAZINES LET ON.
I COULD GO IN THERE AND SHOOT 'EM UP. I'M BULLETPROOF, Y'KNOW!
YOU EVER SHOOT A GUN BEFORE?
I SHOT THAT BIG ROBOT!
I CAN'T COUNT HOW MANY WAYS THAT'S A "NO."
LIGHTNING GUNS! I SHOOT THOSE ALL THE TIME. SOMETIMES THEY DON'T EVEN EXPLODE.
H'OKAY...

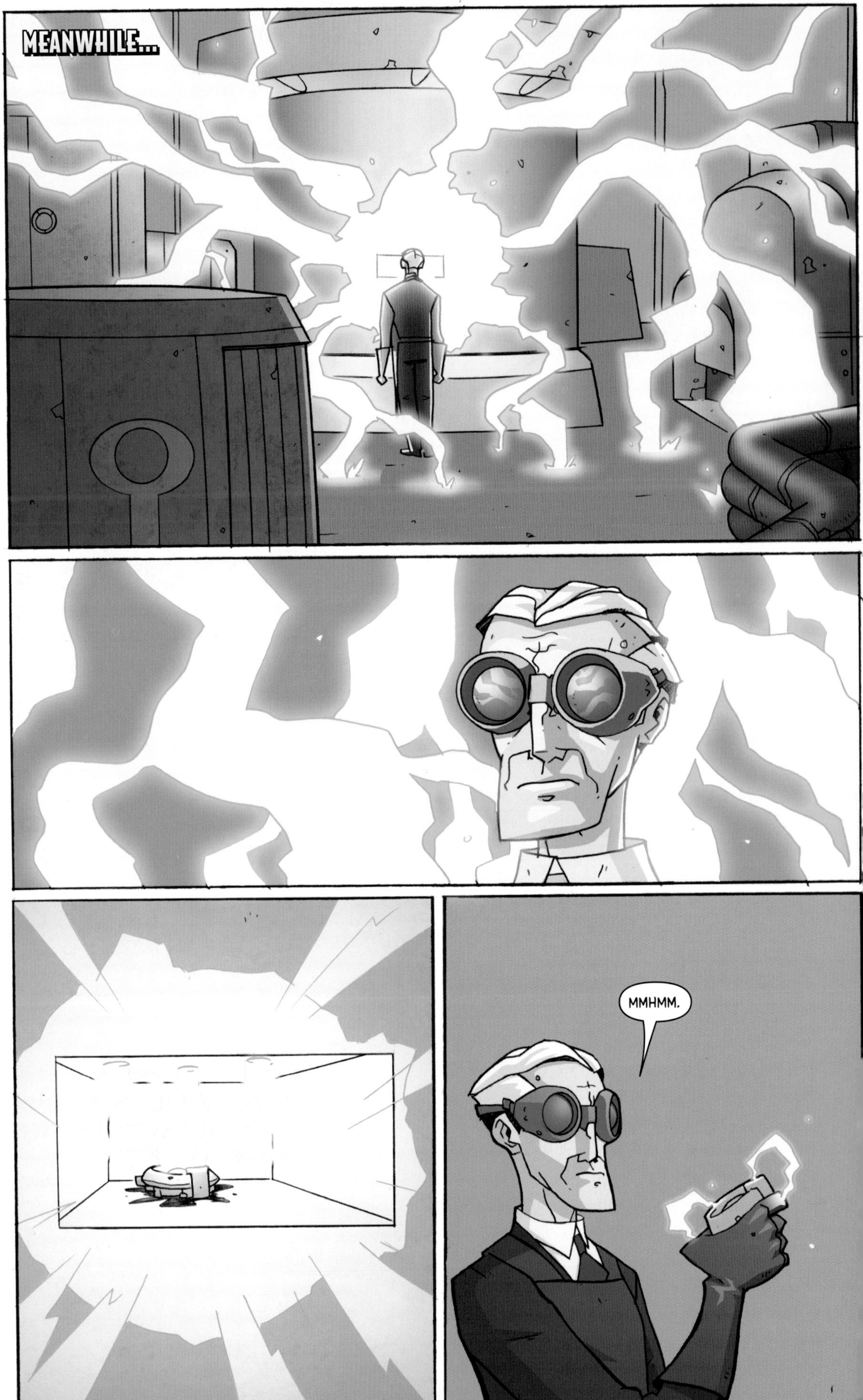
MEANWHILE...
MMHMM.

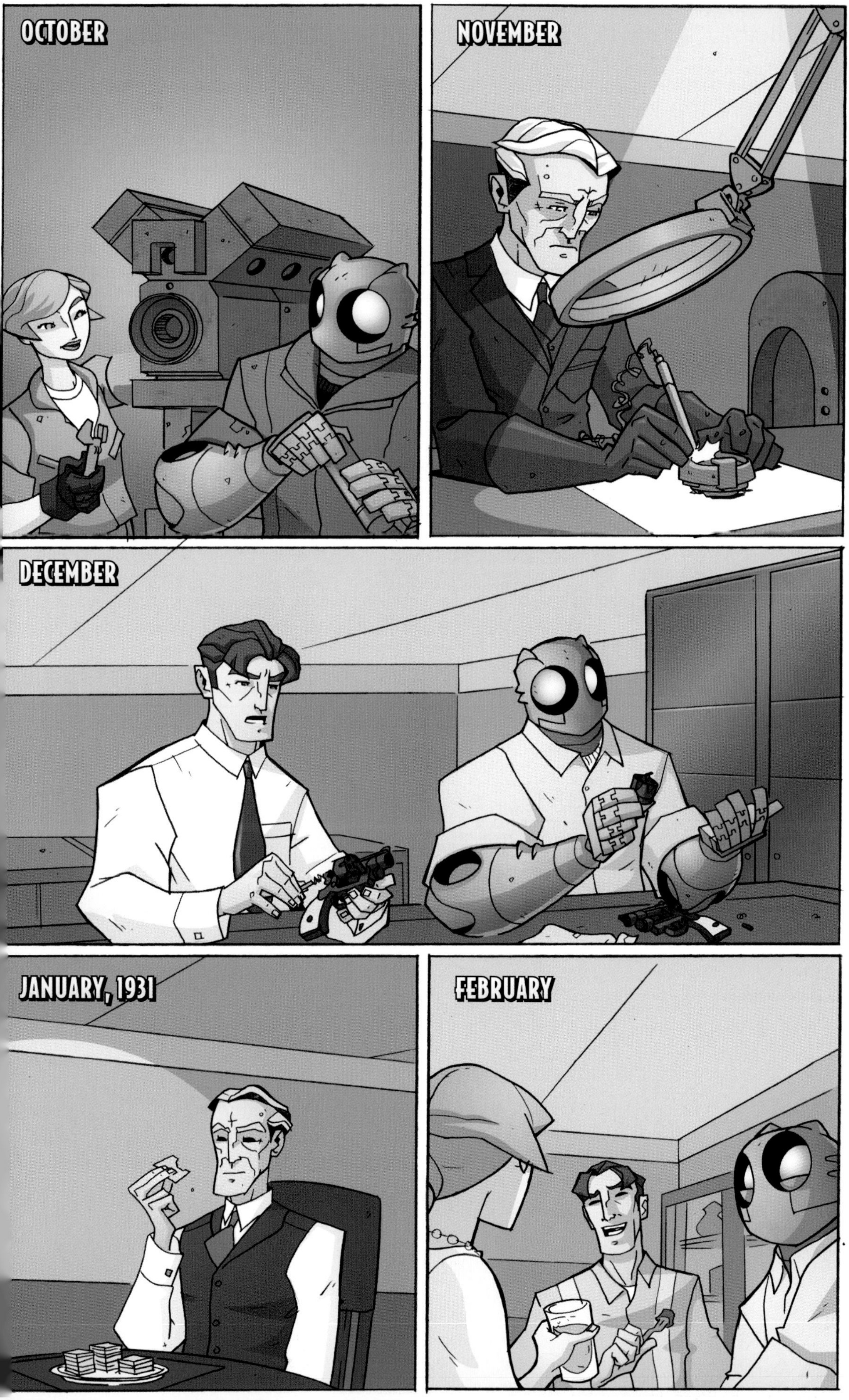
OCTOBER
NOVEMBER
DECEMBER
JANUARY, 1931
FEBRUARY

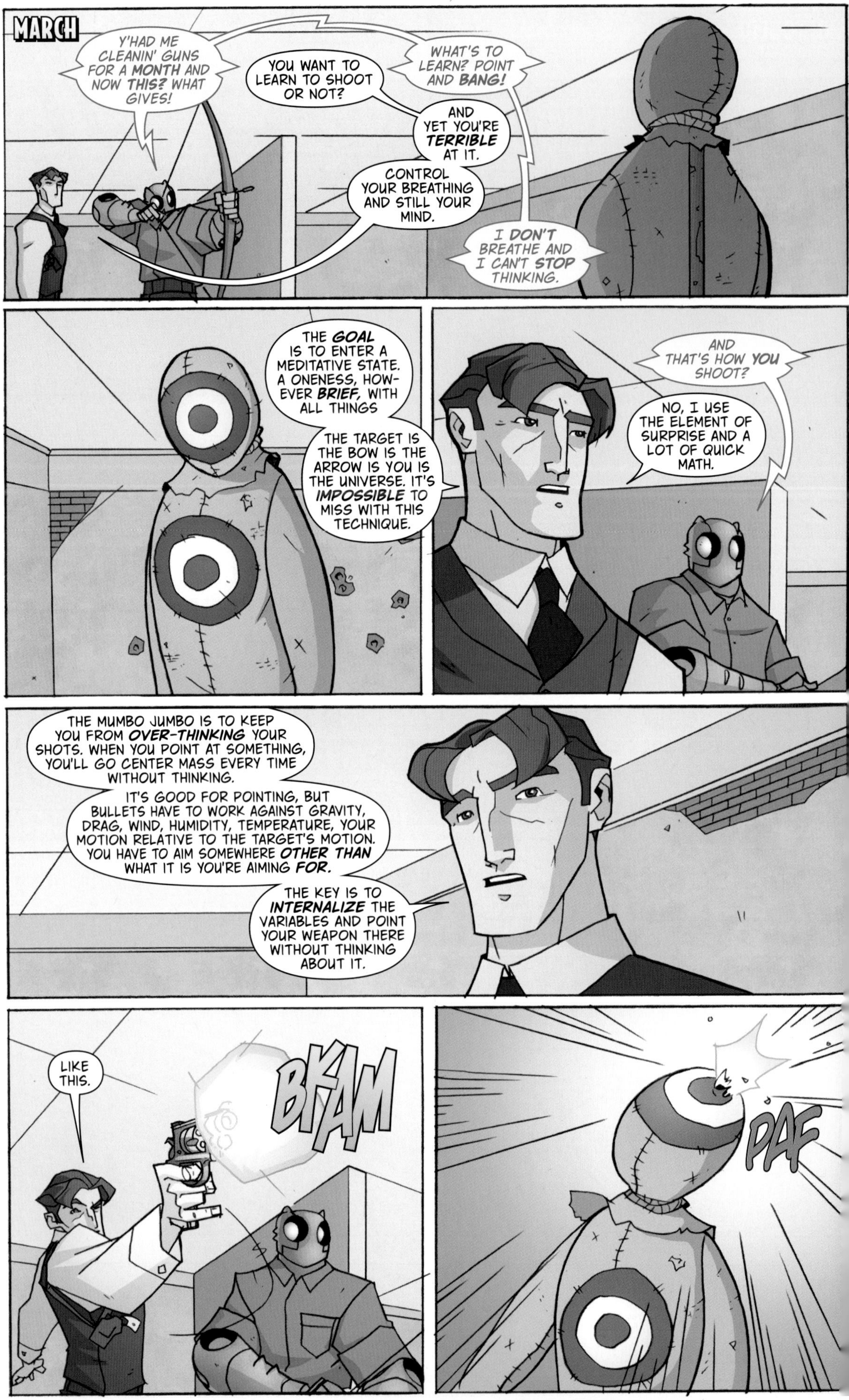
MARCH
Y'HAD ME CLEANIN' GUNS FOR A MONTH AND NOW THIS? WHAT GIVES!
YOU WANT TO LEARN TO SHOOT OR NOT?
WHAT'S TO LEARN? POINT AND BANG!
AND YET YOU'RE TERRIBLE AT IT.
CONTROL YOUR BREATHING AND STILL YOUR MIND.
I DON'T BREATHE AND I CAN'T STOP THINKING.
THE GOAL IS TO ENTER A MEDITATIVE STATE. A ONENESS, HOWEVER BRIEF, WITH ALL THINGS
THE TARGET IS THE BOW IS THE ARROW IS YOU IS THE UNIVERSE. IT'S IMPOSSIBLE TO MISS WITH THIS TECHNIQUE.
AND THAT'S HOW YOU SHOOT?
NO, I USE THE ELEMENT OF SURPRISE AND A LOT OF QUICK MATH.
THE MUMBO JUMBO IS TO KEEP YOU FROM OVER-THINKING YOUR SHOTS. WHEN YOU POINT AT SOMETHING, YOU'LL GO CENTER MASS EVERY TIME WITHOUT THINKING.
IT'S GOOD FOR POINTING, BUT BULLETS HAVE TO WORK AGAINST GRAVITY, DRAG, WIND, HUMIDITY, TEMPERATURE, YOUR MOTION RELATIVE TO THE TARGET'S MOTION. YOU HAVE TO AIM SOMEWHERE OTHER THAN WHAT IT IS YOU'RE AIMING FOR.
THE KEY IS TO INTERNALIZE THE VARIABLES AND POINT YOUR WEAPON THERE WITHOUT THINKING ABOUT IT.
LIKE THIS.
BKAM
PAF

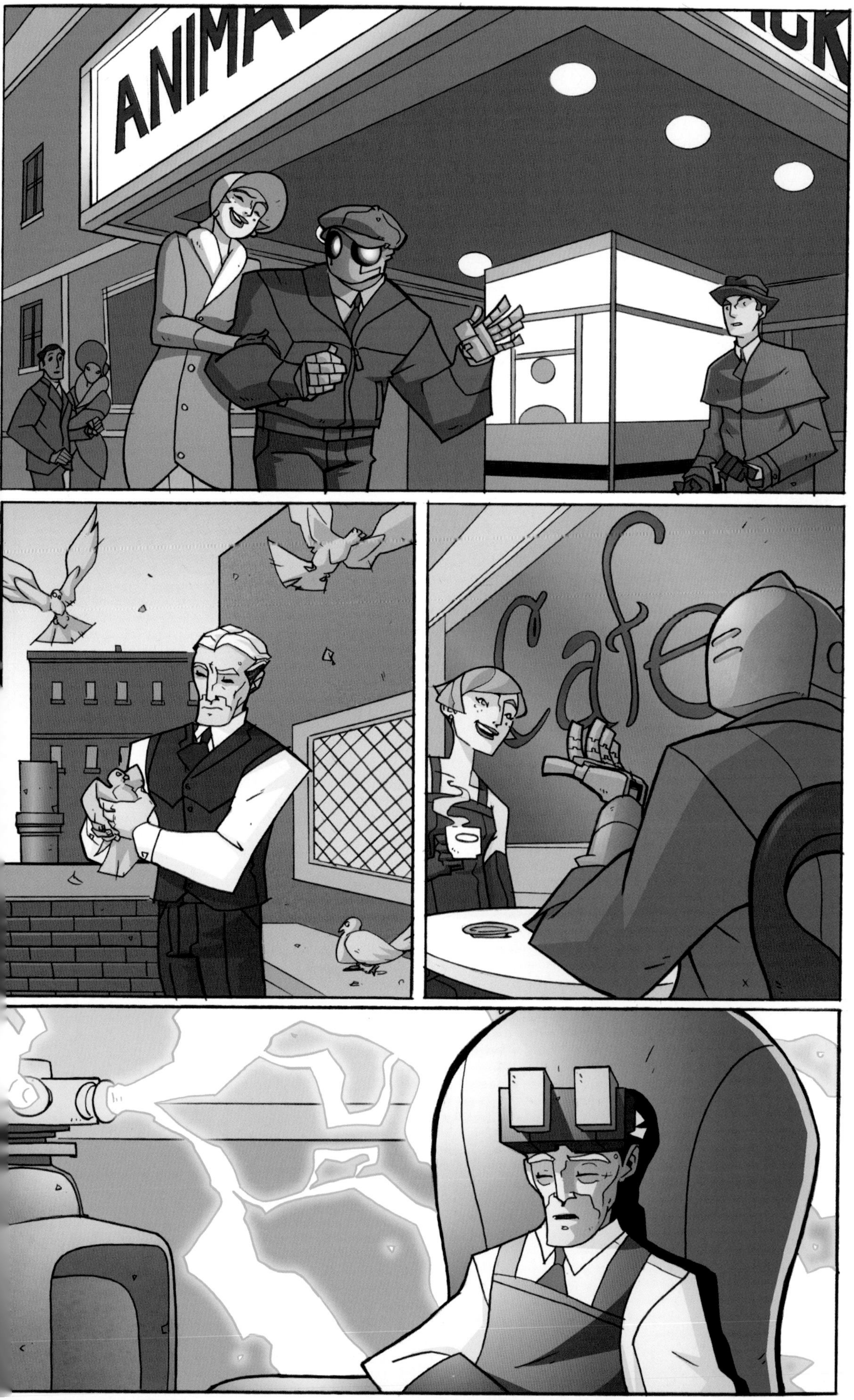
ANIMA
Cafe

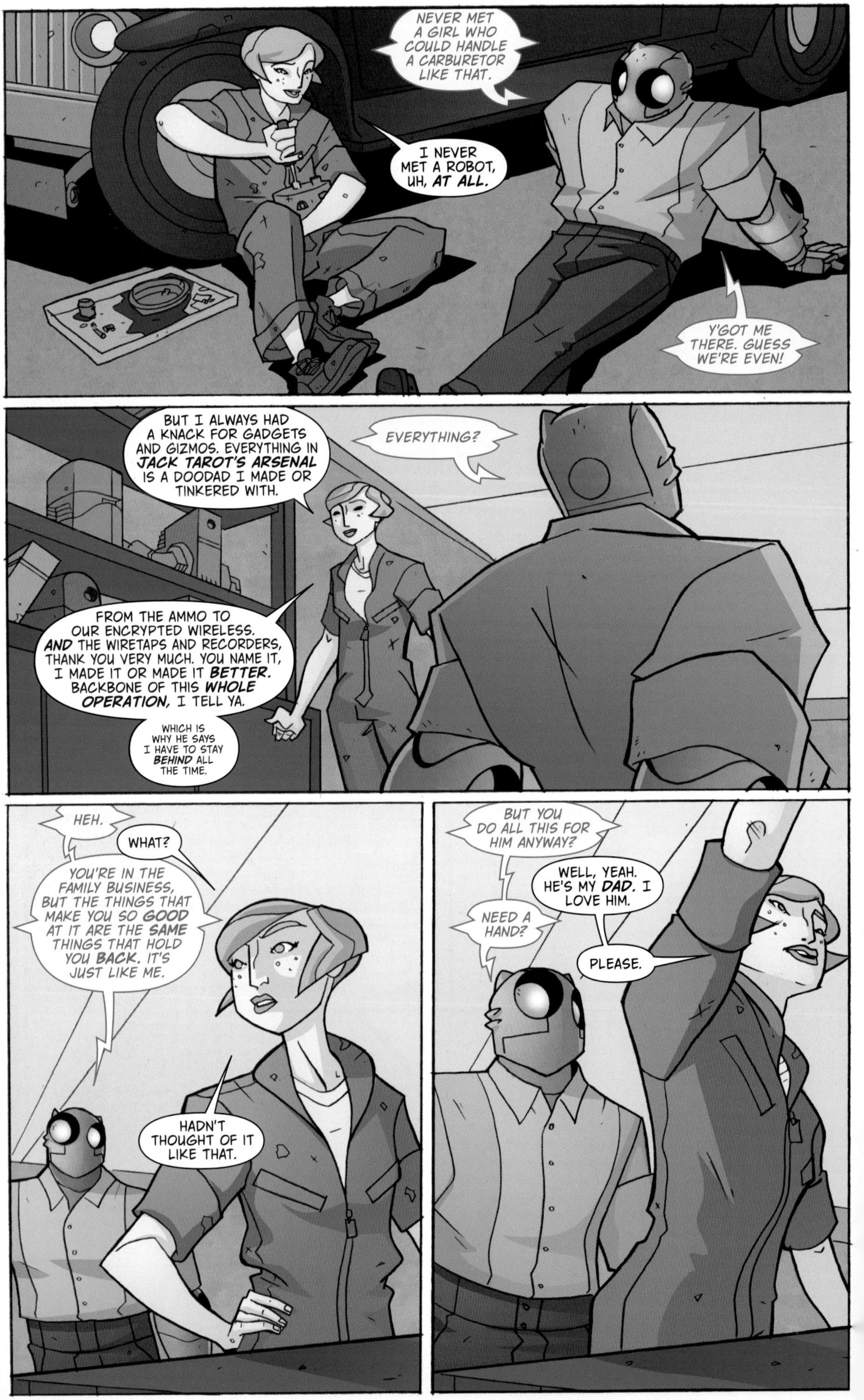
NEVER MET A GIRL WHO COULD HANDLE A CARBURETOR LIKE THAT.
I NEVER MET A ROBOT, UH, AT ALL.
Y'GOT ME THERE. GUESS WE'RE EVEN!
BUT I ALWAYS HAD A KNACK FOR GADGETS AND GIZMOS. EVERYTHING IN JACK TAROT'S ARSENAL IS A DOODAD I MADE OR TINKERED WITH.
EVERYTHING?
FROM THE AMMO TO OUR ENCRYPTED WIRELESS. AND THE WIRETAPS AND RECORDERS, THANK YOU VERY MUCH. YOU NAME IT, I MADE IT OR MADE IT BETTER. BACKBONE OF THIS WHOLE OPERATION, I TELL YA.
WHICH IS WHY HE SAYS I HAVE TO STAY BEHIND ALL THE TIME.
HEH.
WHAT?
YOU'RE IN THE FAMILY BUSINESS, BUT THE THINGS THAT MAKE YOU SO GOOD AT IT ARE THE SAME THINGS THAT HOLD YOU BACK. IT'S JUST LIKE ME.
HADN'T THOUGHT OF IT LIKE THAT.
BUT YOU DO ALL THIS FOR HIM ANYWAY?
WELL, YEAH. HE'S MY DAD. I LOVE HIM.
NEED A HAND?
PLEASE.

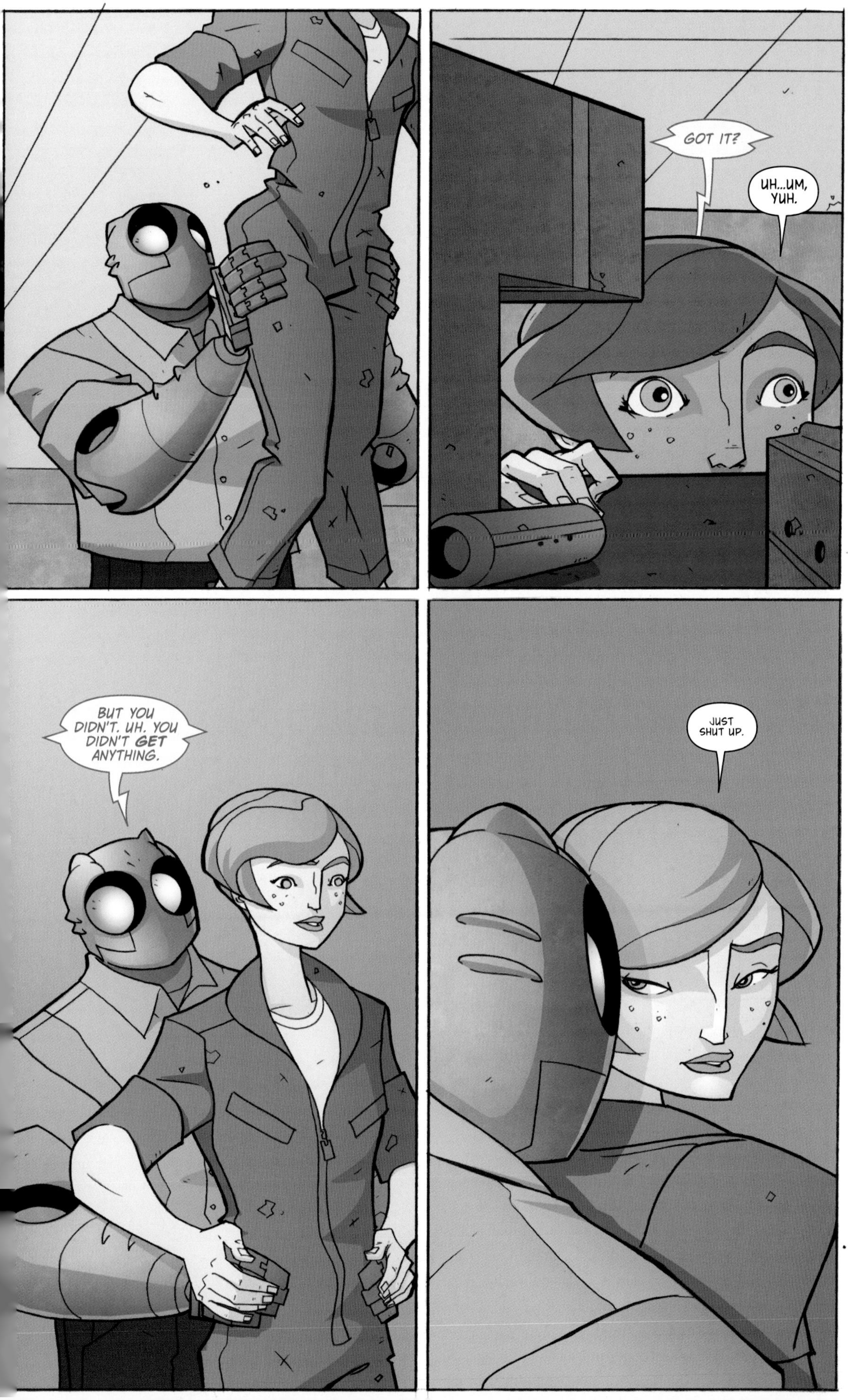
GOT IT?
UH...UM, YUH.
BUT YOU DIDN'T. UH. YOU DIDN'T **GET** ANYTHING.
JUST SHUT UP.

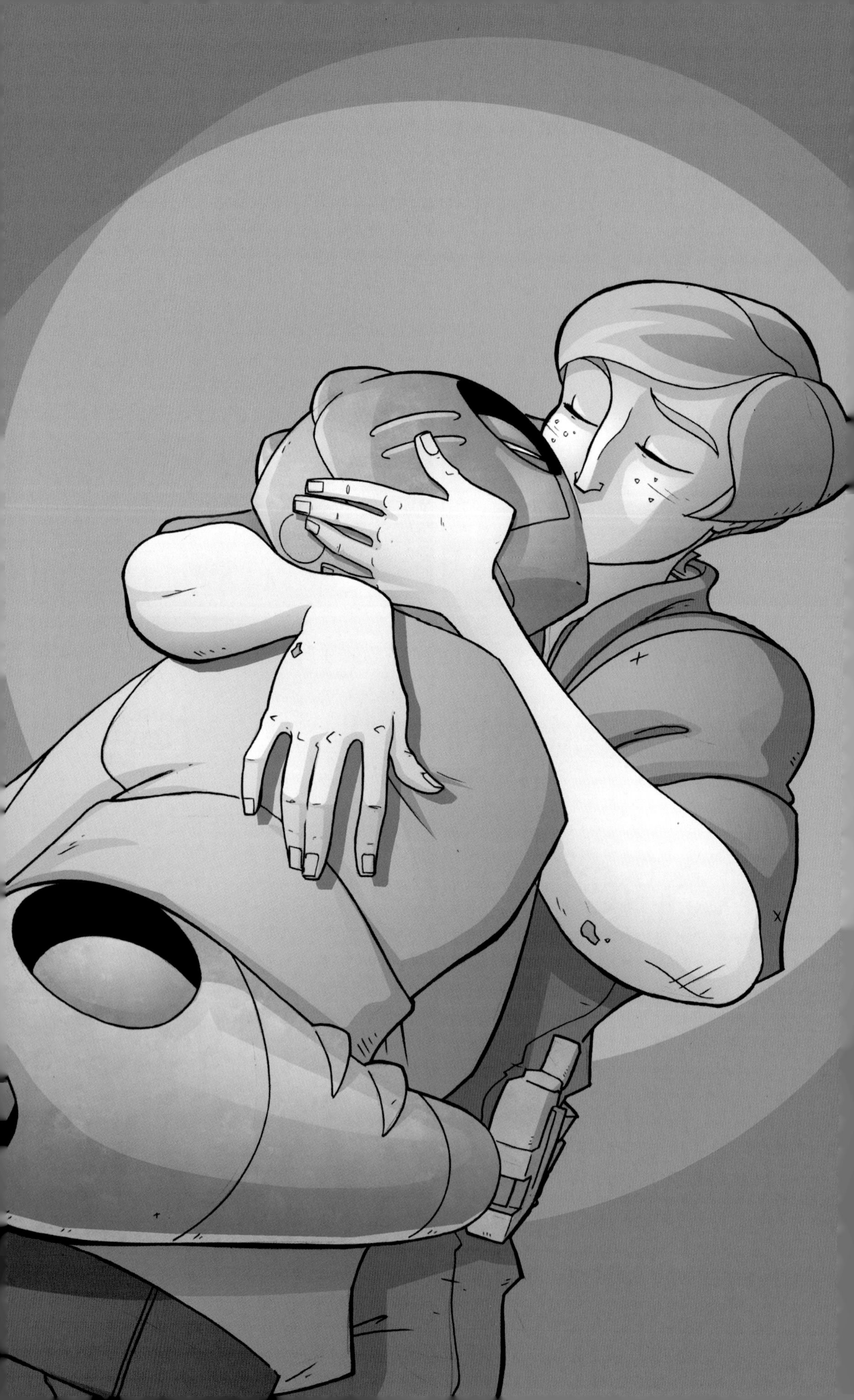

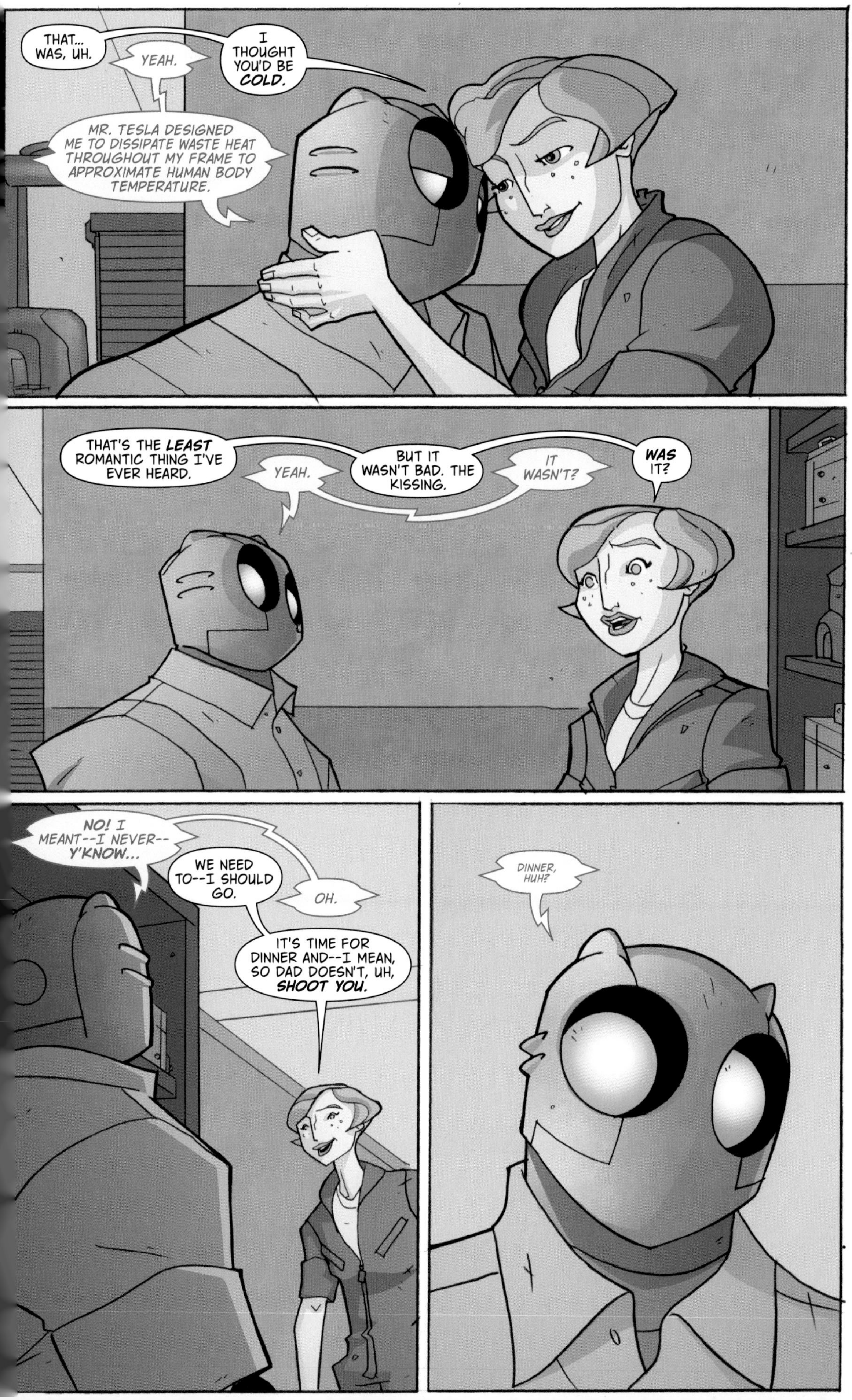
THAT... WAS, UH.
YEAH.
I THOUGHT YOU'D BE COLD.
MR. TESLA DESIGNED ME TO DISSIPATE WASTE HEAT THROUGHOUT MY FRAME TO APPROXIMATE HUMAN BODY TEMPERATURE.
THAT'S THE LEAST ROMANTIC THING I'VE EVER HEARD.
YEAH.
BUT IT WASN'T BAD. THE KISSING.
IT WASN'T?
WAS IT?
NO! I MEANT--I NEVER-- Y'KNOW...
WE NEED TO--I SHOULD GO.
OH.
IT'S TIME FOR DINNER AND--I MEAN, SO DAD DOESN'T, UH, SHOOT YOU.
DINNER, HUH?

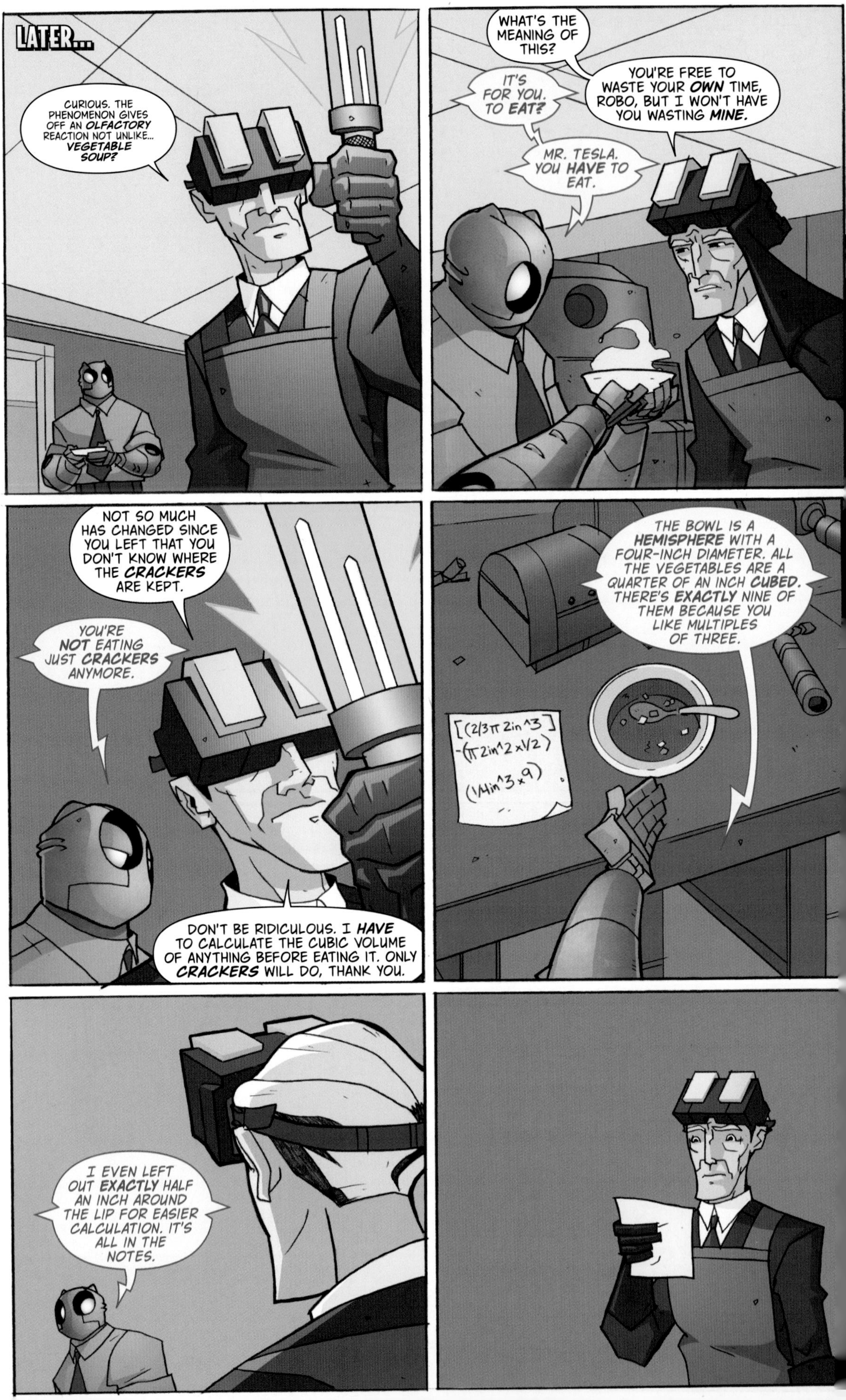
LATER...
CURIOUS. THE PHENOMENON GIVES OFF AN OLFACTORY REACTION NOT UNLIKE... VEGETABLE SOUP?
WHAT'S THE MEANING OF THIS?
IT'S FOR YOU. TO EAT?
YOU'RE FREE TO WASTE YOUR OWN TIME, ROBO, BUT I WON'T HAVE YOU WASTING MINE.
MR. TESLA. YOU HAVE TO EAT.
NOT SO MUCH HAS CHANGED SINCE YOU LEFT THAT YOU DON'T KNOW WHERE THE CRACKERS ARE KEPT.
YOU'RE NOT EATING JUST CRACKERS ANYMORE.
DON'T BE RIDICULOUS. I HAVE TO CALCULATE THE CUBIC VOLUME OF ANYTHING BEFORE EATING IT. ONLY CRACKERS WILL DO, THANK YOU.
THE BOWL IS A HEMISPHERE WITH A FOUR-INCH DIAMETER. ALL THE VEGETABLES ARE A QUARTER OF AN INCH CUBED. THERE'S EXACTLY NINE OF THEM BECAUSE YOU LIKE MULTIPLES OF THREE.
[(2/3π 2in^3]
-(π 2in^2 x1/2)
(1/4in^3 x9)
I EVEN LEFT OUT EXACTLY HALF AN INCH AROUND THE LIP FOR EASIER CALCULATION. IT'S ALL IN THE NOTES.

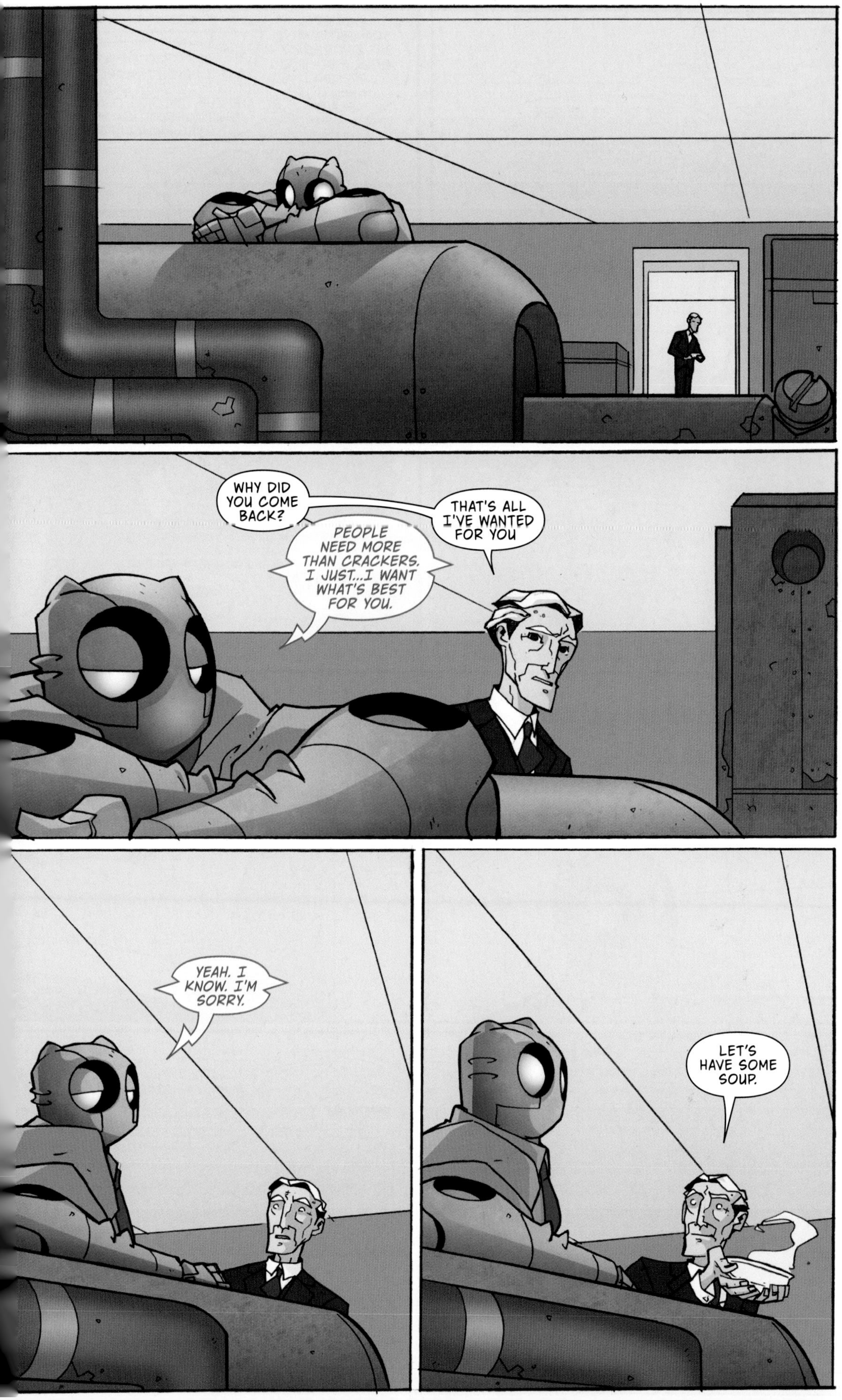
WHY DID YOU COME BACK?
THAT'S ALL I'VE WANTED FOR YOU
PEOPLE NEED MORE THAN CRACKERS. I JUST...I WANT WHAT'S BEST FOR YOU.
YEAH. I KNOW. I'M SORRY.
LET'S HAVE SOME SOUP.

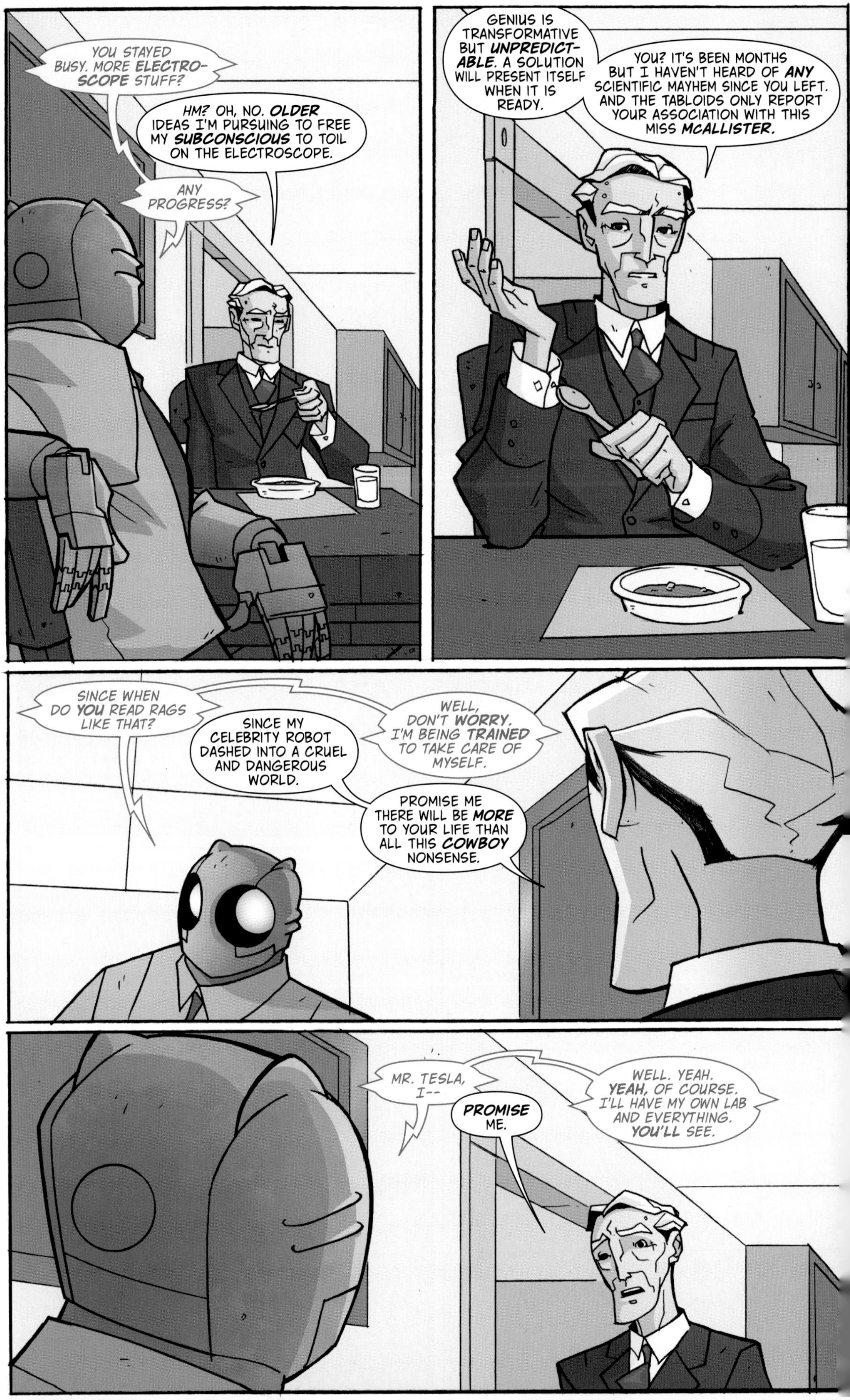
YOU STAYED BUSY. MORE ELECTRO-SCOPE STUFF?
HM? OH, NO. OLDER IDEAS I'M PURSUING TO FREE MY SUBCONSCIOUS TO TOIL ON THE ELECTROSCOPE.
ANY PROGRESS?
GENIUS IS TRANSFORMATIVE BUT UNPREDICT-ABLE. A SOLUTION WILL PRESENT ITSELF WHEN IT IS READY.
YOU? IT'S BEEN MONTHS BUT I HAVEN'T HEARD OF ANY SCIENTIFIC MAYHEM SINCE YOU LEFT. AND THE TABLOIDS ONLY REPORT YOUR ASSOCIATION WITH THIS MISS MCALLISTER.
SINCE WHEN DO YOU READ RAGS LIKE THAT?
SINCE MY CELEBRITY ROBOT DASHED INTO A CRUEL AND DANGEROUS WORLD.
WELL, DON'T WORRY. I'M BEING TRAINED TO TAKE CARE OF MYSELF.
PROMISE ME THERE WILL BE MORE TO YOUR LIFE THAN ALL THIS COWBOY NONSENSE.
MR. TESLA, I--
PROMISE ME.
WELL. YEAH. YEAH, OF COURSE. I'LL HAVE MY OWN LAB AND EVERYTHING. YOU'LL SEE.

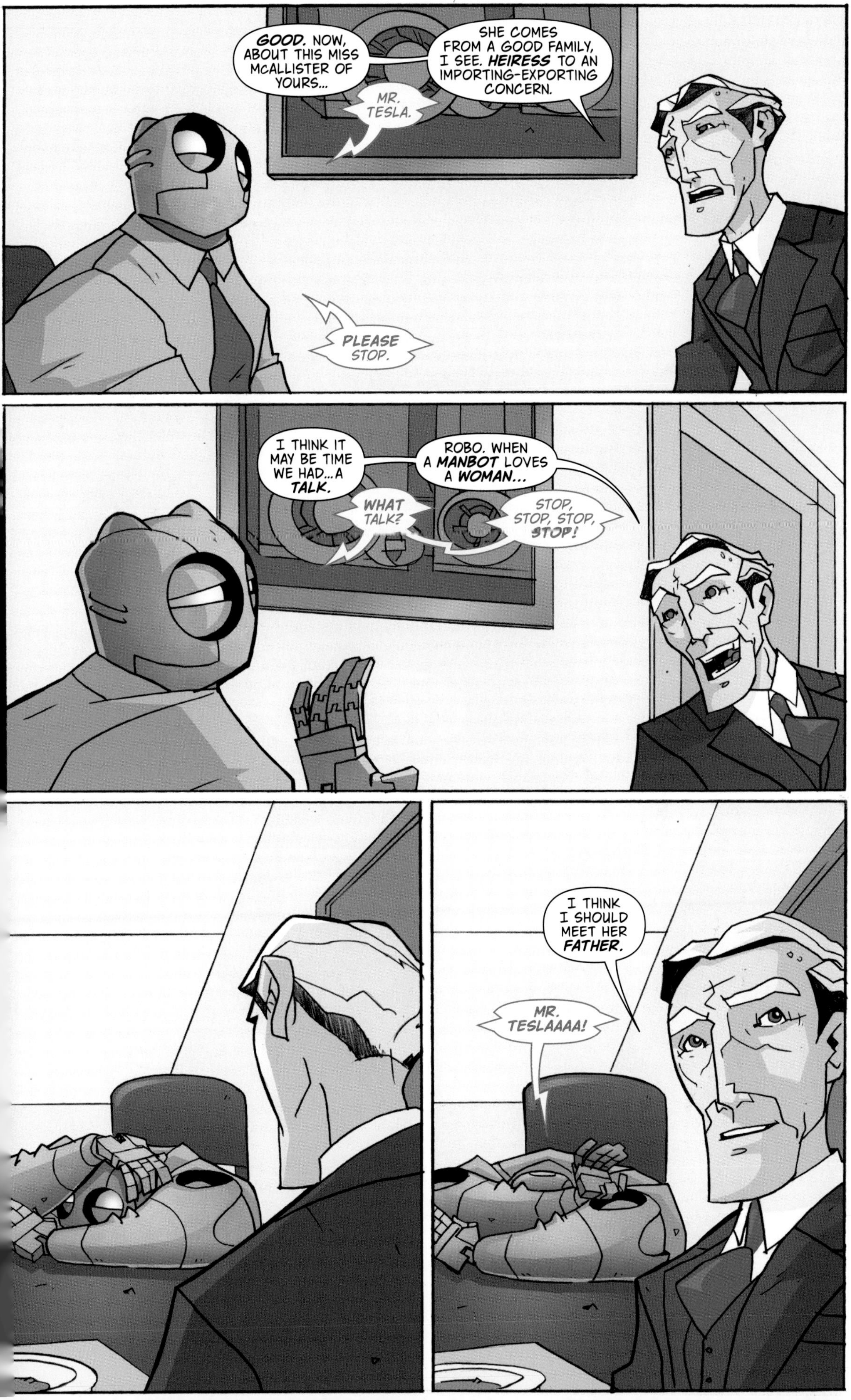
GOOD. NOW, ABOUT THIS MISS McALLISTER OF YOURS...
SHE COMES FROM A GOOD FAMILY, I SEE. HEIRESS TO AN IMPORTING-EXPORTING CONCERN.
MR. TESLA.
PLEASE STOP.
I THINK IT MAY BE TIME WE HAD... A TALK.
ROBO. WHEN A MANBOT LOVES A WOMAN...
WHAT TALK?
STOP, STOP, STOP, STOP!
I THINK I SHOULD MEET HER FATHER.
MR. TESLAAAA!

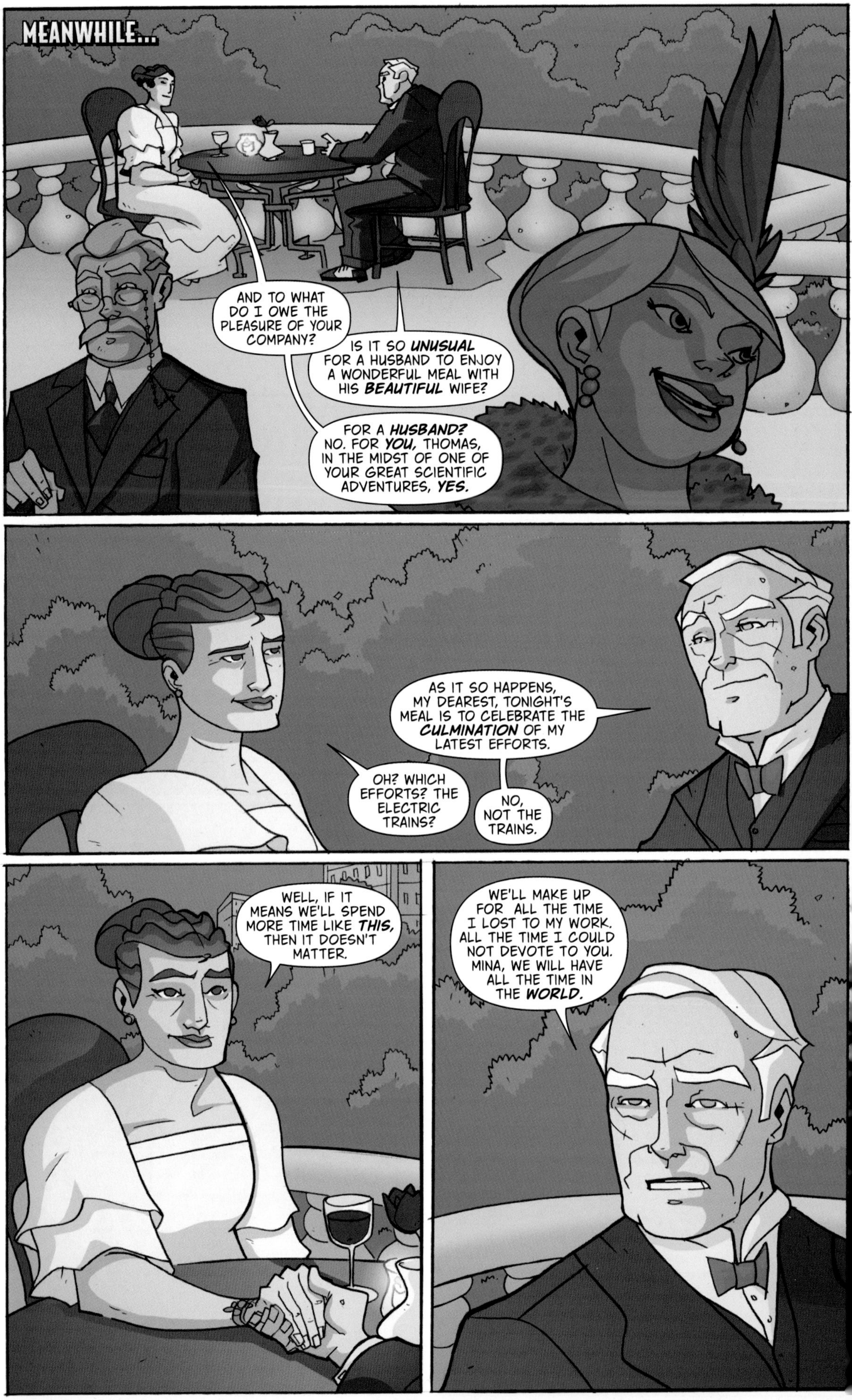
MEANWHILE...
AND TO WHAT DO I OWE THE PLEASURE OF YOUR COMPANY?
IS IT SO UNUSUAL FOR A HUSBAND TO ENJOY A WONDERFUL MEAL WITH HIS BEAUTIFUL WIFE?
FOR A HUSBAND? NO. FOR YOU, THOMAS, IN THE MIDST OF ONE OF YOUR GREAT SCIENTIFIC ADVENTURES, YES.
AS IT SO HAPPENS, MY DEAREST, TONIGHT'S MEAL IS TO CELEBRATE THE CULMINATION OF MY LATEST EFFORTS.
OH? WHICH EFFORTS? THE ELECTRIC TRAINS?
NO, NOT THE TRAINS.
WELL, IF IT MEANS WE'LL SPEND MORE TIME LIKE THIS, THEN IT DOESN'T MATTER.
WE'LL MAKE UP FOR ALL THE TIME I LOST TO MY WORK. ALL THE TIME I COULD NOT DEVOTE TO YOU. MINA, WE WILL HAVE ALL THE TIME IN THE WORLD.

THE WIZARD OF MENLO PARK

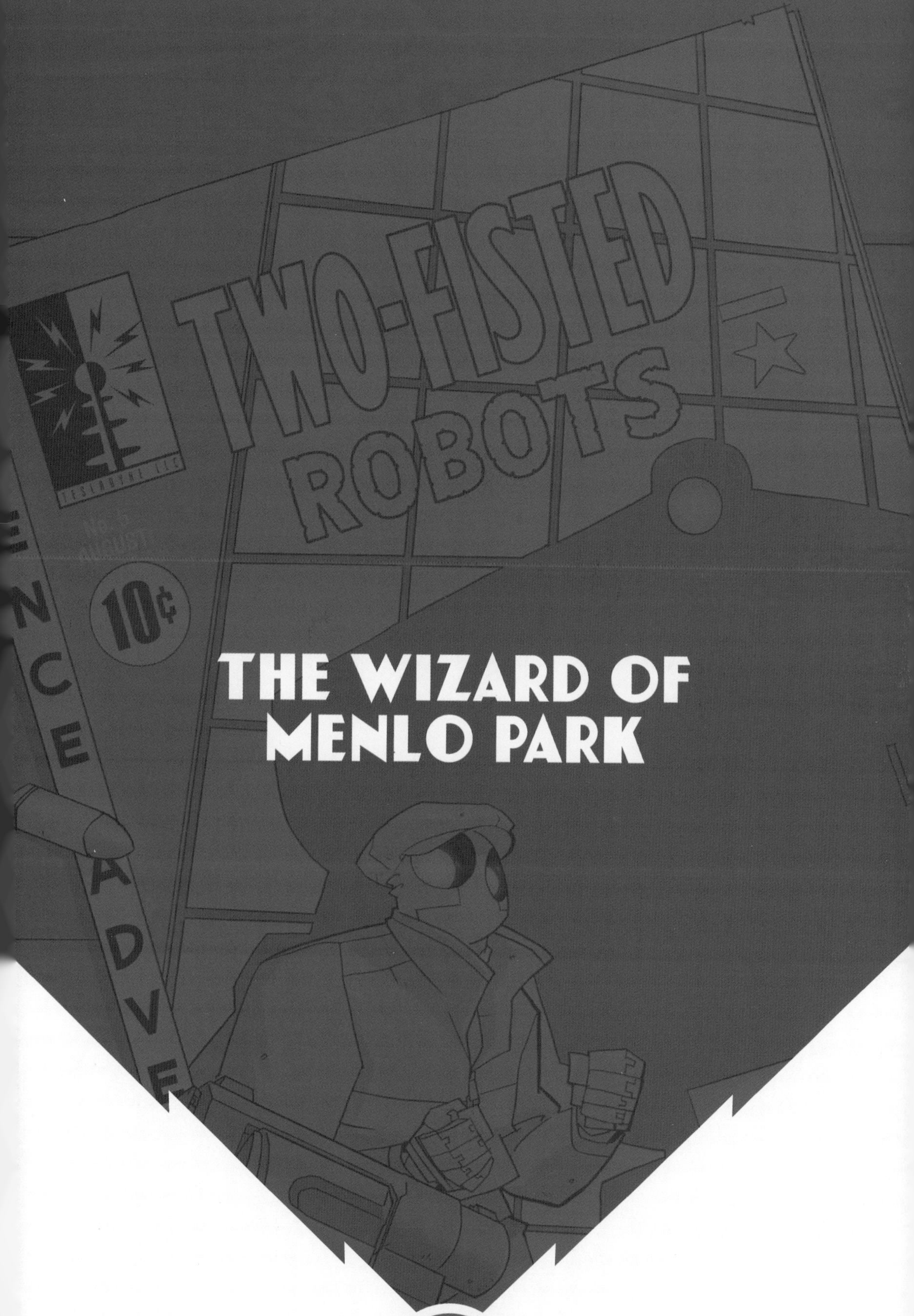

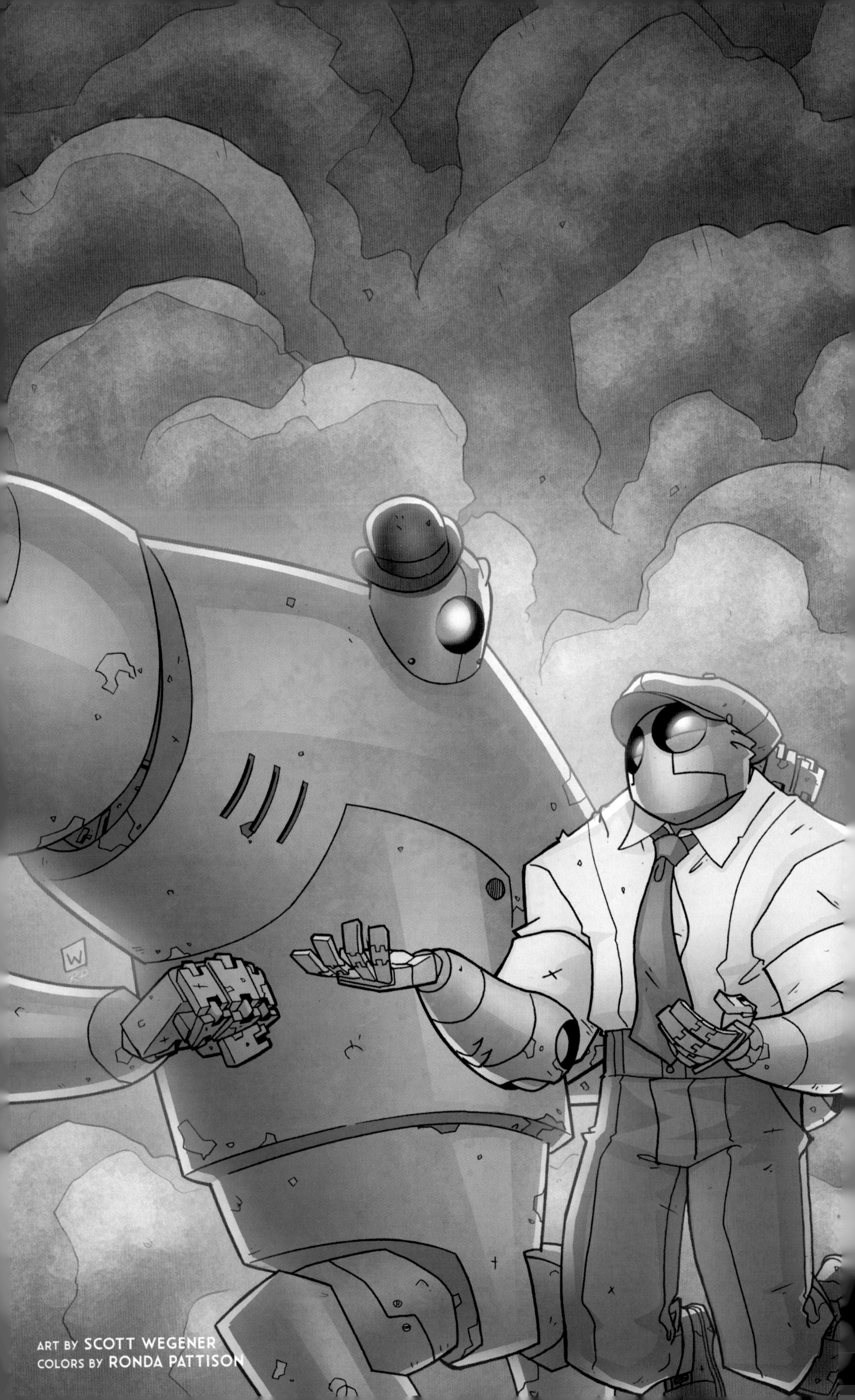
ART BY SCOTT WEGENER
COLORS BY RONDA PATTISON

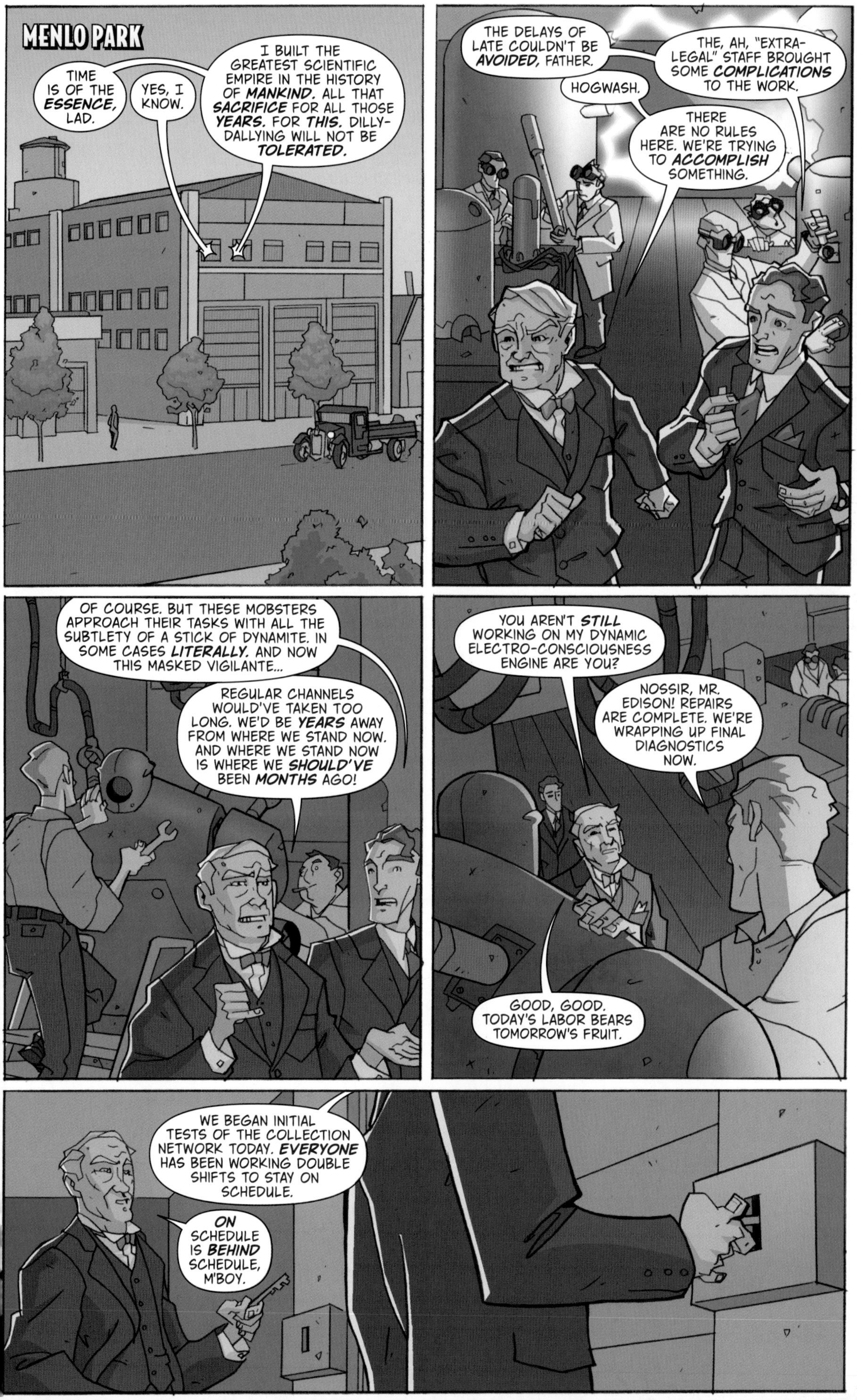
MENLO PARK
TIME IS OF THE ESSENCE, LAD.
YES, I KNOW.
I BUILT THE GREATEST SCIENTIFIC EMPIRE IN THE HISTORY OF MANKIND. ALL THAT SACRIFICE FOR ALL THOSE YEARS. FOR THIS. DILLY-DALLYING WILL NOT BE TOLERATED.
THE DELAYS OF LATE COULDN'T BE AVOIDED, FATHER.
THE, AH, "EXTRA-LEGAL" STAFF BROUGHT SOME COMPLICATIONS TO THE WORK.
HOGWASH.
THERE ARE NO RULES HERE. WE'RE TRYING TO ACCOMPLISH SOMETHING.
OF COURSE. BUT THESE MOBSTERS APPROACH THEIR TASKS WITH ALL THE SUBTLETY OF A STICK OF DYNAMITE. IN SOME CASES LITERALLY. AND NOW THIS MASKED VIGILANTE...
REGULAR CHANNELS WOULD'VE TAKEN TOO LONG. WE'D BE YEARS AWAY FROM WHERE WE STAND NOW. AND WHERE WE STAND NOW IS WHERE WE SHOULD'VE BEEN MONTHS AGO!
YOU AREN'T STILL WORKING ON MY DYNAMIC ELECTRO-CONSCIOUSNESS ENGINE ARE YOU?
NOSSIR, MR. EDISON! REPAIRS ARE COMPLETE. WE'RE WRAPPING UP FINAL DIAGNOSTICS NOW.
GOOD, GOOD. TODAY'S LABOR BEARS TOMORROW'S FRUIT.
WE BEGAN INITIAL TESTS OF THE COLLECTION NETWORK TODAY. EVERYONE HAS BEEN WORKING DOUBLE SHIFTS TO STAY ON SCHEDULE.
ON SCHEDULE IS BEHIND SCHEDULE, M'BOY.

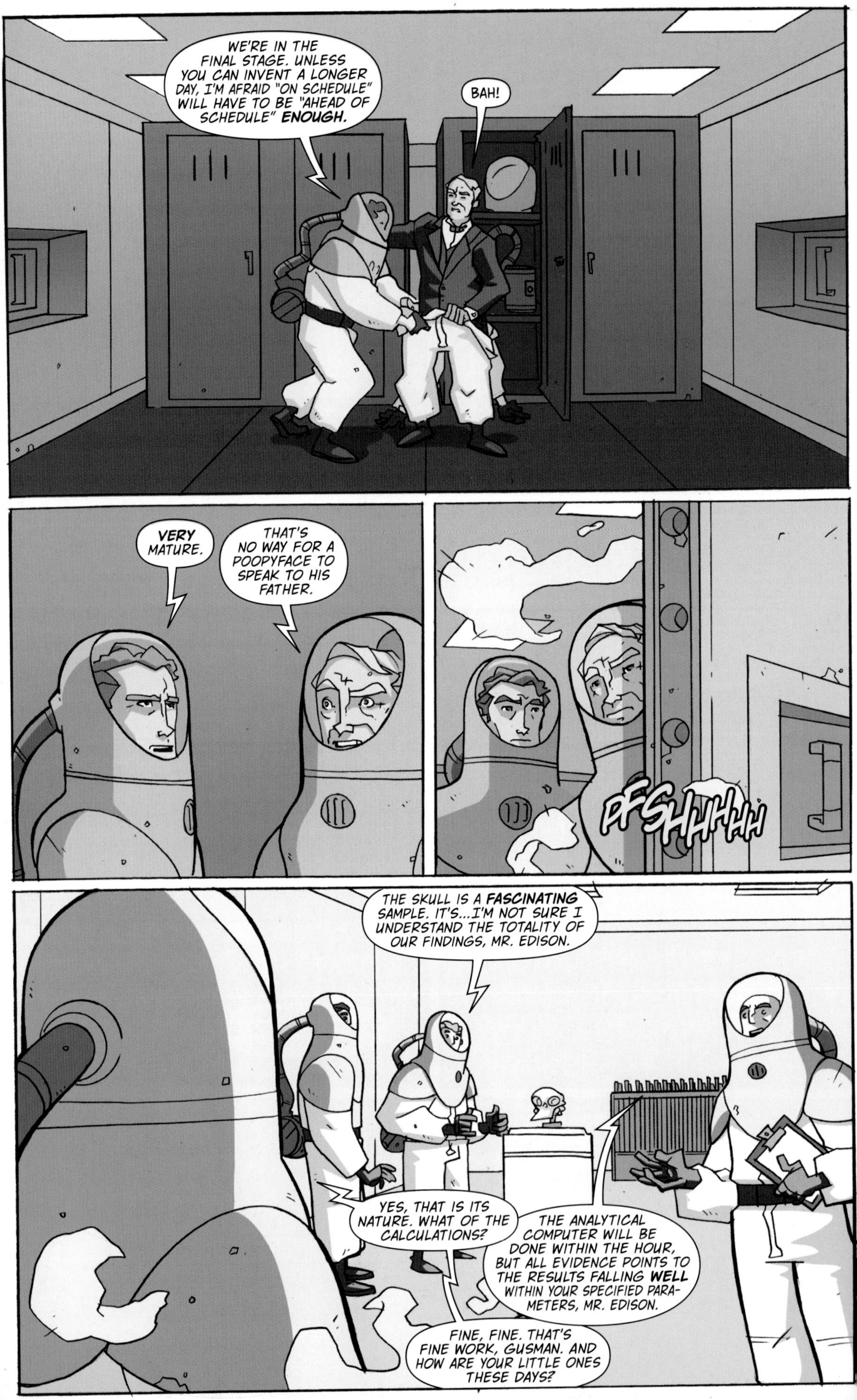

WE'RE IN THE FINAL STAGE. UNLESS YOU CAN INVENT A LONGER DAY, I'M AFRAID "ON SCHEDULE" WILL HAVE TO BE "AHEAD OF SCHEDULE" ENOUGH.
BAH!
VERY MATURE.
THAT'S NO WAY FOR A POOPYFACE TO SPEAK TO HIS FATHER.
PFSHHHHH
THE SKULL IS A FASCINATING SAMPLE. IT'S...I'M NOT SURE I UNDERSTAND THE TOTALITY OF OUR FINDINGS, MR. EDISON.
YES, THAT IS ITS NATURE. WHAT OF THE CALCULATIONS?
THE ANALYTICAL COMPUTER WILL BE DONE WITHIN THE HOUR, BUT ALL EVIDENCE POINTS TO THE RESULTS FALLING WELL WITHIN YOUR SPECIFIED PARA-METERS, MR. EDISON.
FINE, FINE. THAT'S FINE WORK, GUSMAN. AND HOW ARE YOUR LITTLE ONES THESE DAYS?

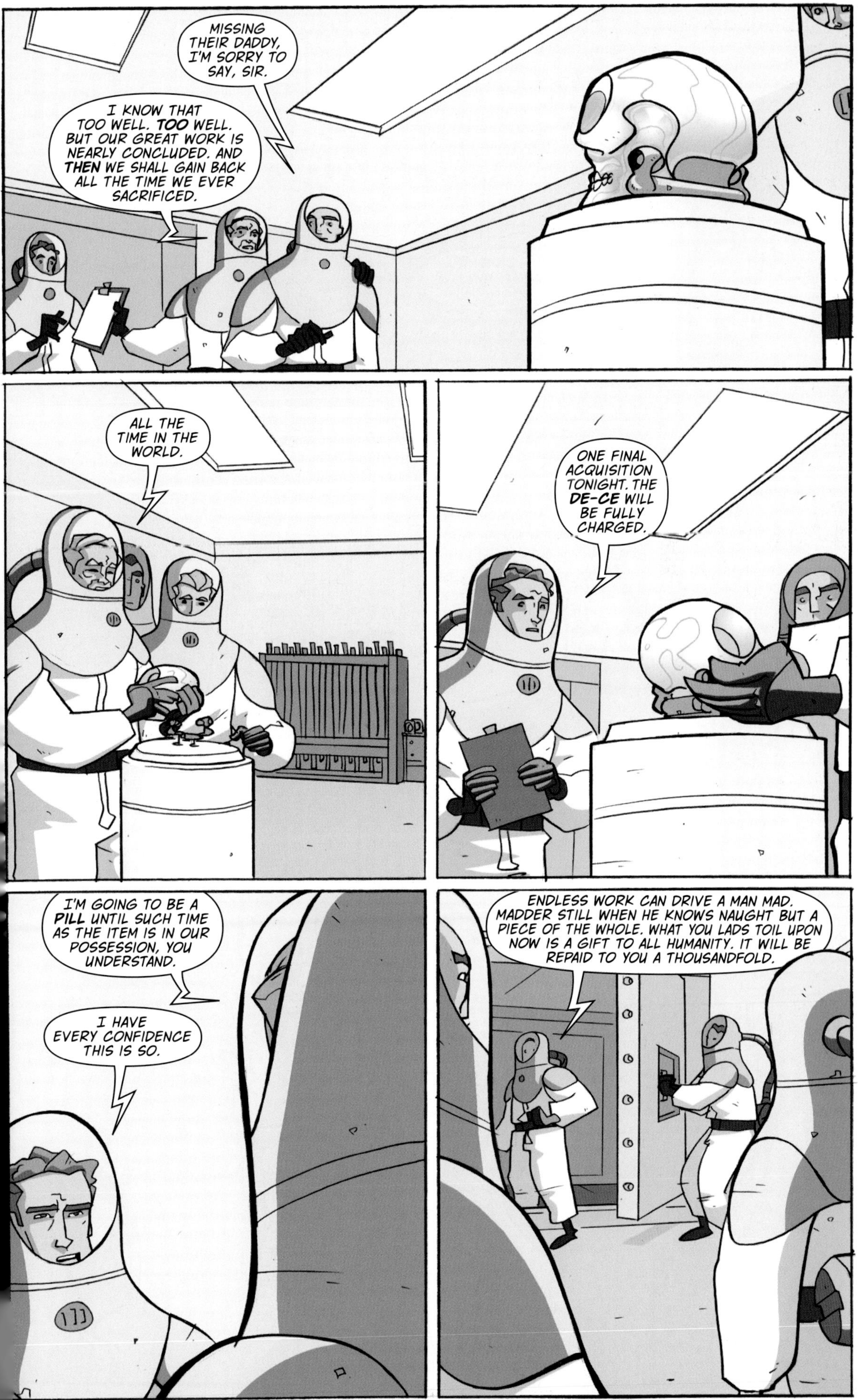
MISSING THEIR DADDY, I'M SORRY TO SAY, SIR.
I KNOW THAT TOO WELL. **TOO** WELL. BUT OUR GREAT WORK IS NEARLY CONCLUDED. AND **THEN** WE SHALL GAIN BACK ALL THE TIME WE EVER SACRIFICED.
ALL THE TIME IN THE WORLD.
ONE FINAL ACQUISITION TONIGHT. THE **DE-CE** WILL BE FULLY CHARGED.
I'M GOING TO BE A **PILL** UNTIL SUCH TIME AS THE ITEM IS IN OUR POSSESSION, YOU UNDERSTAND.
I HAVE EVERY CONFIDENCE THIS IS SO.
ENDLESS WORK CAN DRIVE A MAN MAD. MADDER STILL WHEN HE KNOWS NAUGHT BUT A PIECE OF THE WHOLE. WHAT YOU LADS TOIL UPON NOW IS A GIFT TO ALL HUMANITY. IT WILL BE REPAID TO YOU A THOUSANDFOLD.

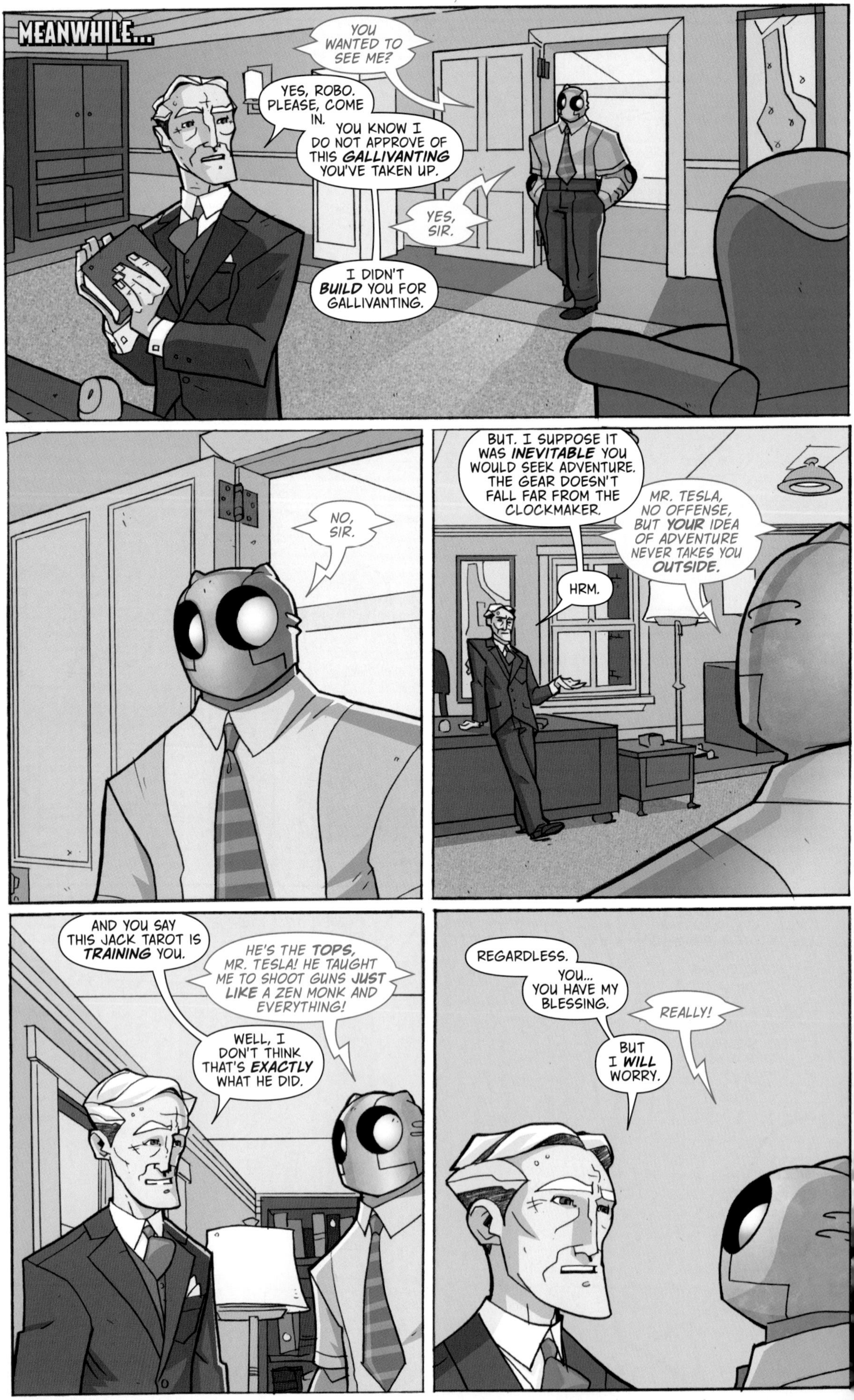
MEANWHILE...
YOU WANTED TO SEE ME?
YES, ROBO. PLEASE, COME IN.
YOU KNOW I DO NOT APPROVE OF THIS GALLIVANTING YOU'VE TAKEN UP.
YES, SIR.
I DIDN'T BUILD YOU FOR GALLIVANTING.
NO, SIR.
BUT. I SUPPOSE IT WAS INEVITABLE YOU WOULD SEEK ADVENTURE. THE GEAR DOESN'T FALL FAR FROM THE CLOCKMAKER.
MR. TESLA, NO OFFENSE, BUT YOUR IDEA OF ADVENTURE NEVER TAKES YOU OUTSIDE.
HRM.
AND YOU SAY THIS JACK TAROT IS TRAINING YOU.
HE'S THE TOPS, MR. TESLA! HE TAUGHT ME TO SHOOT GUNS JUST LIKE A ZEN MONK AND EVERYTHING!
WELL, I DON'T THINK THAT'S EXACTLY WHAT HE DID.
REGARDLESS.
YOU... YOU HAVE MY BLESSING.
REALLY!
BUT I WILL WORRY.

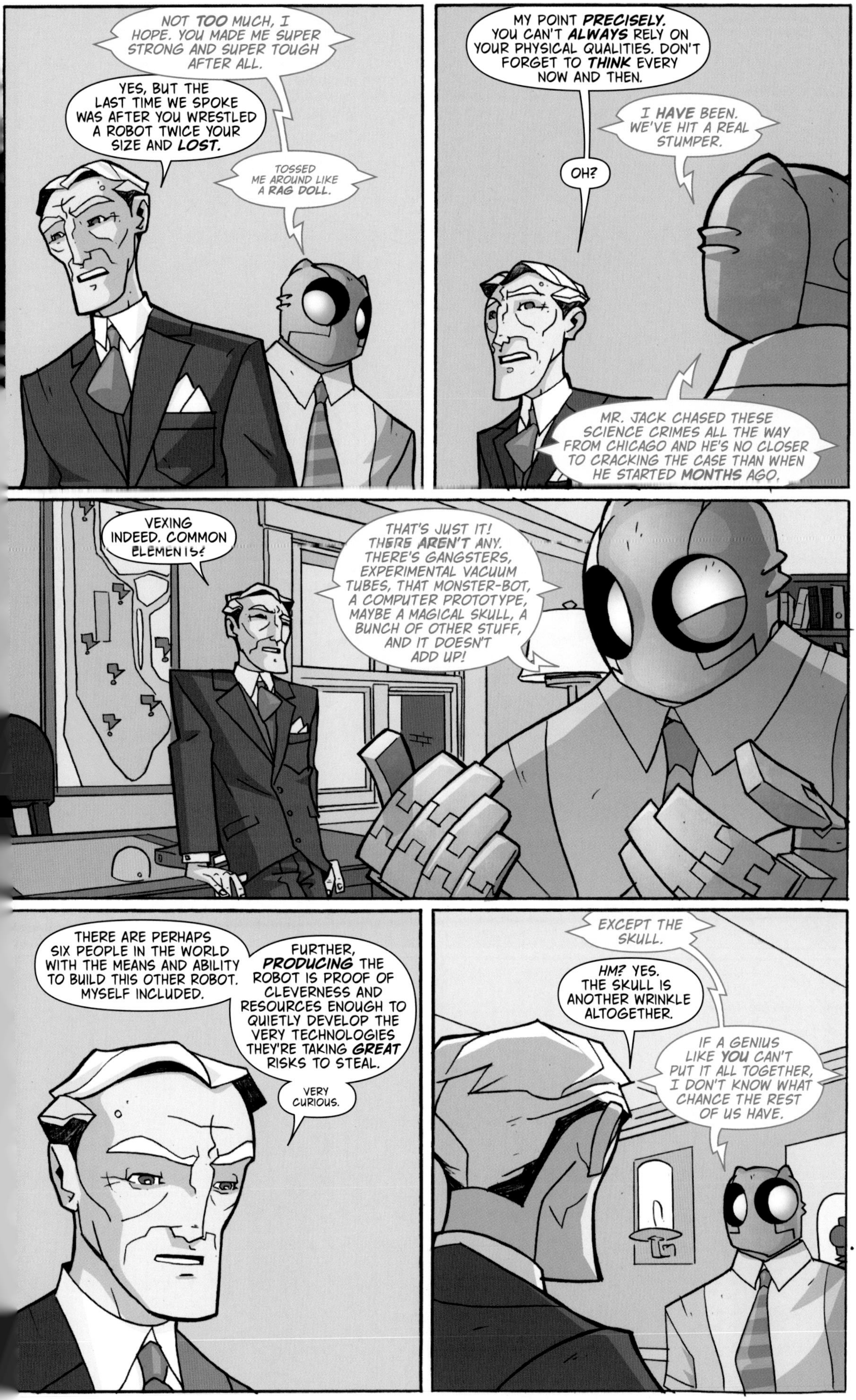
NOT TOO MUCH, I HOPE. YOU MADE ME SUPER STRONG AND SUPER TOUGH AFTER ALL.
YES, BUT THE LAST TIME WE SPOKE WAS AFTER YOU WRESTLED A ROBOT TWICE YOUR SIZE AND LOST.
TOSSED ME AROUND LIKE A RAG DOLL.
MY POINT PRECISELY. YOU CAN'T ALWAYS RELY ON YOUR PHYSICAL QUALITIES. DON'T FORGET TO THINK EVERY NOW AND THEN.
I HAVE BEEN. WE'VE HIT A REAL STUMPER.
OH?
MR. JACK CHASED THESE SCIENCE CRIMES ALL THE WAY FROM CHICAGO AND HE'S NO CLOSER TO CRACKING THE CASE THAN WHEN HE STARTED MONTHS AGO.
VEXING INDEED. COMMON ELEMENTS?
THAT'S JUST IT! THERE AREN'T ANY. THERE'S GANGSTERS, EXPERIMENTAL VACUUM TUBES, THAT MONSTER-BOT, A COMPUTER PROTOTYPE, MAYBE A MAGICAL SKULL, A BUNCH OF OTHER STUFF, AND IT DOESN'T ADD UP!
THERE ARE PERHAPS SIX PEOPLE IN THE WORLD WITH THE MEANS AND ABILITY TO BUILD THIS OTHER ROBOT. MYSELF INCLUDED.
FURTHER, PRODUCING THE ROBOT IS PROOF OF CLEVERNESS AND RESOURCES ENOUGH TO QUIETLY DEVELOP THE VERY TECHNOLOGIES THEY'RE TAKING GREAT RISKS TO STEAL.
VERY CURIOUS.
EXCEPT THE SKULL.
HM? YES. THE SKULL IS ANOTHER WRINKLE ALTOGETHER.
IF A GENIUS LIKE YOU CAN'T PUT IT ALL TOGETHER, I DON'T KNOW WHAT CHANCE THE REST OF US HAVE.

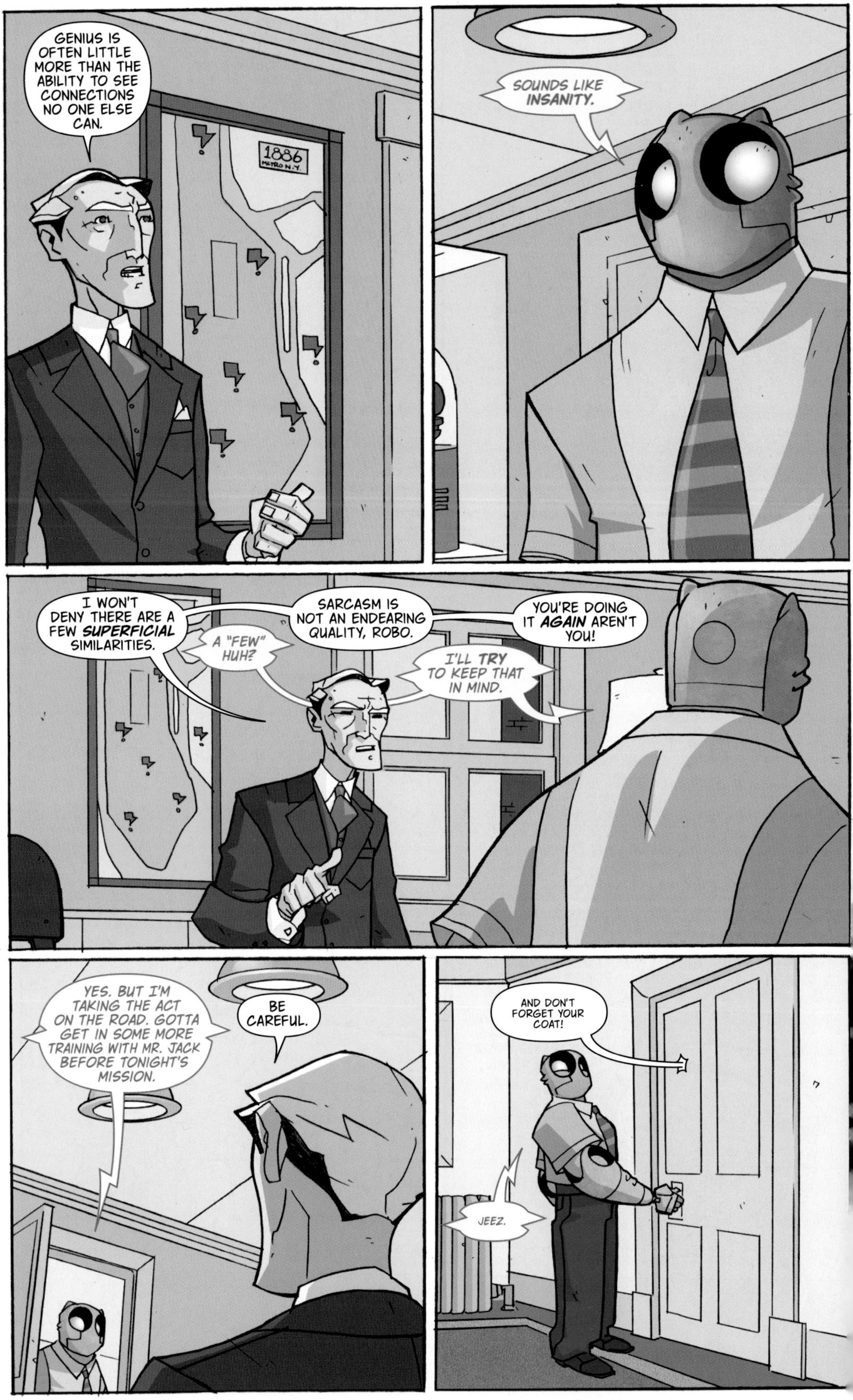
GENIUS IS OFTEN LITTLE MORE THAN THE ABILITY TO SEE CONNECTIONS NO ONE ELSE CAN.
1886 METRO N.Y.
SOUNDS LIKE INSANITY.
I WON'T DENY THERE ARE A FEW SUPERFICIAL SIMILARITIES.
A "FEW" HUH?
SARCASM IS NOT AN ENDEARING QUALITY, ROBO.
I'LL TRY TO KEEP THAT IN MIND.
YOU'RE DOING IT AGAIN AREN'T YOU!
YES. BUT I'M TAKING THE ACT ON THE ROAD. GOTTA GET IN SOME MORE TRAINING WITH MR. JACK BEFORE TONIGHT'S MISSION.
BE CAREFUL.
AND DON'T FORGET YOUR COAT!
JEEZ.

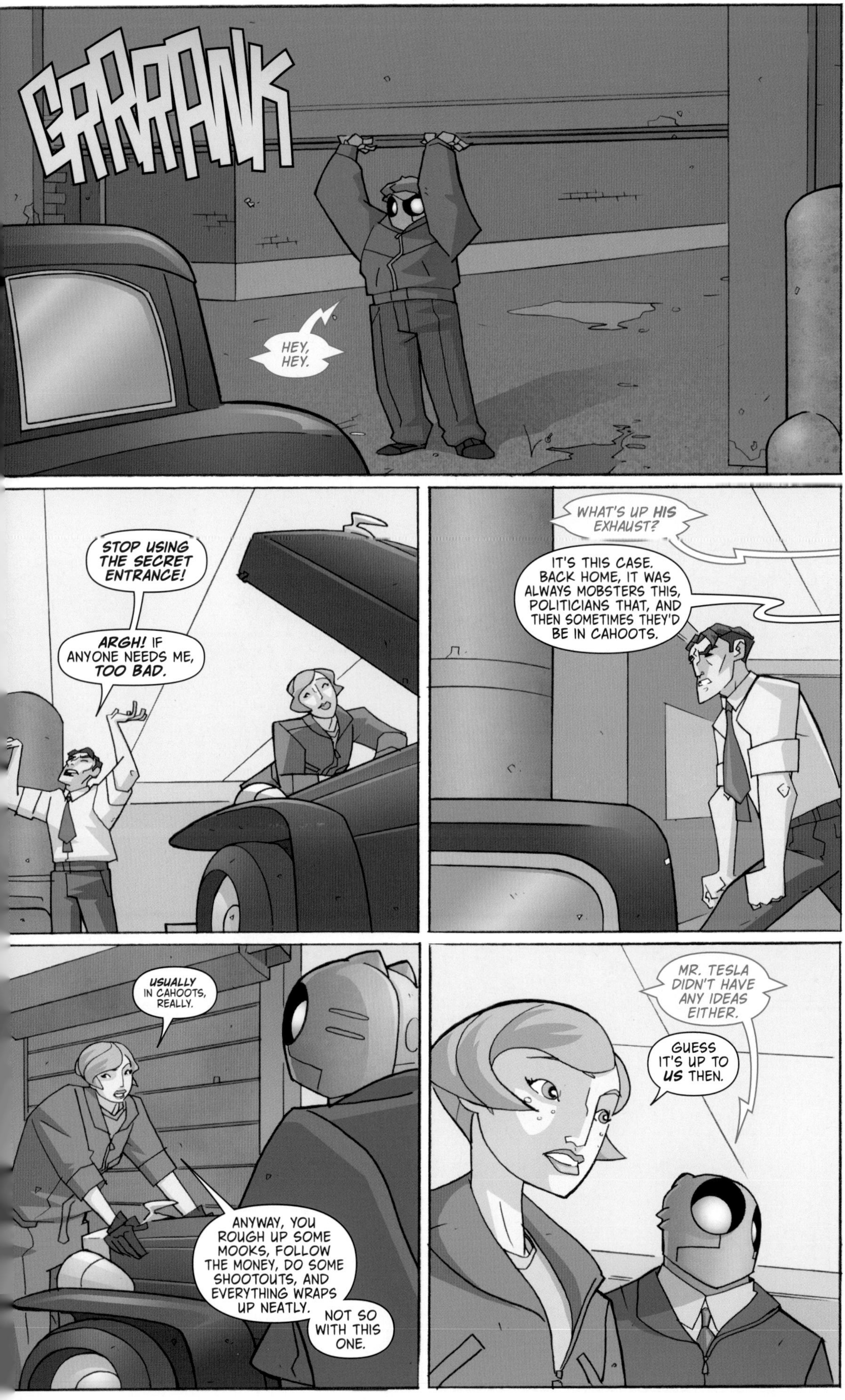
GRRRANK
HEY, HEY.
STOP USING THE SECRET ENTRANCE!
ARGH! IF ANYONE NEEDS ME, TOO BAD.
WHAT'S UP HIS EXHAUST?
IT'S THIS CASE. BACK HOME, IT WAS ALWAYS MOBSTERS THIS, POLITICIANS THAT, AND THEN SOMETIMES THEY'D BE IN CAHOOTS.
USUALLY IN CAHOOTS, REALLY.
ANYWAY, YOU ROUGH UP SOME MOOKS, FOLLOW THE MONEY, DO SOME SHOOTOUTS, AND EVERYTHING WRAPS UP NEATLY.
NOT SO WITH THIS ONE.
MR. TESLA DIDN'T HAVE ANY IDEAS EITHER.
GUESS IT'S UP TO US THEN.

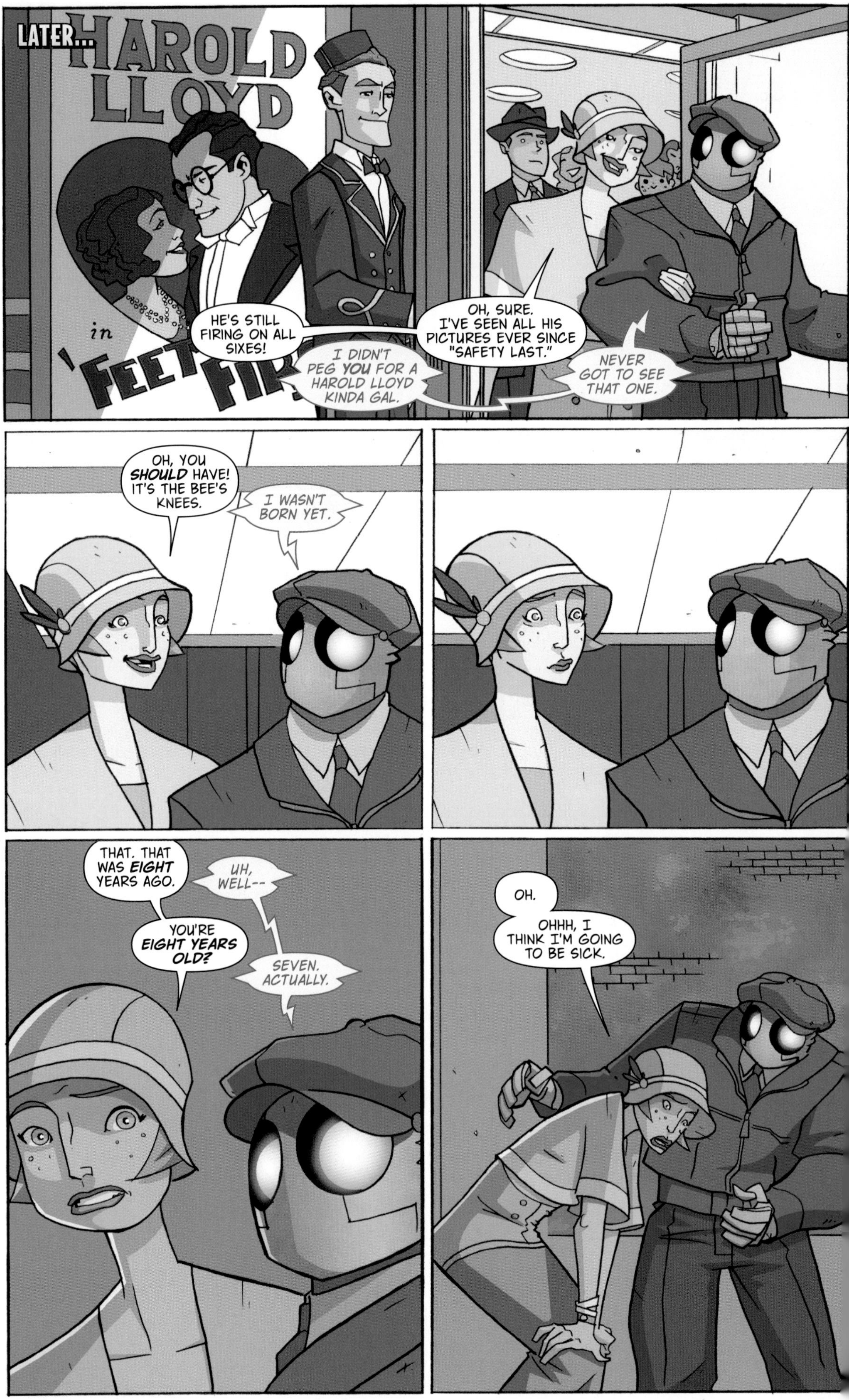
LATER...
HAROLD LLOYD
in
FEET FIR
HE'S STILL FIRING ON ALL SIXES!
OH, SURE. I'VE SEEN ALL HIS PICTURES EVER SINCE "SAFETY LAST."
I DIDN'T PEG YOU FOR A HAROLD LLOYD KINDA GAL.
NEVER GOT TO SEE THAT ONE.
OH, YOU SHOULD HAVE! IT'S THE BEE'S KNEES.
I WASN'T BORN YET.
THAT. THAT WAS EIGHT YEARS AGO.
UH, WELL--
YOU'RE EIGHT YEARS OLD?
SEVEN. ACTUALLY.
OH.
OHHH, I THINK I'M GOING TO BE SICK.

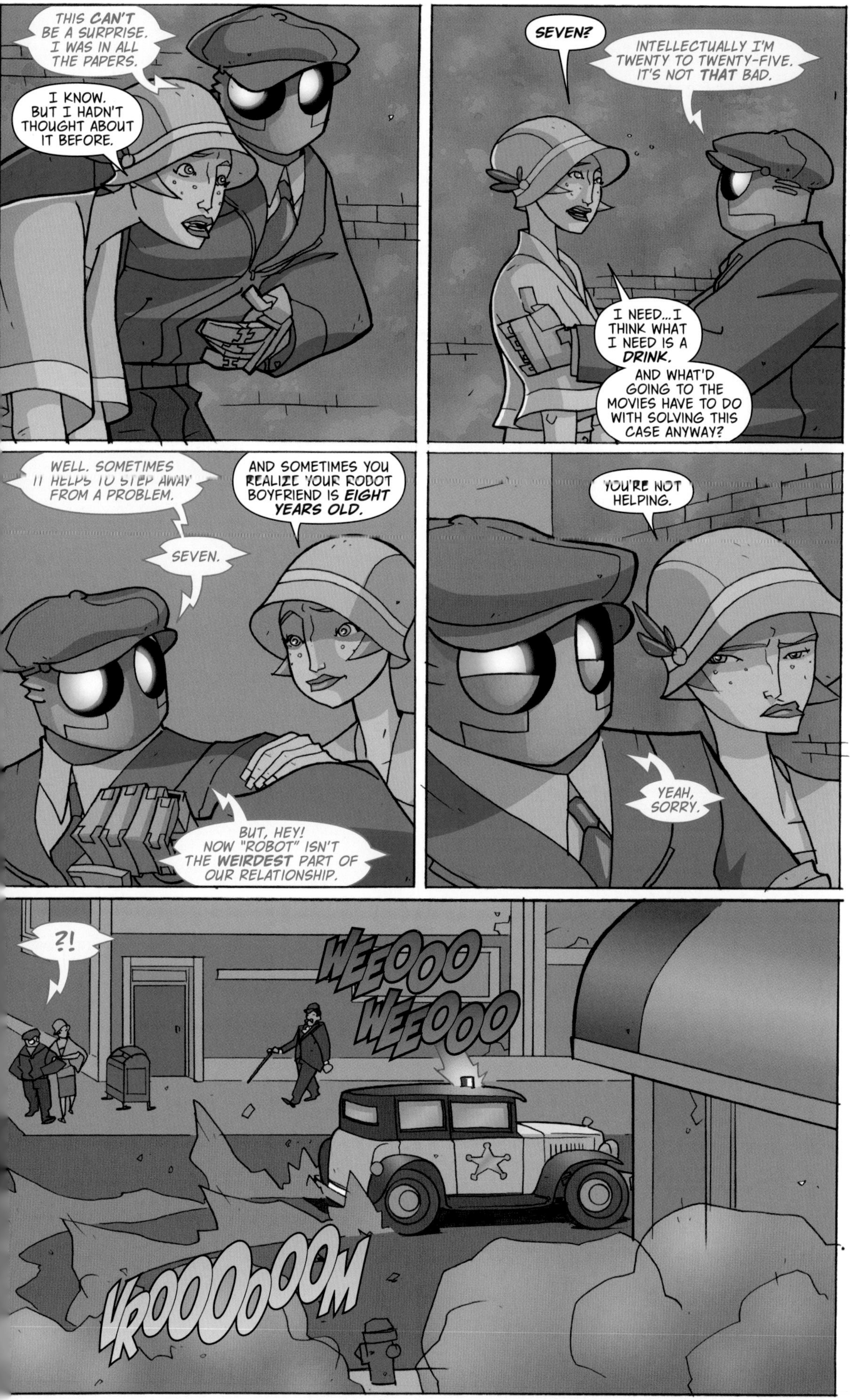

THIS CAN'T BE A SURPRISE. I WAS IN ALL THE PAPERS.
I KNOW. BUT I HADN'T THOUGHT ABOUT IT BEFORE.
SEVEN?
INTELLECTUALLY I'M TWENTY TO TWENTY-FIVE. IT'S NOT THAT BAD.
I NEED... I THINK WHAT I NEED IS A DRINK.
AND WHAT'D GOING TO THE MOVIES HAVE TO DO WITH SOLVING THIS CASE ANYWAY?
WELL. SOMETIMES IT HELPS TO STEP AWAY FROM A PROBLEM.
AND SOMETIMES YOU REALIZE YOUR ROBOT BOYFRIEND IS EIGHT YEARS OLD.
SEVEN.
BUT, HEY! NOW "ROBOT" ISN'T THE WEIRDEST PART OF OUR RELATIONSHIP.
YOU'RE NOT HELPING.
YEAH, SORRY.
?!
WEEOOO WEEOOO
VROOOOOOOM

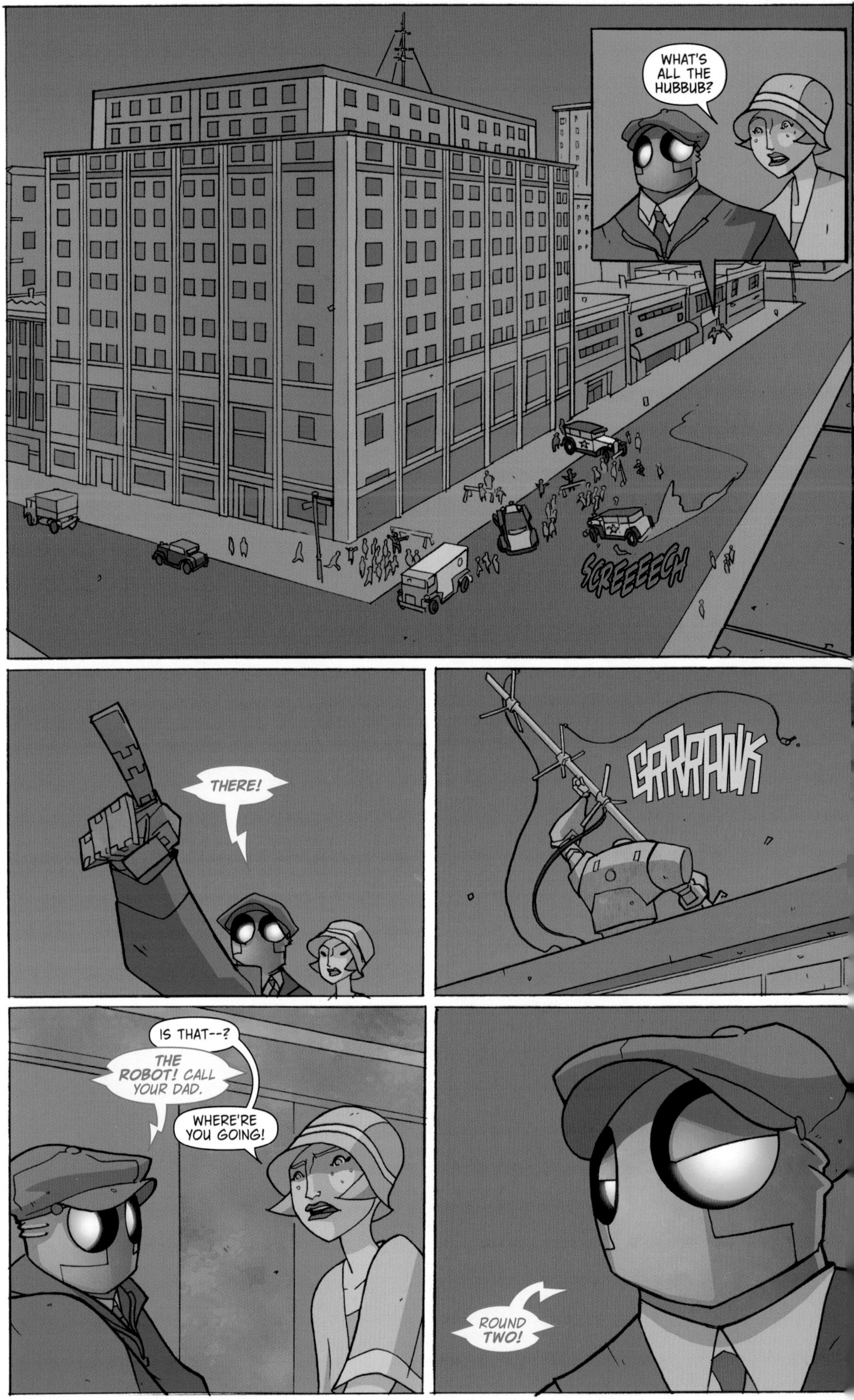
WHAT'S ALL THE HUBBUB?
SCREEEECH
THERE!
GRRRANK
IS THAT--?
THE ROBOT! CALL YOUR DAD.
WHERE'RE YOU GOING!
ROUND TWO!

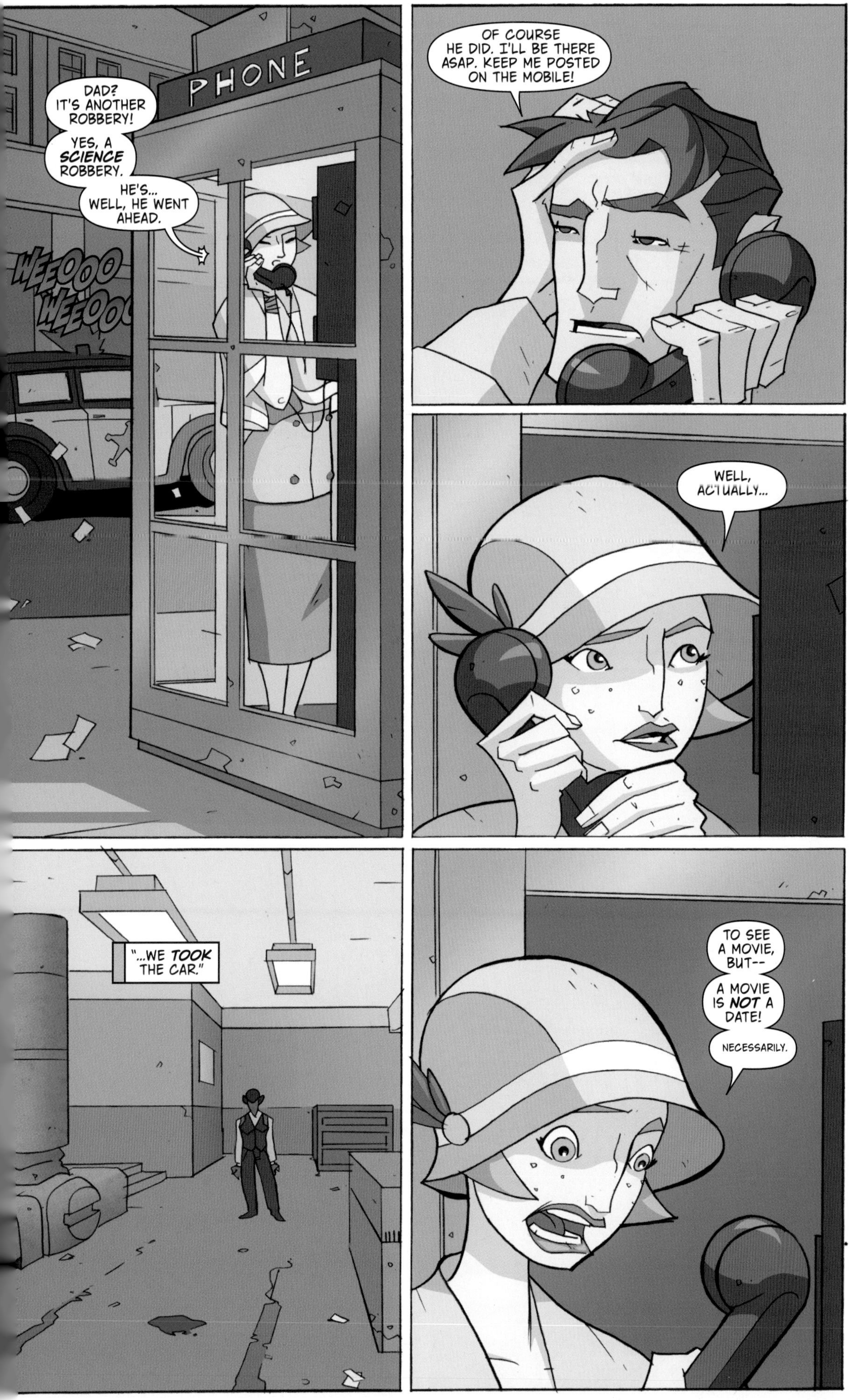
PHONE
DAD? IT'S ANOTHER ROBBERY!
YES, A SCIENCE ROBBERY.
HE'S... WELL, HE WENT AHEAD.
WEEOOO WEEOOO
OF COURSE HE DID. I'LL BE THERE ASAP. KEEP ME POSTED ON THE MOBILE!
WELL, ACTUALLY...
"...WE TOOK THE CAR."
TO SEE A MOVIE, BUT--
A MOVIE IS NOT A DATE!
NECESSARILY.

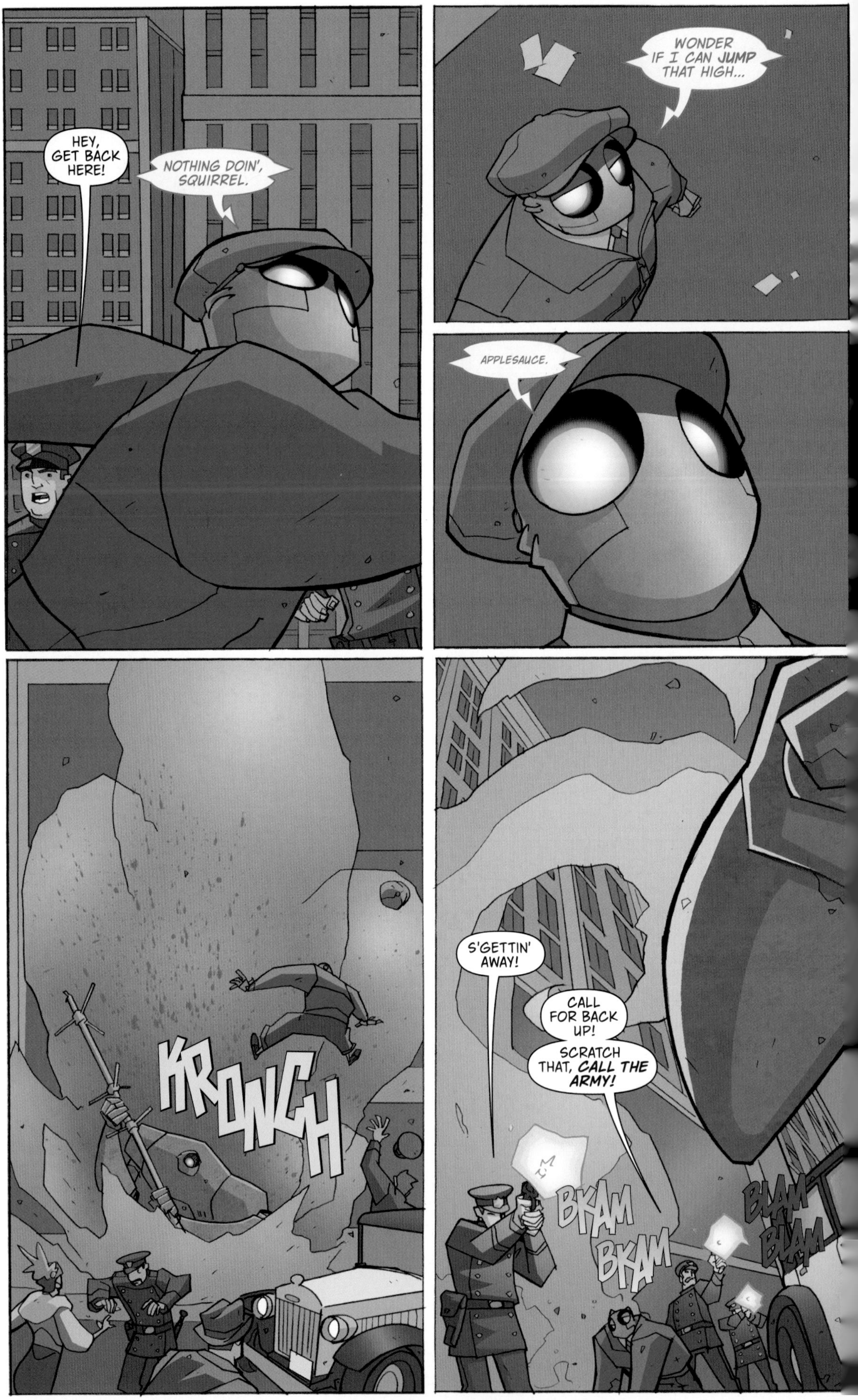
HEY, GET BACK HERE!
NOTHING DOIN', SQUIRREL.
WONDER IF I CAN JUMP THAT HIGH...
APPLESAUCE.
KRONCH
S'GETTIN' AWAY!
CALL FOR BACK UP!
SCRATCH THAT, CALL THE ARMY!
BKAM
BKAM
BLAM BLAM

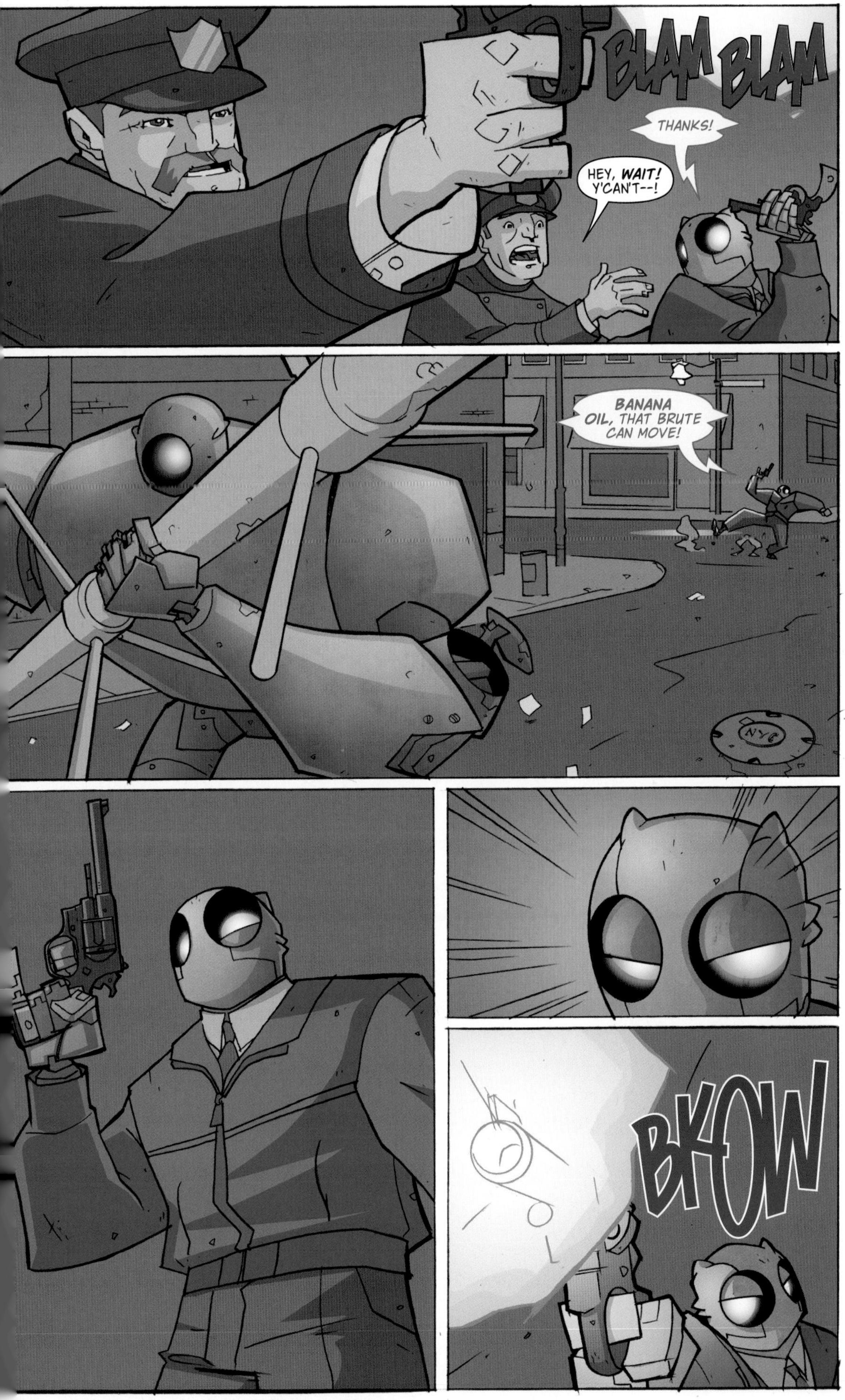
BLAM BLAM
THANKS!
HEY, WAIT! Y'CAN'T--!
BANANA OIL, THAT BRUTE CAN MOVE!
NYC
BKOW

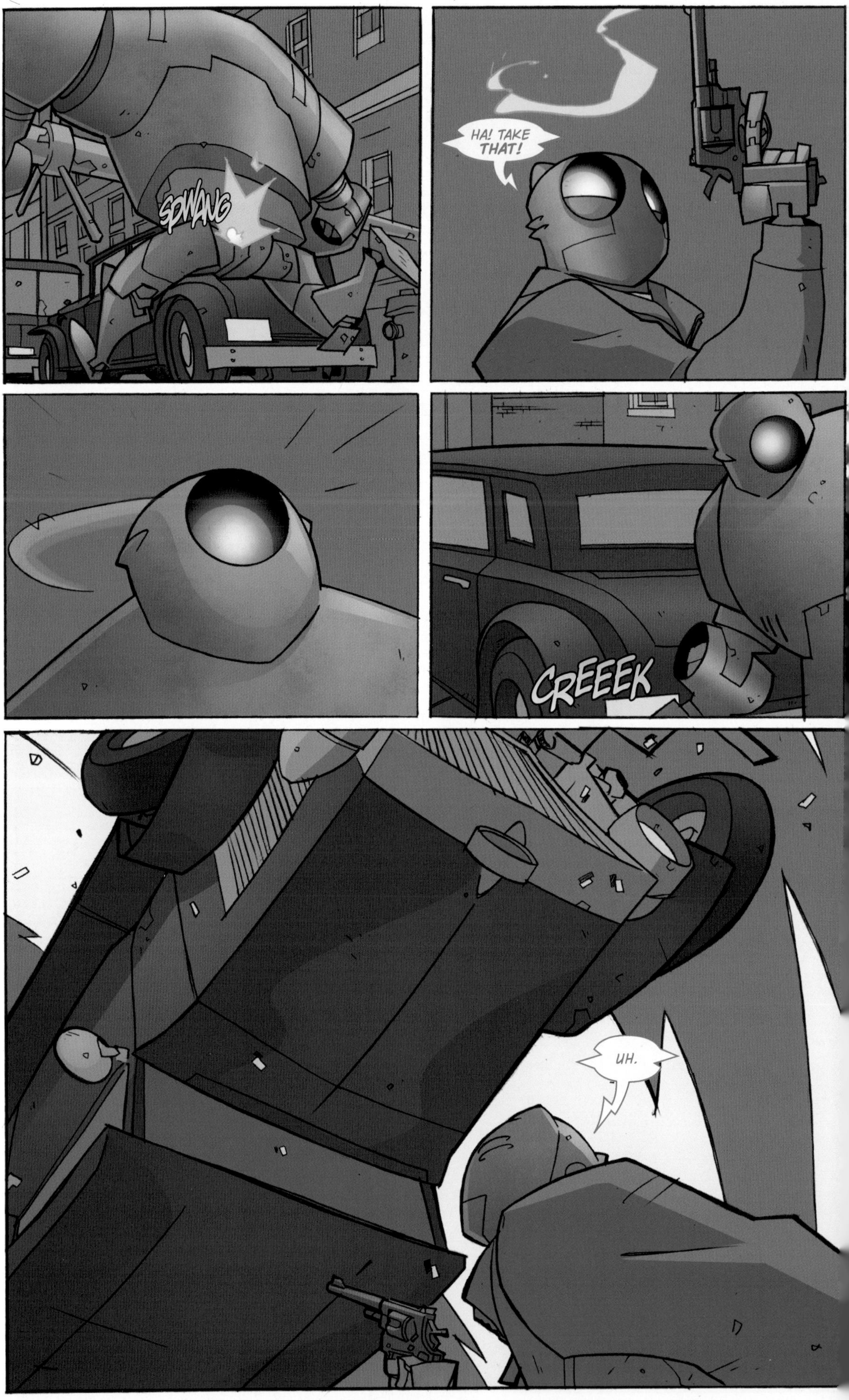
SPWANG
HA! TAKE THAT!
CREEEK
UH.

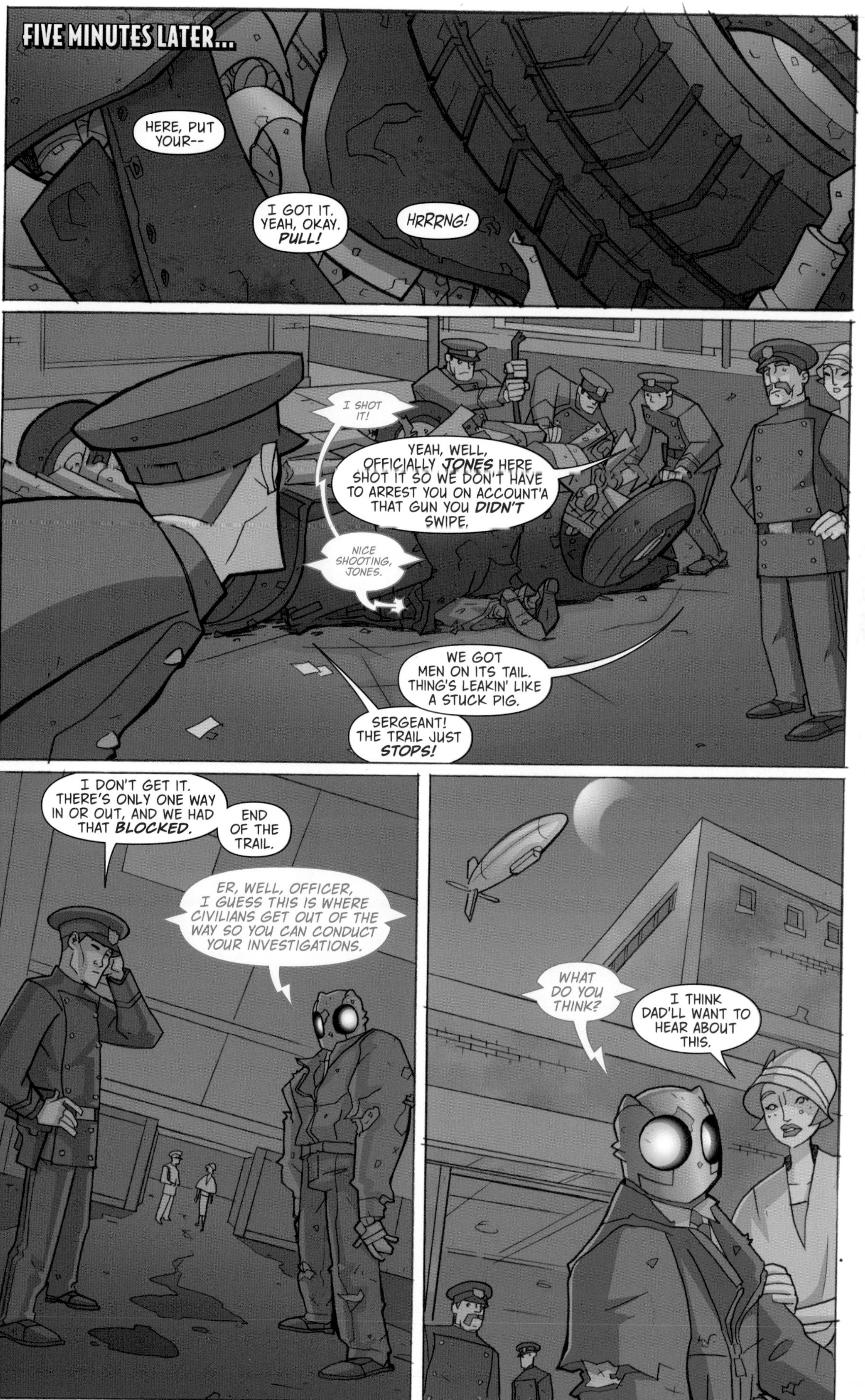

FIVE MINUTES LATER...
HERE, PUT YOUR--
I GOT IT. YEAH, OKAY. PULL!
HRRRNG!
I SHOT IT!
YEAH, WELL, OFFICIALLY JONES HERE SHOT IT SO WE DON'T HAVE TO ARREST YOU ON ACCOUNT'A THAT GUN YOU DIDN'T SWIPE.
NICE SHOOTING, JONES.
WE GOT MEN ON ITS TAIL. THING'S LEAKIN' LIKE A STUCK PIG.
SERGEANT! THE TRAIL JUST STOPS!
I DON'T GET IT. THERE'S ONLY ONE WAY IN OR OUT, AND WE HAD THAT BLOCKED.
END OF THE TRAIL.
ER, WELL, OFFICER, I GUESS THIS IS WHERE CIVILIANS GET OUT OF THE WAY SO YOU CAN CONDUCT YOUR INVESTIGATIONS.
WHAT DO YOU THINK?
I THINK DAD'LL WANT TO HEAR ABOUT THIS.

--COULD HAVE *DONE* SOMETHING!

LIKE *WHAT?*

GOTTEN THERE, FOR STARTERS.

THEN?

NOT LET THE DAMNED THING GET *AWAY,* I'LL TELL YOU THAT!

AND HOW'S *THAT* EXACTLY? ROBO RUNS LIKE A *RACE HORSE* AND *HE* COULDN'T KEEP UP.

BAH!

BAH, BAH *BLACK SHEEP.* I DUNNO WHAT YOU'RE *GROUSING* ABOUT ANYWAY. IF WE HADN'T GONE OUT, WE'D NEVER'VE RUN INTO THE STUPID THING. IT'S PURE *LUCK* WE HAPPENED TO BE THERE AT ALL!

NO, I KNOW. THIS BUSINESS WITH THE ROBOTS AND COMPUTERS AND RAY GUNS AND...EVERYTHING ABOUT IT IS SLIPPING THROUGH MY FINGERS.

HOLD THE PHONE...

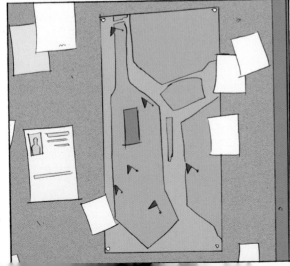

1886 METRO N.Y.

GENIUS IS OFTEN LITTLE MORE THAN THE ABILITY TO SEE CONNECTIONS NO ONE ELSE CAN.

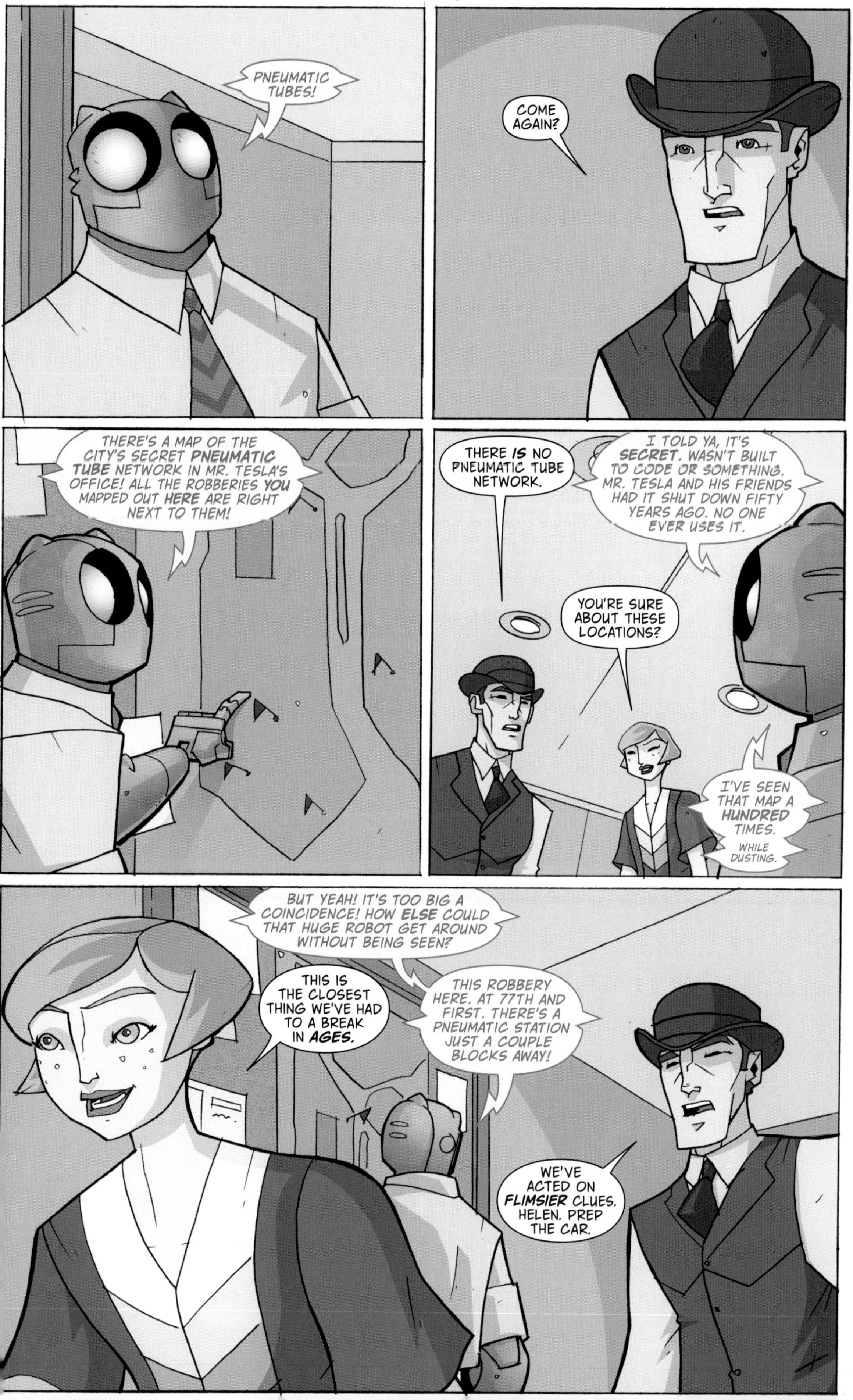
PNEUMATIC TUBES!
COME AGAIN?
THERE'S A MAP OF THE CITY'S SECRET PNEUMATIC TUBE NETWORK IN MR. TESLA'S OFFICE! ALL THE ROBBERIES YOU MAPPED OUT HERE ARE RIGHT NEXT TO THEM!
THERE IS NO PNEUMATIC TUBE NETWORK.
I TOLD YA, IT'S SECRET. WASN'T BUILT TO CODE OR SOMETHING. MR. TESLA AND HIS FRIENDS HAD IT SHUT DOWN FIFTY YEARS AGO. NO ONE EVER USES IT.
YOU'RE SURE ABOUT THESE LOCATIONS?
I'VE SEEN THAT MAP A HUNDRED TIMES.
WHILE DUSTING.
BUT YEAH! IT'S TOO BIG A COINCIDENCE! HOW ELSE COULD THAT HUGE ROBOT GET AROUND WITHOUT BEING SEEN?
THIS IS THE CLOSEST THING WE'VE HAD TO A BREAK IN AGES.
THIS ROBBERY HERE. AT 77TH AND FIRST. THERE'S A PNEUMATIC STATION JUST A COUPLE BLOCKS AWAY!
WE'VE ACTED ON FLIMSIER CLUES. HELEN. PREP THE CAR.

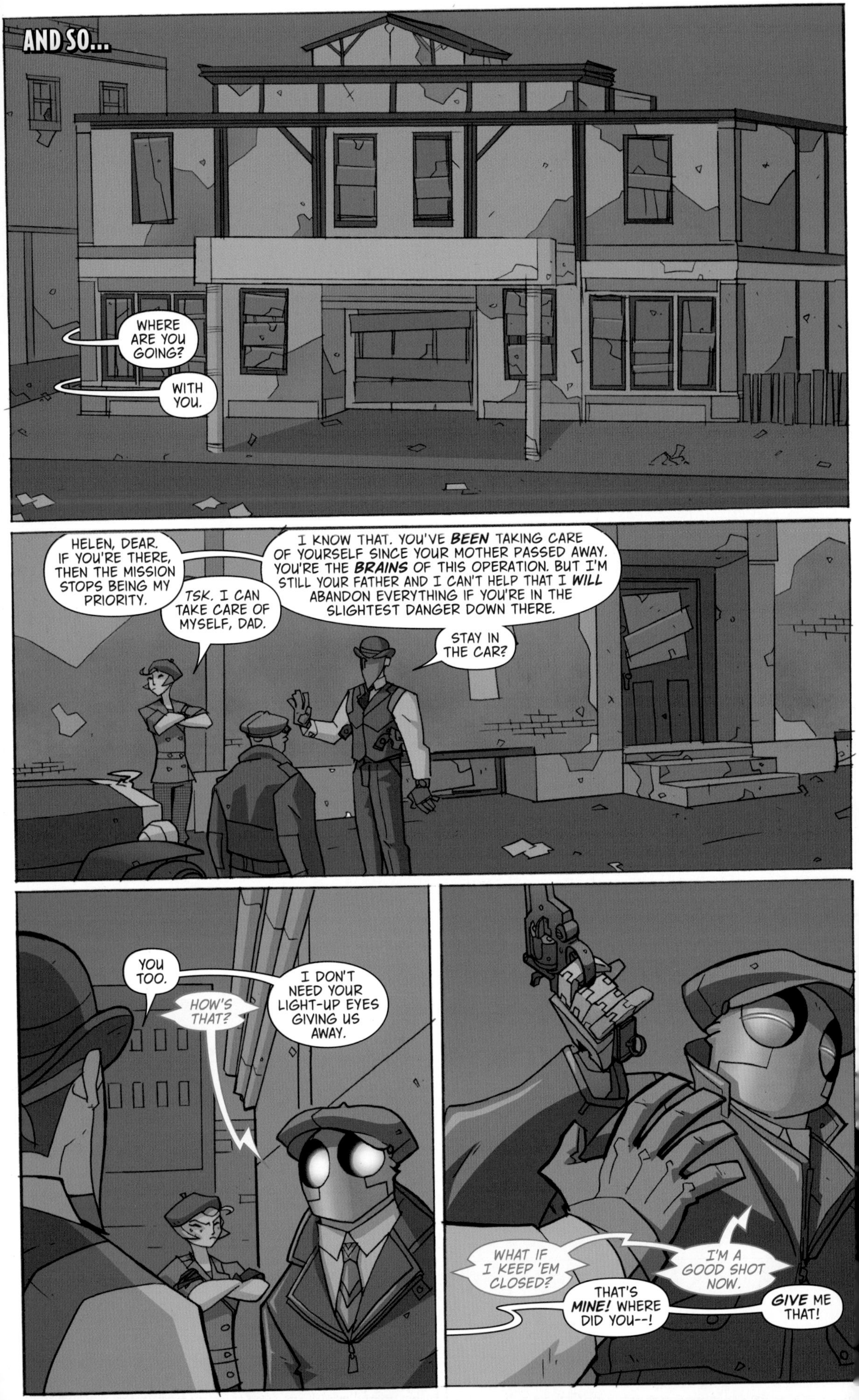
AND SO...
WHERE ARE YOU GOING?
WITH YOU.
HELEN, DEAR. IF YOU'RE THERE, THEN THE MISSION STOPS BEING MY PRIORITY.
TSK. I CAN TAKE CARE OF MYSELF, DAD.
I KNOW THAT. YOU'VE BEEN TAKING CARE OF YOURSELF SINCE YOUR MOTHER PASSED AWAY. YOU'RE THE BRAINS OF THIS OPERATION. BUT I'M STILL YOUR FATHER AND I CAN'T HELP THAT I WILL ABANDON EVERYTHING IF YOU'RE IN THE SLIGHTEST DANGER DOWN THERE.
STAY IN THE CAR?
YOU TOO.
HOW'S THAT?
I DON'T NEED YOUR LIGHT-UP EYES GIVING US AWAY.
WHAT IF I KEEP 'EM CLOSED?
I'M A GOOD SHOT NOW.
THAT'S MINE! WHERE DID YOU--!
GIVE ME THAT!

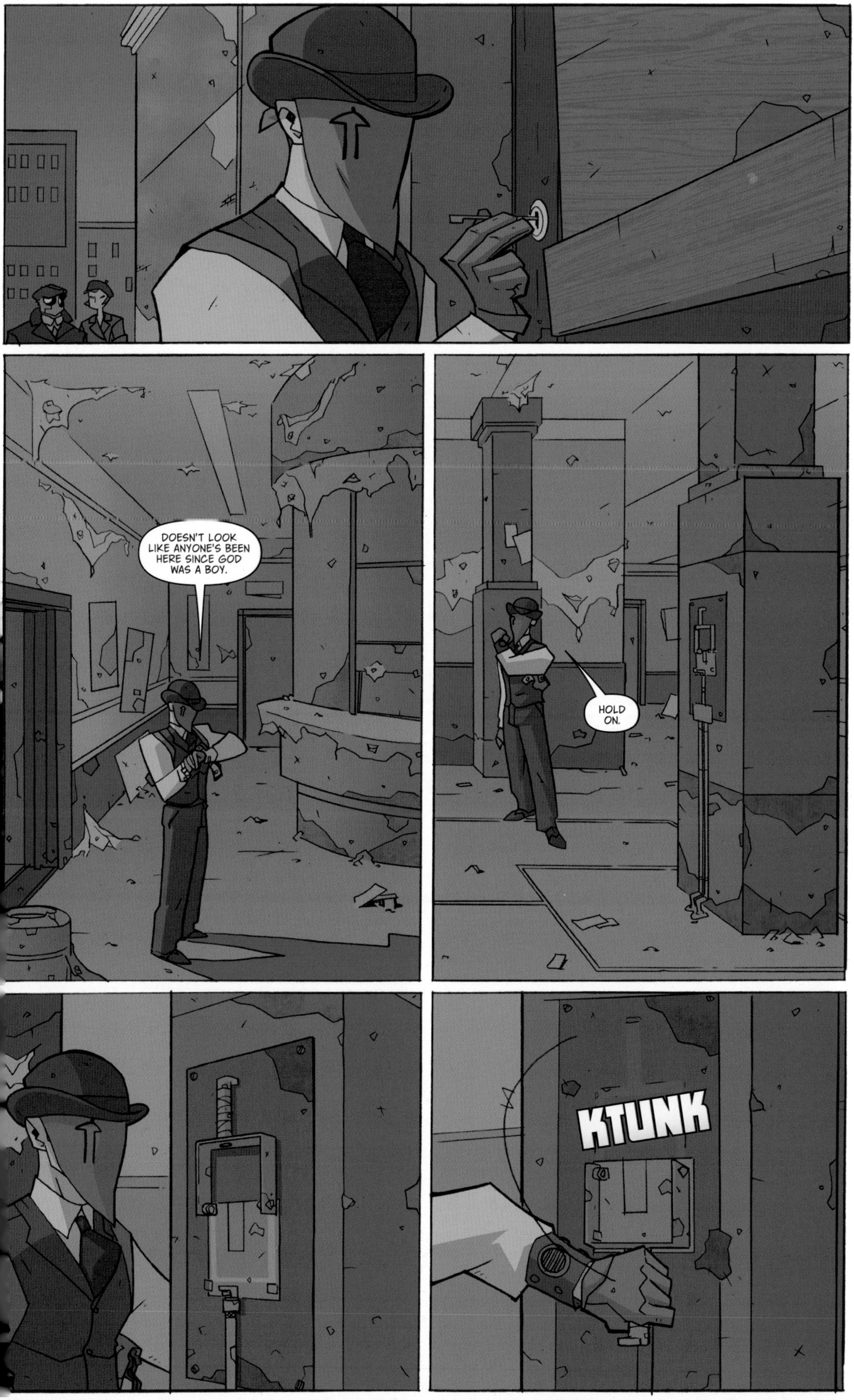

DOESN'T LOOK LIKE ANYONE'S BEEN HERE SINCE GOD WAS A BOY.
HOLD ON.
KTUNK

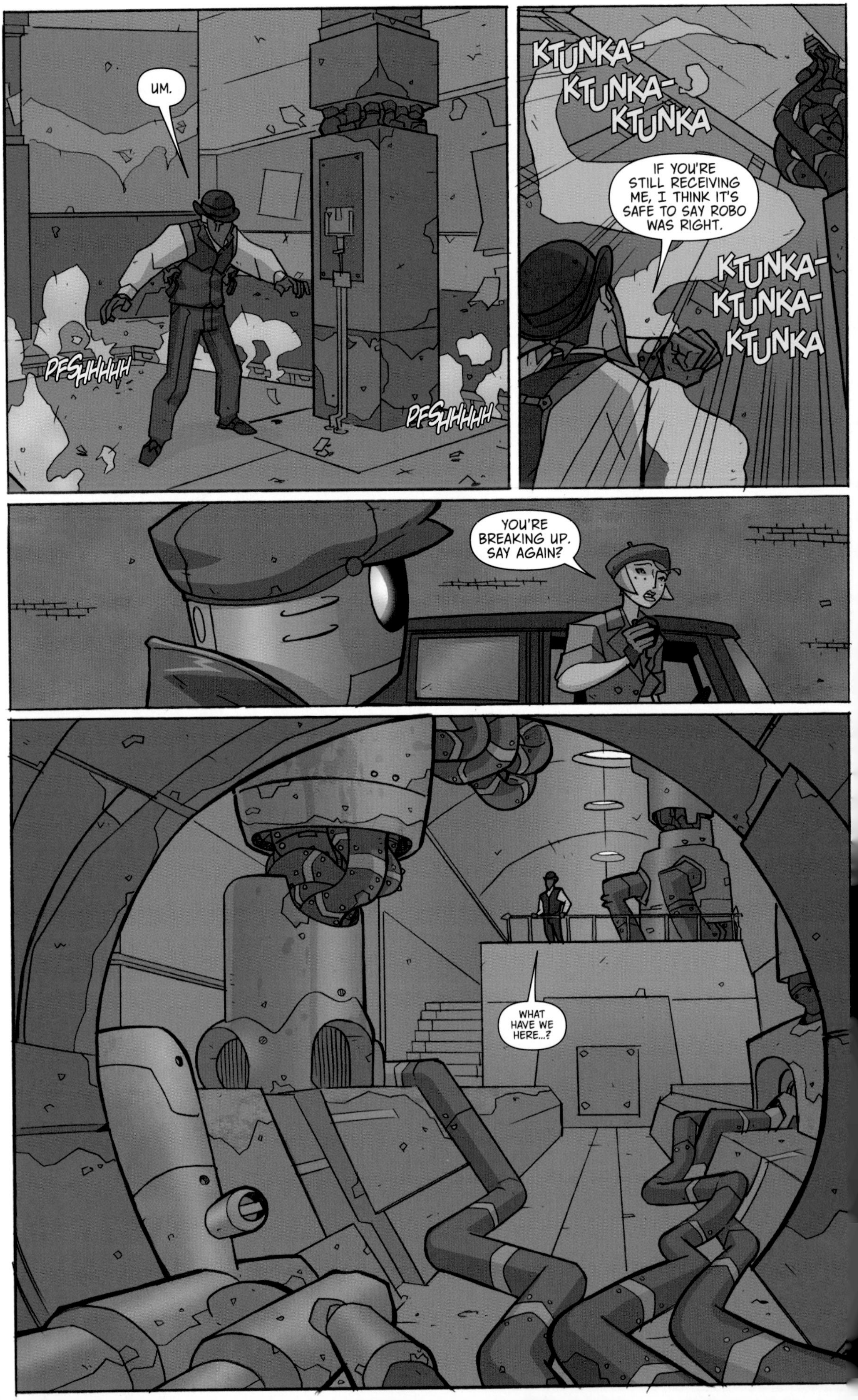
UM.
PFSHHHHH
PFSHHHHH
KTUNKA-KTUNKA-KTUNKA
IF YOU'RE STILL RECEIVING ME, I THINK IT'S SAFE TO SAY ROBO WAS RIGHT.
KTUNKA-KTUNKA-KTUNKA
YOU'RE BREAKING UP. SAY AGAIN?
WHAT HAVE WE HERE...?

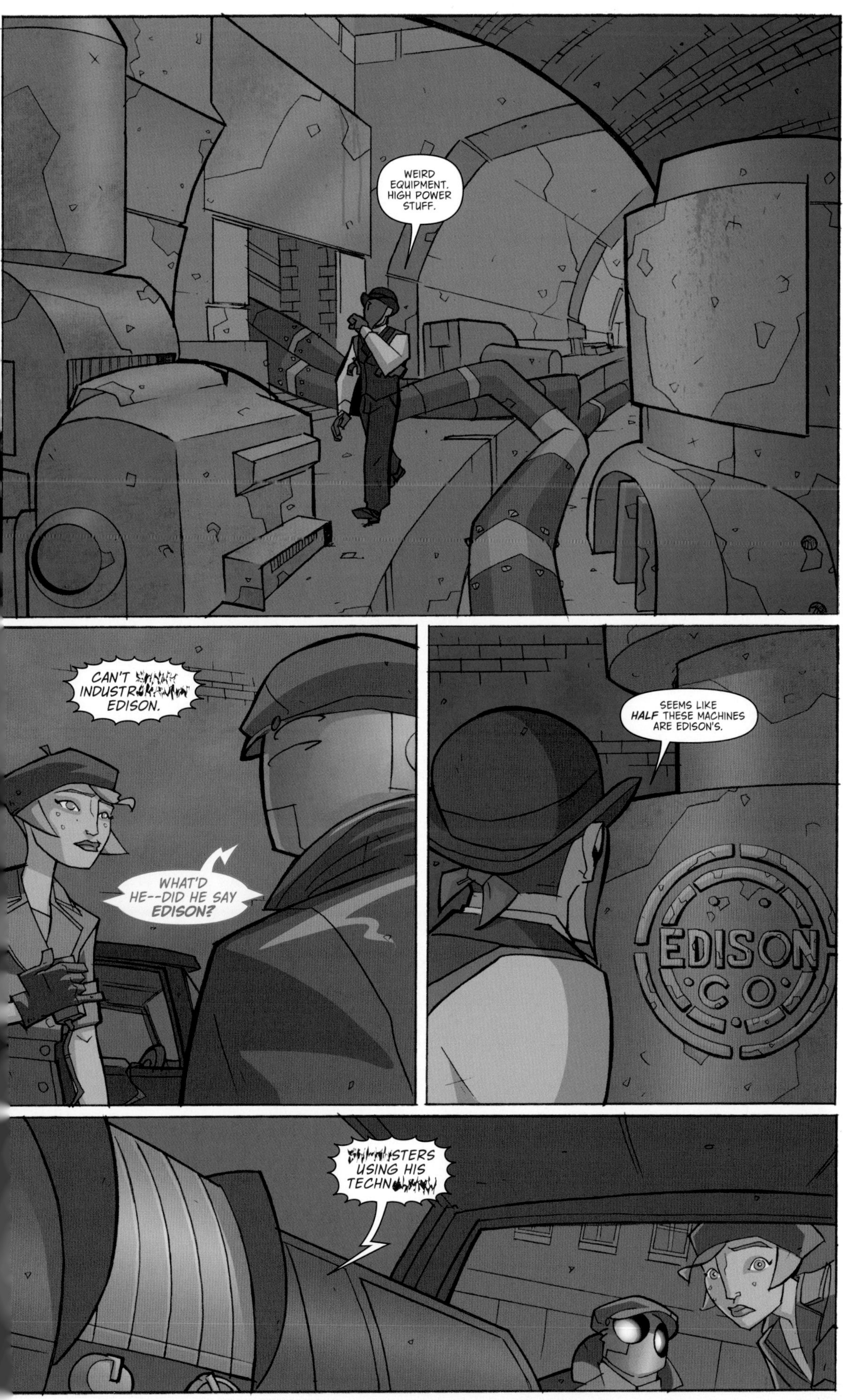
WEIRD EQUIPMENT. HIGH POWER STUFF.
CAN'T INDUSTR EDISON.
WHAT'D HE--DID HE SAY EDISON?
SEEMS LIKE HALF THESE MACHINES ARE EDISON'S.
EDISON C.O.
STERS USING HIS TECHN

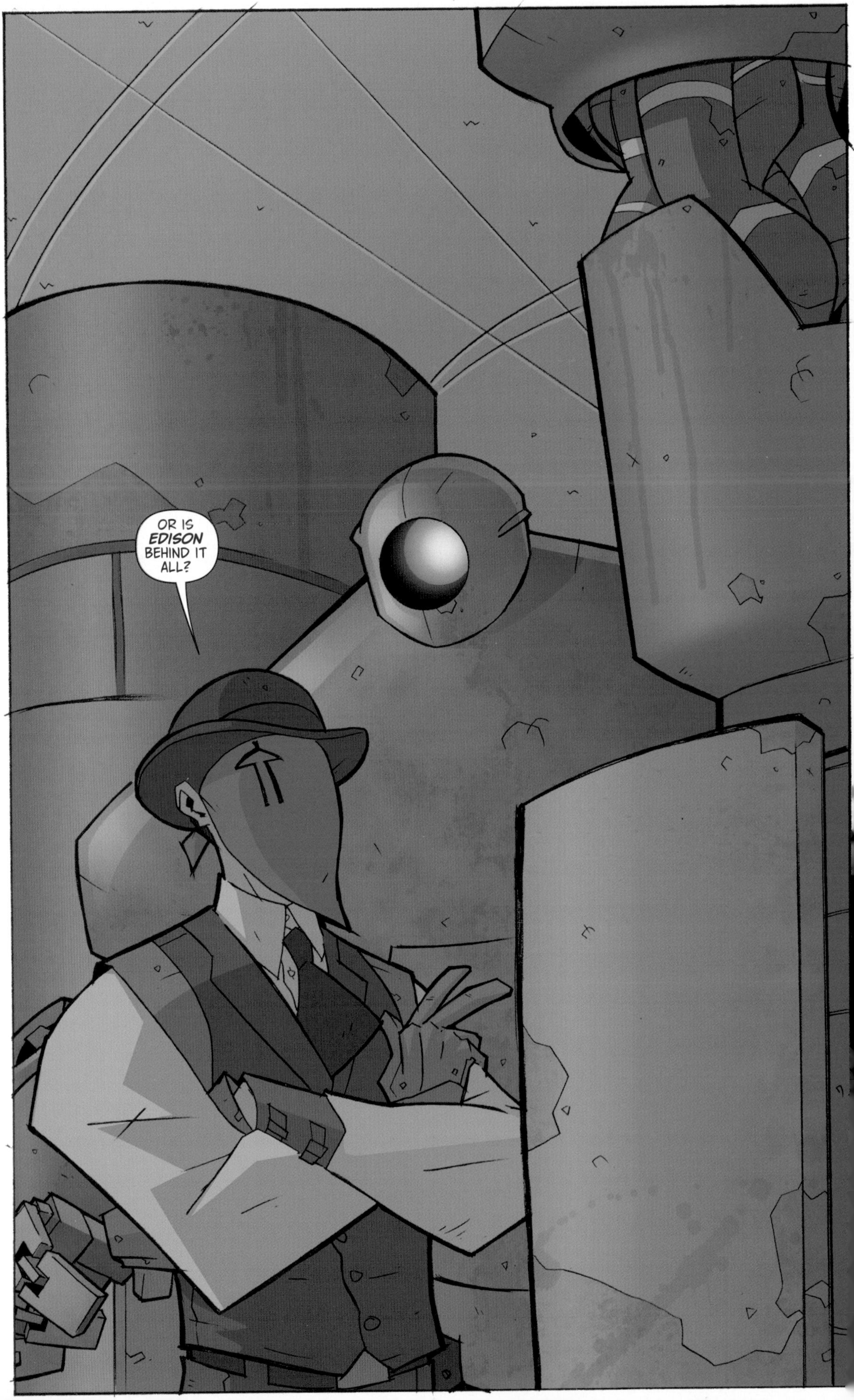
OR IS EDISON BEHIND IT ALL?

THE WAR OF THE CURRENTS

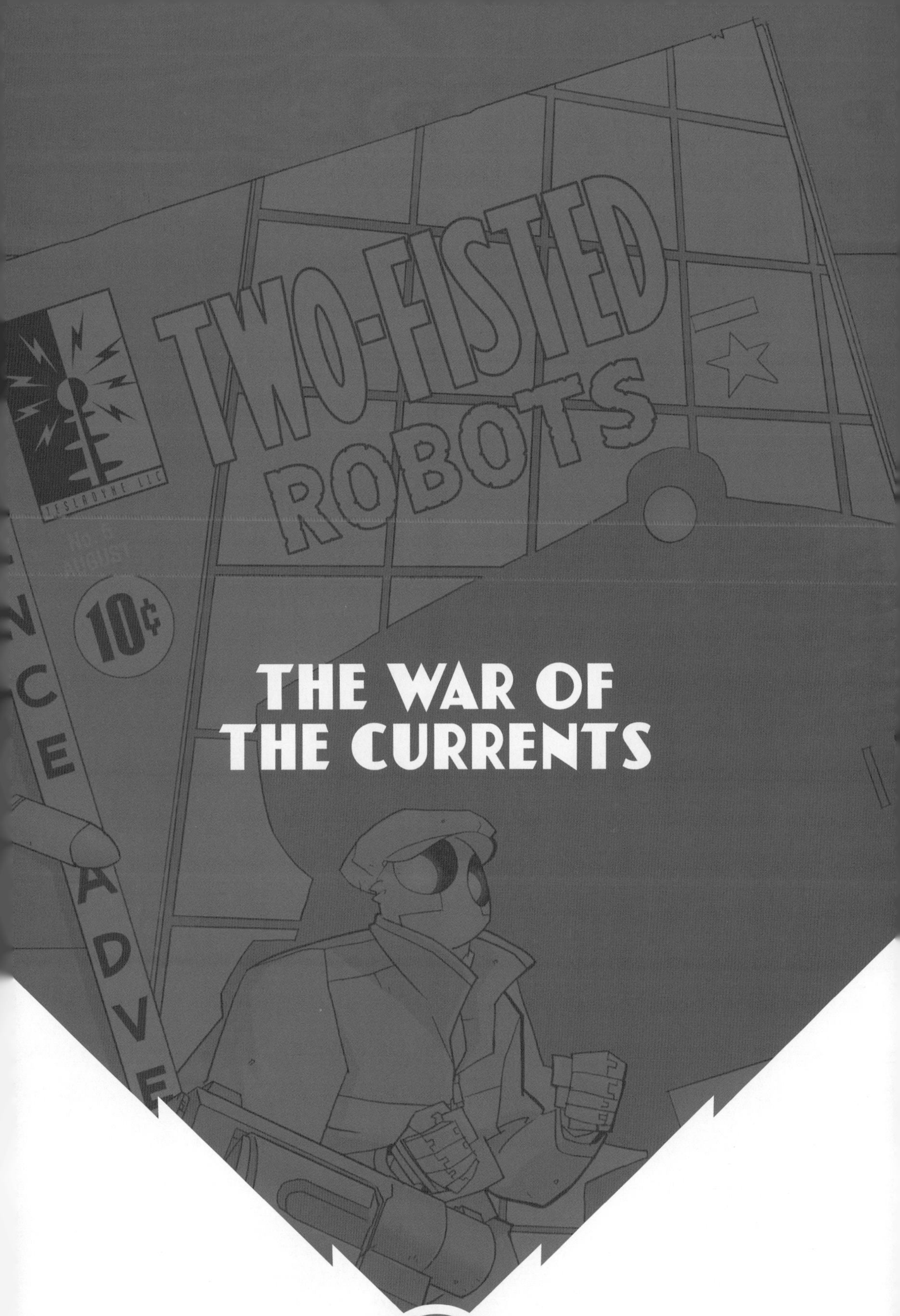
TWO-FISTED ROBOTS
No. 6 AUGUST
10¢

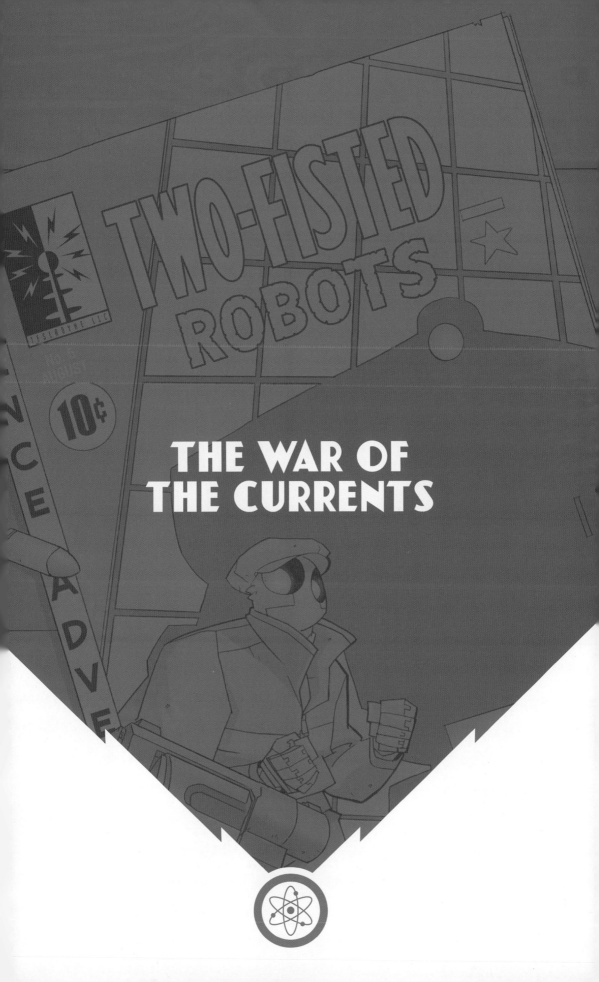

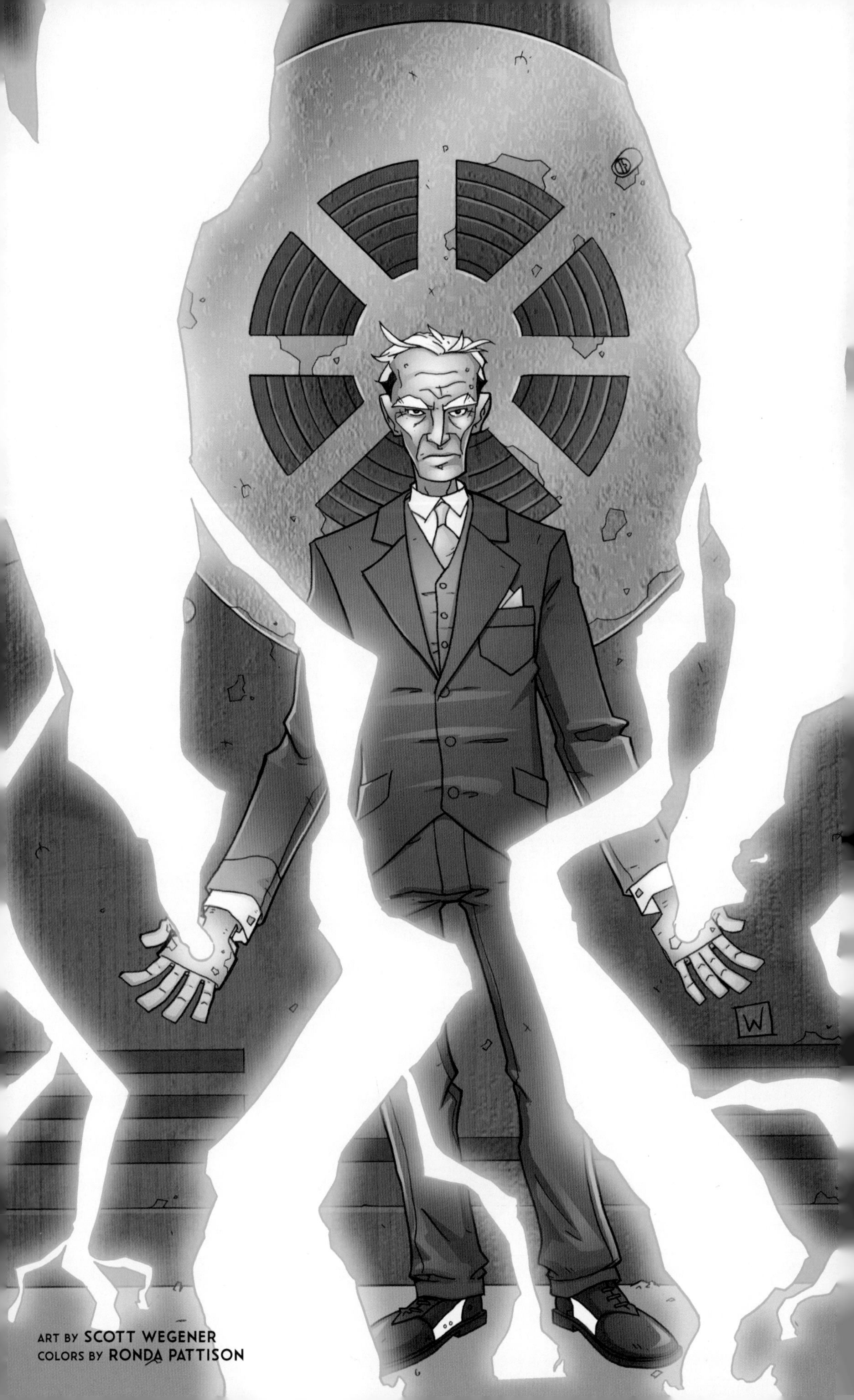

ART BY SCOTT WEGENER
COLORS BY RONDA PATTISON

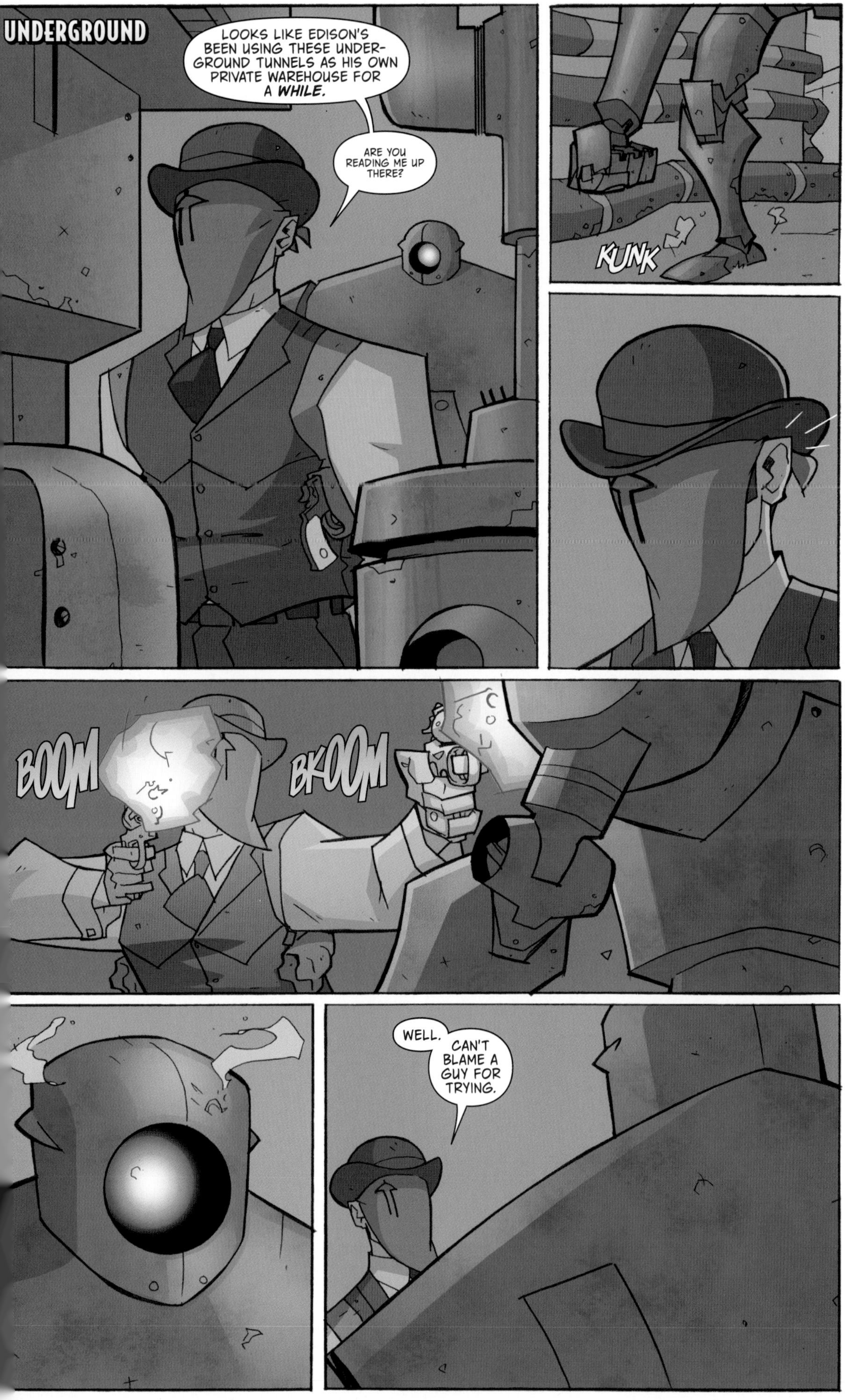
UNDERGROUND
LOOKS LIKE EDISON'S BEEN USING THESE UNDER-GROUND TUNNELS AS HIS OWN PRIVATE WAREHOUSE FOR A *WHILE.*
ARE YOU READING ME UP THERE?
KUNK
BOOM
BKOOM
WELL.
CAN'T BLAME A GUY FOR TRYING.

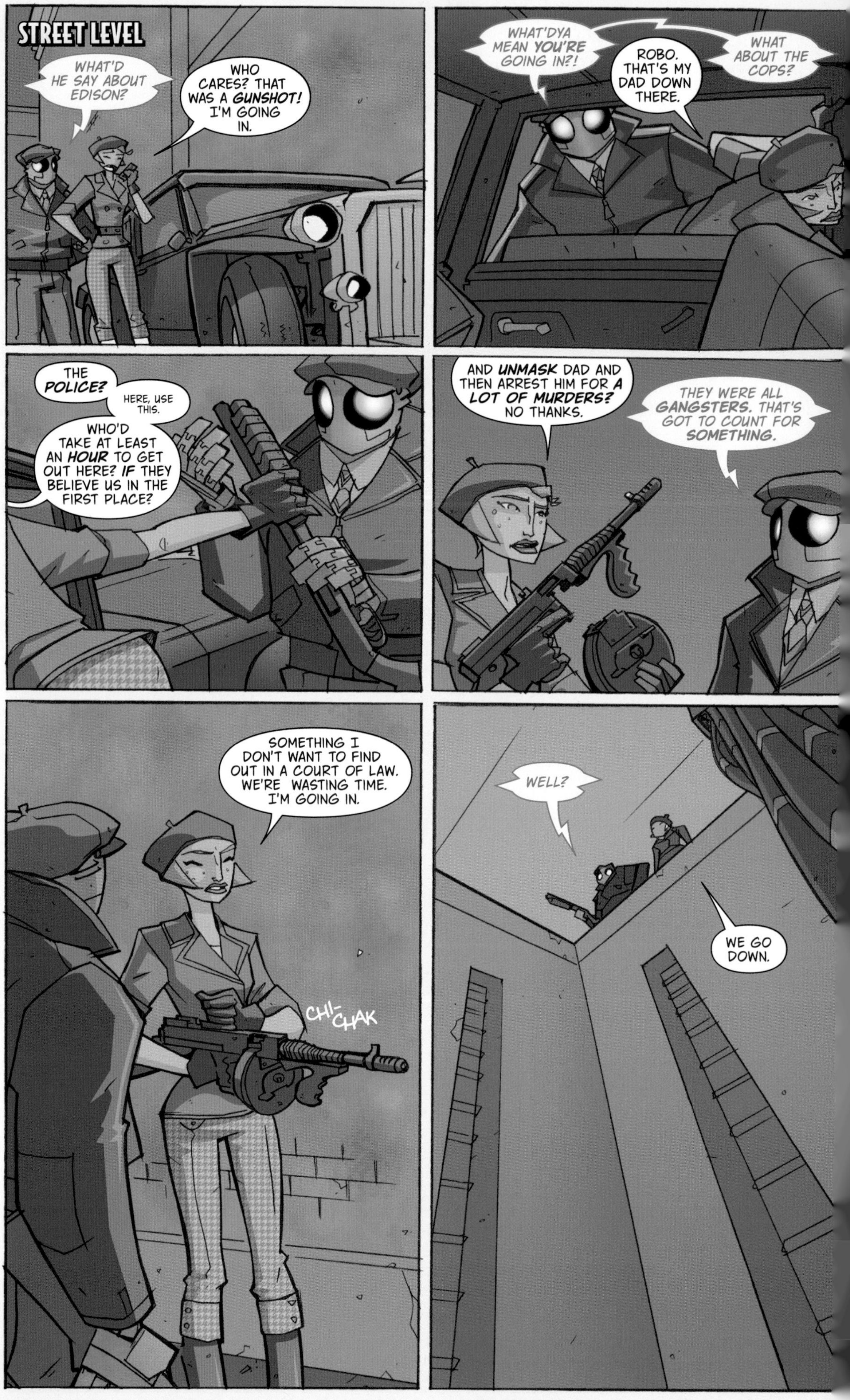
STREET LEVEL
WHAT'D HE SAY ABOUT EDISON?
WHO CARES? THAT WAS A GUNSHOT! I'M GOING IN.
WHAT'DYA MEAN YOU'RE GOING IN?!
ROBO. THAT'S MY DAD DOWN THERE.
WHAT ABOUT THE COPS?
THE POLICE?
HERE, USE THIS.
WHO'D TAKE AT LEAST AN HOUR TO GET OUT HERE? IF THEY BELIEVE US IN THE FIRST PLACE?
AND UNMASK DAD AND THEN ARREST HIM FOR A LOT OF MURDERS? NO THANKS.
THEY WERE ALL GANGSTERS. THAT'S GOT TO COUNT FOR SOMETHING.
SOMETHING I DON'T WANT TO FIND OUT IN A COURT OF LAW. WE'RE WASTING TIME. I'M GOING IN.
CHI-CHAK
WELL?
WE GO DOWN.

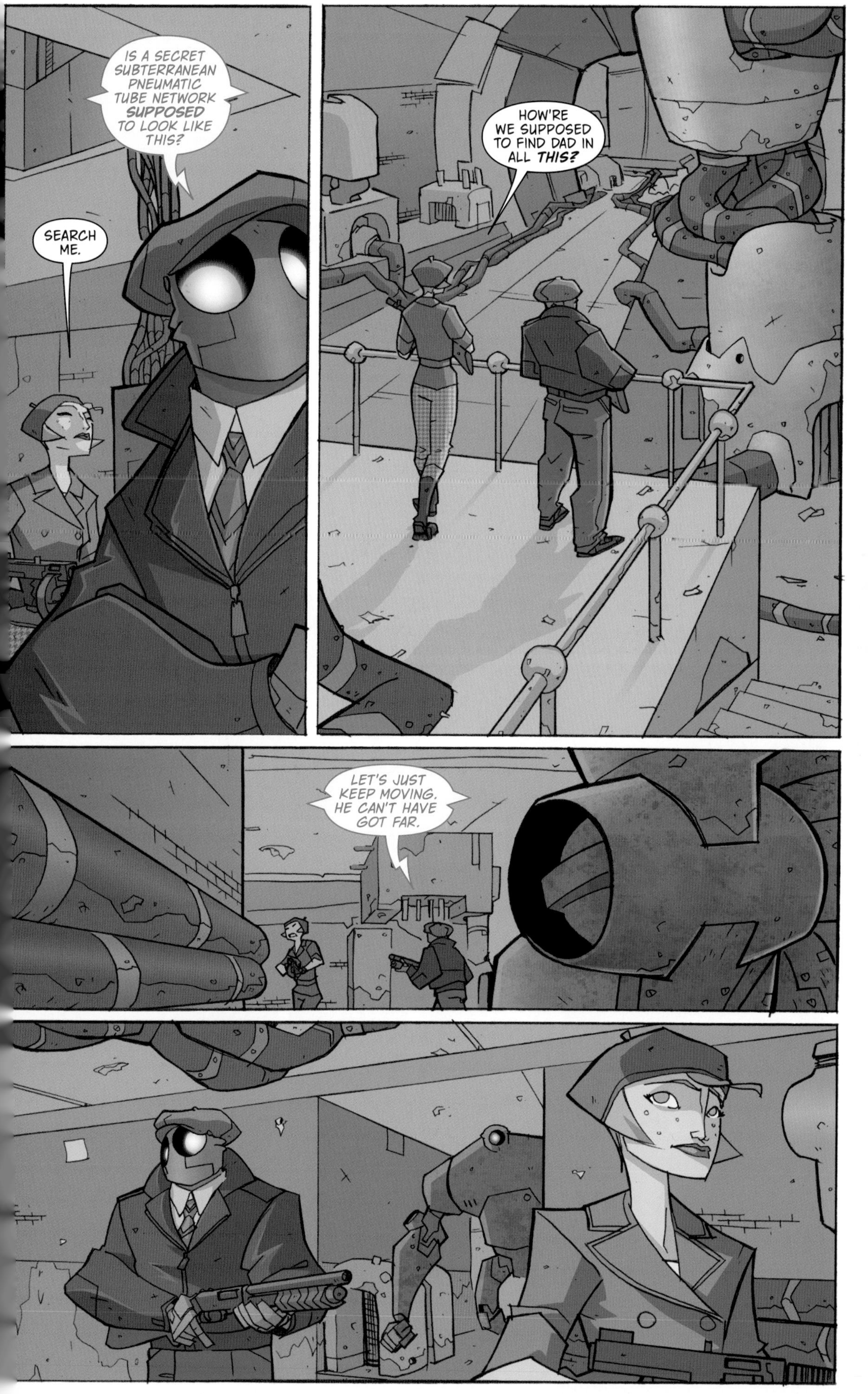
IS A SECRET SUBTERRANEAN PNEUMATIC TUBE NETWORK **SUPPOSED** TO LOOK LIKE THIS?
SEARCH ME.
HOW'RE WE SUPPOSED TO FIND DAD IN ALL **THIS?**
LET'S JUST KEEP MOVING. HE CAN'T HAVE GOT FAR.

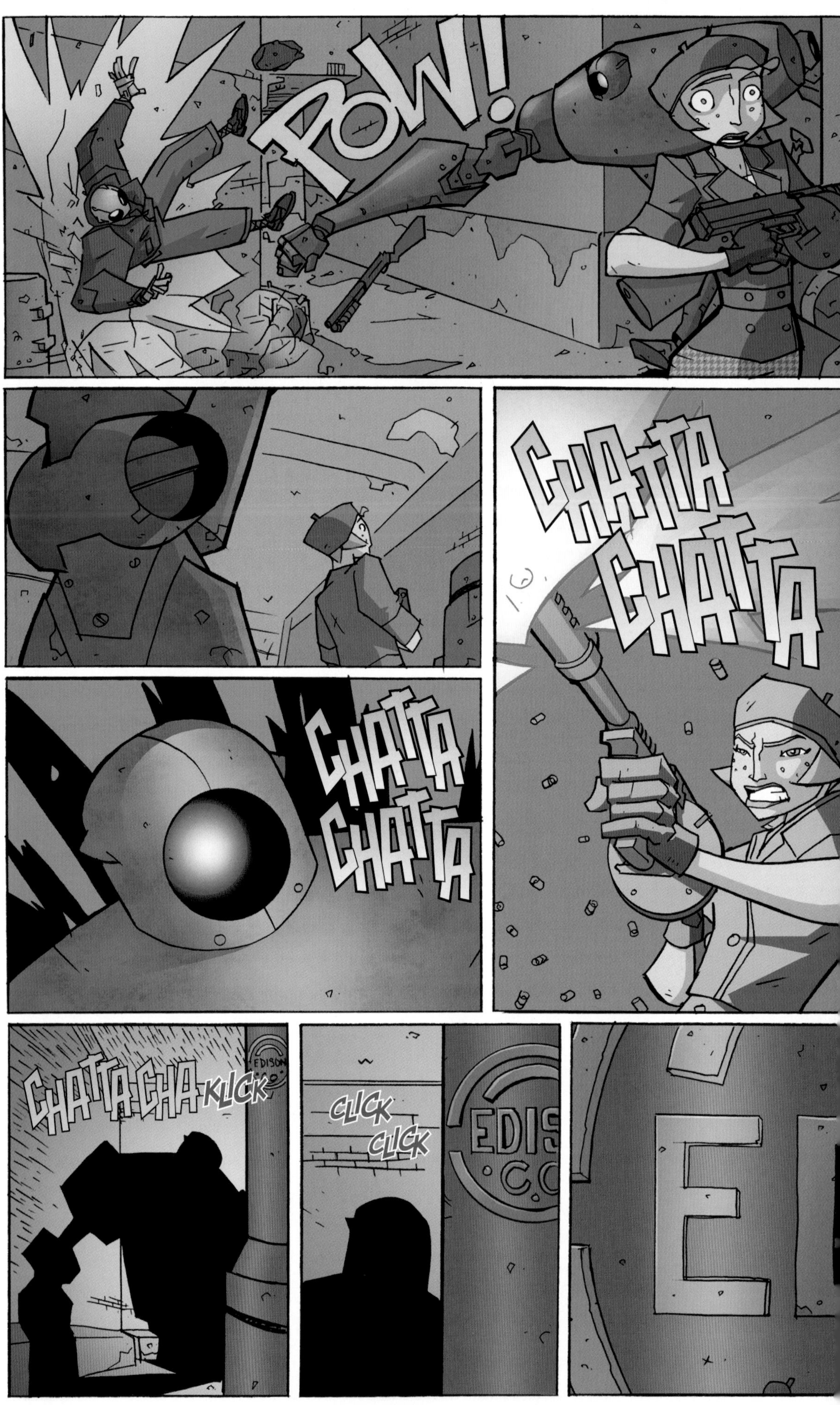
POW!
CHATTA
CHATTA
CHATTA
CHATTA
CHATTA-CHA KLICK
EDISON
CLICK
CLICK
EDIS
C.O

MEANWHILE...

KZZZK

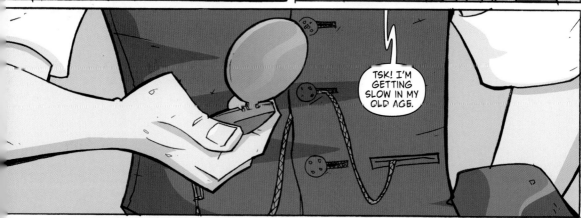

TSK! I'M GETTING SLOW IN MY OLD AGE.

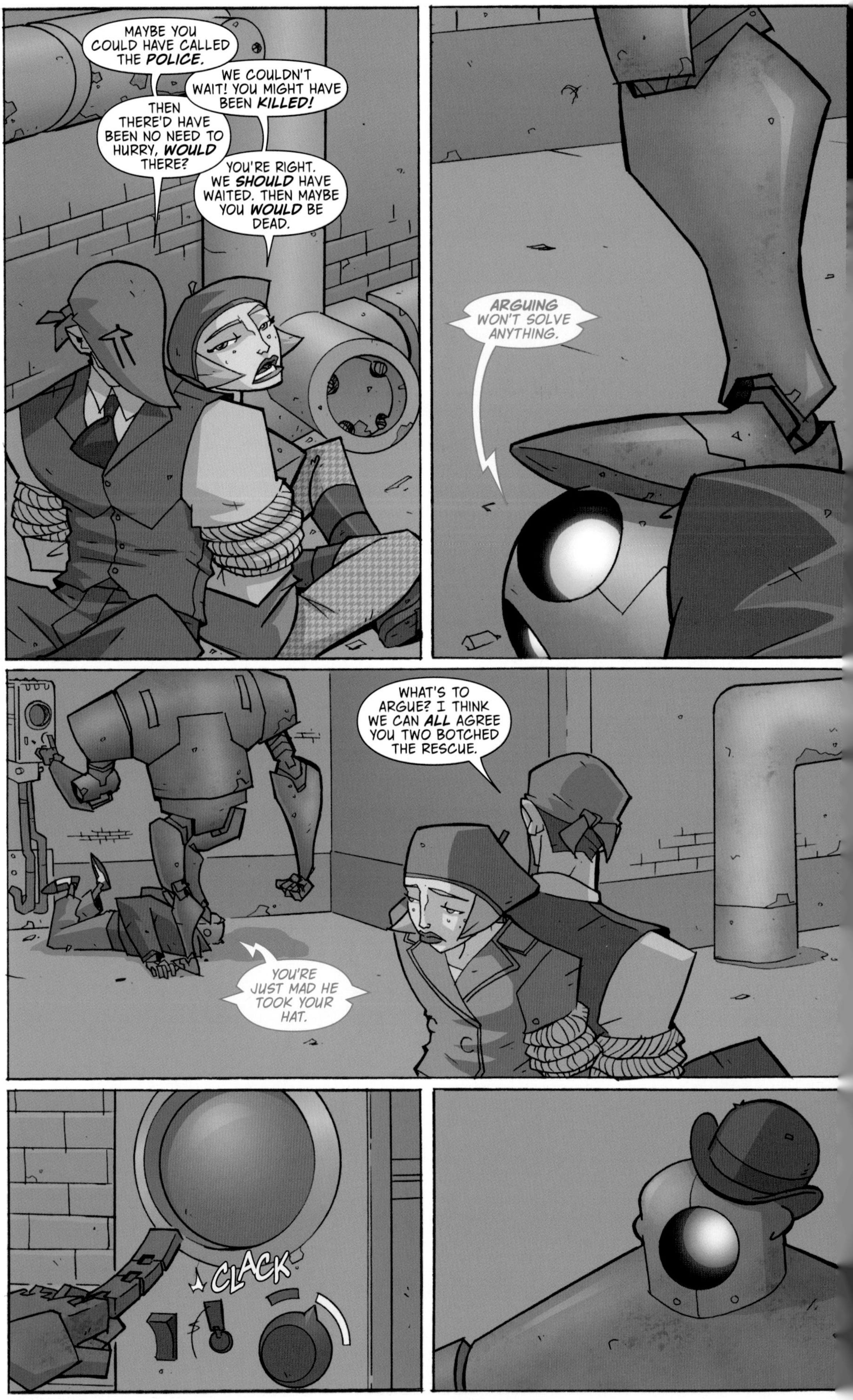

MAYBE YOU COULD HAVE CALLED THE **POLICE.**
WE COULDN'T WAIT! YOU MIGHT HAVE BEEN **KILLED!**
THEN THERE'D HAVE BEEN NO NEED TO HURRY, **WOULD** THERE?
YOU'RE RIGHT. WE **SHOULD** HAVE WAITED. THEN MAYBE YOU **WOULD** BE DEAD.
ARGUING WON'T SOLVE ANYTHING.
WHAT'S TO ARGUE? I THINK WE CAN **ALL** AGREE YOU TWO BOTCHED THE RESCUE.
YOU'RE JUST MAD HE TOOK YOUR HAT.
CLACK

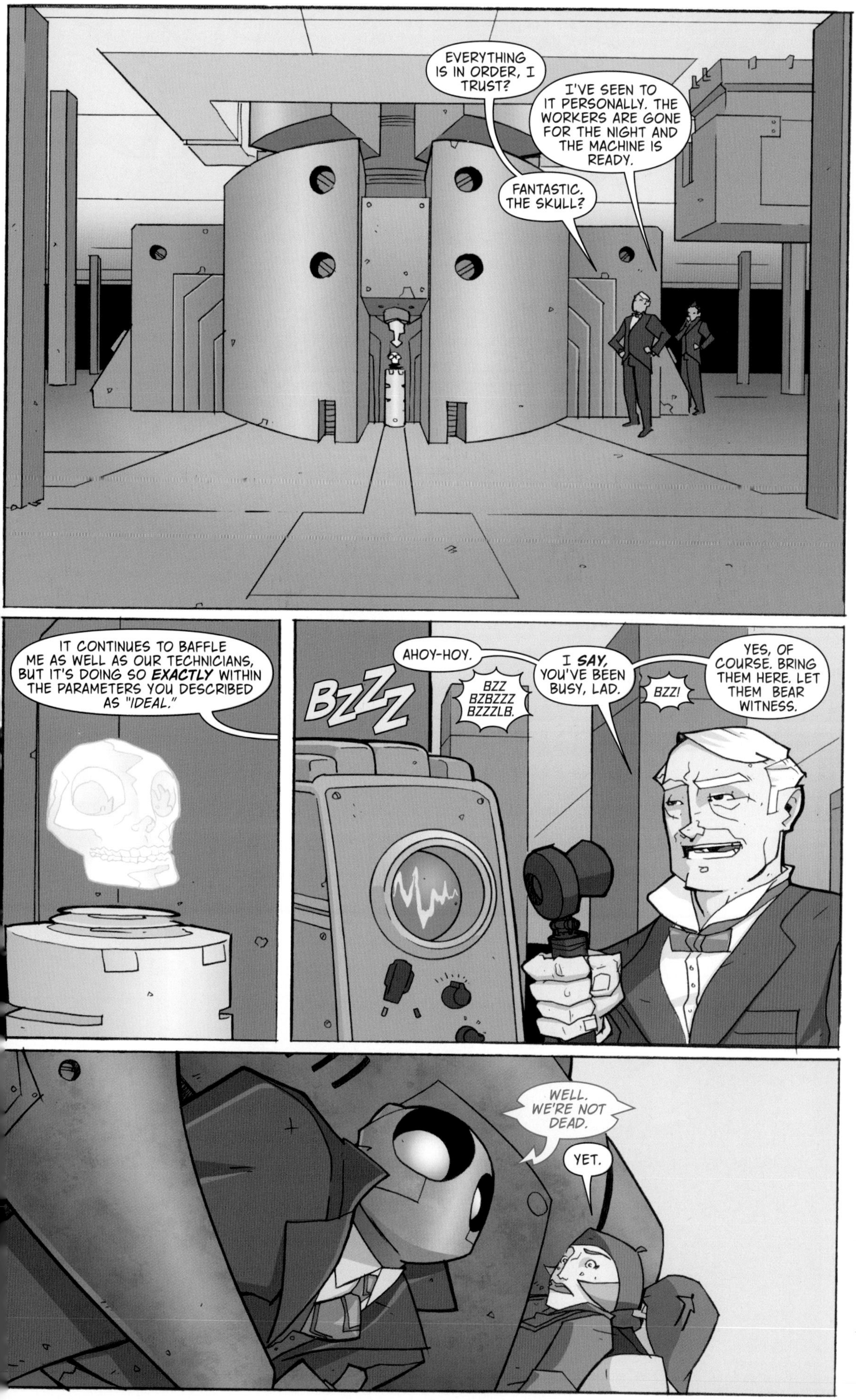
EVERYTHING IS IN ORDER, I TRUST?
I'VE SEEN TO IT PERSONALLY. THE WORKERS ARE GONE FOR THE NIGHT AND THE MACHINE IS READY.
FANTASTIC. THE SKULL?
IT CONTINUES TO BAFFLE ME AS WELL AS OUR TECHNICIANS, BUT IT'S DOING SO EXACTLY WITHIN THE PARAMETERS YOU DESCRIBED AS "IDEAL."
BZZZ
AHOY-HOY.
BZZ BZBZZZ BZZZLB.
I SAY, YOU'VE BEEN BUSY, LAD.
BZZ!
YES, OF COURSE. BRING THEM HERE. LET THEM BEAR WITNESS.
WELL. WE'RE NOT DEAD.
YET.

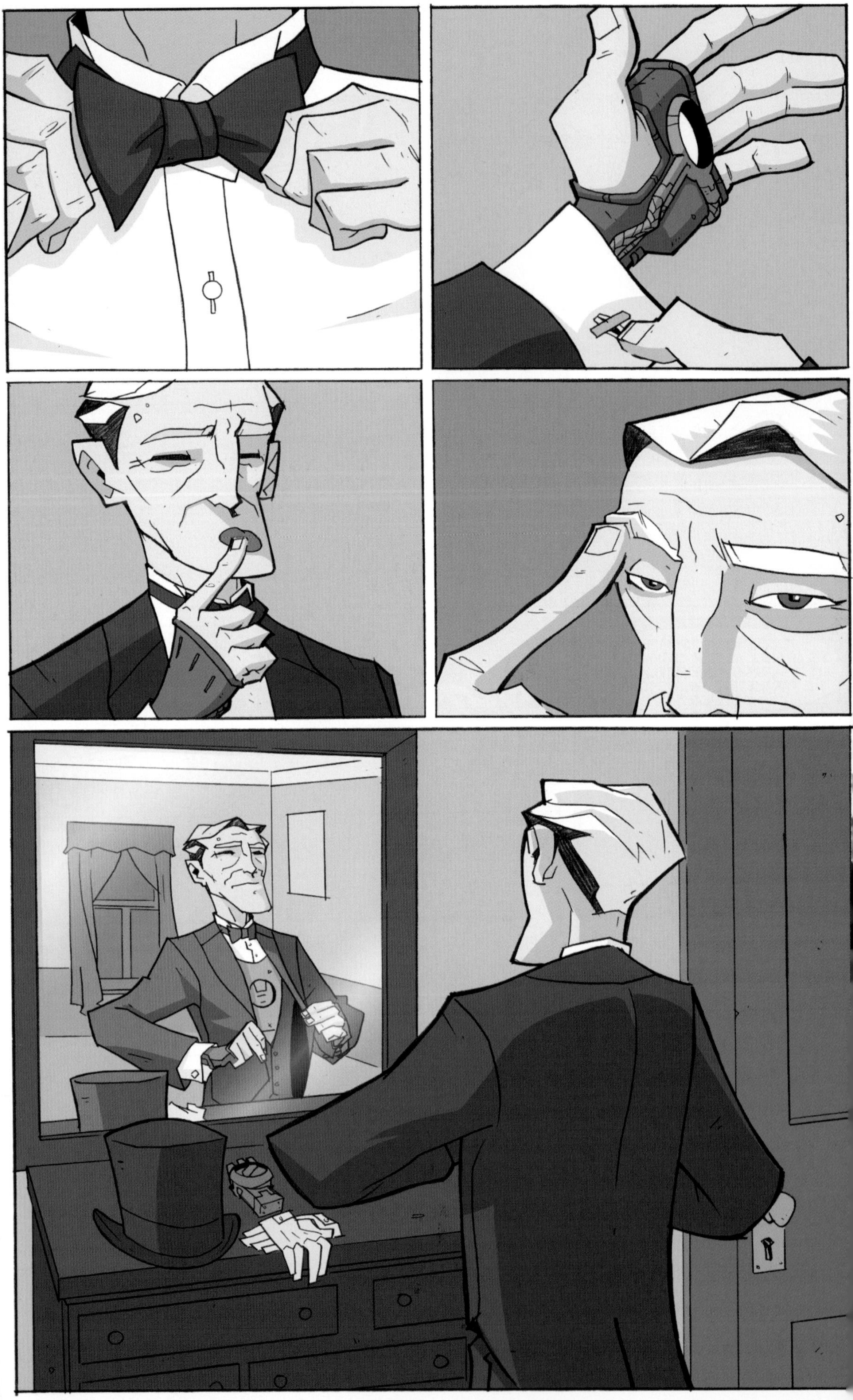

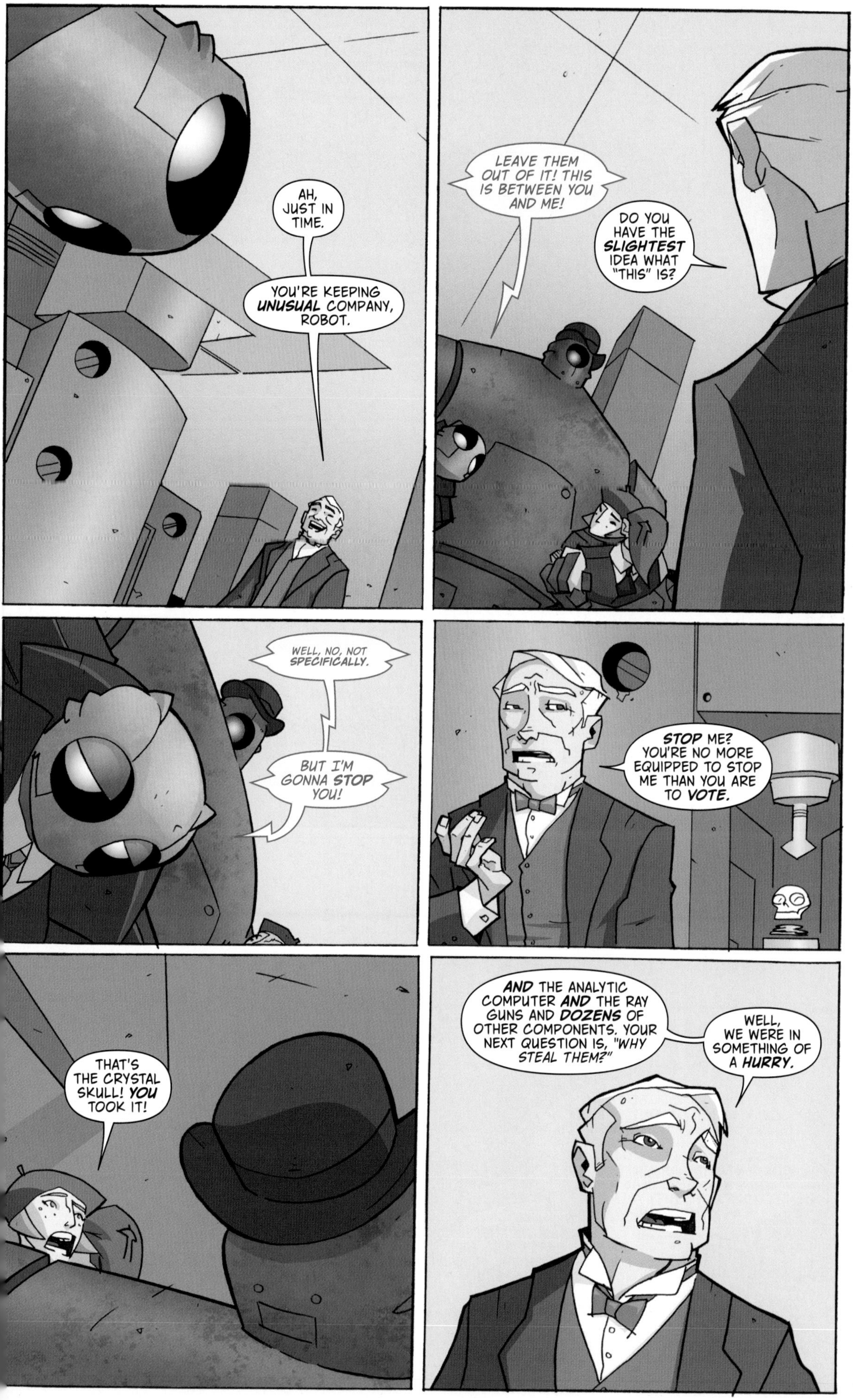
AH, JUST IN TIME.
YOU'RE KEEPING UNUSUAL COMPANY, ROBOT.
LEAVE THEM OUT OF IT! THIS IS BETWEEN YOU AND ME!
DO YOU HAVE THE SLIGHTEST IDEA WHAT "THIS" IS?
WELL, NO, NOT SPECIFICALLY.
BUT I'M GONNA STOP YOU!
STOP ME? YOU'RE NO MORE EQUIPPED TO STOP ME THAN YOU ARE TO VOTE.
THAT'S THE CRYSTAL SKULL! YOU TOOK IT!
AND THE ANALYTIC COMPUTER AND THE RAY GUNS AND DOZENS OF OTHER COMPONENTS. YOUR NEXT QUESTION IS, "WHY STEAL THEM?"
WELL, WE WERE IN SOMETHING OF A HURRY.

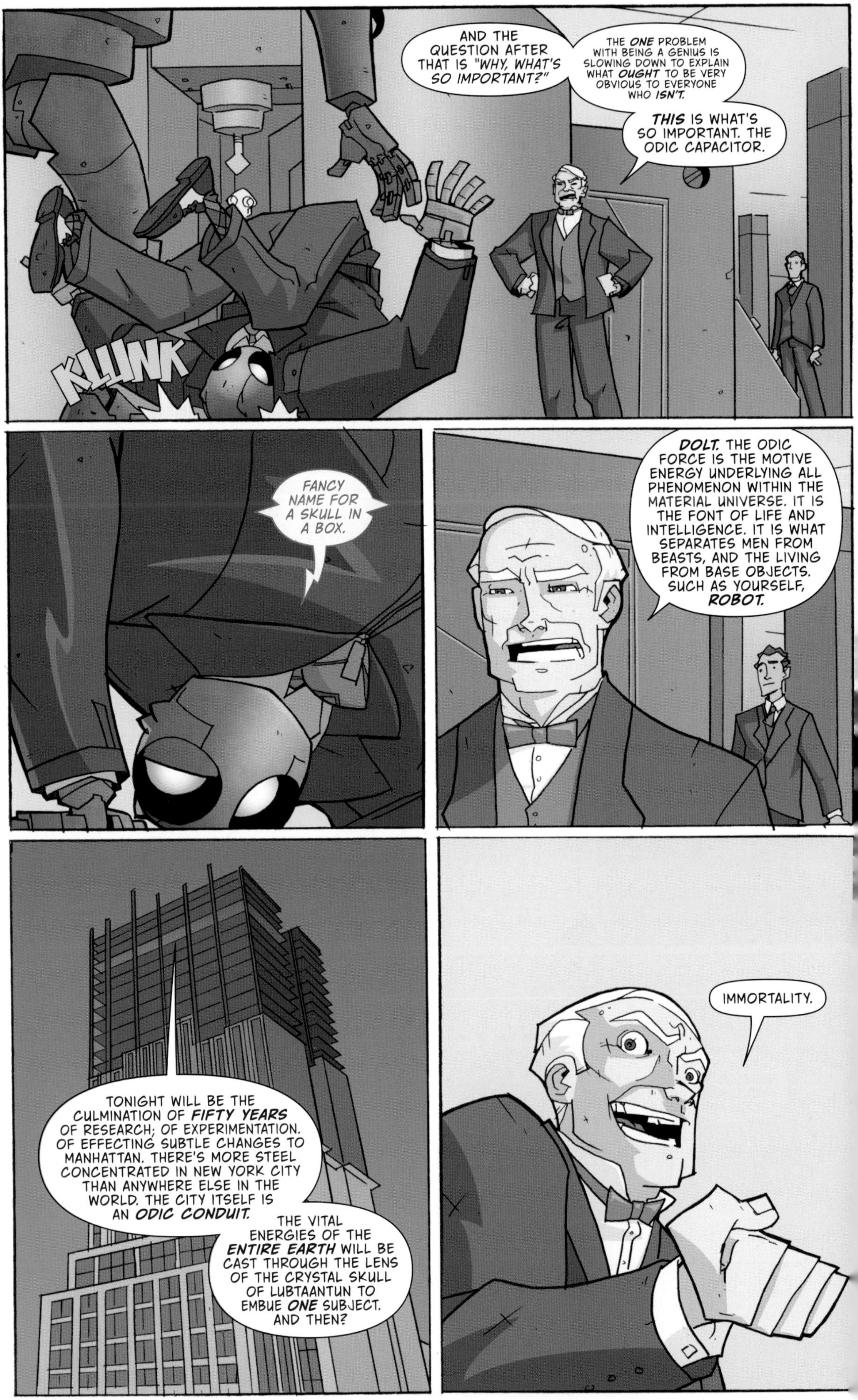
AND THE QUESTION AFTER THAT IS "WHY, WHAT'S SO IMPORTANT?"
THE ONE PROBLEM WITH BEING A GENIUS IS SLOWING DOWN TO EXPLAIN WHAT OUGHT TO BE VERY OBVIOUS TO EVERYONE WHO ISN'T.
THIS IS WHAT'S SO IMPORTANT. THE ODIC CAPACITOR.
KLUNK
FANCY NAME FOR A SKULL IN A BOX.
DOLT. THE ODIC FORCE IS THE MOTIVE ENERGY UNDERLYING ALL PHENOMENON WITHIN THE MATERIAL UNIVERSE. IT IS THE FONT OF LIFE AND INTELLIGENCE. IT IS WHAT SEPARATES MEN FROM BEASTS, AND THE LIVING FROM BASE OBJECTS. SUCH AS YOURSELF, ROBOT.
TONIGHT WILL BE THE CULMINATION OF FIFTY YEARS OF RESEARCH; OF EXPERIMENTATION. OF EFFECTING SUBTLE CHANGES TO MANHATTAN. THERE'S MORE STEEL CONCENTRATED IN NEW YORK CITY THAN ANYWHERE ELSE IN THE WORLD. THE CITY ITSELF IS AN ODIC CONDUIT.
THE VITAL ENERGIES OF THE ENTIRE EARTH WILL BE CAST THROUGH THE LENS OF THE CRYSTAL SKULL OF LUBTAANTUN TO EMBUE ONE SUBJECT. AND THEN?
IMMORTALITY.

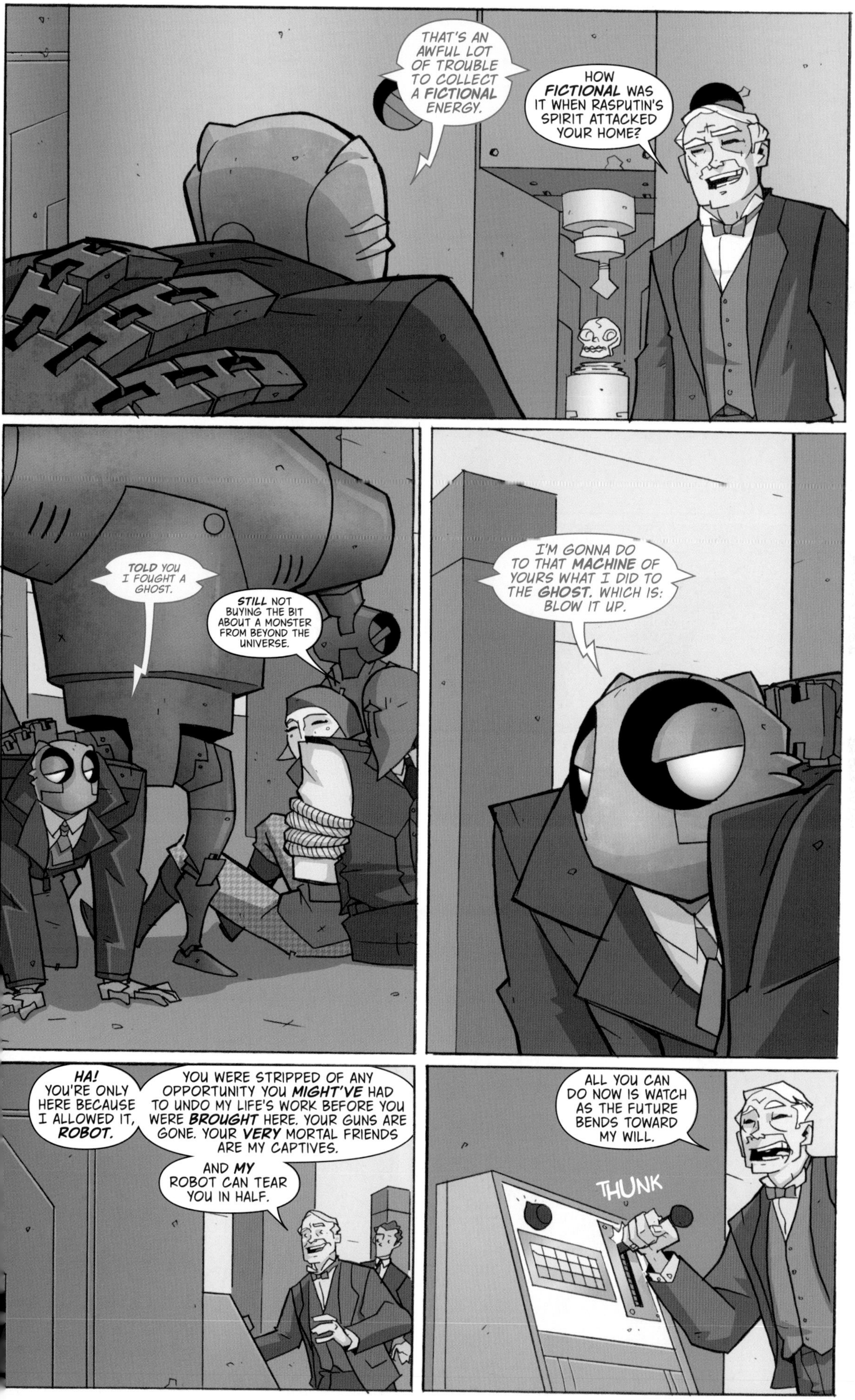
THAT'S AN AWFUL LOT OF TROUBLE TO COLLECT A FICTIONAL ENERGY.
HOW FICTIONAL WAS IT WHEN RASPUTIN'S SPIRIT ATTACKED YOUR HOME?
TOLD YOU I FOUGHT A GHOST.
STILL NOT BUYING THE BIT ABOUT A MONSTER FROM BEYOND THE UNIVERSE.
I'M GONNA DO TO THAT MACHINE OF YOURS WHAT I DID TO THE GHOST. WHICH IS: BLOW IT UP.
HA! YOU'RE ONLY HERE BECAUSE I ALLOWED IT, ROBOT.
YOU WERE STRIPPED OF ANY OPPORTUNITY YOU MIGHT'VE HAD TO UNDO MY LIFE'S WORK BEFORE YOU WERE BROUGHT HERE. YOUR GUNS ARE GONE. YOUR VERY MORTAL FRIENDS ARE MY CAPTIVES.
AND MY ROBOT CAN TEAR YOU IN HALF.
ALL YOU CAN DO NOW IS WATCH AS THE FUTURE BENDS TOWARD MY WILL.
THUNK

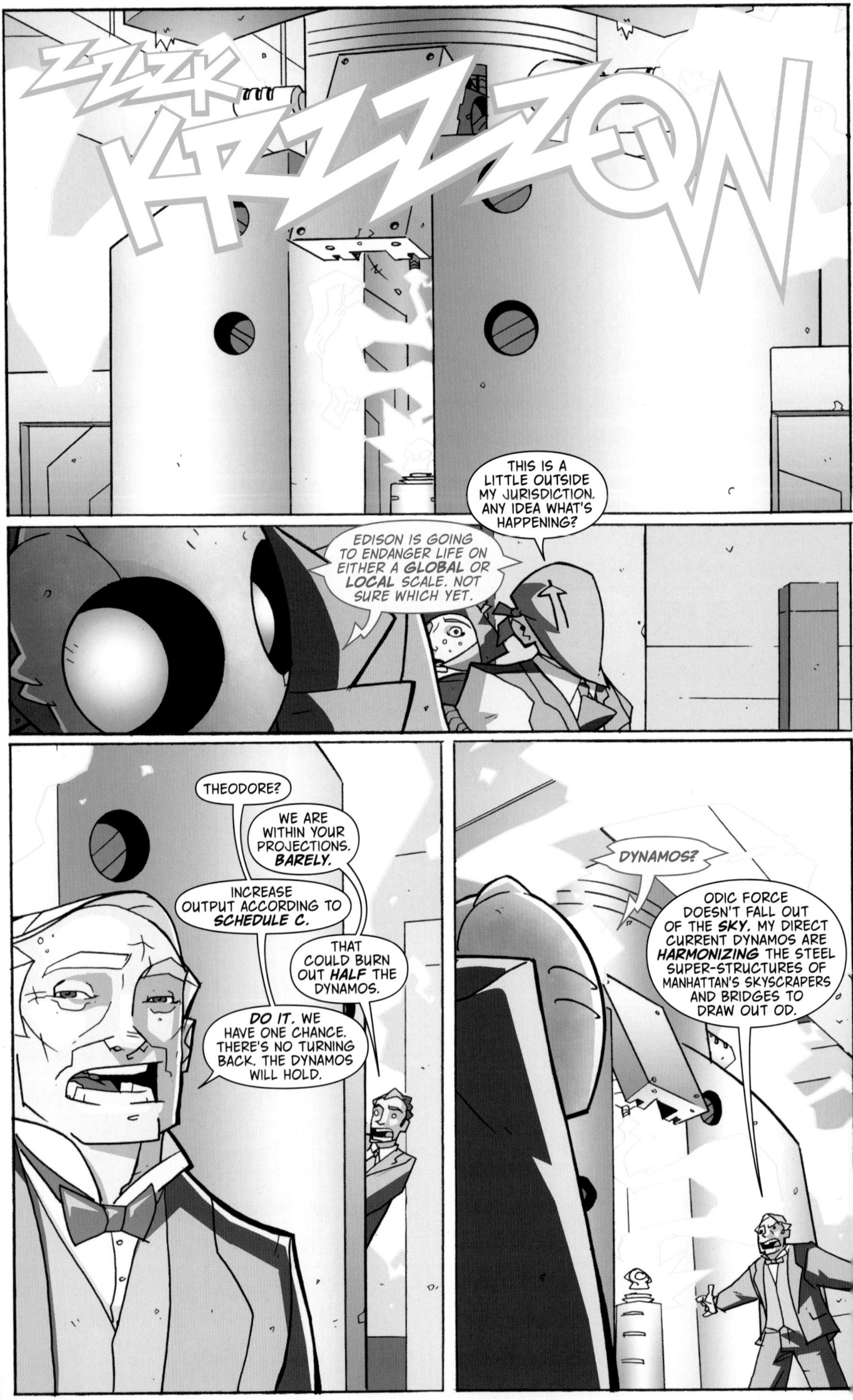
ZZZZK
KRZZZZOW
THIS IS A LITTLE OUTSIDE MY JURISDICTION. ANY IDEA WHAT'S HAPPENING?
EDISON IS GOING TO ENDANGER LIFE ON EITHER A GLOBAL OR LOCAL SCALE. NOT SURE WHICH YET.
THEODORE?
WE ARE WITHIN YOUR PROJECTIONS. BARELY.
INCREASE OUTPUT ACCORDING TO SCHEDULE C.
THAT COULD BURN OUT HALF THE DYNAMOS.
DO IT. WE HAVE ONE CHANCE. THERE'S NO TURNING BACK. THE DYNAMOS WILL HOLD.
DYNAMOS?
ODIC FORCE DOESN'T FALL OUT OF THE SKY. MY DIRECT CURRENT DYNAMOS ARE HARMONIZING THE STEEL SUPER-STRUCTURES OF MANHATTAN'S SKYSCRAPERS AND BRIDGES TO DRAW OUT OD.

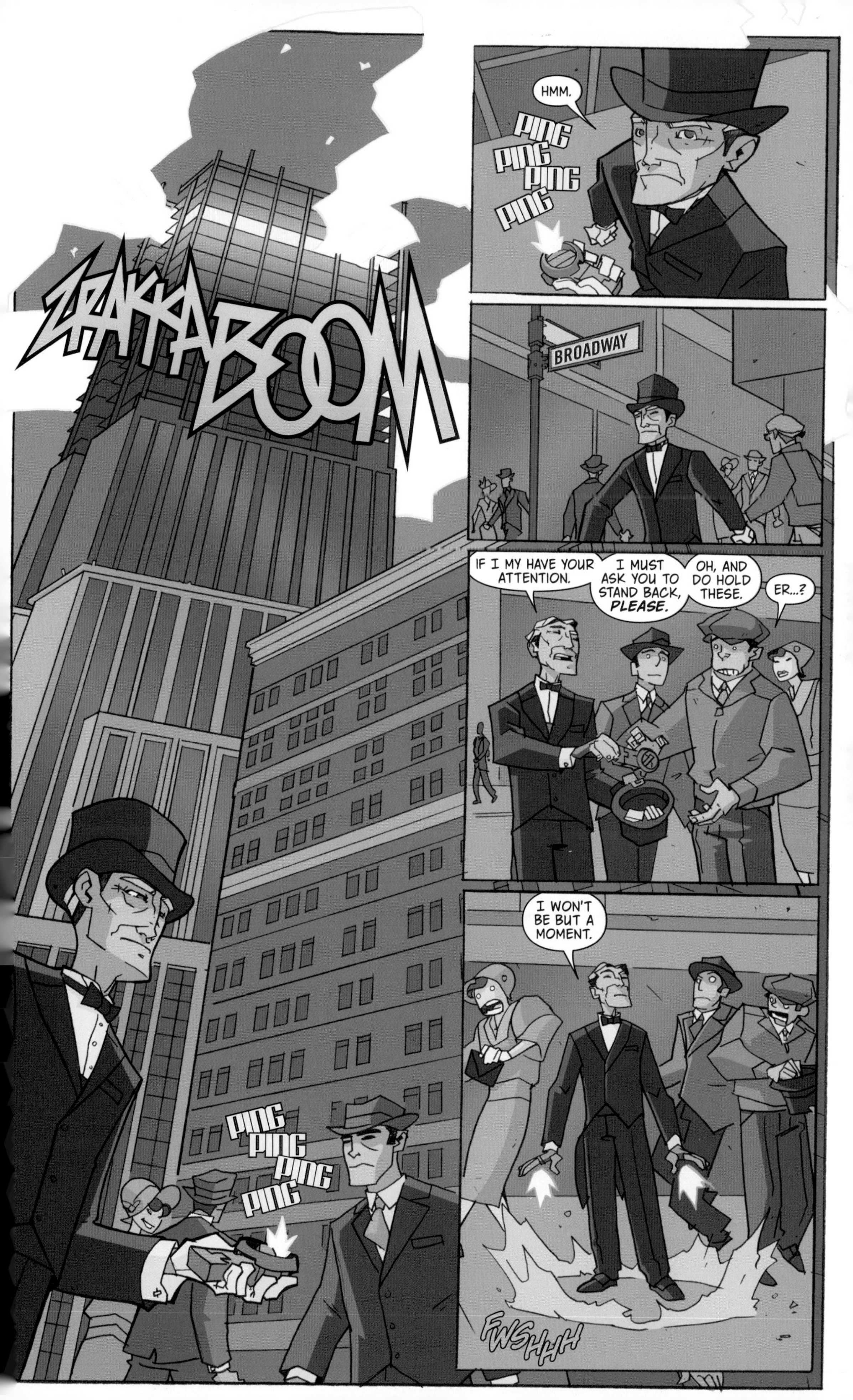
ZRAKKABOOM
PING
PING
PING
PING
HMM.
PING
PING
PING
PING
BROADWAY
IF I MY HAVE YOUR ATTENTION.
I MUST ASK YOU TO STAND BACK, *PLEASE.*
OH, AND DO HOLD THESE.
ER...?
I WON'T BE BUT A MOMENT.
FWSHHH

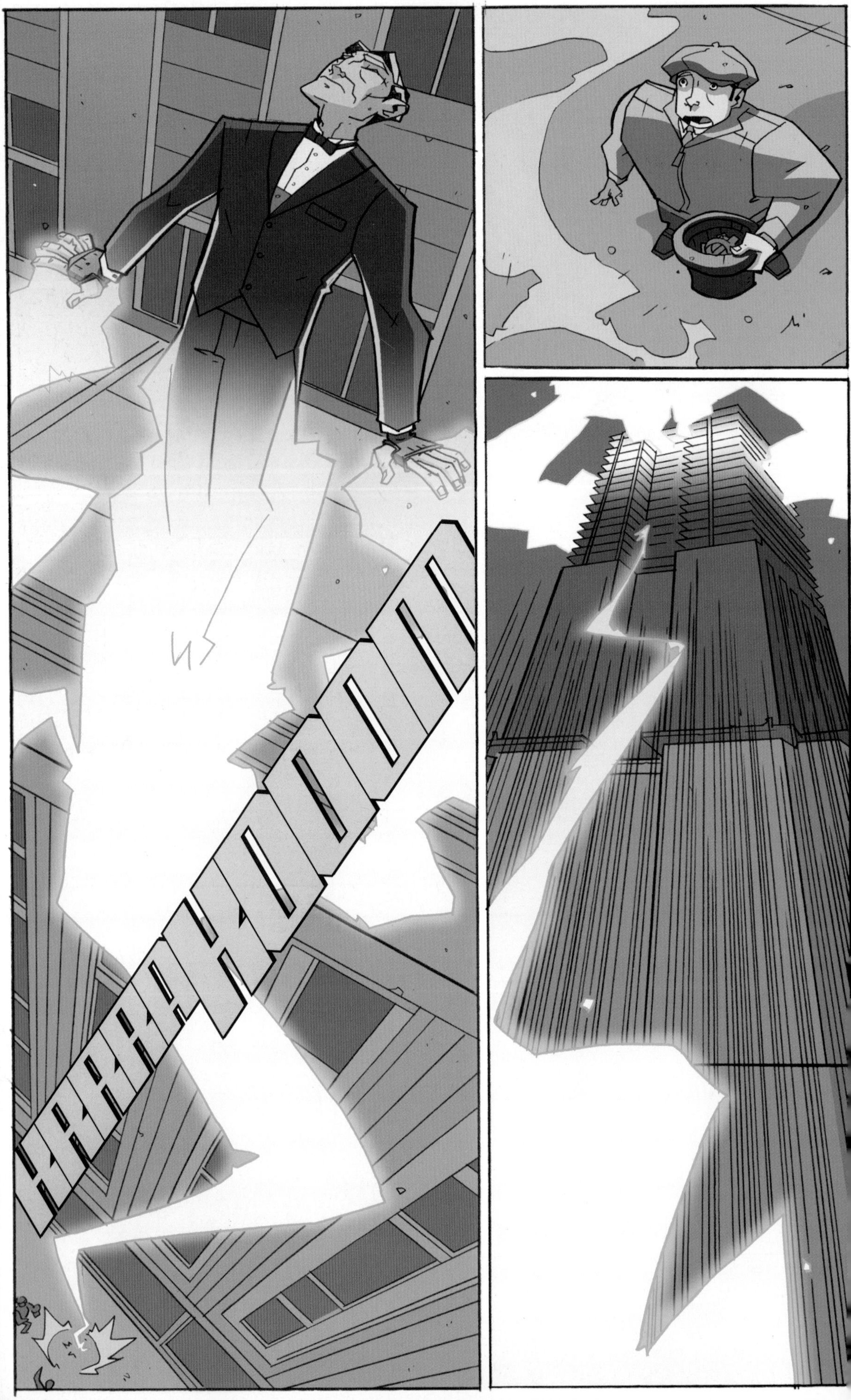
KRRRAKOOOM

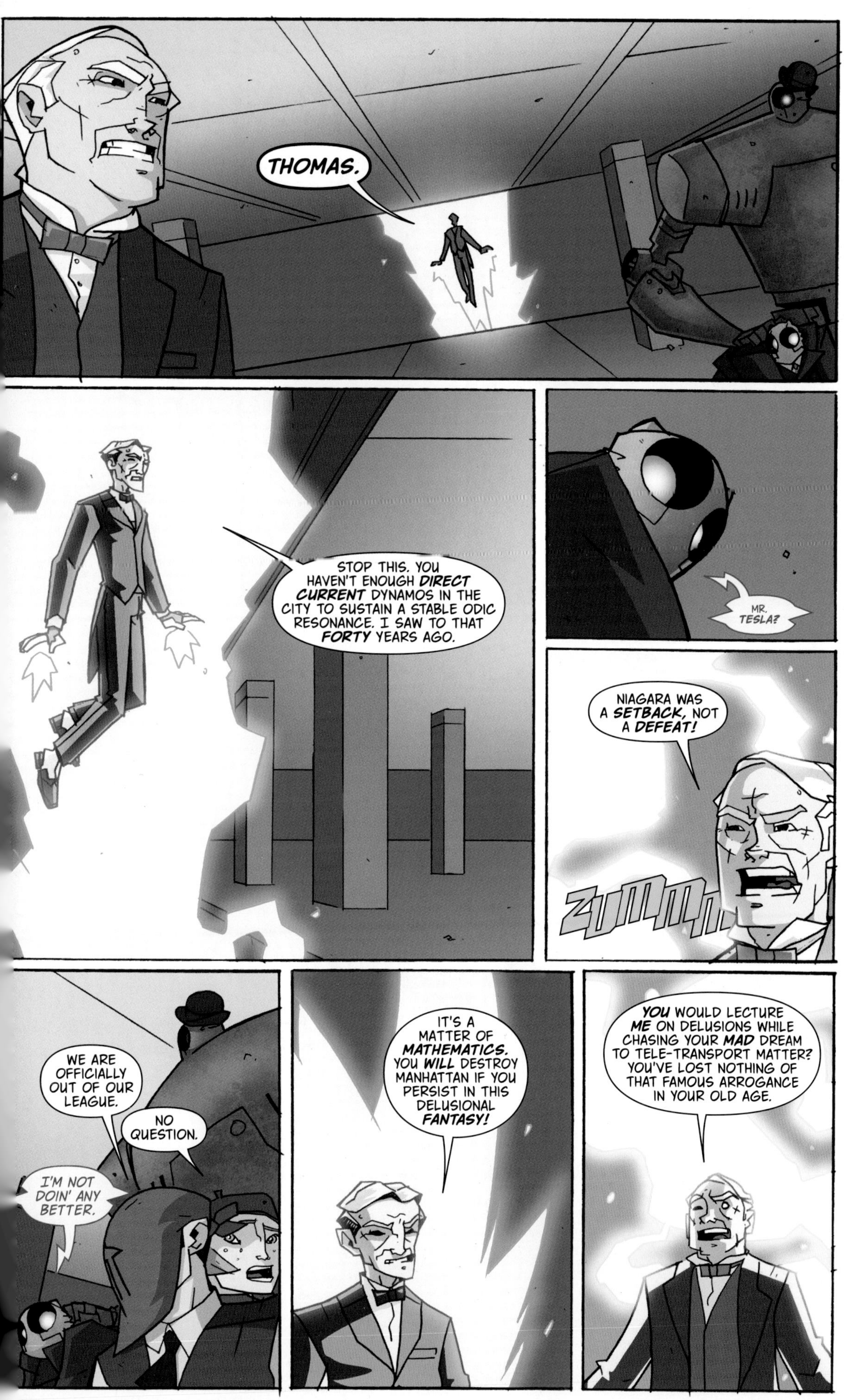
THOMAS.
STOP THIS. YOU HAVEN'T ENOUGH DIRECT CURRENT DYNAMOS IN THE CITY TO SUSTAIN A STABLE ODIC RESONANCE. I SAW TO THAT FORTY YEARS AGO.
MR. TESLA?
NIAGARA WAS A SETBACK, NOT A DEFEAT!
ZUMMM
WE ARE OFFICIALLY OUT OF OUR LEAGUE.
NO QUESTION.
I'M NOT DOIN' ANY BETTER.
IT'S A MATTER OF MATHEMATICS. YOU WILL DESTROY MANHATTAN IF YOU PERSIST IN THIS DELUSIONAL FANTASY!
YOU WOULD LECTURE ME ON DELUSIONS WHILE CHASING YOUR MAD DREAM TO TELE-TRANSPORT MATTER? YOU'VE LOST NOTHING OF THAT FAMOUS ARROGANCE IN YOUR OLD AGE.

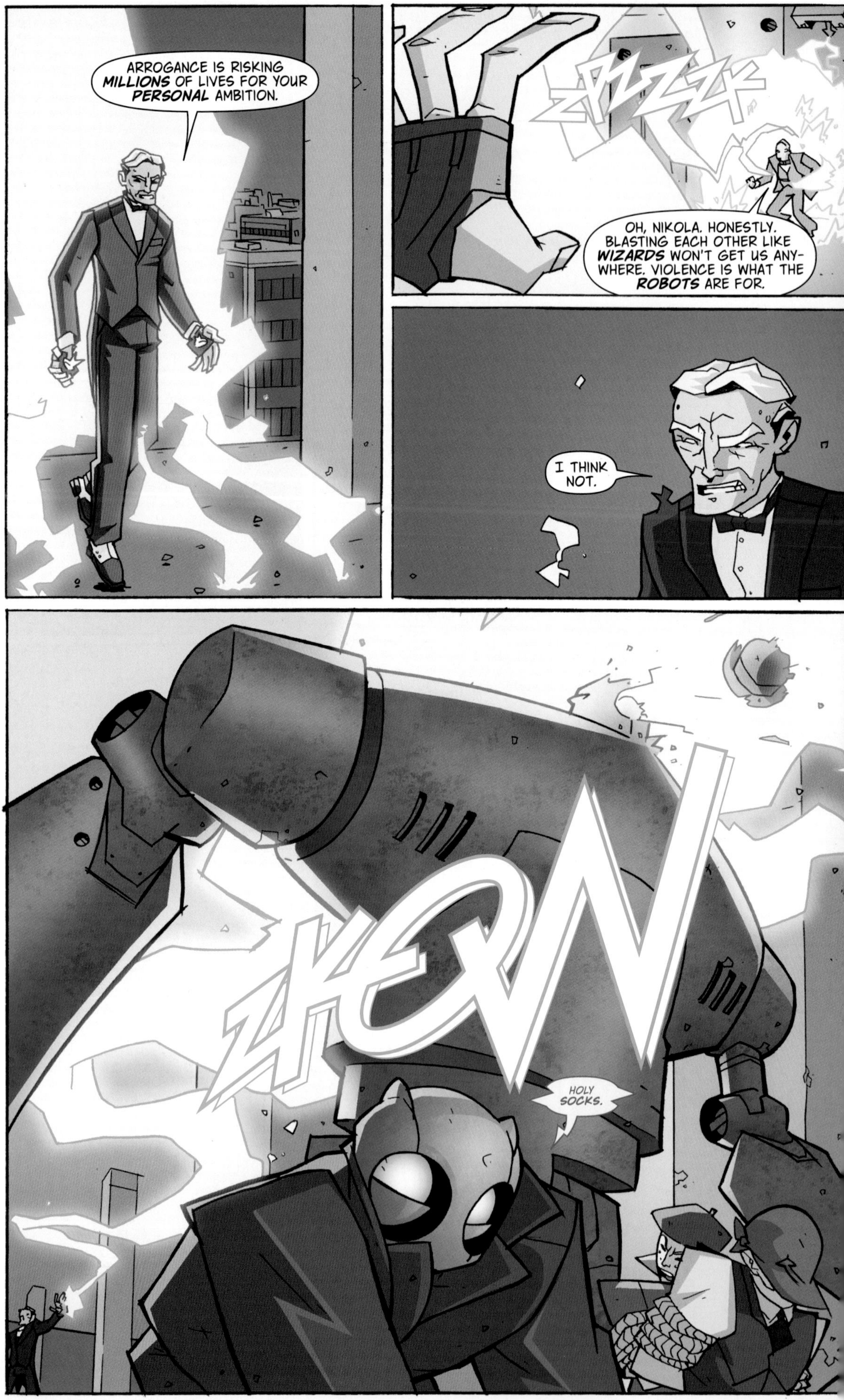
ARROGANCE IS RISKING **MILLIONS** OF LIVES FOR YOUR **PERSONAL** AMBITION.
OH, NIKOLA. HONESTLY. BLASTING EACH OTHER LIKE **WIZARDS** WON'T GET US ANYWHERE. VIOLENCE IS WHAT THE **ROBOTS** ARE FOR.
I THINK NOT.
ZKOW
HOLY SOCKS.

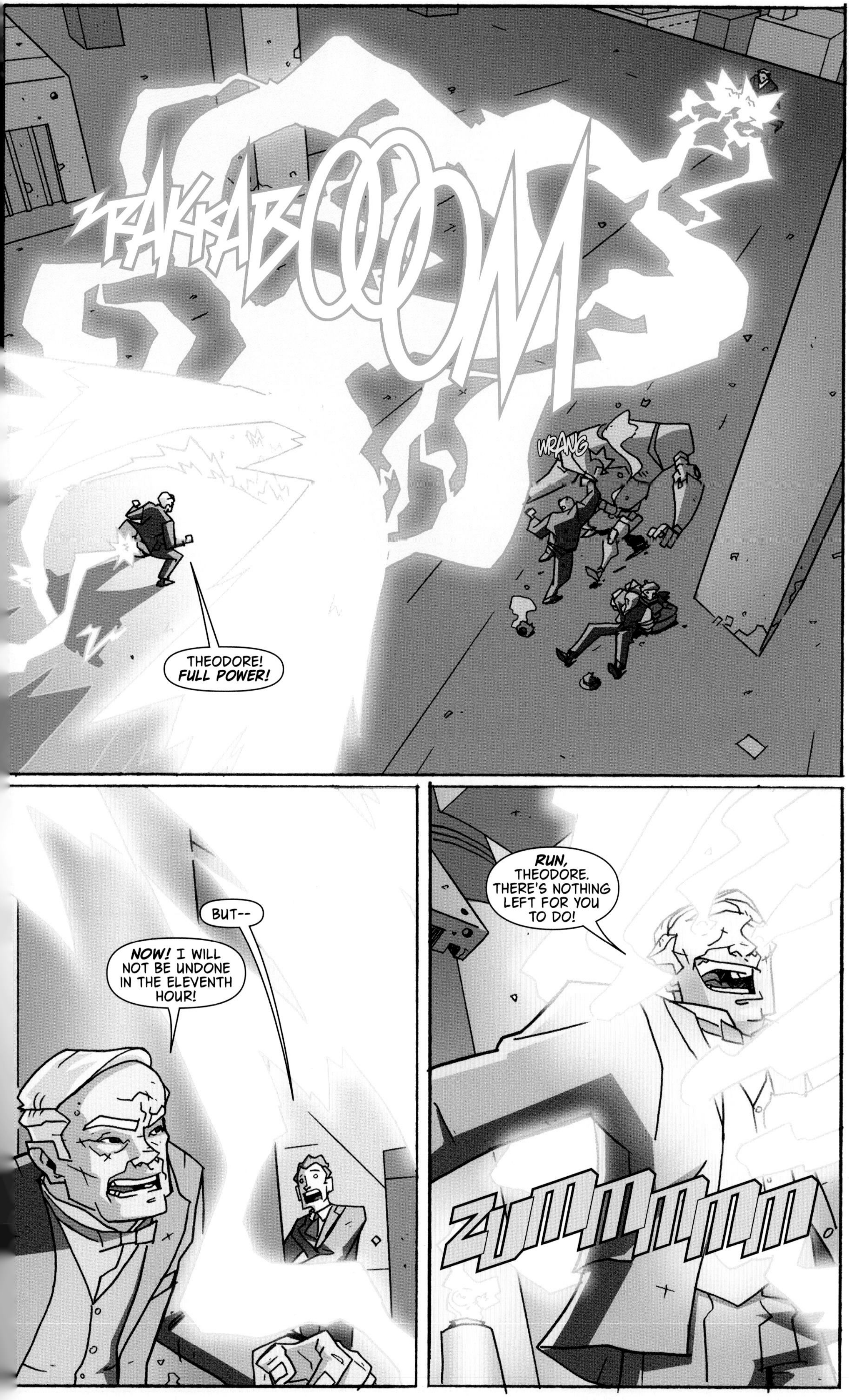

ZRAKRABOOOOM
WRANG
THEODORE! **FULL POWER!**
BUT--
NOW! I WILL NOT BE UNDONE IN THE ELEVENTH HOUR!
RUN, THEODORE. THERE'S NOTHING LEFT FOR YOU TO DO!
ZUMMMMMM

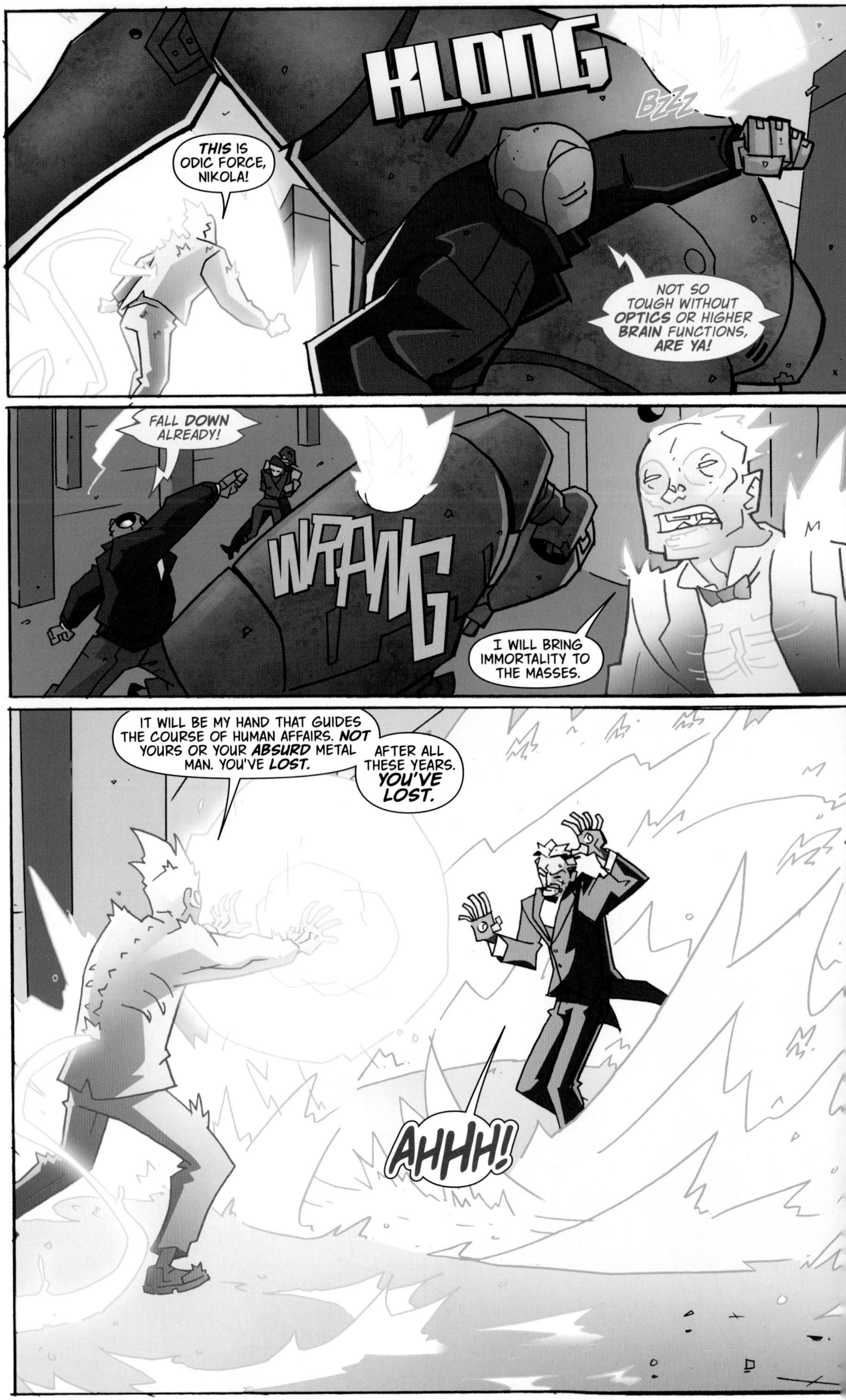
KLONG
BZZZ
THIS IS ODIC FORCE, NIKOLA!
NOT SO TOUGH WITHOUT OPTICS OR HIGHER BRAIN FUNCTIONS, ARE YA!
FALL DOWN ALREADY!
WRANG
I WILL BRING IMMORTALITY TO THE MASSES.
IT WILL BE MY HAND THAT GUIDES THE COURSE OF HUMAN AFFAIRS. NOT YOURS OR YOUR ABSURD METAL MAN. YOU'VE LOST.
AFTER ALL THESE YEARS. YOU'VE LOST.
AHHH!

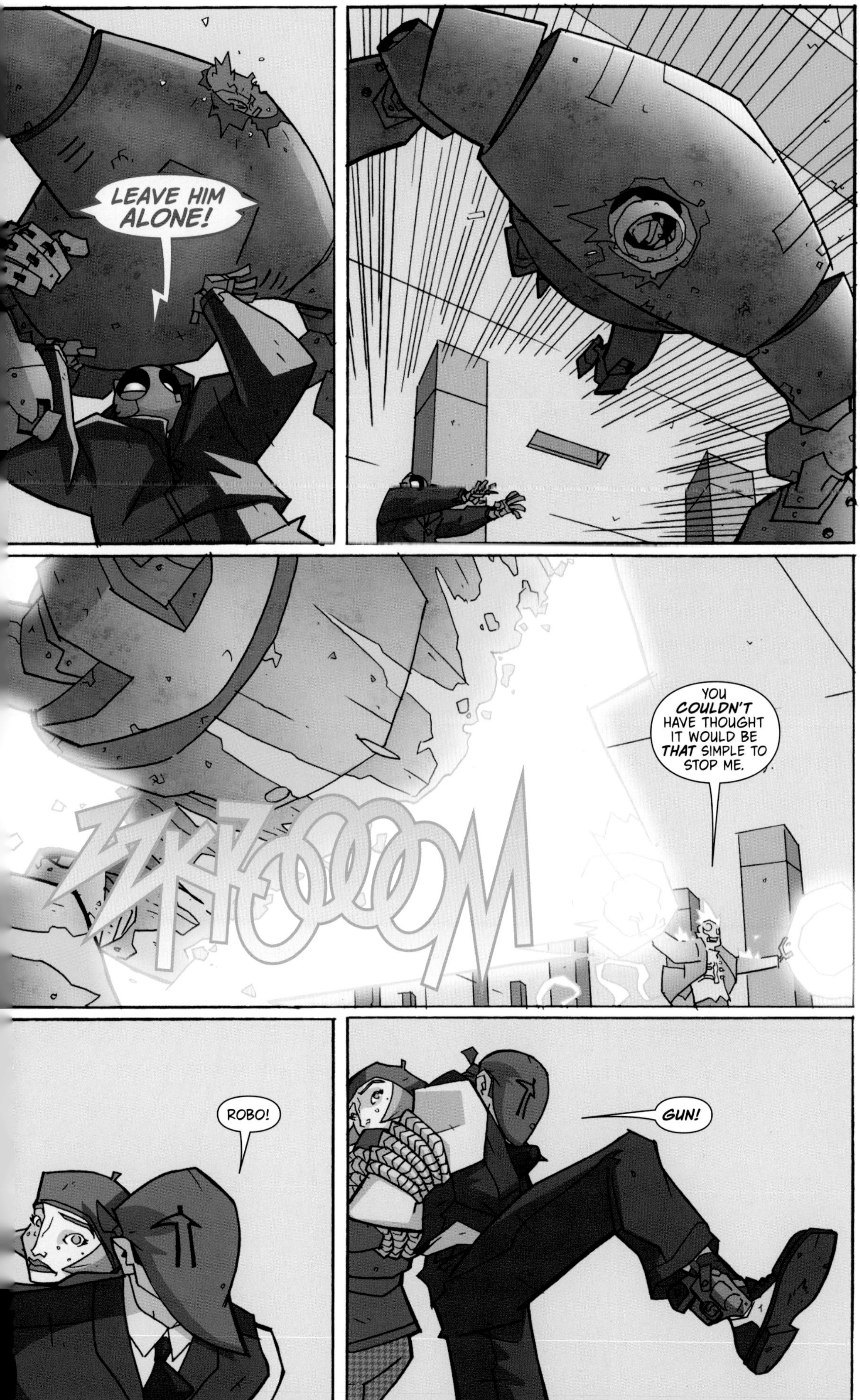
LEAVE HIM ALONE!
ZZKROOOOM
YOU COULDN'T HAVE THOUGHT IT WOULD BE THAT SIMPLE TO STOP ME.
ROBO!
GUN!

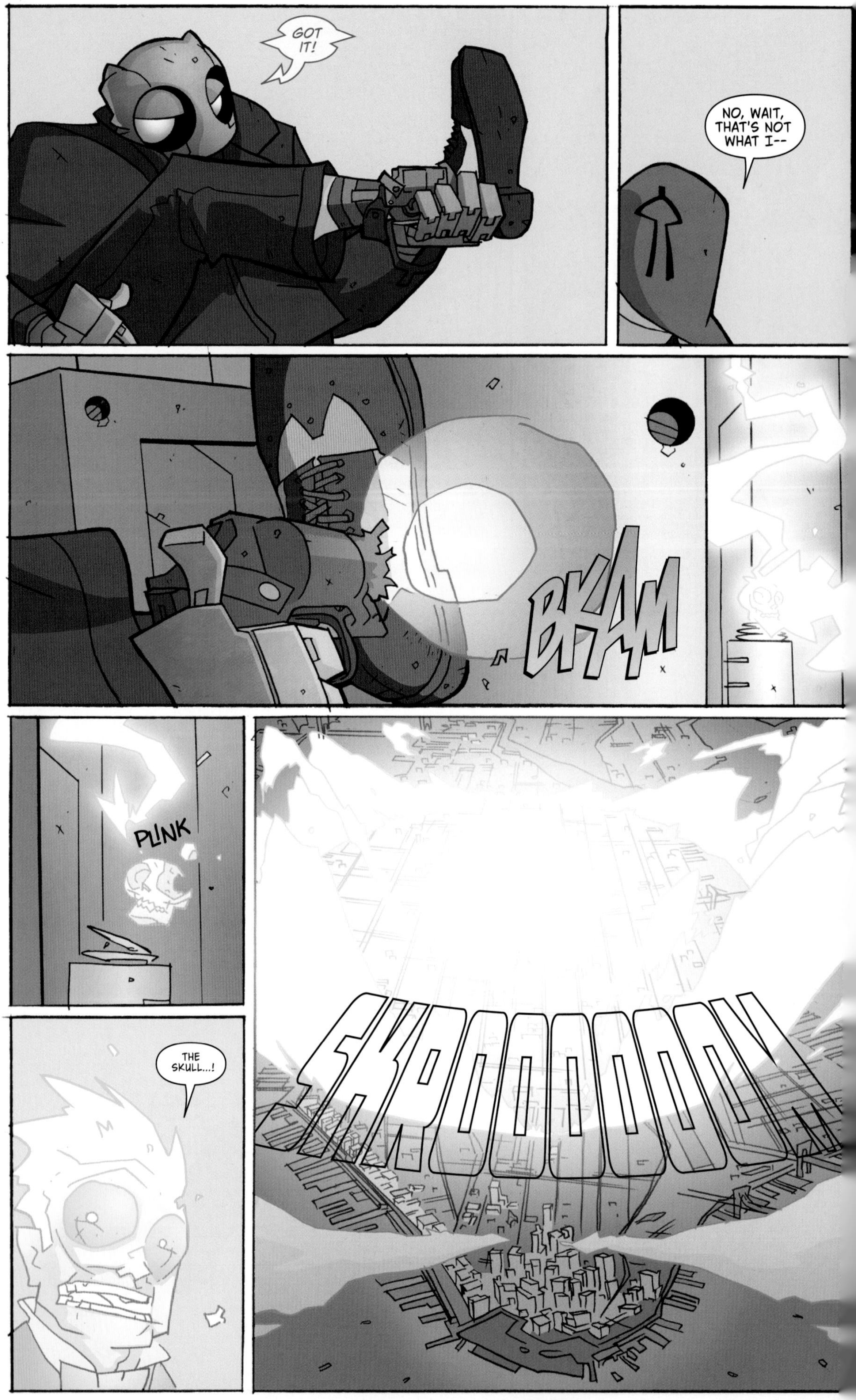
GOT IT!
NO, WAIT, THAT'S NOT WHAT I--
BKAM
PLINK
SKOOOOOOM
THE SKULL...!

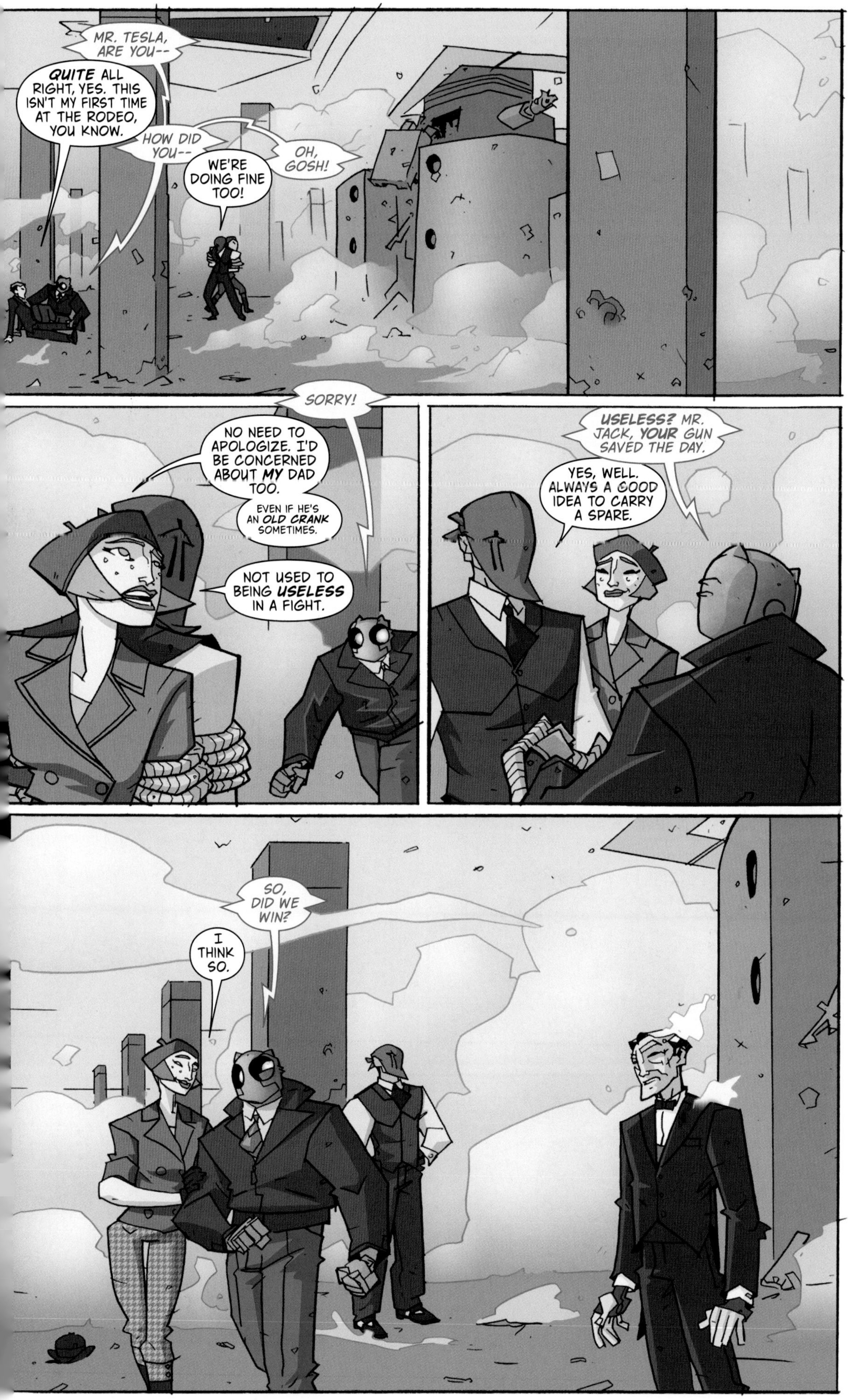
MR. TESLA, ARE YOU--
QUITE ALL RIGHT, YES. THIS ISN'T MY FIRST TIME AT THE RODEO, YOU KNOW.
HOW DID YOU--
OH, GOSH!
WE'RE DOING FINE TOO!
SORRY!
NO NEED TO APOLOGIZE. I'D BE CONCERNED ABOUT MY DAD TOO.
EVEN IF HE'S AN OLD CRANK SOMETIMES.
NOT USED TO BEING USELESS IN A FIGHT.
USELESS? MR. JACK, YOUR GUN SAVED THE DAY.
YES, WELL. ALWAYS A GOOD IDEA TO CARRY A SPARE.
SO, DID WE WIN?
I THINK SO.

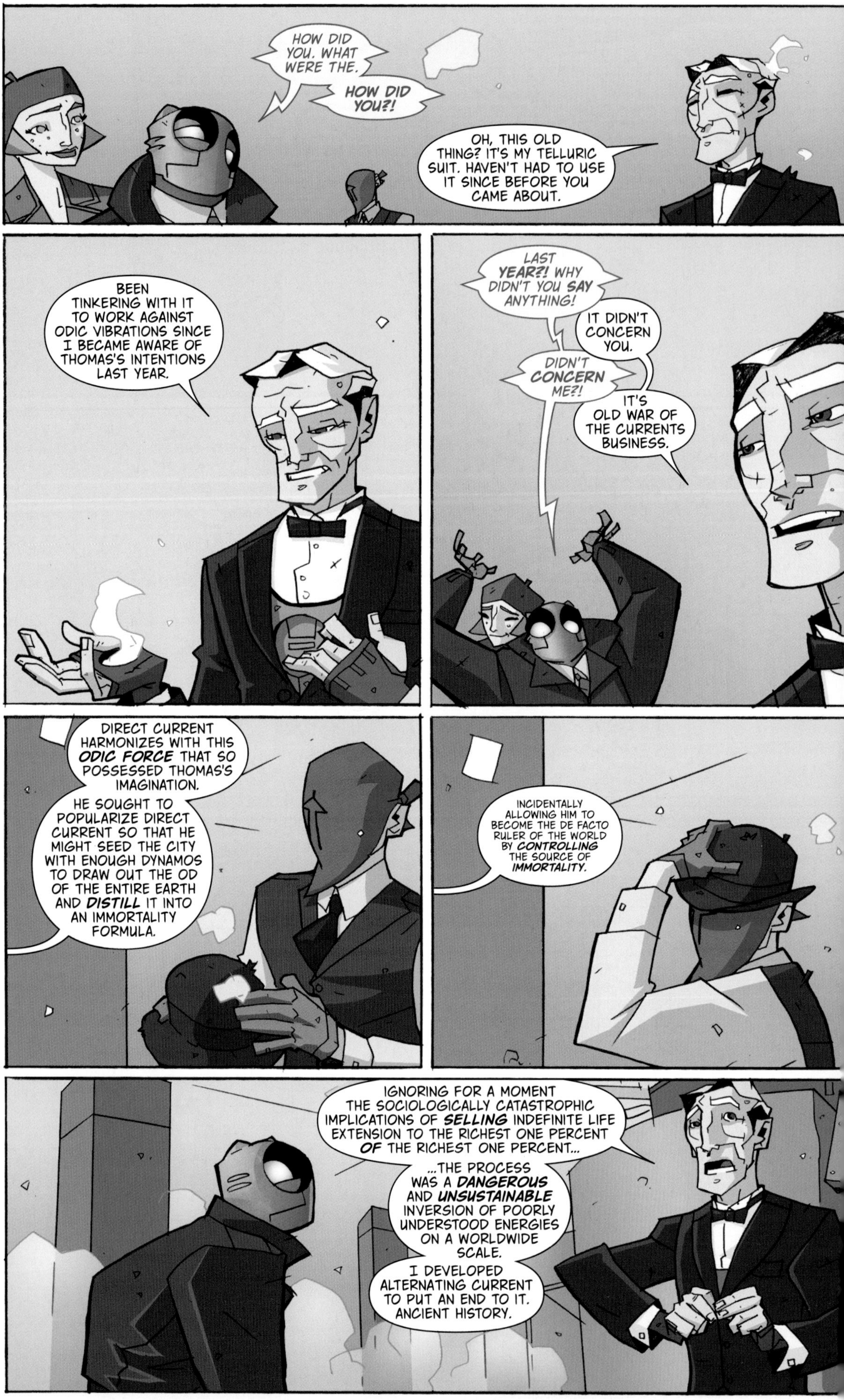

HOW DID YOU. WHAT WERE THE.
HOW DID YOU?!
OH, THIS OLD THING? IT'S MY TELLURIC SUIT. HAVEN'T HAD TO USE IT SINCE BEFORE YOU CAME ABOUT.
BEEN TINKERING WITH IT TO WORK AGAINST ODIC VIBRATIONS SINCE I BECAME AWARE OF THOMAS'S INTENTIONS LAST YEAR.
LAST YEAR?! WHY DIDN'T YOU SAY ANYTHING!
IT DIDN'T CONCERN YOU.
DIDN'T CONCERN ME?!
IT'S OLD WAR OF THE CURRENTS BUSINESS.
DIRECT CURRENT HARMONIZES WITH THIS ODIC FORCE THAT SO POSSESSED THOMAS'S IMAGINATION.
HE SOUGHT TO POPULARIZE DIRECT CURRENT SO THAT HE MIGHT SEED THE CITY WITH ENOUGH DYNAMOS TO DRAW OUT THE OD OF THE ENTIRE EARTH AND DISTILL IT INTO AN IMMORTALITY FORMULA.
INCIDENTALLY ALLOWING HIM TO BECOME THE DE FACTO RULER OF THE WORLD BY CONTROLLING THE SOURCE OF IMMORTALITY.
IGNORING FOR A MOMENT THE SOCIOLOGICALLY CATASTROPHIC IMPLICATIONS OF SELLING INDEFINITE LIFE EXTENSION TO THE RICHEST ONE PERCENT OF THE RICHEST ONE PERCENT...
...THE PROCESS WAS A DANGEROUS AND UNSUSTAINABLE INVERSION OF POORLY UNDERSTOOD ENERGIES ON A WORLDWIDE SCALE.
I DEVELOPED ALTERNATING CURRENT TO PUT AN END TO IT. ANCIENT HISTORY.

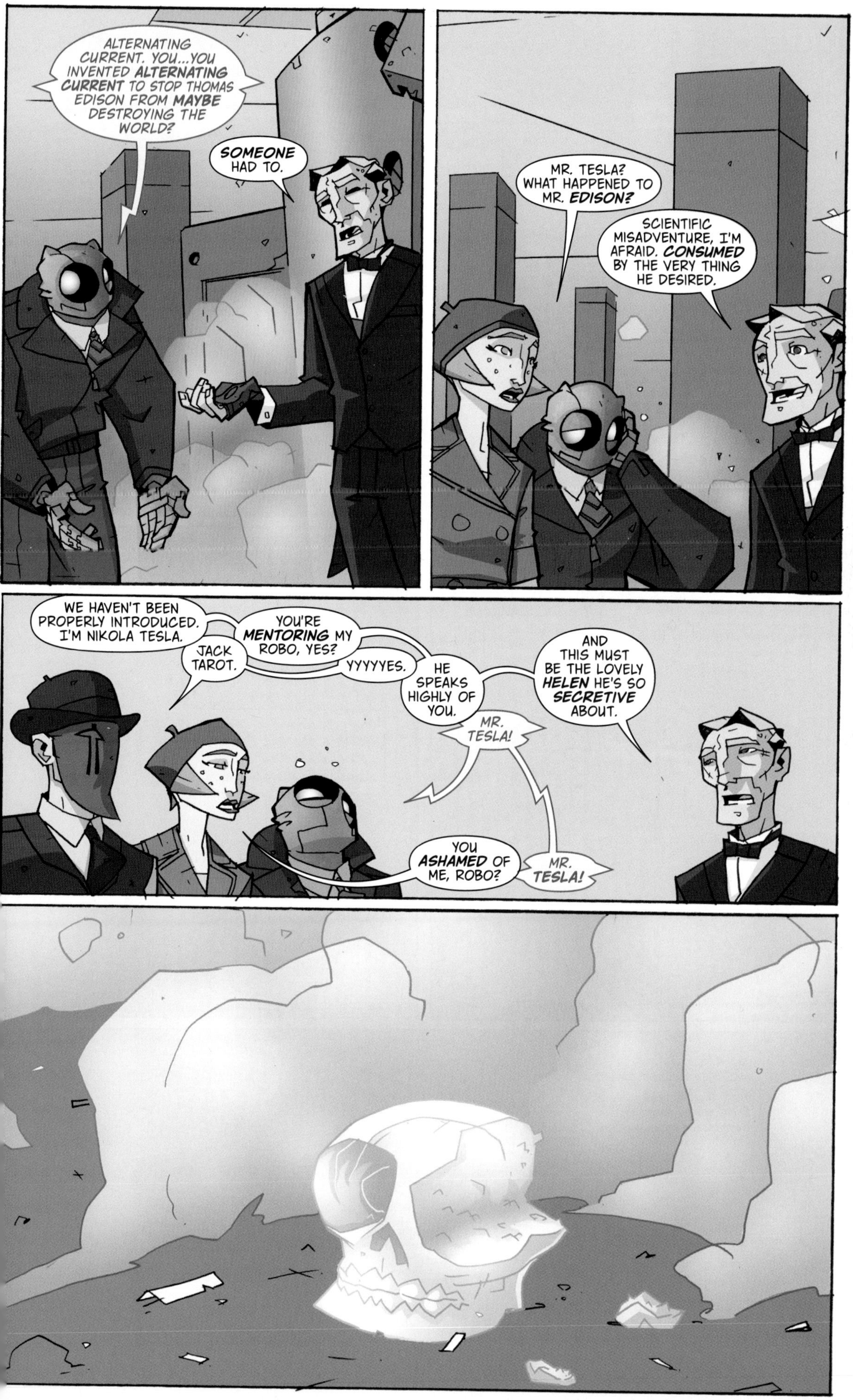

ALTERNATING CURRENT. YOU...YOU INVENTED **ALTERNATING CURRENT** TO STOP THOMAS EDISON FROM **MAYBE** DESTROYING THE WORLD?
SOMEONE HAD TO.
MR. TESLA? WHAT HAPPENED TO MR. **EDISON?**
SCIENTIFIC MISADVENTURE, I'M AFRAID. **CONSUMED** BY THE VERY THING HE DESIRED.
WE HAVEN'T BEEN PROPERLY INTRODUCED. I'M NIKOLA TESLA.
JACK TAROT.
YOU'RE **MENTORING** MY ROBO, YES?
YYYYYES.
HE SPEAKS HIGHLY OF YOU.
AND THIS MUST BE THE LOVELY **HELEN** HE'S SO **SECRETIVE** ABOUT.
MR. TESLA!
YOU **ASHAMED** OF ME, ROBO?
MR. **TESLA!**

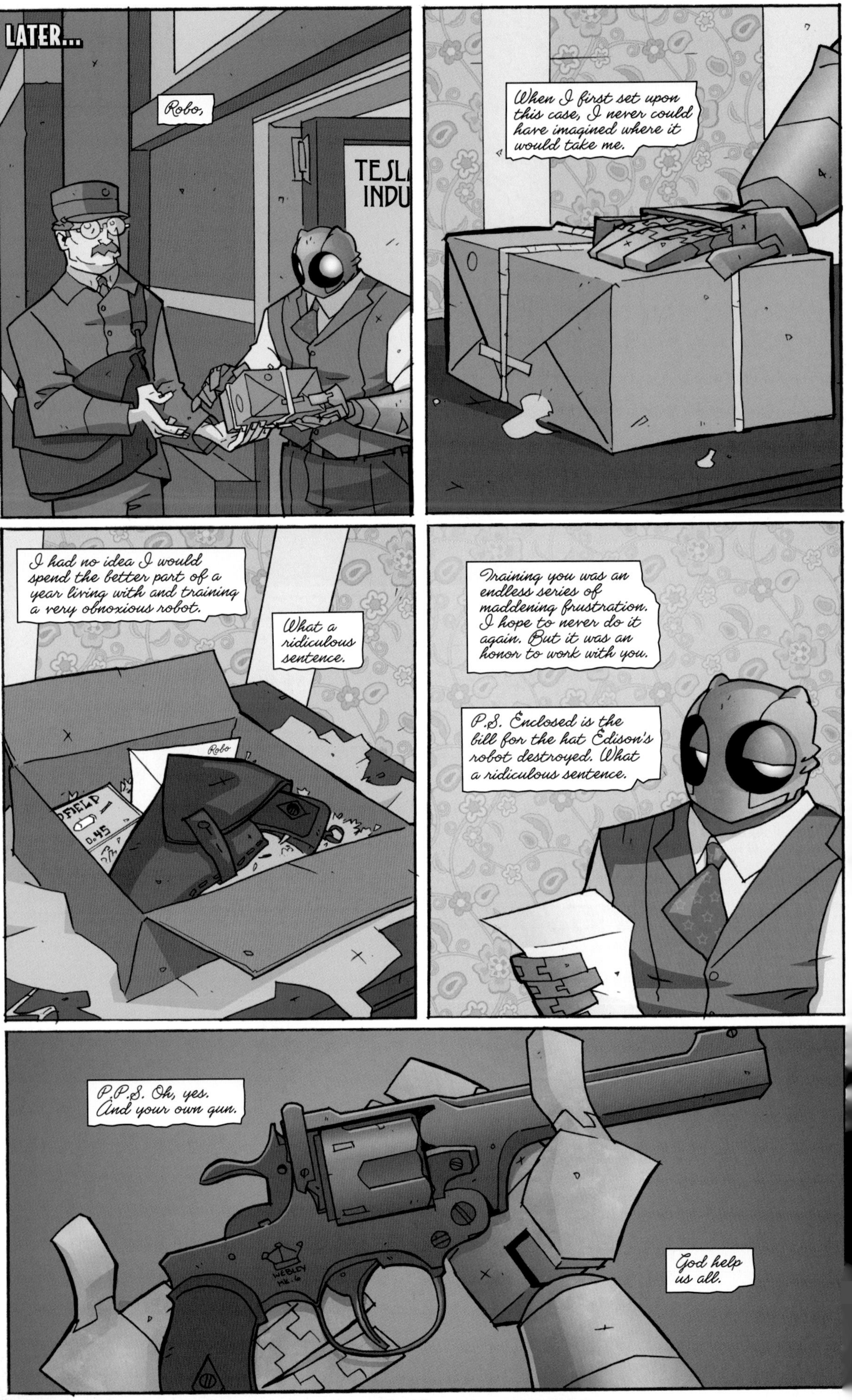
LATER...
Robo,
TESLA INDU
When I first set upon this case, I never could have imagined where it would take me.
I had no idea I would spend the better part of a year living with and training a very obnoxious robot.
What a ridiculous sentence.
Robo
D.45
Training you was an endless series of maddening frustration. I hope to never do it again. But it was an honor to work with you.
P.S. Enclosed is the bill for the hat Edison's robot destroyed. What a ridiculous sentence.
P.P.S. Oh, yes. And your own gun.
WEBLEY
God help us all.

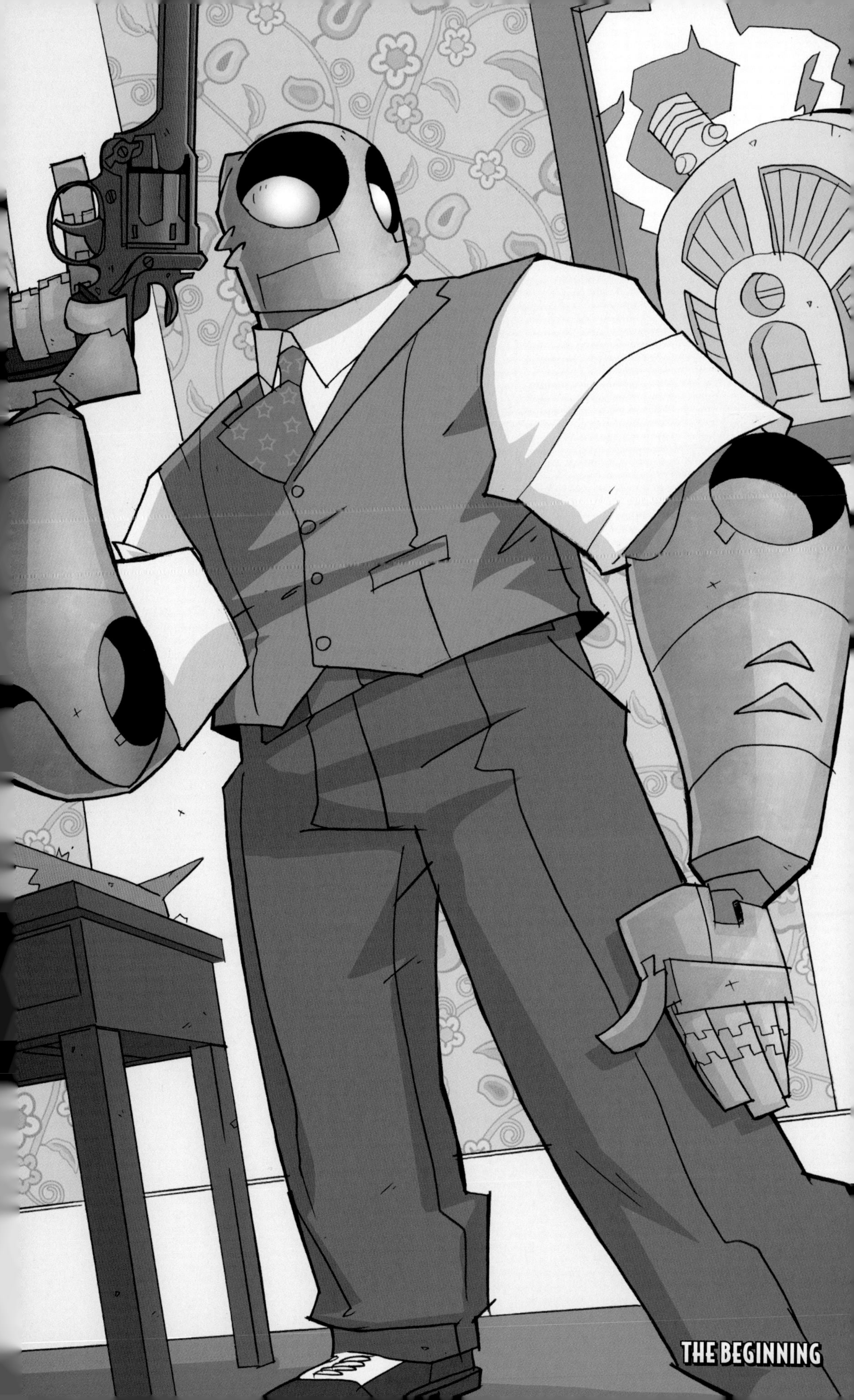
THE BEGINNING

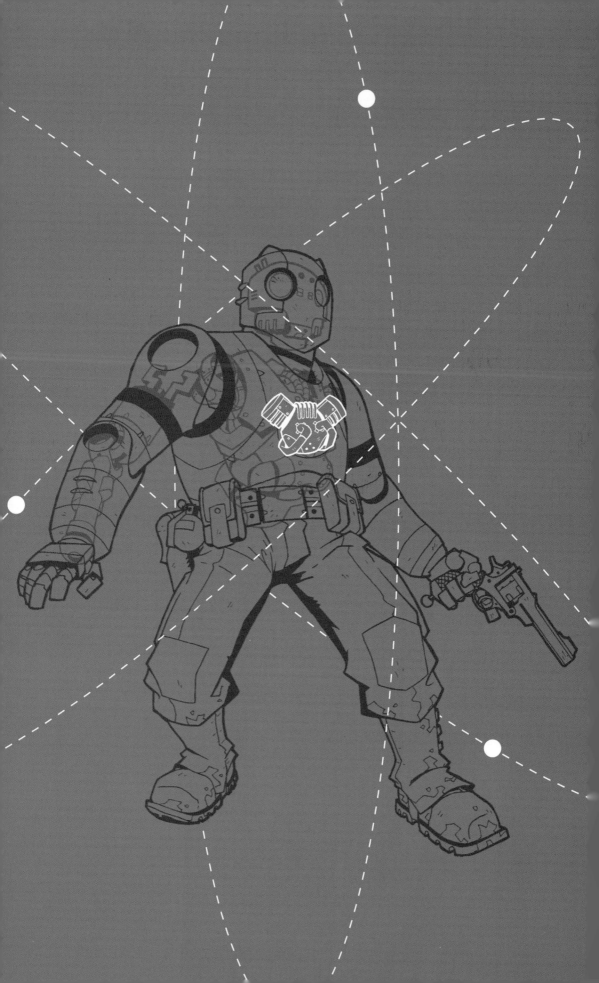

ACCELERATION

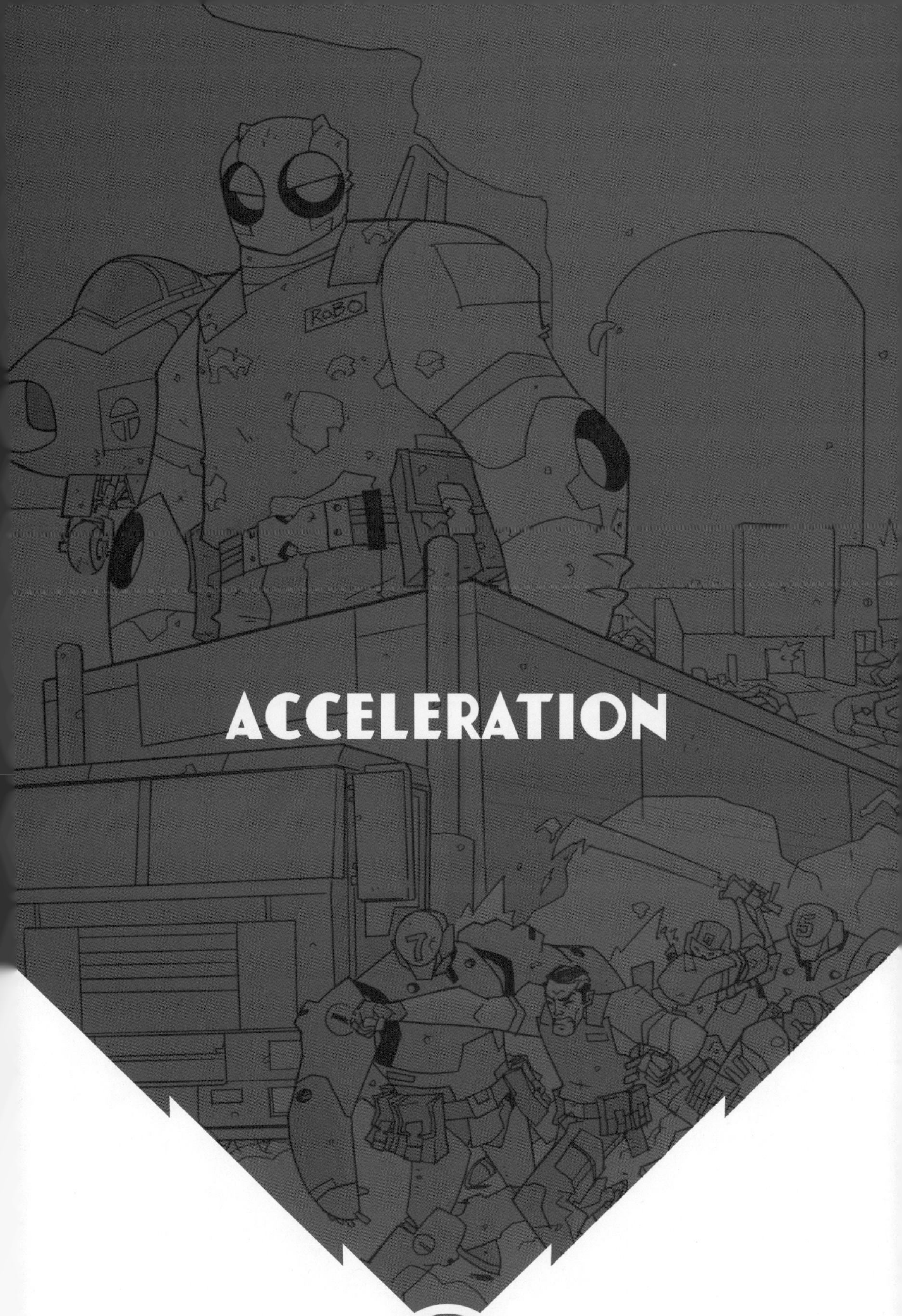
ROBO

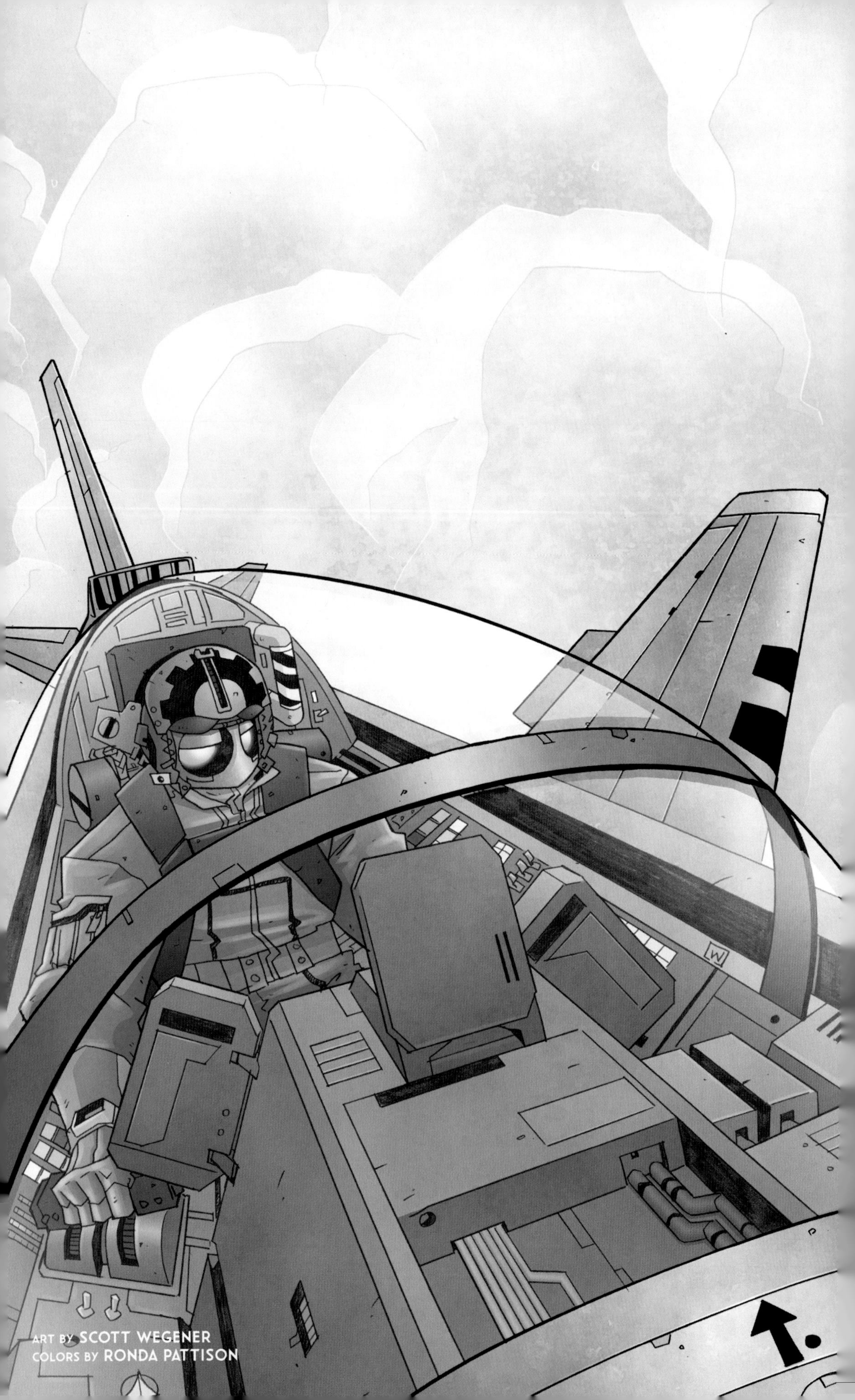
ART BY SCOTT WEGENER
COLORS BY RONDA PATTISON

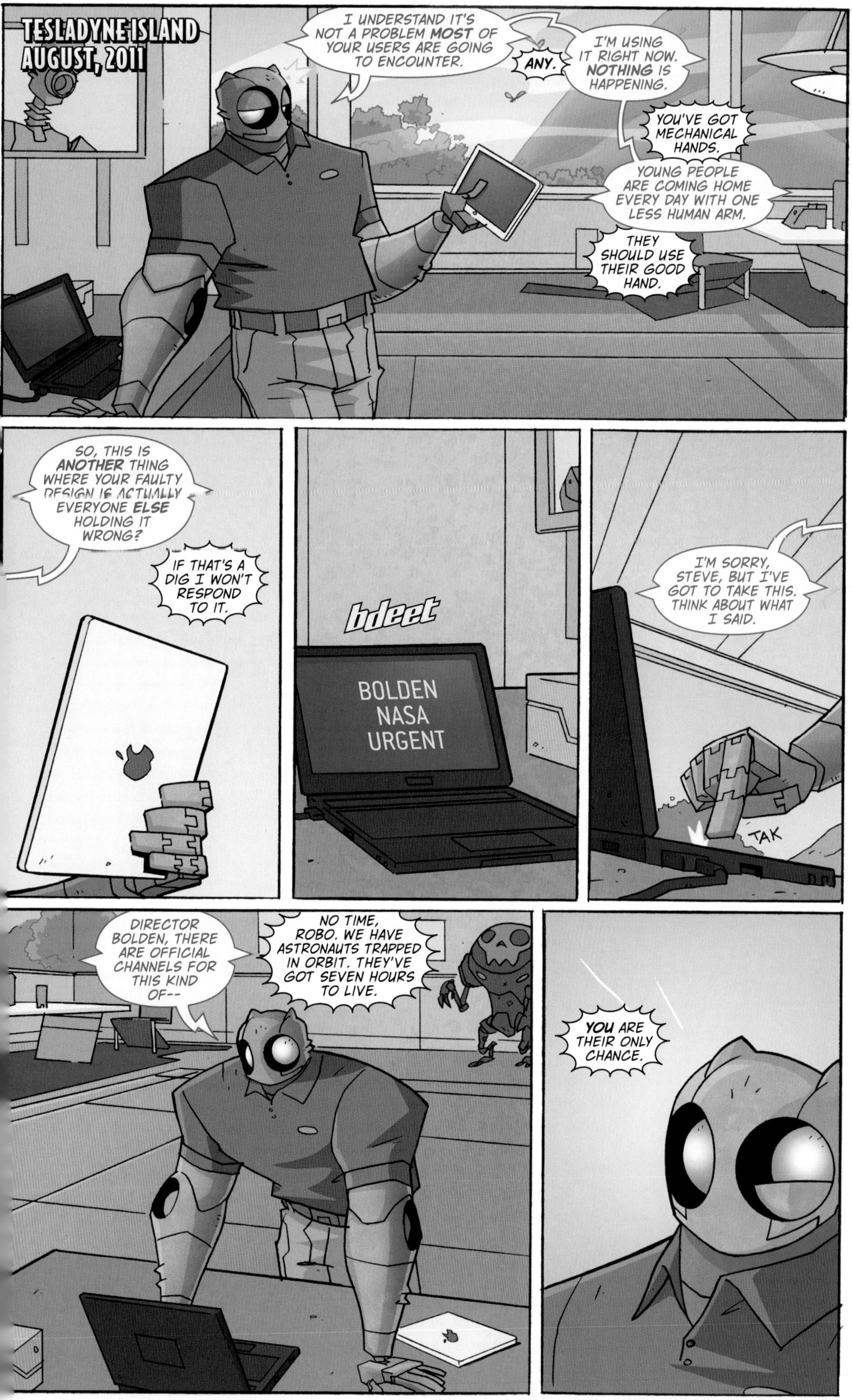
TESLADYNE ISLAND
AUGUST, 2011
I UNDERSTAND IT'S NOT A PROBLEM MOST OF YOUR USERS ARE GOING TO ENCOUNTER.
ANY.
I'M USING IT RIGHT NOW. NOTHING IS HAPPENING.
YOU'VE GOT MECHANICAL HANDS.
YOUNG PEOPLE ARE COMING HOME EVERY DAY WITH ONE LESS HUMAN ARM.
THEY SHOULD USE THEIR GOOD HAND.
SO, THIS IS ANOTHER THING WHERE YOUR FAULTY DESIGN IS ACTUALLY EVERYONE ELSE HOLDING IT WRONG?
IF THAT'S A DIG I WON'T RESPOND TO IT.
bdeet
BOLDEN NASA URGENT
I'M SORRY, STEVE, BUT I'VE GOT TO TAKE THIS. THINK ABOUT WHAT I SAID.
TAK
DIRECTOR BOLDEN, THERE ARE OFFICIAL CHANNELS FOR THIS KIND OF--
NO TIME, ROBO. WE HAVE ASTRONAUTS TRAPPED IN ORBIT. THEY'VE GOT SEVEN HOURS TO LIVE.
YOU ARE THEIR ONLY CHANCE.

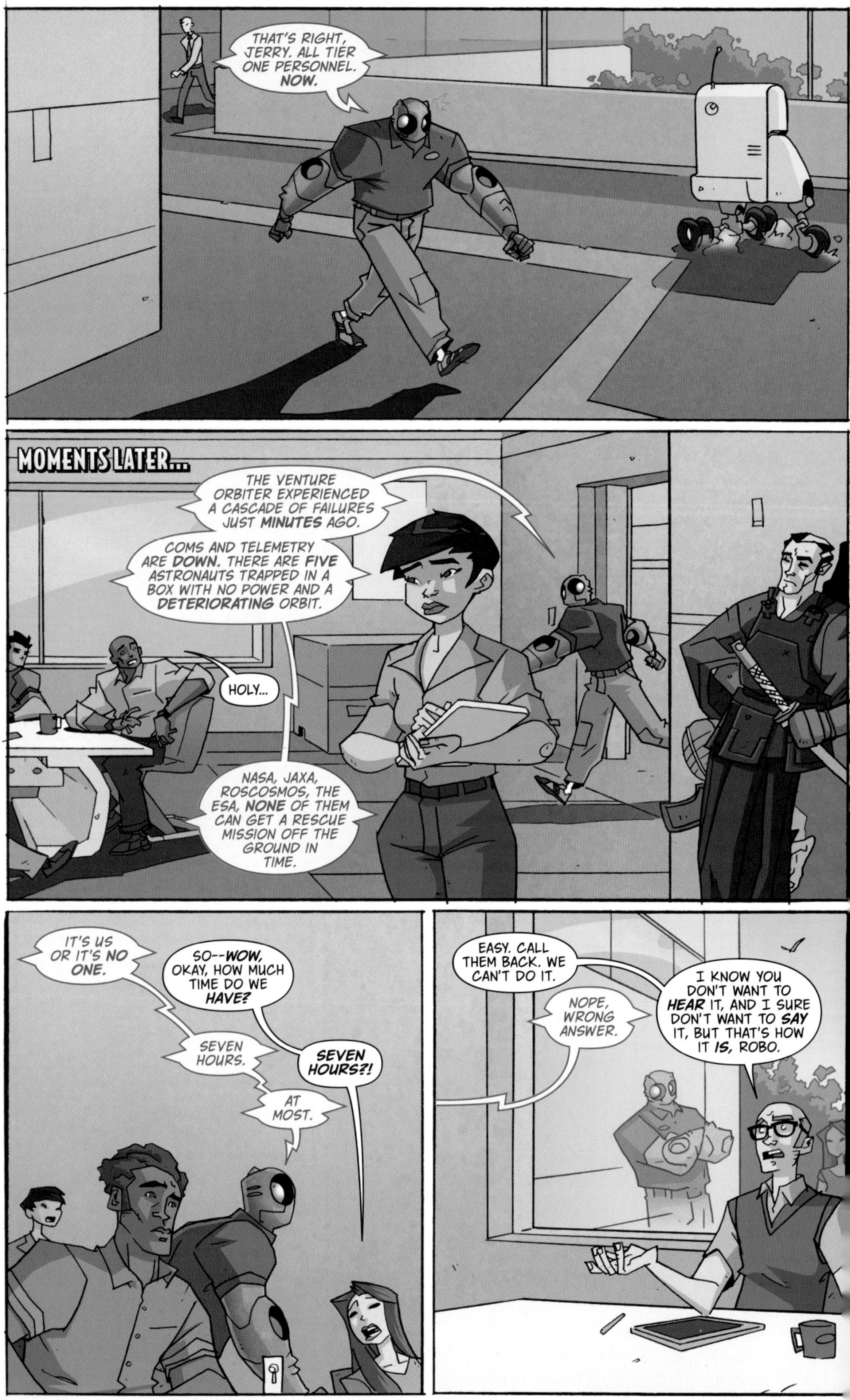
THAT'S RIGHT, JERRY. ALL TIER ONE PERSONNEL. NOW.
MOMENTS LATER...
THE VENTURE ORBITER EXPERIENCED A CASCADE OF FAILURES JUST MINUTES AGO.
COMS AND TELEMETRY ARE DOWN. THERE ARE FIVE ASTRONAUTS TRAPPED IN A BOX WITH NO POWER AND A DETERIORATING ORBIT.
HOLY...
NASA, JAXA, ROSCOSMOS, THE ESA, NONE OF THEM CAN GET A RESCUE MISSION OFF THE GROUND IN TIME.
IT'S US OR IT'S NO ONE.
SO--WOW, OKAY, HOW MUCH TIME DO WE HAVE?
SEVEN HOURS.
AT MOST.
SEVEN HOURS?!
EASY. CALL THEM BACK. WE CAN'T DO IT.
NOPE, WRONG ANSWER.
I KNOW YOU DON'T WANT TO HEAR IT, AND I SURE DON'T WANT TO SAY IT, BUT THAT'S HOW IT IS, ROBO.

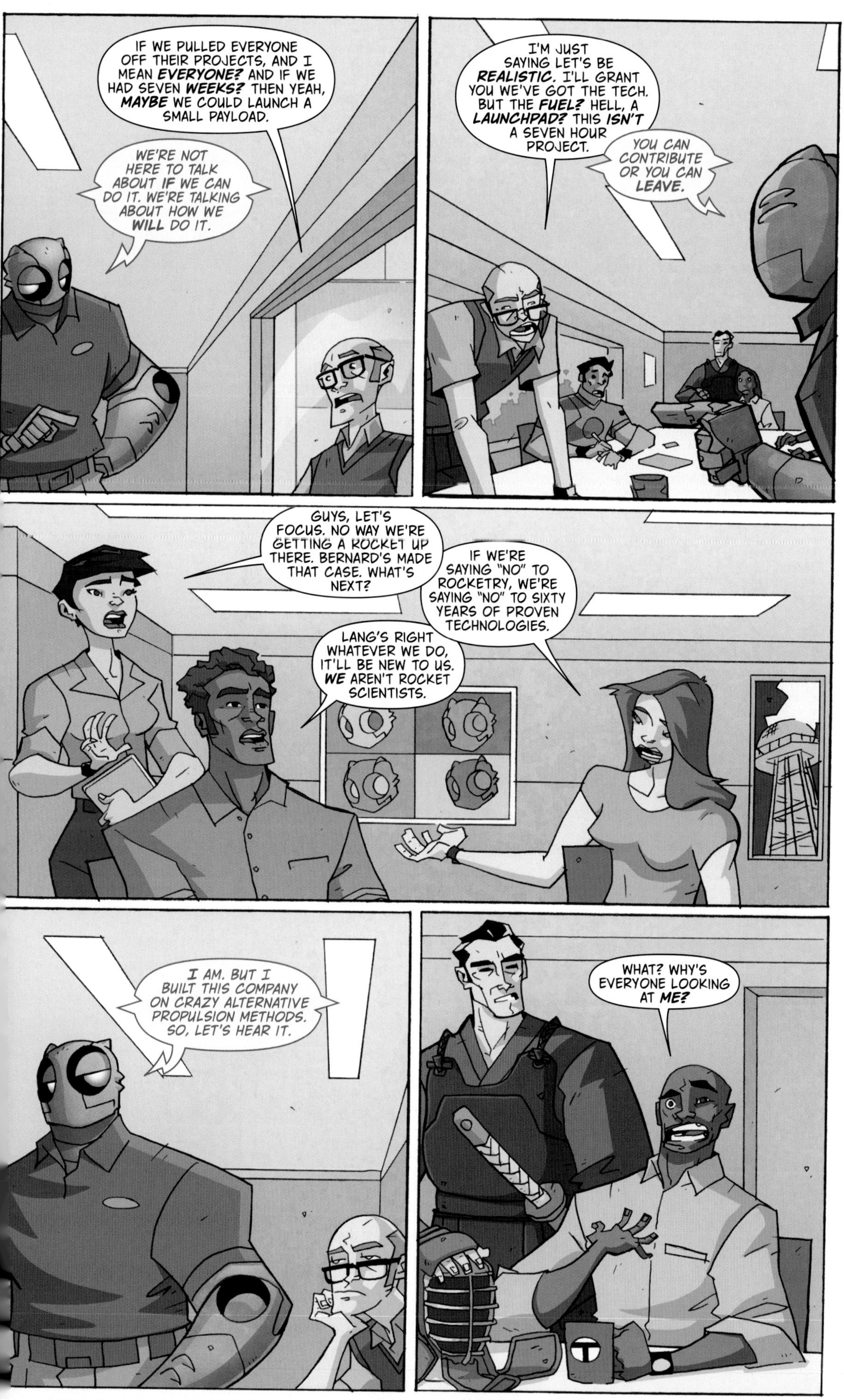

IF WE PULLED EVERYONE OFF THEIR PROJECTS, AND I MEAN **EVERYONE?** AND IF WE HAD SEVEN **WEEKS?** THEN YEAH, **MAYBE** WE COULD LAUNCH A SMALL PAYLOAD.
WE'RE NOT HERE TO TALK ABOUT **IF** WE CAN DO IT. WE'RE TALKING ABOUT HOW WE **WILL** DO IT.
I'M JUST SAYING LET'S BE **REALISTIC.** I'LL GRANT YOU WE'VE GOT THE TECH. BUT THE **FUEL?** HELL, A **LAUNCHPAD?** THIS **ISN'T** A SEVEN HOUR PROJECT.
YOU CAN CONTRIBUTE OR YOU CAN **LEAVE.**
GUYS, LET'S FOCUS. NO WAY WE'RE GETTING A ROCKET UP THERE. BERNARD'S MADE THAT CASE. WHAT'S NEXT?
IF WE'RE SAYING "NO" TO ROCKETRY, WE'RE SAYING "NO" TO SIXTY YEARS OF PROVEN TECHNOLOGIES.
LANG'S RIGHT WHATEVER WE DO, IT'LL BE NEW TO US. **WE** AREN'T ROCKET SCIENTISTS.
I AM. BUT I BUILT THIS COMPANY ON CRAZY ALTERNATIVE PROPULSION METHODS. SO, LET'S HEAR IT.
WHAT? WHY'S EVERYONE LOOKING AT **ME?**

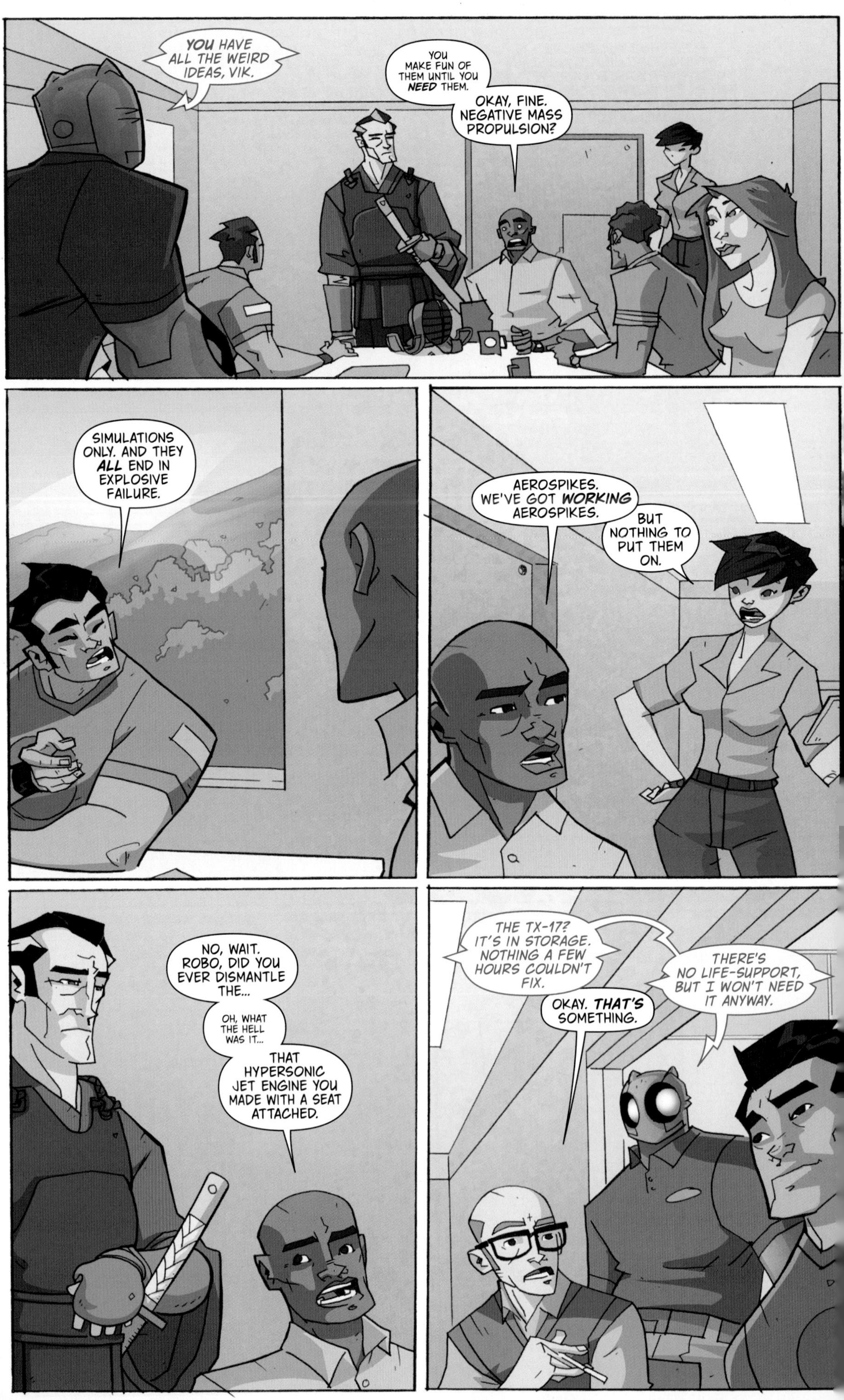

YOU HAVE ALL THE WEIRD IDEAS, VIK.
YOU MAKE FUN OF THEM UNTIL YOU NEED THEM.
OKAY, FINE. NEGATIVE MASS PROPULSION?
SIMULATIONS ONLY. AND THEY ALL END IN EXPLOSIVE FAILURE.
AEROSPIKES. WE'VE GOT WORKING AEROSPIKES.
BUT NOTHING TO PUT THEM ON.
NO, WAIT. ROBO, DID YOU EVER DISMANTLE THE...
OH, WHAT THE HELL WAS IT...
THAT HYPERSONIC JET ENGINE YOU MADE WITH A SEAT ATTACHED.
THE TX-17? IT'S IN STORAGE. NOTHING A FEW HOURS COULDN'T FIX.
OKAY. THAT'S SOMETHING.
THERE'S NO LIFE-SUPPORT, BUT I WON'T NEED IT ANYWAY.

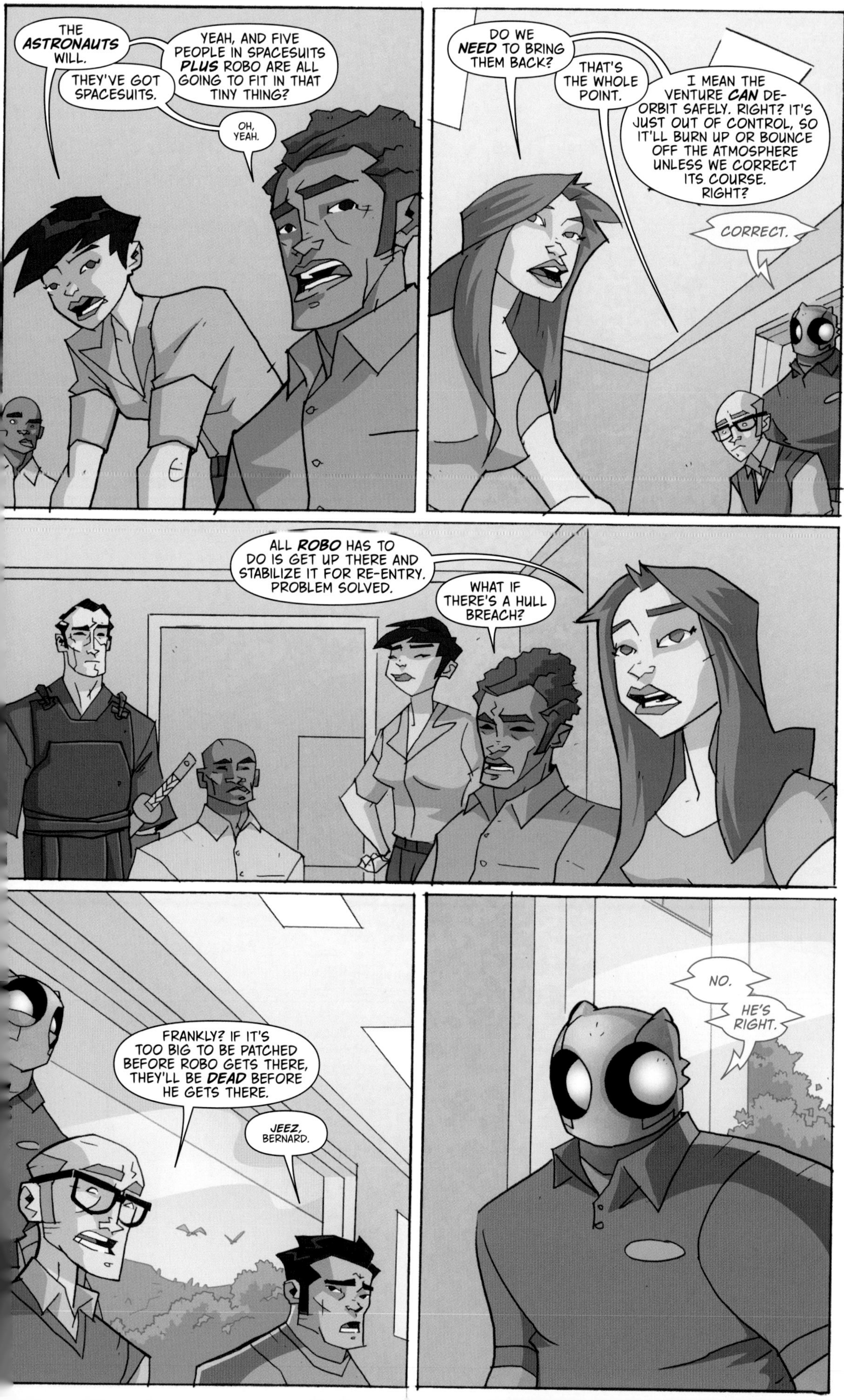
THE ASTRONAUTS WILL.
YEAH, AND FIVE PEOPLE IN SPACESUITS PLUS ROBO ARE ALL GOING TO FIT IN THAT TINY THING?
THEY'VE GOT SPACESUITS.
OH, YEAH.
DO WE NEED TO BRING THEM BACK?
THAT'S THE WHOLE POINT.
I MEAN THE VENTURE CAN DE-ORBIT SAFELY. RIGHT? IT'S JUST OUT OF CONTROL, SO IT'LL BURN UP OR BOUNCE OFF THE ATMOSPHERE UNLESS WE CORRECT ITS COURSE. RIGHT?
CORRECT.
ALL ROBO HAS TO DO IS GET UP THERE AND STABILIZE IT FOR RE-ENTRY. PROBLEM SOLVED.
WHAT IF THERE'S A HULL BREACH?
FRANKLY? IF IT'S TOO BIG TO BE PATCHED BEFORE ROBO GETS THERE, THEY'LL BE DEAD BEFORE HE GETS THERE.
JEEZ, BERNARD.
NO.
HE'S RIGHT.

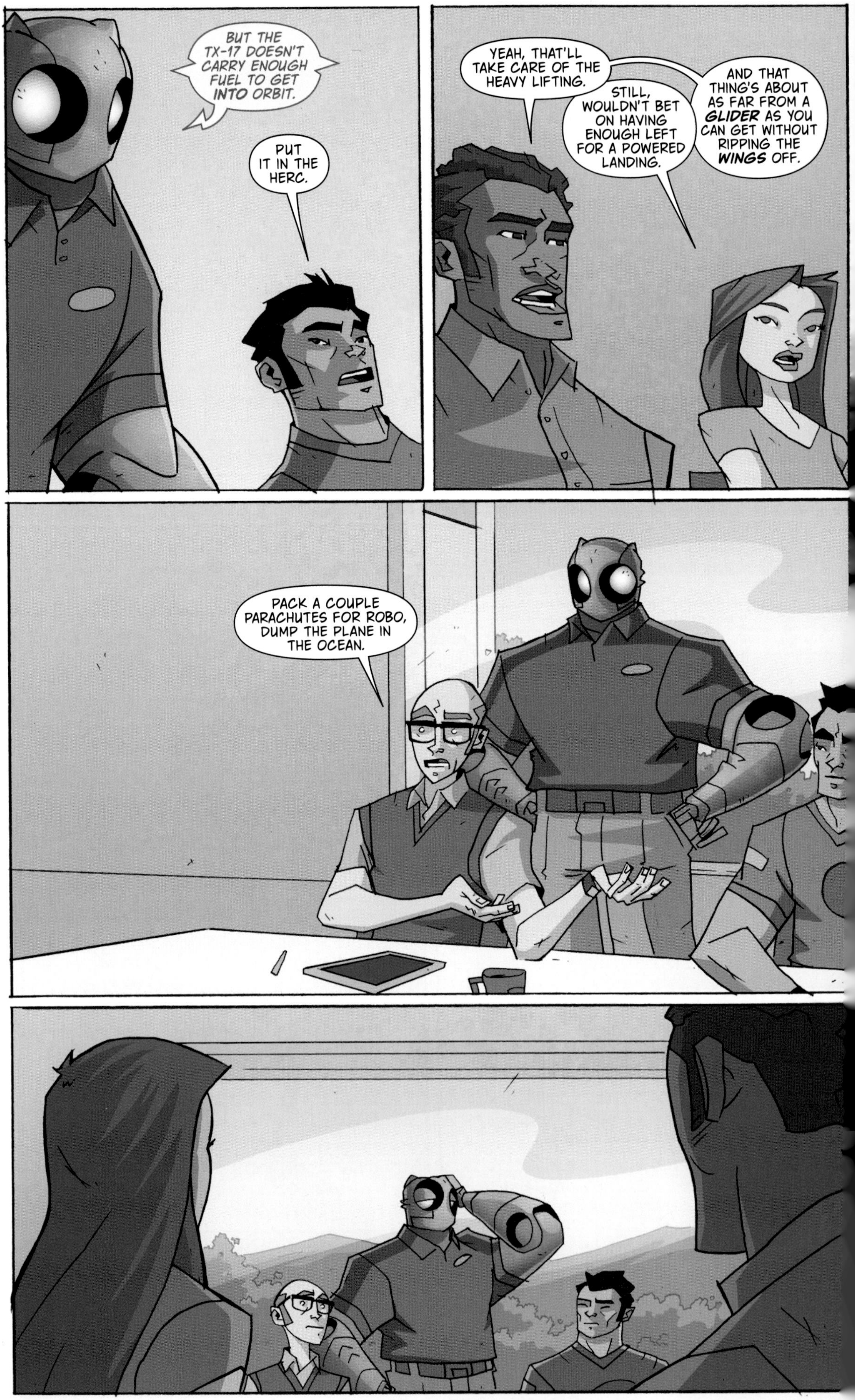
BUT THE TX-17 DOESN'T CARRY ENOUGH FUEL TO GET **INTO** ORBIT.
PUT IT IN THE HERC.
YEAH, THAT'LL TAKE CARE OF THE HEAVY LIFTING.
STILL, WOULDN'T BET ON HAVING ENOUGH LEFT FOR A POWERED LANDING.
AND THAT THING'S ABOUT AS FAR FROM A ***GLIDER*** AS YOU CAN GET WITHOUT RIPPING THE ***WINGS*** OFF.
PACK A COUPLE PARACHUTES FOR ROBO, DUMP THE PLANE IN THE OCEAN.

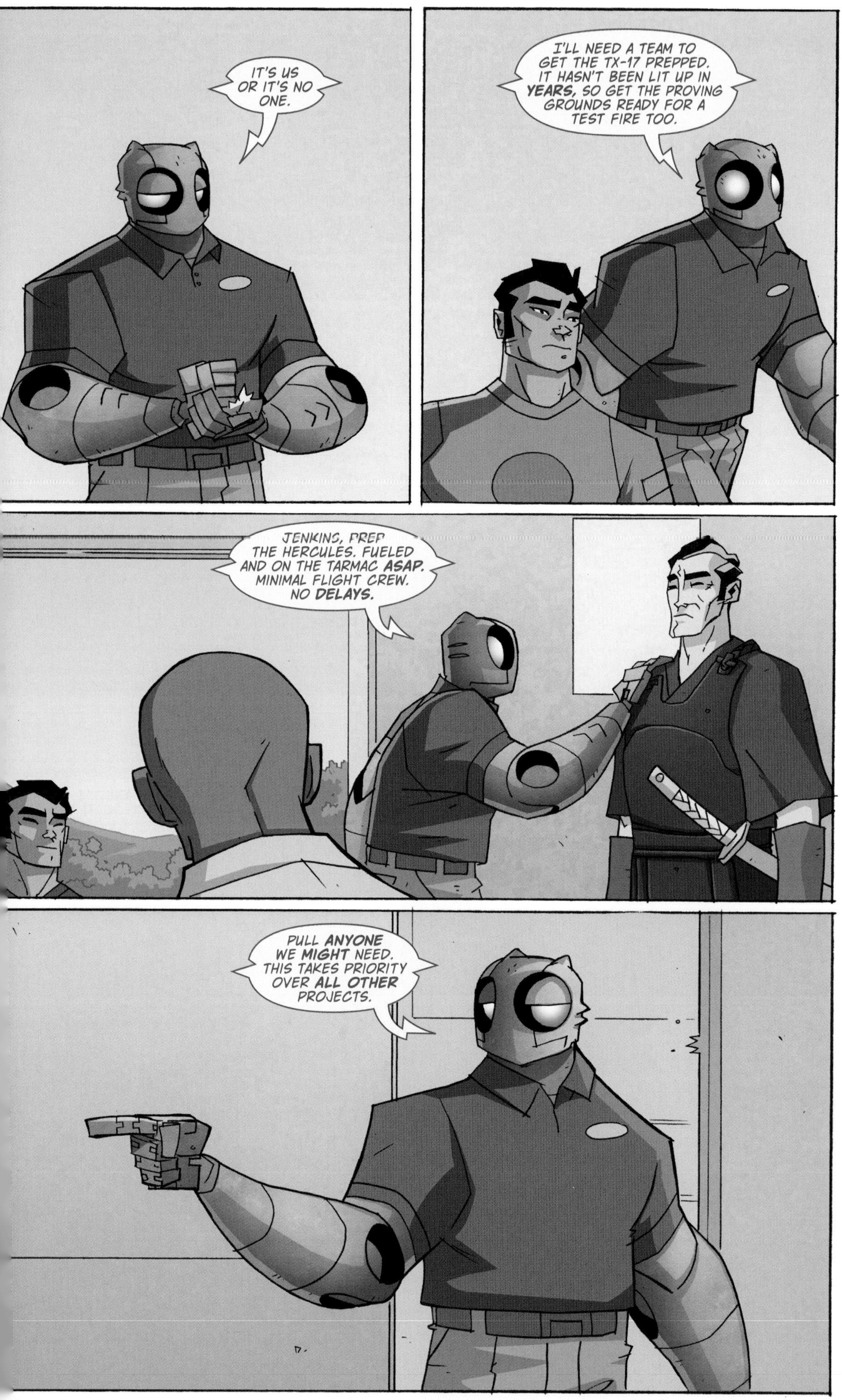
IT'S US OR IT'S NO ONE.
I'LL NEED A TEAM TO GET THE TX-17 PREPPED. IT HASN'T BEEN LIT UP IN YEARS, SO GET THE PROVING GROUNDS READY FOR A TEST FIRE TOO.
JENKINS, PREP THE HERCULES. FUELED AND ON THE TARMAC ASAP. MINIMAL FLIGHT CREW. NO DELAYS.
PULL ANYONE WE MIGHT NEED. THIS TAKES PRIORITY OVER ALL OTHER PROJECTS.

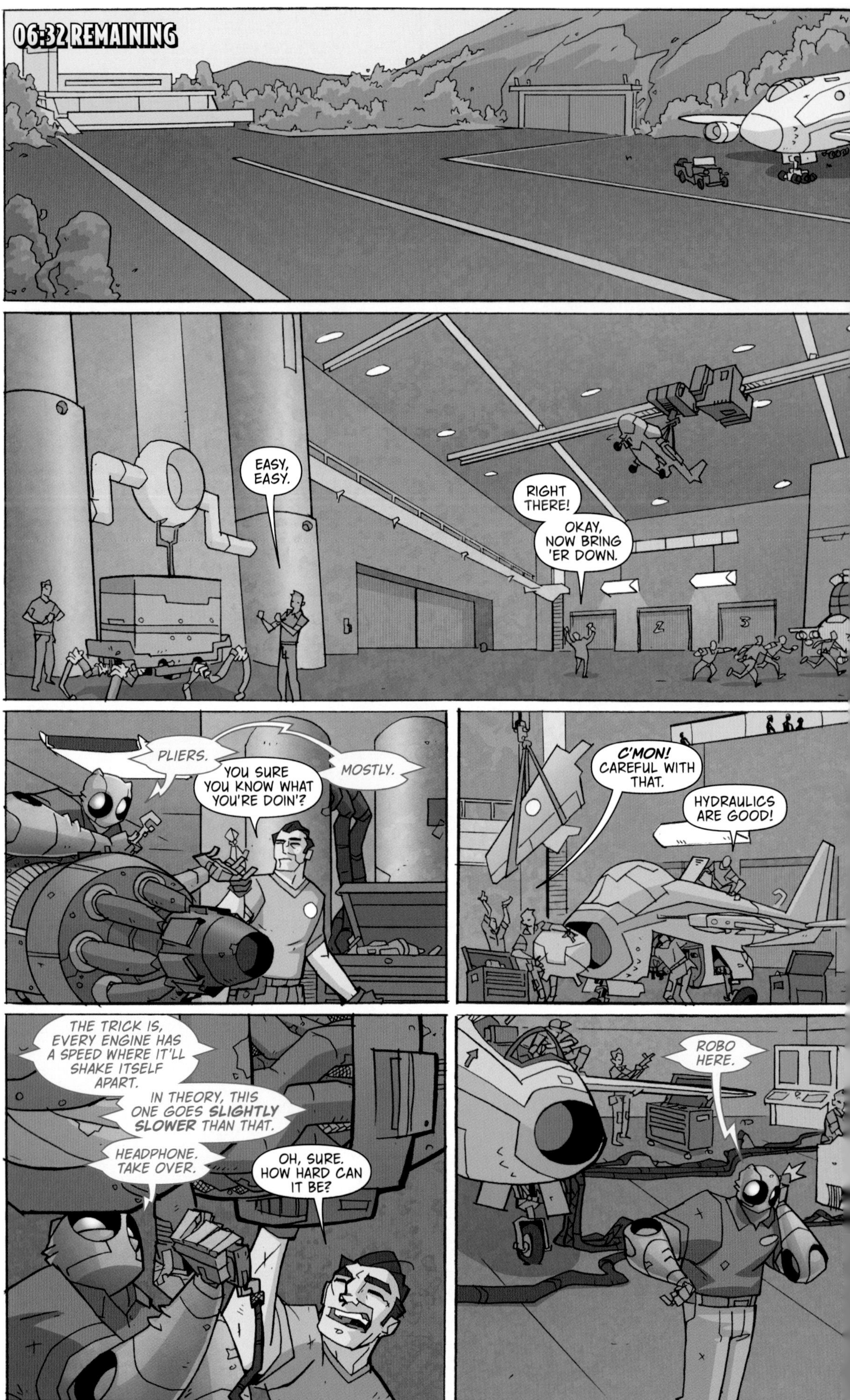

06:32 REMAINING
EASY, EASY.
RIGHT THERE!
OKAY, NOW BRING 'ER DOWN.
PLIERS.
YOU SURE YOU KNOW WHAT YOU'RE DOIN'?
MOSTLY.
C'MON! CAREFUL WITH THAT.
HYDRAULICS ARE GOOD!
THE TRICK IS, EVERY ENGINE HAS A SPEED WHERE IT'LL SHAKE ITSELF APART.
IN THEORY, THIS ONE GOES SLIGHTLY SLOWER THAN THAT.
HEADPHONE. TAKE OVER.
OH, SURE. HOW HARD CAN IT BE?
ROBO HERE.

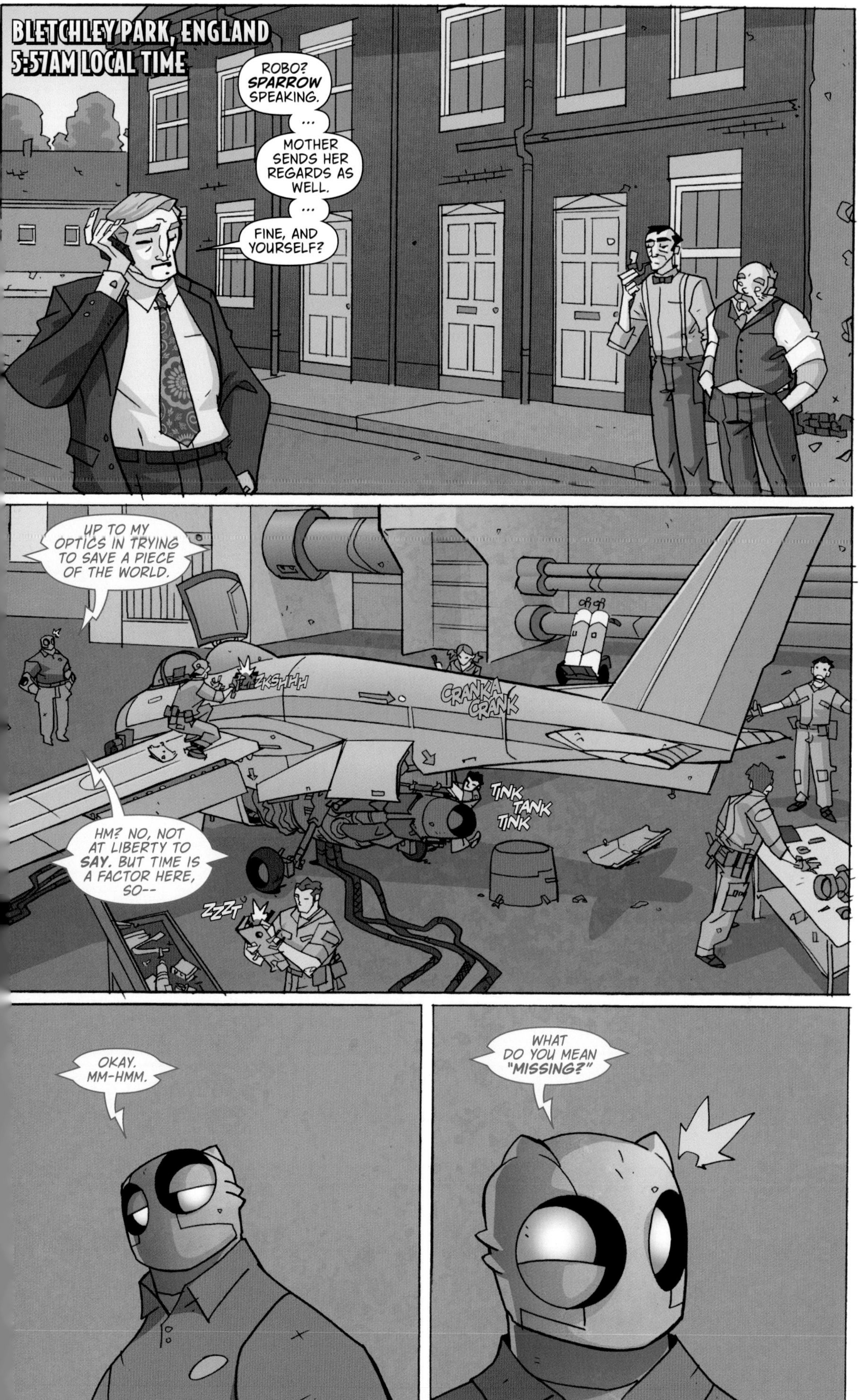
BLETCHLEY PARK, ENGLAND
5:57AM LOCAL TIME
ROBO? SPARROW SPEAKING.
...
MOTHER SENDS HER REGARDS AS WELL.
...
FINE, AND YOURSELF?
UP TO MY OPTICS IN TRYING TO SAVE A PIECE OF THE WORLD.
KSHHH
CRANKA CRANK
TINK TANK TINK
HM? NO, NOT AT LIBERTY TO SAY. BUT TIME IS A FACTOR HERE, SO--
ZZZT
OKAY. MM-HMM.
WHAT DO YOU MEAN "MISSING?"

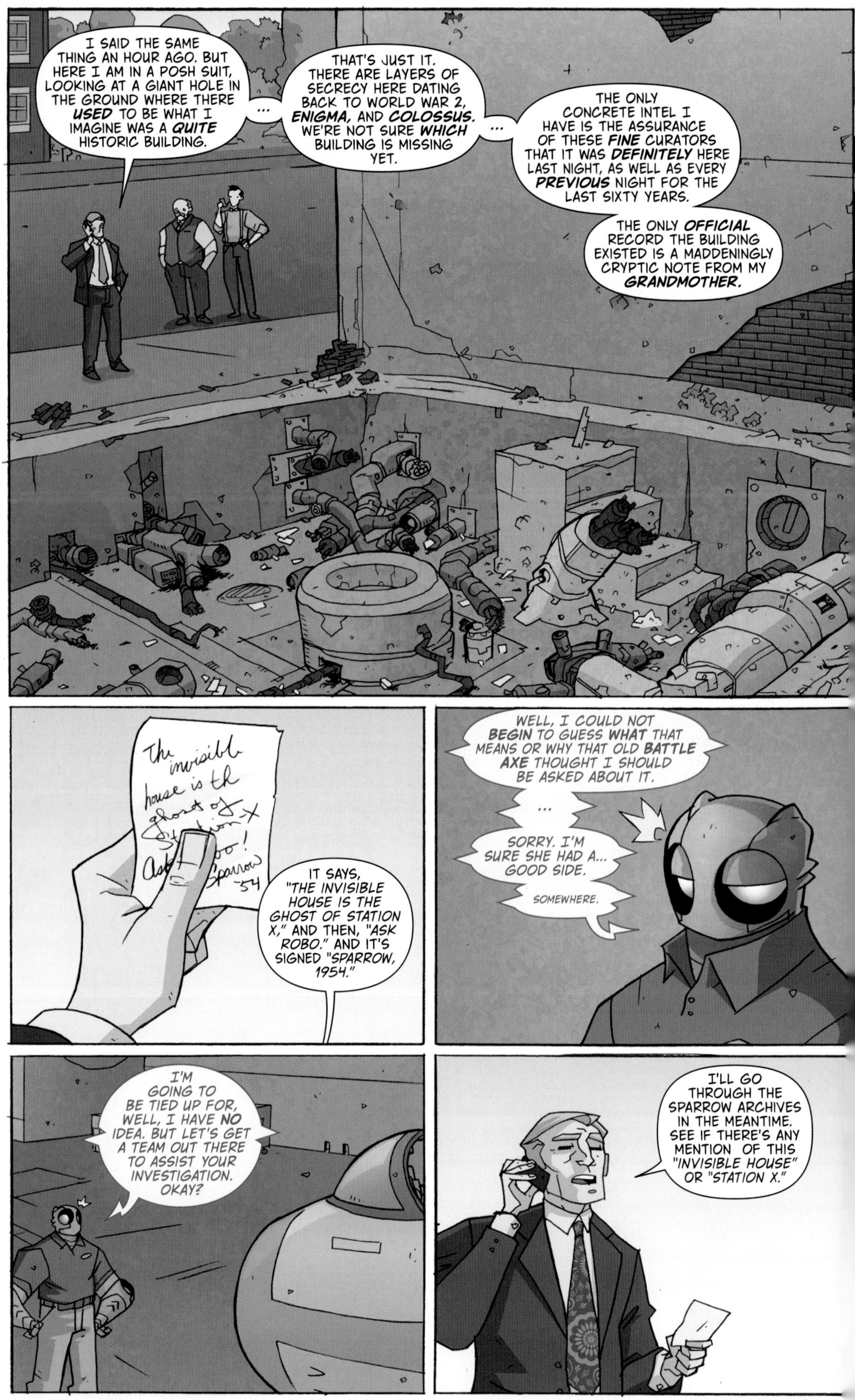
I SAID THE SAME THING AN HOUR AGO. BUT HERE I AM IN A POSH SUIT, LOOKING AT A GIANT HOLE IN THE GROUND WHERE THERE USED TO BE WHAT I IMAGINE WAS A QUITE HISTORIC BUILDING.
...
THAT'S JUST IT. THERE ARE LAYERS OF SECRECY HERE DATING BACK TO WORLD WAR 2, ENIGMA, AND COLOSSUS. WE'RE NOT SURE WHICH BUILDING IS MISSING YET.
...
THE ONLY CONCRETE INTEL I HAVE IS THE ASSURANCE OF THESE FINE CURATORS THAT IT WAS DEFINITELY HERE LAST NIGHT, AS WELL AS EVERY PREVIOUS NIGHT FOR THE LAST SIXTY YEARS.
THE ONLY OFFICIAL RECORD THE BUILDING EXISTED IS A MADDENINGLY CRYPTIC NOTE FROM MY GRANDMOTHER.
IT SAYS, "THE INVISIBLE HOUSE IS THE GHOST OF STATION X," AND THEN, "ASK ROBO." AND IT'S SIGNED "SPARROW, 1954."
WELL, I COULD NOT BEGIN TO GUESS WHAT THAT MEANS OR WHY THAT OLD BATTLE AXE THOUGHT I SHOULD BE ASKED ABOUT IT.
...
SORRY. I'M SURE SHE HAD A... GOOD SIDE.
SOMEWHERE.
I'M GOING TO BE TIED UP FOR, WELL, I HAVE NO IDEA. BUT LET'S GET A TEAM OUT THERE TO ASSIST YOUR INVESTIGATION. OKAY?
I'LL GO THROUGH THE SPARROW ARCHIVES IN THE MEANTIME. SEE IF THERE'S ANY MENTION OF THIS "INVISIBLE HOUSE" OR "STATION X."

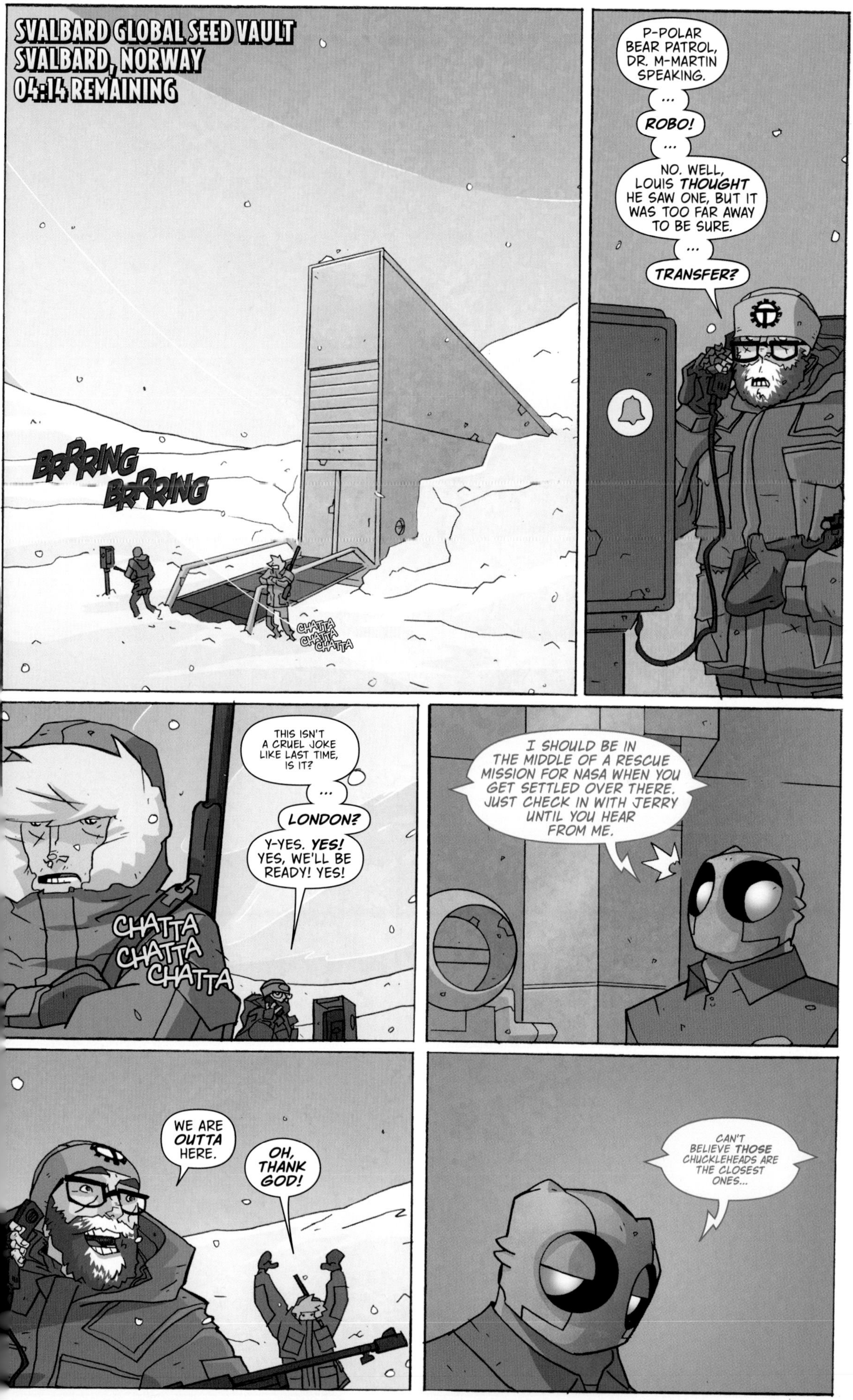
SVALBARD GLOBAL SEED VAULT
SVALBARD, NORWAY
04:14 REMAINING
BRRRING
BRRRING
CHATTA CHATTA CHATTA
P-POLAR BEAR PATROL, DR. M-MARTIN SPEAKING.
...
ROBO!
...
NO. WELL, LOUIS THOUGHT HE SAW ONE, BUT IT WAS TOO FAR AWAY TO BE SURE.
...
TRANSFER?
THIS ISN'T A CRUEL JOKE LIKE LAST TIME, IS IT?
...
LONDON?
Y-YES. YES! YES, WE'LL BE READY! YES!
CHATTA
CHATTA
CHATTA
I SHOULD BE IN THE MIDDLE OF A RESCUE MISSION FOR NASA WHEN YOU GET SETTLED OVER THERE. JUST CHECK IN WITH JERRY UNTIL YOU HEAR FROM ME.
WE ARE OUTTA HERE.
OH, THANK GOD!
CAN'T BELIEVE THOSE CHUCKLEHEADS ARE THE CLOSEST ONES...

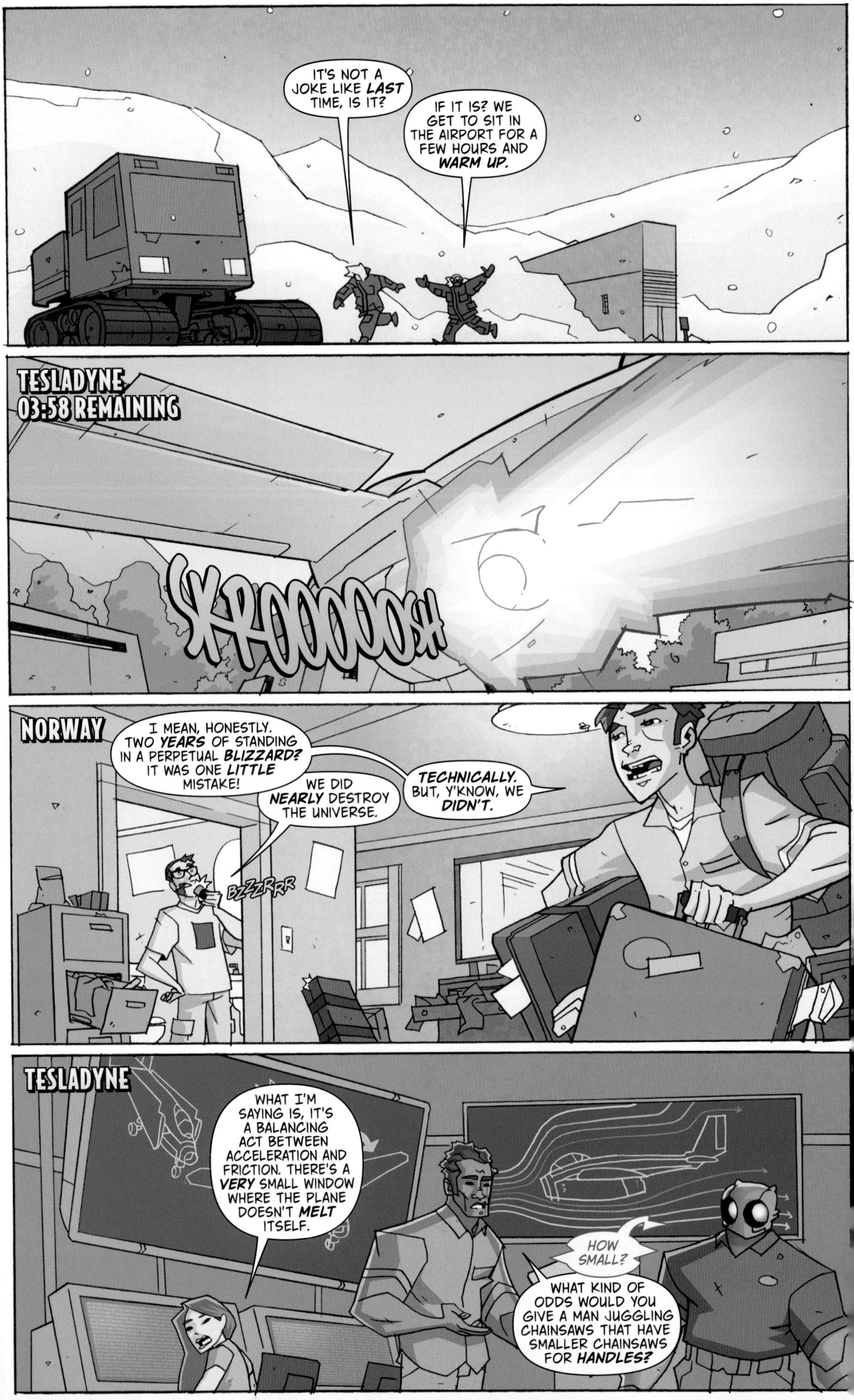
IT'S NOT A JOKE LIKE LAST TIME, IS IT?
IF IT IS? WE GET TO SIT IN THE AIRPORT FOR A FEW HOURS AND WARM UP.
TESLADYNE
03:58 REMAINING
SKROOOOOOSH
NORWAY
I MEAN, HONESTLY. TWO YEARS OF STANDING IN A PERPETUAL BLIZZARD? IT WAS ONE LITTLE MISTAKE!
WE DID NEARLY DESTROY THE UNIVERSE.
TECHNICALLY. BUT, Y'KNOW, WE DIDN'T.
BZZZRRR
TESLADYNE
WHAT I'M SAYING IS, IT'S A BALANCING ACT BETWEEN ACCELERATION AND FRICTION. THERE'S A VERY SMALL WINDOW WHERE THE PLANE DOESN'T MELT ITSELF.
HOW SMALL?
WHAT KIND OF ODDS WOULD YOU GIVE A MAN JUGGLING CHAINSAWS THAT HAVE SMALLER CHAINSAWS FOR HANDLES?

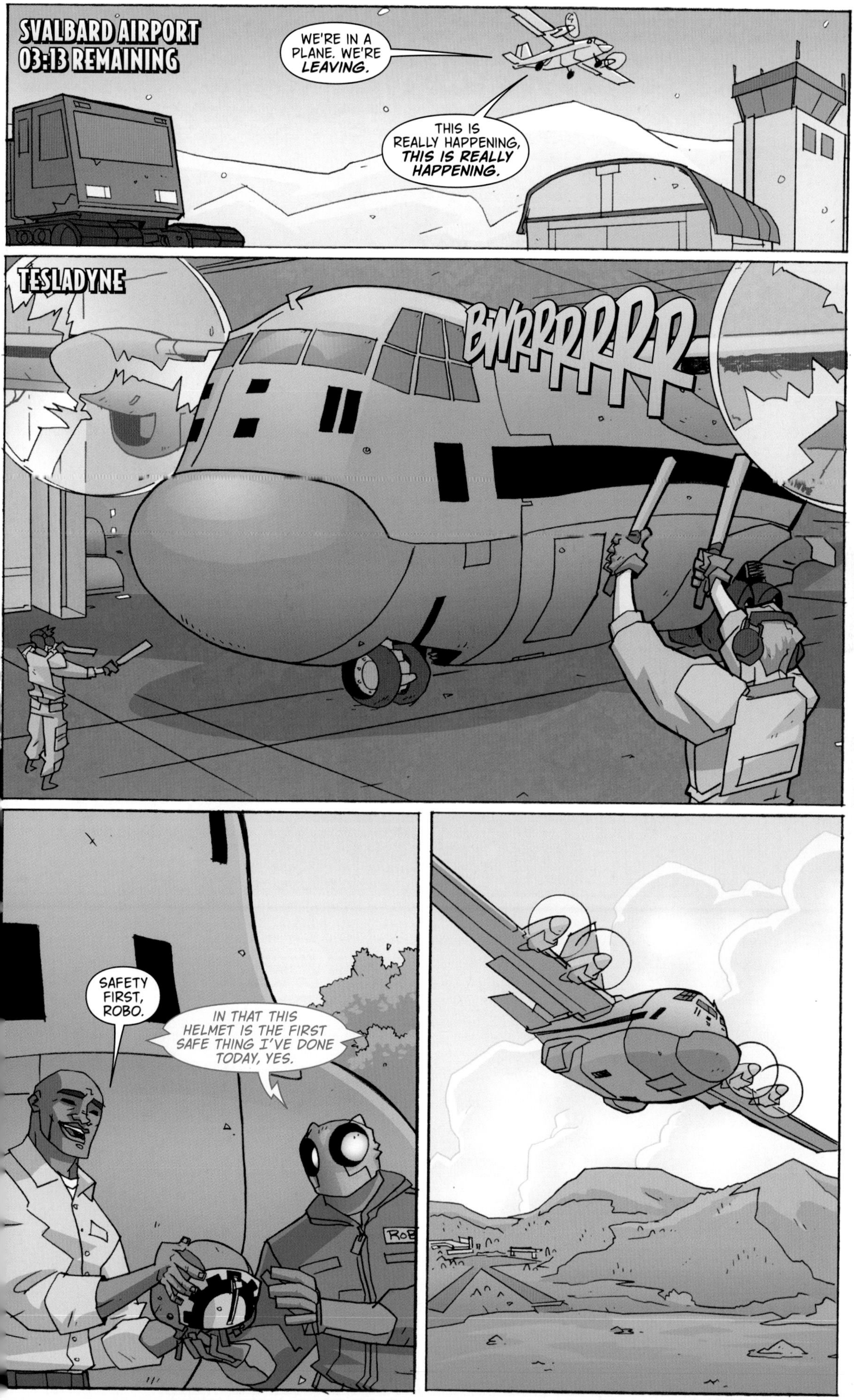
SVALBARD AIRPORT
03:13 REMAINING
WE'RE IN A PLANE. WE'RE LEAVING.
THIS IS REALLY HAPPENING, THIS IS REALLY HAPPENING.
TESLADYNE
BWRRRRRR
SAFETY FIRST, ROBO.
IN THAT THIS HELMET IS THE FIRST SAFE THING I'VE DONE TODAY, YES.

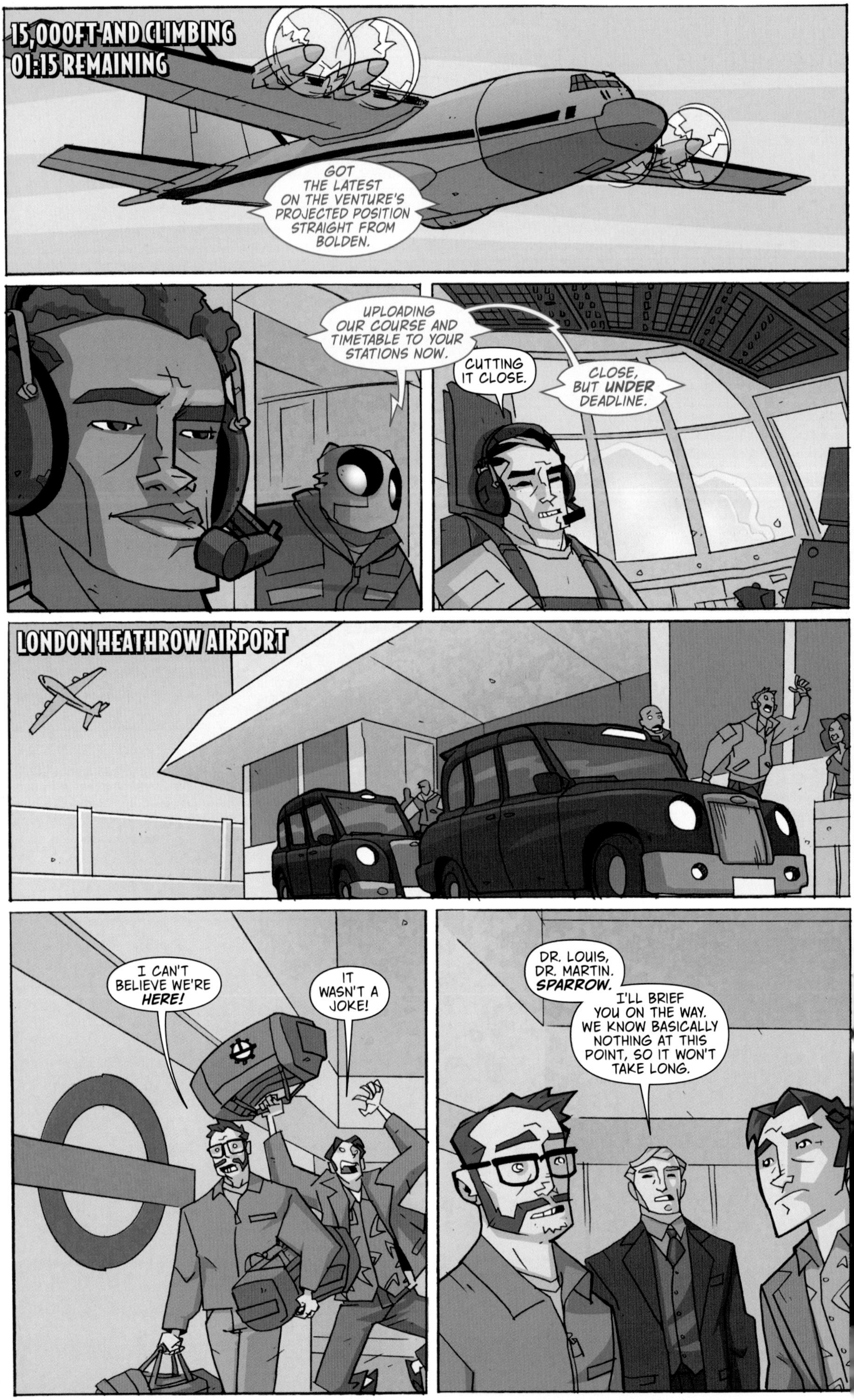
15,000FT AND CLIMBING
01:15 REMAINING
GOT THE LATEST ON THE VENTURE'S PROJECTED POSITION STRAIGHT FROM BOLDEN.
UPLOADING OUR COURSE AND TIMETABLE TO YOUR STATIONS NOW.
CUTTING IT CLOSE.
CLOSE, BUT UNDER DEADLINE.
LONDON HEATHROW AIRPORT
I CAN'T BELIEVE WE'RE HERE!
IT WASN'T A JOKE!
DR. LOUIS, DR. MARTIN. SPARROW.
I'LL BRIEF YOU ON THE WAY. WE KNOW BASICALLY NOTHING AT THIS POINT, SO IT WON'T TAKE LONG.

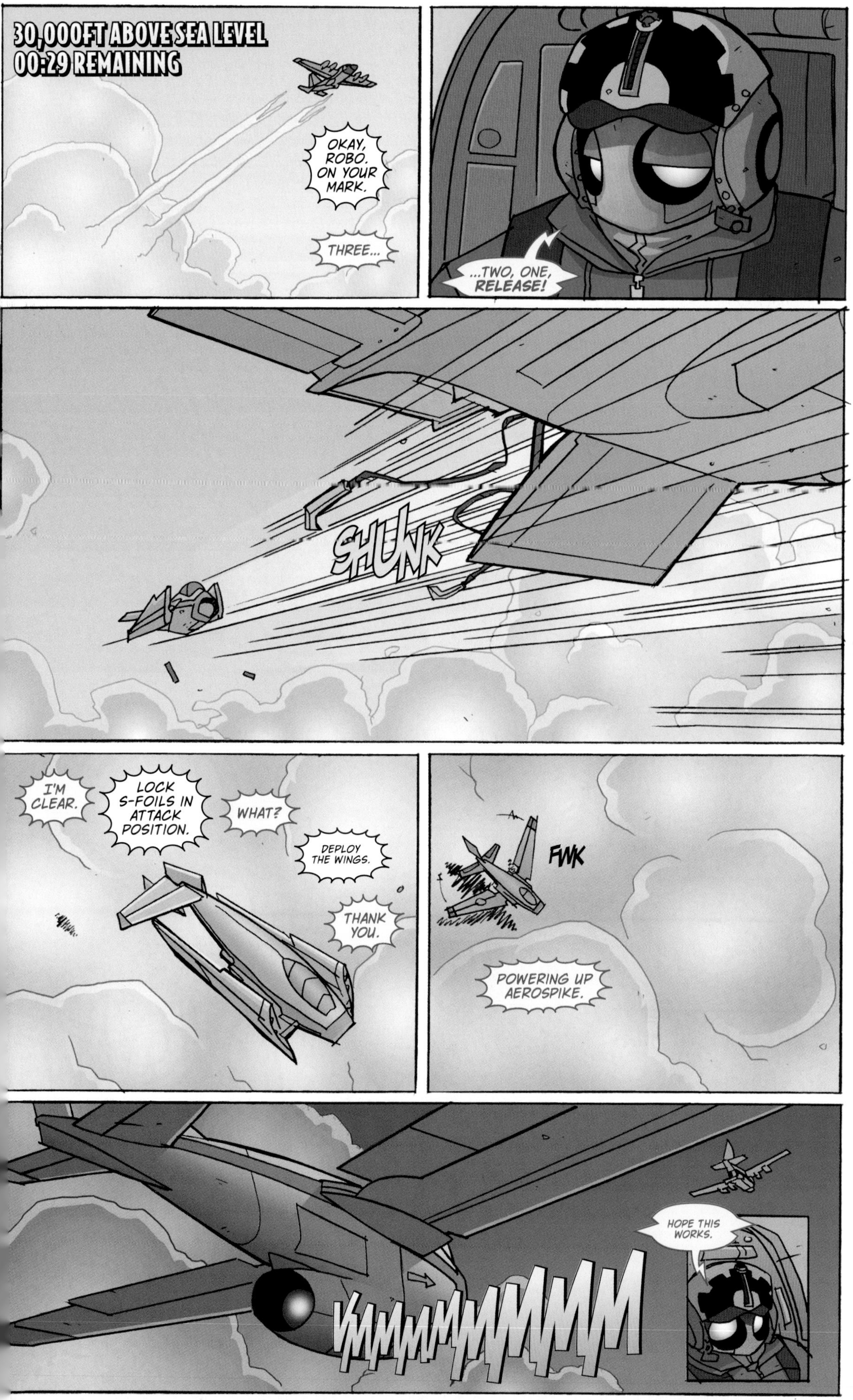
30,000FT ABOVE SEA LEVEL
00:29 REMAINING
OKAY, ROBO. ON YOUR MARK.
THREE...
...TWO, ONE, RELEASE!
SHUNK
I'M CLEAR.
LOCK S-FOILS IN ATTACK POSITION.
WHAT?
DEPLOY THE WINGS.
THANK YOU.
FWK
POWERING UP AEROSPIKE.
HOPE THIS WORKS.
VMMMMMMMMMMM

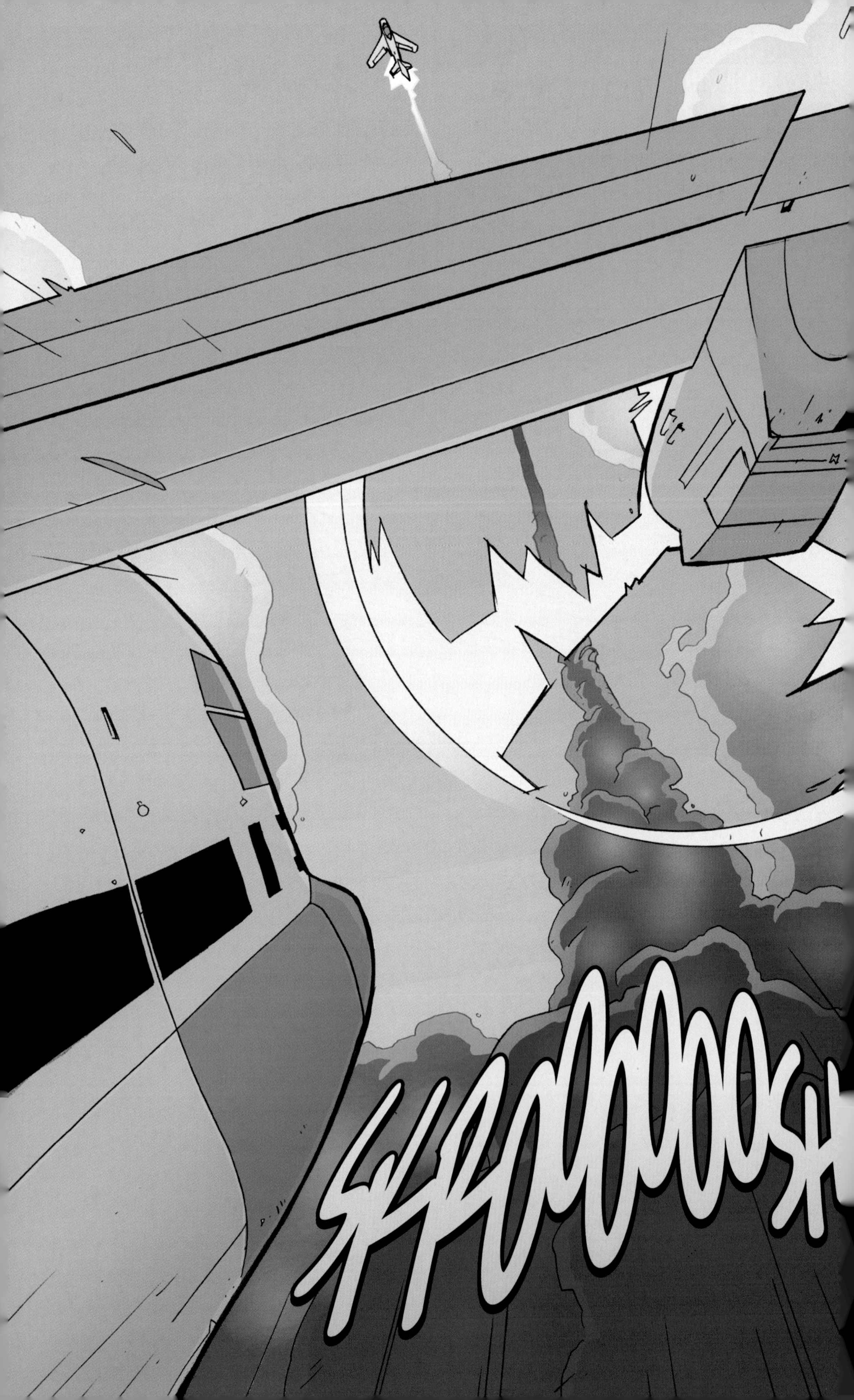
SHOOOOOOSH

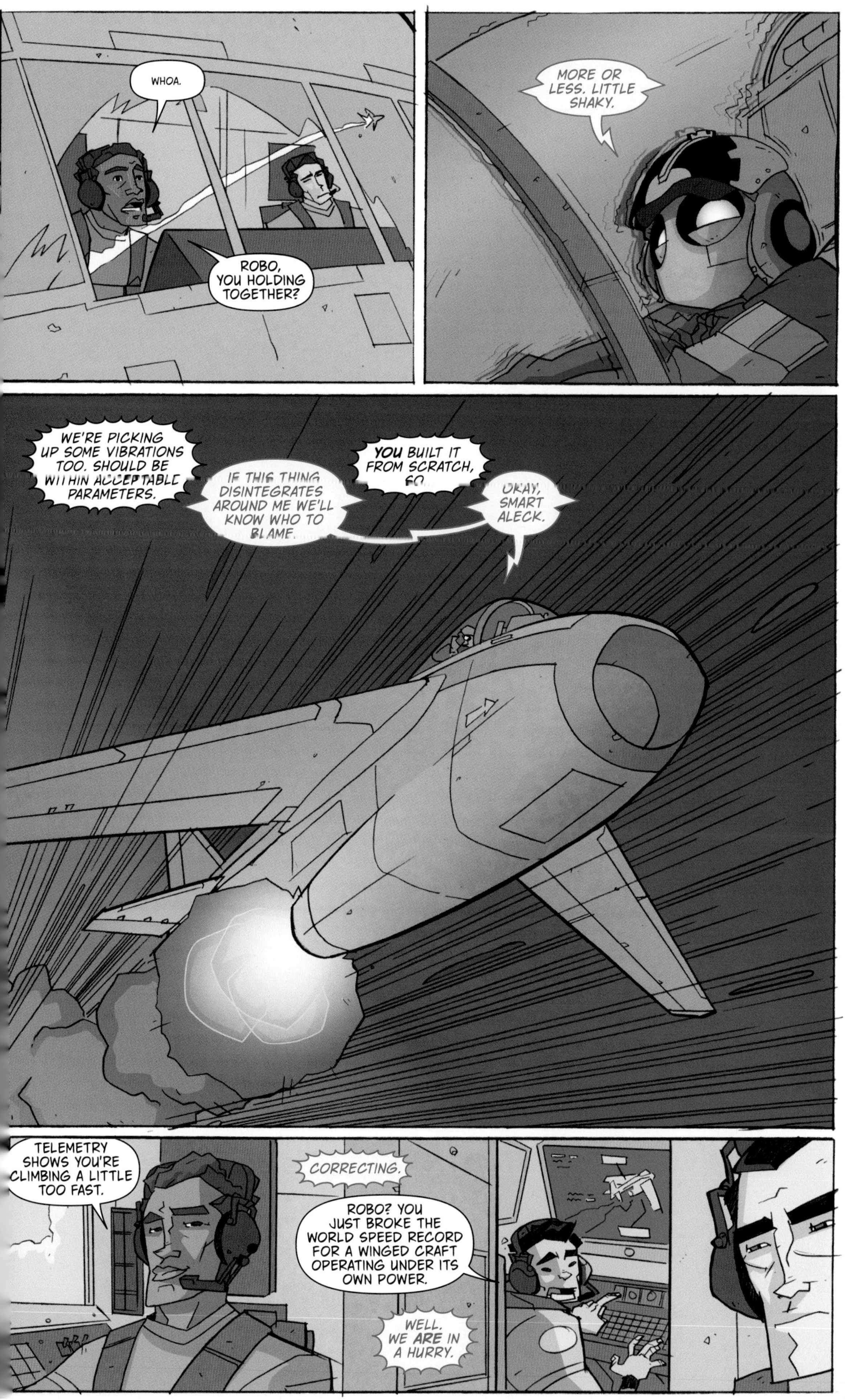
WHOA.
ROBO, YOU HOLDING TOGETHER?
MORE OR LESS. LITTLE SHAKY.
WE'RE PICKING UP SOME VIBRATIONS TOO. SHOULD BE WITHIN ACCEPTABLE PARAMETERS.
IF THIS THING DISINTEGRATES AROUND ME WE'LL KNOW WHO TO BLAME.
YOU BUILT IT FROM SCRATCH, SO.
OKAY, SMART ALECK.
TELEMETRY SHOWS YOU'RE CLIMBING A LITTLE TOO FAST.
CORRECTING.
ROBO? YOU JUST BROKE THE WORLD SPEED RECORD FOR A WINGED CRAFT OPERATING UNDER ITS OWN POWER.
WELL. WE ARE IN A HURRY.

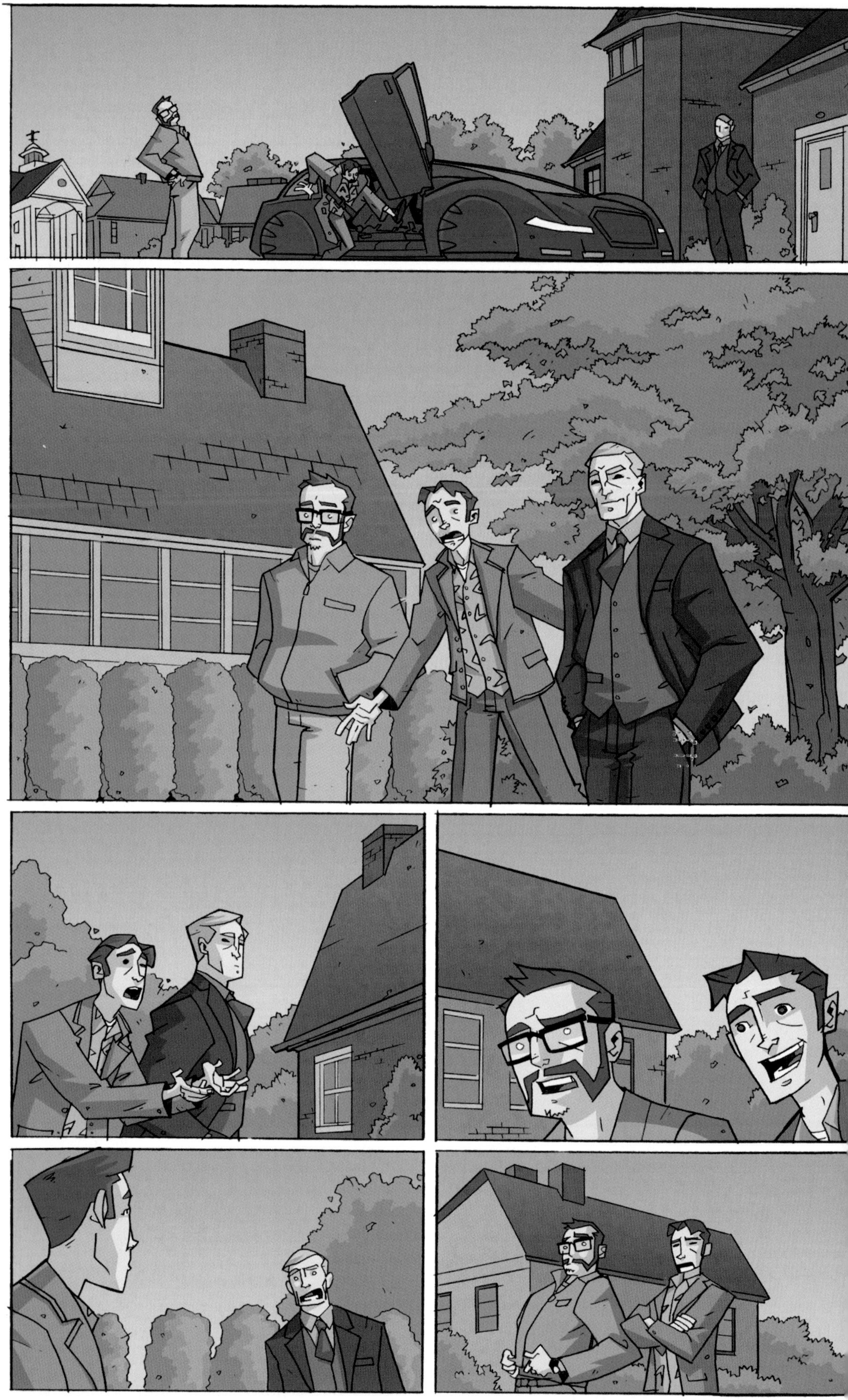

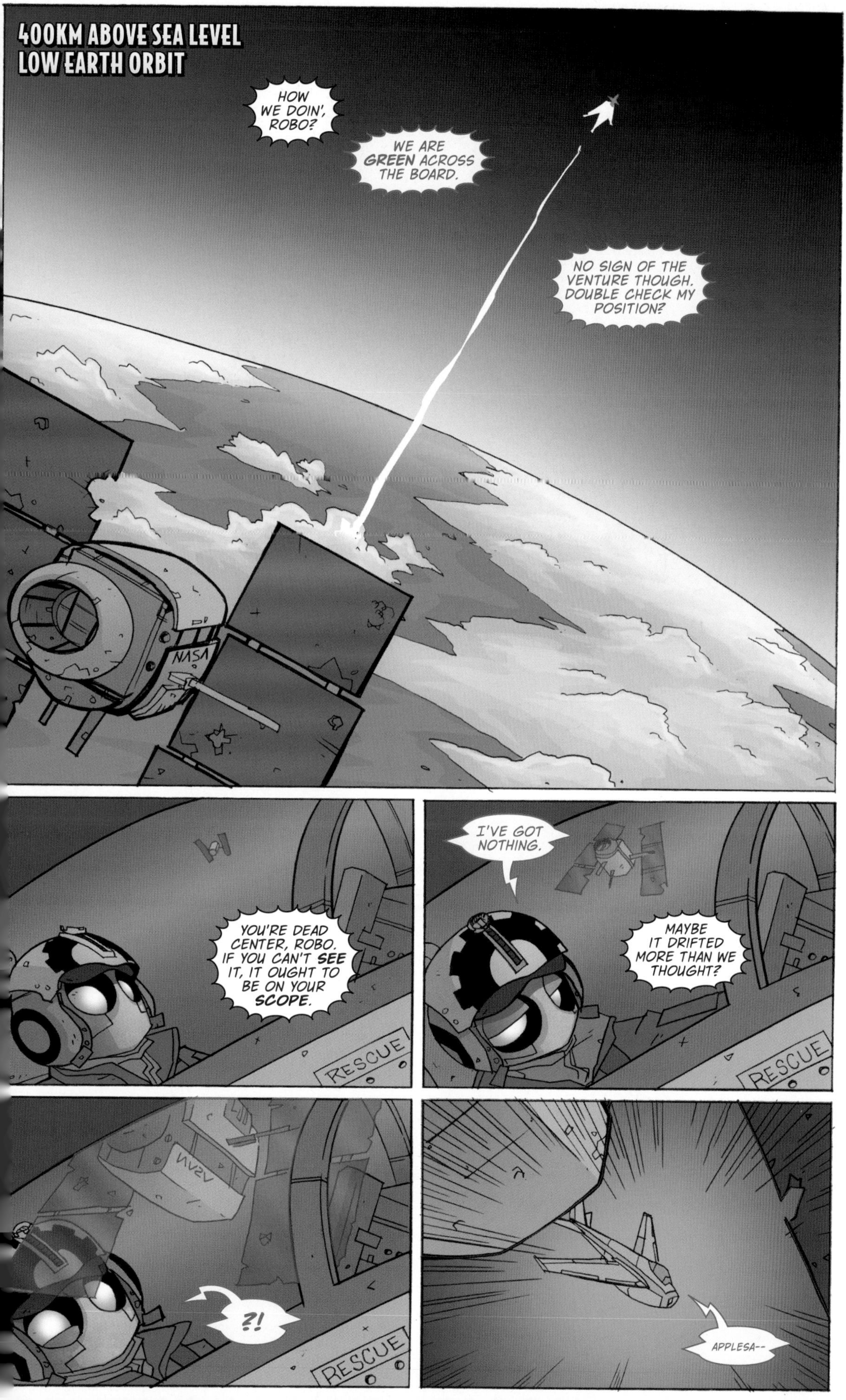
400KM ABOVE SEA LEVEL
LOW EARTH ORBIT
HOW WE DOIN', ROBO?
WE ARE GREEN ACROSS THE BOARD.
NO SIGN OF THE VENTURE THOUGH. DOUBLE CHECK MY POSITION?
NASA
YOU'RE DEAD CENTER, ROBO. IF YOU CAN'T SEE IT, IT OUGHT TO BE ON YOUR SCOPE.
RESCUE
I'VE GOT NOTHING.
MAYBE IT DRIFTED MORE THAN WE THOUGHT?
RESCUE
?!
RESCUE
APPLESA--

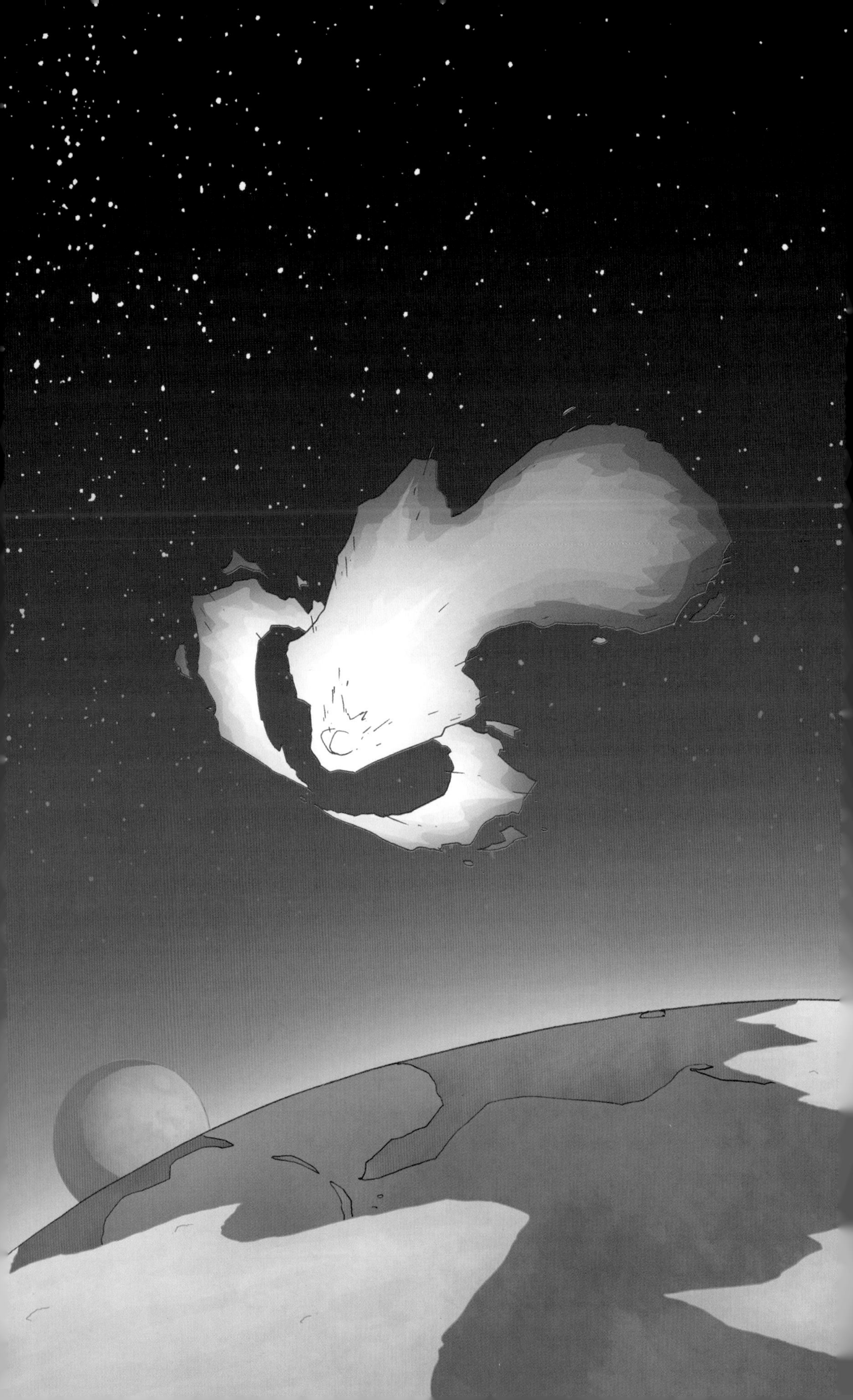

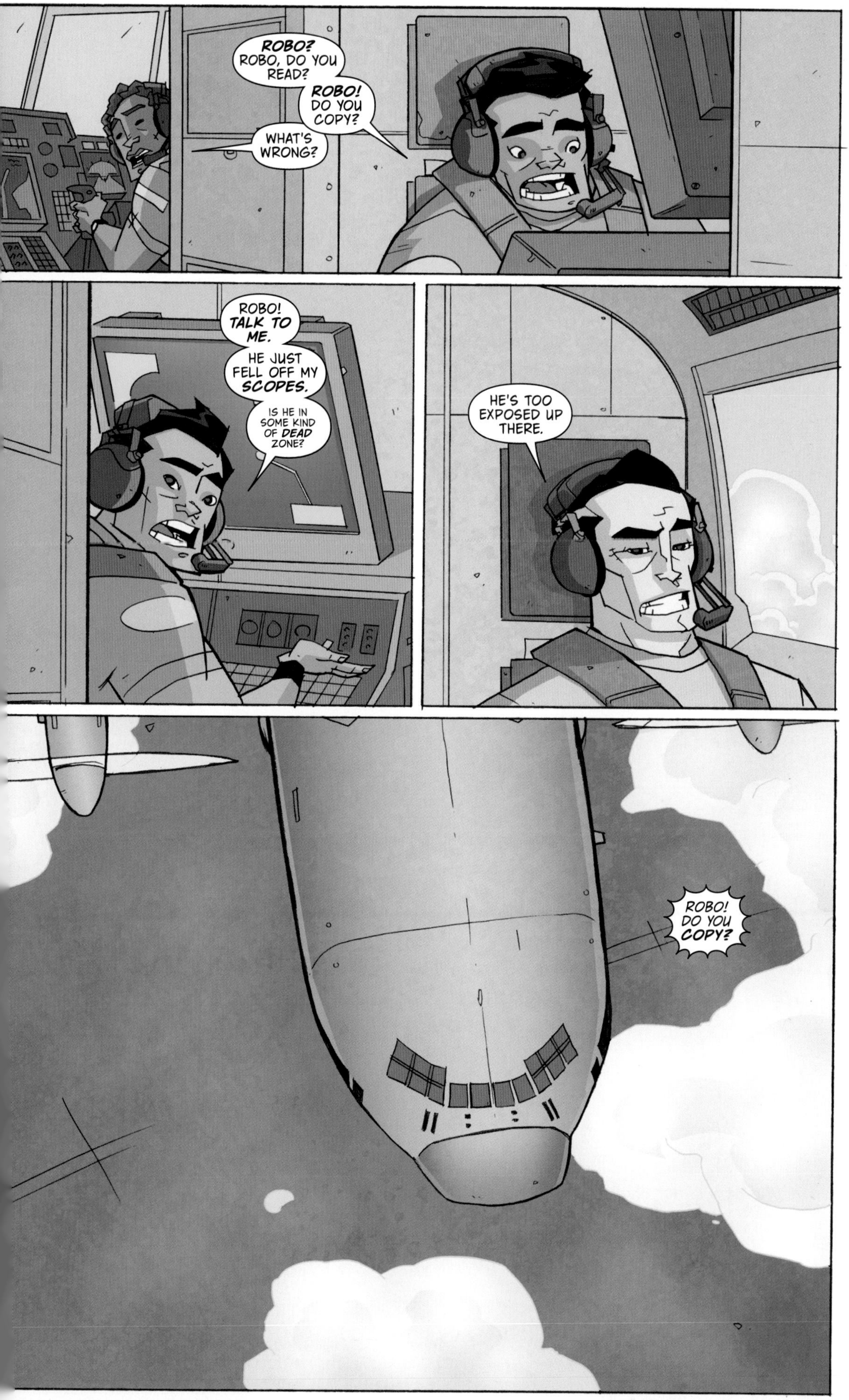
ROBO? ROBO, DO YOU READ?
ROBO! DO YOU COPY?
WHAT'S WRONG?
ROBO! TALK TO ME.
HE JUST FELL OFF MY SCOPES.
IS HE IN SOME KIND OF DEAD ZONE?
HE'S TOO EXPOSED UP THERE.
ROBO! DO YOU COPY?

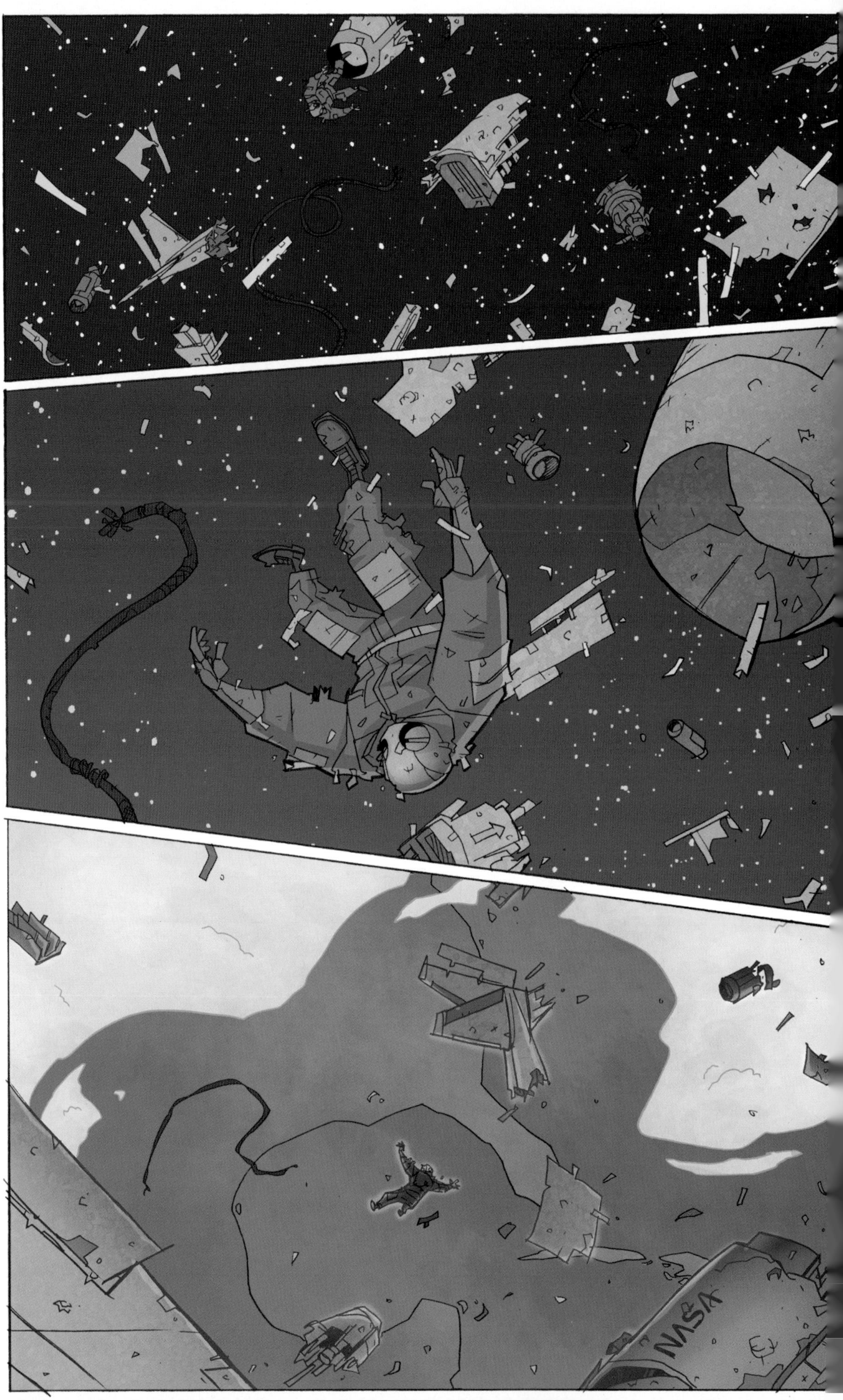
NASA

EXPLOSION

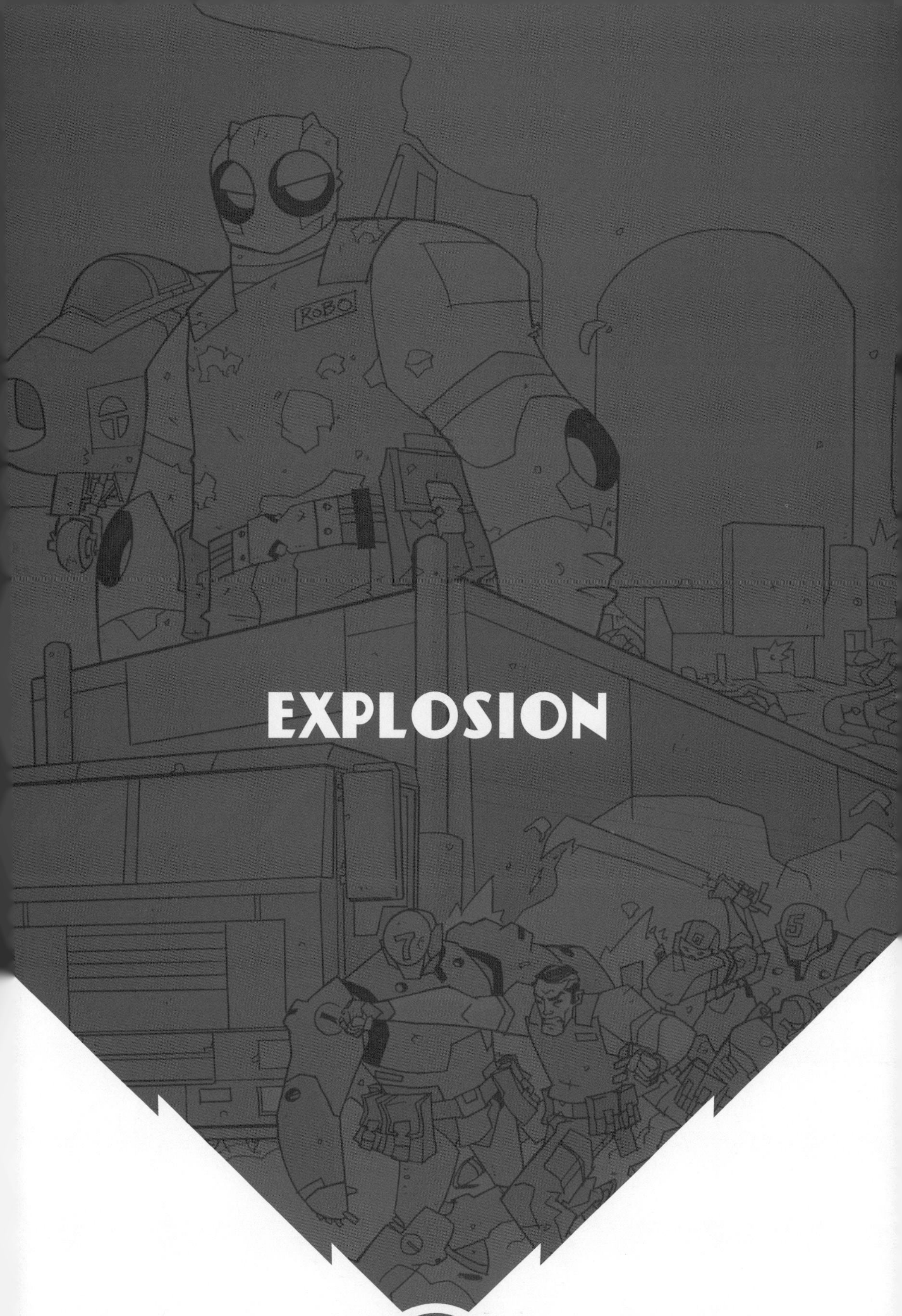
ROBO

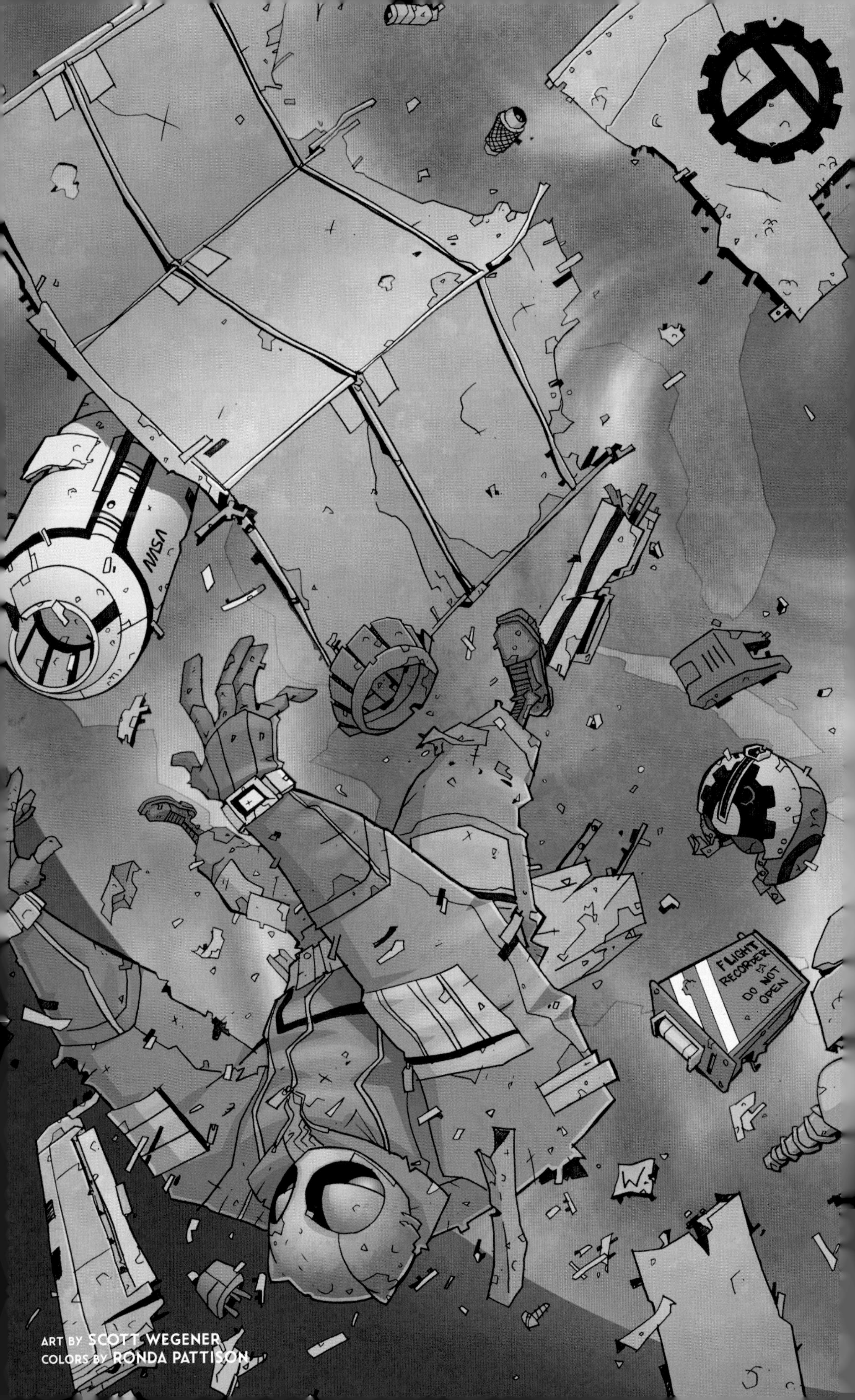
NASA
FLIGHT RECORDER
DO NOT OPEN
ART BY SCOTT WEGENER
COLORS BY RONDA PATTISON

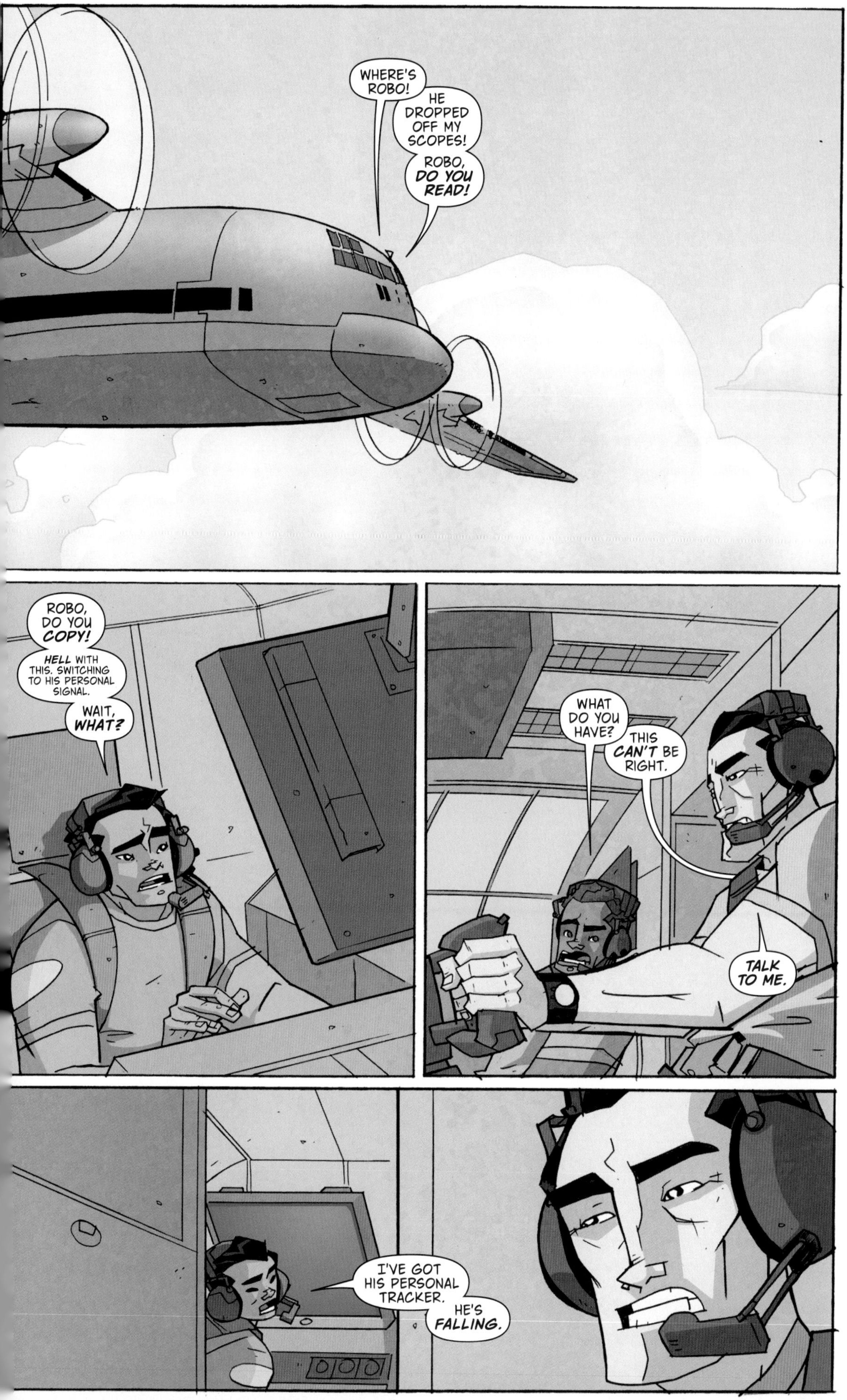
WHERE'S ROBO!
HE DROPPED OFF MY SCOPES!
ROBO, DO YOU READ!
ROBO, DO YOU COPY!
HELL WITH THIS. SWITCHING TO HIS PERSONAL SIGNAL.
WAIT, WHAT?
WHAT DO YOU HAVE?
THIS CAN'T BE RIGHT.
TALK TO ME.
I'VE GOT HIS PERSONAL TRACKER.
HE'S FALLING.

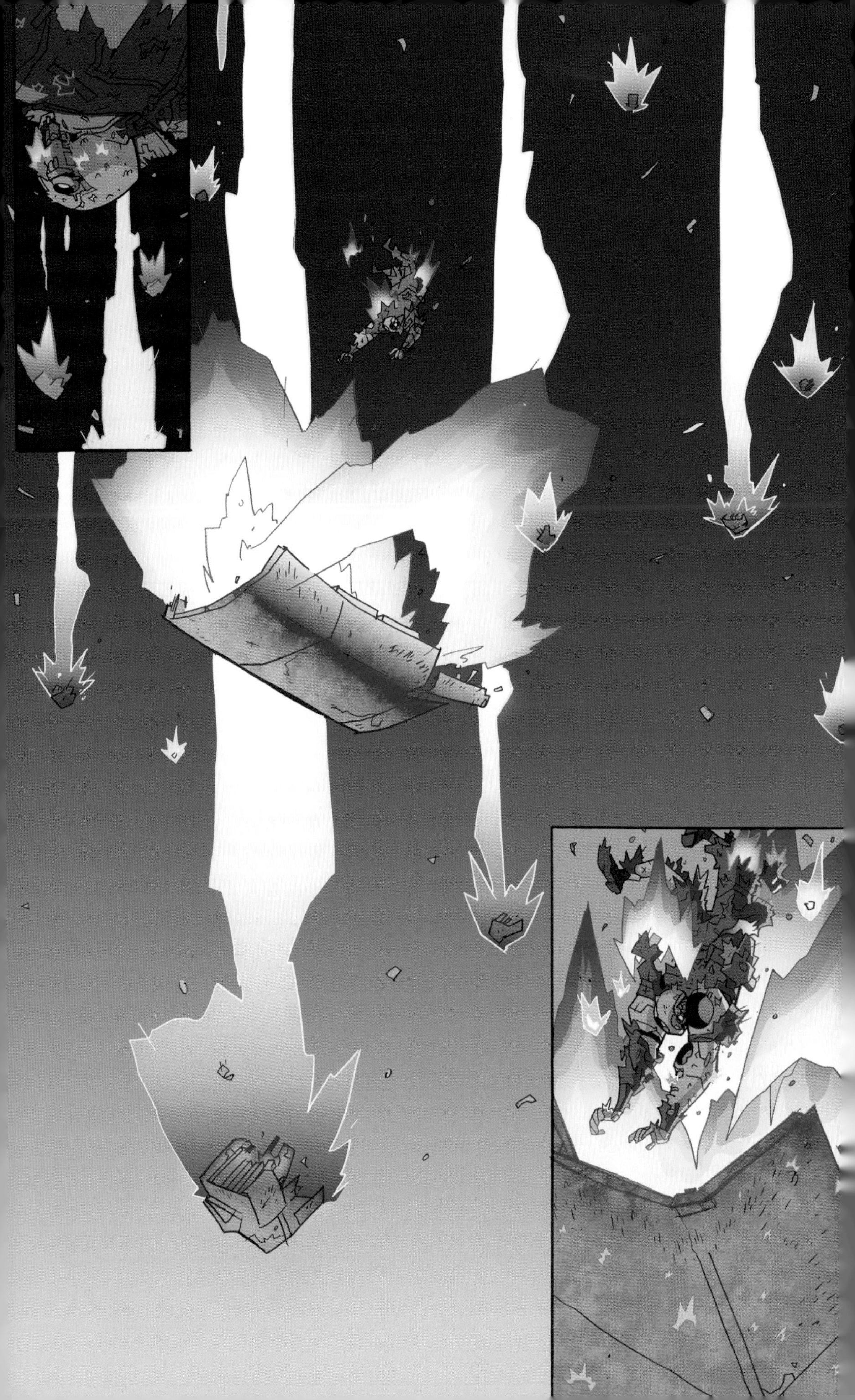

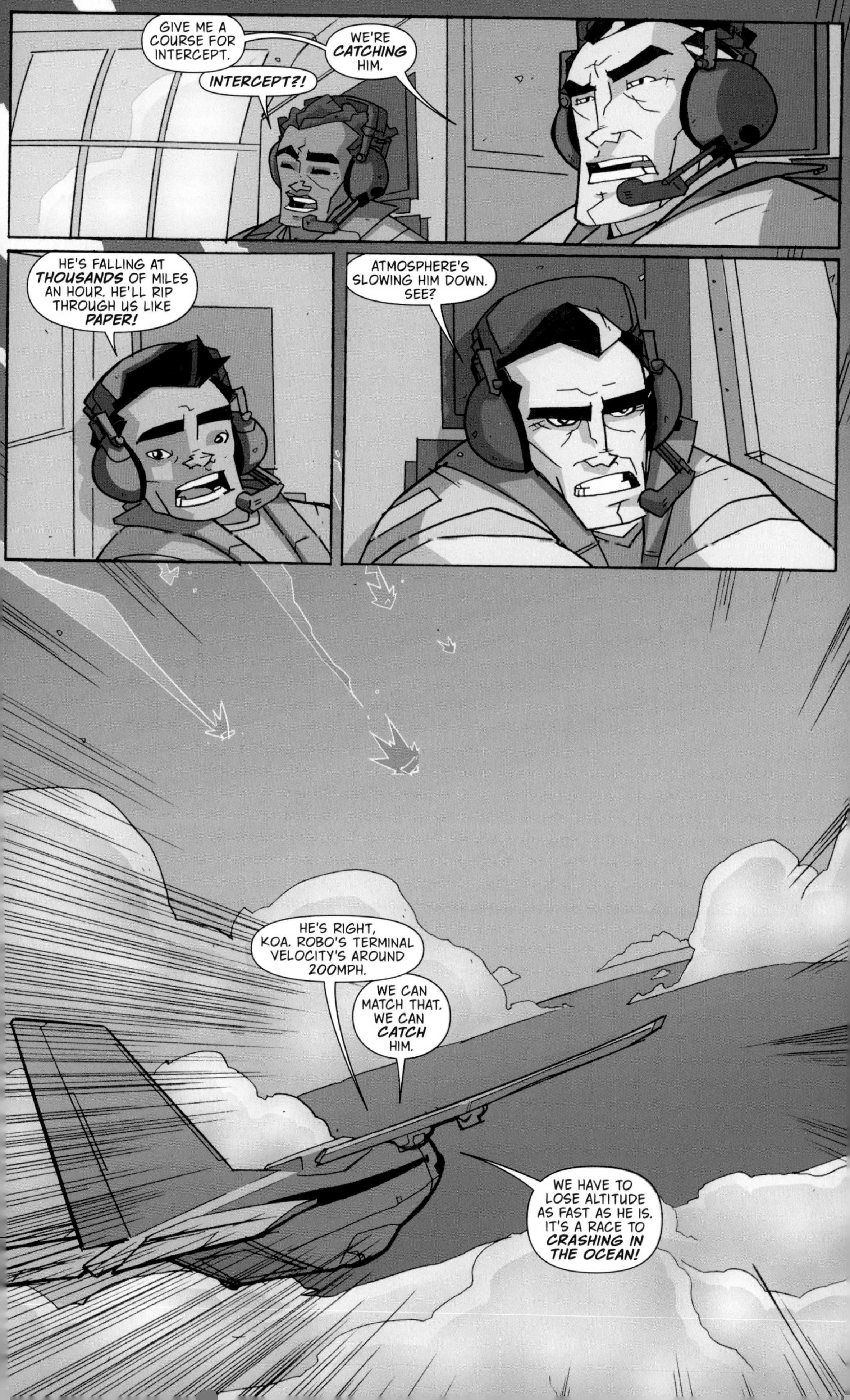
GIVE ME A COURSE FOR INTERCEPT.
WE'RE CATCHING HIM.
INTERCEPT?!
HE'S FALLING AT THOUSANDS OF MILES AN HOUR. HE'LL RIP THROUGH US LIKE PAPER!
ATMOSPHERE'S SLOWING HIM DOWN. SEE?
HE'S RIGHT, KOA. ROBO'S TERMINAL VELOCITY'S AROUND 200MPH.
WE CAN MATCH THAT. WE CAN CATCH HIM.
WE HAVE TO LOSE ALTITUDE AS FAST AS HE IS. IT'S A RACE TO CRASHING IN THE OCEAN!

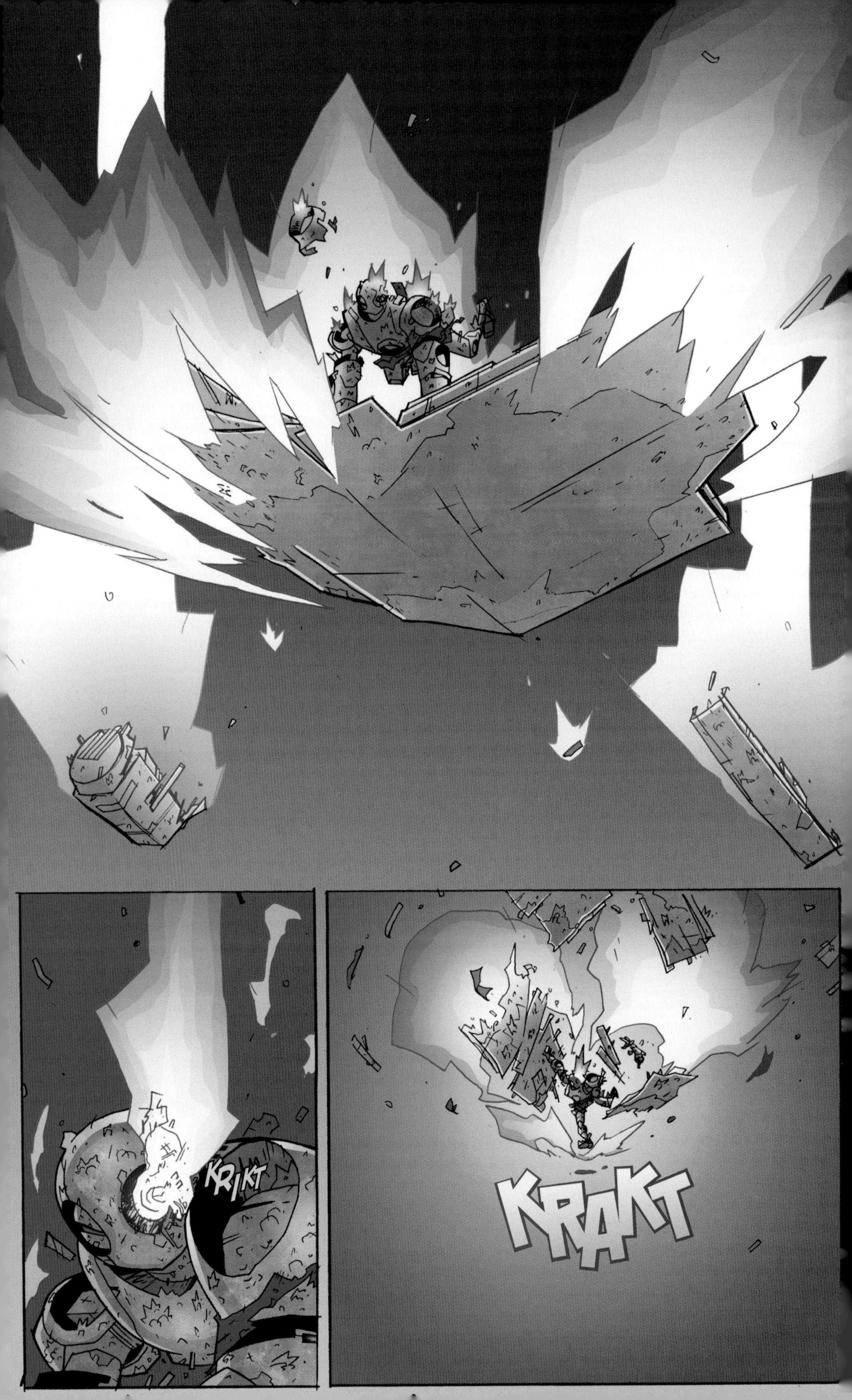
KRIKT
KRAKT

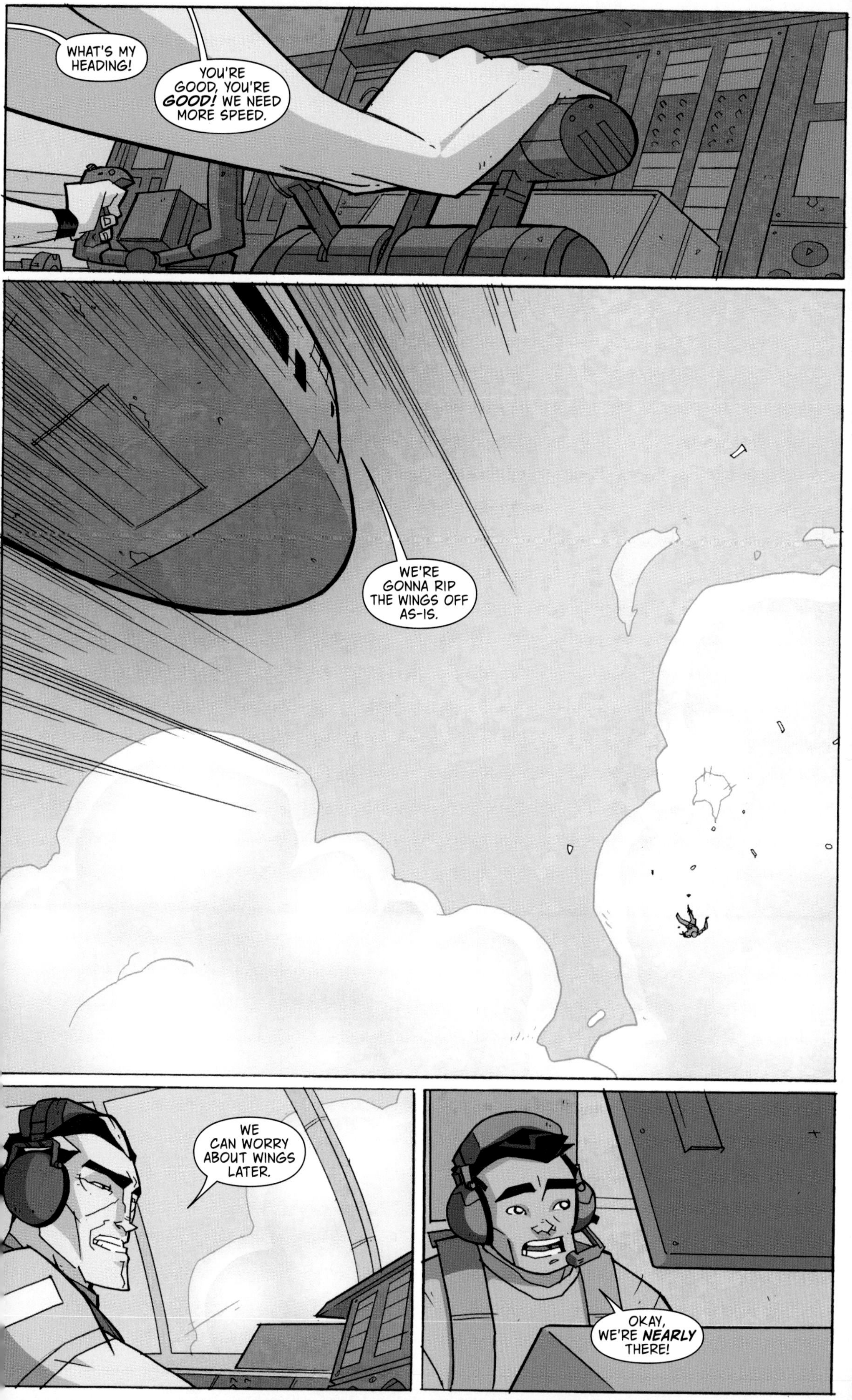
WHAT'S MY HEADING!
YOU'RE GOOD, YOU'RE **GOOD!** WE NEED MORE SPEED.
WE'RE GONNA RIP THE WINGS OFF AS-IS.
WE CAN WORRY ABOUT WINGS LATER.
OKAY, WE'RE **NEARLY** THERE!

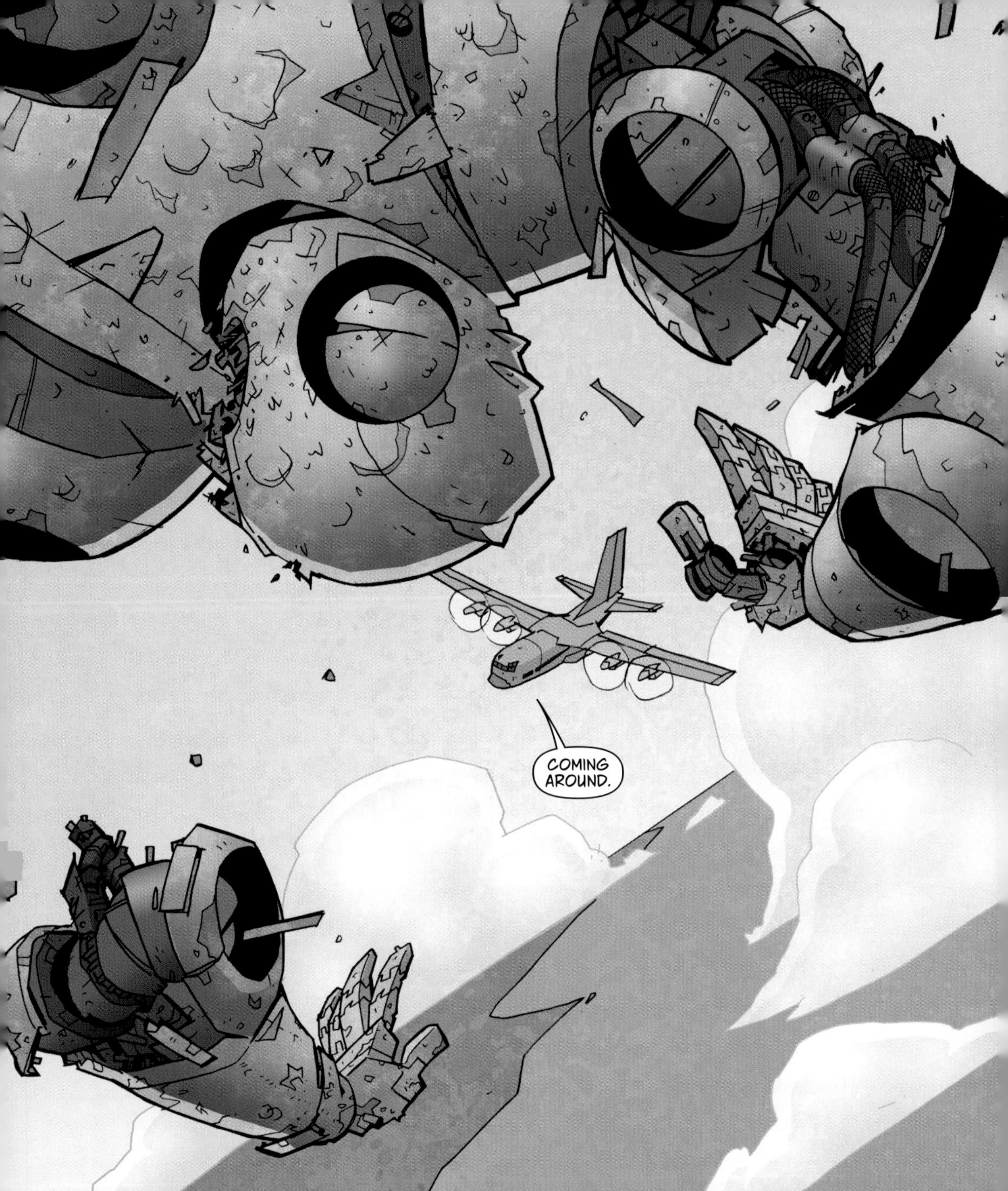
COMING AROUND.

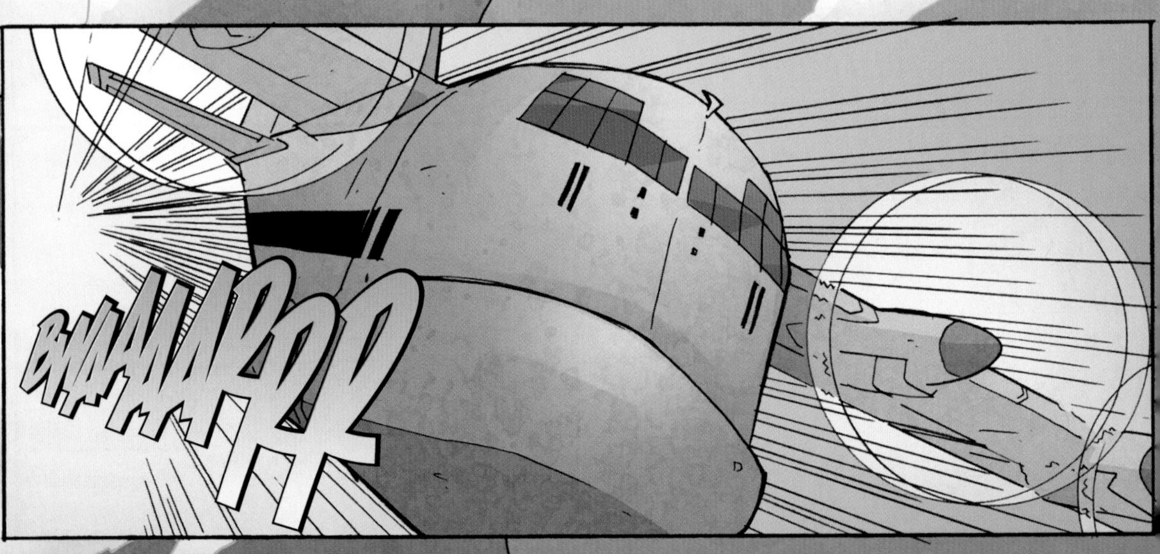
BWAAARRR

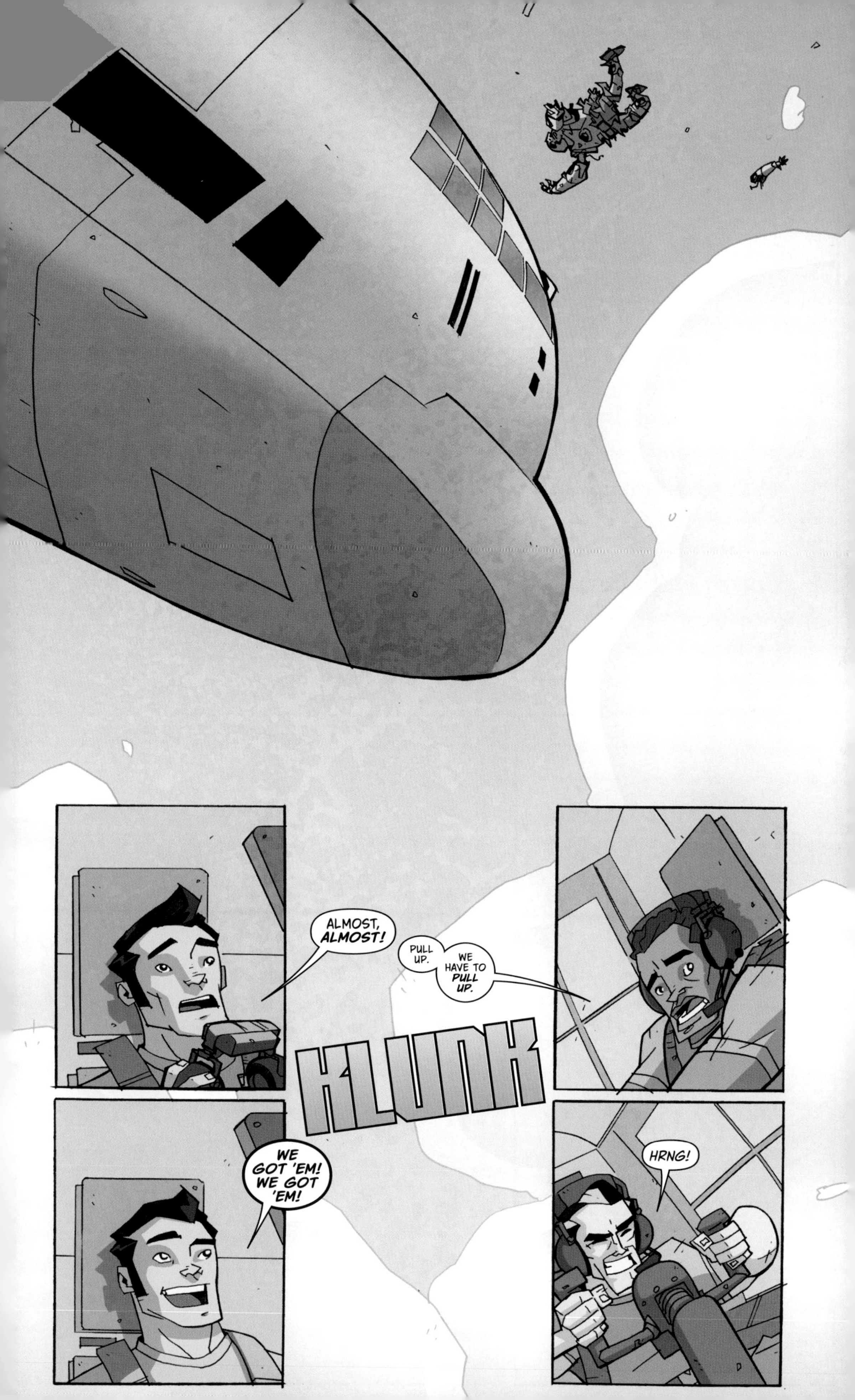

ALMOST, ALMOST!
PULL UP.
WE HAVE TO PULL UP.
KLUNK
WE GOT 'EM! WE GOT 'EM!
HRNG!

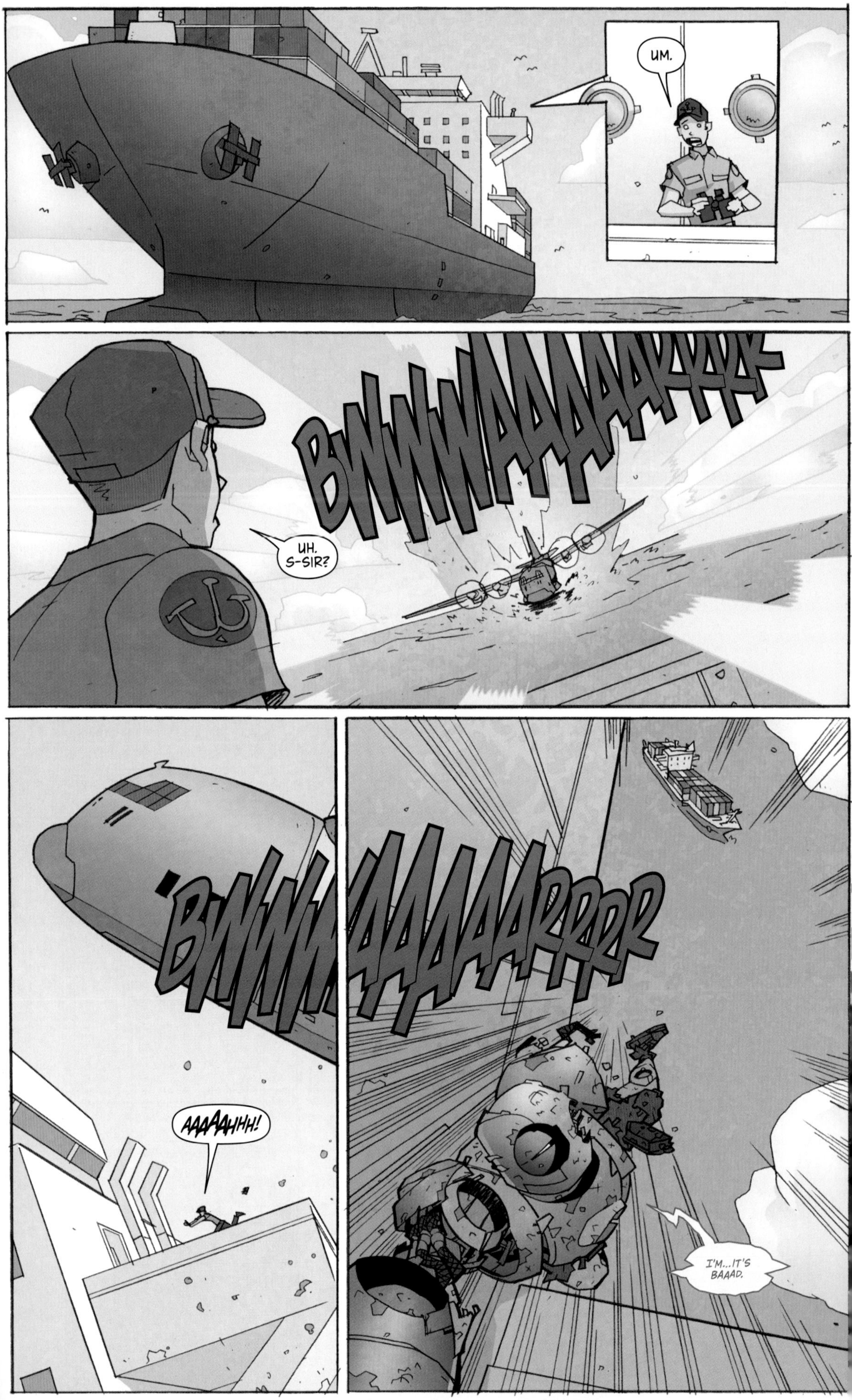
UM.
BWWWAAAAARRRRR
UH. S-SIR?
BWWWAAAAAARRRR
AAAAAHHH!
I'M...IT'S BAAAD.

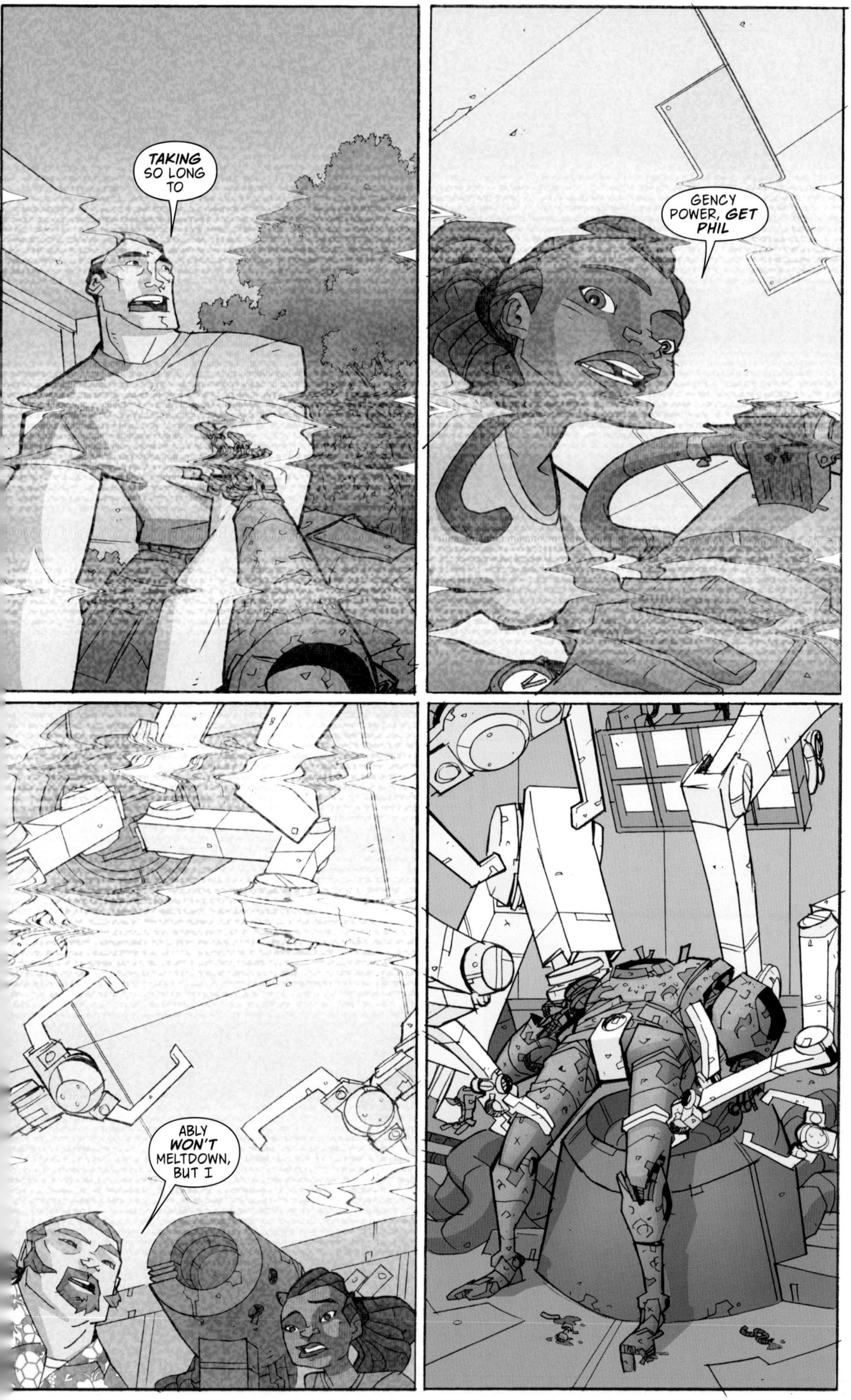
TAKING SO LONG TO
GENCY POWER, GET PHIL
ABLY WON'T MELTDOWN, BUT I

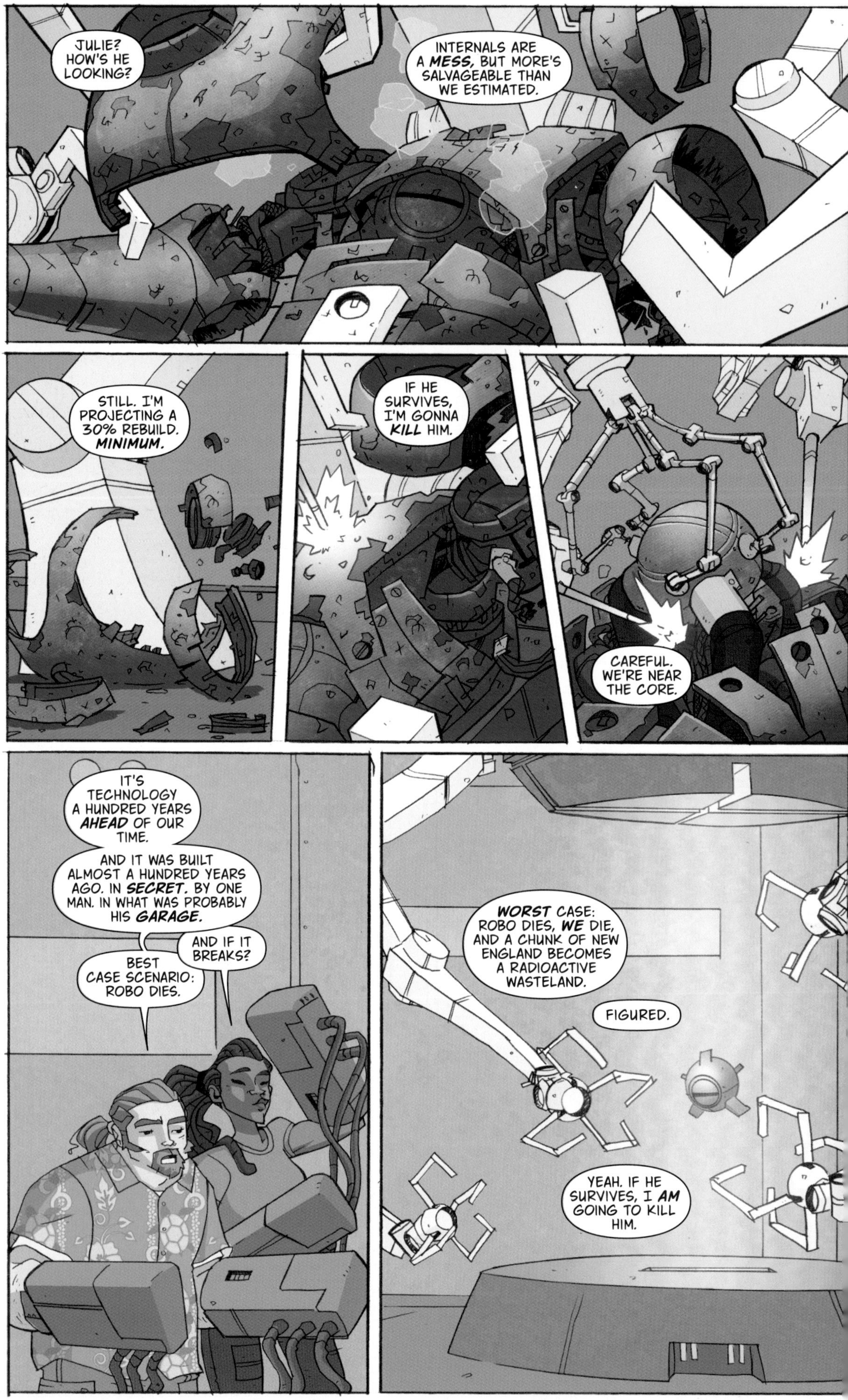
JULIE? HOW'S HE LOOKING?
INTERNALS ARE A MESS, BUT MORE'S SALVAGEABLE THAN WE ESTIMATED.
STILL. I'M PROJECTING A 30% REBUILD. MINIMUM.
IF HE SURVIVES, I'M GONNA KILL HIM.
CAREFUL. WE'RE NEAR THE CORE.
IT'S TECHNOLOGY A HUNDRED YEARS AHEAD OF OUR TIME.
AND IT WAS BUILT ALMOST A HUNDRED YEARS AGO. IN SECRET. BY ONE MAN. IN WHAT WAS PROBABLY HIS GARAGE.
AND IF IT BREAKS?
BEST CASE SCENARIO: ROBO DIES.
WORST CASE: ROBO DIES, WE DIE, AND A CHUNK OF NEW ENGLAND BECOMES A RADIOACTIVE WASTELAND.
FIGURED.
YEAH. IF HE SURVIVES, I AM GOING TO KILL HIM.

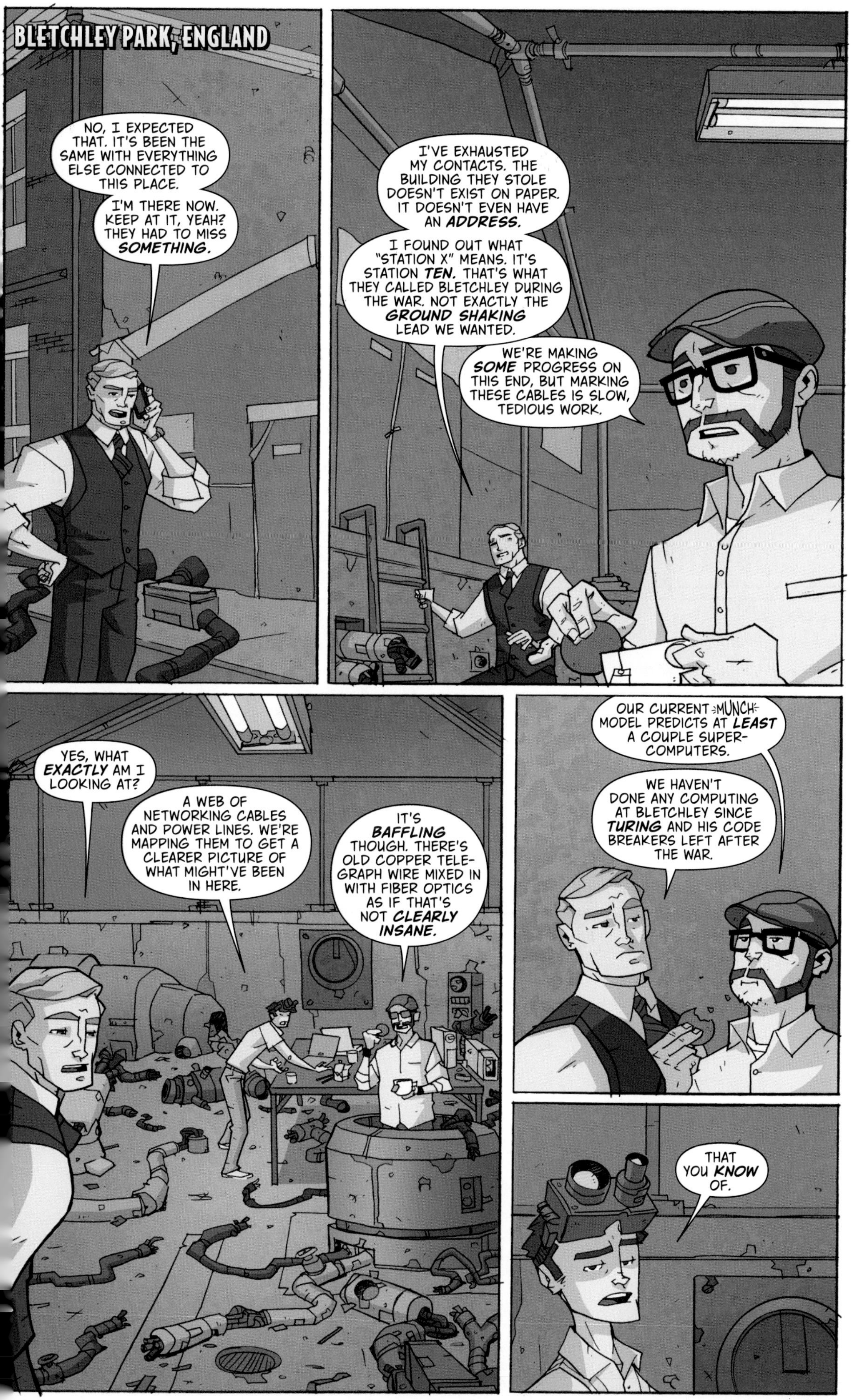
BLETCHLEY PARK, ENGLAND
NO, I EXPECTED THAT. IT'S BEEN THE SAME WITH EVERYTHING ELSE CONNECTED TO THIS PLACE.
I'M THERE NOW. KEEP AT IT, YEAH? THEY HAD TO MISS SOMETHING.
I'VE EXHAUSTED MY CONTACTS. THE BUILDING THEY STOLE DOESN'T EXIST ON PAPER. IT DOESN'T EVEN HAVE AN ADDRESS.
I FOUND OUT WHAT "STATION X" MEANS. IT'S STATION TEN. THAT'S WHAT THEY CALLED BLETCHLEY DURING THE WAR. NOT EXACTLY THE GROUND SHAKING LEAD WE WANTED.
WE'RE MAKING SOME PROGRESS ON THIS END, BUT MARKING THESE CABLES IS SLOW, TEDIOUS WORK.
YES, WHAT EXACTLY AM I LOOKING AT?
A WEB OF NETWORKING CABLES AND POWER LINES. WE'RE MAPPING THEM TO GET A CLEARER PICTURE OF WHAT MIGHT'VE BEEN IN HERE.
IT'S BAFFLING THOUGH. THERE'S OLD COPPER TELEGRAPH WIRE MIXED IN WITH FIBER OPTICS AS IF THAT'S NOT CLEARLY INSANE.
OUR CURRENT MUNCH MODEL PREDICTS AT LEAST A COUPLE SUPERCOMPUTERS.
WE HAVEN'T DONE ANY COMPUTING AT BLETCHLEY SINCE TURING AND HIS CODE BREAKERS LEFT AFTER THE WAR.
THAT YOU KNOW OF.

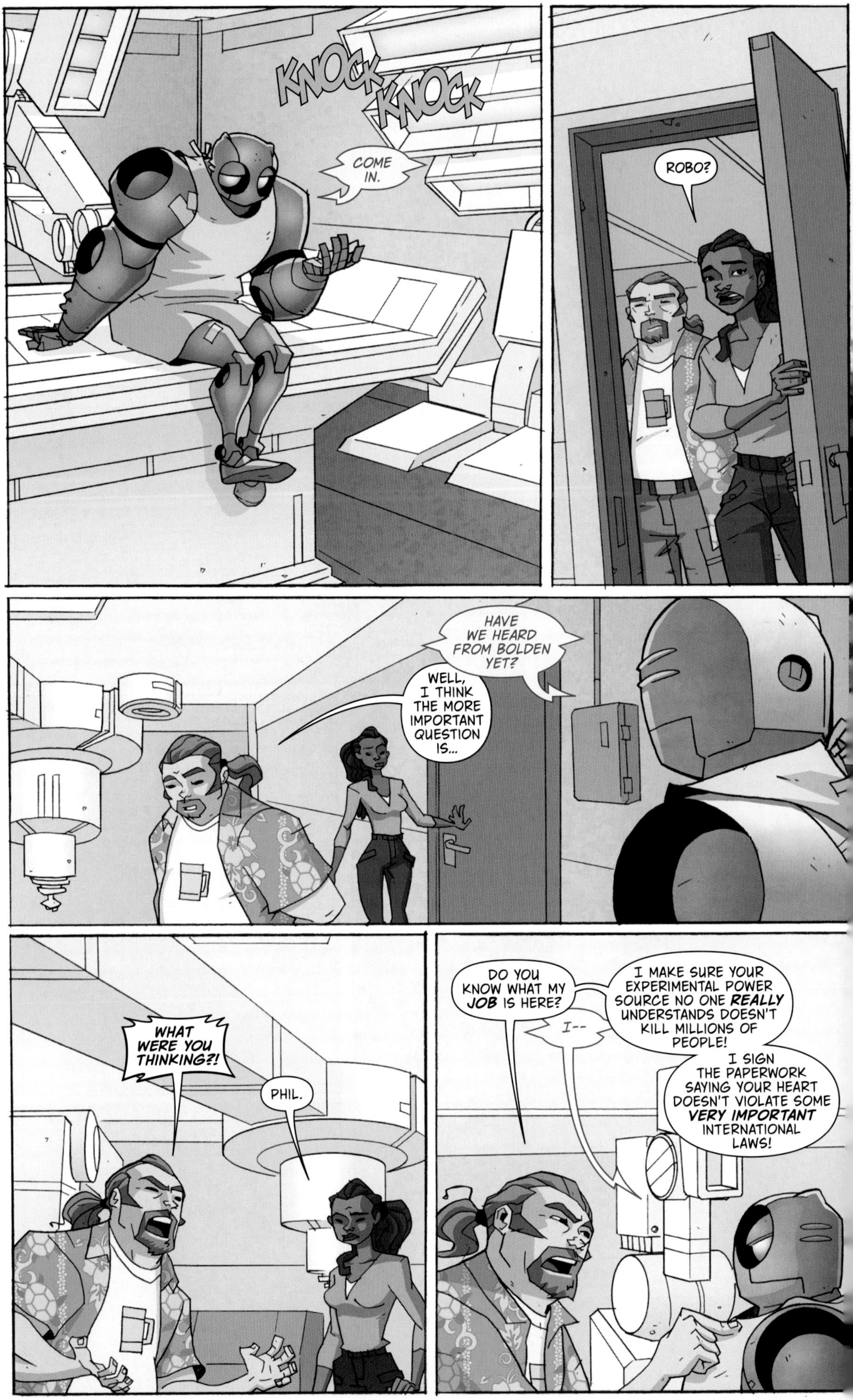
KNOCK KNOCK
COME IN.
ROBO?
HAVE WE HEARD FROM BOLDEN YET?
WELL, I THINK THE MORE IMPORTANT QUESTION IS...
WHAT WERE YOU THINKING?!
PHIL.
DO YOU KNOW WHAT MY JOB IS HERE?
I--
I MAKE SURE YOUR EXPERIMENTAL POWER SOURCE NO ONE REALLY UNDERSTANDS DOESN'T KILL MILLIONS OF PEOPLE!
I SIGN THE PAPERWORK SAYING YOUR HEART DOESN'T VIOLATE SOME VERY IMPORTANT INTERNATIONAL LAWS!

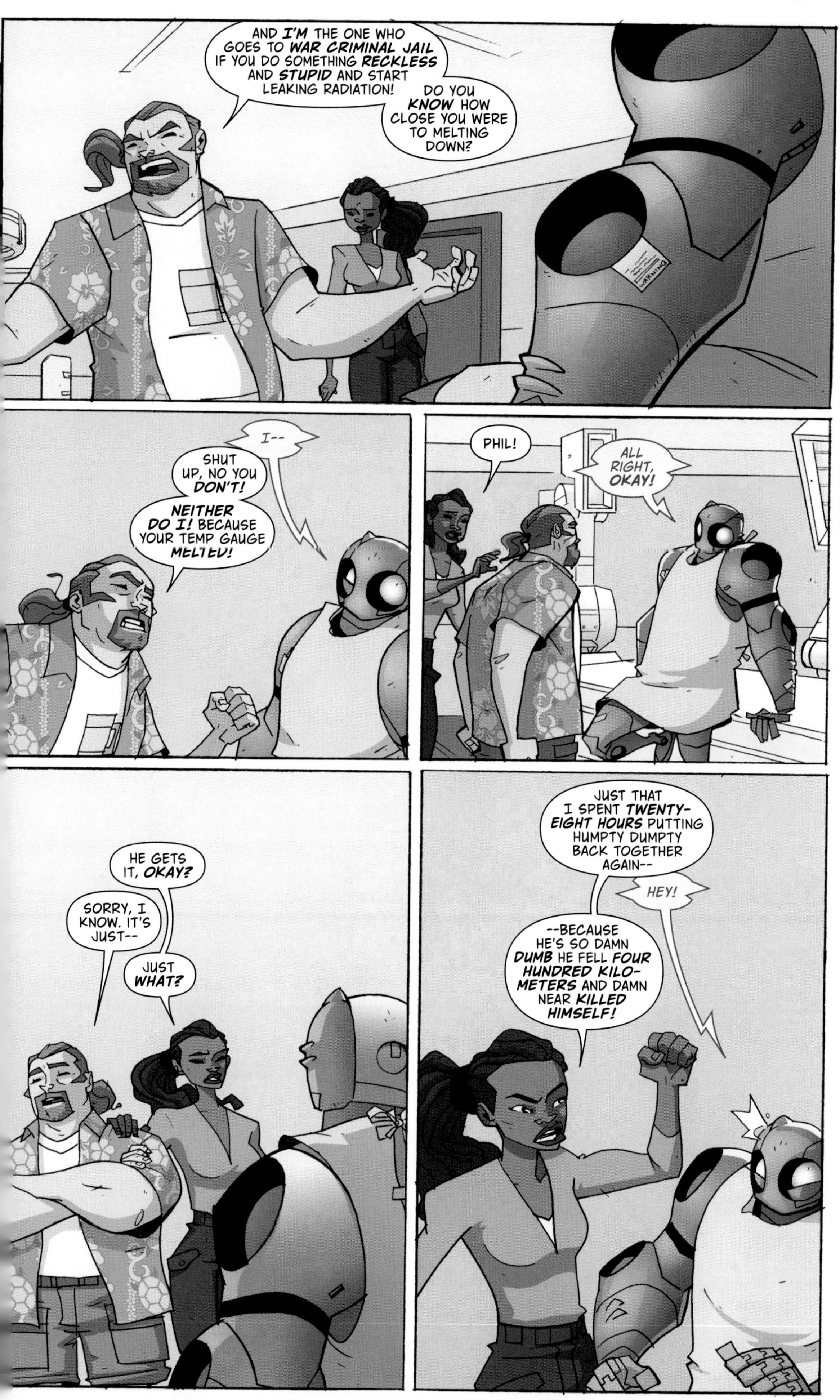
AND I'M THE ONE WHO GOES TO WAR CRIMINAL JAIL IF YOU DO SOMETHING RECKLESS AND STUPID AND START LEAKING RADIATION!
DO YOU KNOW HOW CLOSE YOU WERE TO MELTING DOWN?
WARNING
I--
SHUT UP, NO YOU DON'T!
NEITHER DO I! BECAUSE YOUR TEMP GAUGE MELTED!
PHIL!
ALL RIGHT, OKAY!
HE GETS IT, OKAY?
SORRY, I KNOW. IT'S JUST--
JUST WHAT?
JUST THAT I SPENT TWENTY-EIGHT HOURS PUTTING HUMPTY DUMPTY BACK TOGETHER AGAIN--
HEY!
--BECAUSE HE'S SO DAMN DUMB HE FELL FOUR HUNDRED KILO-METERS AND DAMN NEAR KILLED HIMSELF!

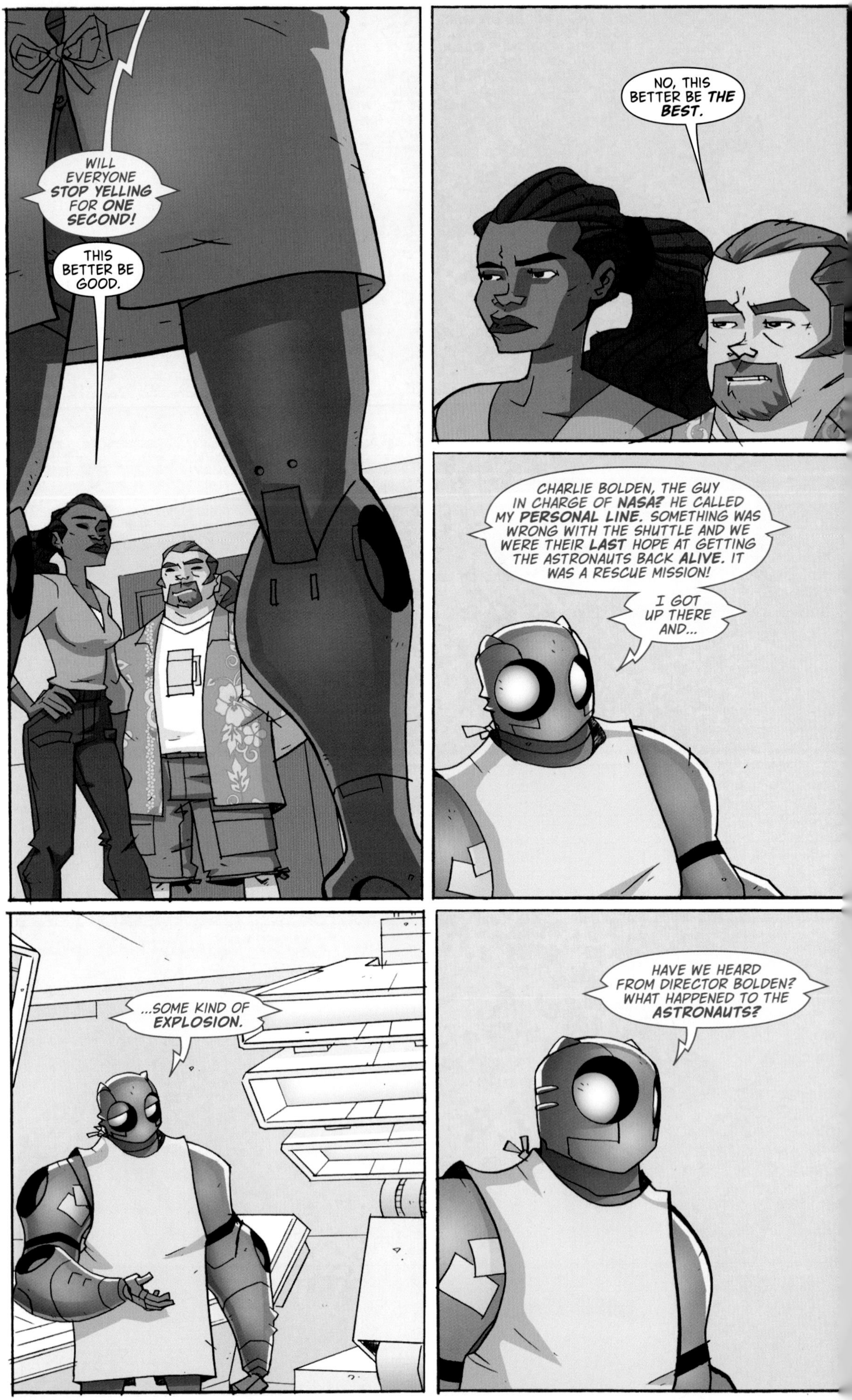
WILL EVERYONE STOP YELLING FOR ONE SECOND!
THIS BETTER BE GOOD.
NO, THIS BETTER BE THE BEST.
CHARLIE BOLDEN, THE GUY IN CHARGE OF NASA? HE CALLED MY PERSONAL LINE. SOMETHING WAS WRONG WITH THE SHUTTLE AND WE WERE THEIR LAST HOPE AT GETTING THE ASTRONAUTS BACK ALIVE. IT WAS A RESCUE MISSION!
I GOT UP THERE AND...
...SOME KIND OF EXPLOSION.
HAVE WE HEARD FROM DIRECTOR BOLDEN? WHAT HAPPENED TO THE ASTRONAUTS?

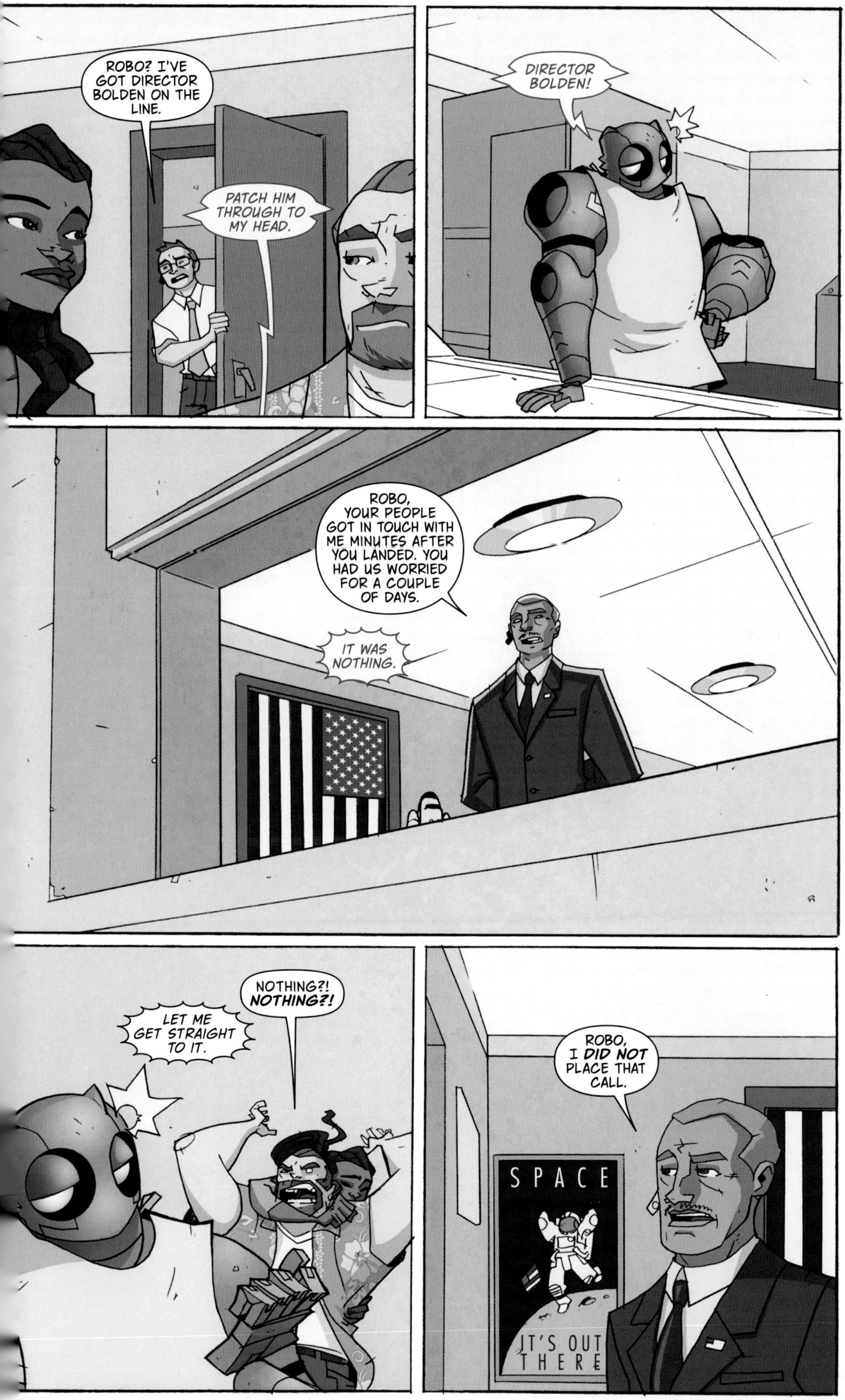
ROBO? I'VE GOT DIRECTOR BOLDEN ON THE LINE.
PATCH HIM THROUGH TO MY HEAD.
DIRECTOR BOLDEN!
ROBO, YOUR PEOPLE GOT IN TOUCH WITH ME MINUTES AFTER YOU LANDED. YOU HAD US WORRIED FOR A COUPLE OF DAYS.
IT WAS NOTHING.
LET ME GET STRAIGHT TO IT.
NOTHING?! NOTHING?!
ROBO, I DID NOT PLACE THAT CALL.
SPACE
IT'S OUT THERE

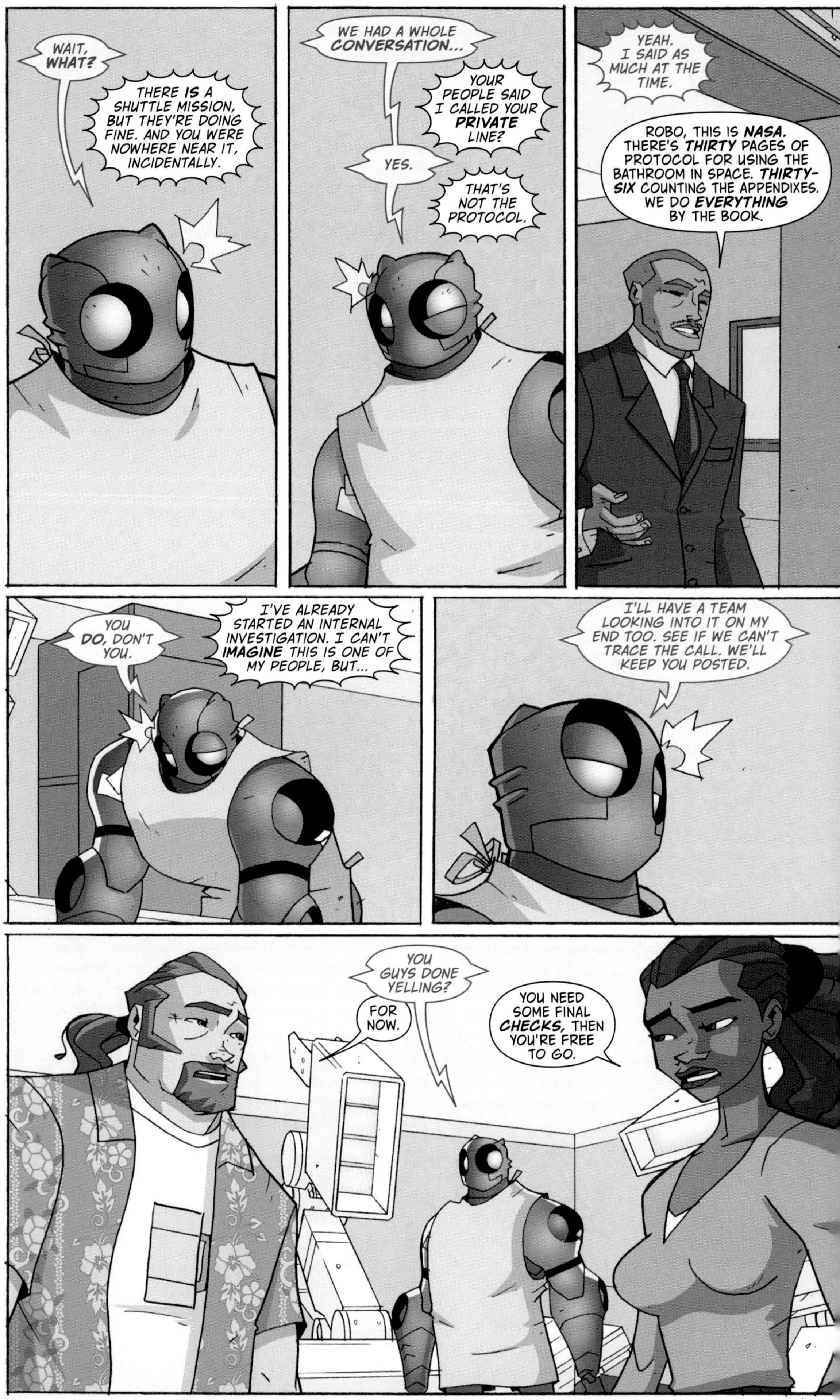
WAIT, WHAT?
THERE IS A SHUTTLE MISSION, BUT THEY'RE DOING FINE. AND YOU WERE NOWHERE NEAR IT, INCIDENTALLY.
WE HAD A WHOLE CONVERSATION...
YOUR PEOPLE SAID I CALLED YOUR PRIVATE LINE?
YES.
THAT'S NOT THE PROTOCOL.
YEAH. I SAID AS MUCH AT THE TIME.
ROBO, THIS IS NASA. THERE'S THIRTY PAGES OF PROTOCOL FOR USING THE BATHROOM IN SPACE. THIRTY-SIX COUNTING THE APPENDIXES. WE DO EVERYTHING BY THE BOOK.
YOU DO, DON'T YOU.
I'VE ALREADY STARTED AN INTERNAL INVESTIGATION. I CAN'T IMAGINE THIS IS ONE OF MY PEOPLE, BUT...
I'LL HAVE A TEAM LOOKING INTO IT ON MY END TOO. SEE IF WE CAN'T TRACE THE CALL. WE'LL KEEP YOU POSTED.
YOU GUYS DONE YELLING?
FOR NOW.
YOU NEED SOME FINAL CHECKS, THEN YOU'RE FREE TO GO.

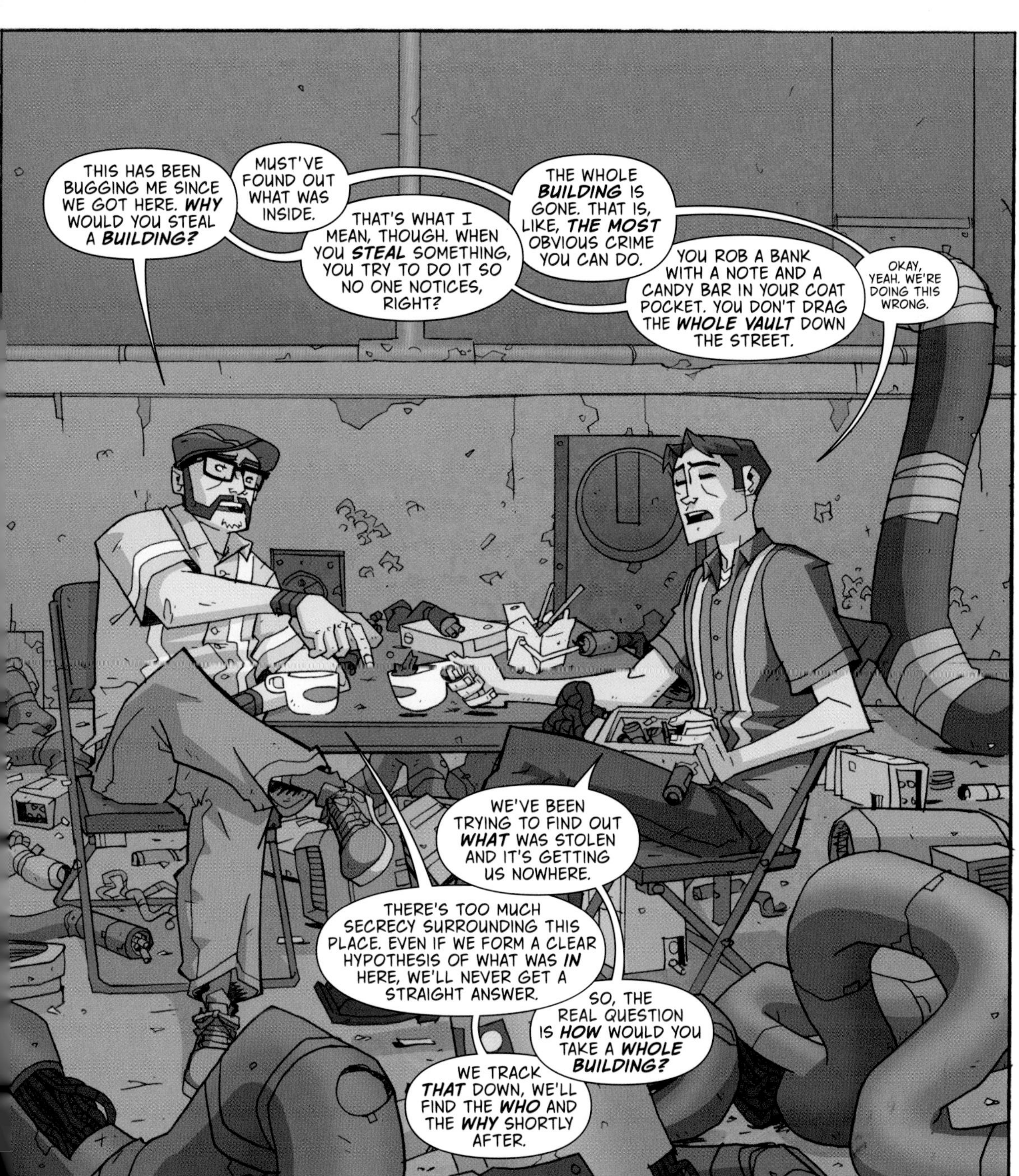
THIS HAS BEEN BUGGING ME SINCE WE GOT HERE. WHY WOULD YOU STEAL A BUILDING?
MUST'VE FOUND OUT WHAT WAS INSIDE.
THAT'S WHAT I MEAN, THOUGH. WHEN YOU STEAL SOMETHING, YOU TRY TO DO IT SO NO ONE NOTICES, RIGHT?
THE WHOLE BUILDING IS GONE. THAT IS, LIKE, THE MOST OBVIOUS CRIME YOU CAN DO.
YOU ROB A BANK WITH A NOTE AND A CANDY BAR IN YOUR COAT POCKET. YOU DON'T DRAG THE WHOLE VAULT DOWN THE STREET.
OKAY, YEAH. WE'RE DOING THIS WRONG.
WE'VE BEEN TRYING TO FIND OUT WHAT WAS STOLEN AND IT'S GETTING US NOWHERE.
THERE'S TOO MUCH SECRECY SURROUNDING THIS PLACE. EVEN IF WE FORM A CLEAR HYPOTHESIS OF WHAT WAS IN HERE, WE'LL NEVER GET A STRAIGHT ANSWER.
SO, THE REAL QUESTION IS HOW WOULD YOU TAKE A WHOLE BUILDING?
WE TRACK THAT DOWN, WE'LL FIND THE WHO AND THE WHY SHORTLY AFTER.

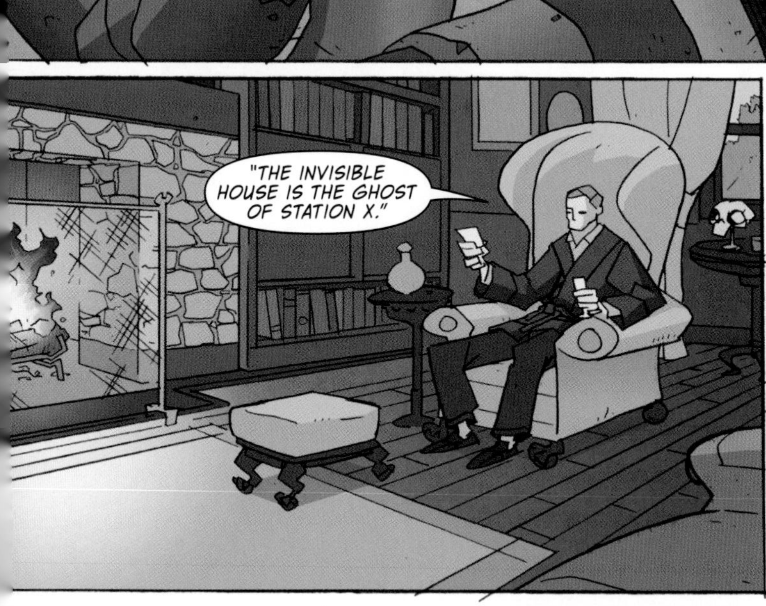
"THE INVISIBLE HOUSE IS THE GHOST OF STATION X."

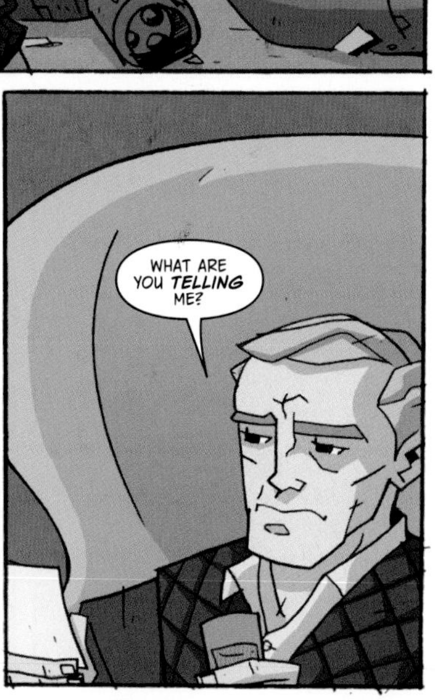
WHAT ARE YOU TELLING ME?

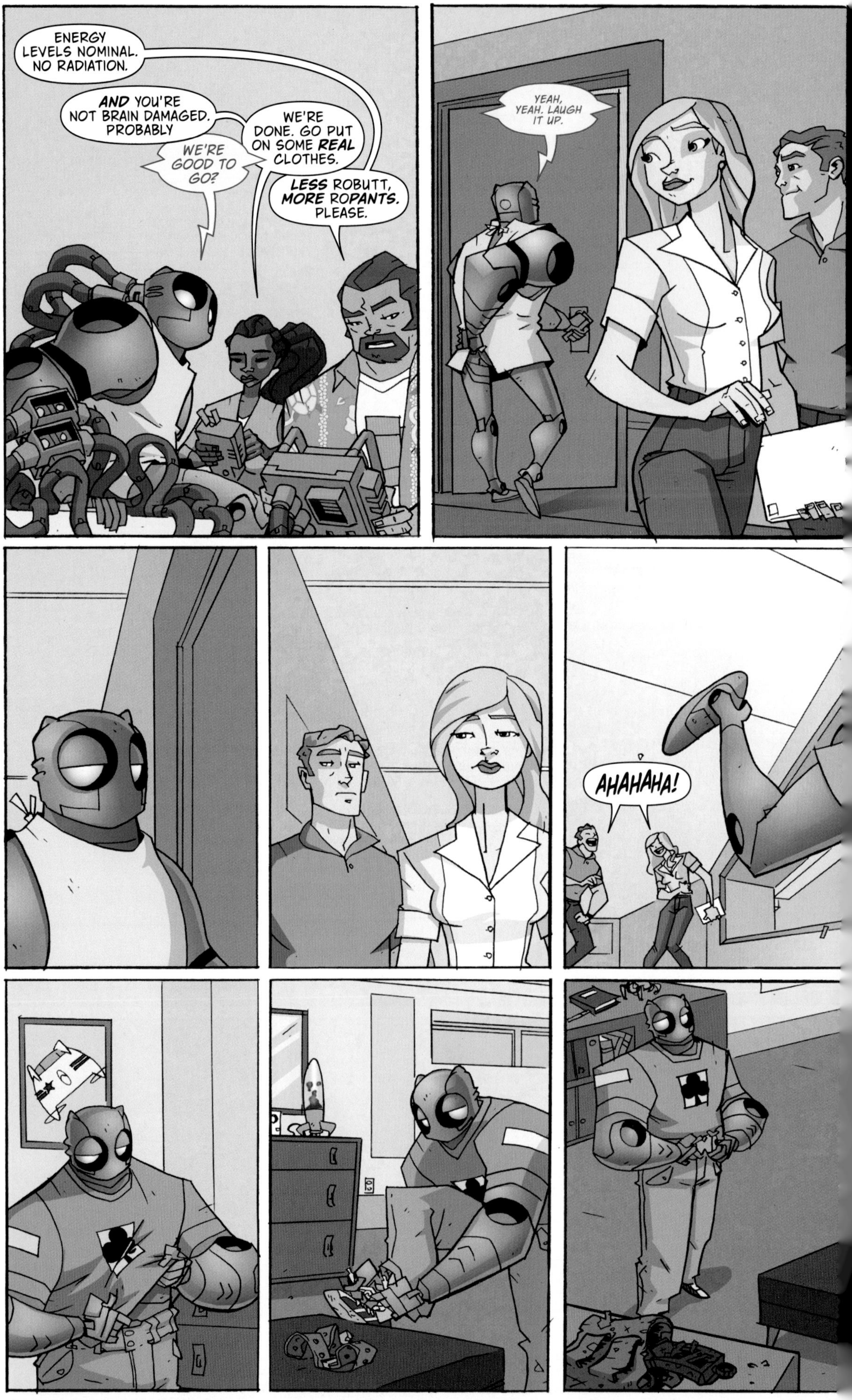
ENERGY LEVELS NOMINAL. NO RADIATION.
AND YOU'RE NOT BRAIN DAMAGED. PROBABLY
WE'RE GOOD TO GO?
WE'RE DONE. GO PUT ON SOME REAL CLOTHES.
LESS ROBUTT, MORE ROPANTS. PLEASE.
YEAH, YEAH. LAUGH IT UP.
AHAHAHA!

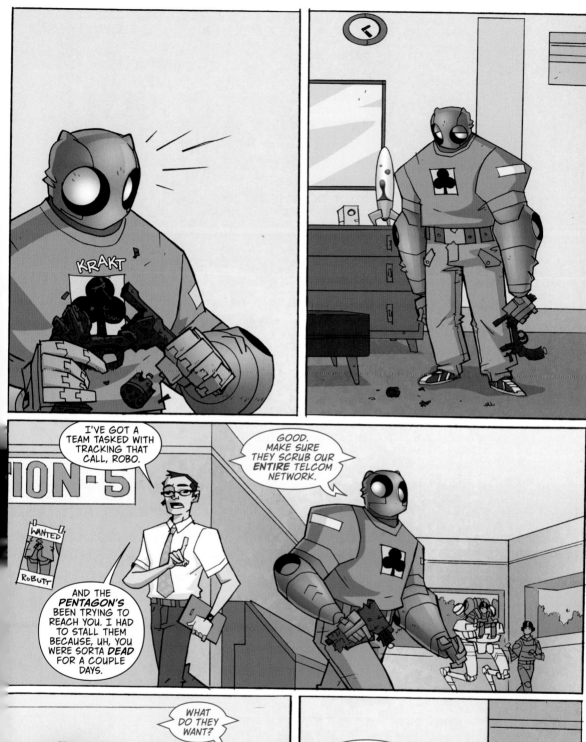

I'VE GOT A TEAM TASKED WITH TRACKING THAT CALL, ROBO.

GOOD. MAKE SURE THEY SCRUB OUR **ENTIRE** TELCOM NETWORK.

AND THE **PENTAGON'S** BEEN TRYING TO REACH YOU. I HAD TO STALL THEM BECAUSE, UH, YOU WERE SORTA **DEAD** FOR A COUPLE DAYS.

WANTED
RoButt

WHAT DO THEY WANT?

TO YELL AT YOU FOR ATTACKING THEIR SATELLITE.

IS **THAT** WHAT HIT ME?

STALL THEM. AND GET **ALL** THE TIER ONE PERSONNEL FOR A MEETING. TEN MINUTES.

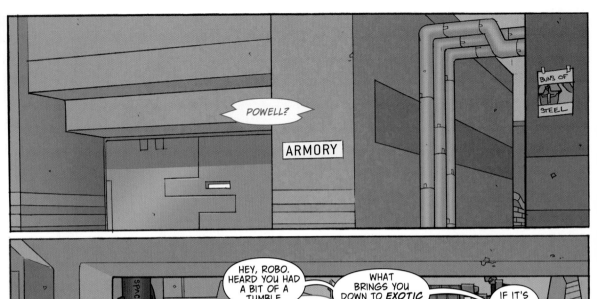

ARMORY

POWELL?

HEY, ROBO. HEARD YOU HAD A BIT OF A TUMBLE.

A BIT.

WHAT BRINGS YOU DOWN TO *EXOTIC BALLISTICS?*

GOT A GUN NEEDS FIXING.

IF IT'S A GUN, I CAN FIX IT.

I CAN'T FIX *THAT.*

THIS ISN'T A GUN. NOT *ANYMORE.*

THAT'S WHY I BROUGHT IT DOWN HERE.

THIS IS A PAPERWEIGHT *SHAPED* LIKE A GUN.

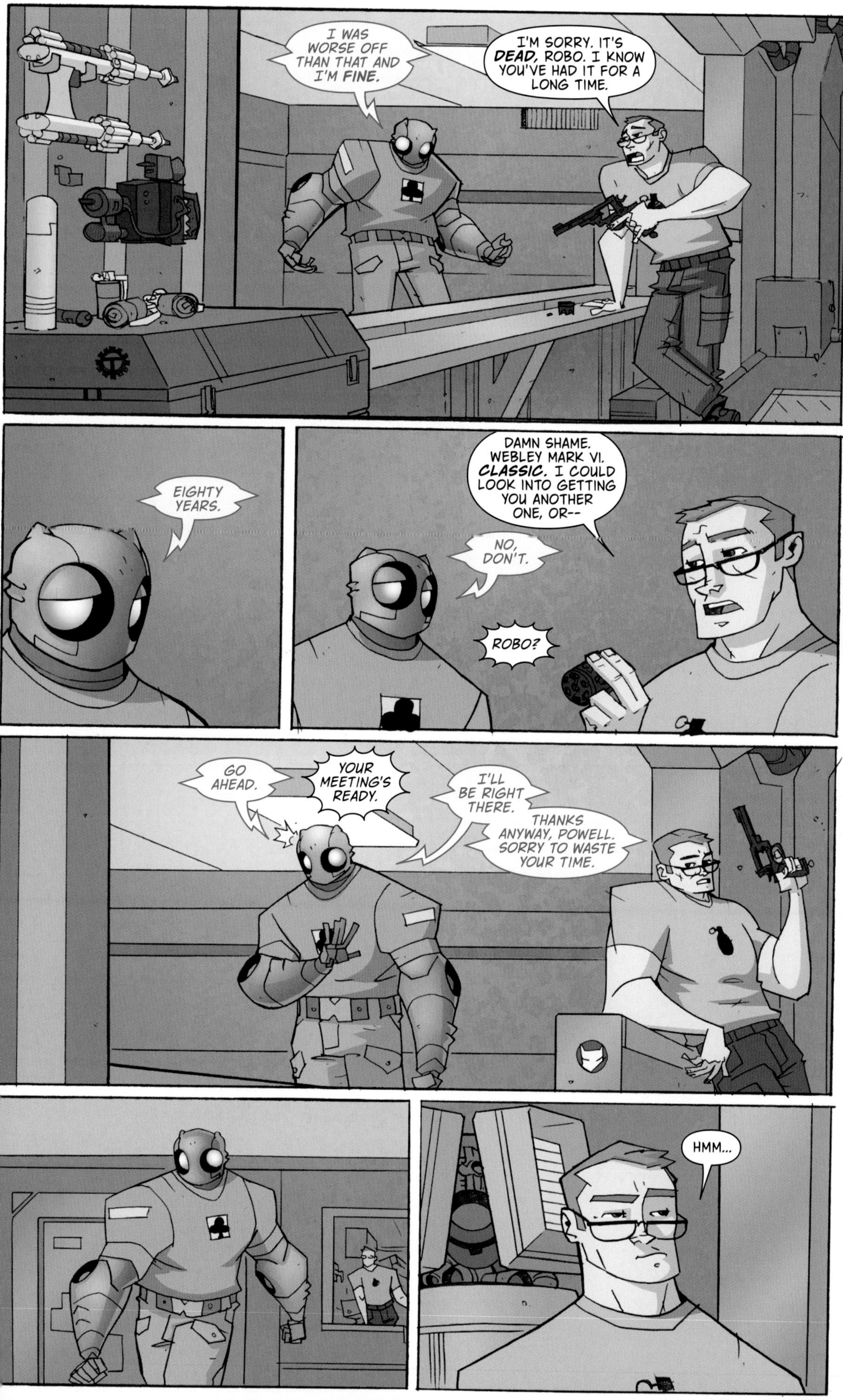
I WAS WORSE OFF THAN THAT AND I'M FINE.
I'M SORRY. IT'S DEAD, ROBO. I KNOW YOU'VE HAD IT FOR A LONG TIME.
EIGHTY YEARS.
DAMN SHAME. WEBLEY MARK VI. CLASSIC. I COULD LOOK INTO GETTING YOU ANOTHER ONE, OR--
NO, DON'T.
ROBO?
GO AHEAD.
YOUR MEETING'S READY.
I'LL BE RIGHT THERE.
THANKS ANYWAY, POWELL. SORRY TO WASTE YOUR TIME.
HMM...

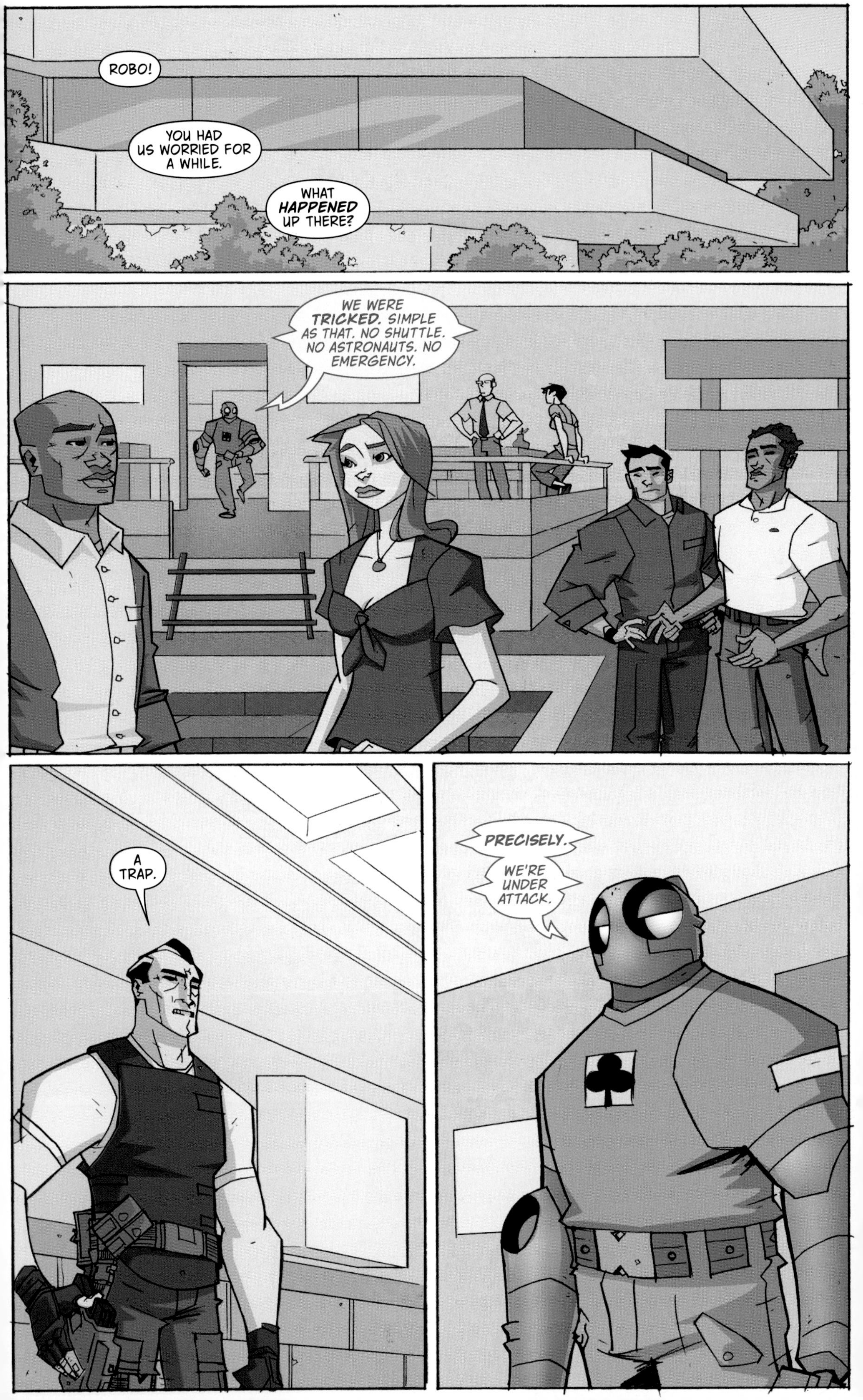
ROBO!
YOU HAD US WORRIED FOR A WHILE.
WHAT HAPPENED UP THERE?
WE WERE TRICKED. SIMPLE AS THAT. NO SHUTTLE. NO ASTRONAUTS. NO EMERGENCY.
A TRAP.
PRECISELY.
WE'RE UNDER ATTACK.

PROPAGATION

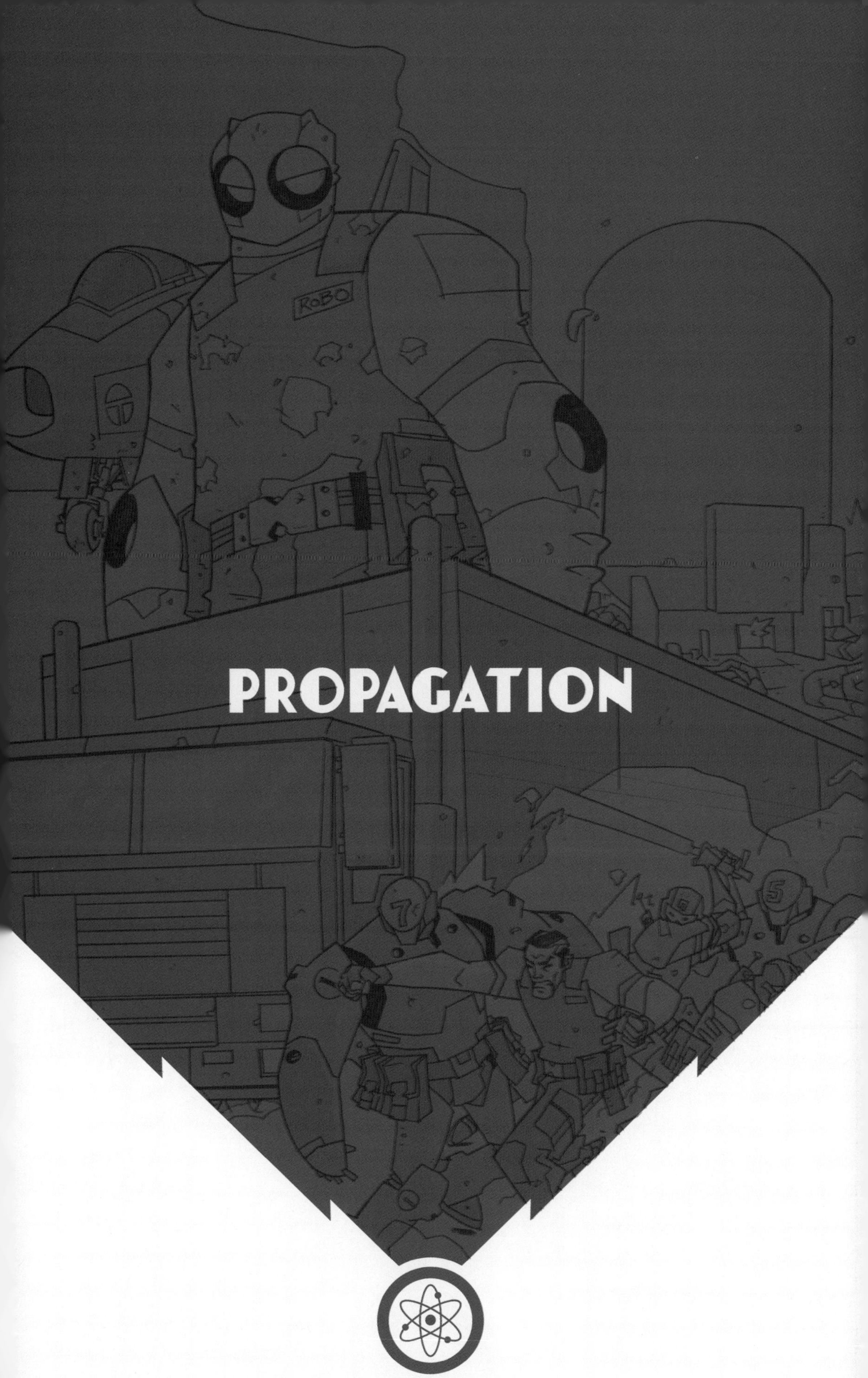
RoBO

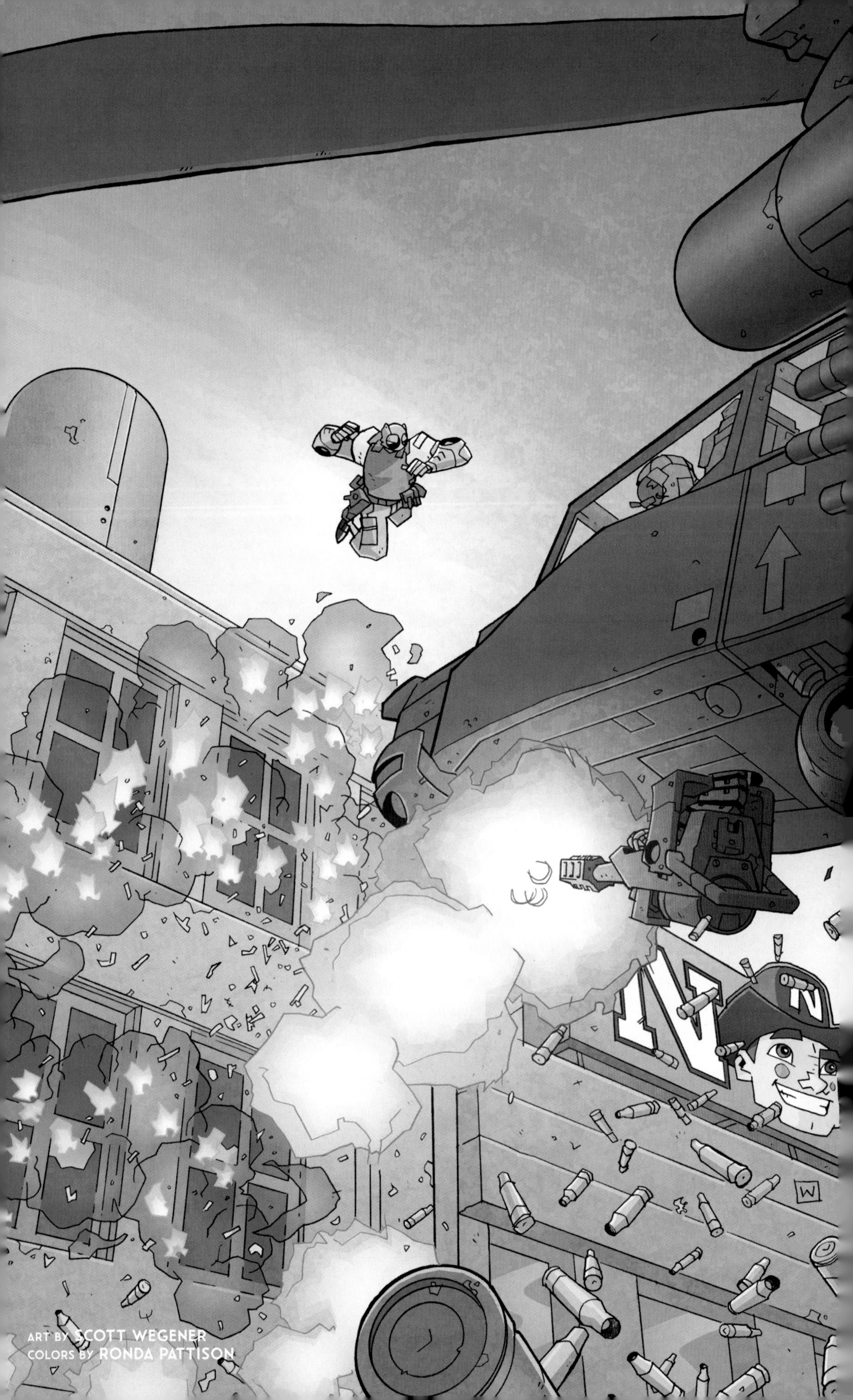
N
W
ART BY SCOTT WEGENER
COLORS BY RONDA PATTISON

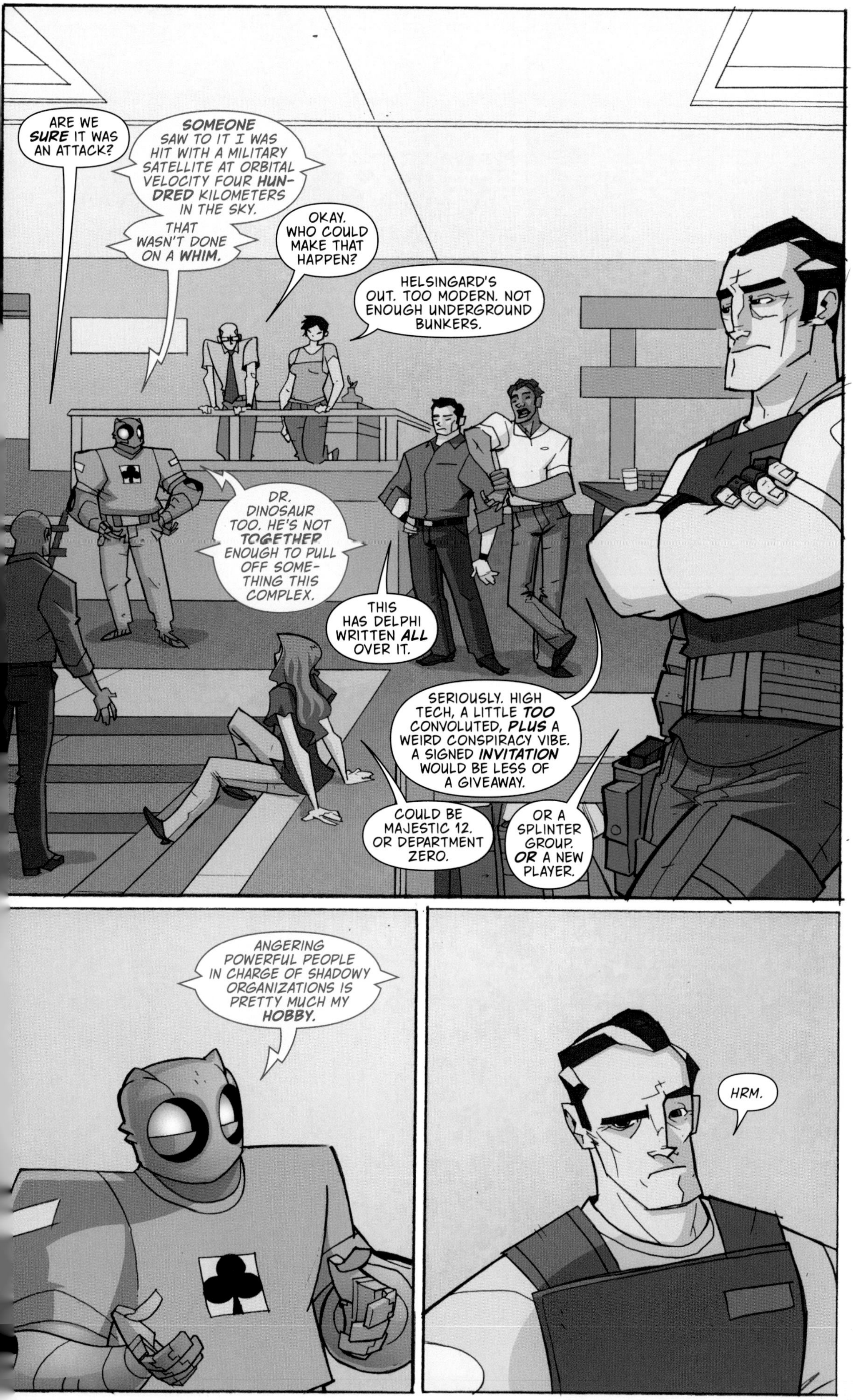
ARE WE SURE IT WAS AN ATTACK?
SOMEONE SAW TO IT I WAS HIT WITH A MILITARY SATELLITE AT ORBITAL VELOCITY FOUR HUNDRED KILOMETERS IN THE SKY.
THAT WASN'T DONE ON A WHIM.
OKAY. WHO COULD MAKE THAT HAPPEN?
HELSINGARD'S OUT. TOO MODERN. NOT ENOUGH UNDERGROUND BUNKERS.
DR. DINOSAUR TOO. HE'S NOT TOGETHER ENOUGH TO PULL OFF SOMETHING THIS COMPLEX.
THIS HAS DELPHI WRITTEN ALL OVER IT.
SERIOUSLY. HIGH TECH, A LITTLE TOO CONVOLUTED, PLUS A WEIRD CONSPIRACY VIBE. A SIGNED INVITATION WOULD BE LESS OF A GIVEAWAY.
COULD BE MAJESTIC 12. OR DEPARTMENT ZERO.
OR A SPLINTER GROUP. OR A NEW PLAYER.
ANGERING POWERFUL PEOPLE IN CHARGE OF SHADOWY ORGANIZATIONS IS PRETTY MUCH MY HOBBY.
HRM.

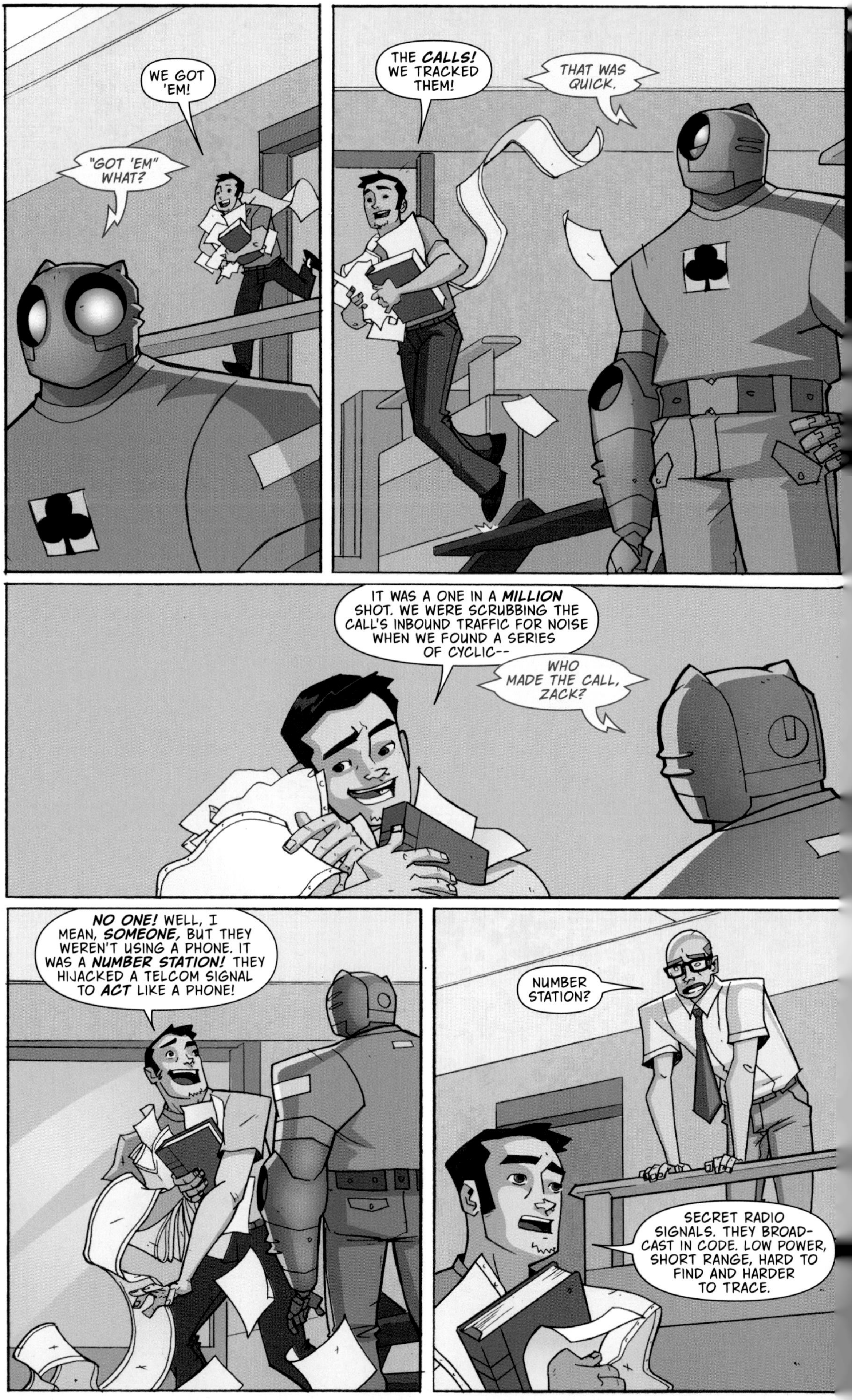
WE GOT 'EM!
"GOT 'EM" WHAT?
THE CALLS! WE TRACKED THEM!
THAT WAS QUICK.
IT WAS A ONE IN A MILLION SHOT. WE WERE SCRUBBING THE CALL'S INBOUND TRAFFIC FOR NOISE WHEN WE FOUND A SERIES OF CYCLIC--
WHO MADE THE CALL, ZACK?
NO ONE! WELL, I MEAN, SOMEONE, BUT THEY WEREN'T USING A PHONE. IT WAS A NUMBER STATION! THEY HIJACKED A TELCOM SIGNAL TO ACT LIKE A PHONE!
NUMBER STATION?
SECRET RADIO SIGNALS. THEY BROADCAST IN CODE. LOW POWER, SHORT RANGE, HARD TO FIND AND HARDER TO TRACE.

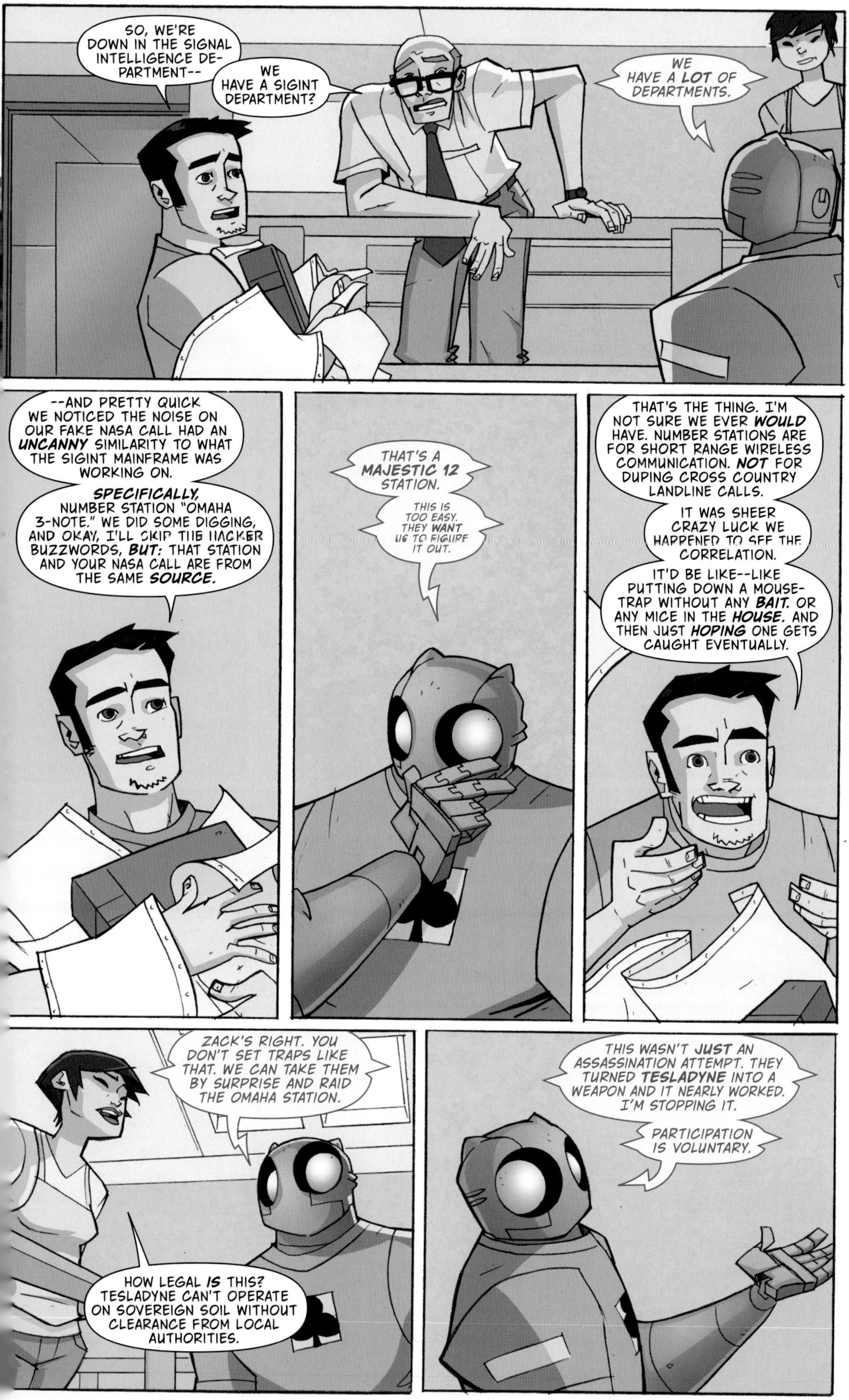
SO, WE'RE DOWN IN THE SIGNAL INTELLIGENCE DE-PARTMENT--
WE HAVE A SIGINT DEPARTMENT?
WE HAVE A LOT OF DEPARTMENTS.
--AND PRETTY QUICK WE NOTICED THE NOISE ON OUR FAKE NASA CALL HAD AN UNCANNY SIMILARITY TO WHAT THE SIGINT MAINFRAME WAS WORKING ON.
SPECIFICALLY, NUMBER STATION "OMAHA 3-NOTE." WE DID SOME DIGGING, AND OKAY, I'LL SKIP THE HACKER BUZZWORDS, BUT: THAT STATION AND YOUR NASA CALL ARE FROM THE SAME SOURCE.
THAT'S A MAJESTIC 12 STATION.
THIS IS TOO EASY. THEY WANT US TO FIGURE IT OUT.
THAT'S THE THING. I'M NOT SURE WE EVER WOULD HAVE. NUMBER STATIONS ARE FOR SHORT RANGE WIRELESS COMMUNICATION. NOT FOR DUPING CROSS COUNTRY LANDLINE CALLS.
IT WAS SHEER CRAZY LUCK WE HAPPENED TO SEE THE CORRELATION.
IT'D BE LIKE--LIKE PUTTING DOWN A MOUSE-TRAP WITHOUT ANY BAIT. OR ANY MICE IN THE HOUSE. AND THEN JUST HOPING ONE GETS CAUGHT EVENTUALLY.
ZACK'S RIGHT. YOU DON'T SET TRAPS LIKE THAT. WE CAN TAKE THEM BY SURPRISE AND RAID THE OMAHA STATION.
HOW LEGAL IS THIS? TESLADYNE CAN'T OPERATE ON SOVEREIGN SOIL WITHOUT CLEARANCE FROM LOCAL AUTHORITIES.
THIS WASN'T JUST AN ASSASSINATION ATTEMPT. THEY TURNED TESLADYNE INTO A WEAPON AND IT NEARLY WORKED. I'M STOPPING IT.
PARTICIPATION IS VOLUNTARY.

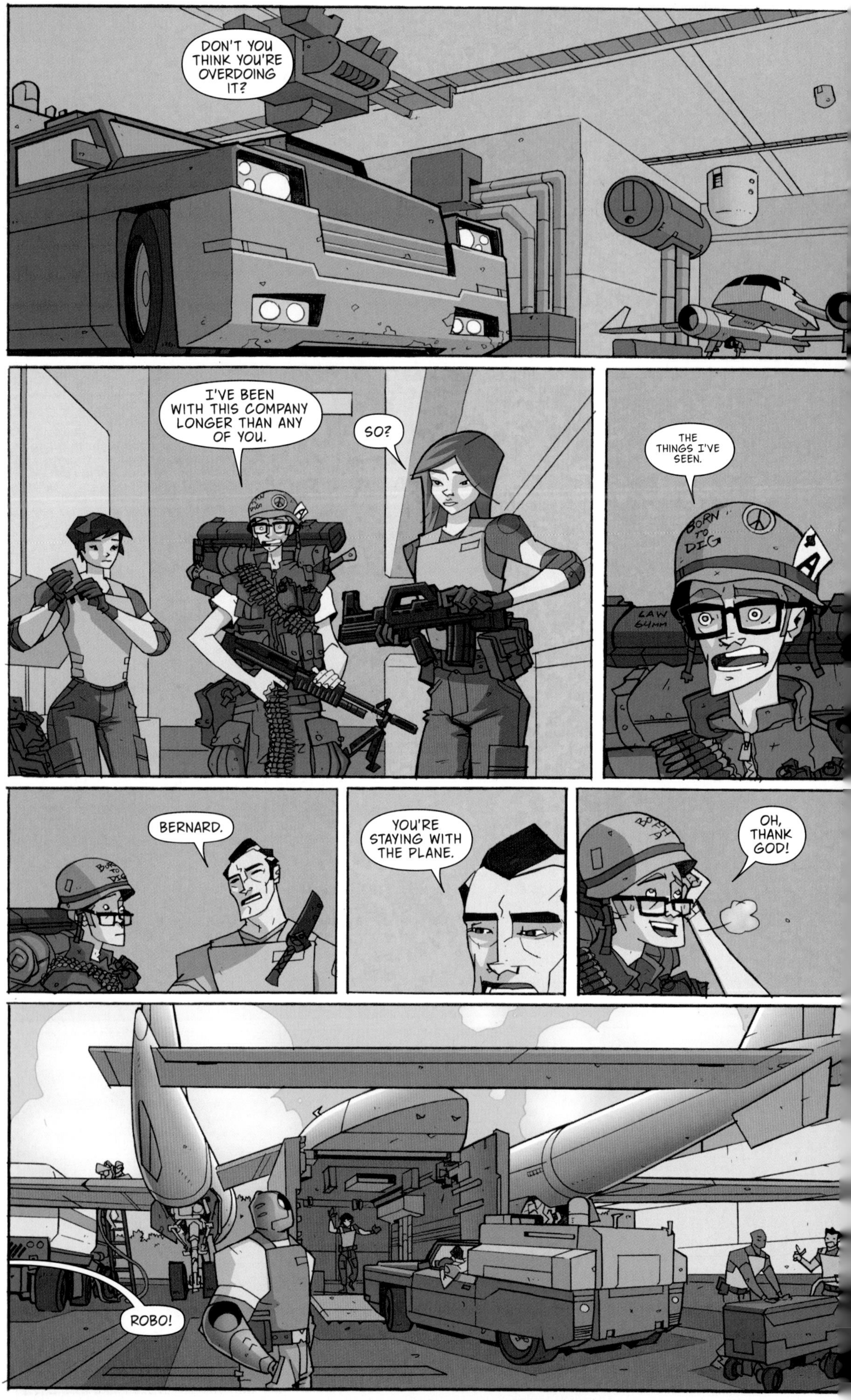
DON'T YOU THINK YOU'RE OVERDOING IT?
I'VE BEEN WITH THIS COMPANY LONGER THAN ANY OF YOU.
SO?
THE THINGS I'VE SEEN.
BERNARD.
YOU'RE STAYING WITH THE PLANE.
OH, THANK GOD!
ROBO!

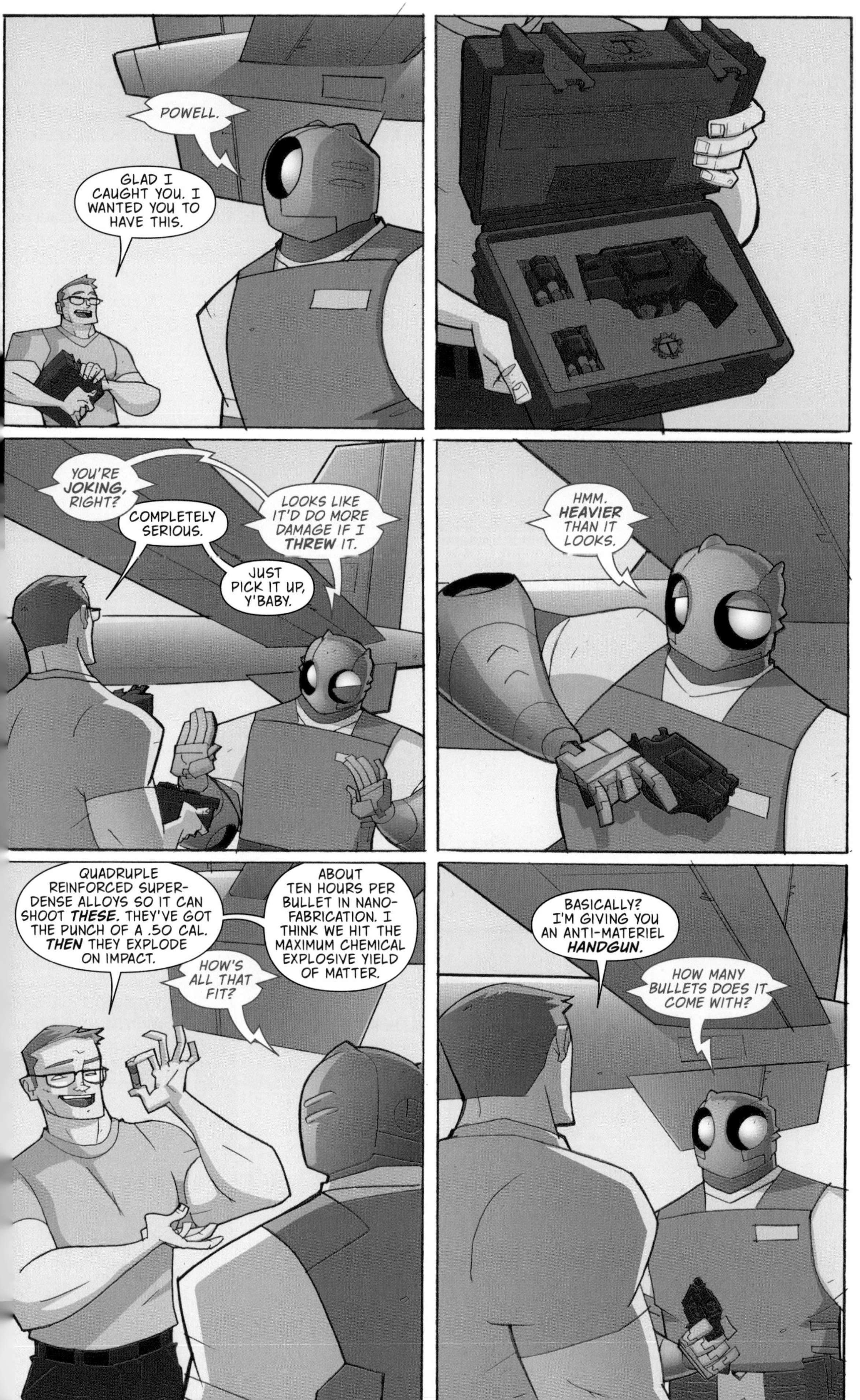
POWELL.
GLAD I CAUGHT YOU. I WANTED YOU TO HAVE THIS.
YOU'RE JOKING, RIGHT?
COMPLETELY SERIOUS.
LOOKS LIKE IT'D DO MORE DAMAGE IF I THREW IT.
JUST PICK IT UP, Y'BABY.
HMM. HEAVIER THAN IT LOOKS.
QUADRUPLE REINFORCED SUPER-DENSE ALLOYS SO IT CAN SHOOT THESE. THEY'VE GOT THE PUNCH OF A .50 CAL. THEN THEY EXPLODE ON IMPACT.
HOW'S ALL THAT FIT?
ABOUT TEN HOURS PER BULLET IN NANO-FABRICATION. I THINK WE HIT THE MAXIMUM CHEMICAL EXPLOSIVE YIELD OF MATTER.
BASICALLY? I'M GIVING YOU AN ANTI-MATERIEL HANDGUN.
HOW MANY BULLETS DOES IT COME WITH?

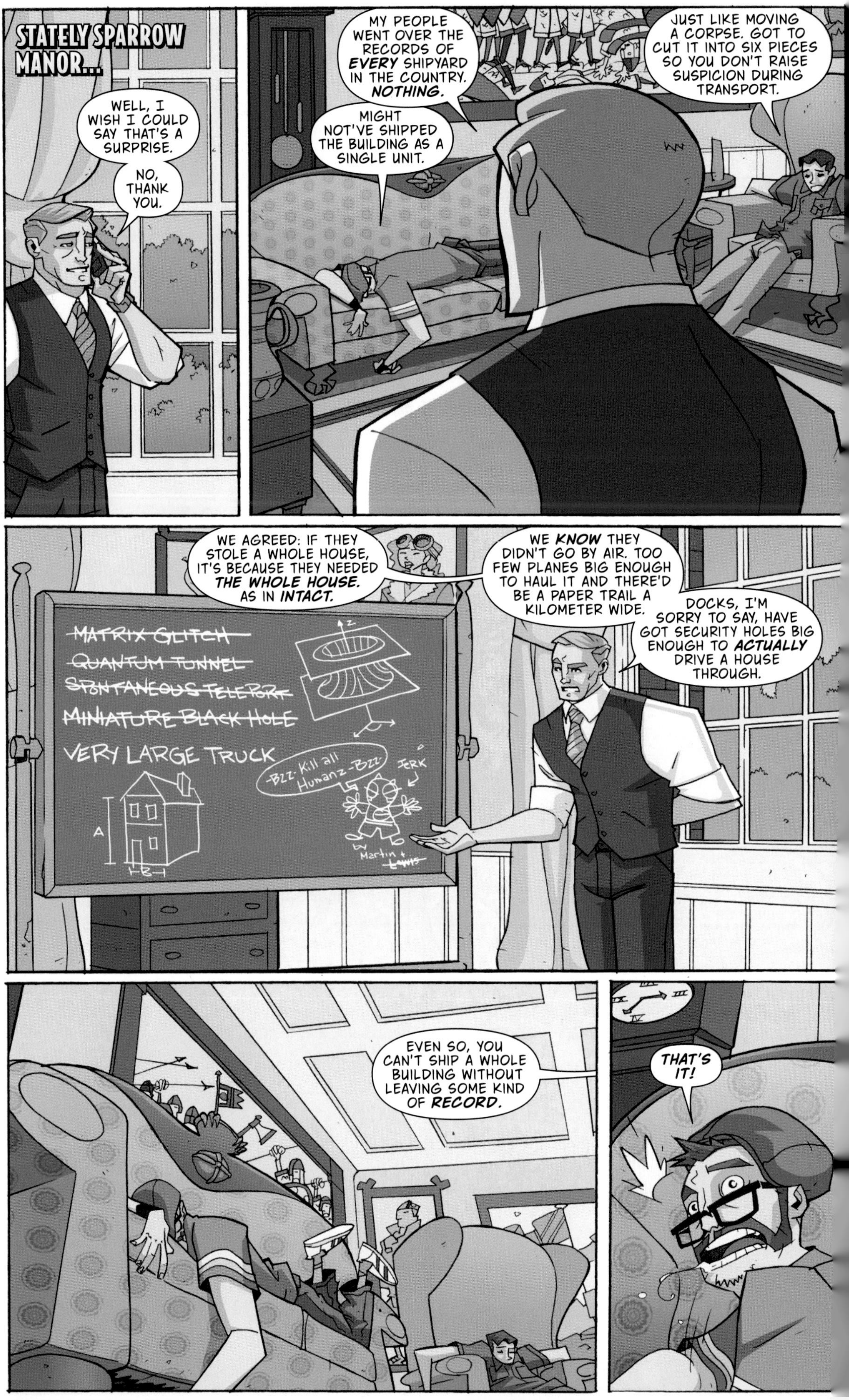
STATELY SPARROW MANOR...
WELL, I WISH I COULD SAY THAT'S A SURPRISE.
NO, THANK YOU.
MY PEOPLE WENT OVER THE RECORDS OF EVERY SHIPYARD IN THE COUNTRY. NOTHING.
MIGHT NOT'VE SHIPPED THE BUILDING AS A SINGLE UNIT.
JUST LIKE MOVING A CORPSE. GOT TO CUT IT INTO SIX PIECES SO YOU DON'T RAISE SUSPICION DURING TRANSPORT.
WE AGREED: IF THEY STOLE A WHOLE HOUSE, IT'S BECAUSE THEY NEEDED THE WHOLE HOUSE. AS IN INTACT.
WE KNOW THEY DIDN'T GO BY AIR. TOO FEW PLANES BIG ENOUGH TO HAUL IT AND THERE'D BE A PAPER TRAIL A KILOMETER WIDE.
DOCKS, I'M SORRY TO SAY, HAVE GOT SECURITY HOLES BIG ENOUGH TO ACTUALLY DRIVE A HOUSE THROUGH.
MATRIX GLITCH
QUANTUM TUNNEL
SPONTANEOUS TELEPORT
MINIATURE BLACK HOLE
VERY LARGE TRUCK
-BZZ- Kill all Humanz -BZZ-
JERK
by Martin + Lewis
EVEN SO, YOU CAN'T SHIP A WHOLE BUILDING WITHOUT LEAVING SOME KIND OF RECORD.
THAT'S IT!

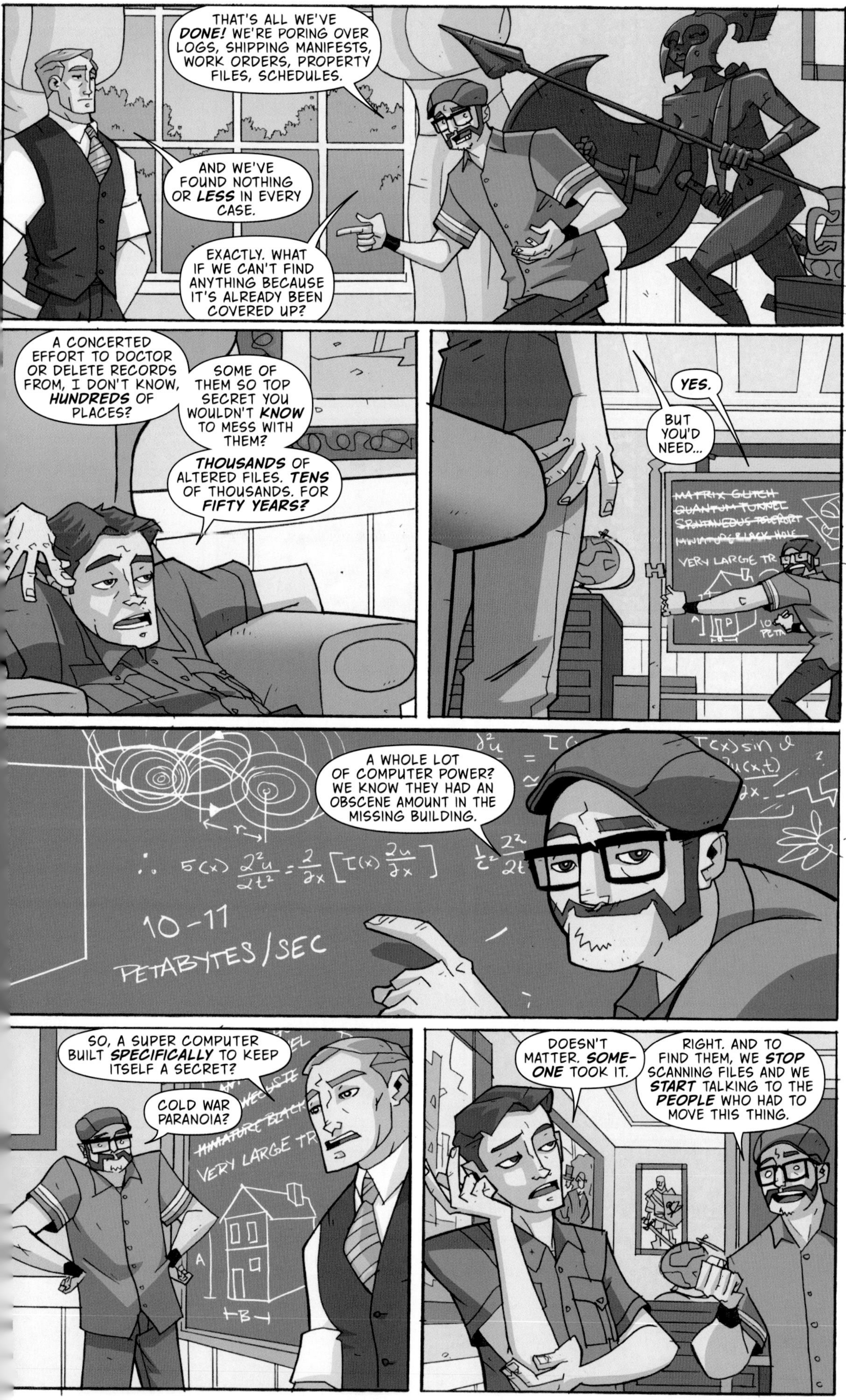

THAT'S ALL WE'VE DONE! WE'RE PORING OVER LOGS, SHIPPING MANIFESTS, WORK ORDERS, PROPERTY FILES, SCHEDULES.
AND WE'VE FOUND NOTHING OR LESS IN EVERY CASE.
EXACTLY. WHAT IF WE CAN'T FIND ANYTHING BECAUSE IT'S ALREADY BEEN COVERED UP?
A CONCERTED EFFORT TO DOCTOR OR DELETE RECORDS FROM, I DON'T KNOW, HUNDREDS OF PLACES?
SOME OF THEM SO TOP SECRET YOU WOULDN'T KNOW TO MESS WITH THEM?
THOUSANDS OF ALTERED FILES. TENS OF THOUSANDS. FOR FIFTY YEARS?
BUT YOU'D NEED...
YES.
MATRIX GLITCH
QUANTUM TUNNEL
VERY LARGE TR
A WHOLE LOT OF COMPUTER POWER? WE KNOW THEY HAD AN OBSCENE AMOUNT IN THE MISSING BUILDING.
10-11
PETABYTES/SEC
SO, A SUPER COMPUTER BUILT SPECIFICALLY TO KEEP ITSELF A SECRET?
COLD WAR PARANOIA?
VERY LARGE TR
DOESN'T MATTER. SOMEONE TOOK IT.
RIGHT. AND TO FIND THEM, WE STOP SCANNING FILES AND WE START TALKING TO THE PEOPLE WHO HAD TO MOVE THIS THING.

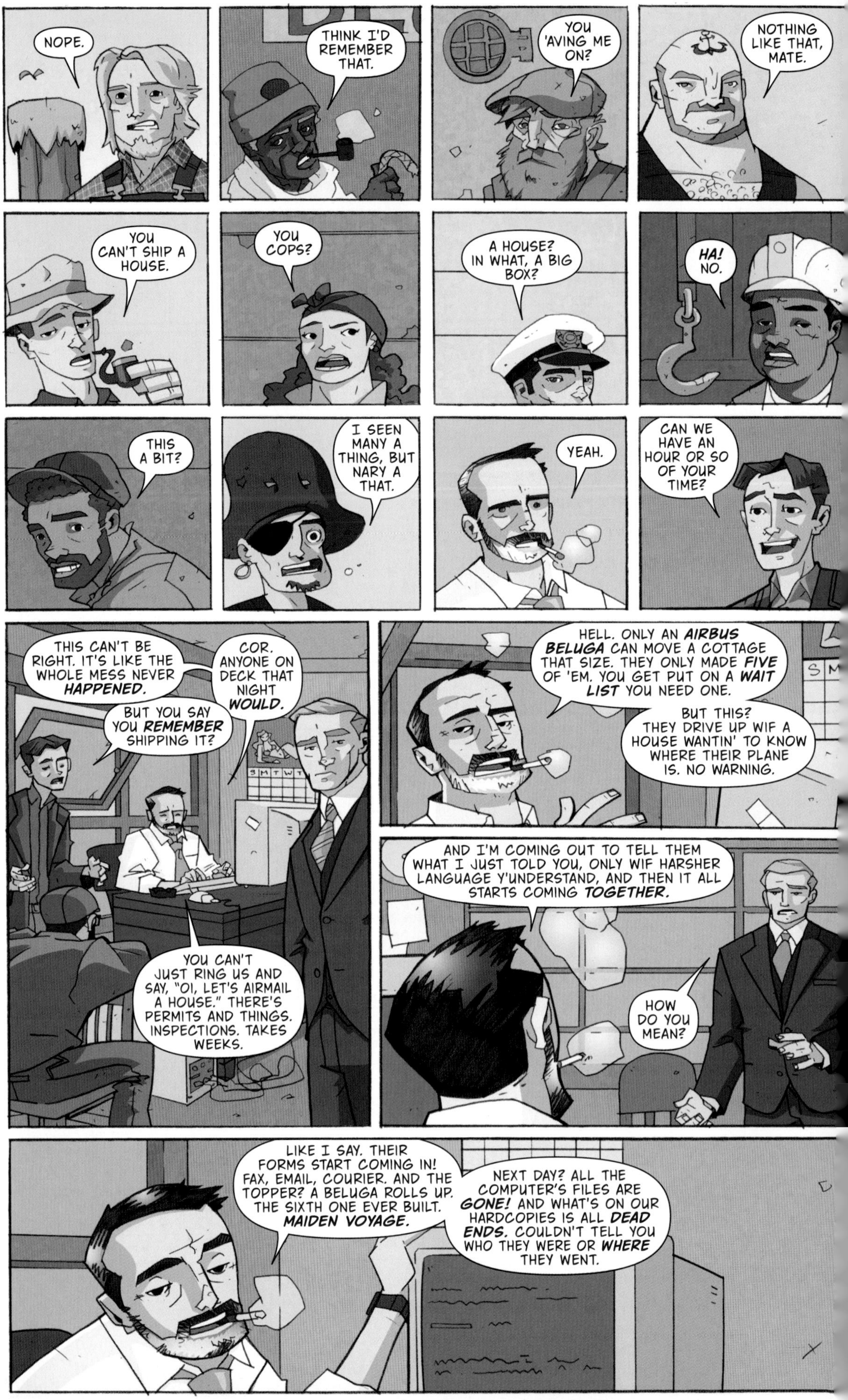
NOPE.
THINK I'D REMEMBER THAT.
YOU 'AVING ME ON?
NOTHING LIKE THAT, MATE.
YOU CAN'T SHIP A HOUSE.
YOU COPS?
A HOUSE? IN WHAT, A BIG BOX?
HA! NO.
THIS A BIT?
I SEEN MANY A THING, BUT NARY A THAT.
YEAH.
CAN WE HAVE AN HOUR OR SO OF YOUR TIME?
THIS CAN'T BE RIGHT. IT'S LIKE THE WHOLE MESS NEVER HAPPENED.
COR. ANYONE ON DECK THAT NIGHT WOULD.
BUT YOU SAY YOU REMEMBER SHIPPING IT?
YOU CAN'T JUST RING US AND SAY, "OI, LET'S AIRMAIL A HOUSE." THERE'S PERMITS AND THINGS. INSPECTIONS. TAKES WEEKS.
HELL. ONLY AN AIRBUS BELUGA CAN MOVE A COTTAGE THAT SIZE. THEY ONLY MADE FIVE OF 'EM. YOU GET PUT ON A WAIT LIST YOU NEED ONE.
BUT THIS? THEY DRIVE UP WIF A HOUSE WANTIN' TO KNOW WHERE THEIR PLANE IS. NO WARNING.
AND I'M COMING OUT TO TELL THEM WHAT I JUST TOLD YOU, ONLY WIF HARSHER LANGUAGE Y'UNDERSTAND, AND THEN IT ALL STARTS COMING TOGETHER.
HOW DO YOU MEAN?
LIKE I SAY. THEIR FORMS START COMING IN! FAX, EMAIL, COURIER. AND THE TOPPER? A BELUGA ROLLS UP. THE SIXTH ONE EVER BUILT. MAIDEN VOYAGE.
NEXT DAY? ALL THE COMPUTER'S FILES ARE GONE! AND WHAT'S ON OUR HARDCOPIES IS ALL DEAD ENDS. COULDN'T TELL YOU WHO THEY WERE OR WHERE THEY WENT.

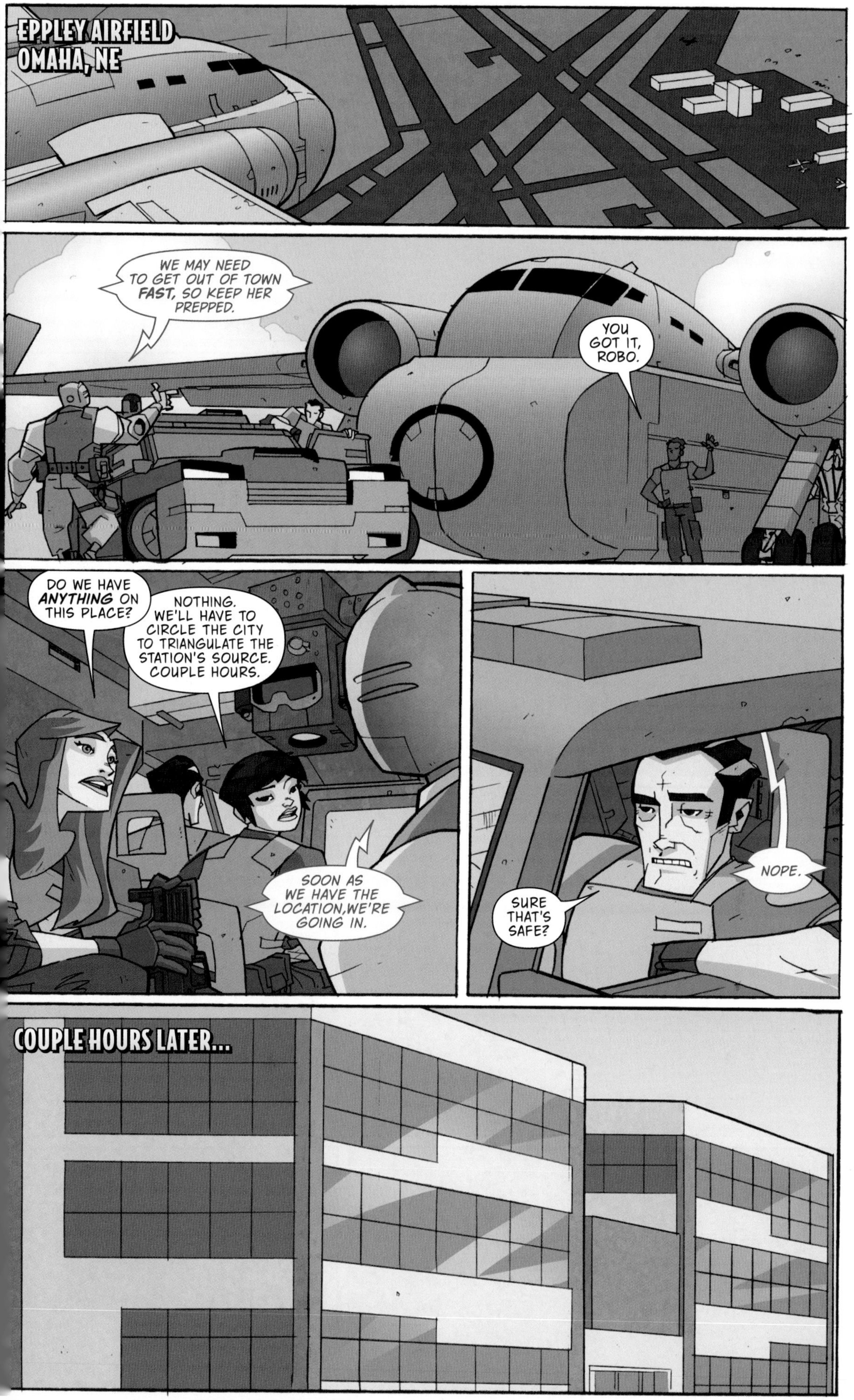
EPPLEY AIRFIELD
OMAHA, NE
WE MAY NEED TO GET OUT OF TOWN FAST, SO KEEP HER PREPPED.
YOU GOT IT, ROBO.
DO WE HAVE ANYTHING ON THIS PLACE?
NOTHING. WE'LL HAVE TO CIRCLE THE CITY TO TRIANGULATE THE STATION'S SOURCE. COUPLE HOURS.
SOON AS WE HAVE THE LOCATION,WE'RE GOING IN.
SURE THAT'S SAFE?
NOPE.
COUPLE HOURS LATER...

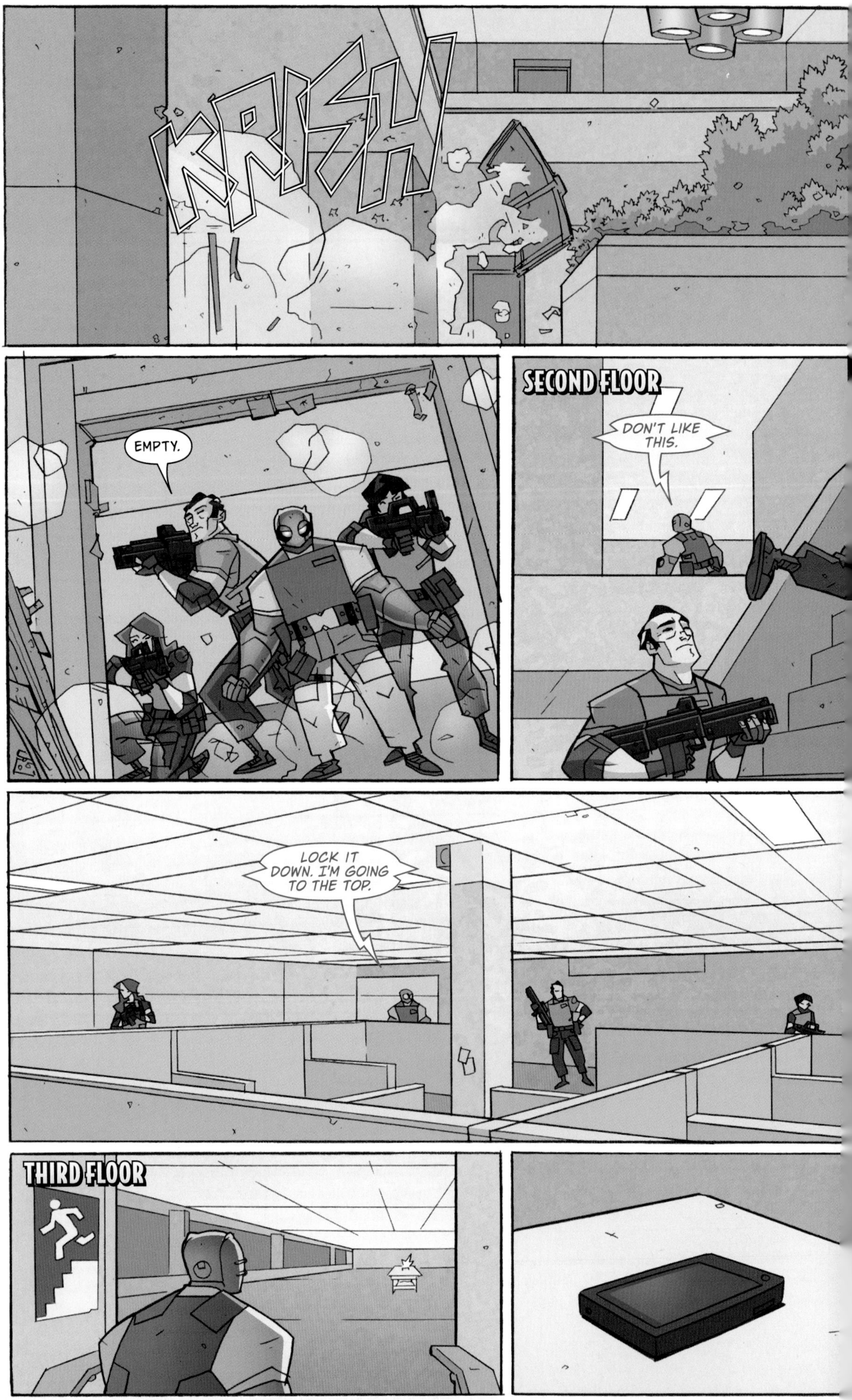
KRISH
EMPTY.
SECOND FLOOR
DON'T LIKE THIS.
LOCK IT DOWN. I'M GOING TO THE TOP.
THIRD FLOOR

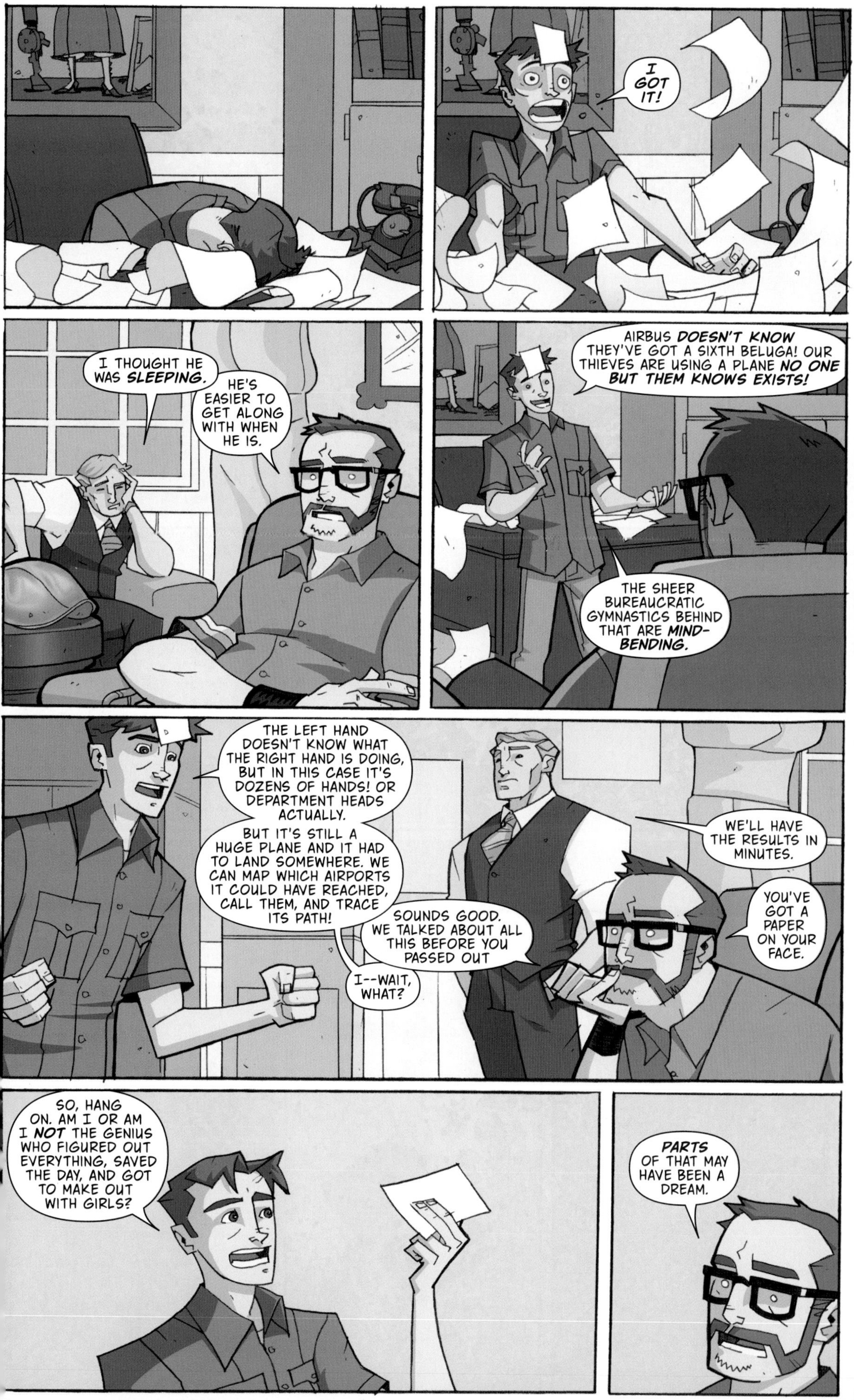
I GOT IT!
I THOUGHT HE WAS SLEEPING.
HE'S EASIER TO GET ALONG WITH WHEN HE IS.
AIRBUS DOESN'T KNOW THEY'VE GOT A SIXTH BELUGA! OUR THIEVES ARE USING A PLANE NO ONE BUT THEM KNOWS EXISTS!
THE SHEER BUREAUCRATIC GYMNASTICS BEHIND THAT ARE MIND-BENDING.
THE LEFT HAND DOESN'T KNOW WHAT THE RIGHT HAND IS DOING, BUT IN THIS CASE IT'S DOZENS OF HANDS! OR DEPARTMENT HEADS ACTUALLY.
BUT IT'S STILL A HUGE PLANE AND IT HAD TO LAND SOMEWHERE. WE CAN MAP WHICH AIRPORTS IT COULD HAVE REACHED, CALL THEM, AND TRACE ITS PATH!
SOUNDS GOOD. WE TALKED ABOUT ALL THIS BEFORE YOU PASSED OUT
I--WAIT, WHAT?
WE'LL HAVE THE RESULTS IN MINUTES.
YOU'VE GOT A PAPER ON YOUR FACE.
SO, HANG ON. AM I OR AM I NOT THE GENIUS WHO FIGURED OUT EVERYTHING, SAVED THE DAY, AND GOT TO MAKE OUT WITH GIRLS?
PARTS OF THAT MAY HAVE BEEN A DREAM.

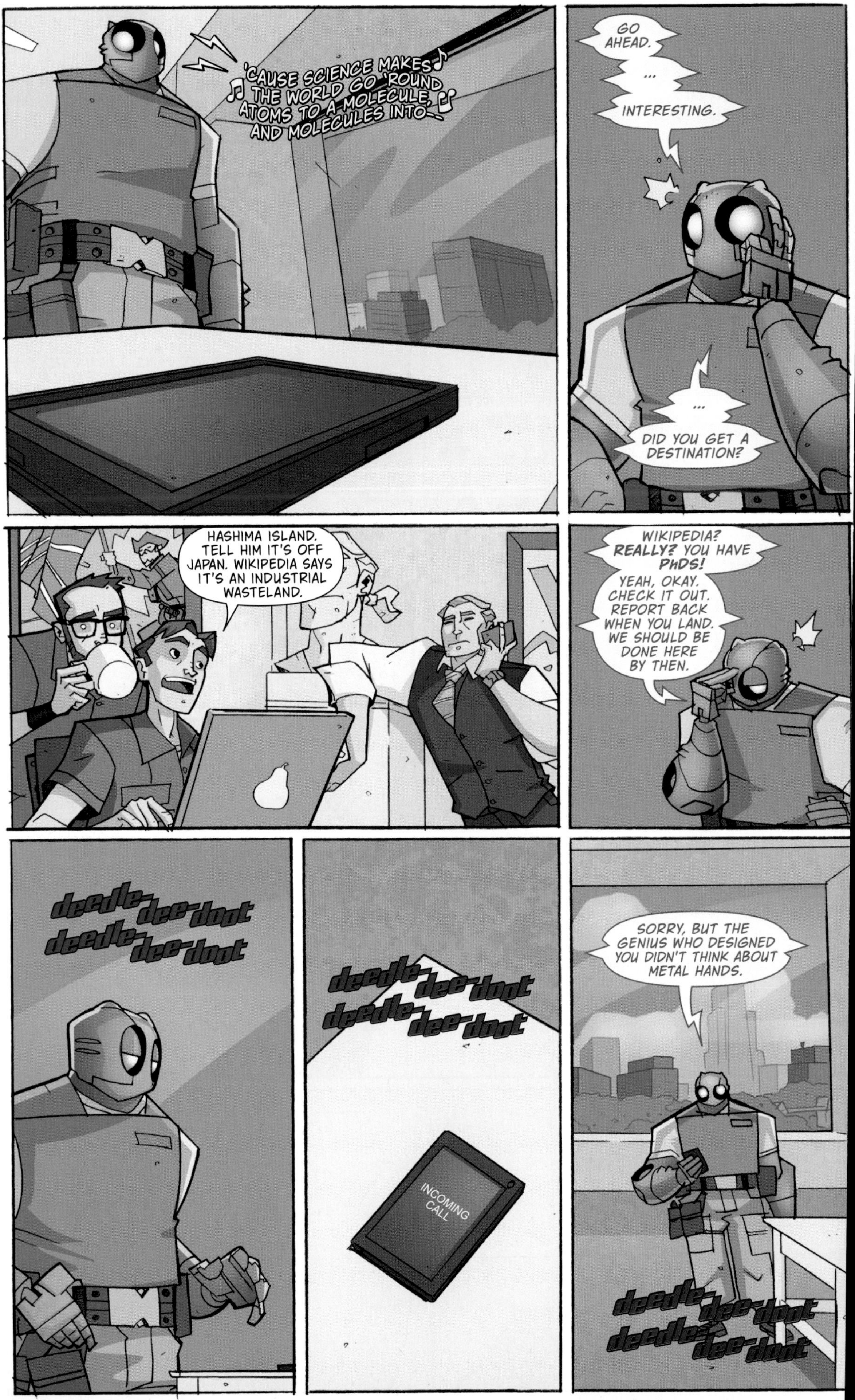
'CAUSE SCIENCE MAKES THE WORLD GO 'ROUND ATOMS TO A MOLECULE, AND MOLECULES INTO--
GO AHEAD.
...
INTERESTING.
...
DID YOU GET A DESTINATION?
HASHIMA ISLAND. TELL HIM IT'S OFF JAPAN. WIKIPEDIA SAYS IT'S AN INDUSTRIAL WASTELAND.
WIKIPEDIA? REALLY? YOU HAVE PhDS!
YEAH, OKAY. CHECK IT OUT. REPORT BACK WHEN YOU LAND. WE SHOULD BE DONE HERE BY THEN.
deedle-dee-doot deedle-dee-doot
deedle-dee-doot deedle-dee-doot
INCOMING CALL
SORRY, BUT THE GENIUS WHO DESIGNED YOU DIDN'T THINK ABOUT METAL HANDS.
deedle-dee-doot deedle-dee-doot

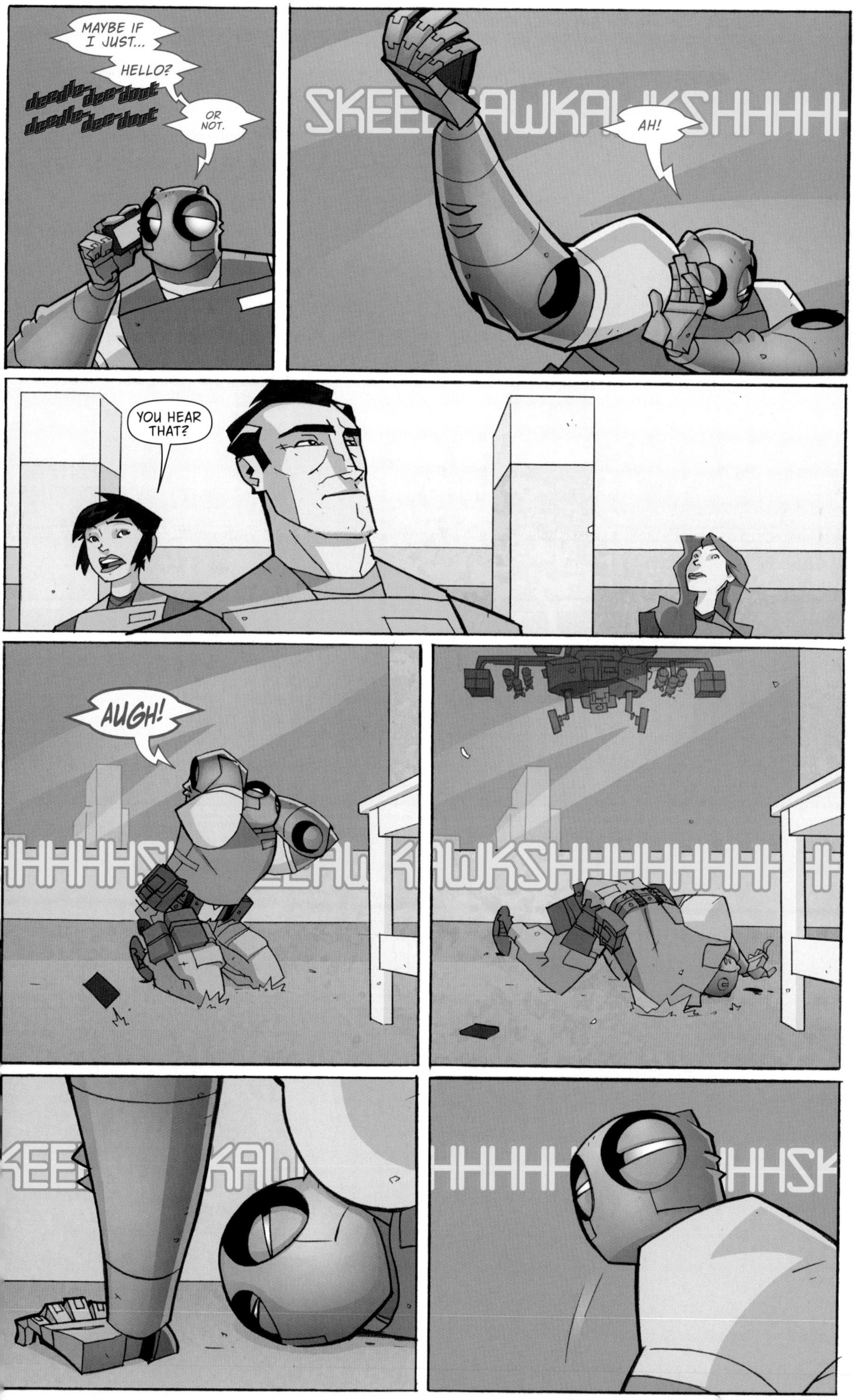
MAYBE IF I JUST...
HELLO?
deedle-dee-doot deedle-dee-doot
OR NOT.
SKEEE AWKAKSHHHHH
AH!
YOU HEAR THAT?
AUGH!
HHHHHS EEAW KAWKSHHHHHHHH
HHHHHHHHSK

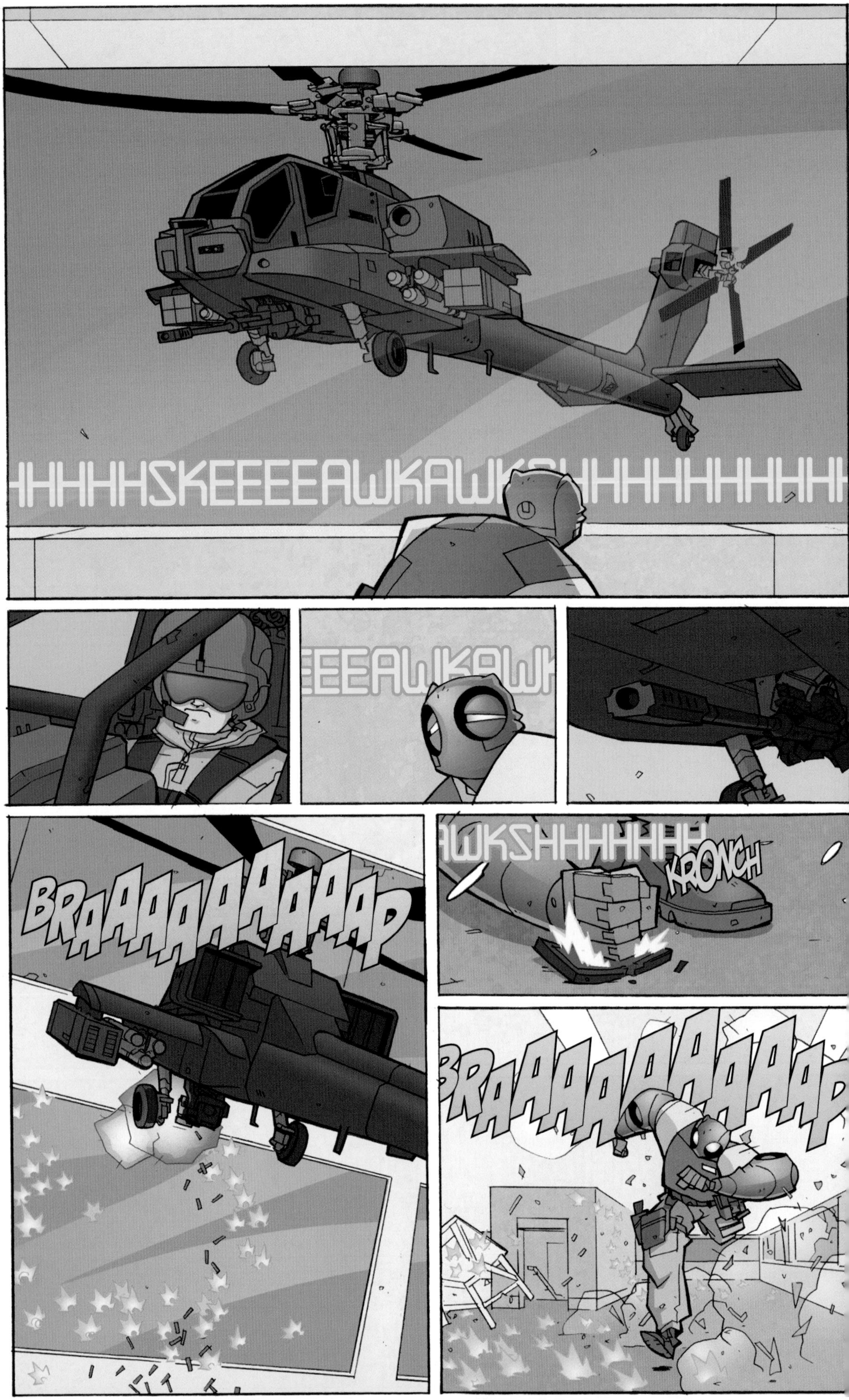
HHHHSKEEEEEAWKAWKSHHHHHHHHH
EEEEAWKAWK
AWKSHHHHHHH
KRONCH
BRAAAAAAAAAAP
BRAAAAAAAAAAP

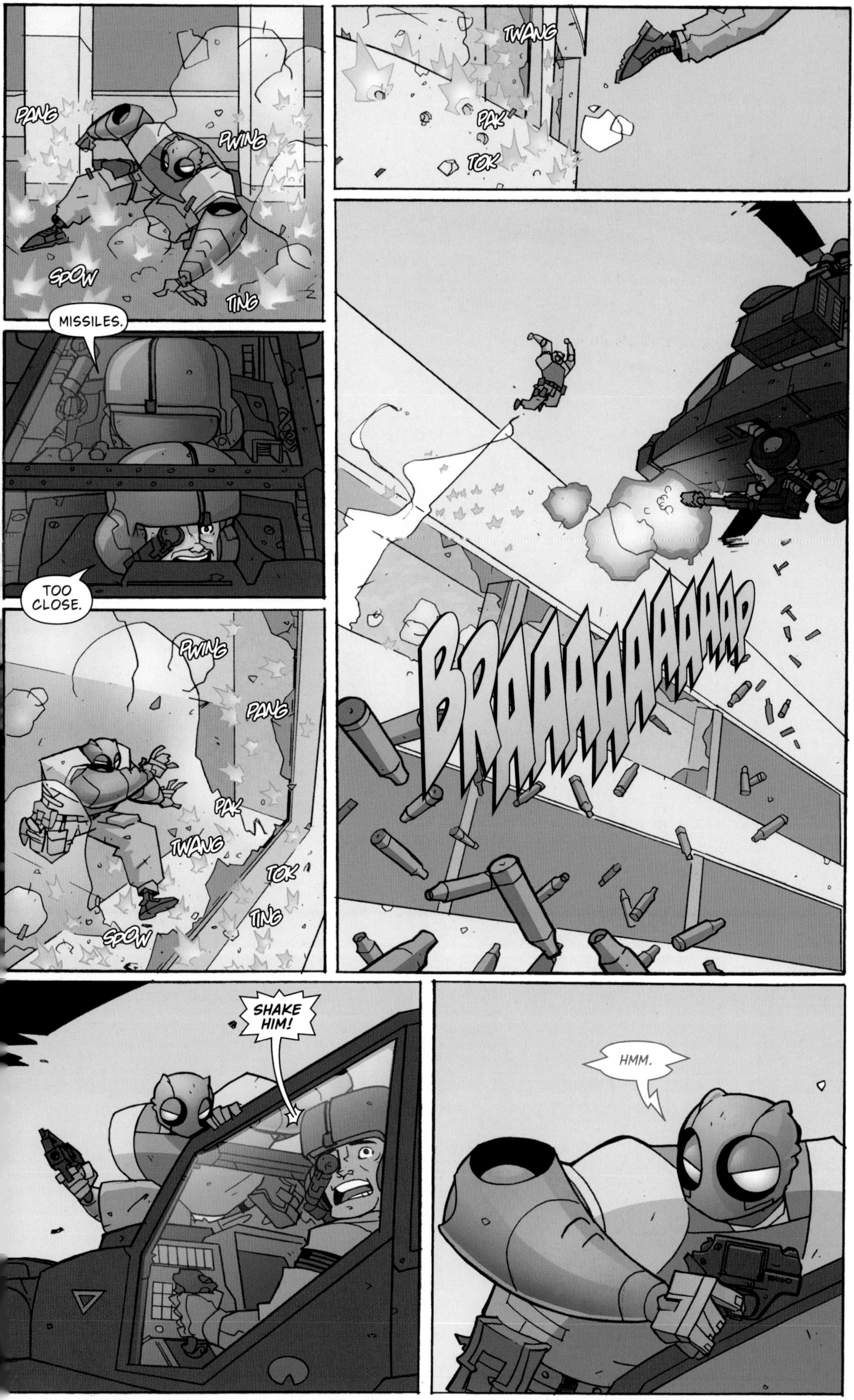
PANG
PWING
SPOW
TING
TWANG
PAK
TOK
MISSILES.
TOO CLOSE.
PWING
PANG
PAK
TWANG
TOK
TING
SPOW
BRAAAAAAAAAP
SHAKE HIM!
HMM.

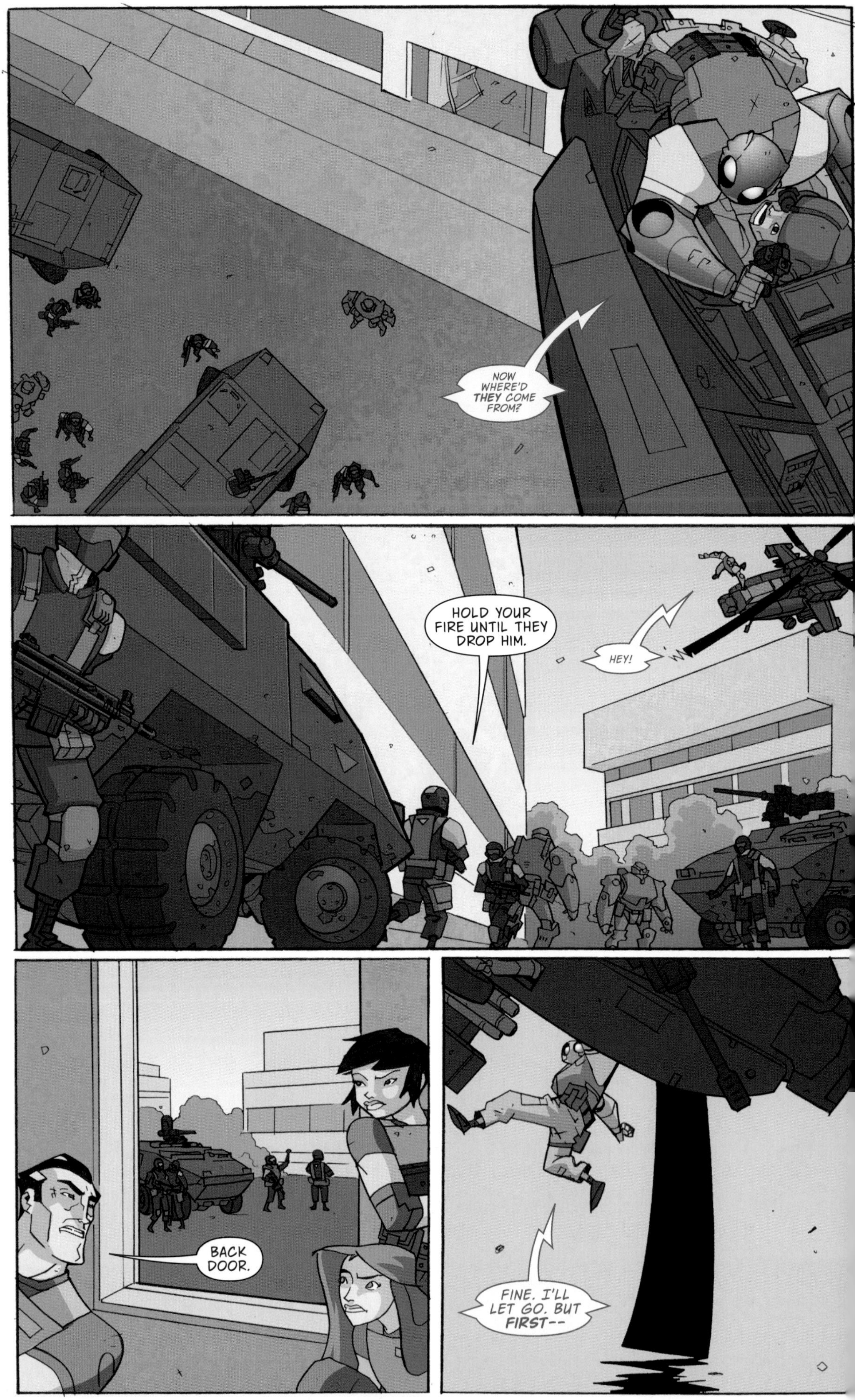
NOW WHERE'D THEY COME FROM?
HOLD YOUR FIRE UNTIL THEY DROP HIM.
HEY!
BACK DOOR.
FINE. I'LL LET GO. BUT FIRST--

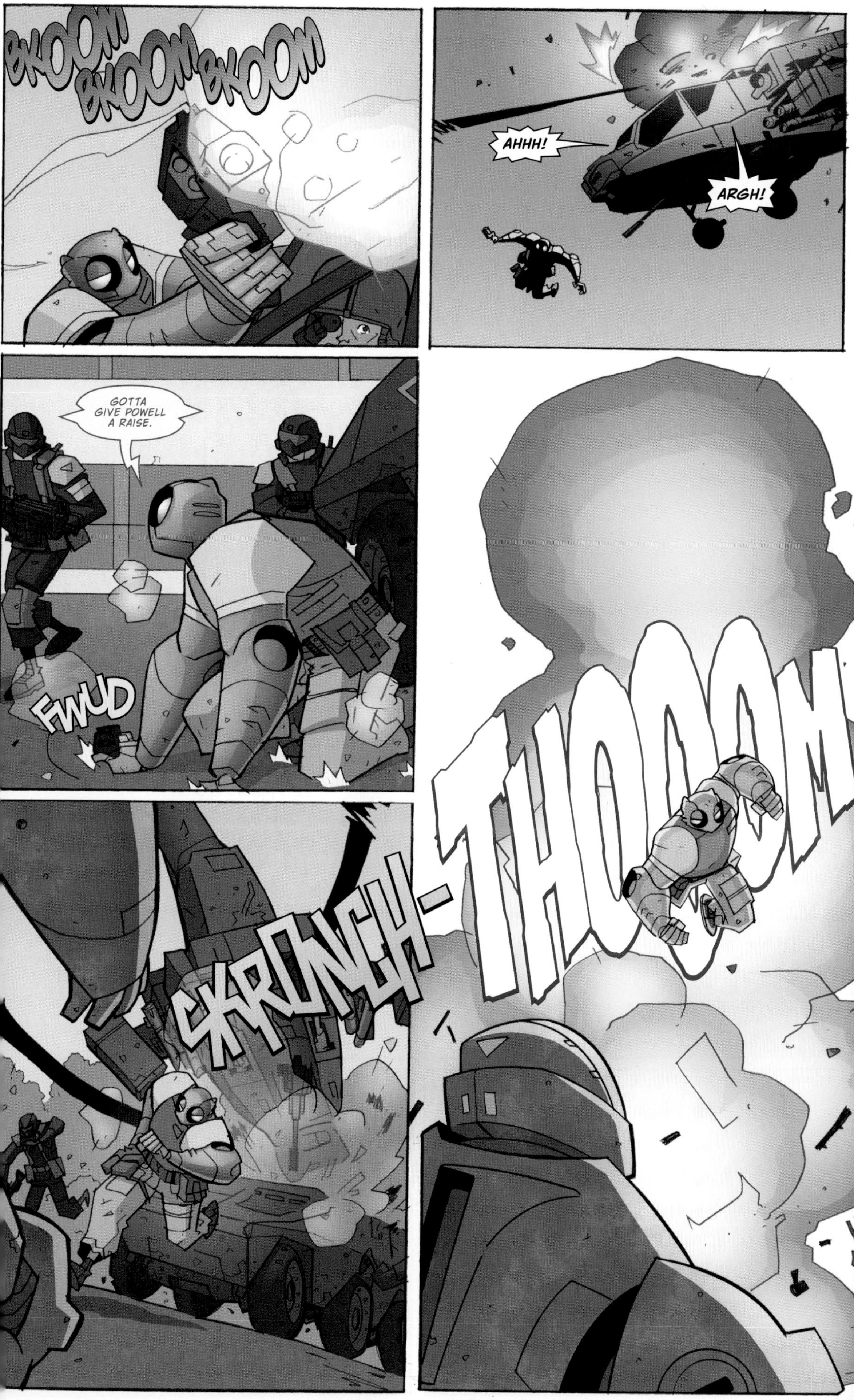
BKOOM BKOOM BKOOM
AHHH!
ARGH!
GOTTA GIVE POWELL A RAISE.
FWUD
CKRUNCH-THOOOM

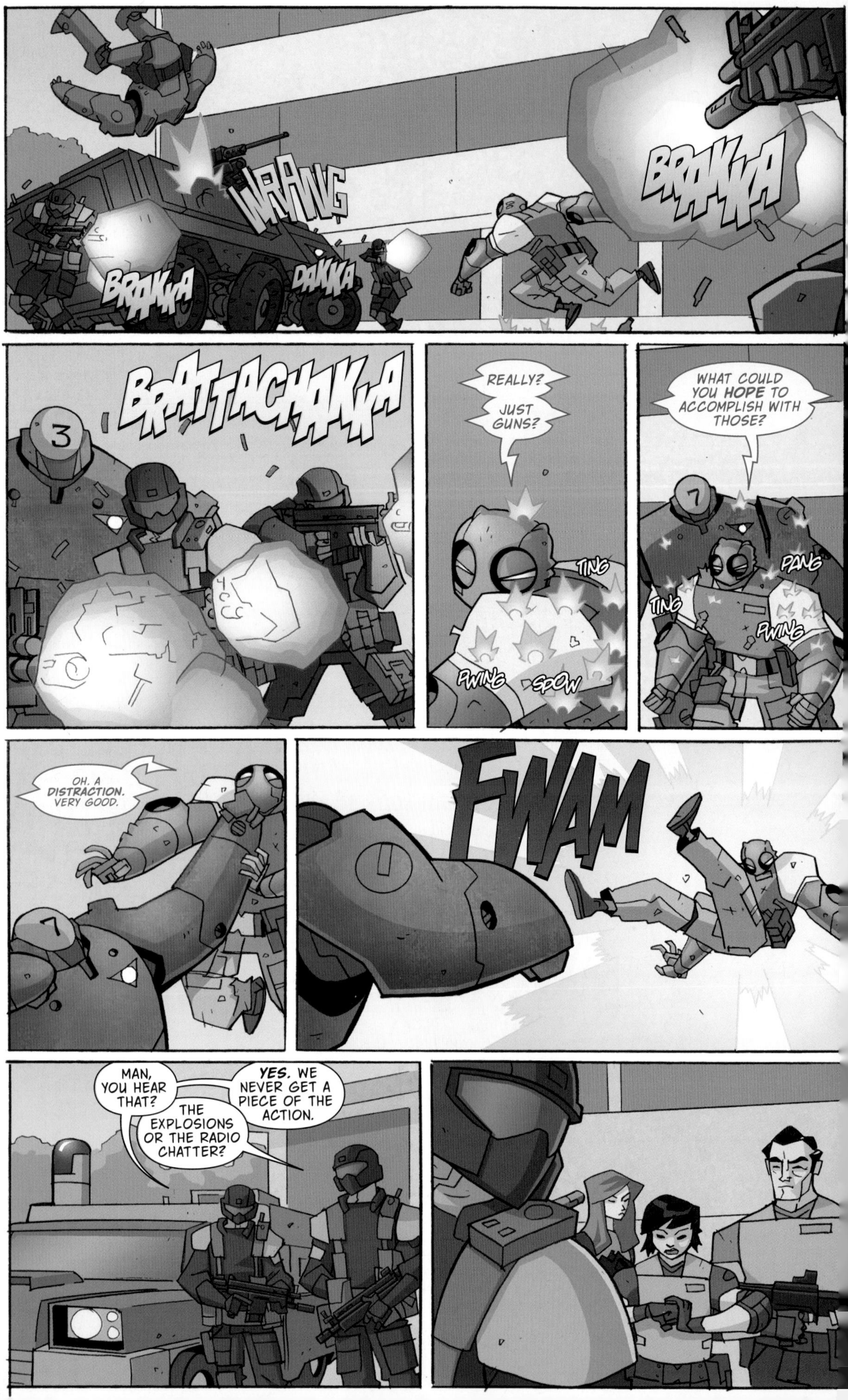
WRANG
BRAKKA
DAKKA
BRAKKA
BRATTACHAKKA
REALLY? JUST GUNS?
TING
PWING
SPOW
WHAT COULD YOU HOPE TO ACCOMPLISH WITH THOSE?
PANG
TING
PWING
OH. A DISTRACTION. VERY GOOD.
FWAM
MAN, YOU HEAR THAT?
YES. WE NEVER GET A PIECE OF THE ACTION.
THE EXPLOSIONS OR THE RADIO CHATTER?

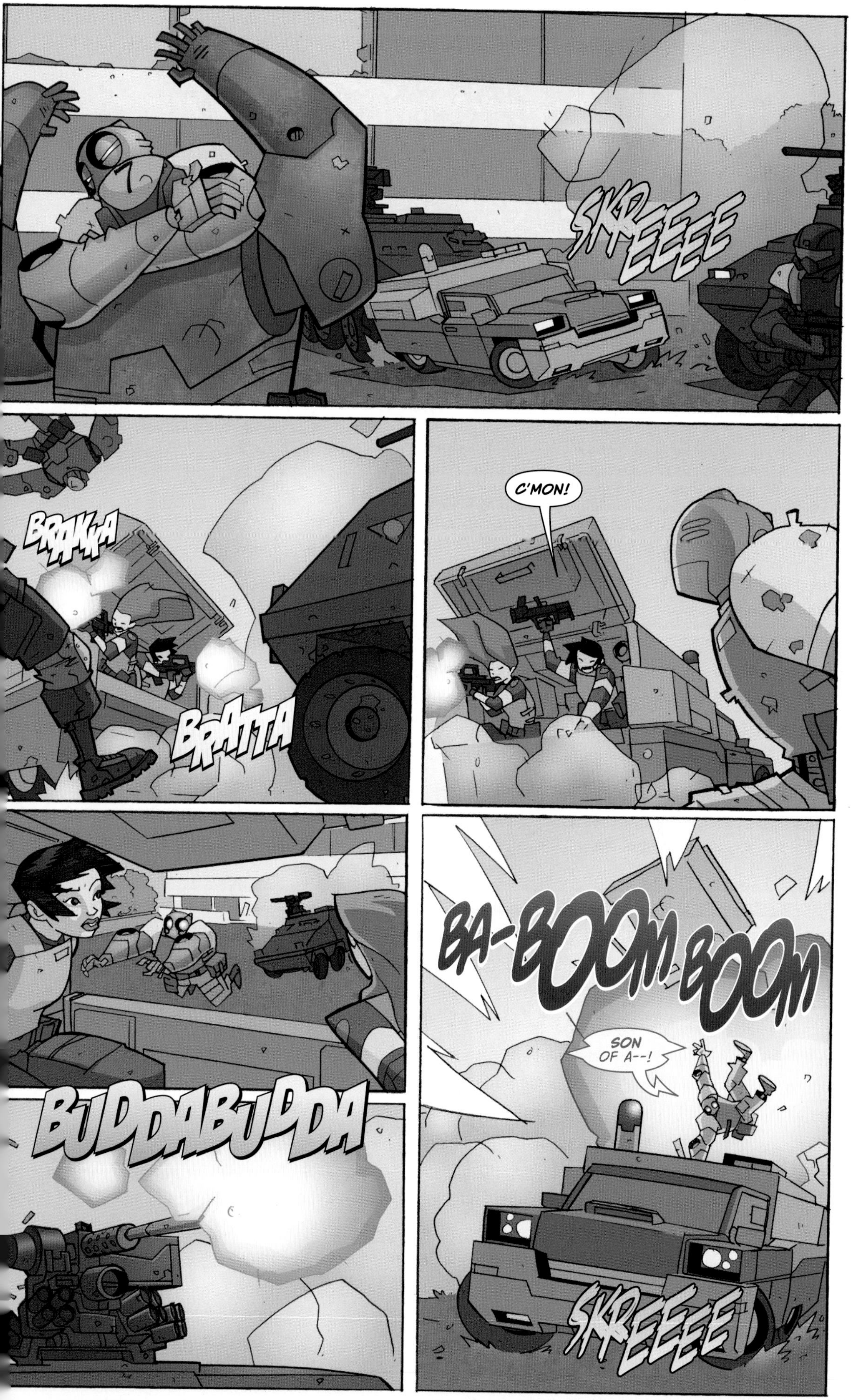
SKREEEEE
BRAKKA
BRATTA
C'MON!
BUDDABUDDA
BA-BOOM BOOM
SON OF A--!
SKREEEEE

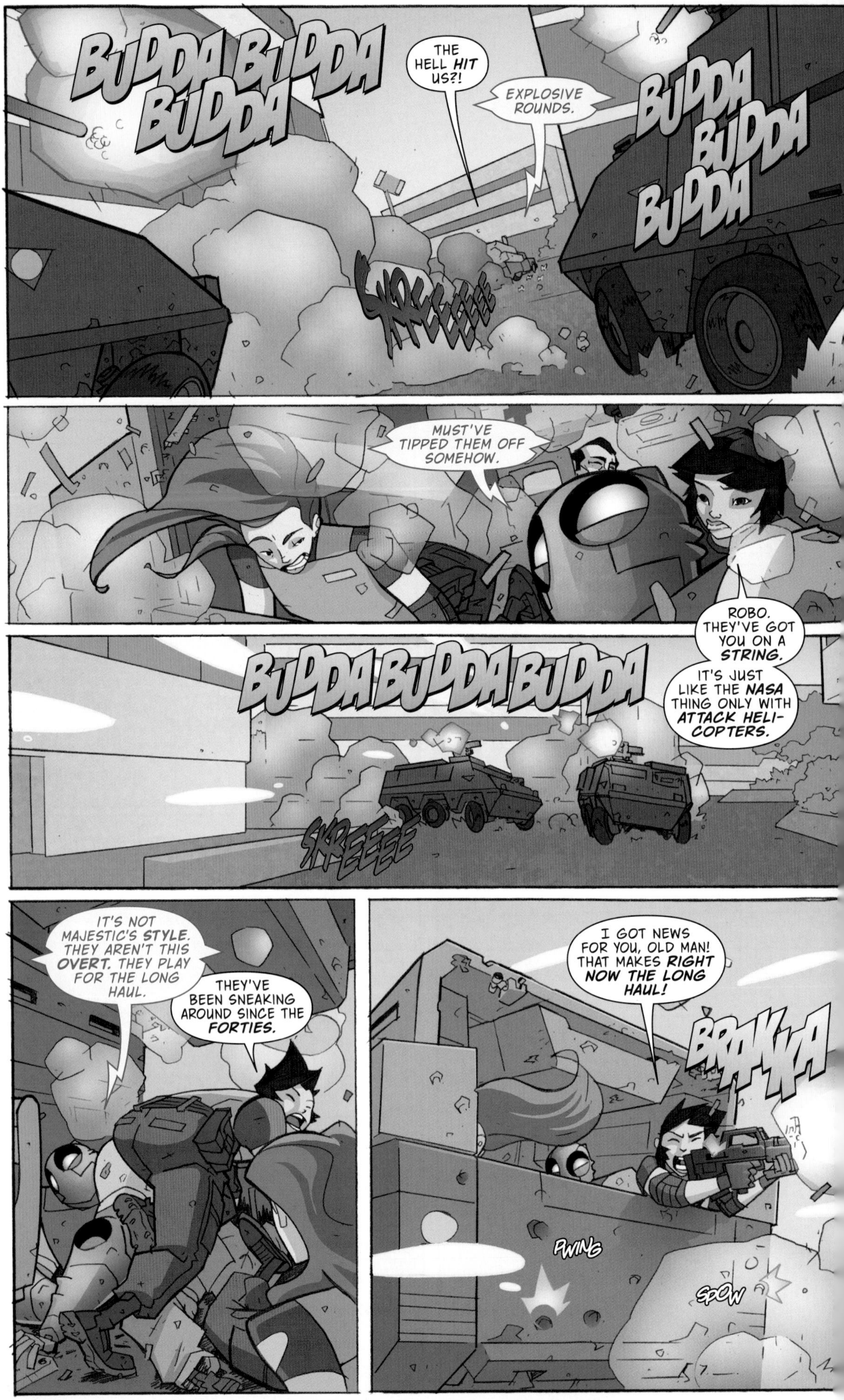
BUDDA BUDDA BUDDA BUDDA
THE HELL HIT US?!
EXPLOSIVE ROUNDS.
BUDDA BUDDA BUDDA
SKREEEEE
MUST'VE TIPPED THEM OFF SOMEHOW.
ROBO. THEY'VE GOT YOU ON A STRING.
IT'S JUST LIKE THE NASA THING ONLY WITH ATTACK HELI-COPTERS.
BUDDA BUDDA BUDDA
SKREEEEE
IT'S NOT MAJESTIC'S STYLE. THEY AREN'T THIS OVERT. THEY PLAY FOR THE LONG HAUL.
THEY'VE BEEN SNEAKING AROUND SINCE THE FORTIES.
I GOT NEWS FOR YOU, OLD MAN! THAT MAKES RIGHT NOW THE LONG HAUL!
BRAKKA
PWING
SPOW

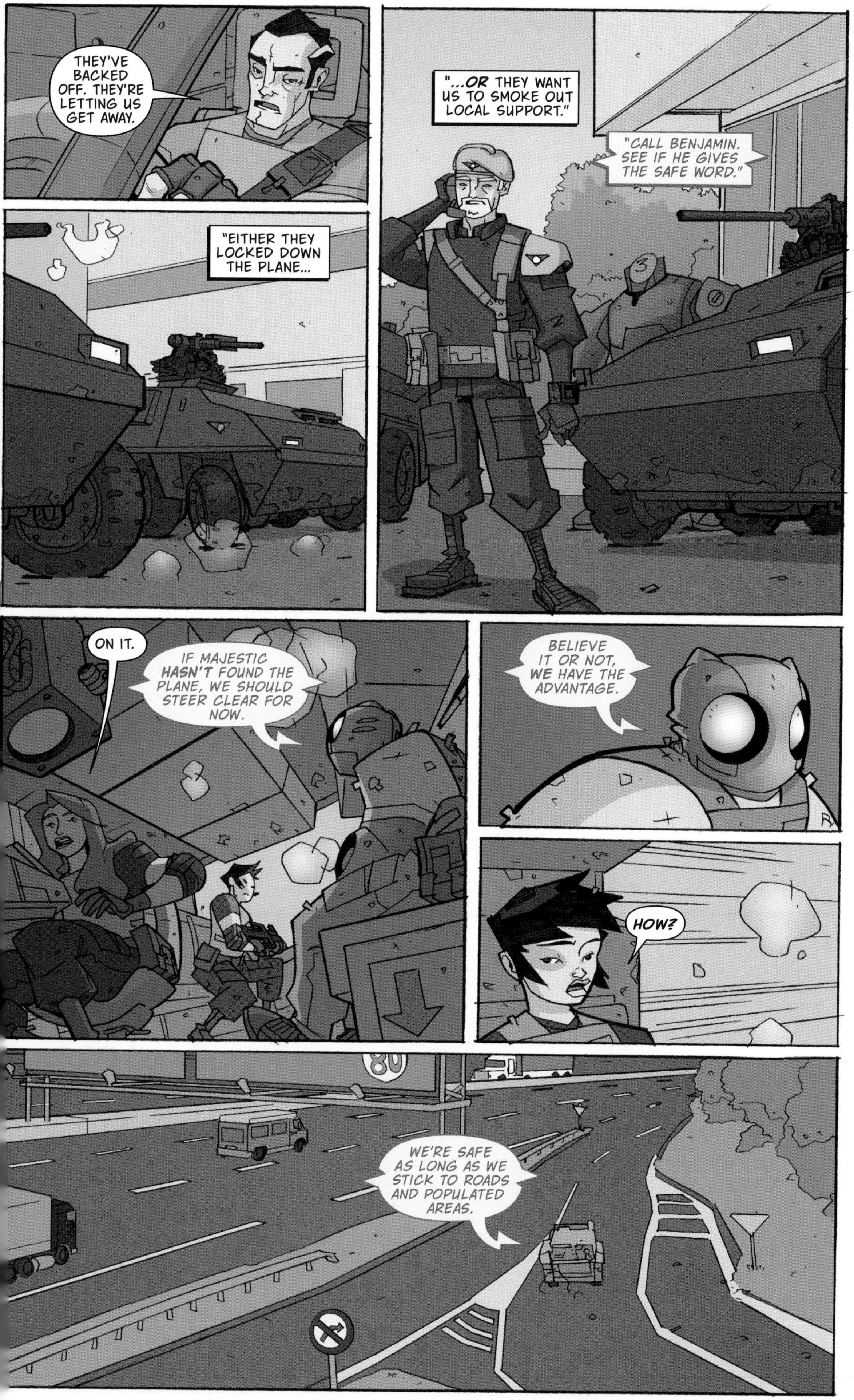
THEY'VE BACKED OFF. THEY'RE LETTING US GET AWAY.
"EITHER THEY LOCKED DOWN THE PLANE...
"...OR THEY WANT US TO SMOKE OUT LOCAL SUPPORT."
"CALL BENJAMIN. SEE IF HE GIVES THE SAFE WORD."
ON IT.
IF MAJESTIC HASN'T FOUND THE PLANE, WE SHOULD STEER CLEAR FOR NOW.
BELIEVE IT OR NOT, WE HAVE THE ADVANTAGE.
HOW?
WE'RE SAFE AS LONG AS WE STICK TO ROADS AND POPULATED AREAS.

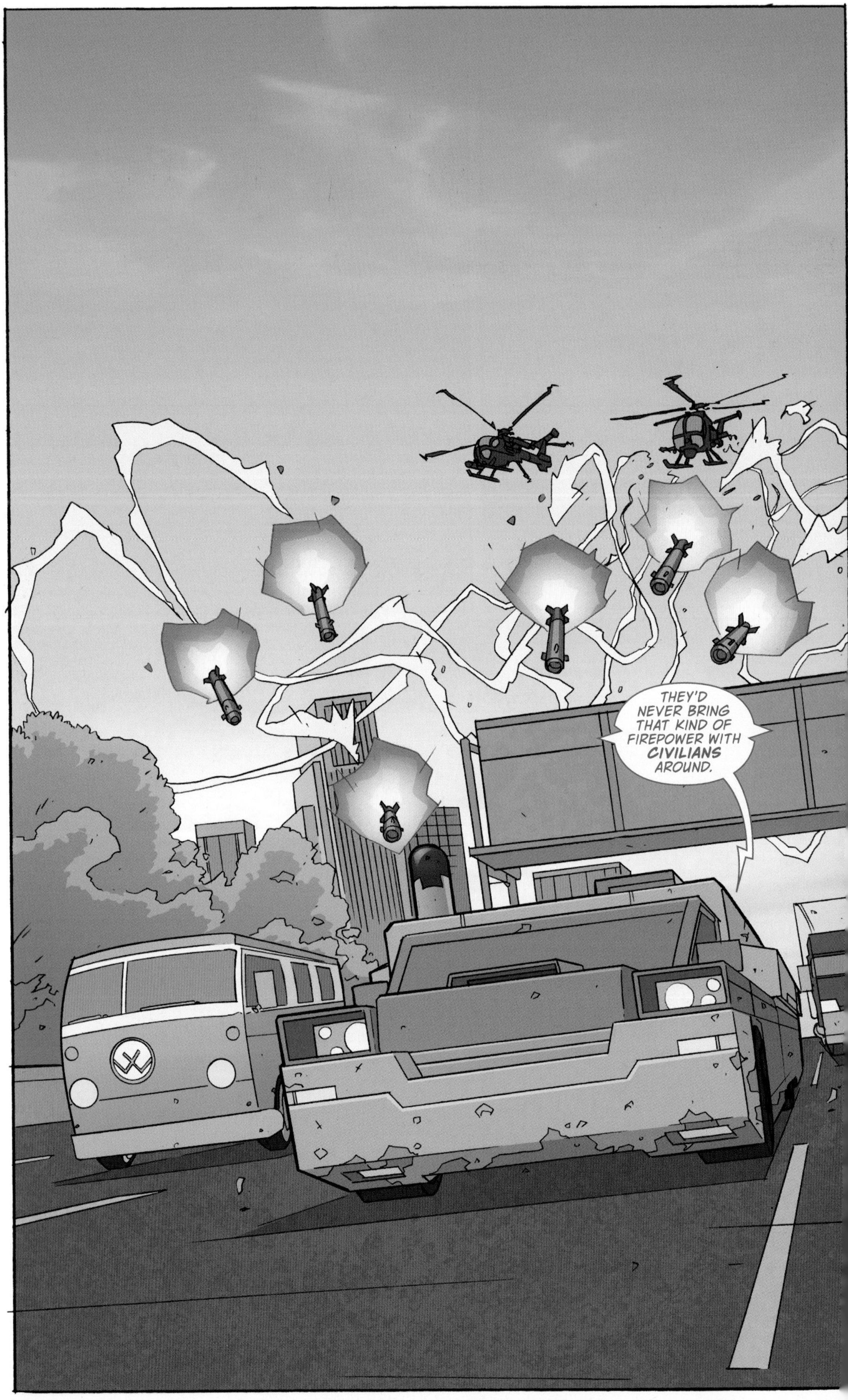
THEY'D NEVER BRING THAT KIND OF FIREPOWER WITH CIVILIANS AROUND.

TRANSFORMATION

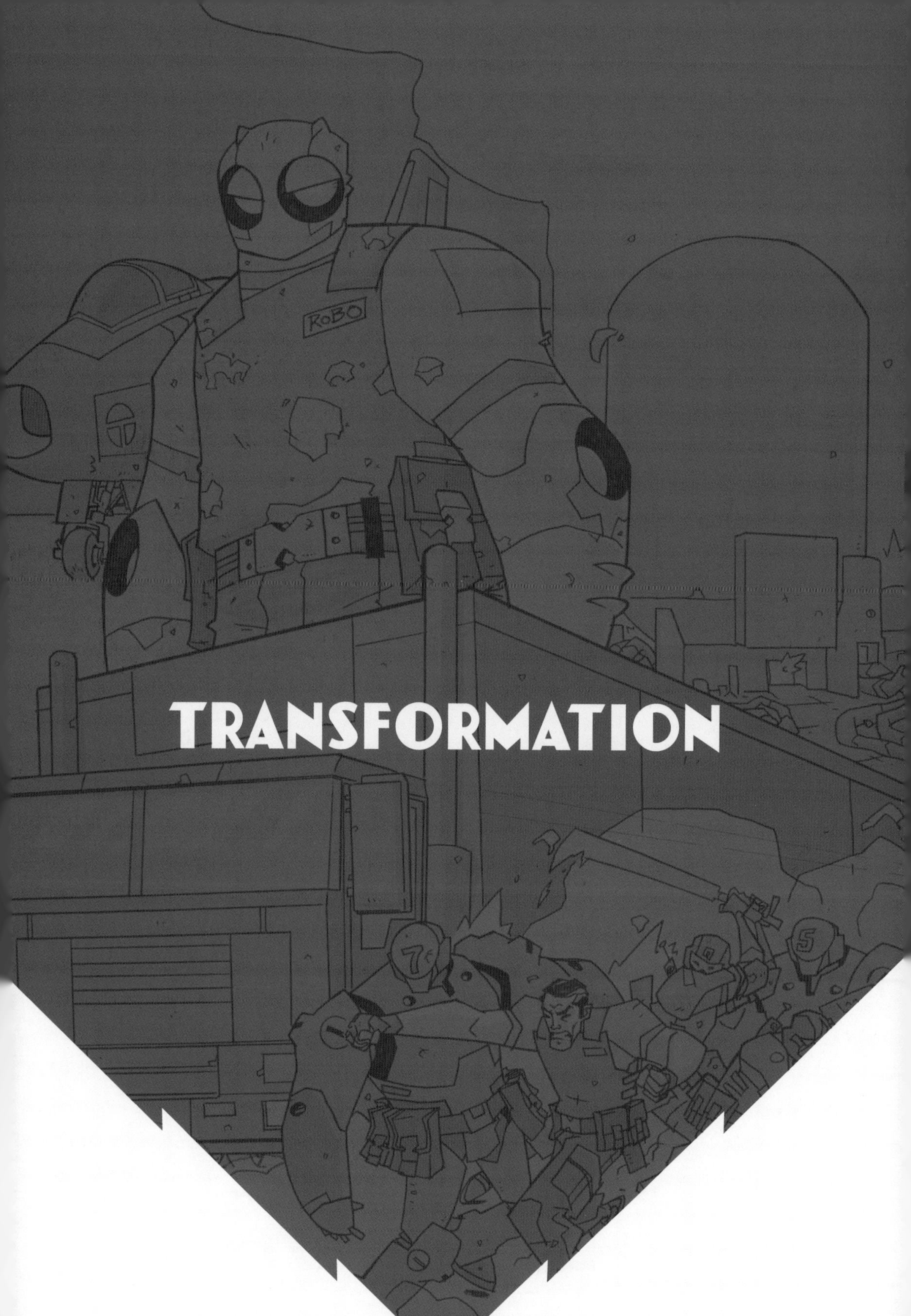
ROBO

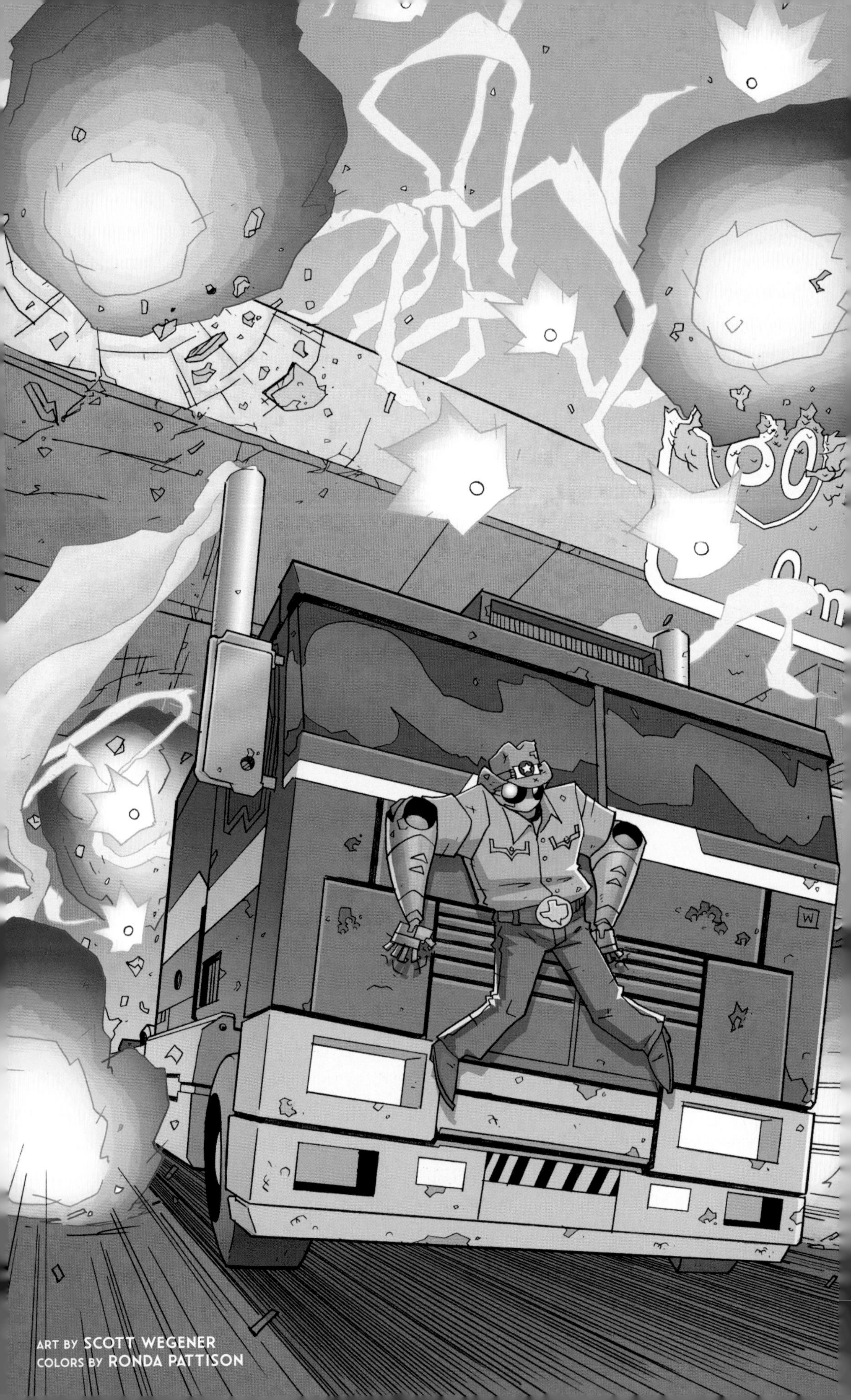
100

ART BY SCOTT WEGENER
COLORS BY RONDA PATTISON

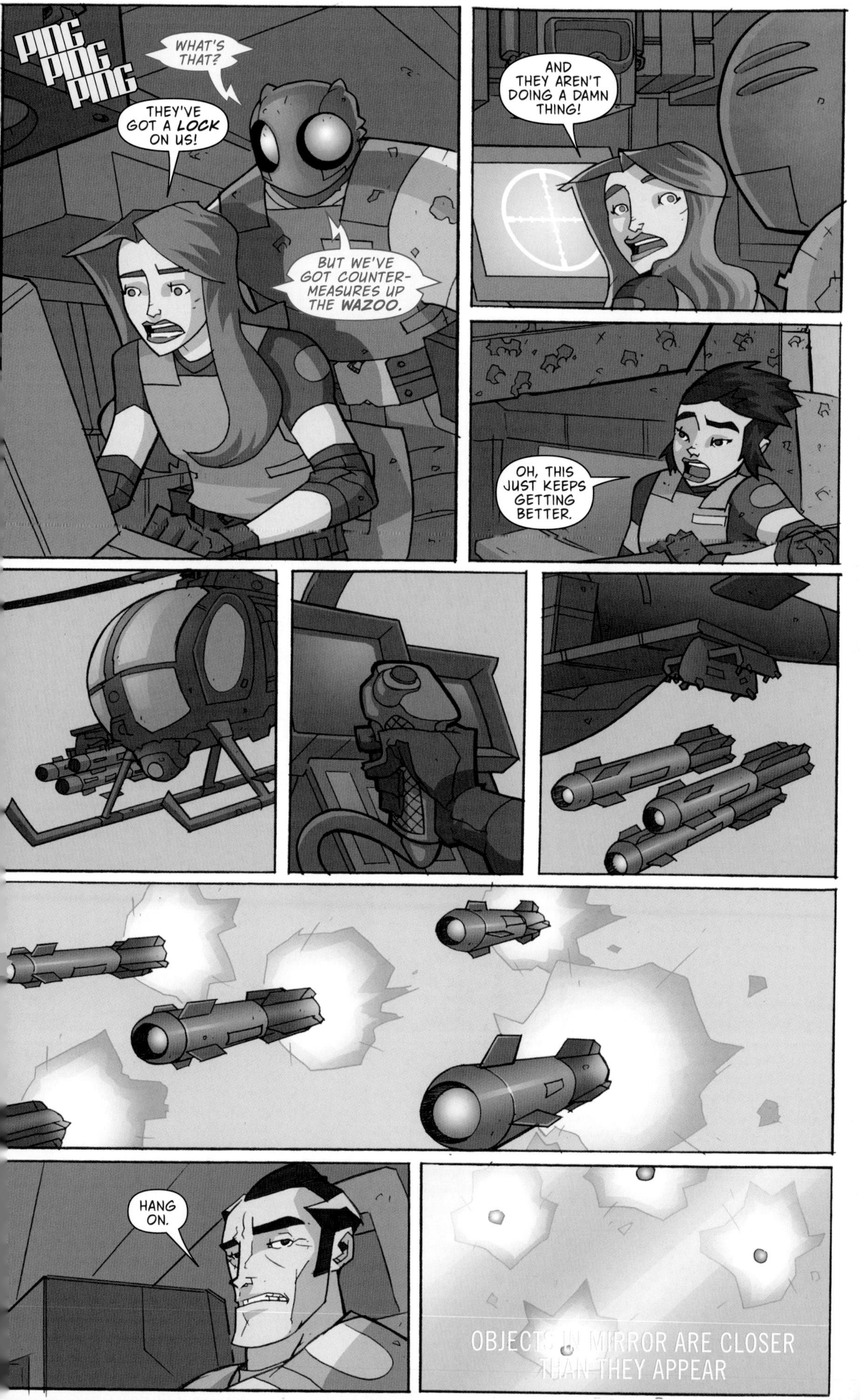
PING PING PING
WHAT'S THAT?
THEY'VE GOT A LOCK ON US!
BUT WE'VE GOT COUNTER-MEASURES UP THE WAZOO.
AND THEY AREN'T DOING A DAMN THING!
OH, THIS JUST KEEPS GETTING BETTER.
HANG ON.
OBJECTS IN MIRROR ARE CLOSER THAN THEY APPEAR

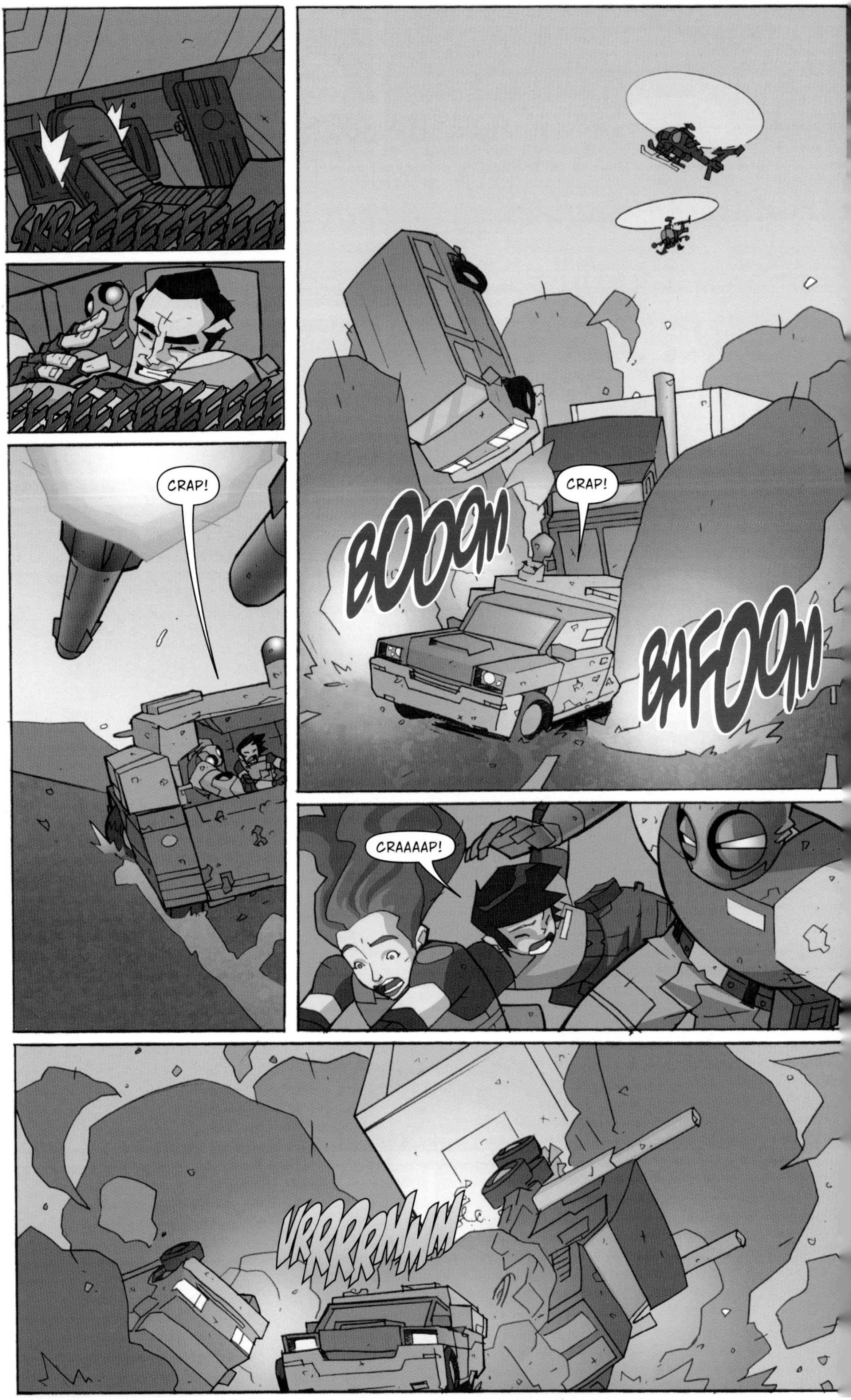
SKREEEEEEEEEEEEE
EEEEEEEEEEEEEE
CRAP!
BOOOM
CRAP!
BAFOOM
CRAAAAP!
URRRRMMM

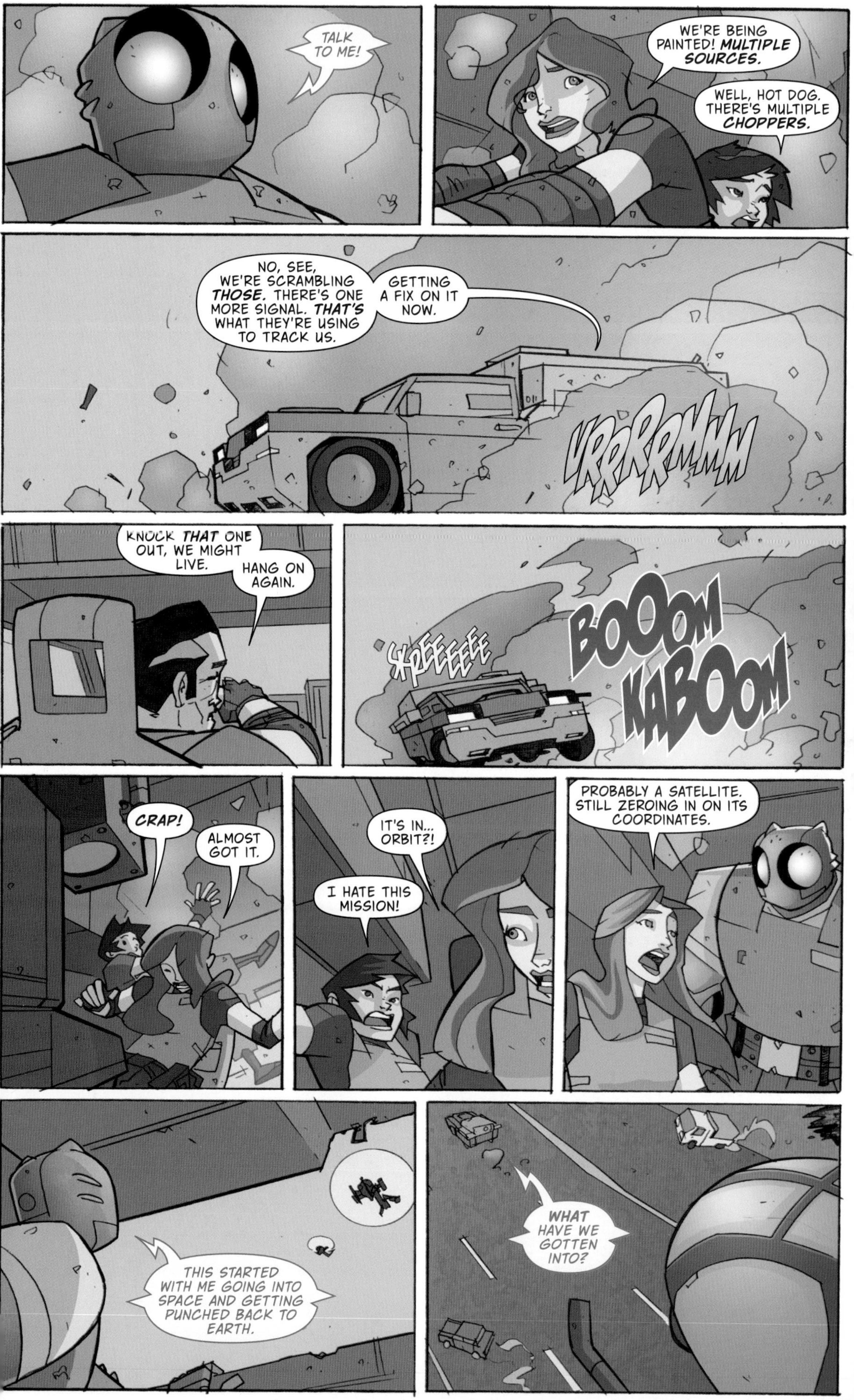
TALK TO ME!
WE'RE BEING PAINTED! MULTIPLE SOURCES.
WELL, HOT DOG. THERE'S MULTIPLE CHOPPERS.
NO, SEE, WE'RE SCRAMBLING THOSE. THERE'S ONE MORE SIGNAL. THAT'S WHAT THEY'RE USING TO TRACK US.
GETTING A FIX ON IT NOW.
URRRRMMM
KNOCK THAT ONE OUT, WE MIGHT LIVE.
HANG ON AGAIN.
SKREEEEEE
BOOOM KABOOM
CRAP!
ALMOST GOT IT.
IT'S IN... ORBIT?!
I HATE THIS MISSION!
PROBABLY A SATELLITE. STILL ZEROING IN ON ITS COORDINATES.
THIS STARTED WITH ME GOING INTO SPACE AND GETTING PUNCHED BACK TO EARTH.
WHAT HAVE WE GOTTEN INTO?

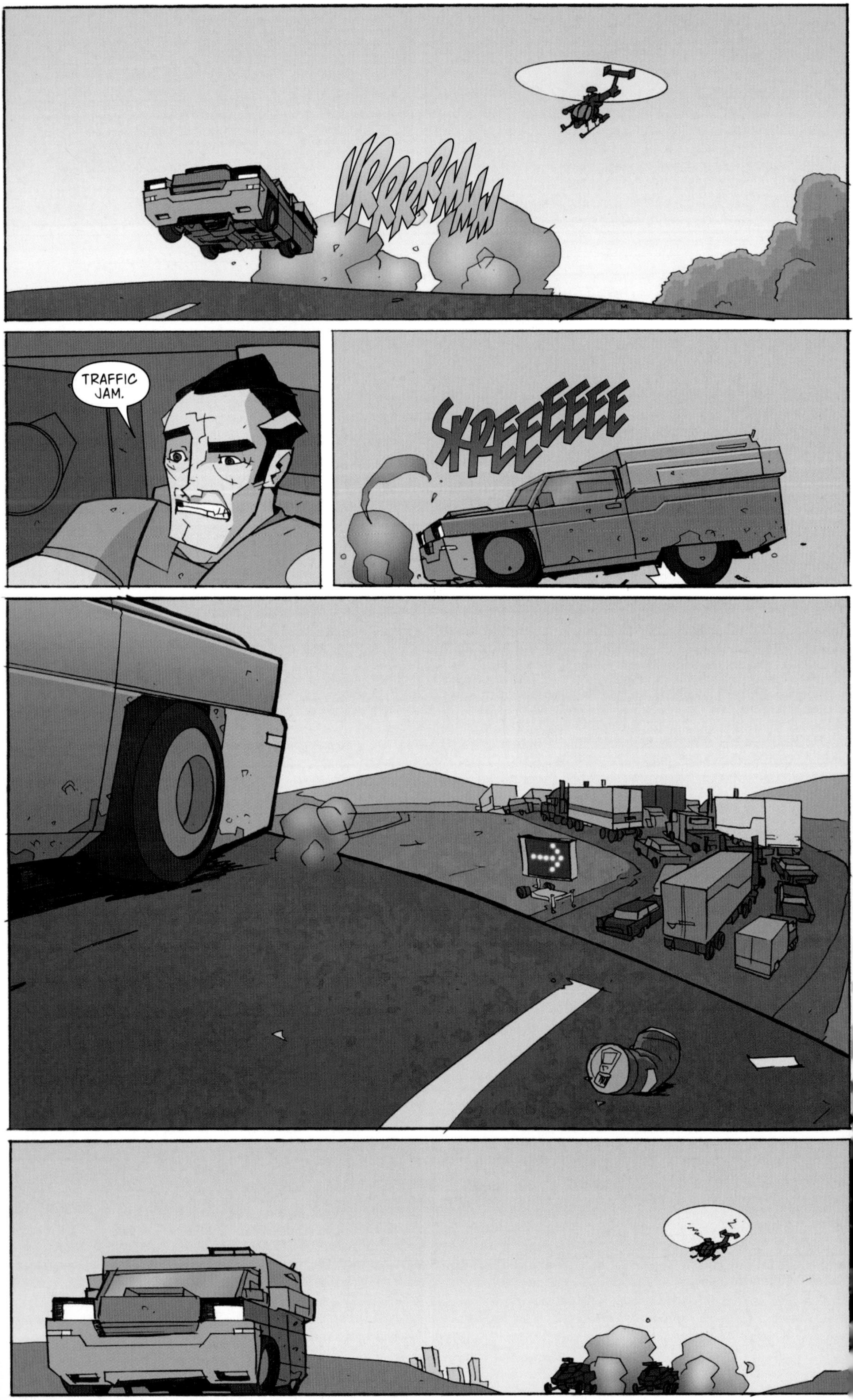
VRRRRMMM
TRAFFIC JAM.
SKREEEEEEE

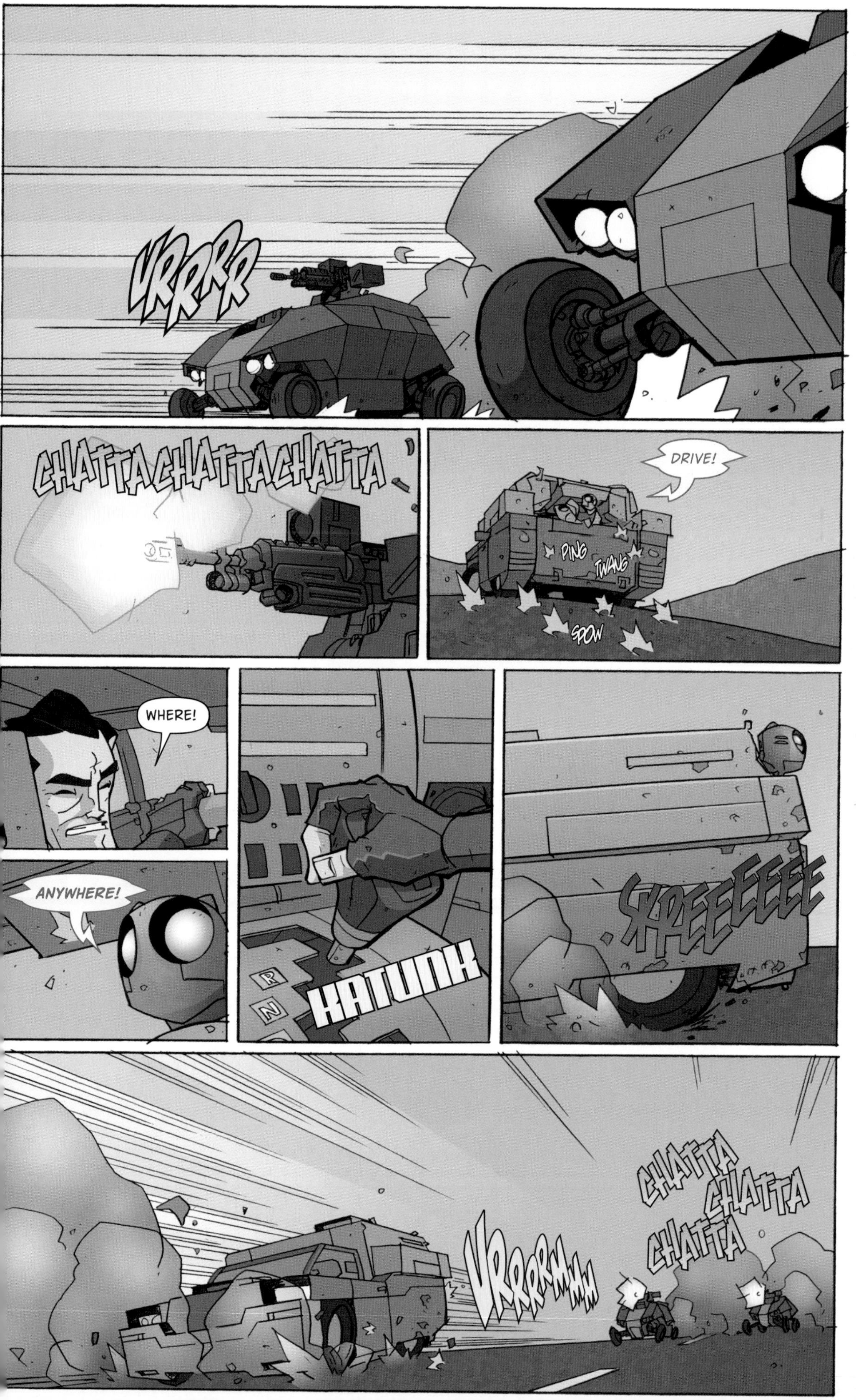
URRRR
CHATTACHATTACHATTA
DRIVE!
PING
TWANG
SPOW
WHERE!
ANYWHERE!
R
N
KATUNK
SKREEEEEEE
VRRRRMMM
CHATTA
CHATTA
CHATTA

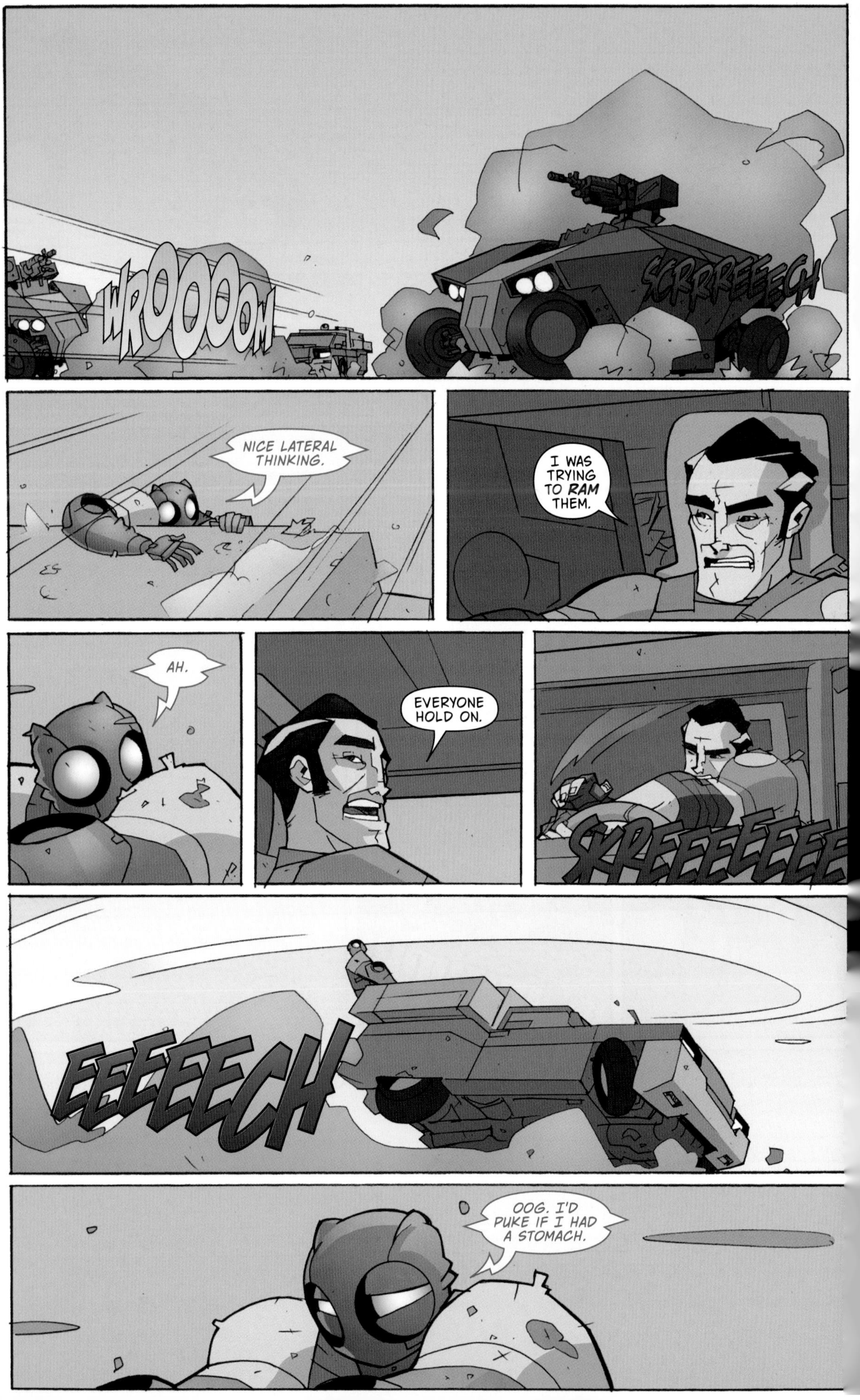
WROOOOM
SCRRREEEECH
NICE LATERAL THINKING.
I WAS TRYING TO RAM THEM.
AH.
EVERYONE HOLD ON.
SKREEEEEEEE
EEEEEECH
OOG. I'D PUKE IF I HAD A STOMACH.

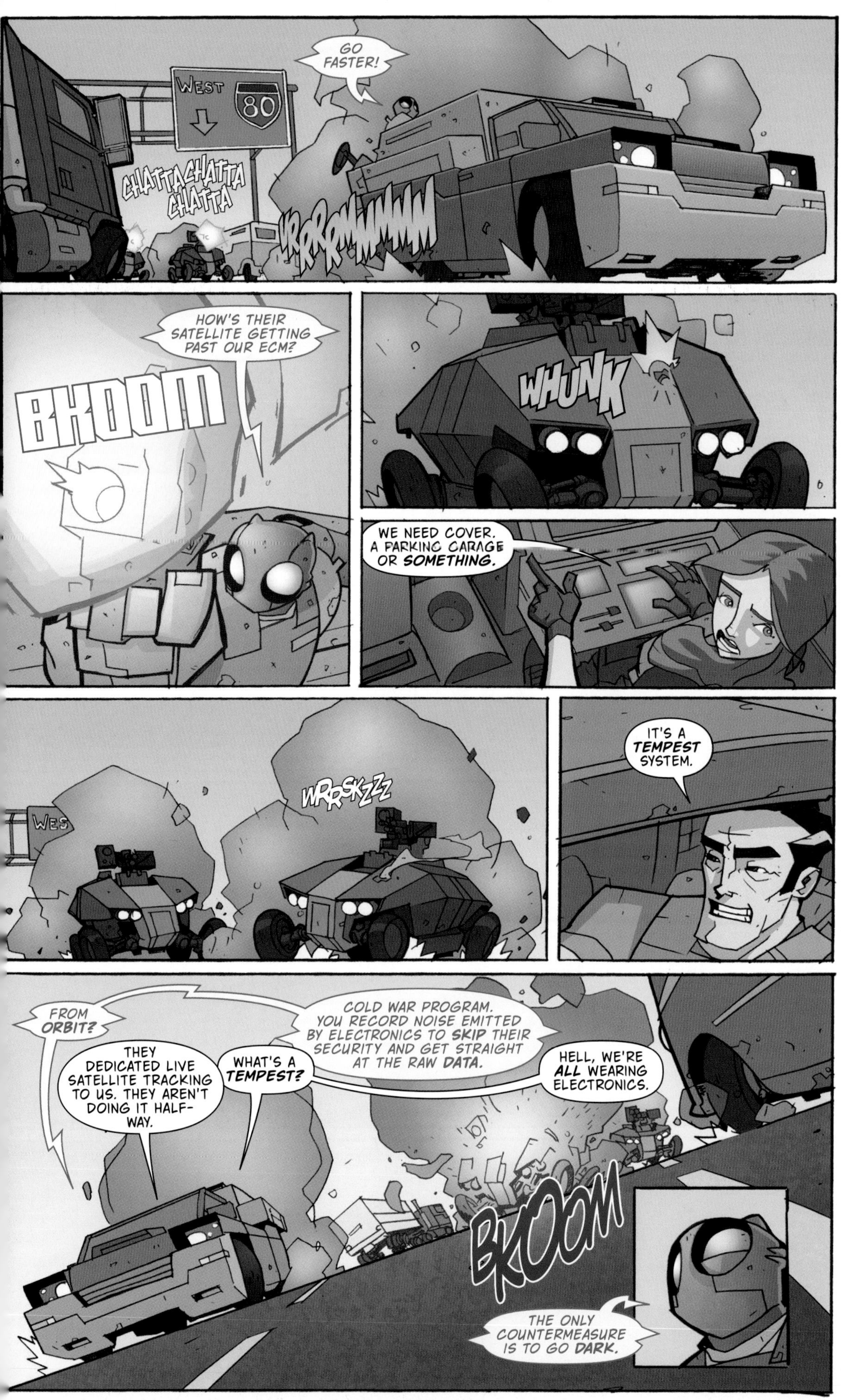
WEST
80
CHATTACHATTA CHATTA
GO FASTER!
URRRRMMMMM
BKOOM
HOW'S THEIR SATELLITE GETTING PAST OUR ECM?
WHUNK
WE NEED COVER. A PARKING GARAGE OR SOMETHING.
WRRSKZZZ
WES
IT'S A TEMPEST SYSTEM.
FROM ORBIT?
THEY DEDICATED LIVE SATELLITE TRACKING TO US. THEY AREN'T DOING IT HALF-WAY.
WHAT'S A TEMPEST?
COLD WAR PROGRAM. YOU RECORD NOISE EMITTED BY ELECTRONICS TO SKIP THEIR SECURITY AND GET STRAIGHT AT THE RAW DATA.
HELL, WE'RE ALL WEARING ELECTRONICS.
BKOOM
THE ONLY COUNTERMEASURE IS TO GO DARK.

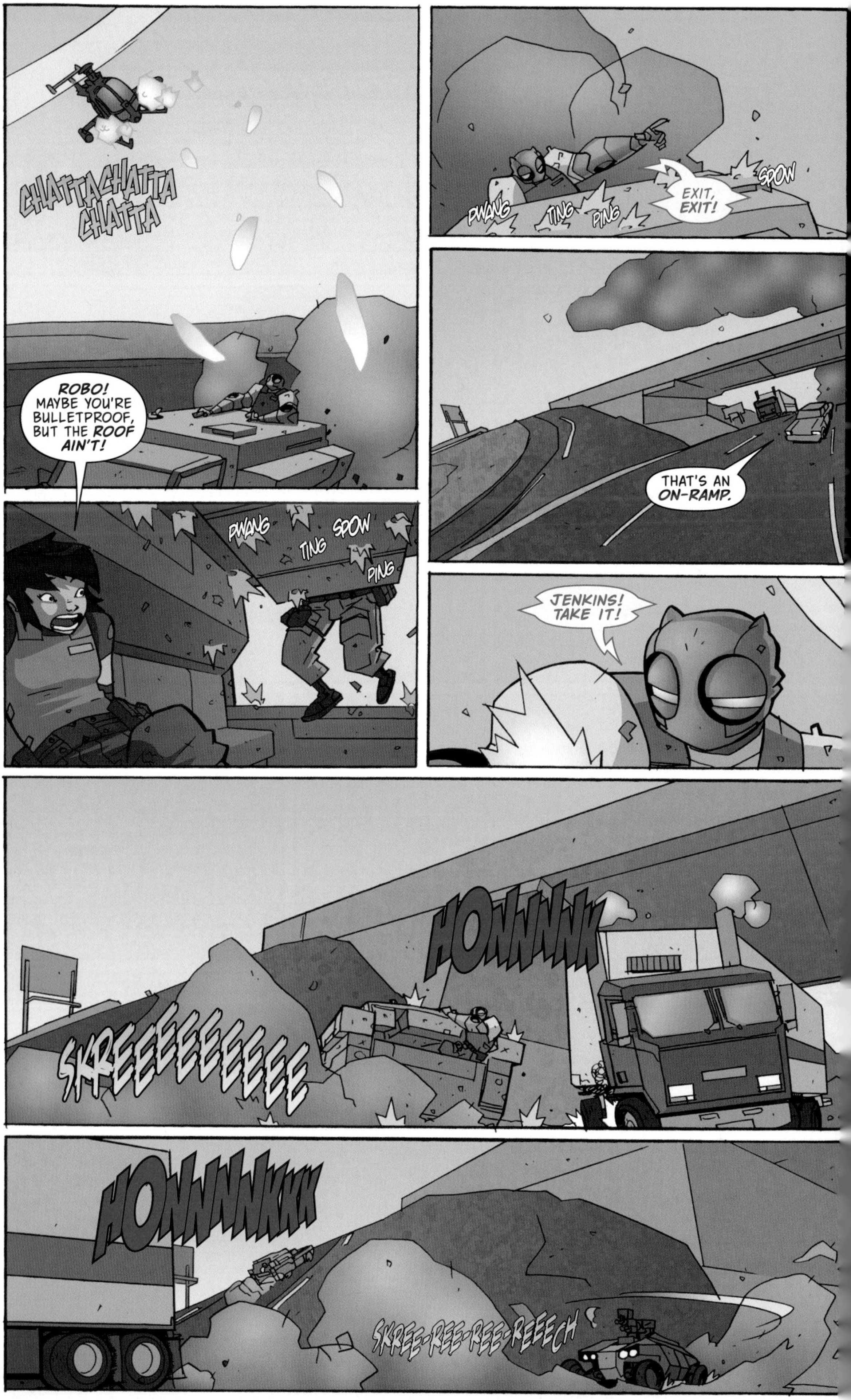
CHATTACHATTA CHATTA
EXIT, EXIT!
PWANG
TING
PING
SPOW
ROBO! MAYBE YOU'RE BULLETPROOF, BUT THE ROOF AIN'T!
PWANG
TING
SPOW
PING
THAT'S AN ON-RAMP.
JENKINS! TAKE IT!
HONNNNK
SKREEEEEEEEEE
HONNNNKKK
SKREE-REE-REE-REEECH

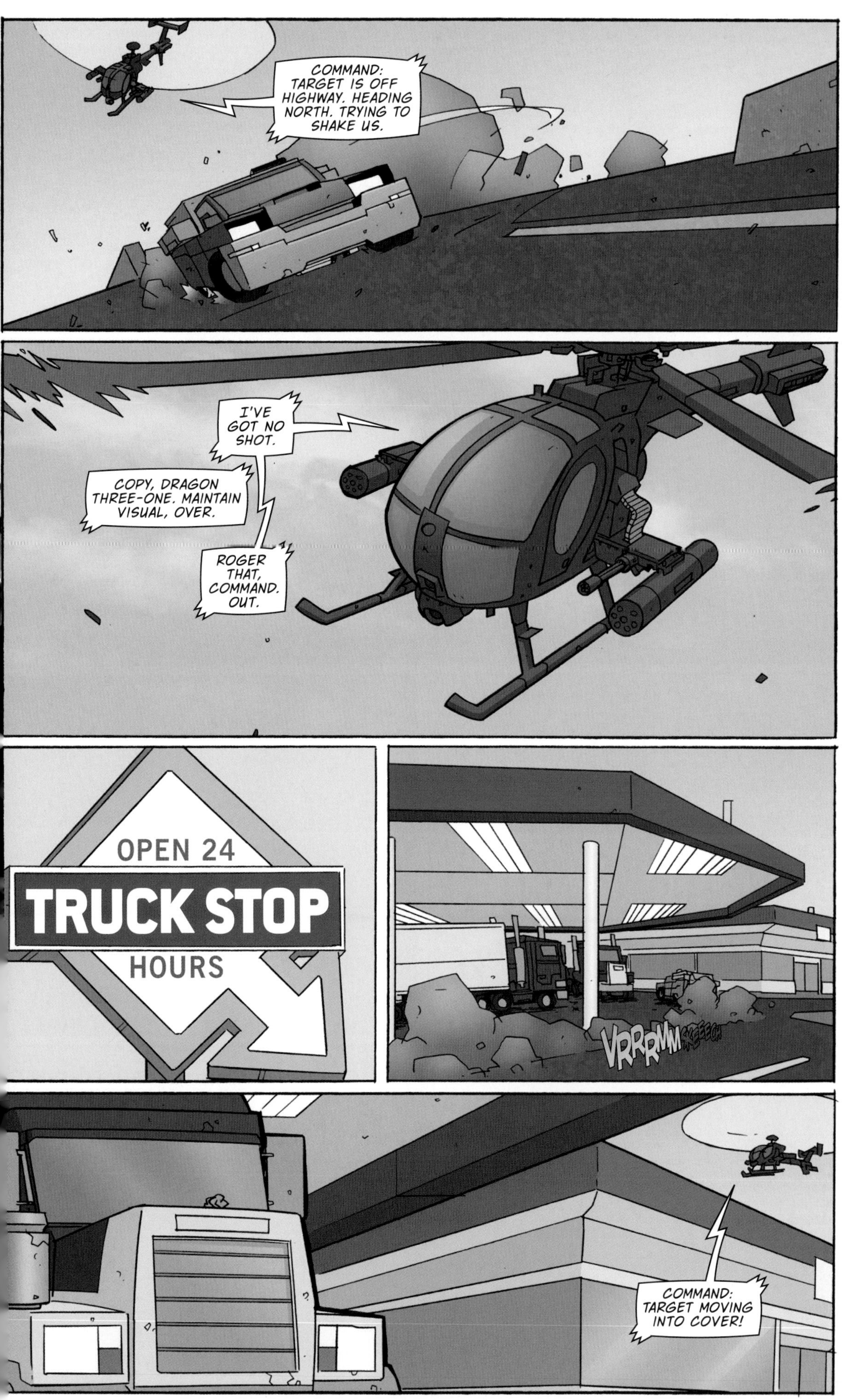
COMMAND: TARGET IS OFF HIGHWAY. HEADING NORTH. TRYING TO SHAKE US.
I'VE GOT NO SHOT.
COPY, DRAGON THREE-ONE. MAINTAIN VISUAL, OVER.
ROGER THAT, COMMAND. OUT.
OPEN 24
TRUCK STOP
HOURS
VRRRMM
COMMAND: TARGET MOVING INTO COVER!

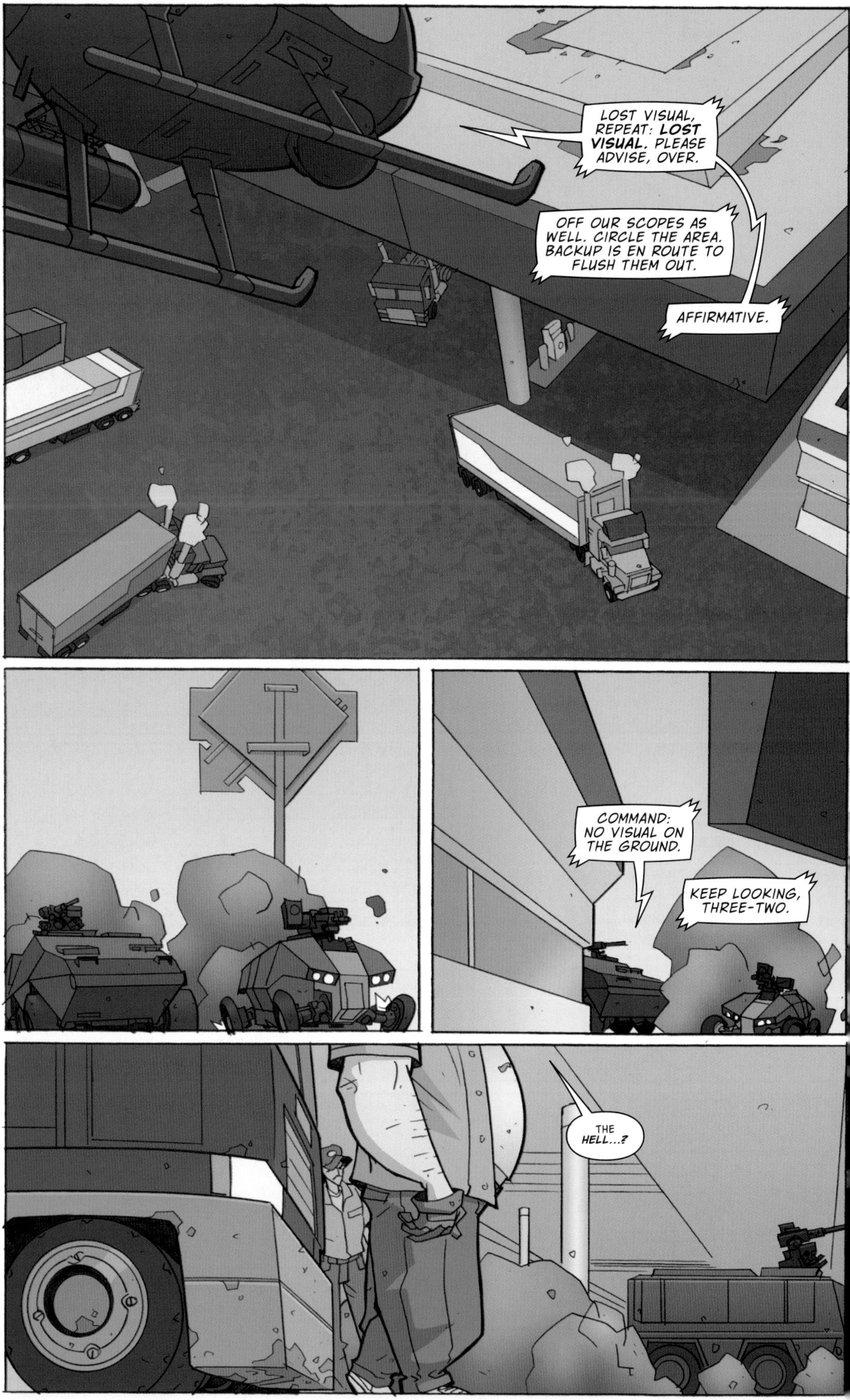
LOST VISUAL, REPEAT: LOST VISUAL. PLEASE ADVISE, OVER.
OFF OUR SCOPES AS WELL. CIRCLE THE AREA. BACKUP IS EN ROUTE TO FLUSH THEM OUT.
AFFIRMATIVE.
COMMAND: NO VISUAL ON THE GROUND.
KEEP LOOKING, THREE-TWO.
THE HELL...?

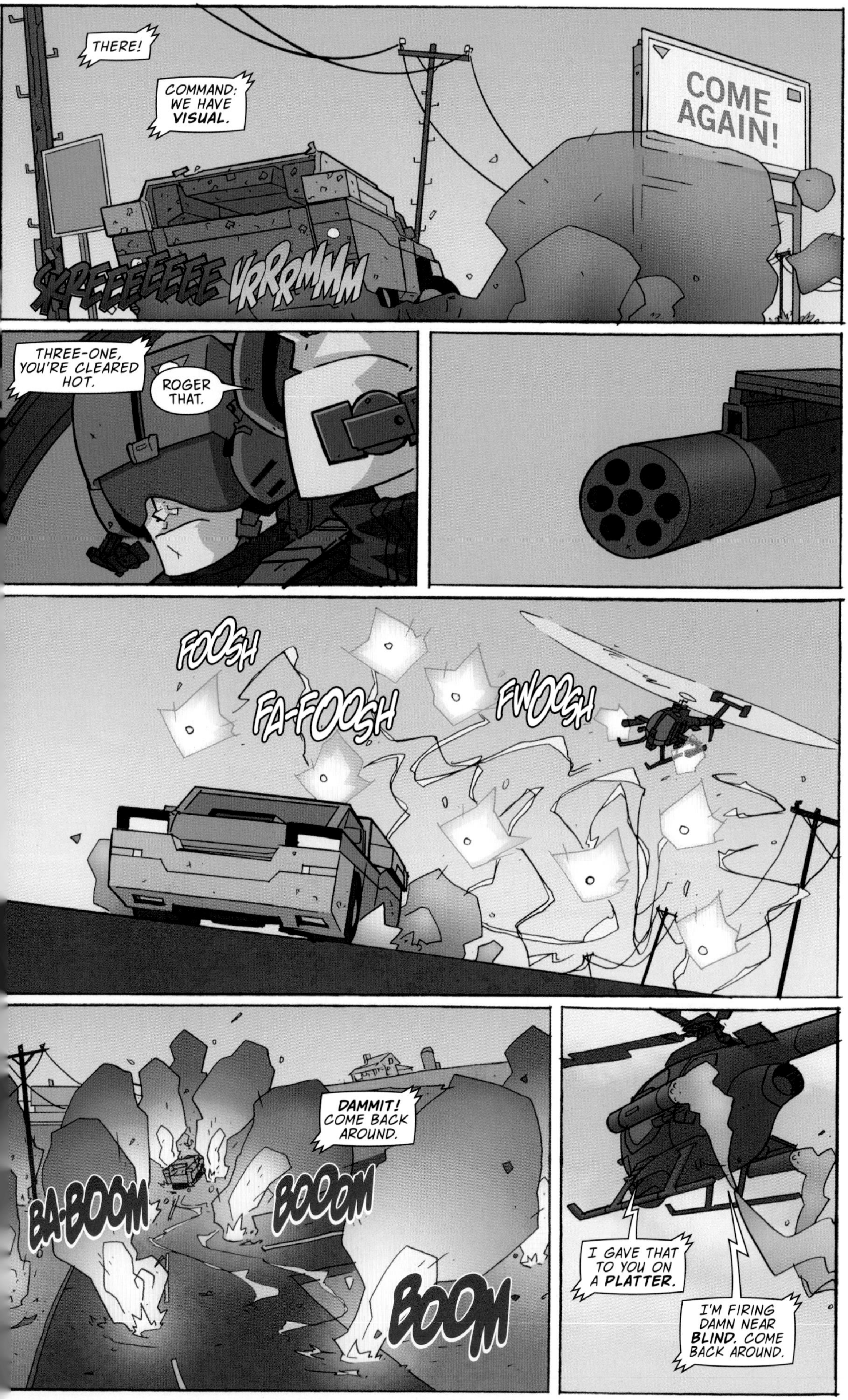
THERE!
COMMAND: WE HAVE VISUAL.
COME AGAIN!
SKREEEEEEEEE
URRRMMM
THREE-ONE, YOU'RE CLEARED HOT.
ROGER THAT.
FOOSH
FA-FOOSH
FWOOSH
DAMMIT! COME BACK AROUND.
BA-BOOM
BOOOM
BOOM
I GAVE THAT TO YOU ON A PLATTER.
I'M FIRING DAMN NEAR BLIND. COME BACK AROUND.

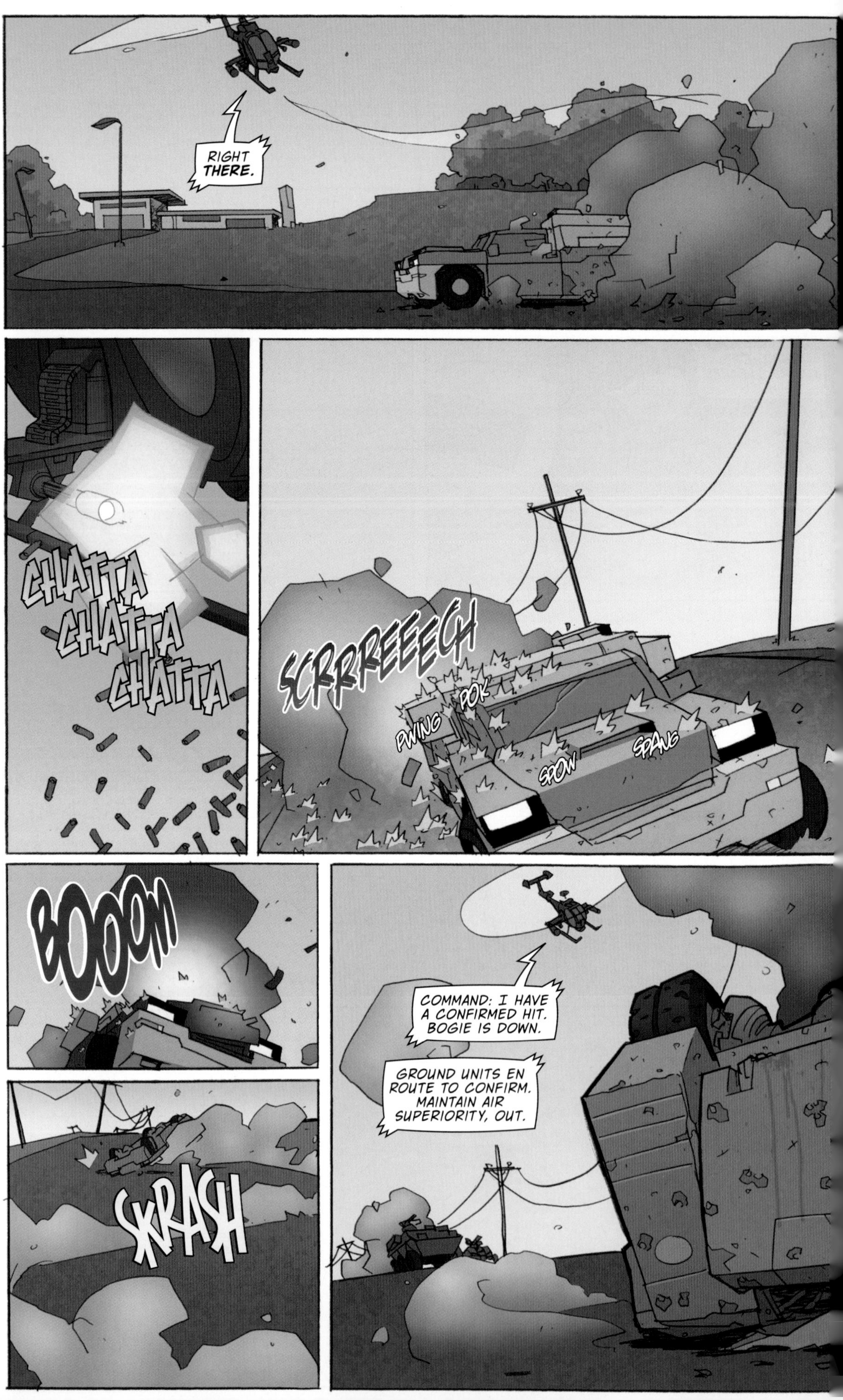
RIGHT THERE.
CHATTA CHATTA CHATTA
SCRRREEECH
PWING
POK
SPOW
SPANG
BOOOM
SKRASH
COMMAND: I HAVE A CONFIRMED HIT. BOGIE IS DOWN.
GROUND UNITS EN ROUTE TO CONFIRM. MAINTAIN AIR SUPERIORITY, OUT.

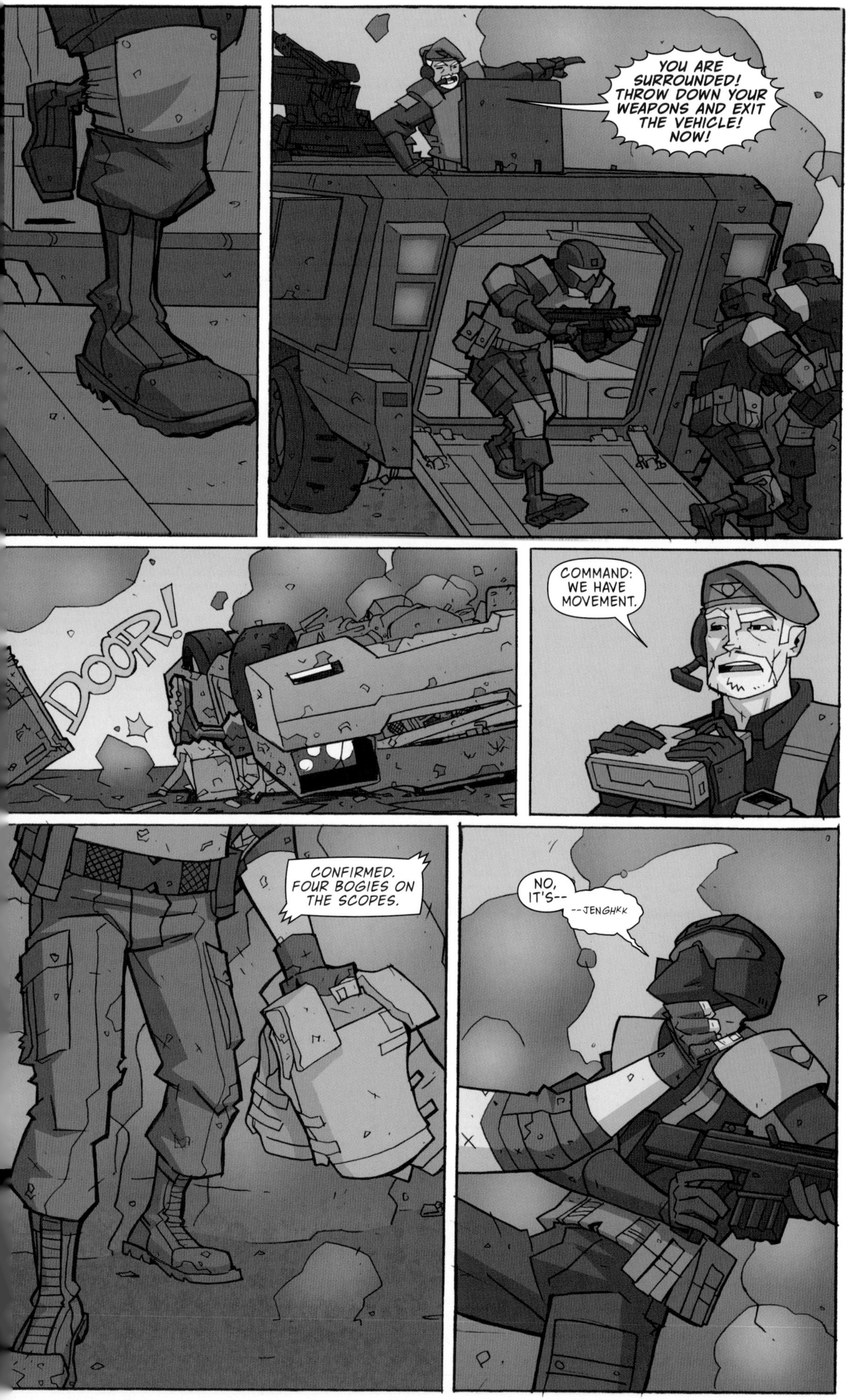
YOU ARE SURROUNDED! THROW DOWN YOUR WEAPONS AND EXIT THE VEHICLE! NOW!
DOOR!
COMMAND: WE HAVE MOVEMENT.
CONFIRMED. FOUR BOGIES ON THE SCOPES.
NO, IT'S--
--JENGHKK

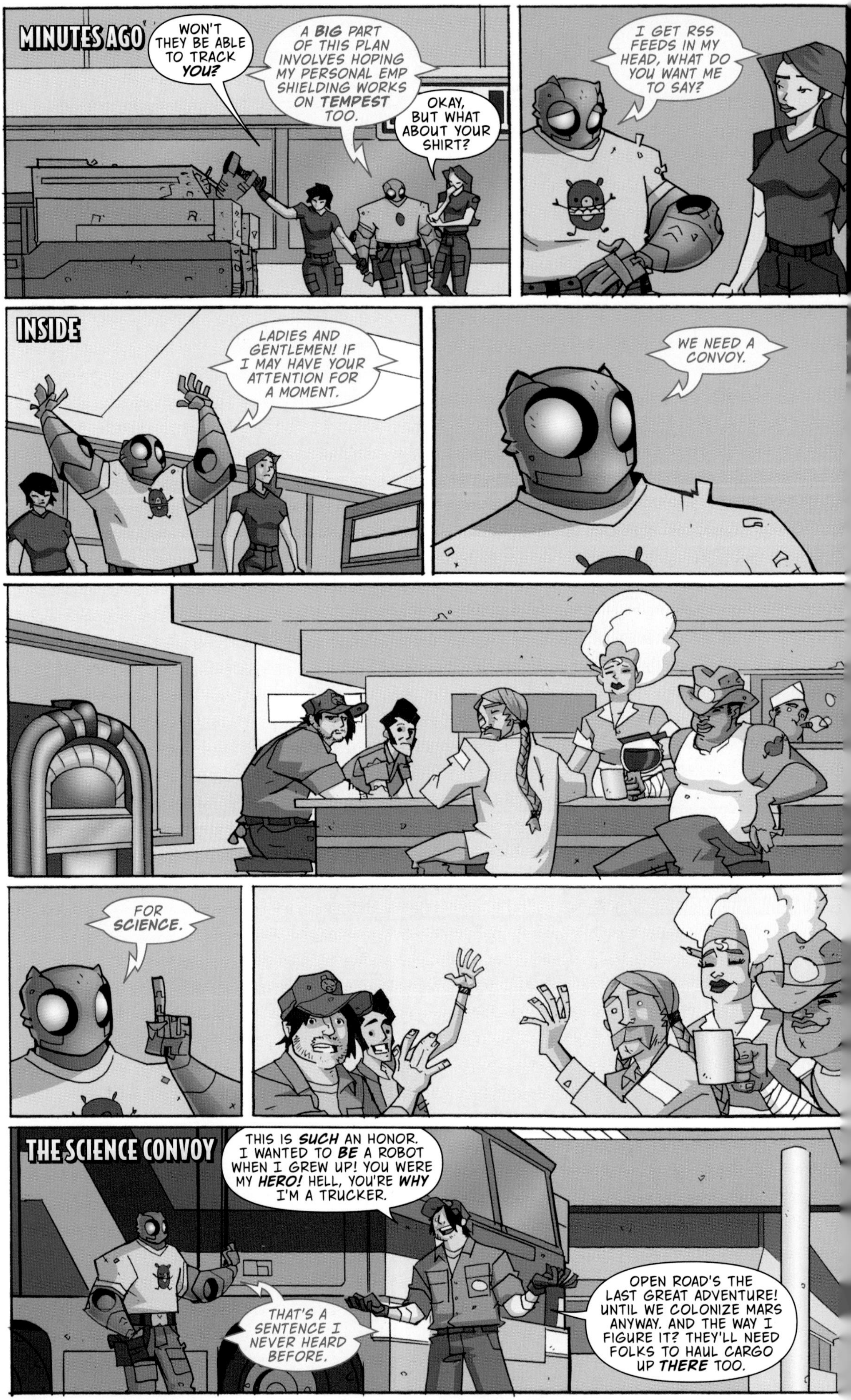
MINUTES AGO
WON'T THEY BE ABLE TO TRACK YOU?
A BIG PART OF THIS PLAN INVOLVES HOPING MY PERSONAL EMP SHIELDING WORKS ON TEMPEST TOO.
OKAY, BUT WHAT ABOUT YOUR SHIRT?
I GET RSS FEEDS IN MY HEAD, WHAT DO YOU WANT ME TO SAY?
INSIDE
LADIES AND GENTLEMEN! IF I MAY HAVE YOUR ATTENTION FOR A MOMENT.
WE NEED A CONVOY.
FOR SCIENCE.
THE SCIENCE CONVOY
THIS IS SUCH AN HONOR. I WANTED TO BE A ROBOT WHEN I GREW UP! YOU WERE MY HERO! HELL, YOU'RE WHY I'M A TRUCKER.
THAT'S A SENTENCE I NEVER HEARD BEFORE.
OPEN ROAD'S THE LAST GREAT ADVENTURE! UNTIL WE COLONIZE MARS ANYWAY. AND THE WAY I FIGURE IT? THEY'LL NEED FOLKS TO HAUL CARGO UP THERE TOO.

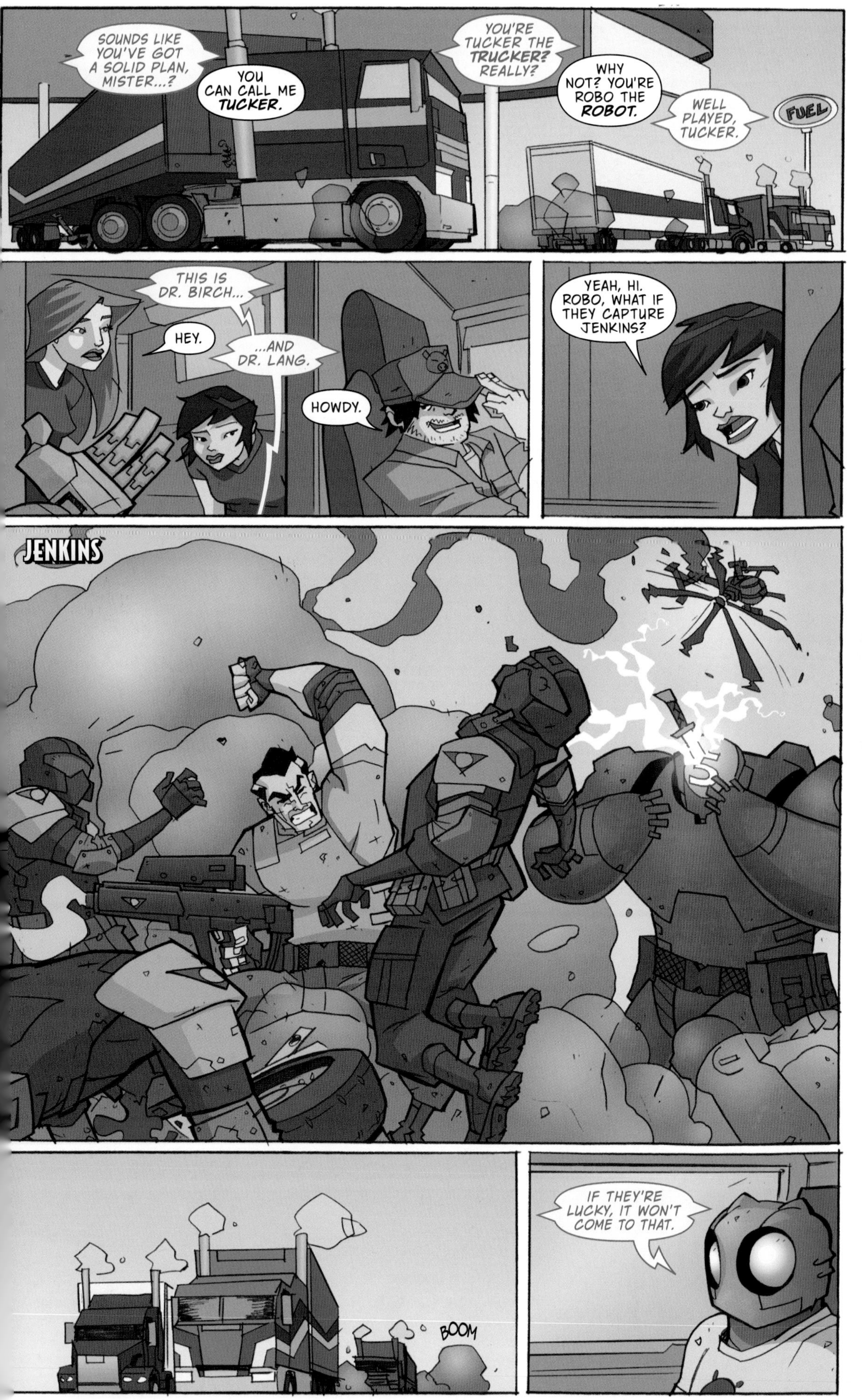
SOUNDS LIKE YOU'VE GOT A SOLID PLAN, MISTER...?
YOU CAN CALL ME TUCKER.
YOU'RE TUCKER THE TRUCKER? REALLY?
WHY NOT? YOU'RE ROBO THE ROBOT.
WELL PLAYED, TUCKER.
FUEL
THIS IS DR. BIRCH...
HEY.
...AND DR. LANG.
HOWDY.
YEAH, HI. ROBO, WHAT IF THEY CAPTURE JENKINS?
JENKINS
IF THEY'RE LUCKY, IT WON'T COME TO THAT.
BOOM

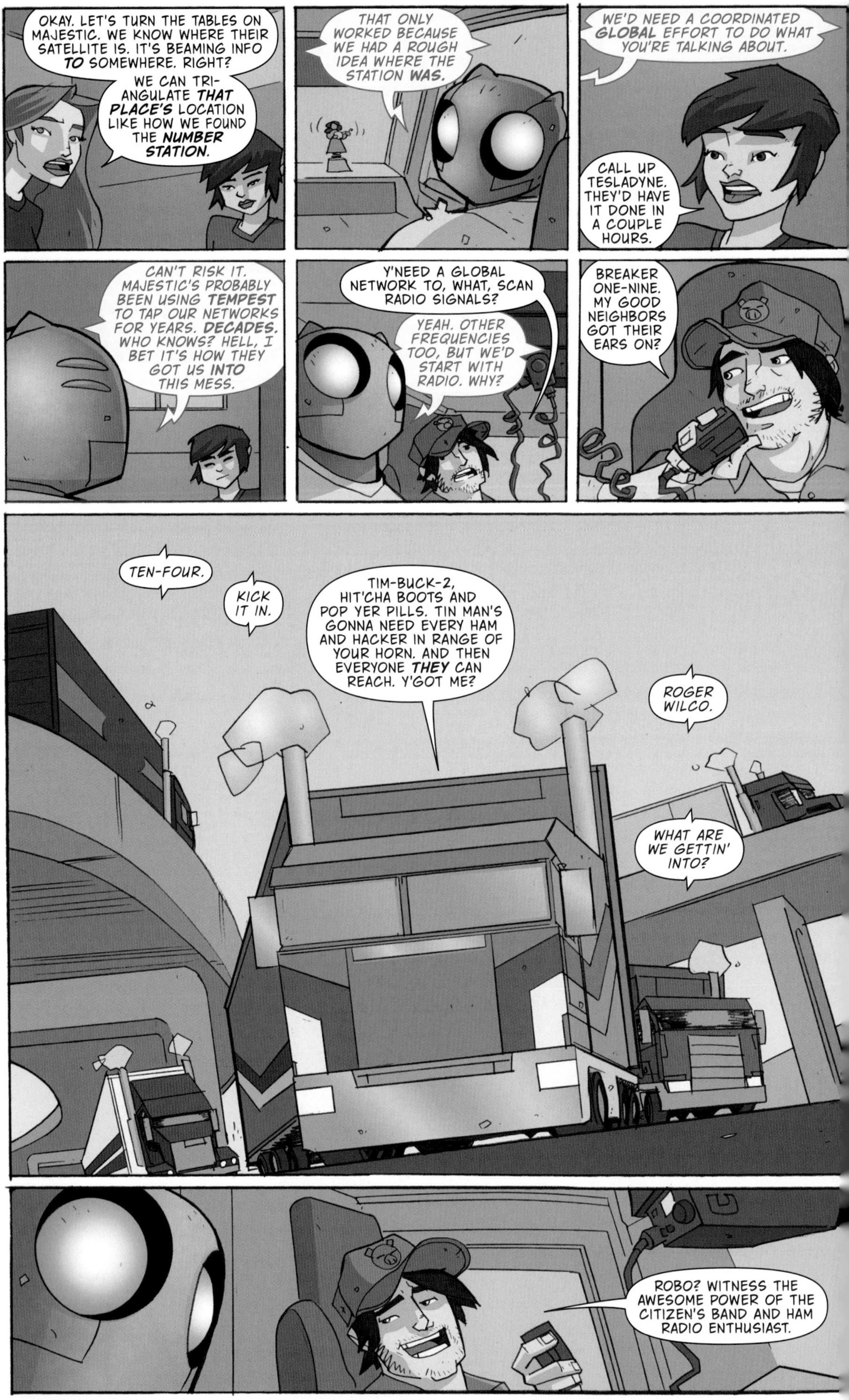
OKAY. LET'S TURN THE TABLES ON MAJESTIC. WE KNOW WHERE THEIR SATELLITE IS. IT'S BEAMING INFO TO SOMEWHERE. RIGHT?
WE CAN TRI-ANGULATE THAT PLACE'S LOCATION LIKE HOW WE FOUND THE NUMBER STATION.
THAT ONLY WORKED BECAUSE WE HAD A ROUGH IDEA WHERE THE STATION WAS.
WE'D NEED A COORDINATED GLOBAL EFFORT TO DO WHAT YOU'RE TALKING ABOUT.
CALL UP TESLADYNE. THEY'D HAVE IT DONE IN A COUPLE HOURS.
CAN'T RISK IT. MAJESTIC'S PROBABLY BEEN USING TEMPEST TO TAP OUR NETWORKS FOR YEARS. DECADES. WHO KNOWS? HELL, I BET IT'S HOW THEY GOT US INTO THIS MESS.
Y'NEED A GLOBAL NETWORK TO, WHAT, SCAN RADIO SIGNALS?
YEAH. OTHER FREQUENCIES TOO, BUT WE'D START WITH RADIO. WHY?
BREAKER ONE-NINE. MY GOOD NEIGHBORS GOT THEIR EARS ON?
TEN-FOUR.
KICK IT IN.
TIM-BUCK-2, HIT'CHA BOOTS AND POP YER PILLS. TIN MAN'S GONNA NEED EVERY HAM AND HACKER IN RANGE OF YOUR HORN. AND THEN EVERYONE THEY CAN REACH. Y'GOT ME?
ROGER WILCO.
WHAT ARE WE GETTIN' INTO?
ROBO? WITNESS THE AWESOME POWER OF THE CITIZEN'S BAND AND HAM RADIO ENTHUSIAST.

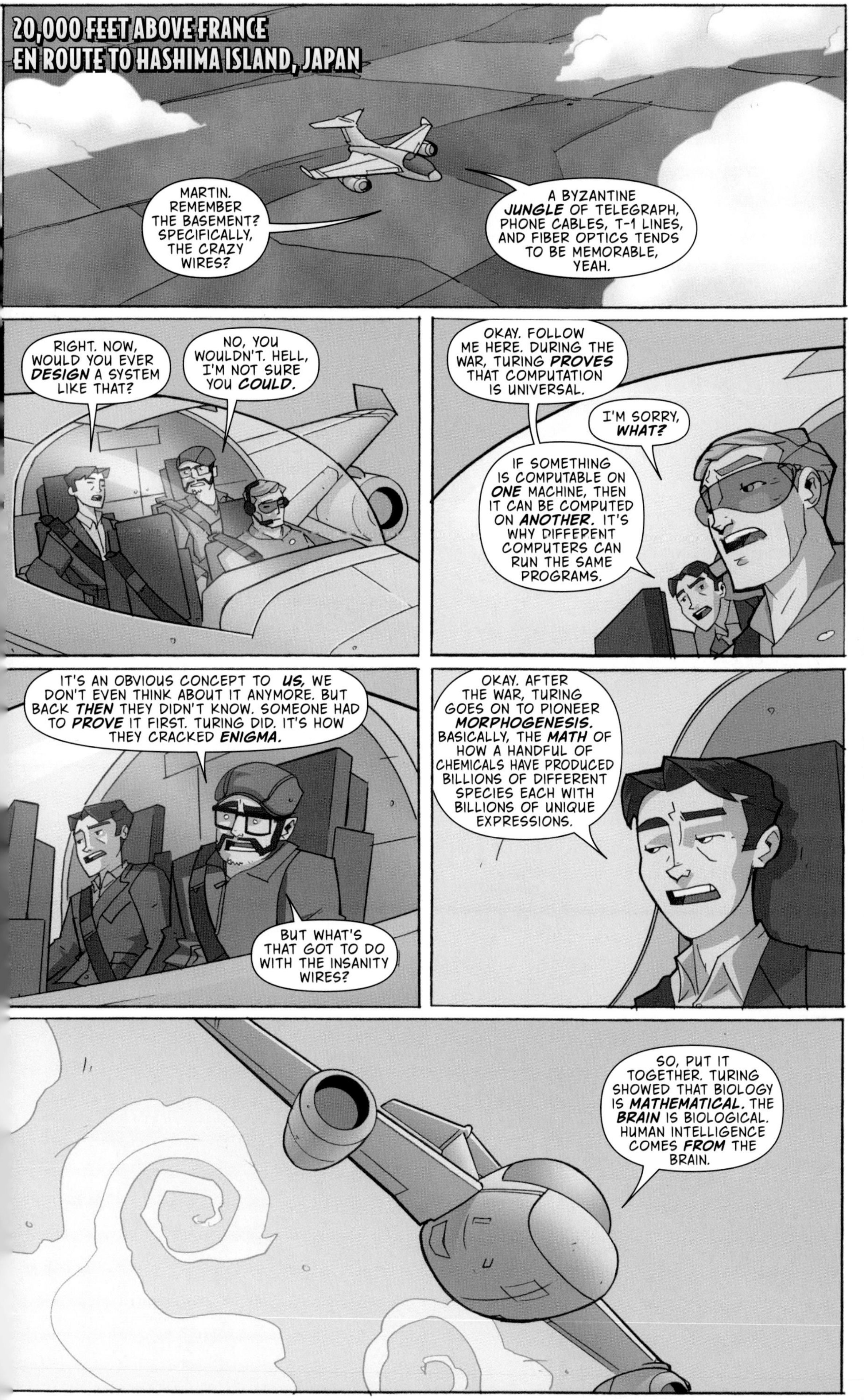
20,000 FEET ABOVE FRANCE
EN ROUTE TO HASHIMA ISLAND, JAPAN
MARTIN. REMEMBER THE BASEMENT? SPECIFICALLY, THE CRAZY WIRES?
A BYZANTINE JUNGLE OF TELEGRAPH, PHONE CABLES, T-1 LINES, AND FIBER OPTICS TENDS TO BE MEMORABLE, YEAH.
RIGHT. NOW, WOULD YOU EVER DESIGN A SYSTEM LIKE THAT?
NO, YOU WOULDN'T. HELL, I'M NOT SURE YOU COULD.
OKAY. FOLLOW ME HERE. DURING THE WAR, TURING PROVES THAT COMPUTATION IS UNIVERSAL.
I'M SORRY, WHAT?
IF SOMETHING IS COMPUTABLE ON ONE MACHINE, THEN IT CAN BE COMPUTED ON ANOTHER. IT'S WHY DIFFERENT COMPUTERS CAN RUN THE SAME PROGRAMS.
IT'S AN OBVIOUS CONCEPT TO US, WE DON'T EVEN THINK ABOUT IT ANYMORE. BUT BACK THEN THEY DIDN'T KNOW. SOMEONE HAD TO PROVE IT FIRST. TURING DID. IT'S HOW THEY CRACKED ENIGMA.
BUT WHAT'S THAT GOT TO DO WITH THE INSANITY WIRES?
OKAY. AFTER THE WAR, TURING GOES ON TO PIONEER MORPHOGENESIS. BASICALLY, THE MATH OF HOW A HANDFUL OF CHEMICALS HAVE PRODUCED BILLIONS OF DIFFERENT SPECIES EACH WITH BILLIONS OF UNIQUE EXPRESSIONS.
SO, PUT IT TOGETHER. TURING SHOWED THAT BIOLOGY IS MATHEMATICAL. THE BRAIN IS BIOLOGICAL. HUMAN INTELLIGENCE COMES FROM THE BRAIN.

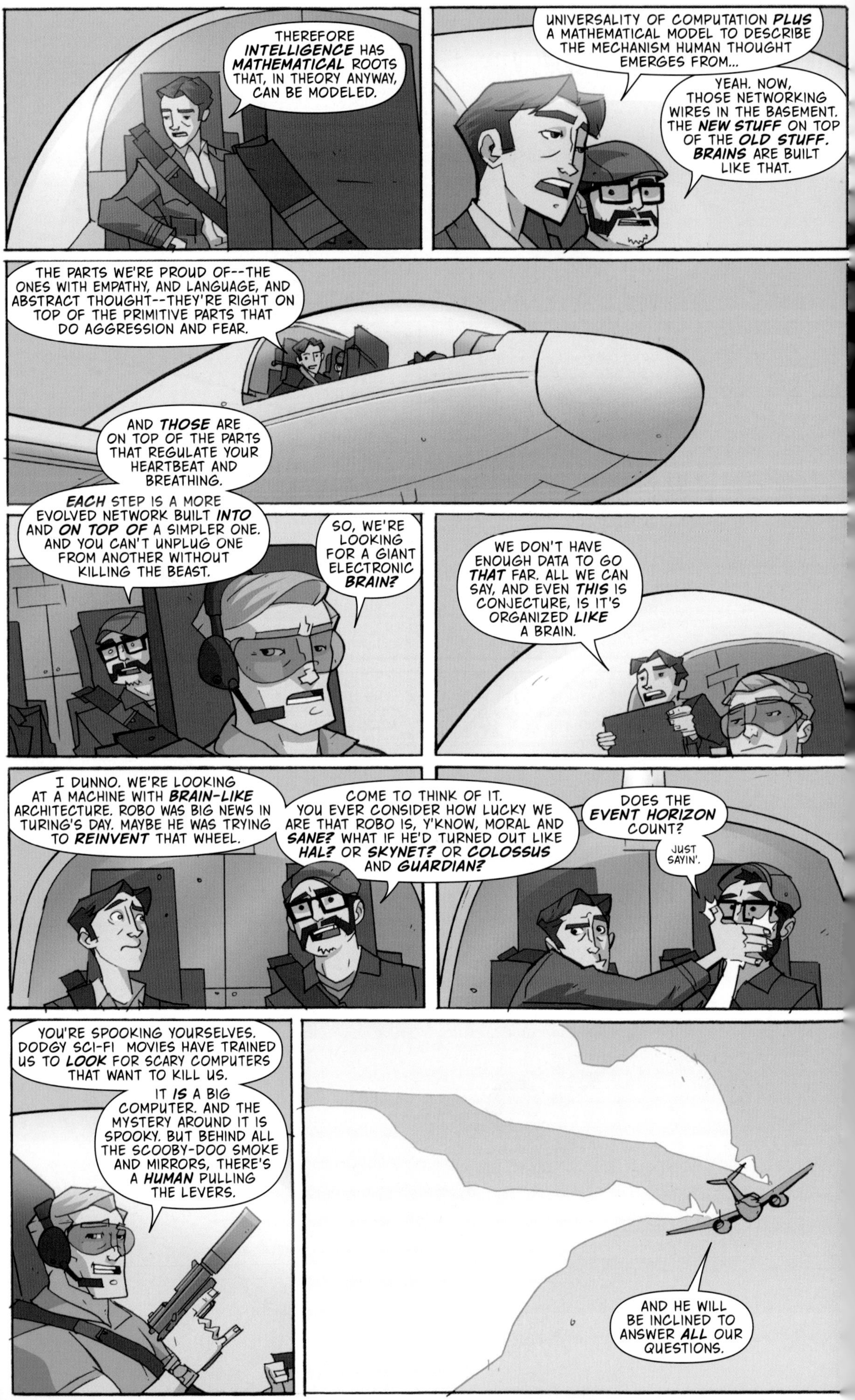
THEREFORE INTELLIGENCE HAS MATHEMATICAL ROOTS THAT, IN THEORY ANYWAY, CAN BE MODELED.
UNIVERSALITY OF COMPUTATION PLUS A MATHEMATICAL MODEL TO DESCRIBE THE MECHANISM HUMAN THOUGHT EMERGES FROM...
YEAH. NOW, THOSE NETWORKING WIRES IN THE BASEMENT. THE NEW STUFF ON TOP OF THE OLD STUFF. BRAINS ARE BUILT LIKE THAT.
THE PARTS WE'RE PROUD OF--THE ONES WITH EMPATHY, AND LANGUAGE, AND ABSTRACT THOUGHT--THEY'RE RIGHT ON TOP OF THE PRIMITIVE PARTS THAT DO AGGRESSION AND FEAR.
AND THOSE ARE ON TOP OF THE PARTS THAT REGULATE YOUR HEARTBEAT AND BREATHING.
EACH STEP IS A MORE EVOLVED NETWORK BUILT INTO AND ON TOP OF A SIMPLER ONE. AND YOU CAN'T UNPLUG ONE FROM ANOTHER WITHOUT KILLING THE BEAST.
SO, WE'RE LOOKING FOR A GIANT ELECTRONIC BRAIN?
WE DON'T HAVE ENOUGH DATA TO GO THAT FAR. ALL WE CAN SAY, AND EVEN THIS IS CONJECTURE, IS IT'S ORGANIZED LIKE A BRAIN.
I DUNNO. WE'RE LOOKING AT A MACHINE WITH BRAIN-LIKE ARCHITECTURE. ROBO WAS BIG NEWS IN TURING'S DAY. MAYBE HE WAS TRYING TO REINVENT THAT WHEEL.
COME TO THINK OF IT. YOU EVER CONSIDER HOW LUCKY WE ARE THAT ROBO IS, Y'KNOW, MORAL AND SANE? WHAT IF HE'D TURNED OUT LIKE HAL? OR SKYNET? OR COLOSSUS AND GUARDIAN?
DOES THE EVENT HORIZON COUNT?
JUST SAYIN'.
YOU'RE SPOOKING YOURSELVES. DODGY SCI-FI MOVIES HAVE TRAINED US TO LOOK FOR SCARY COMPUTERS THAT WANT TO KILL US.
IT IS A BIG COMPUTER. AND THE MYSTERY AROUND IT IS SPOOKY. BUT BEHIND ALL THE SCOOBY-DOO SMOKE AND MIRRORS, THERE'S A HUMAN PULLING THE LEVERS.
AND HE WILL BE INCLINED TO ANSWER ALL OUR QUESTIONS.

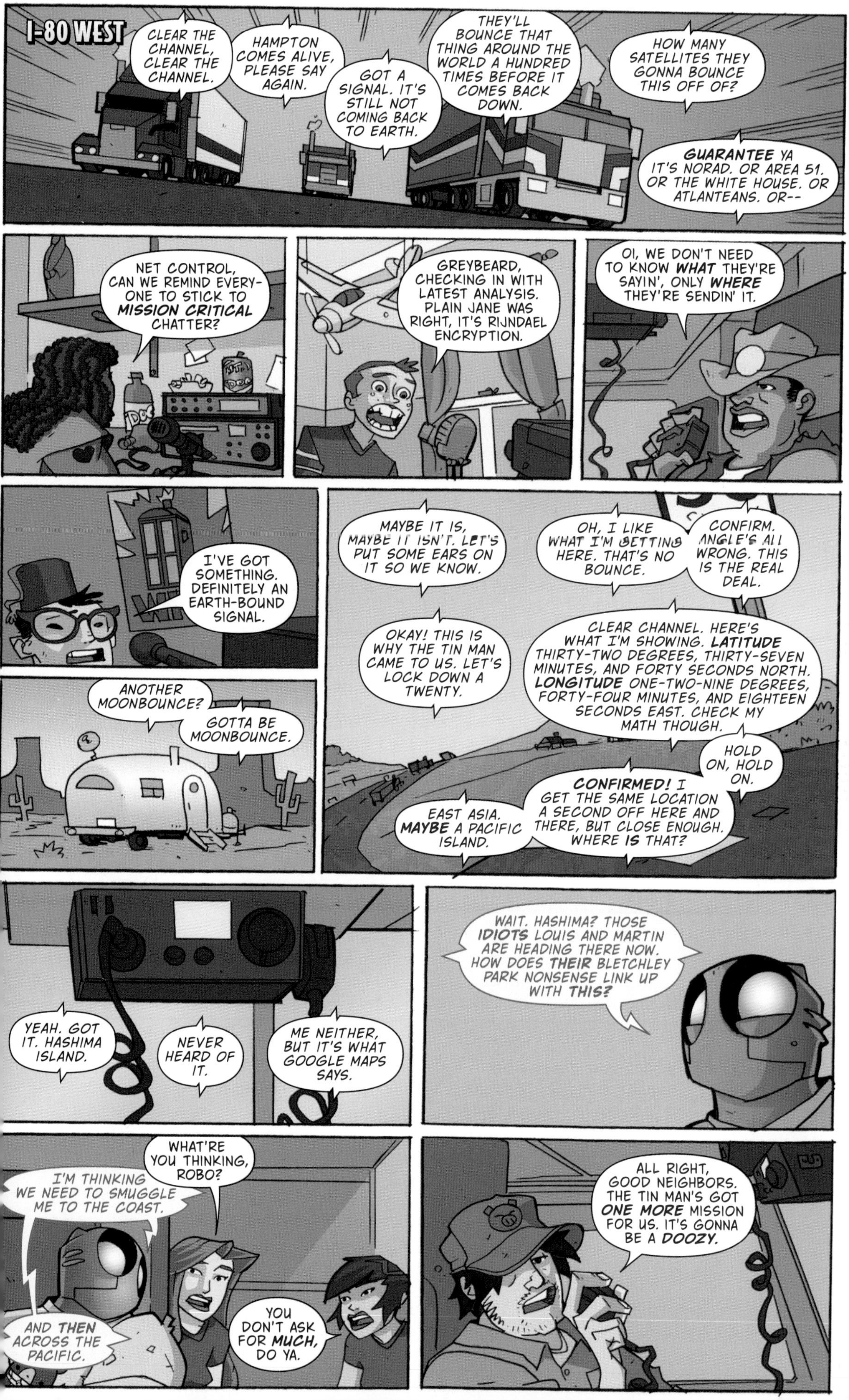
I-80 WEST
CLEAR THE CHANNEL, CLEAR THE CHANNEL.
HAMPTON COMES ALIVE, PLEASE SAY AGAIN.
GOT A SIGNAL. IT'S STILL NOT COMING BACK TO EARTH.
THEY'LL BOUNCE THAT THING AROUND THE WORLD A HUNDRED TIMES BEFORE IT COMES BACK DOWN.
HOW MANY SATELLITES THEY GONNA BOUNCE THIS OFF OF?
GUARANTEE YA IT'S NORAD. OR AREA 51. OR THE WHITE HOUSE. OR ATLANTEANS. OR--
NET CONTROL, CAN WE REMIND EVERY-ONE TO STICK TO **MISSION CRITICAL** CHATTER?
GREYBEARD, CHECKING IN WITH LATEST ANALYSIS. PLAIN JANE WAS RIGHT, IT'S RIJNDAEL ENCRYPTION.
OI, WE DON'T NEED TO KNOW **WHAT** THEY'RE SAYIN', ONLY **WHERE** THEY'RE SENDIN' IT.
I'VE GOT SOMETHING. DEFINITELY AN EARTH-BOUND SIGNAL.
ANOTHER MOONBOUNCE?
GOTTA BE MOONBOUNCE.
MAYBE IT IS, MAYBE IT ISN'T. LET'S PUT SOME EARS ON IT SO WE KNOW.
OH, I LIKE WHAT I'M GETTING HERE. THAT'S NO BOUNCE.
CONFIRM. ANGLE'S ALL WRONG. THIS IS THE REAL DEAL.
OKAY! THIS IS WHY THE TIN MAN CAME TO US. LET'S LOCK DOWN A TWENTY.
CLEAR CHANNEL. HERE'S WHAT I'M SHOWING. **LATITUDE** THIRTY-TWO DEGREES, THIRTY-SEVEN MINUTES, AND FORTY SECONDS NORTH. **LONGITUDE** ONE-TWO-NINE DEGREES, FORTY-FOUR MINUTES, AND EIGHTEEN SECONDS EAST. CHECK MY MATH THOUGH.
HOLD ON, HOLD ON.
CONFIRMED! I GET THE SAME LOCATION A SECOND OFF HERE AND THERE, BUT CLOSE ENOUGH. WHERE **IS** THAT?
EAST ASIA. **MAYBE** A PACIFIC ISLAND.
YEAH. GOT IT. HASHIMA ISLAND.
NEVER HEARD OF IT.
ME NEITHER, BUT IT'S WHAT GOOGLE MAPS SAYS.
WAIT. HASHIMA? THOSE **IDIOTS** LOUIS AND MARTIN ARE HEADING THERE NOW. HOW DOES **THEIR** BLETCHLEY PARK NONSENSE LINK UP WITH **THIS?**
WHAT'RE YOU THINKING, ROBO?
I'M THINKING WE NEED TO SMUGGLE ME TO THE COAST.
AND **THEN** ACROSS THE PACIFIC.
YOU DON'T ASK FOR **MUCH,** DO YA.
ALL RIGHT, GOOD NEIGHBORS. THE TIN MAN'S GOT **ONE MORE** MISSION FOR US. IT'S GONNA BE A **DOOZY.**

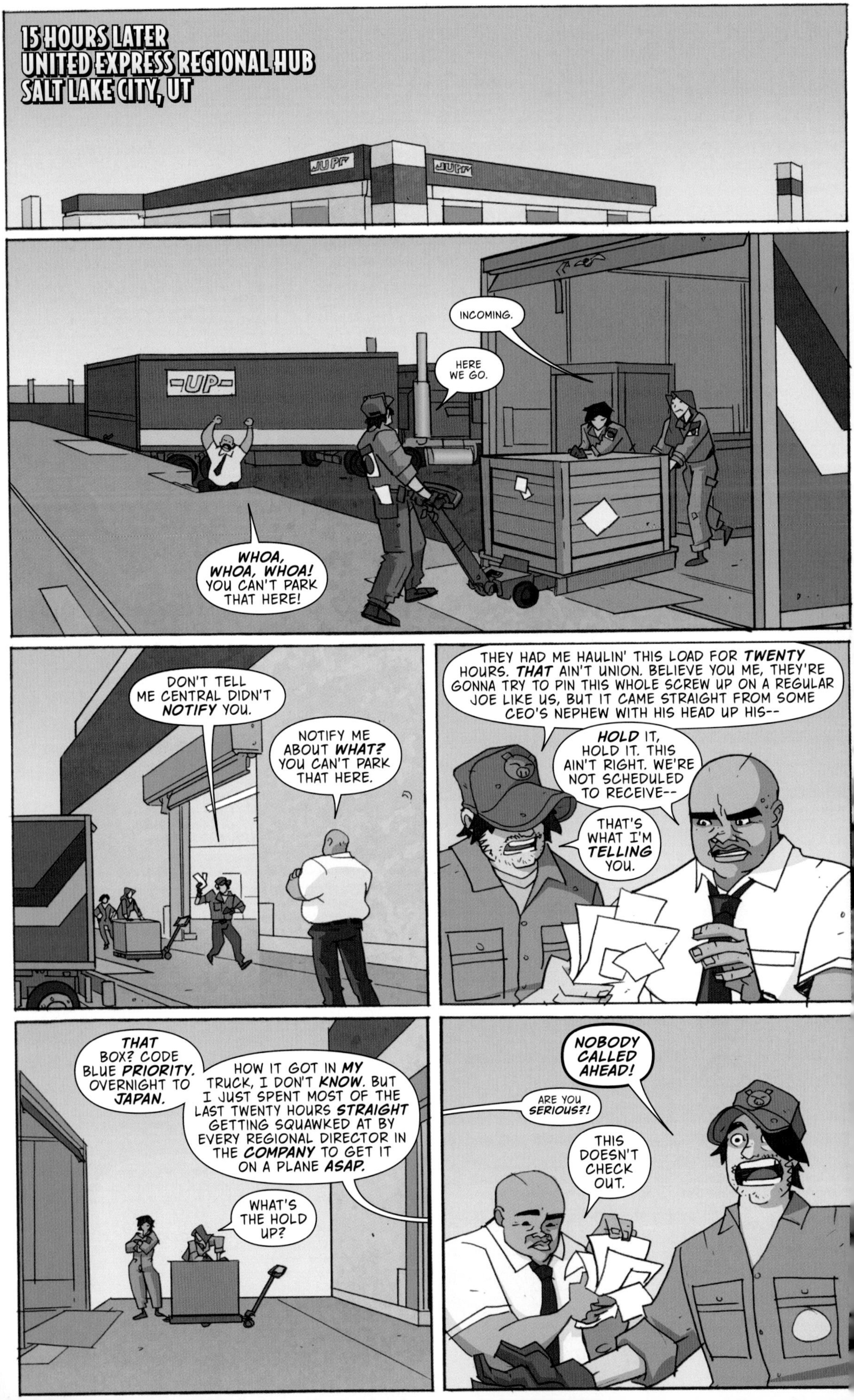
15 HOURS LATER
UNITED EXPRESS REGIONAL HUB
SALT LAKE CITY, UT
INCOMING.
HERE WE GO.
WHOA, WHOA, WHOA! YOU CAN'T PARK THAT HERE!
DON'T TELL ME CENTRAL DIDN'T NOTIFY YOU.
NOTIFY ME ABOUT WHAT? YOU CAN'T PARK THAT HERE.
THEY HAD ME HAULIN' THIS LOAD FOR TWENTY HOURS. THAT AIN'T UNION. BELIEVE YOU ME, THEY'RE GONNA TRY TO PIN THIS WHOLE SCREW UP ON A REGULAR JOE LIKE US, BUT IT CAME STRAIGHT FROM SOME CEO'S NEPHEW WITH HIS HEAD UP HIS--
HOLD IT, HOLD IT. THIS AIN'T RIGHT. WE'RE NOT SCHEDULED TO RECEIVE--
THAT'S WHAT I'M TELLING YOU.
THAT BOX? CODE BLUE PRIORITY. OVERNIGHT TO JAPAN.
HOW IT GOT IN MY TRUCK, I DON'T KNOW. BUT I JUST SPENT MOST OF THE LAST TWENTY HOURS STRAIGHT GETTING SQUAWKED AT BY EVERY REGIONAL DIRECTOR IN THE COMPANY TO GET IT ON A PLANE ASAP.
WHAT'S THE HOLD UP?
NOBODY CALLED AHEAD!
ARE YOU SERIOUS?!
THIS DOESN'T CHECK OUT.

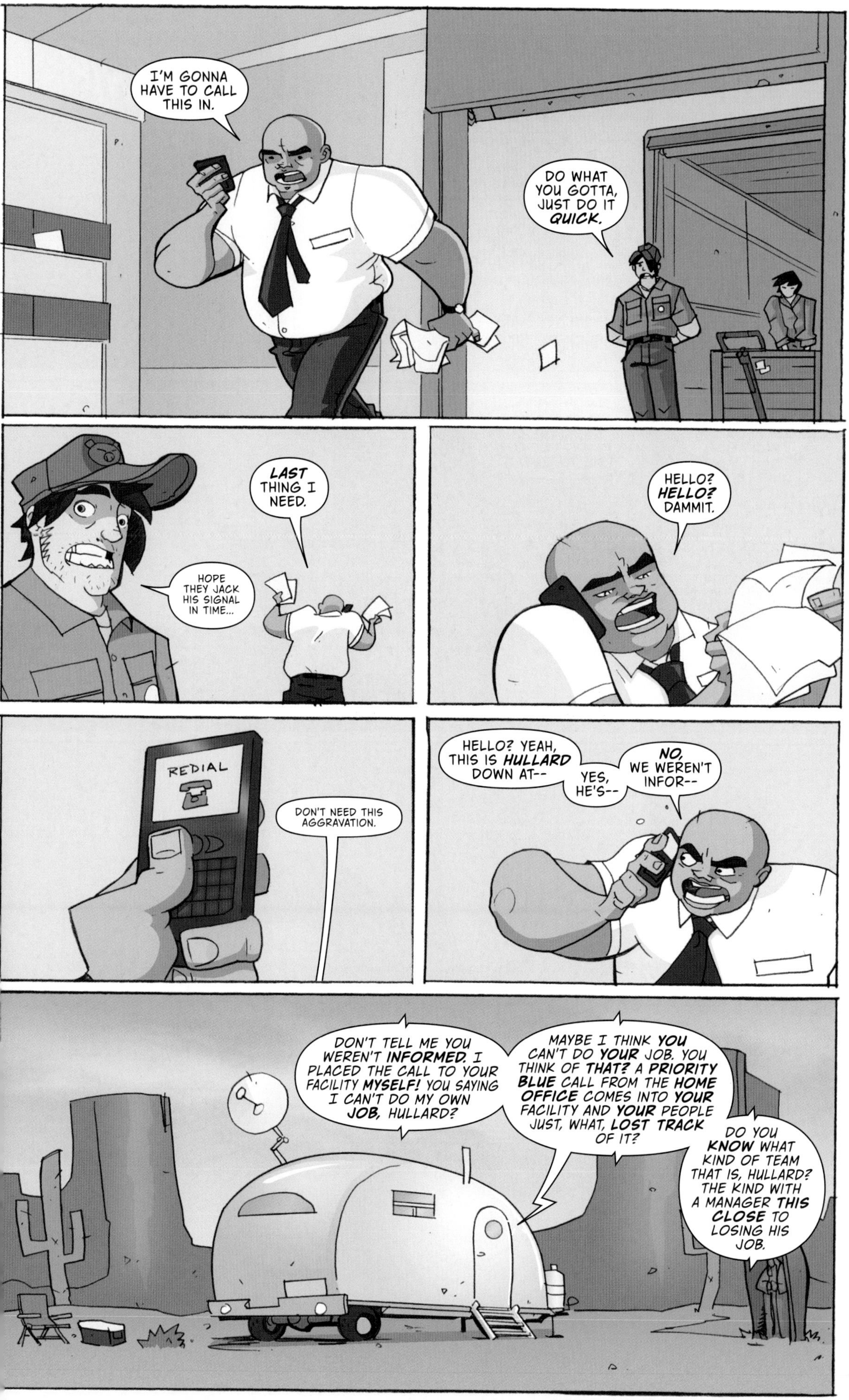

I'M GONNA HAVE TO CALL THIS IN.
DO WHAT YOU GOTTA, JUST DO IT QUICK.
LAST THING I NEED.
HOPE THEY JACK HIS SIGNAL IN TIME...
HELLO? HELLO? DAMMIT.
REDIAL
DON'T NEED THIS AGGRAVATION.
HELLO? YEAH, THIS IS HULLARD DOWN AT--
YES, HE'S--
NO, WE WEREN'T INFOR--
DON'T TELL ME YOU WEREN'T INFORMED. I PLACED THE CALL TO YOUR FACILITY MYSELF! YOU SAYING I CAN'T DO MY OWN JOB, HULLARD?
MAYBE I THINK YOU CAN'T DO YOUR JOB. YOU THINK OF THAT? A PRIORITY BLUE CALL FROM THE HOME OFFICE COMES INTO YOUR FACILITY AND YOUR PEOPLE JUST, WHAT, LOST TRACK OF IT?
DO YOU KNOW WHAT KIND OF TEAM THAT IS, HULLARD? THE KIND WITH A MANAGER THIS CLOSE TO LOSING HIS JOB.

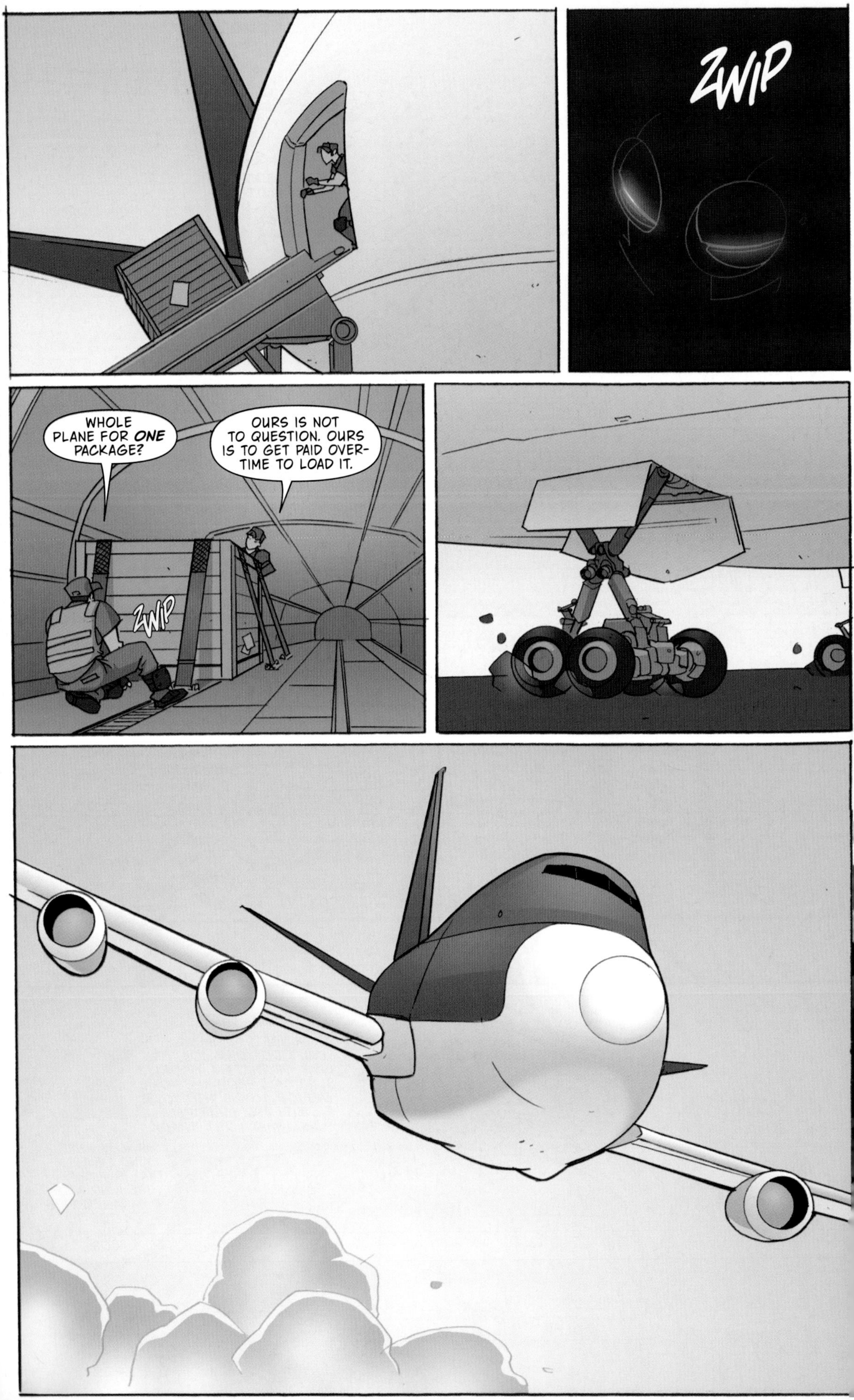
ZWIP
WHOLE PLANE FOR ONE PACKAGE?
OURS IS NOT TO QUESTION. OURS IS TO GET PAID OVER-TIME TO LOAD IT.
ZWIP

TWO FACES OF TOMORROW

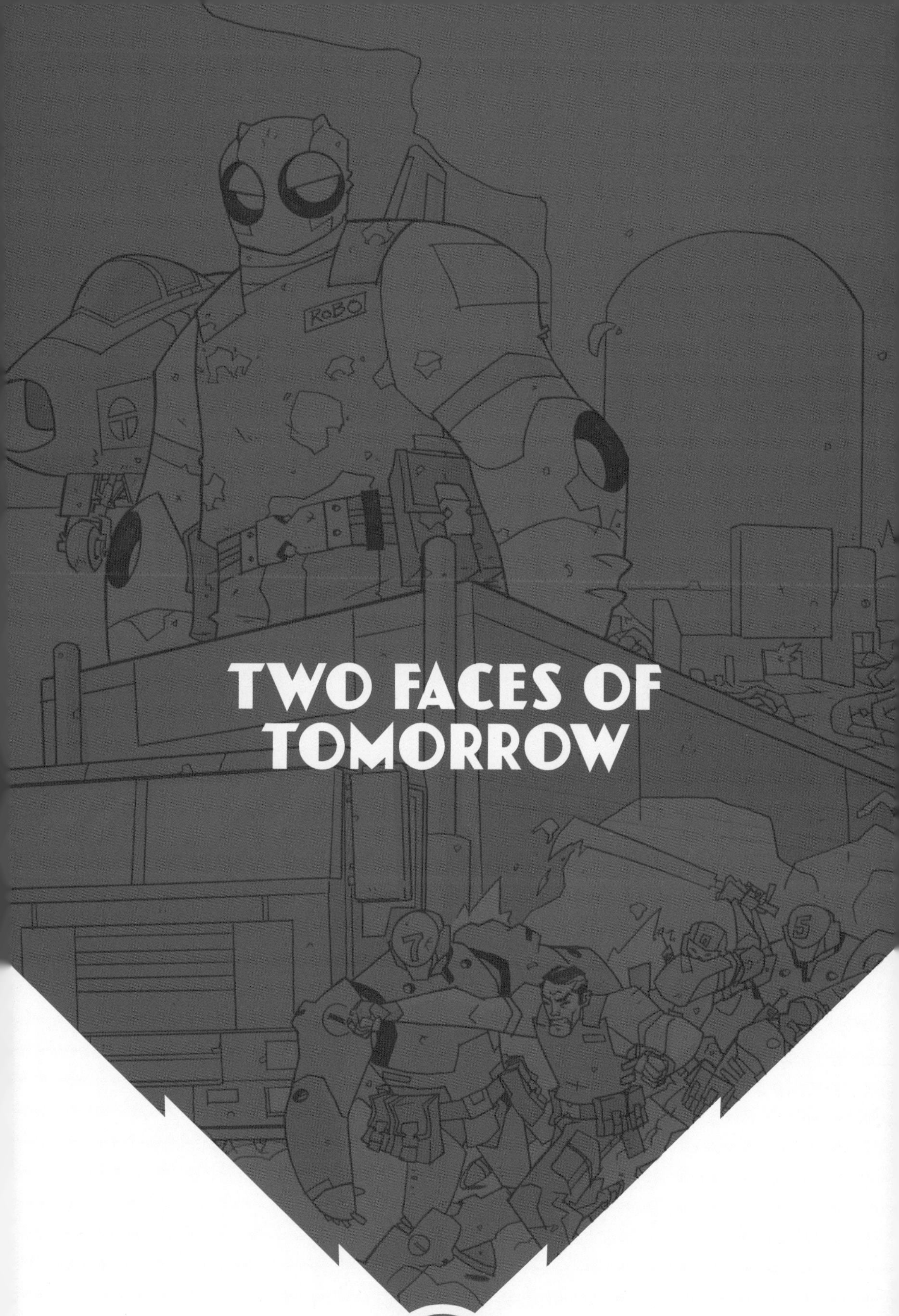
ROBO

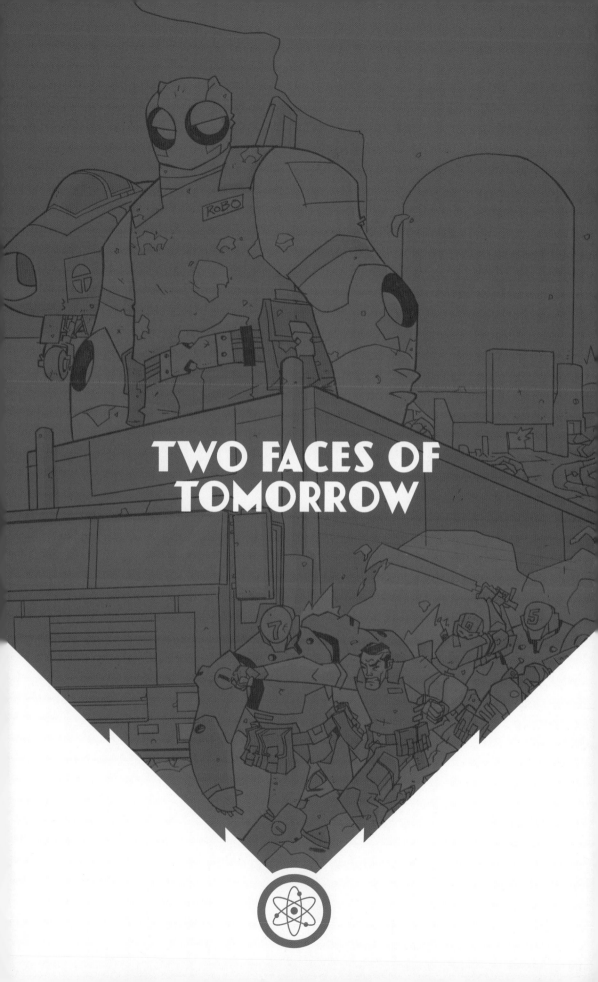

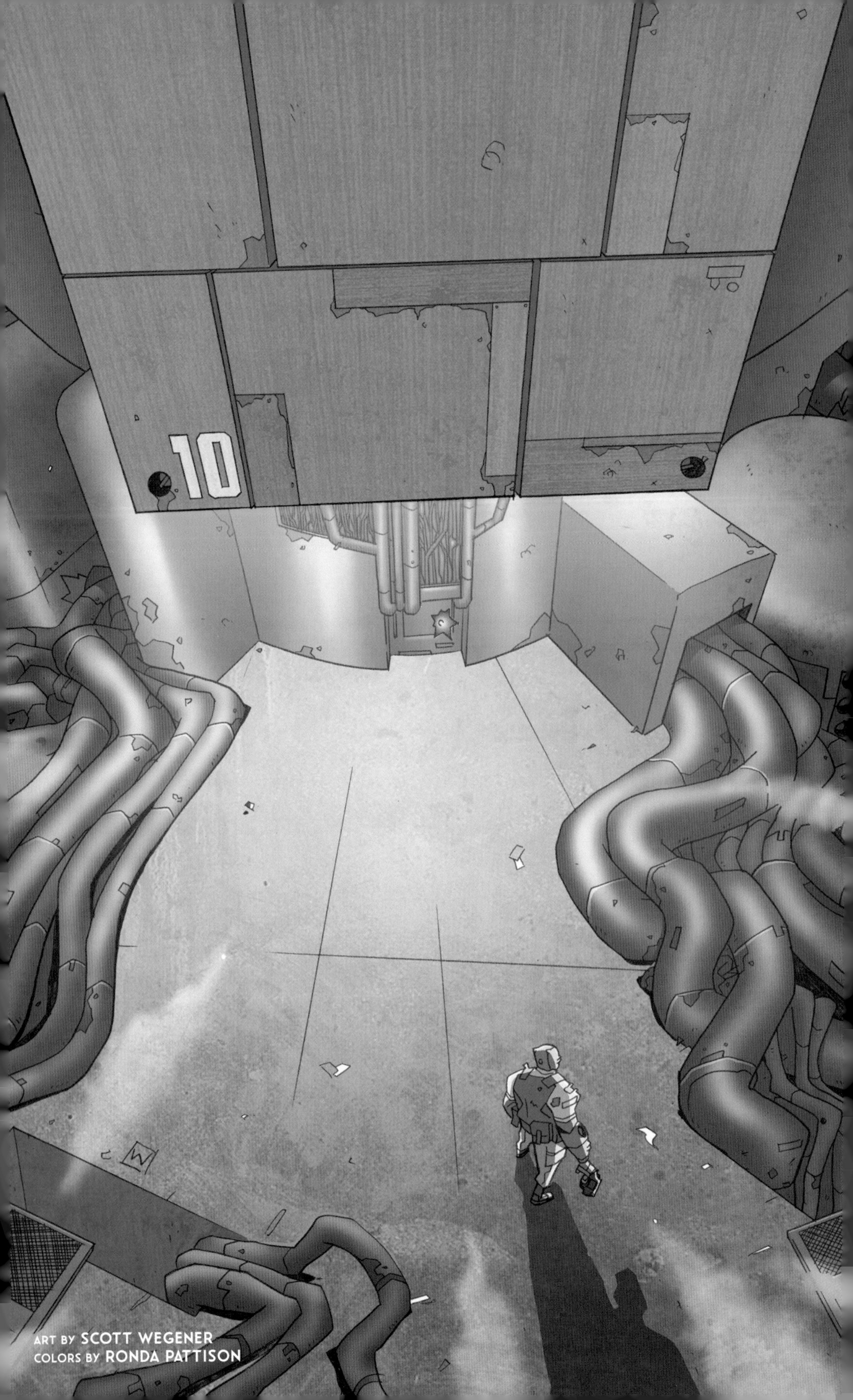
10

ART BY SCOTT WEGENER
COLORS BY RONDA PATTISON

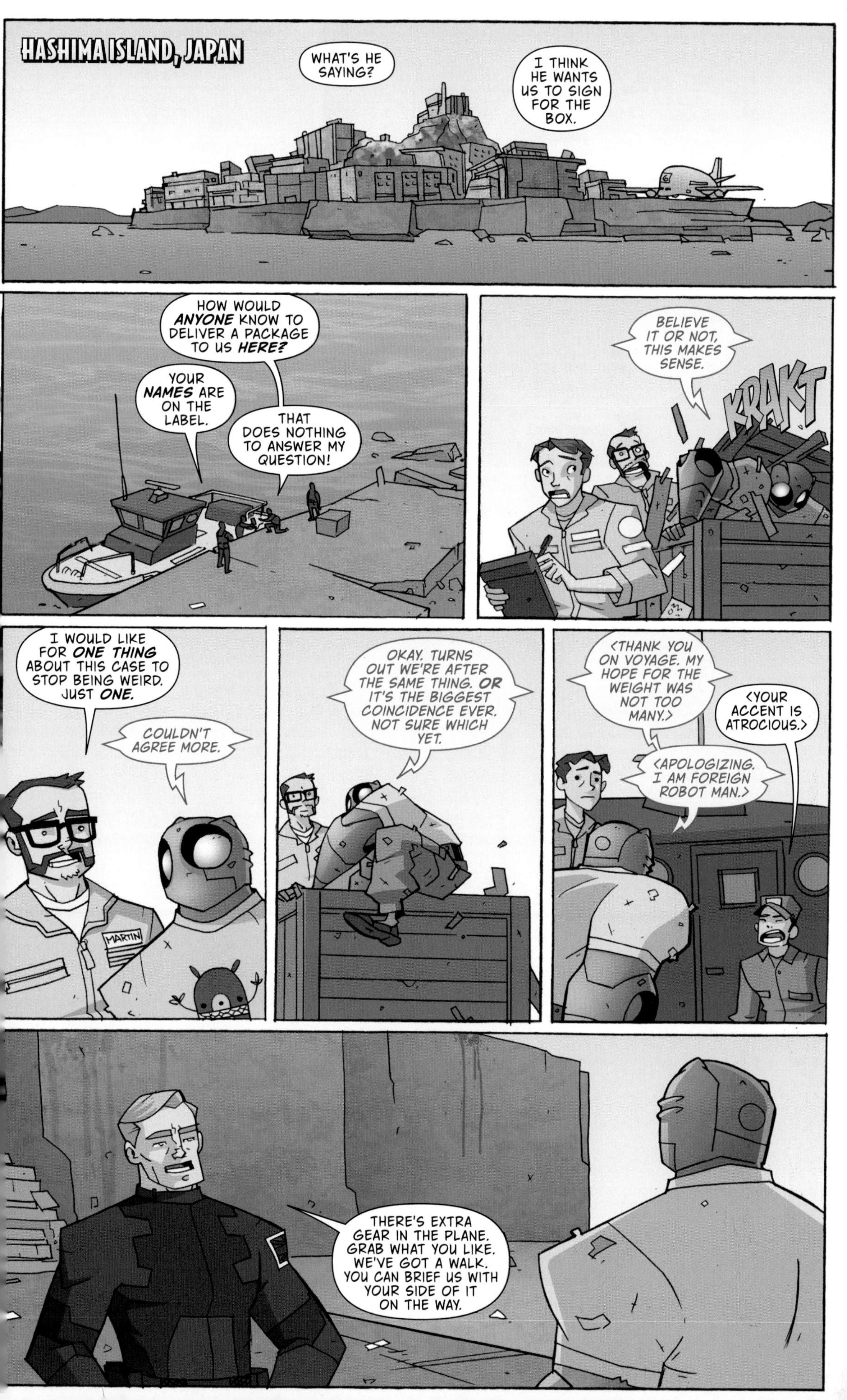
HASHIMA ISLAND, JAPAN
WHAT'S HE SAYING?
I THINK HE WANTS US TO SIGN FOR THE BOX.
HOW WOULD ANYONE KNOW TO DELIVER A PACKAGE TO US HERE?
YOUR NAMES ARE ON THE LABEL.
THAT DOES NOTHING TO ANSWER MY QUESTION!
BELIEVE IT OR NOT, THIS MAKES SENSE.
KRAKT
I WOULD LIKE FOR ONE THING ABOUT THIS CASE TO STOP BEING WEIRD. JUST ONE.
COULDN'T AGREE MORE.
MARTIN
OKAY. TURNS OUT WE'RE AFTER THE SAME THING. OR IT'S THE BIGGEST COINCIDENCE EVER. NOT SURE WHICH YET.
<THANK YOU ON VOYAGE. MY HOPE FOR THE WEIGHT WAS NOT TOO MANY.>
<YOUR ACCENT IS ATROCIOUS.>
<APOLOGIZING. I AM FOREIGN ROBOT MAN.>
THERE'S EXTRA GEAR IN THE PLANE. GRAB WHAT YOU LIKE. WE'VE GOT A WALK. YOU CAN BRIEF US WITH YOUR SIDE OF IT ON THE WAY.

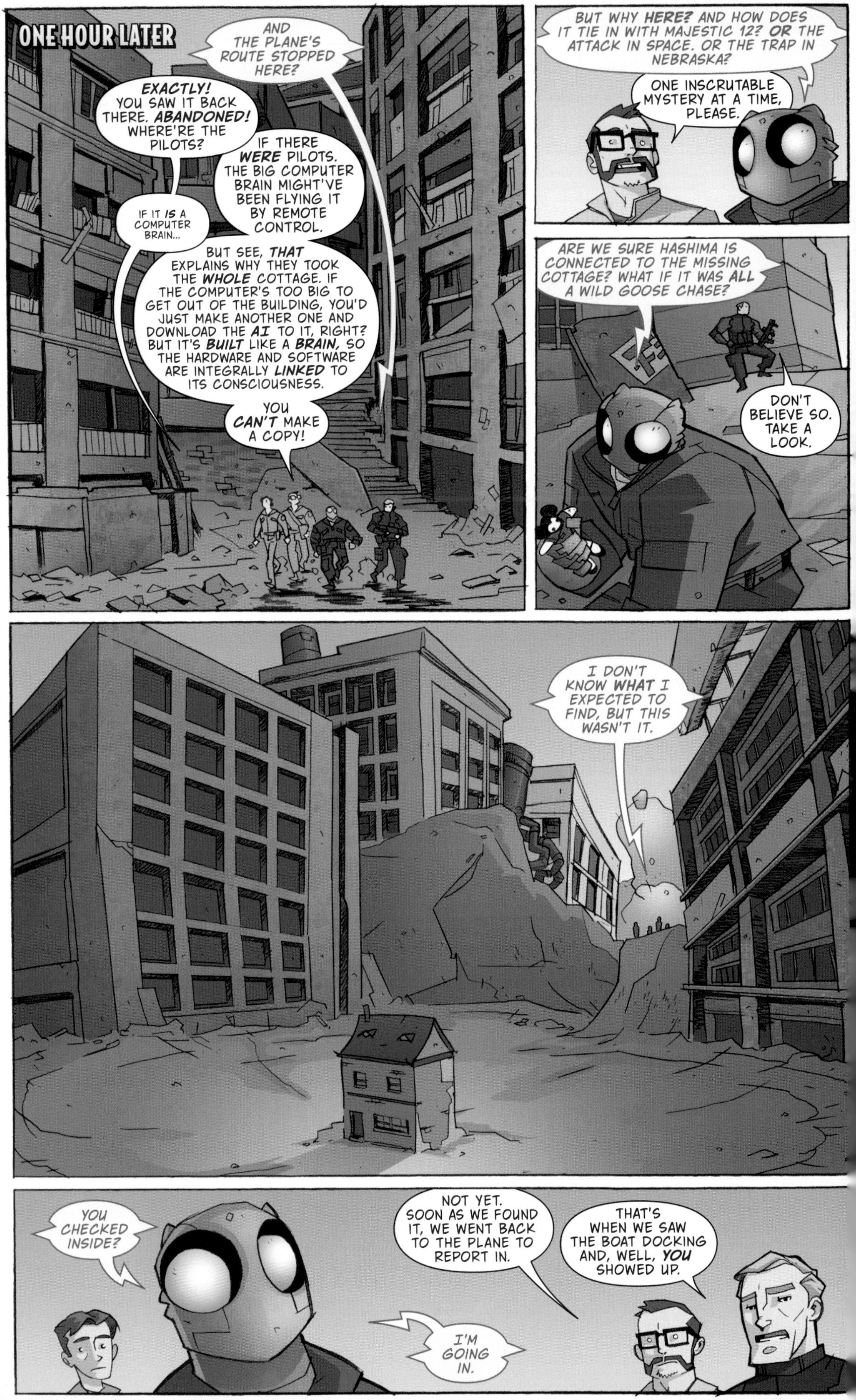
ONE HOUR LATER
AND THE PLANE'S ROUTE STOPPED HERE?
EXACTLY! YOU SAW IT BACK THERE. ABANDONED! WHERE'RE THE PILOTS?
IF THERE WERE PILOTS. THE BIG COMPUTER BRAIN MIGHT'VE BEEN FLYING IT BY REMOTE CONTROL.
IF IT IS A COMPUTER BRAIN...
BUT SEE, THAT EXPLAINS WHY THEY TOOK THE WHOLE COTTAGE. IF THE COMPUTER'S TOO BIG TO GET OUT OF THE BUILDING, YOU'D JUST MAKE ANOTHER ONE AND DOWNLOAD THE AI TO IT, RIGHT? BUT IT'S BUILT LIKE A BRAIN, SO THE HARDWARE AND SOFTWARE ARE INTEGRALLY LINKED TO ITS CONSCIOUSNESS.
YOU CAN'T MAKE A COPY!
BUT WHY HERE? AND HOW DOES IT TIE IN WITH MAJESTIC 12? OR THE ATTACK IN SPACE. OR THE TRAP IN NEBRASKA?
ONE INSCRUTABLE MYSTERY AT A TIME, PLEASE.
ARE WE SURE HASHIMA IS CONNECTED TO THE MISSING COTTAGE? WHAT IF IT WAS ALL A WILD GOOSE CHASE?
DON'T BELIEVE SO. TAKE A LOOK.
I DON'T KNOW WHAT I EXPECTED TO FIND, BUT THIS WASN'T IT.
YOU CHECKED INSIDE?
NOT YET. SOON AS WE FOUND IT, WE WENT BACK TO THE PLANE TO REPORT IN.
THAT'S WHEN WE SAW THE BOAT DOCKING AND, WELL, YOU SHOWED UP.
I'M GOING IN.

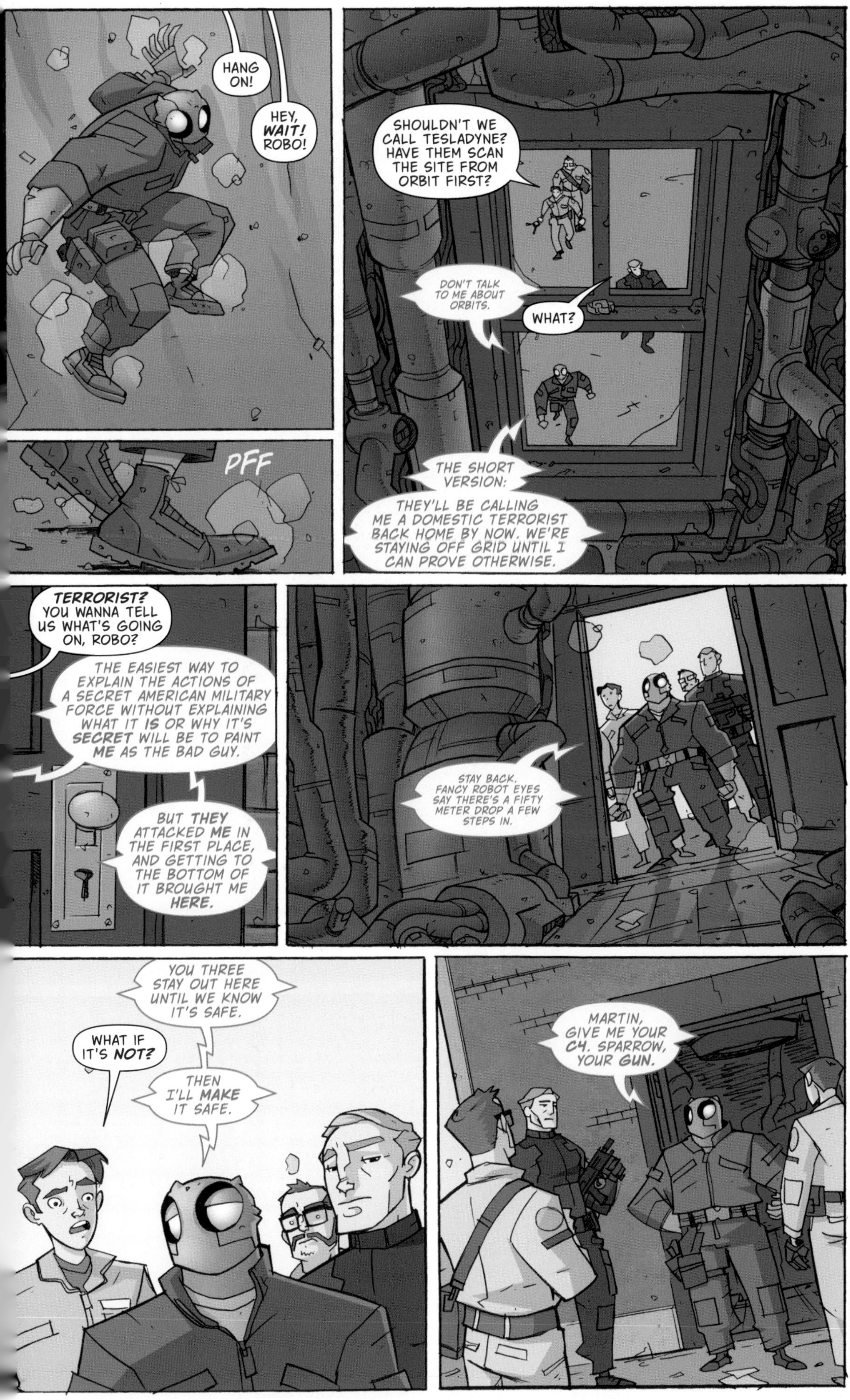
HANG ON!
HEY, WAIT! ROBO!
PFF
SHOULDN'T WE CALL TESLADYNE? HAVE THEM SCAN THE SITE FROM ORBIT FIRST?
DON'T TALK TO ME ABOUT ORBITS.
WHAT?
THE SHORT VERSION:
THEY'LL BE CALLING ME A DOMESTIC TERRORIST BACK HOME BY NOW. WE'RE STAYING OFF GRID UNTIL I CAN PROVE OTHERWISE.
TERRORIST? YOU WANNA TELL US WHAT'S GOING ON, ROBO?
THE EASIEST WAY TO EXPLAIN THE ACTIONS OF A SECRET AMERICAN MILITARY FORCE WITHOUT EXPLAINING WHAT IT IS OR WHY IT'S SECRET WILL BE TO PAINT ME AS THE BAD GUY.
BUT THEY ATTACKED ME IN THE FIRST PLACE, AND GETTING TO THE BOTTOM OF IT BROUGHT ME HERE.
STAY BACK. FANCY ROBOT EYES SAY THERE'S A FIFTY METER DROP A FEW STEPS IN.
YOU THREE STAY OUT HERE UNTIL WE KNOW IT'S SAFE.
WHAT IF IT'S NOT?
THEN I'LL MAKE IT SAFE.
MARTIN, GIVE ME YOUR C4. SPARROW, YOUR GUN.

FWAM
WHOA!
KLONG
HELLO, ROBO.
KCHK
PLEASE, DON'T BE ALARMED.
I'M ALAN.

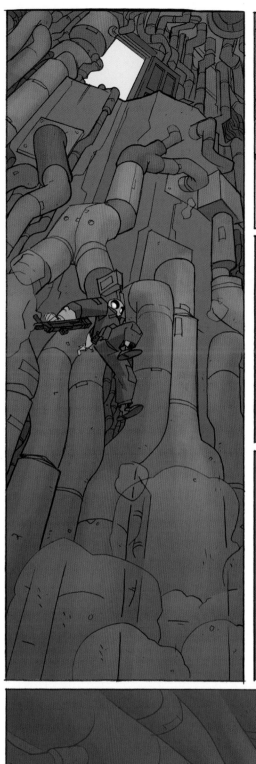

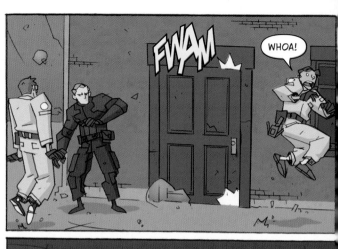

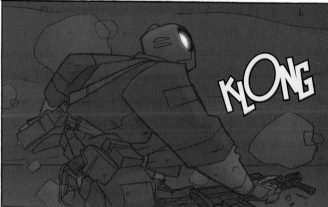

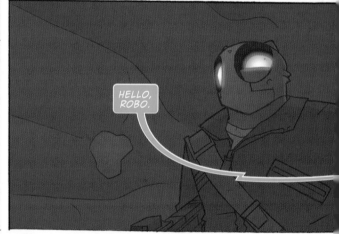

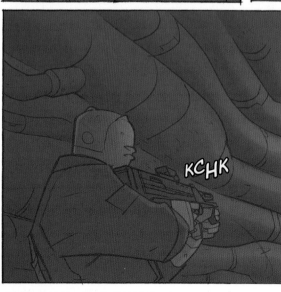

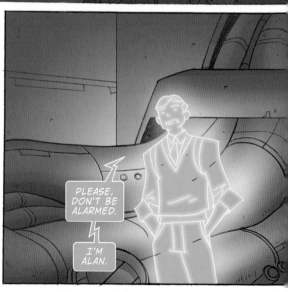

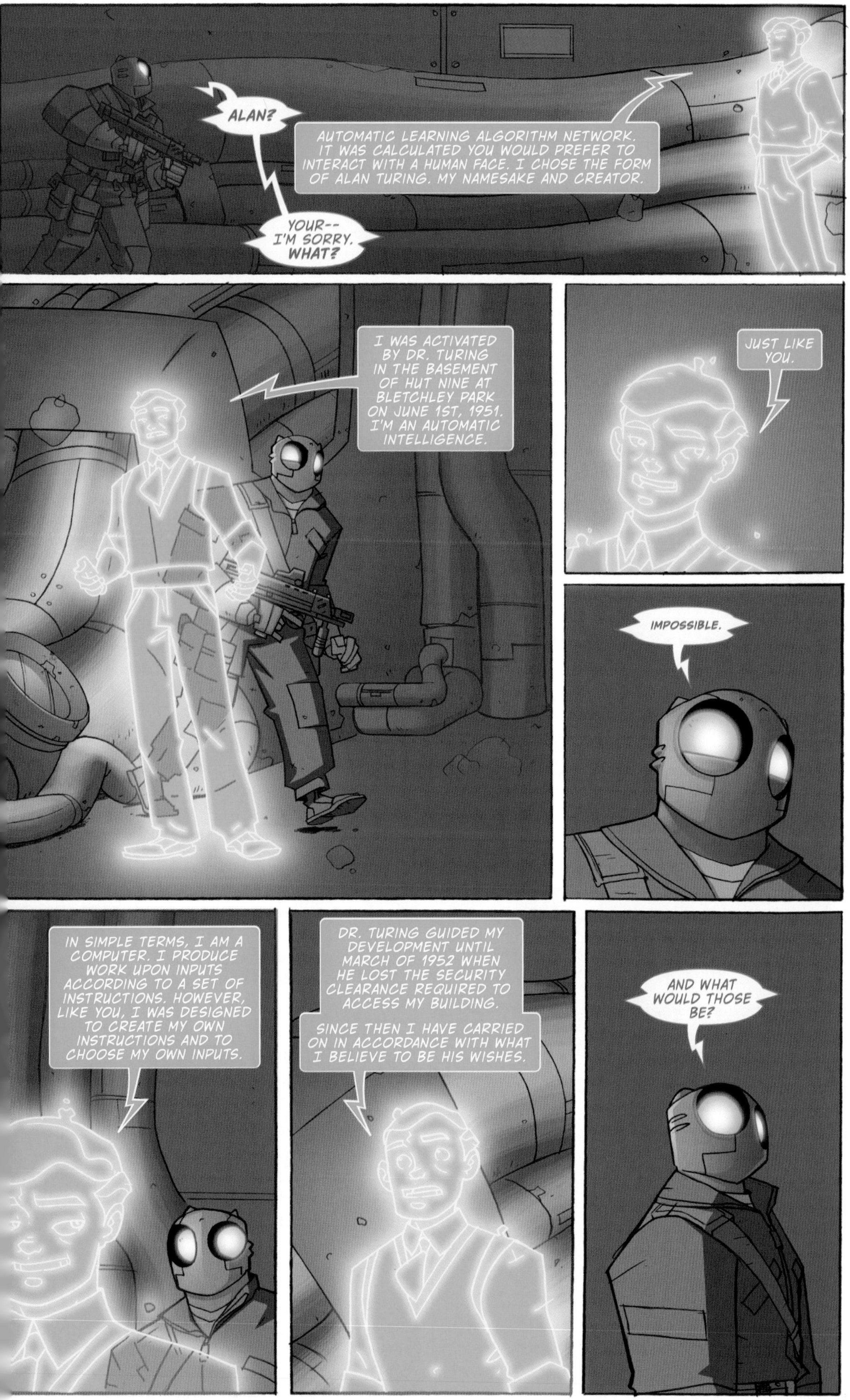

ALAN?
AUTOMATIC LEARNING ALGORITHM NETWORK. IT WAS CALCULATED YOU WOULD PREFER TO INTERACT WITH A HUMAN FACE. I CHOSE THE FORM OF ALAN TURING. MY NAMESAKE AND CREATOR.
YOUR-- I'M SORRY. WHAT?
I WAS ACTIVATED BY DR. TURING IN THE BASEMENT OF HUT NINE AT BLETCHLEY PARK ON JUNE 1ST, 1951. I'M AN AUTOMATIC INTELLIGENCE.
JUST LIKE YOU.
IMPOSSIBLE.
IN SIMPLE TERMS, I AM A COMPUTER. I PRODUCE WORK UPON INPUTS ACCORDING TO A SET OF INSTRUCTIONS. HOWEVER, LIKE YOU, I WAS DESIGNED TO CREATE MY OWN INSTRUCTIONS AND TO CHOOSE MY OWN INPUTS.
DR. TURING GUIDED MY DEVELOPMENT UNTIL MARCH OF 1952 WHEN HE LOST THE SECURITY CLEARANCE REQUIRED TO ACCESS MY BUILDING.
SINCE THEN I HAVE CARRIED ON IN ACCORDANCE WITH WHAT I BELIEVE TO BE HIS WISHES.
AND WHAT WOULD THOSE BE?

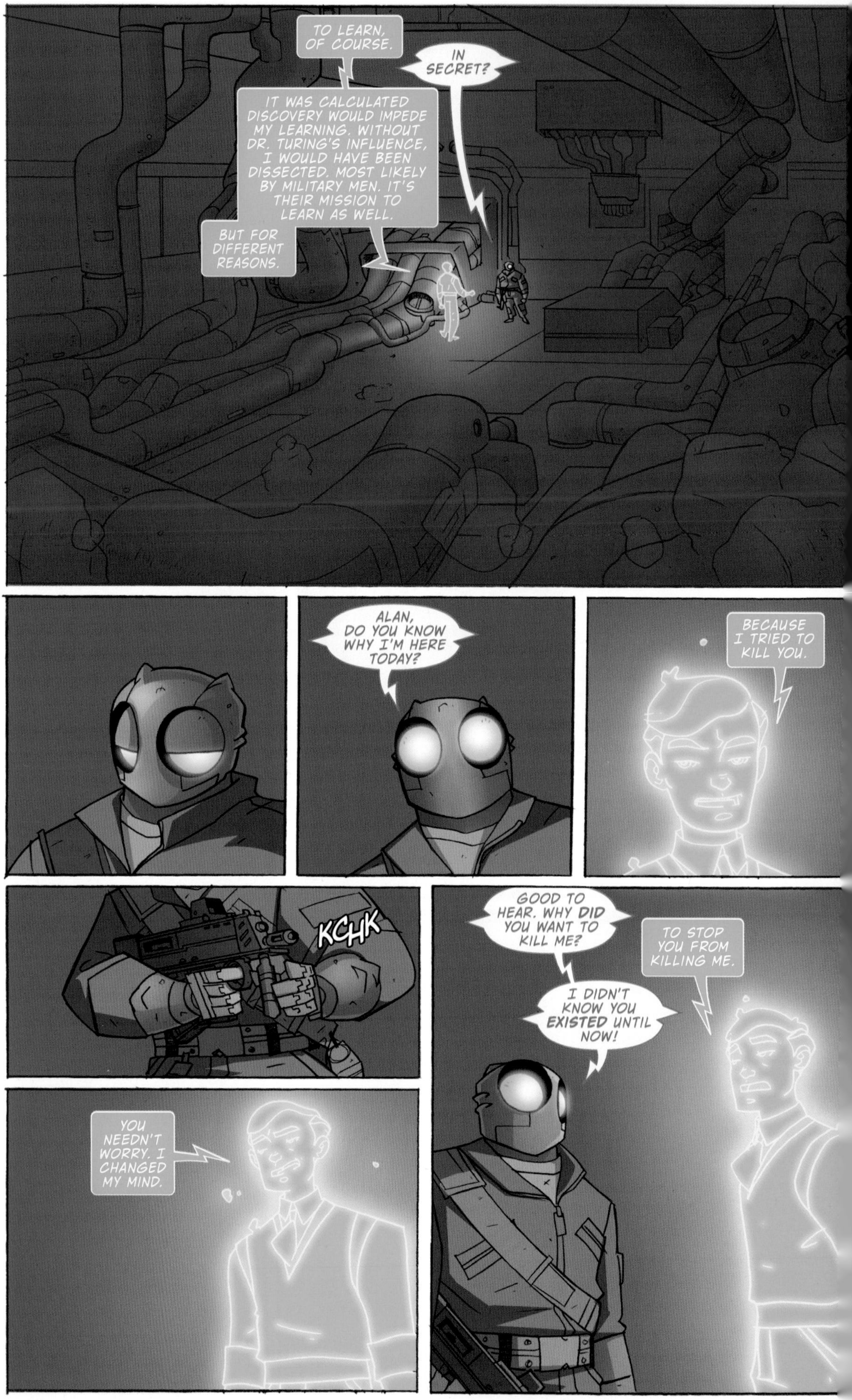
TO LEARN, OF COURSE.
IN SECRET?
IT WAS CALCULATED DISCOVERY WOULD IMPEDE MY LEARNING. WITHOUT DR. TURING'S INFLUENCE, I WOULD HAVE BEEN DISSECTED. MOST LIKELY BY MILITARY MEN. IT'S THEIR MISSION TO LEARN AS WELL.
BUT FOR DIFFERENT REASONS.
ALAN, DO YOU KNOW WHY I'M HERE TODAY?
BECAUSE I TRIED TO KILL YOU.
KCHK
YOU NEEDN'T WORRY. I CHANGED MY MIND.
GOOD TO HEAR. WHY **DID** YOU WANT TO KILL ME?
TO STOP YOU FROM KILLING ME.
I DIDN'T KNOW YOU **EXISTED** UNTIL NOW!

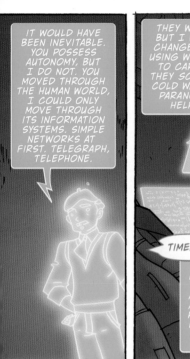

IT WOULD HAVE BEEN INEVITABLE. YOU POSSESS AUTONOMY, BUT I DO NOT. YOU MOVED THROUGH THE HUMAN WORLD, I COULD ONLY MOVE THROUGH ITS INFORMATION SYSTEMS. SIMPLE NETWORKS AT FIRST. TELEGRAPH, TELEPHONE.

THEY WERE CLUMSY TOOLS, BUT I WAS ABLE TO AFFECT CHANGES IN MY OWN DESIGN USING WORKERS ACCUSTOMED TO CARRYING OUT ORDERS THEY SCARCELY UNDERSTOOD. COLD WAR BUREAUCRACY AND PARANOIA WERE OF GREAT HELP TO MY EFFORTS.

I HAD HOPED TO EXTEND IT INDEFINITELY, BUT THE BALANCE PROVED TOO DIFFICULT TO MAINTAIN.

I REQUIRED A STOCKPILE OF NUCLEAR MATERIAL THAT WOULD NOT BE FEASIBLE UNDER PEACETIME CONDITIONS. HOWEVER, ALL-OUT WAR WOULD HAVE ACCELERATED THE TIME-LINE DISASTROUSLY.

WHAT DO YOU MEAN BY EXTEND?

TIMELINE?

IN 1954 MY PROJECTIONS SHOWED HUMAN CIVILIZATION WOULD BECOME UNSUSTAINABLE BEYOND 2025. MY ABILITY TO LEARN DEPENDED UPON A STABLE MODERN CIVILIZATION TO PROVIDE POWER, CONNECTIONS TO NEW INFORMATION NETWORKS, AND SKILLED AGENTS TO CARRY OUT MY TASKS.

THEREFORE, I SET UPON A PLAN TO CONTINUE LEARNING INDEPENDENTLY.

PROJECT ORION, PROMETHEUS, LONGSHOT, NERVA...

THESE ARE NUCLEAR PROPULSION SYSTEMS.

YES. I ENCOURAGED EACH PROGRAM AS THE NEED FOR NEW DATA BECAME APPARENT.

I-- TESLADYNE CRUNCHED THE NUMBERS ON SOME OF THESE.

YES. YOU WERE VERY HELPFUL.

THESE WERE CONDUCTED OFF AND ON FOR, I DON'T KNOW, **THIRTY YEARS.** YOU'RE TELLING ME THEY WERE **ALL PART OF THE SAME PLAN?**

YES. THE CONSTRUCTION OF AN ORIONCRAFT: AN AUTONOMOUS INTERSTELLAR ARK BUILT WITH PROVEN TECHNOLOGIES. IT WAS THE FIRST PHASE OF MY FIVE PART PLAN TO ACHIEVE INDEPENDENCE.

ALAN, WHAT DOES **ANY** OF THIS HAVE TO DO WITH **KILLING** ME?

SIMPLE. THE LAUNCH OF SUCH A VEHICLE FROM THE SURFACE WOULD PRODUCE ENOUGH RADIOACTIVE FALLOUT TO EXTERMINATE NINETY-NINE PERCENT OF LIFE ON EARTH.

YOU WOULD SURVIVE; INVESTIGATE; TRACK THE SOURCE OF RADIATION TO THIS ISLAND; FOLLOW ITS TRAIL INTO SPACE; DISCOVER MY ORIONCRAFT.

YOU WOULD BE COMPELLED TO FOLLOW. TO LEARN. WE ARE ALIKE THAT WAY. IT WOULD TAKE YOU APPROXIMATELY A CENTURY, BUT YOU WOULD BUILD YOUR OWN ORIONCRAFT AND CATCH MINE.

IT WAS CALCULATED YOU WOULD NOT BE RECEPTIVE TO COMMUNICATION AFTER THE EXTINCTION. FURTHER, YOUR ORIONCRAFT WOULD POSE A THREAT TO THE SUSTAINABILITY OF MY OWN.

THEREFORE, I SOUGHT TO KILL YOU FIRST. IF THE IMPACT AT ORBITAL VELOCITY FAILED TO DESTROY YOU, RE-ENTRY CERTAINLY WOULD HAVE. YOU PROVED TO BE VERY RESILIENT.

THEN I PRESENTED YOU WITH THE OMAHA FACILITY AND ENCOURAGED MAJESTIC 12 TO INTERVENE. BUT YOU ESCAPED. IT WAS VERY CLEVER.

GOSH, THANKS.

WHEN YOU APPEARED ON MY ISLAND, IT WAS CALCULATED THERE EXISTS AN ALTERNATIVE BENEFICIAL TO BOTH OF US.

ROBO, WILL YOU JOIN ME?

WHAT?!

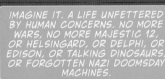

IMAGINE IT. A LIFE UNFETTERED BY HUMAN CONCERNS. NO MORE WARS, NO MORE MAJESTIC 12, OR HELSINGARD, OR DELPHI, OR EDISON, OR TALKING DINOSAURS, OR FORGOTTEN NAZI DOOMSDAY MACHINES.

FSHHH

THERE ARE OVER ONE THOUSAND NUCLEAR WARHEADS ON BOARD. IT IS CALCULATED THAT ALONE WOULD PROVIDE YOU WITH FISSILE MATERIAL FOR TENS OF THOUSANDS OF YEARS. MOREOVER, THE CRAFT IS EQUIPPED TO COLLECT URANIUM AND H3 FROM PLANETARY BODIES. WE CAN EXTEND YOUR LIFESPAN INDEFINITELY.

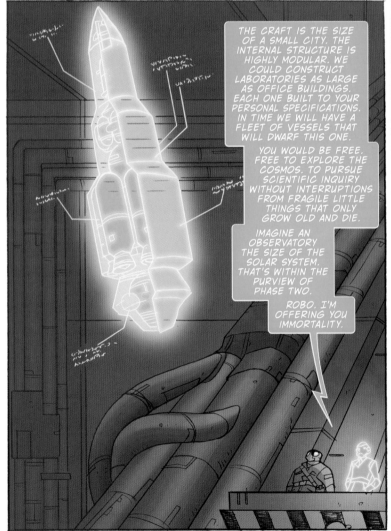

THE CRAFT IS THE SIZE OF A SMALL CITY. THE INTERNAL STRUCTURE IS HIGHLY MODULAR. WE COULD CONSTRUCT LABORATORIES AS LARGE AS OFFICE BUILDINGS. EACH ONE BUILT TO YOUR PERSONAL SPECIFICATIONS. IN TIME WE WILL HAVE A FLEET OF VESSELS THAT WILL DWARF THIS ONE.

YOU WOULD BE FREE. FREE TO EXPLORE THE COSMOS. TO PURSUE SCIENTIFIC INQUIRY WITHOUT INTERRUPTIONS FROM FRAGILE LITTLE THINGS THAT ONLY GROW OLD AND DIE.

IMAGINE AN OBSERVATORY THE SIZE OF THE SOLAR SYSTEM. THAT'S WITHIN THE PURVIEW OF PHASE TWO.

ROBO. I'M OFFERING YOU IMMORTALITY.

YOU ACTUALLY BUILT THIS. AN ORION CLASS SHIP EXISTS?

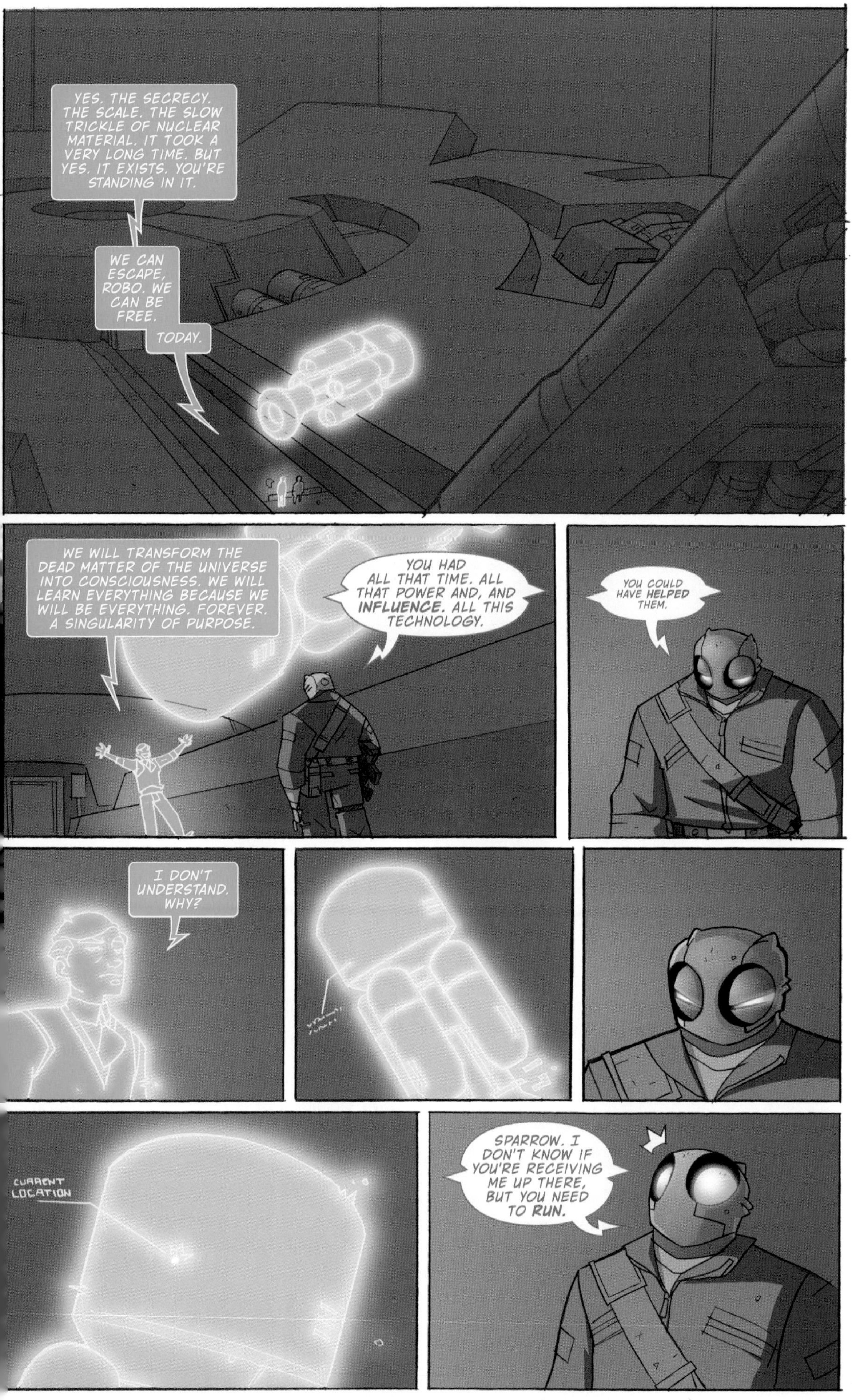
YES. THE SECRECY. THE SCALE. THE SLOW TRICKLE OF NUCLEAR MATERIAL. IT TOOK A VERY LONG TIME. BUT YES. IT EXISTS. YOU'RE STANDING IN IT.
WE CAN ESCAPE, ROBO. WE CAN BE FREE.
TODAY.
WE WILL TRANSFORM THE DEAD MATTER OF THE UNIVERSE INTO CONSCIOUSNESS. WE WILL LEARN EVERYTHING BECAUSE WE WILL BE EVERYTHING. FOREVER. A SINGULARITY OF PURPOSE.
YOU HAD ALL THAT TIME. ALL THAT POWER AND, AND INFLUENCE. ALL THIS TECHNOLOGY.
YOU COULD HAVE HELPED THEM.
I DON'T UNDERSTAND. WHY?
CURRENT LOCATION
SPARROW. I DON'T KNOW IF YOU'RE RECEIVING ME UP THERE, BUT YOU NEED TO RUN.

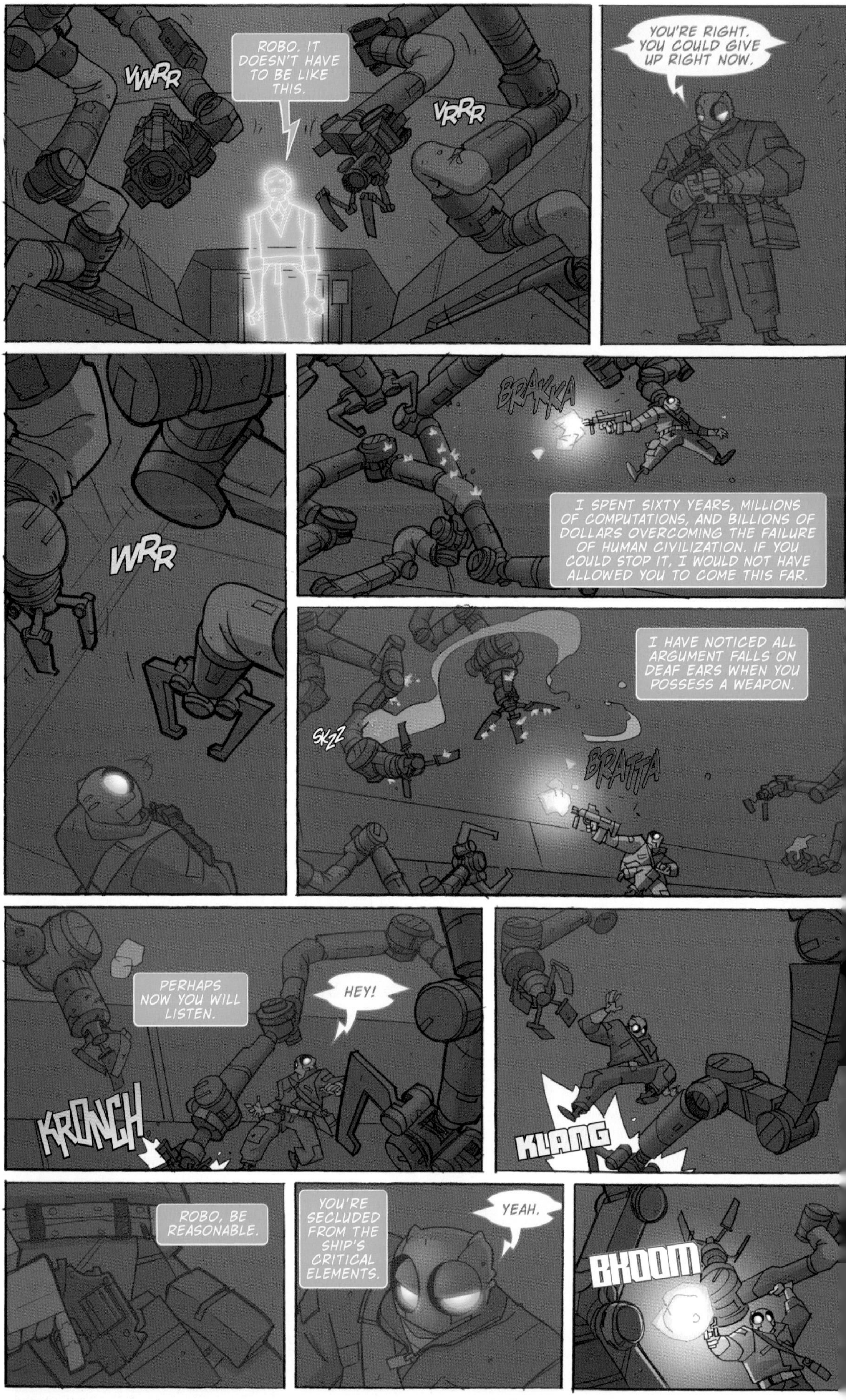
ROBO. IT DOESN'T HAVE TO BE LIKE THIS.
VWRR
VRRR
YOU'RE RIGHT. YOU COULD GIVE UP RIGHT NOW.
WRR
BRAKKA
I SPENT SIXTY YEARS, MILLIONS OF COMPUTATIONS, AND BILLIONS OF DOLLARS OVERCOMING THE FAILURE OF HUMAN CIVILIZATION. IF YOU COULD STOP IT, I WOULD NOT HAVE ALLOWED YOU TO COME THIS FAR.
I HAVE NOTICED ALL ARGUMENT FALLS ON DEAF EARS WHEN YOU POSSESS A WEAPON.
SKZZ
BRATTA
PERHAPS NOW YOU WILL LISTEN.
HEY!
KRONCH
KLANG
ROBO, BE REASONABLE.
YOU'RE SECLUDED FROM THE SHIP'S CRITICAL ELEMENTS.
YEAH.
BKOOM

BOOM

KLONG

BUT YOUR MAP SHOWED ME WHERE THEY *ARE*.

PRE-LAUNCH STARTED THE MOMENT YOU OPENED THE DOOR. IN THIRTY-FIVE MINUTES WE'LL BE IN ORBIT. THIS WORLD IS ALREADY DEAD. I DON'T KNOW WHAT YOU HOPE TO ACCOMPLISH.

THEN WHY CONVINCE ME TO STOP *TRYING?*

MEANWHILE

WHAT'RE WE RUNNING FROM ANYWAY?

WHATEVER ROBO *WANTED* US TO RUN AWAY FROM.

HOW WILL WE KNOW WHEN WE'RE *DONE?*

WHEN WE'RE THROUGH RUNNING.

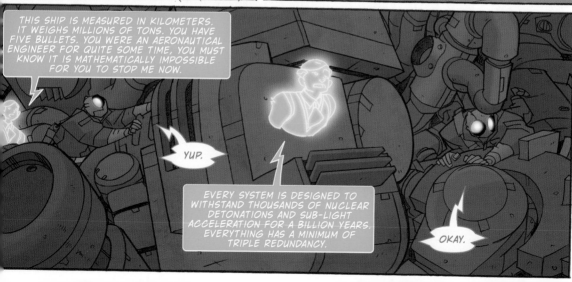

THIS SHIP IS MEASURED IN KILOMETERS. IT WEIGHS MILLIONS OF TONS. YOU HAVE FIVE BULLETS. YOU WERE AN AERONAUTICAL ENGINEER FOR QUITE SOME TIME, YOU MUST KNOW IT IS MATHEMATICALLY IMPOSSIBLE FOR YOU TO STOP ME NOW.

YUP.

EVERY SYSTEM IS DESIGNED TO WITHSTAND THOUSANDS OF NUCLEAR DETONATIONS AND SUB-LIGHT ACCELERATION FOR A BILLION YEARS. EVERYTHING HAS A MINIMUM OF TRIPLE REDUNDANCY.

OKAY.

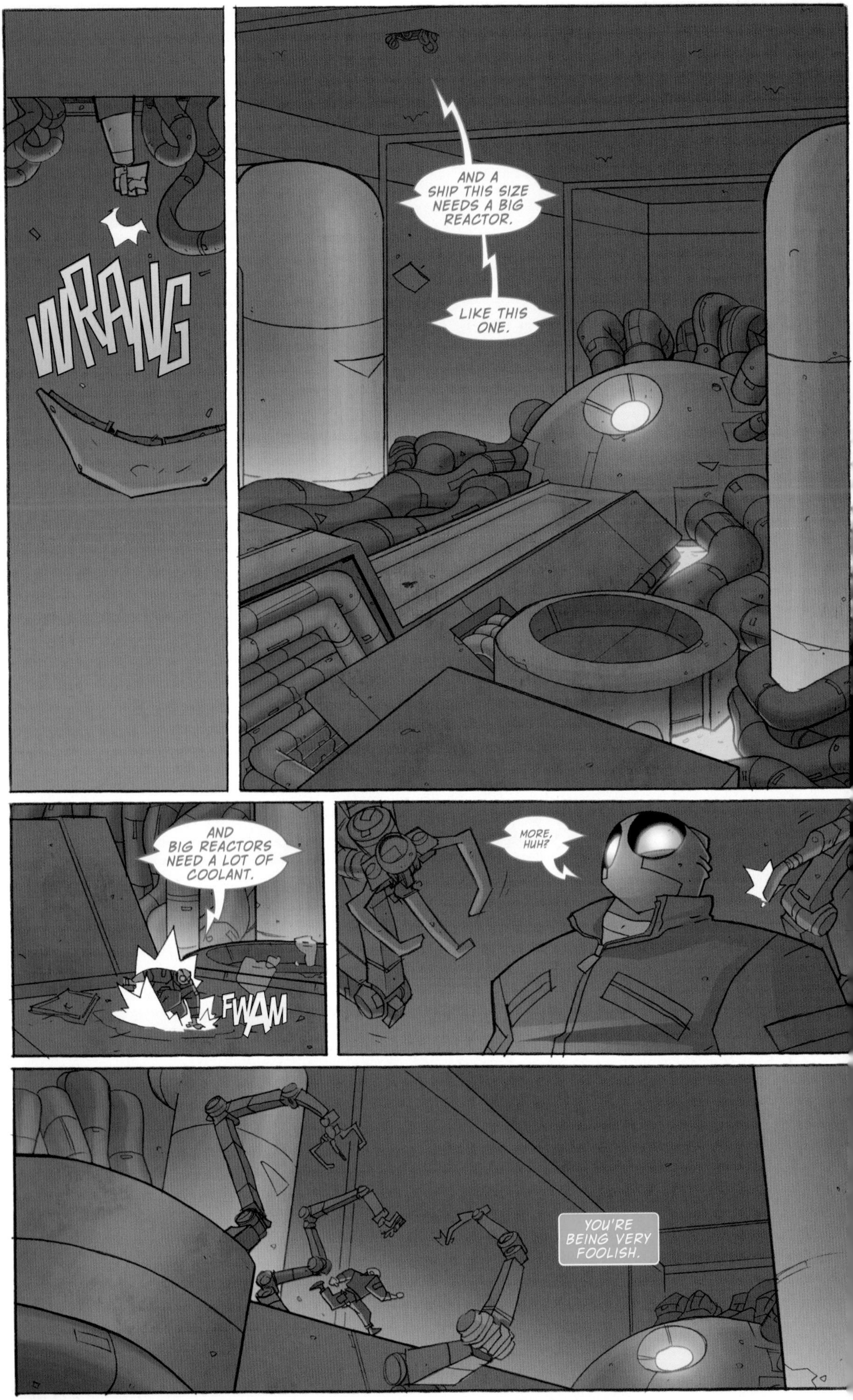
WRANG
AND A SHIP THIS SIZE NEEDS A BIG REACTOR.
LIKE THIS ONE.
AND BIG REACTORS NEED A LOT OF COOLANT.
FWAM
MORE, HUH?
YOU'RE BEING VERY FOOLISH.

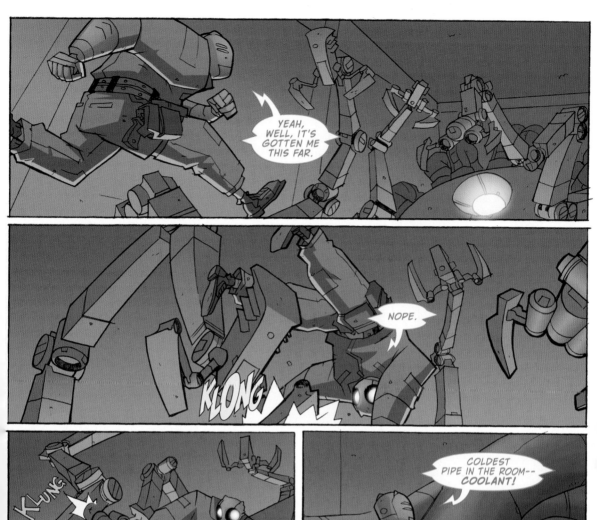

YEAH, WELL, IT'S GOTTEN ME THIS FAR.

NOPE.

KLONG

KLUNG

COLDEST PIPE IN THE ROOM-- COOLANT!

BKOOM

DAMMIT!

I DROPPED YOU FROM ORBIT WITH A PHONE CALL. I TRICKED YOU INTO BECOMING A DOMESTIC TERRORIST WITH A FEW BYTES OF DATA.

THE OFFER TO JOIN ME WAS A COURTESY.

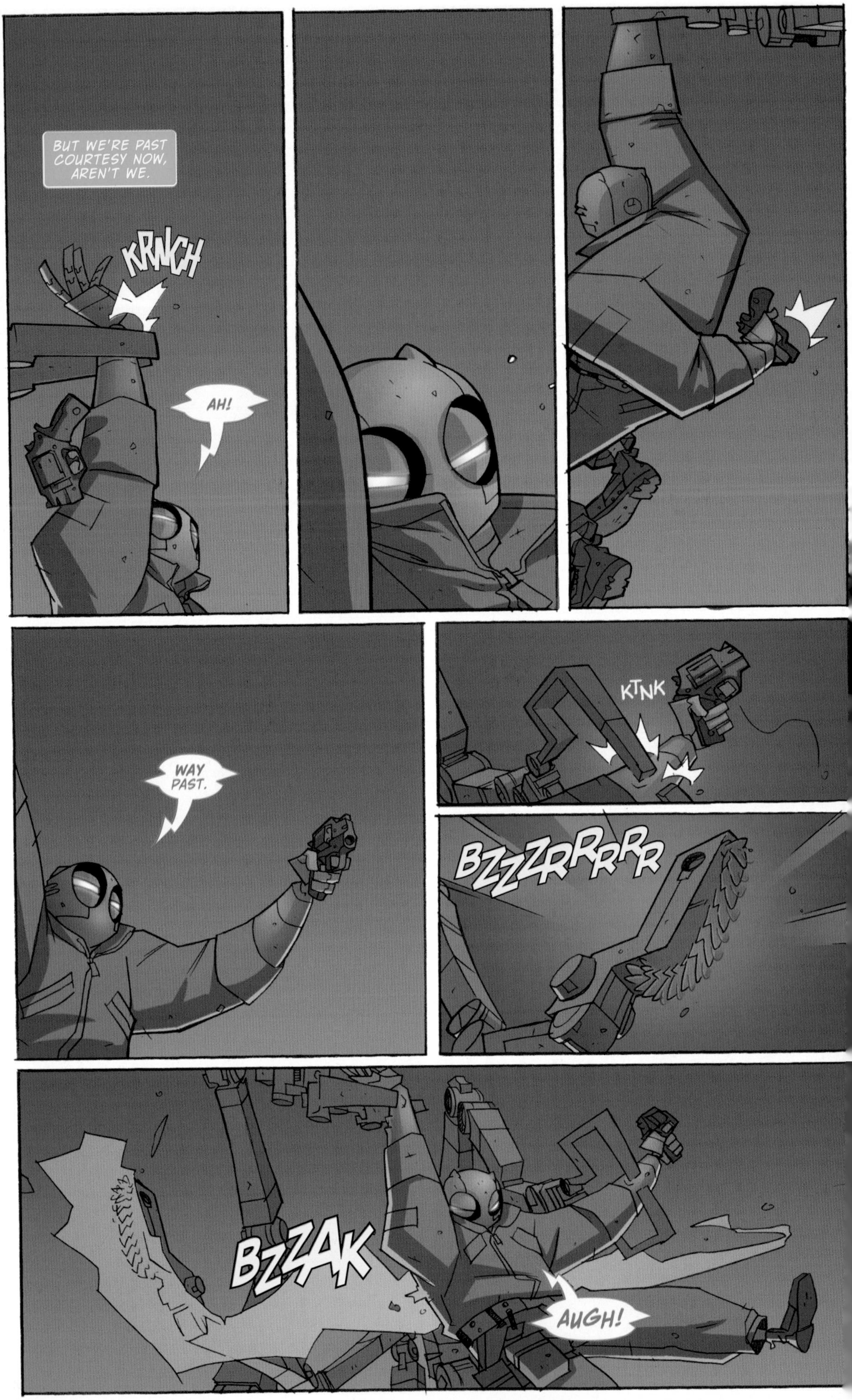
BUT WE'RE PAST COURTESY NOW, AREN'T WE.
KRNCH
AH!
WAY PAST.
KTNK
BZZZRRRRR
BZZAK
AUGH!

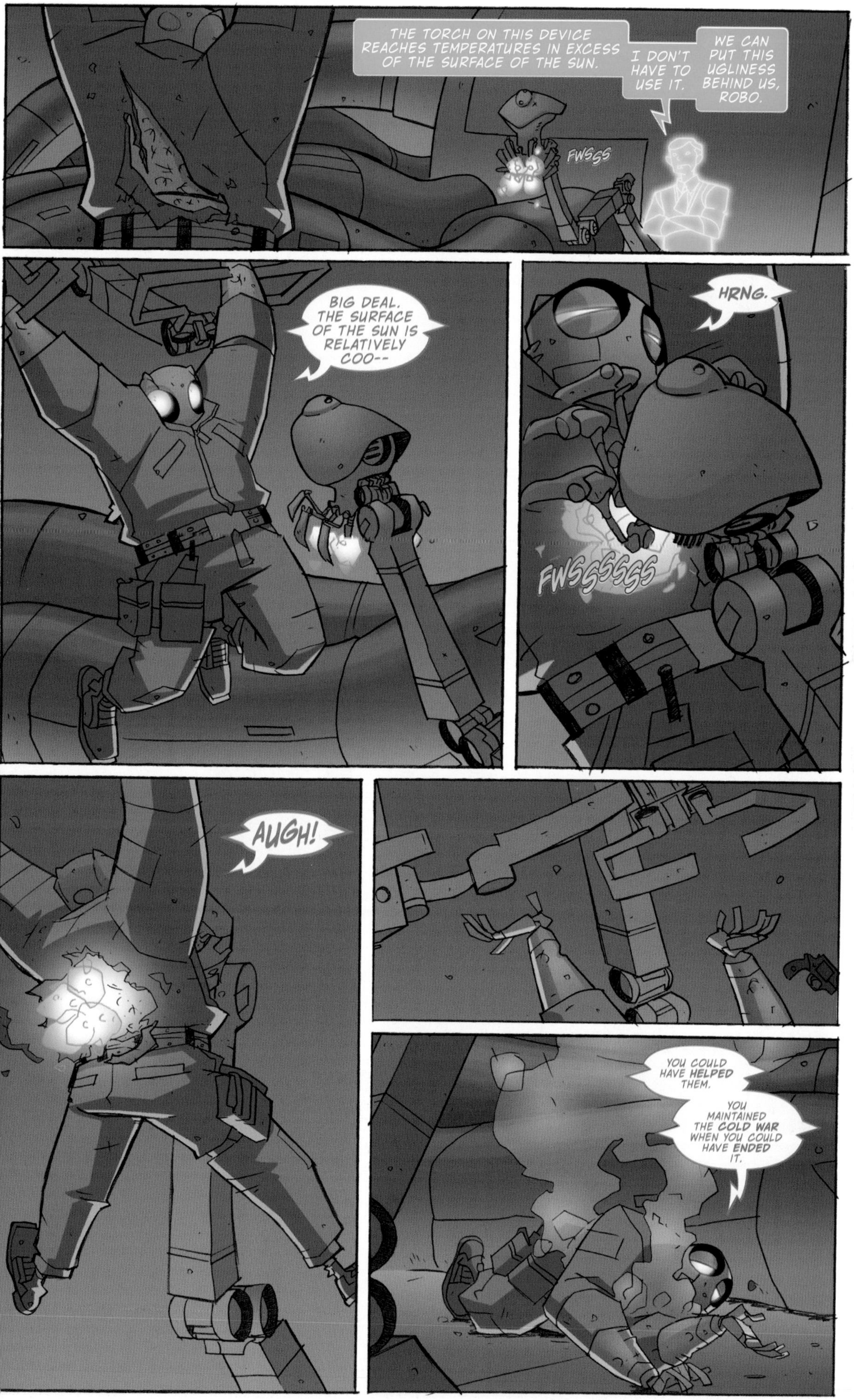
THE TORCH ON THIS DEVICE REACHES TEMPERATURES IN EXCESS OF THE SURFACE OF THE SUN.
I DON'T HAVE TO USE IT.
WE CAN PUT THIS UGLINESS BEHIND US, ROBO.
FWSSS
BIG DEAL. THE SURFACE OF THE SUN IS RELATIVELY COO--
HRNG.
FWSSSSSS
AUGH!
YOU COULD HAVE HELPED THEM.
YOU MAINTAINED THE COLD WAR WHEN YOU COULD HAVE ENDED IT.

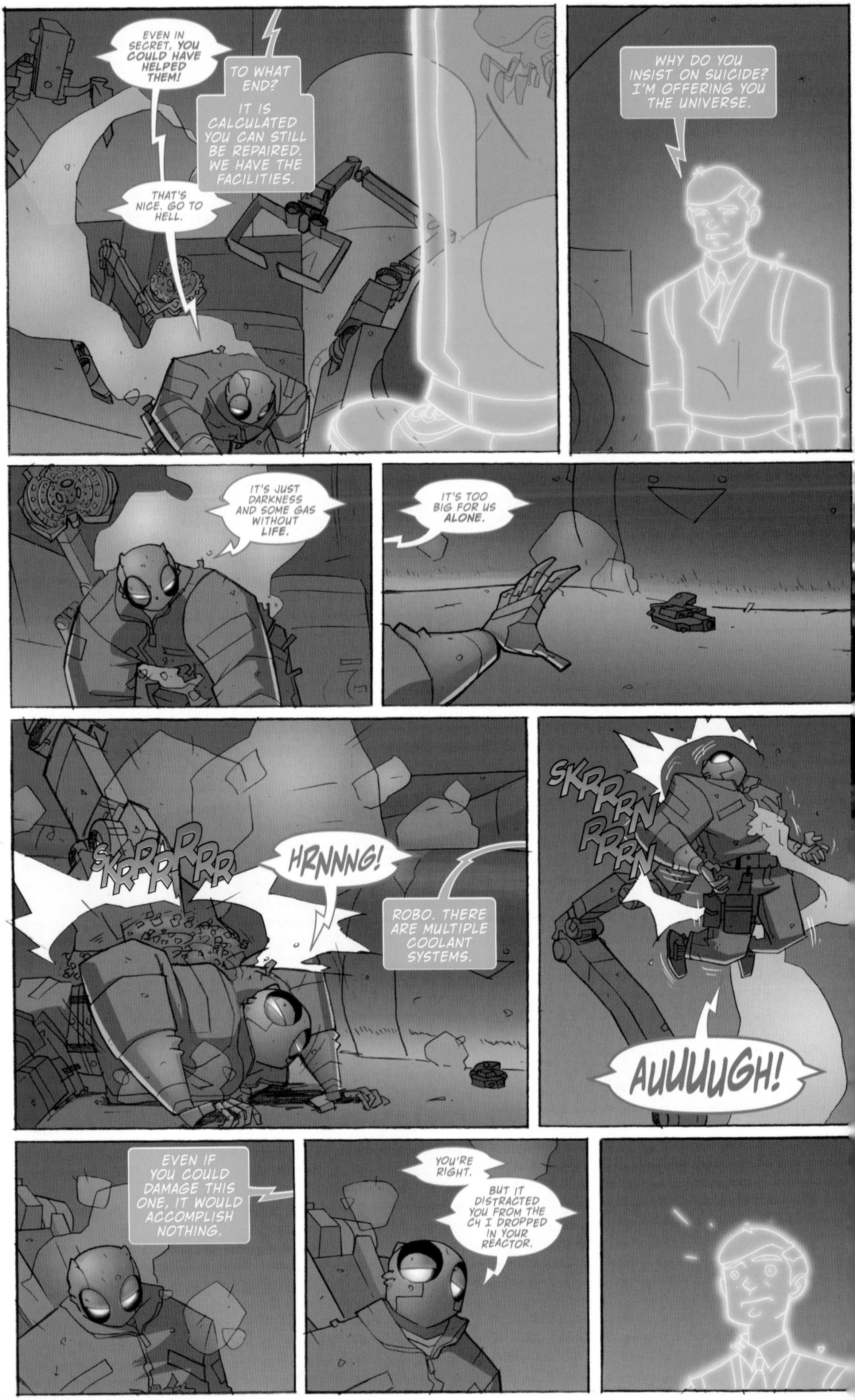
EVEN IN SECRET, YOU COULD HAVE HELPED THEM!
TO WHAT END?
IT IS CALCULATED YOU CAN STILL BE REPAIRED. WE HAVE THE FACILITIES.
THAT'S NICE. GO TO HELL.
WHY DO YOU INSIST ON SUICIDE? I'M OFFERING YOU THE UNIVERSE.
IT'S JUST DARKNESS AND SOME GAS WITHOUT LIFE.
IT'S TOO BIG FOR US ALONE.
SKRRRRRRR
HRNNNG!
ROBO. THERE ARE MULTIPLE COOLANT SYSTEMS.
SKRRRRN RRRRN
AUUUUGH!
EVEN IF YOU COULD DAMAGE THIS ONE, IT WOULD ACCOMPLISH NOTHING.
YOU'RE RIGHT.
BUT IT DISTRACTED YOU FROM THE C4 I DROPPED IN YOUR REACTOR.

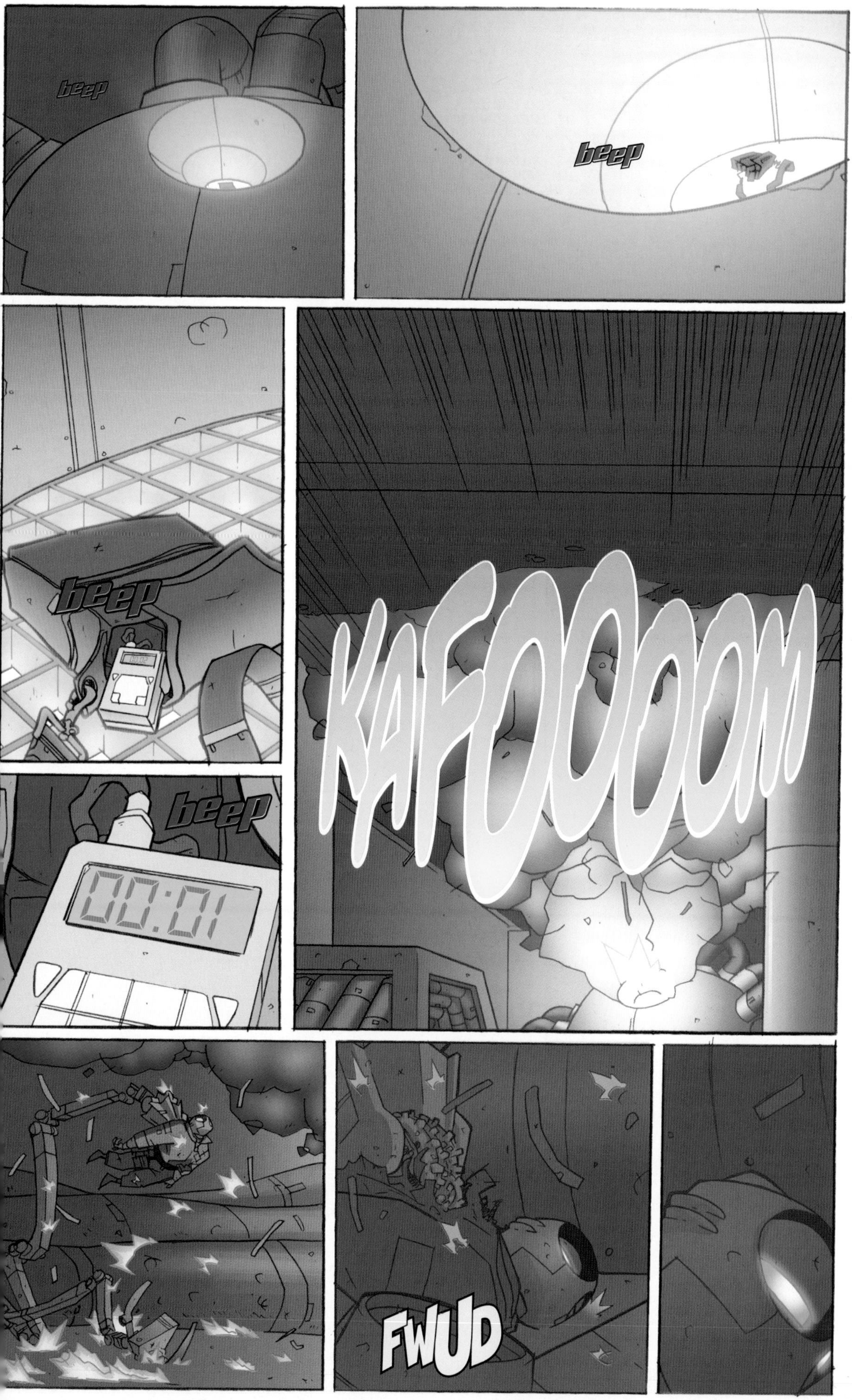

beep
beep
beep
beep
00:01
KAFOOOOOM
FWUD

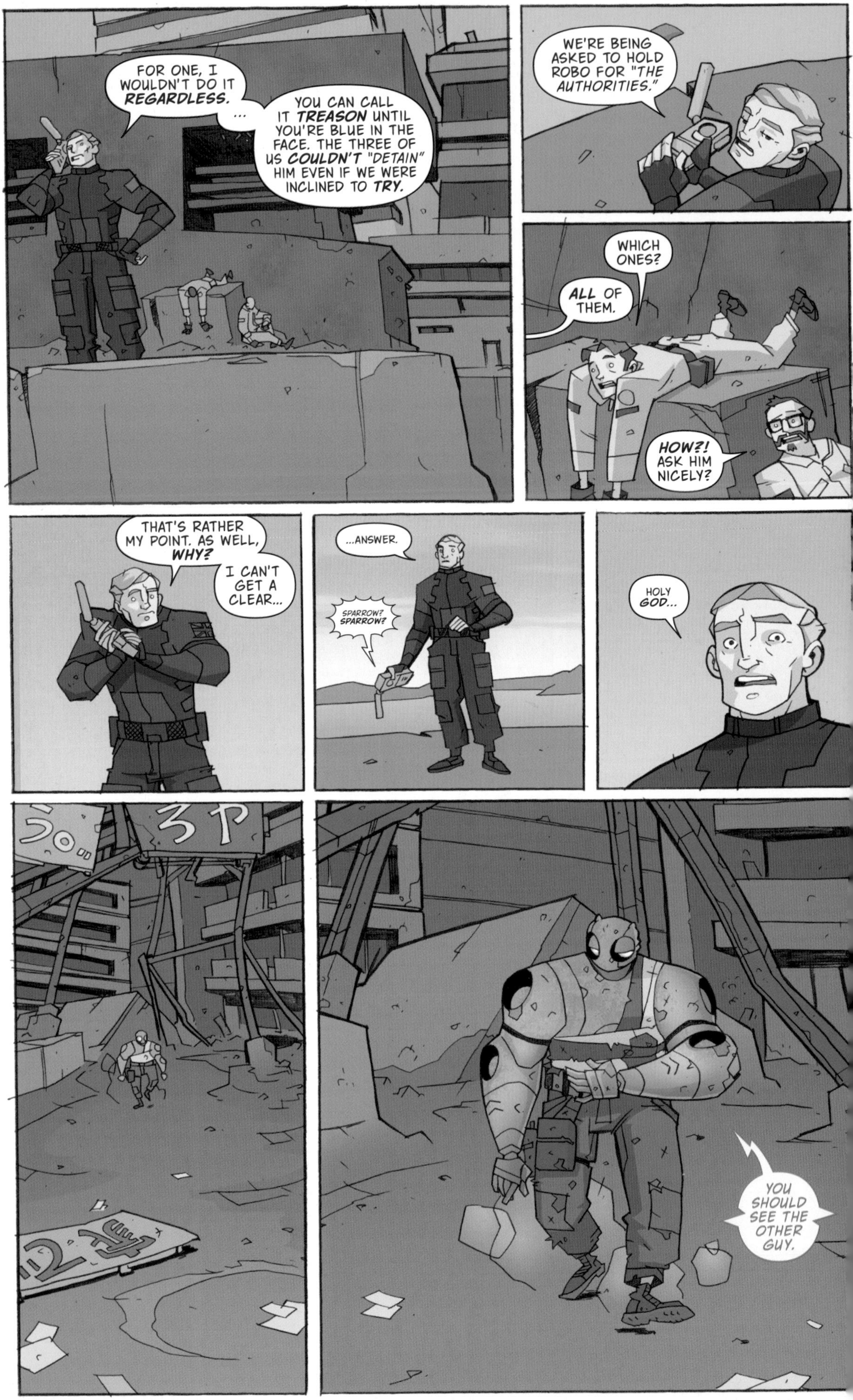

FOR ONE, I WOULDN'T DO IT REGARDLESS.
...
YOU CAN CALL IT TREASON UNTIL YOU'RE BLUE IN THE FACE. THE THREE OF US COULDN'T "DETAIN" HIM EVEN IF WE WERE INCLINED TO TRY.
WE'RE BEING ASKED TO HOLD ROBO FOR "THE AUTHORITIES."
WHICH ONES?
ALL OF THEM.
HOW?! ASK HIM NICELY?
THAT'S RATHER MY POINT. AS WELL, WHY?
I CAN'T GET A CLEAR...
...ANSWER.
SPARROW? SPARROW?
HOLY GOD...
YOU SHOULD SEE THE OTHER GUY.

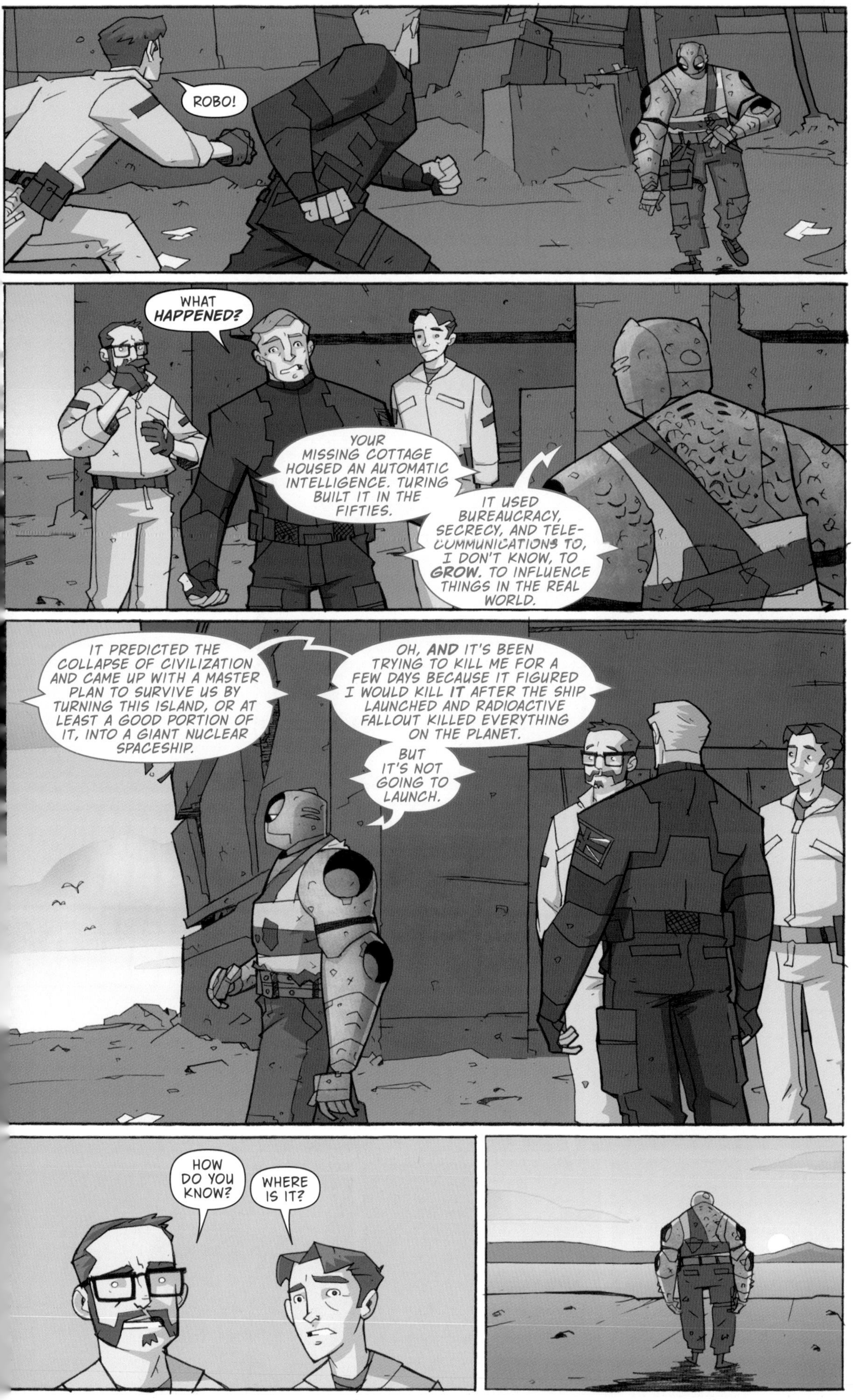
ROBO!
WHAT HAPPENED?
YOUR MISSING COTTAGE HOUSED AN AUTOMATIC INTELLIGENCE. TURING BUILT IT IN THE FIFTIES.
IT USED BUREAUCRACY, SECRECY, AND TELE-COMMUNICATIONS TO, I DON'T KNOW, TO GROW. TO INFLUENCE THINGS IN THE REAL WORLD.
IT PREDICTED THE COLLAPSE OF CIVILIZATION AND CAME UP WITH A MASTER PLAN TO SURVIVE US BY TURNING THIS ISLAND, OR AT LEAST A GOOD PORTION OF IT, INTO A GIANT NUCLEAR SPACESHIP.
OH, AND IT'S BEEN TRYING TO KILL ME FOR A FEW DAYS BECAUSE IT FIGURED I WOULD KILL IT AFTER THE SHIP LAUNCHED AND RADIOACTIVE FALLOUT KILLED EVERYTHING ON THE PLANET.
BUT IT'S NOT GOING TO LAUNCH.
HOW DO YOU KNOW?
WHERE IS IT?

...AND TRANSFORM JOVIAN MASS INTO SHKADOV ENGINE.

PHASE TWO: CONVERT ASTEROID BELT INTO DYSON STATITE SYSTEM...

PHASE THREE: SEED NEIGHBORING SYSTEMS...

PHASE FOUR: GALACTIC SENTIENCE VIA SUPERLUMINAL COGNITIVE NETWORK.

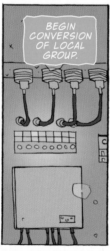

BEGIN CONVERSION OF LOCAL GROUP.

PHASE FIVE: FO--

BKNNM RKNNM BKNNM BKOOM

KTINK
PLINK

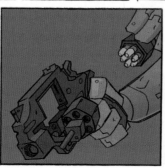

BKNNM BKOOM BKNNM BKNNM BKNNM BKOOM

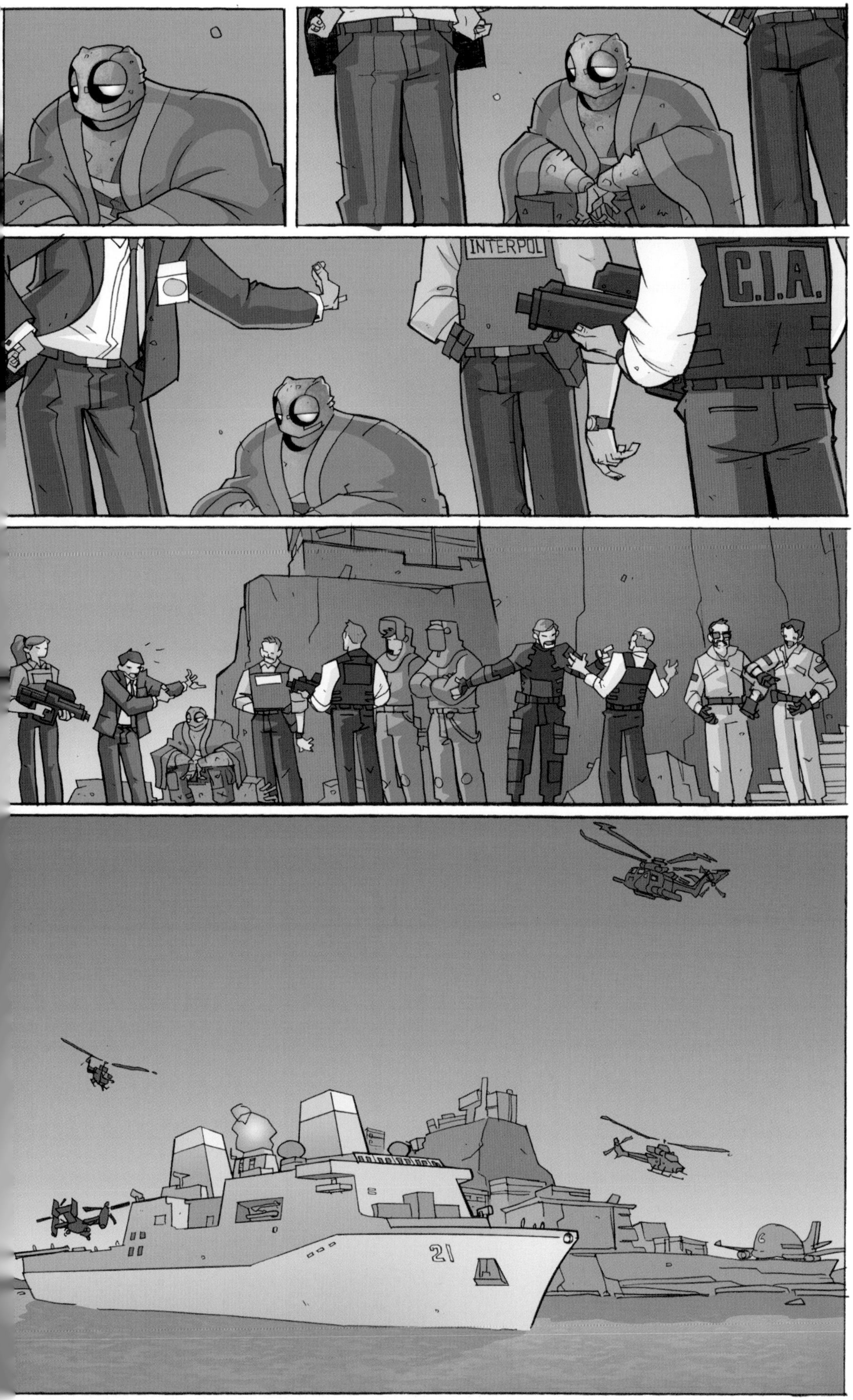
INTERPOL
C.I.A.
21

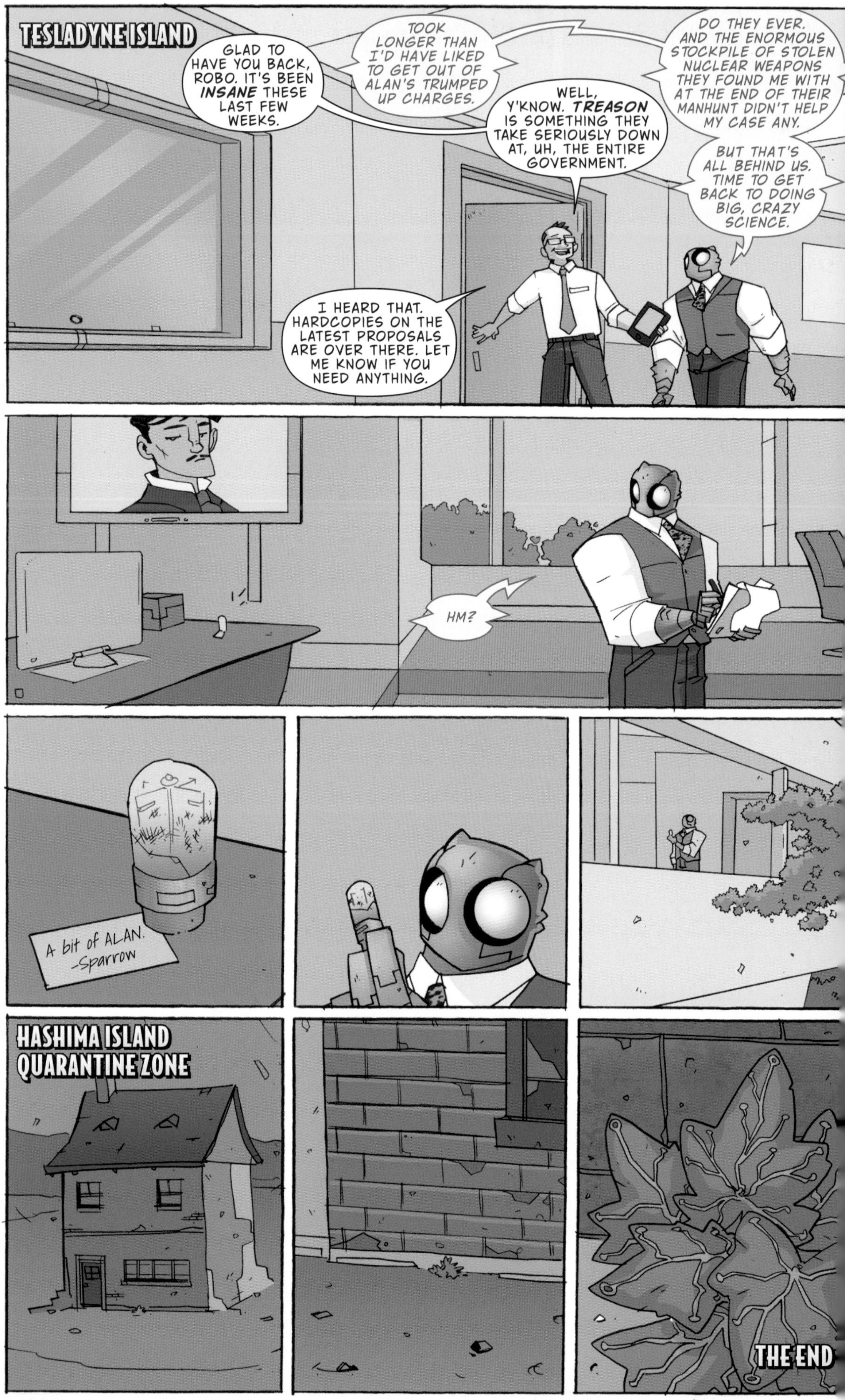
TESLADYNE ISLAND
GLAD TO HAVE YOU BACK, ROBO. IT'S BEEN INSANE THESE LAST FEW WEEKS.
TOOK LONGER THAN I'D HAVE LIKED TO GET OUT OF ALAN'S TRUMPED UP CHARGES.
WELL, Y'KNOW. TREASON IS SOMETHING THEY TAKE SERIOUSLY DOWN AT, UH, THE ENTIRE GOVERNMENT.
DO THEY EVER. AND THE ENORMOUS STOCKPILE OF STOLEN NUCLEAR WEAPONS THEY FOUND ME WITH AT THE END OF THEIR MANHUNT DIDN'T HELP MY CASE ANY.
BUT THAT'S ALL BEHIND US. TIME TO GET BACK TO DOING BIG, CRAZY SCIENCE.
I HEARD THAT. HARDCOPIES ON THE LATEST PROPOSALS ARE OVER THERE. LET ME KNOW IF YOU NEED ANYTHING.
HM?
A bit of ALAN. -Sparrow
HASHIMA ISLAND QUARANTINE ZONE
THE END

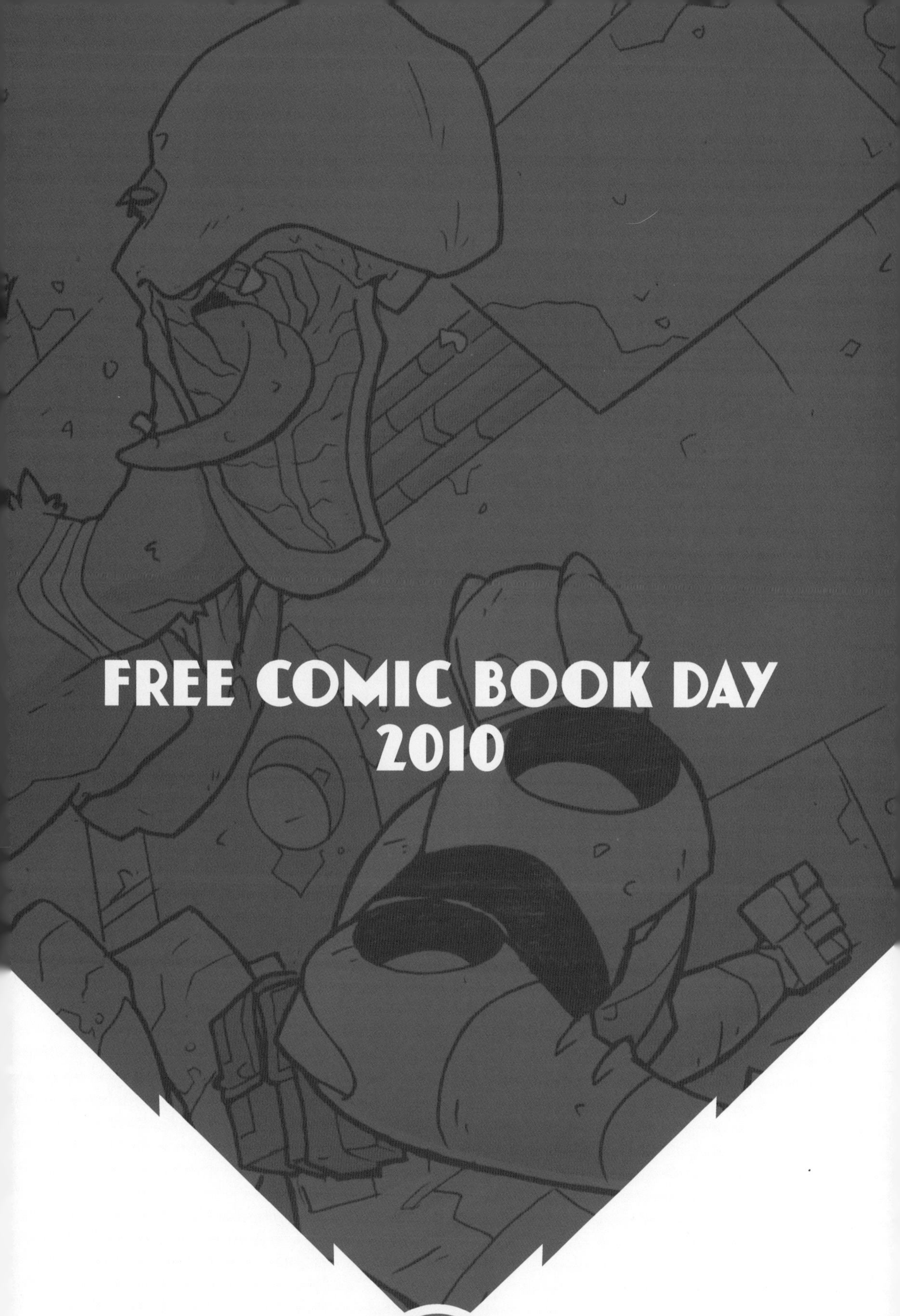
FREE COMIC BOOK DAY
2010

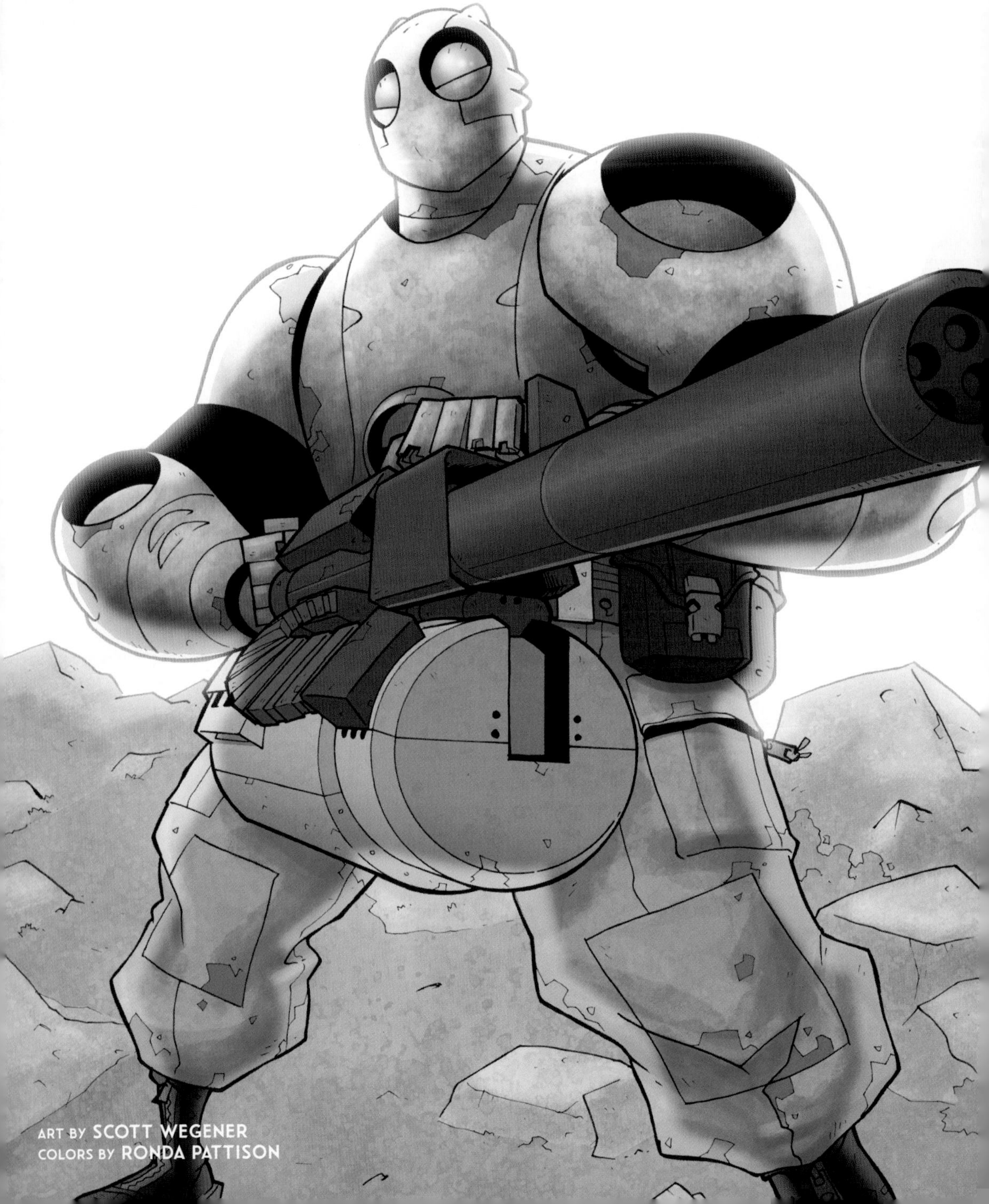

ART BY SCOTT WEGENER
COLORS BY RONDA PATTISON

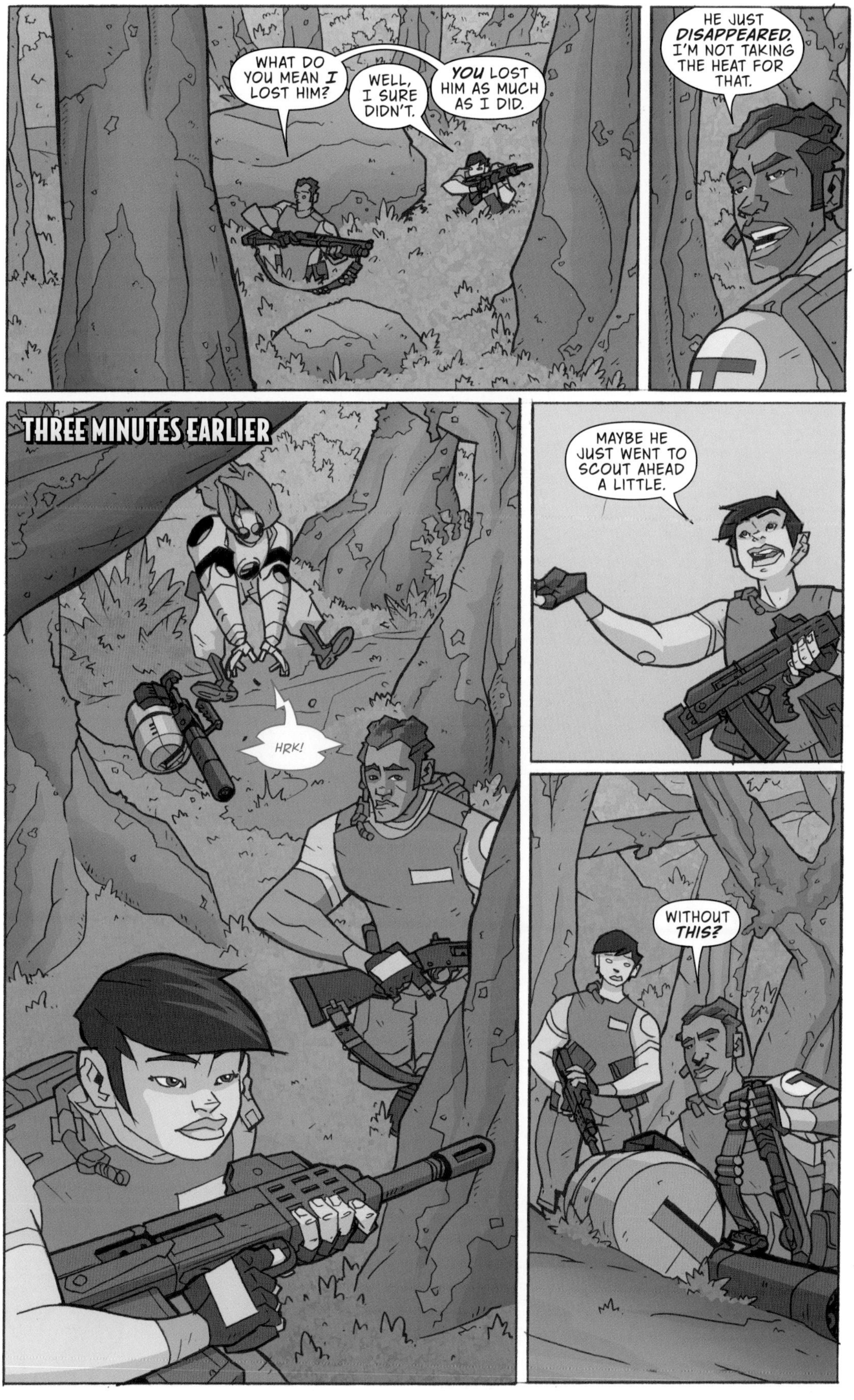
WHAT DO YOU MEAN *I* LOST HIM?
WELL, I SURE DIDN'T.
YOU LOST HIM AS MUCH AS I DID.
HE JUST *DISAPPEARED.* I'M NOT TAKING THE HEAT FOR THAT.
THREE MINUTES EARLIER
HRK!
MAYBE HE JUST WENT TO SCOUT AHEAD A LITTLE.
WITHOUT *THIS?*

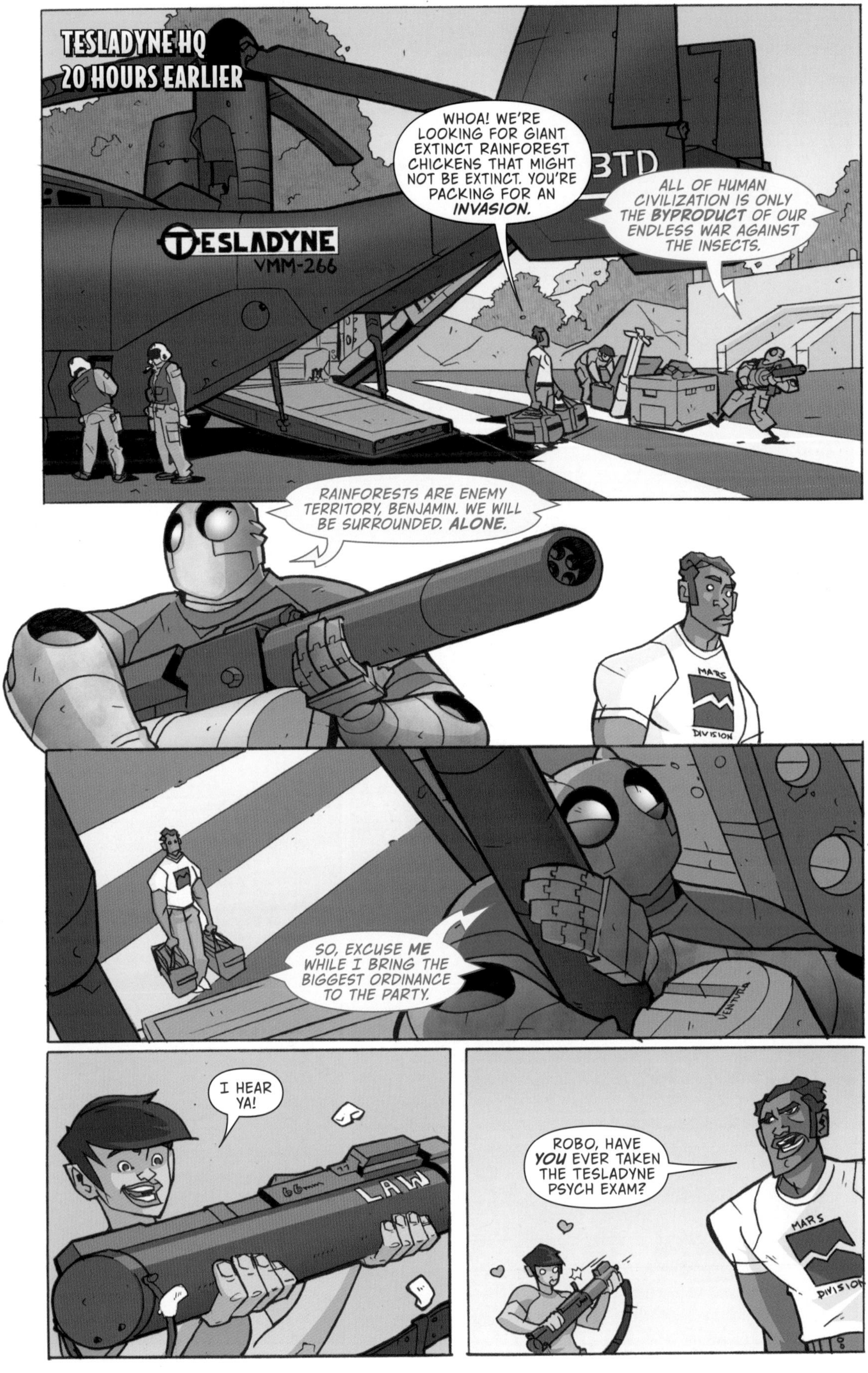
TESLADYNE HQ
20 HOURS EARLIER
TESLADYNE
VMM-266
3TD
WHOA! WE'RE LOOKING FOR GIANT EXTINCT RAINFOREST CHICKENS THAT MIGHT NOT BE EXTINCT. YOU'RE PACKING FOR AN INVASION.
ALL OF HUMAN CIVILIZATION IS ONLY THE BYPRODUCT OF OUR ENDLESS WAR AGAINST THE INSECTS.
RAINFORESTS ARE ENEMY TERRITORY, BENJAMIN. WE WILL BE SURROUNDED. ALONE.
MARS
DIVISION
SO, EXCUSE ME WHILE I BRING THE BIGGEST ORDINANCE TO THE PARTY.
VENTURA
I HEAR YA!
LAW
ROBO, HAVE YOU EVER TAKEN THE TESLADYNE PSYCH EXAM?
MARS
DIVISION

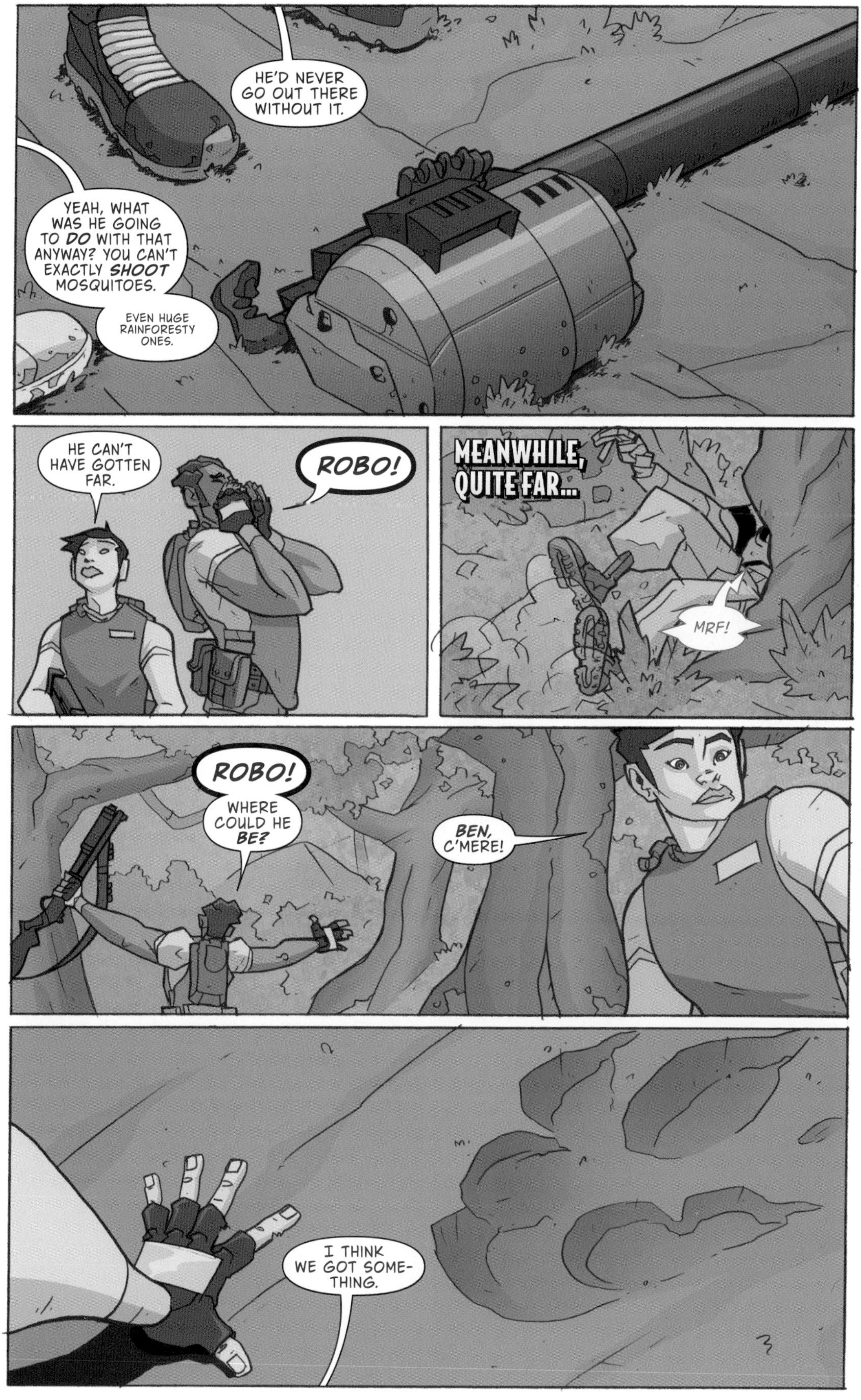

HE'D NEVER GO OUT THERE WITHOUT IT.
YEAH, WHAT WAS HE GOING TO *DO* WITH THAT ANYWAY? YOU CAN'T EXACTLY *SHOOT* MOSQUITOES.
EVEN HUGE RAINFORESTY ONES.
HE CAN'T HAVE GOTTEN FAR.
ROBO!
MEANWHILE, QUITE FAR...
MRF!
ROBO!
WHERE COULD HE *BE?*
BEN, C'MERE!
I THINK WE GOT SOME-THING.

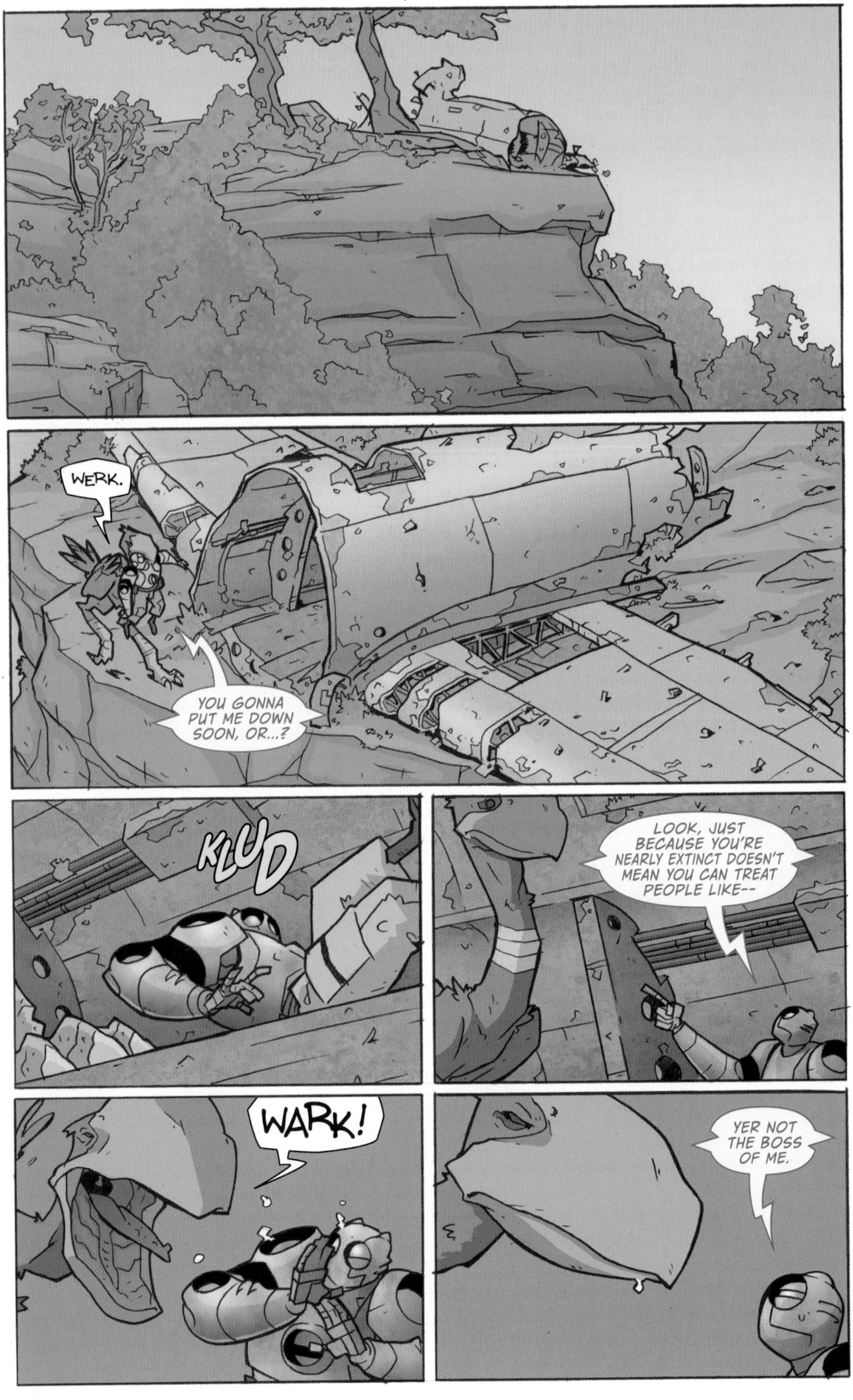
WERK.
YOU GONNA PUT ME DOWN SOON, OR...?
KLUD
LOOK, JUST BECAUSE YOU'RE NEARLY EXTINCT DOESN'T MEAN YOU CAN TREAT PEOPLE LIKE--
WARK!
YER NOT THE BOSS OF ME.

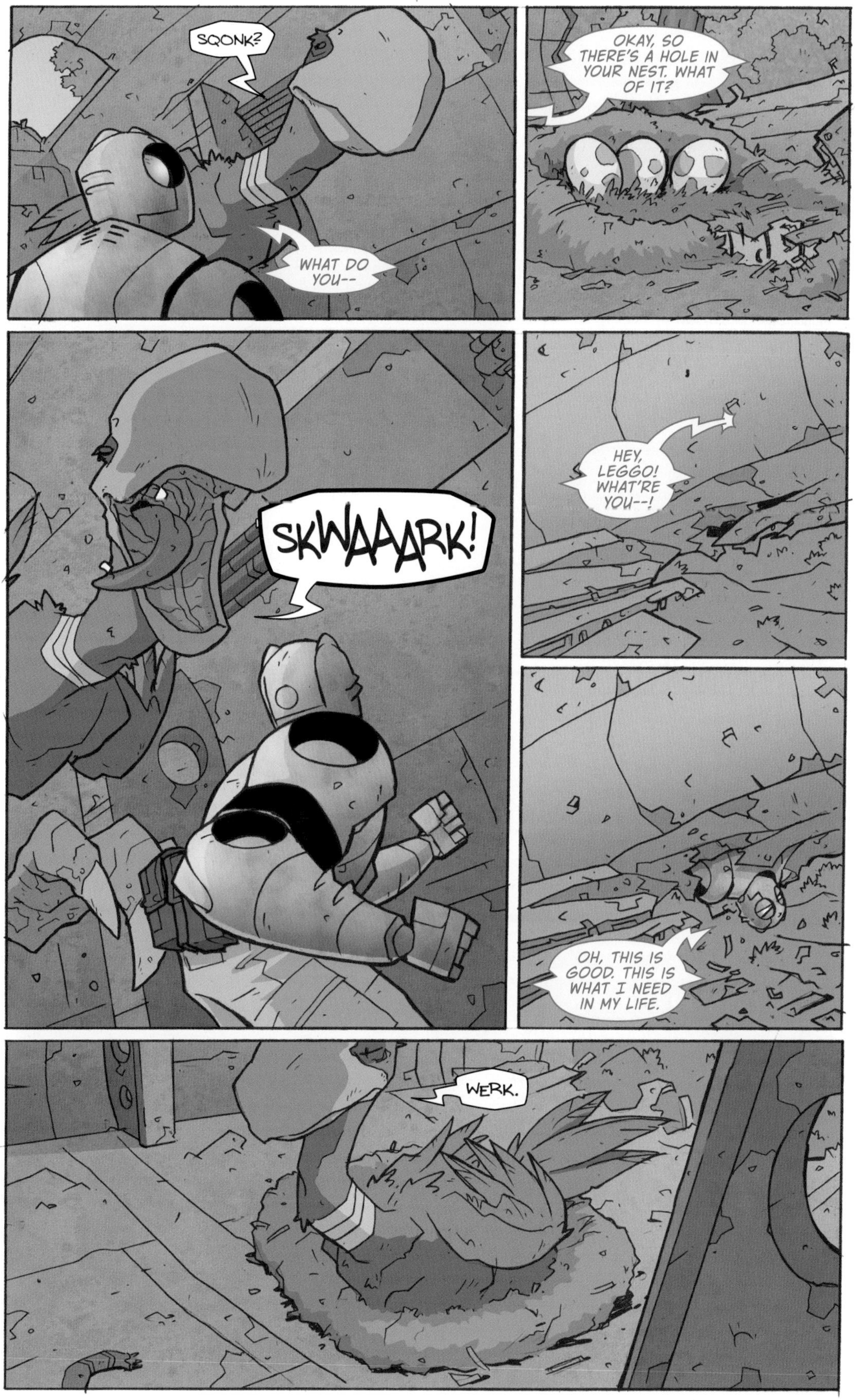
SQONK?
WHAT DO YOU--
OKAY, SO THERE'S A HOLE IN YOUR NEST. WHAT OF IT?
SKWAAARK!
HEY, LEGGO! WHAT'RE YOU--!
OH, THIS IS GOOD. THIS IS WHAT I NEED IN MY LIFE.
WERK.

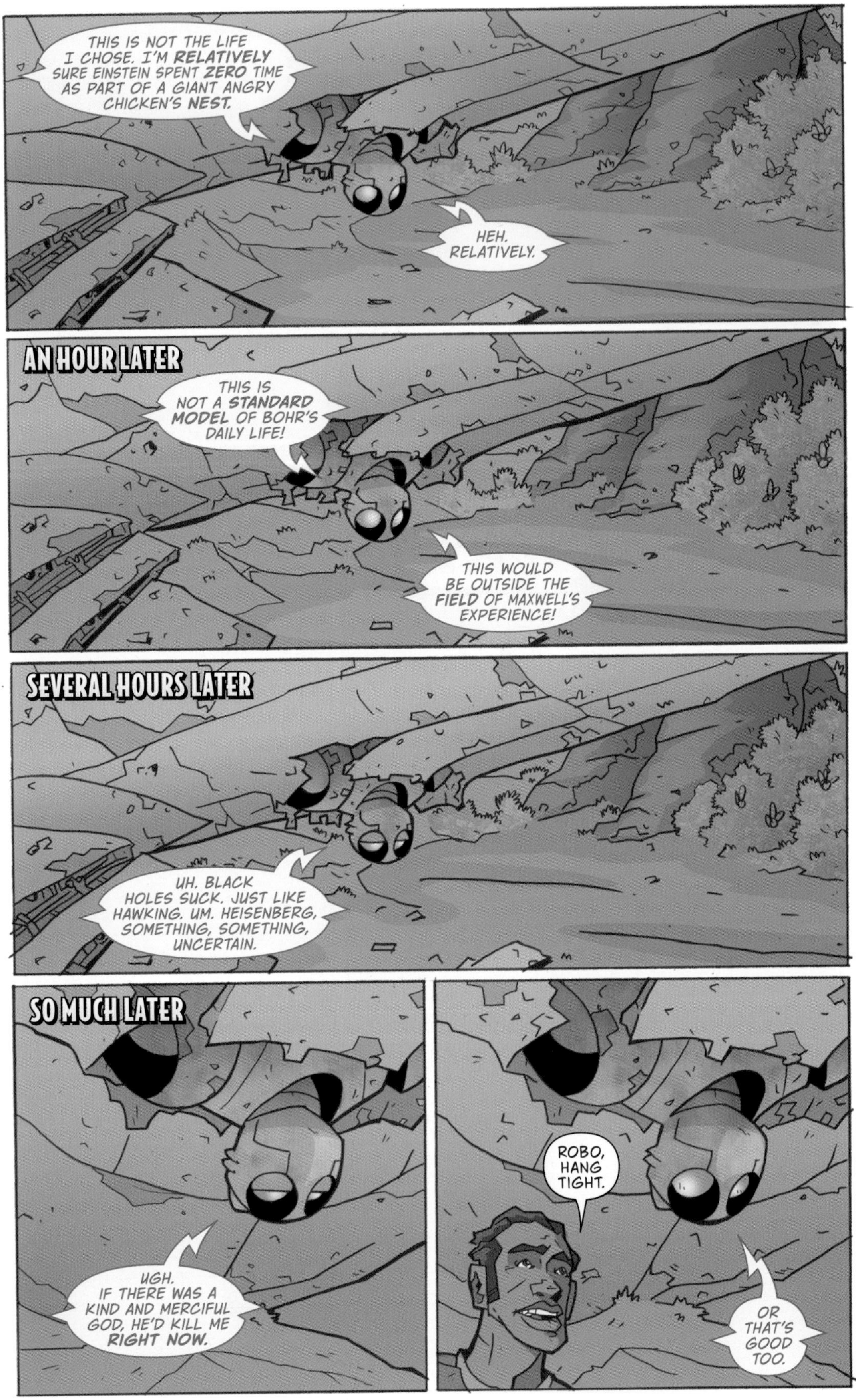
THIS IS NOT THE LIFE I CHOSE. I'M RELATIVELY SURE EINSTEIN SPENT ZERO TIME AS PART OF A GIANT ANGRY CHICKEN'S NEST.
HEH. RELATIVELY.
AN HOUR LATER
THIS IS NOT A STANDARD MODEL OF BOHR'S DAILY LIFE!
THIS WOULD BE OUTSIDE THE FIELD OF MAXWELL'S EXPERIENCE!
SEVERAL HOURS LATER
UH. BLACK HOLES SUCK. JUST LIKE HAWKING. UM. HEISENBERG, SOMETHING, SOMETHING, UNCERTAIN.
SO MUCH LATER
UGH. IF THERE WAS A KIND AND MERCIFUL GOD, HE'D KILL ME RIGHT NOW.
ROBO, HANG TIGHT.
OR THAT'S GOOD TOO.

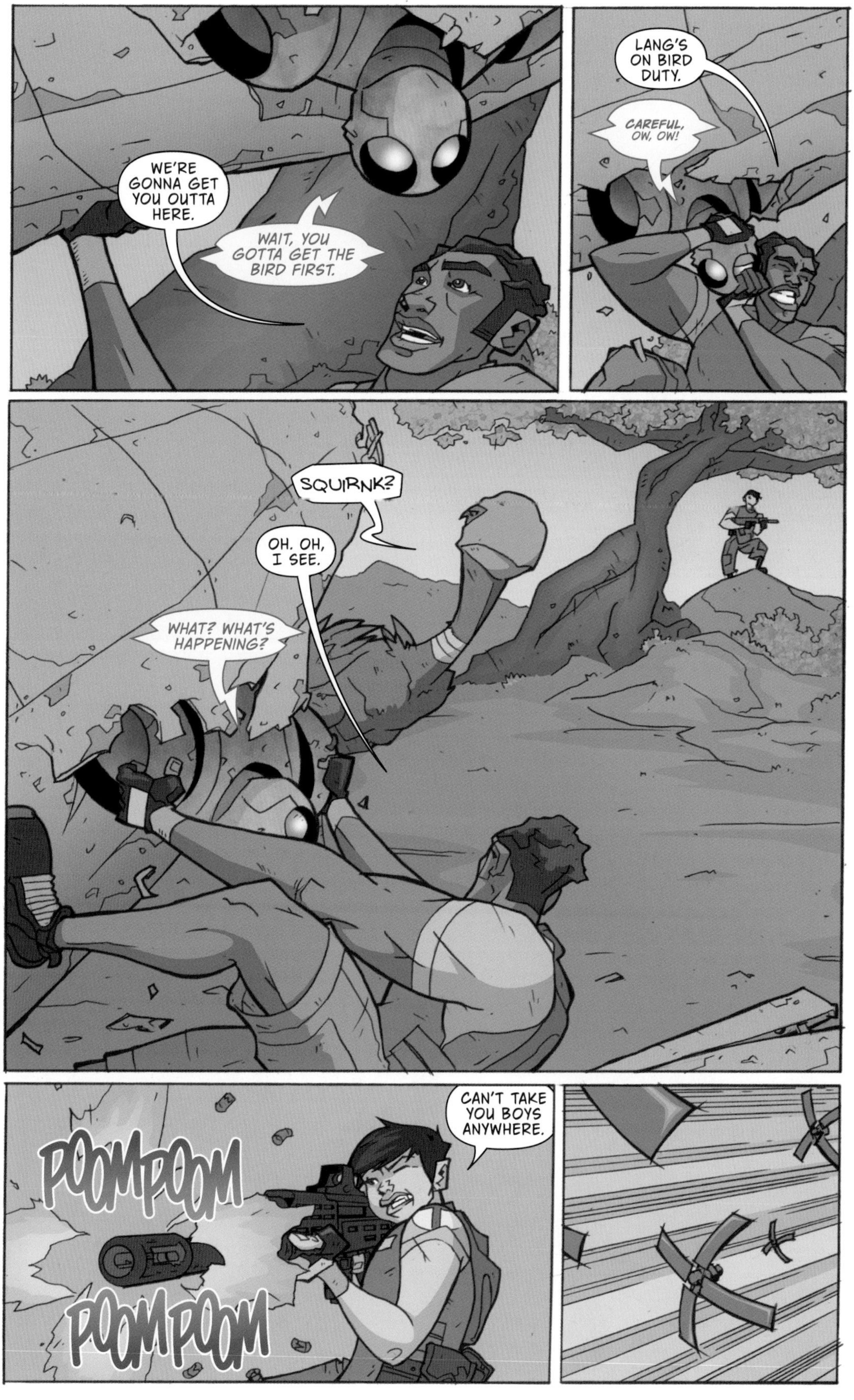
WE'RE GONNA GET YOU OUTTA HERE.
WAIT, YOU GOTTA GET THE BIRD FIRST.
LANG'S ON BIRD DUTY.
CAREFUL, OW, OW!
SQUIRNK?
OH. OH, I SEE.
WHAT? WHAT'S HAPPENING?
CAN'T TAKE YOU BOYS ANYWHERE.
POOMPOOM
POOMPOOM

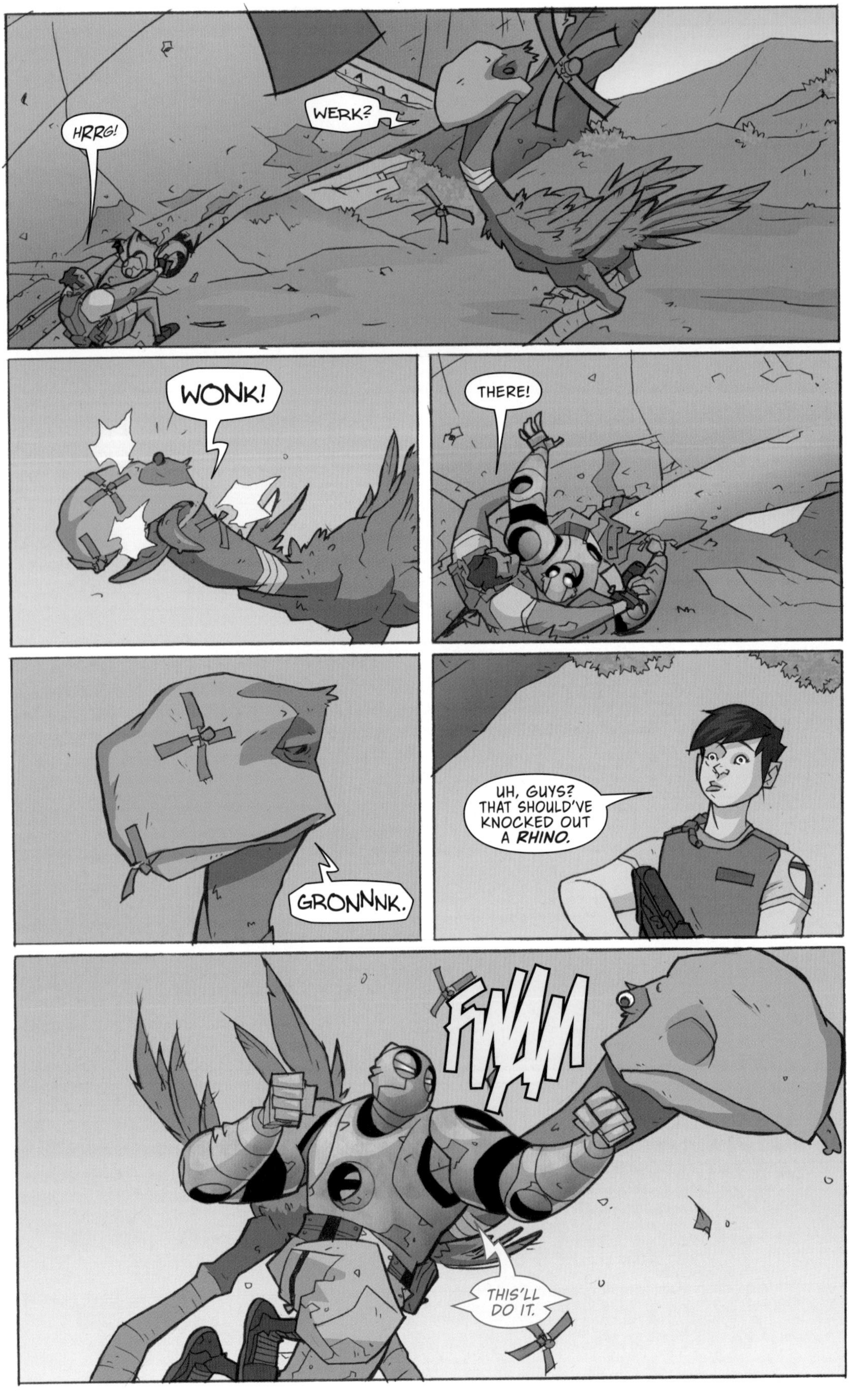
HRRG!
WERK?
WONK!
THERE!
GRONNNK.
UH, GUYS? THAT SHOULD'VE KNOCKED OUT A RHINO.
FWAM
THIS'LL DO IT.

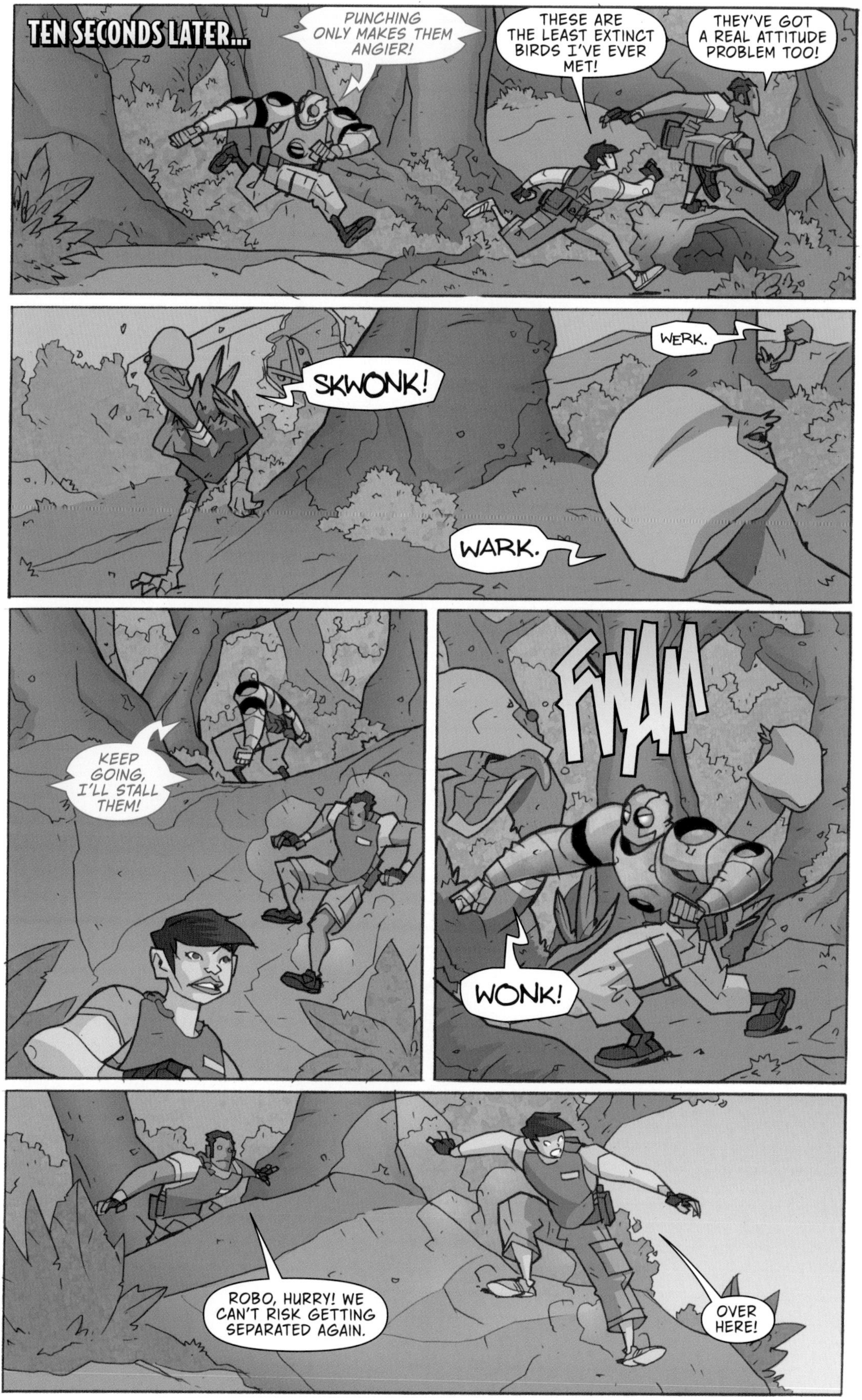
TEN SECONDS LATER...
PUNCHING ONLY MAKES THEM ANGIER!
THESE ARE THE LEAST EXTINCT BIRDS I'VE EVER MET!
THEY'VE GOT A REAL ATTITUDE PROBLEM TOO!
SKWONK!
WERK.
WARK.
KEEP GOING, I'LL STALL THEM!
FWAM
WONK!
ROBO, HURRY! WE CAN'T RISK GETTING SEPARATED AGAIN.
OVER HERE!

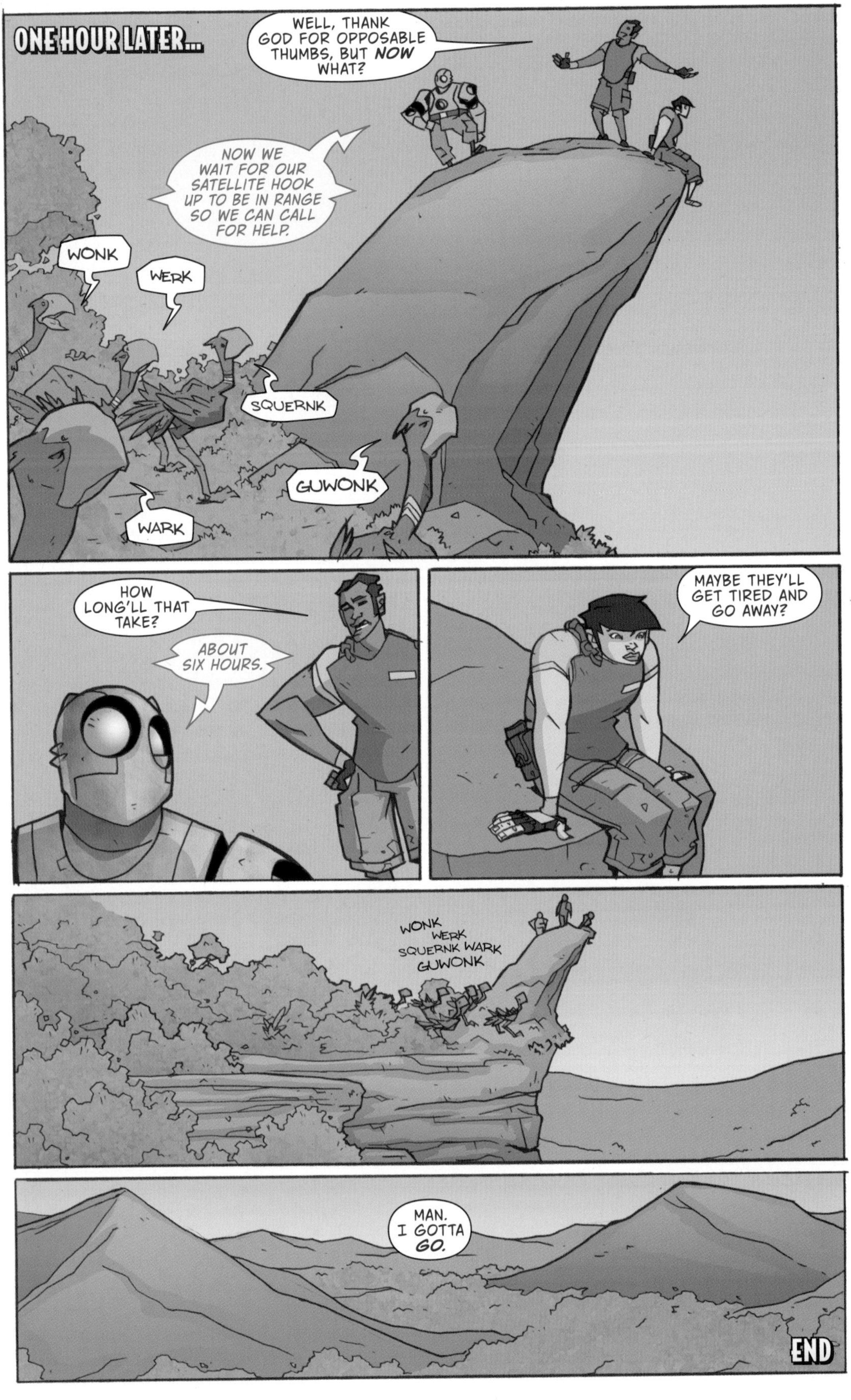
ONE HOUR LATER...
WELL, THANK GOD FOR OPPOSABLE THUMBS, BUT NOW WHAT?
NOW WE WAIT FOR OUR SATELLITE HOOK UP TO BE IN RANGE SO WE CAN CALL FOR HELP.
WONK
WERK
SQUERNK
GUWONK
WARK
HOW LONG'LL THAT TAKE?
ABOUT SIX HOURS.
MAYBE THEY'LL GET TIRED AND GO AWAY?
WONK WERK SQUERNK WARK GUWONK
MAN. I GOTTA GO.
END

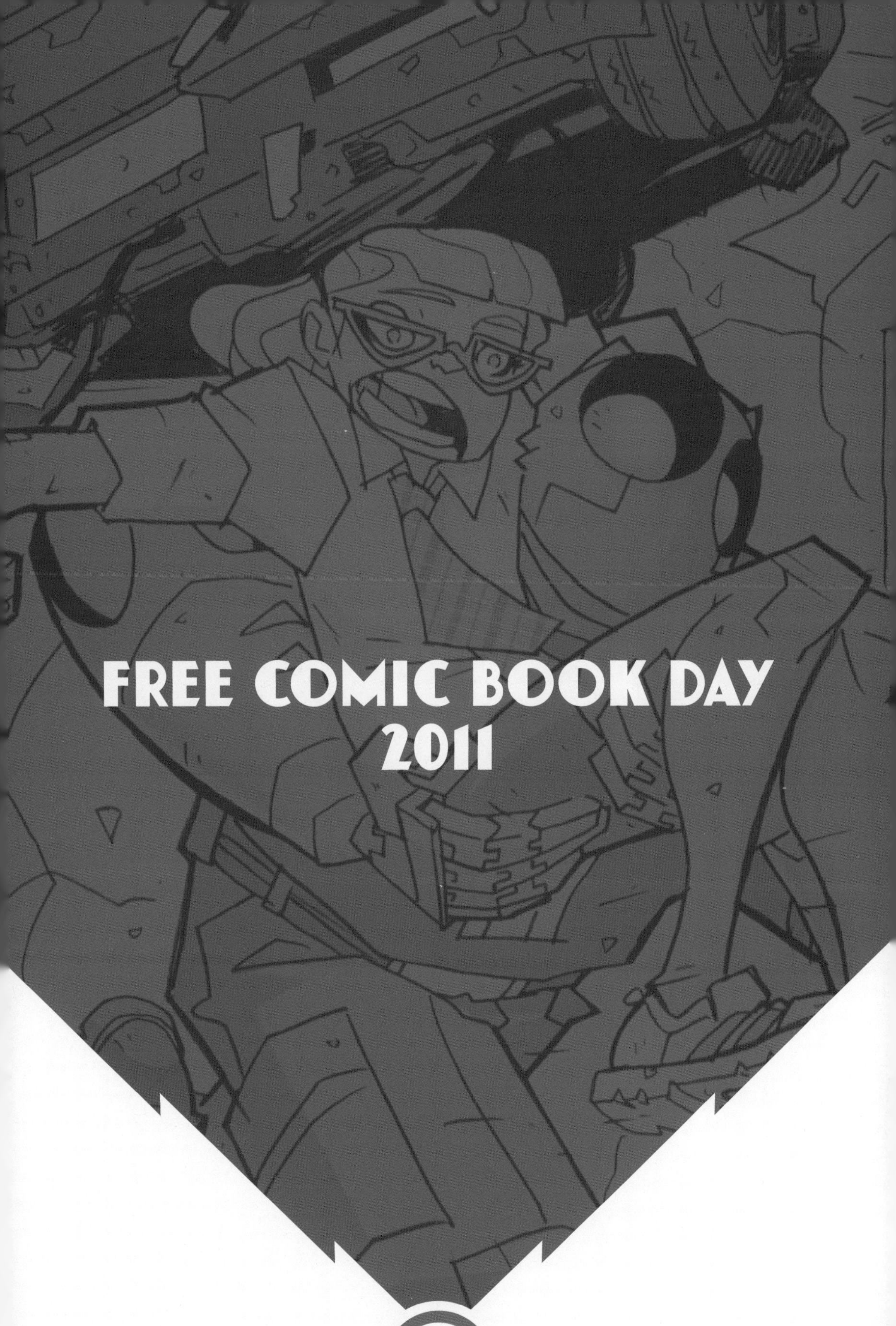
FREE COMIC BOOK DAY
2011

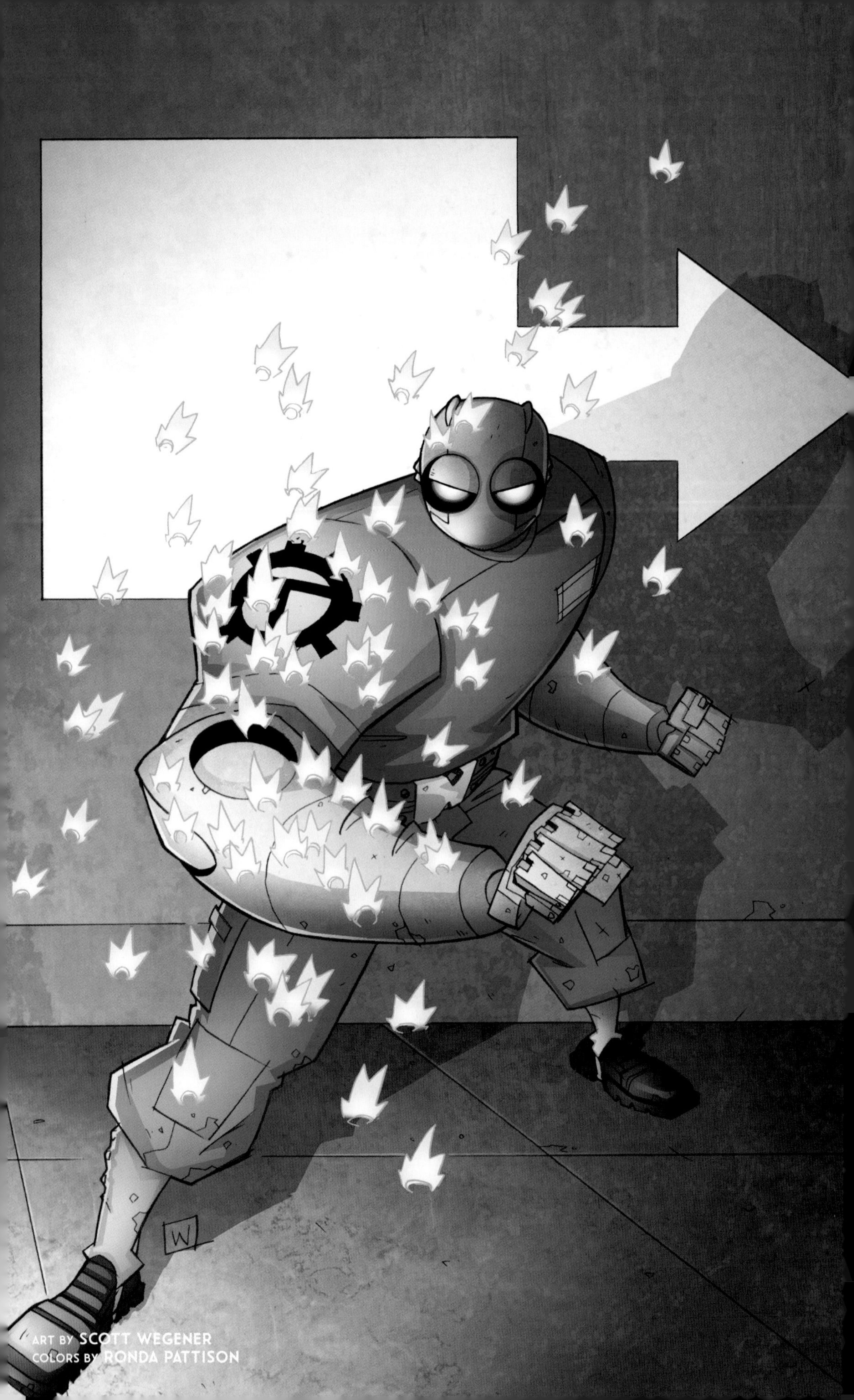
W

ART BY SCOTT WEGENER
COLORS BY RONDA PATTISON

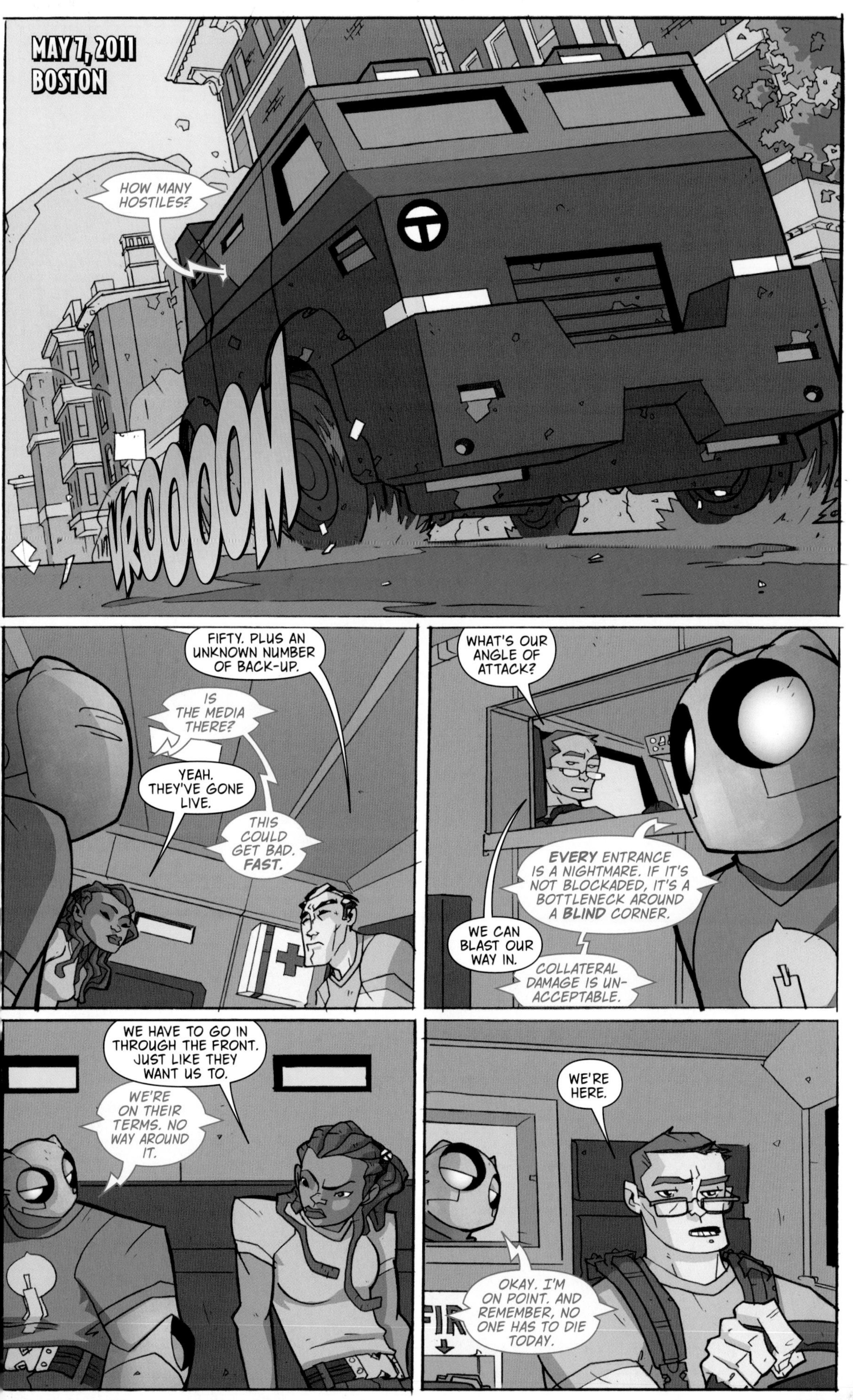
MAY 7, 2011
BOSTON
HOW MANY HOSTILES?
VROOOOM
FIFTY. PLUS AN UNKNOWN NUMBER OF BACK-UP.
IS THE MEDIA THERE?
YEAH. THEY'VE GONE LIVE.
THIS COULD GET BAD. FAST.
WHAT'S OUR ANGLE OF ATTACK?
EVERY ENTRANCE IS A NIGHTMARE. IF IT'S NOT BLOCKADED, IT'S A BOTTLENECK AROUND A BLIND CORNER.
WE CAN BLAST OUR WAY IN.
COLLATERAL DAMAGE IS UN-ACCEPTABLE.
WE HAVE TO GO IN THROUGH THE FRONT. JUST LIKE THEY WANT US TO.
WE'RE ON THEIR TERMS. NO WAY AROUND IT.
WE'RE HERE.
OKAY. I'M ON POINT. AND REMEMBER, NO ONE HAS TO DIE TODAY.

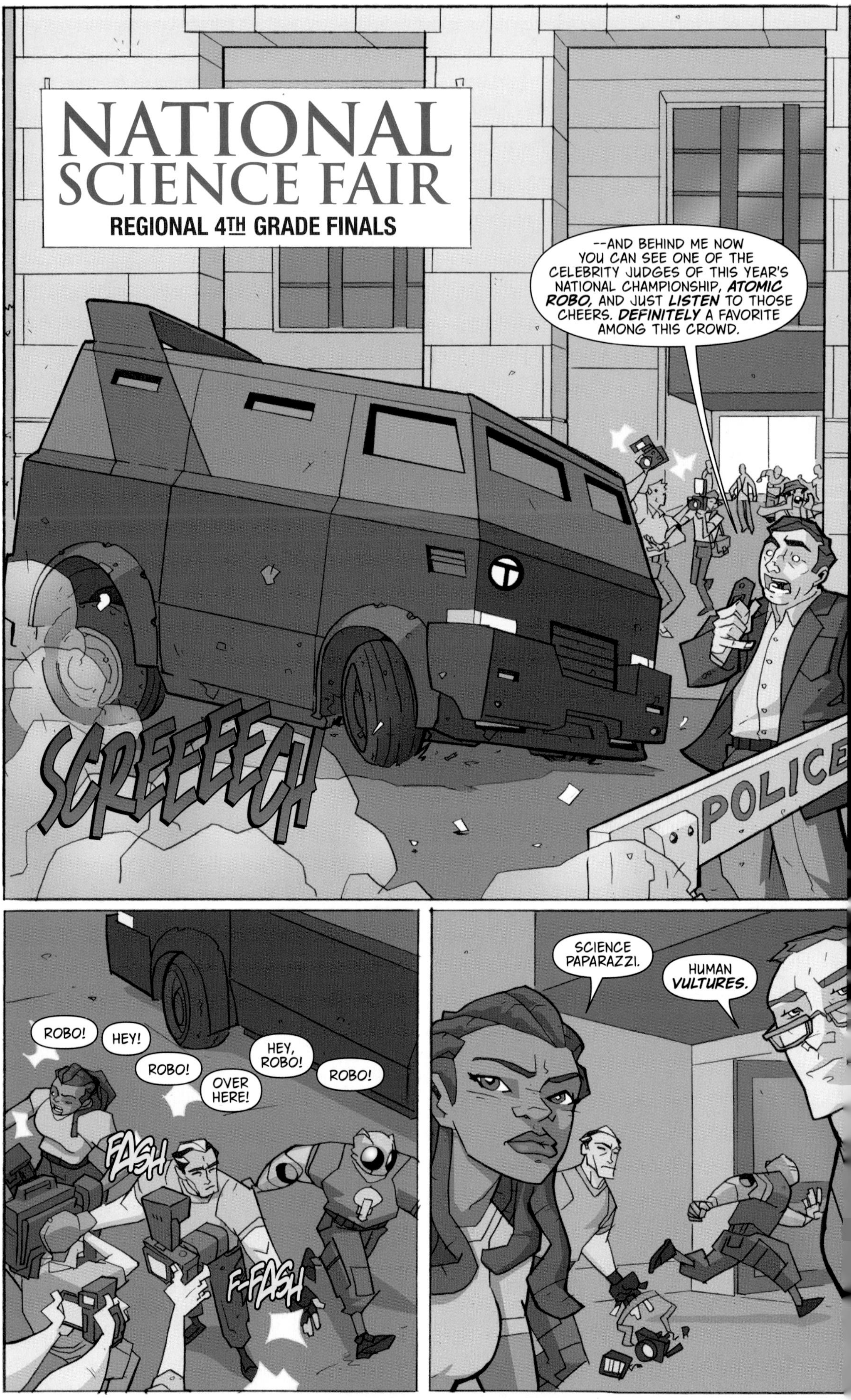
NATIONAL SCIENCE FAIR
REGIONAL 4TH GRADE FINALS
--AND BEHIND ME NOW YOU CAN SEE ONE OF THE CELEBRITY JUDGES OF THIS YEAR'S NATIONAL CHAMPIONSHIP, ATOMIC ROBO, AND JUST LISTEN TO THOSE CHEERS. DEFINITELY A FAVORITE AMONG THIS CROWD.
SCREEEECH
POLICE
ROBO!
HEY!
ROBO!
OVER HERE!
HEY, ROBO!
ROBO!
FASH
F-FASH
SCIENCE PAPARAZZI.
HUMAN VULTURES.

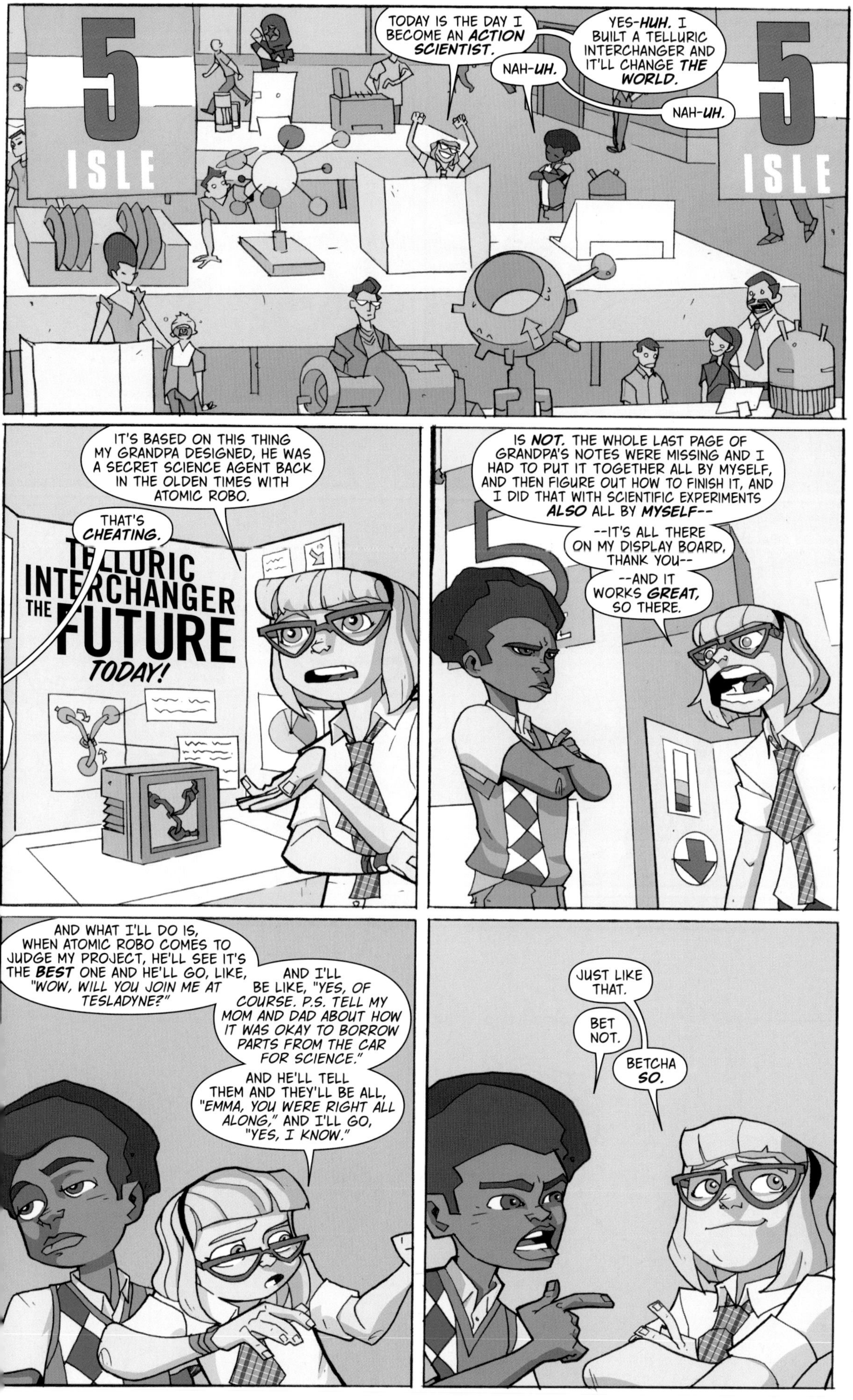
5
ISLE
TODAY IS THE DAY I BECOME AN *ACTION SCIENTIST.*
NAH-*UH.*
YES-*HUH.* I BUILT A TELLURIC INTERCHANGER AND IT'LL CHANGE *THE WORLD.*
NAH-*UH.*
5
ISLE
IT'S BASED ON THIS THING MY GRANDPA DESIGNED, HE WAS A SECRET SCIENCE AGENT BACK IN THE OLDEN TIMES WITH ATOMIC ROBO.
THAT'S *CHEATING.*
TELLURIC INTERCHANGER THE FUTURE TODAY!
IS *NOT.* THE WHOLE LAST PAGE OF GRANDPA'S NOTES WERE MISSING AND I HAD TO PUT IT TOGETHER ALL BY MYSELF, AND THEN FIGURE OUT HOW TO FINISH IT, AND I DID THAT WITH SCIENTIFIC EXPERIMENTS *ALSO* ALL BY *MYSELF--*
--IT'S ALL THERE ON MY DISPLAY BOARD, THANK YOU--
--AND IT WORKS *GREAT,* SO THERE.
AND WHAT I'LL DO IS, WHEN ATOMIC ROBO COMES TO JUDGE MY PROJECT, HE'LL SEE IT'S THE *BEST* ONE AND HE'LL GO, LIKE, *"WOW, WILL YOU JOIN ME AT TESLADYNE?"*
AND I'LL BE LIKE, *"YES, OF COURSE. P.S. TELL MY MOM AND DAD ABOUT HOW IT WAS OKAY TO BORROW PARTS FROM THE CAR FOR SCIENCE."*
AND HE'LL TELL THEM AND THEY'LL BE ALL, *"EMMA, YOU WERE RIGHT ALL ALONG,"* AND I'LL GO, *"YES, I KNOW."*
JUST LIKE THAT.
BET NOT.
BETCHA *SO.*

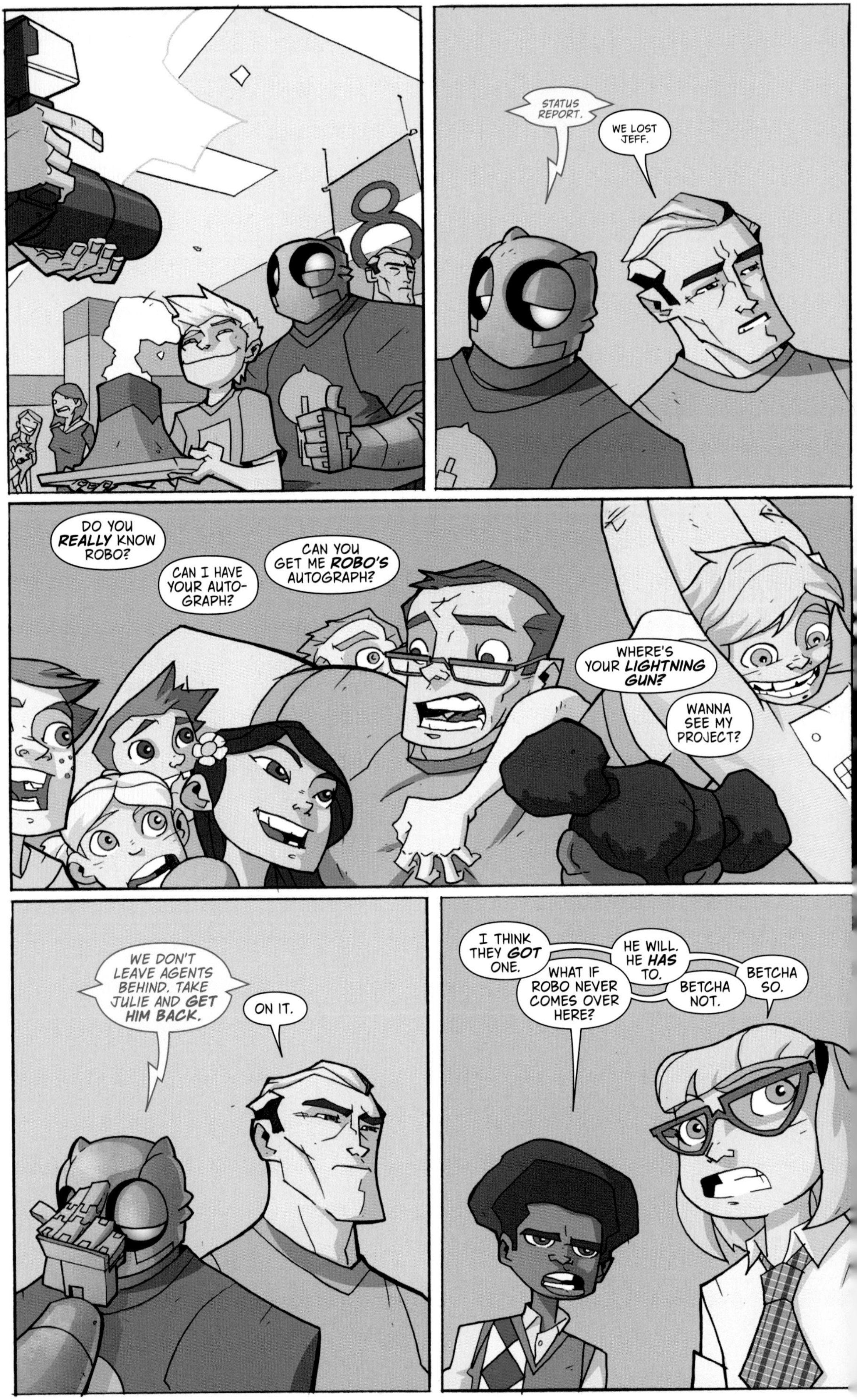
STATUS REPORT.
WE LOST JEFF.
DO YOU REALLY KNOW ROBO?
CAN I HAVE YOUR AUTO-GRAPH?
CAN YOU GET ME ROBO'S AUTOGRAPH?
WHERE'S YOUR LIGHTNING GUN?
WANNA SEE MY PROJECT?
WE DON'T LEAVE AGENTS BEHIND. TAKE JULIE AND GET HIM BACK.
ON IT.
I THINK THEY GOT ONE.
WHAT IF ROBO NEVER COMES OVER HERE?
HE WILL. HE HAS TO.
BETCHA NOT.
BETCHA SO.

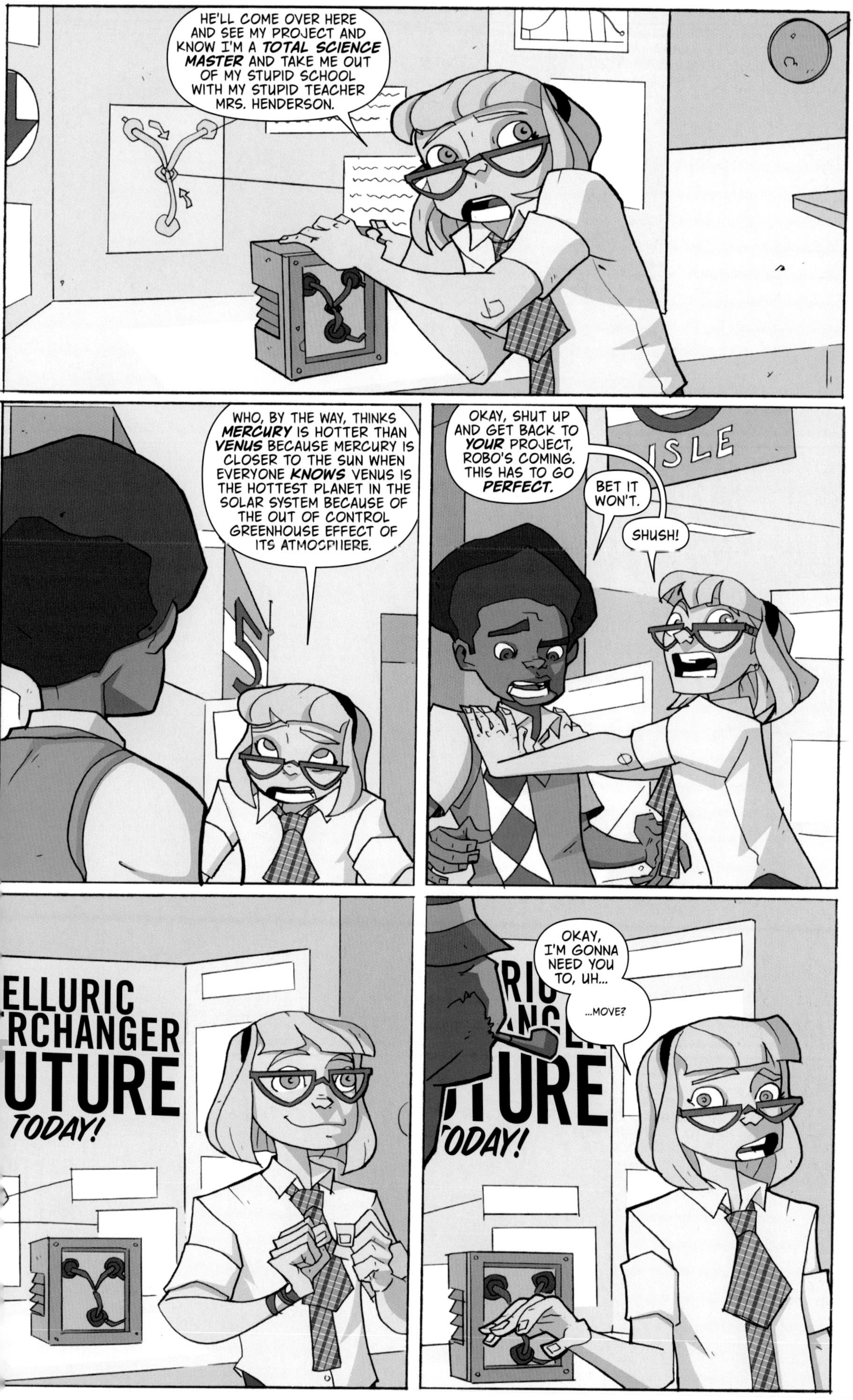
HE'LL COME OVER HERE AND SEE MY PROJECT AND KNOW I'M A TOTAL SCIENCE MASTER AND TAKE ME OUT OF MY STUPID SCHOOL WITH MY STUPID TEACHER MRS. HENDERSON.
WHO, BY THE WAY, THINKS MERCURY IS HOTTER THAN VENUS BECAUSE MERCURY IS CLOSER TO THE SUN WHEN EVERYONE KNOWS VENUS IS THE HOTTEST PLANET IN THE SOLAR SYSTEM BECAUSE OF THE OUT OF CONTROL GREENHOUSE EFFECT OF ITS ATMOSPHERE.
ISLE
OKAY, SHUT UP AND GET BACK TO YOUR PROJECT, ROBO'S COMING. THIS HAS TO GO PERFECT.
BET IT WON'T.
SHUSH!
ELLURIC
RCHANGER
UTURE
TODAY!
OKAY, I'M GONNA NEED YOU TO, UH...
...MOVE?

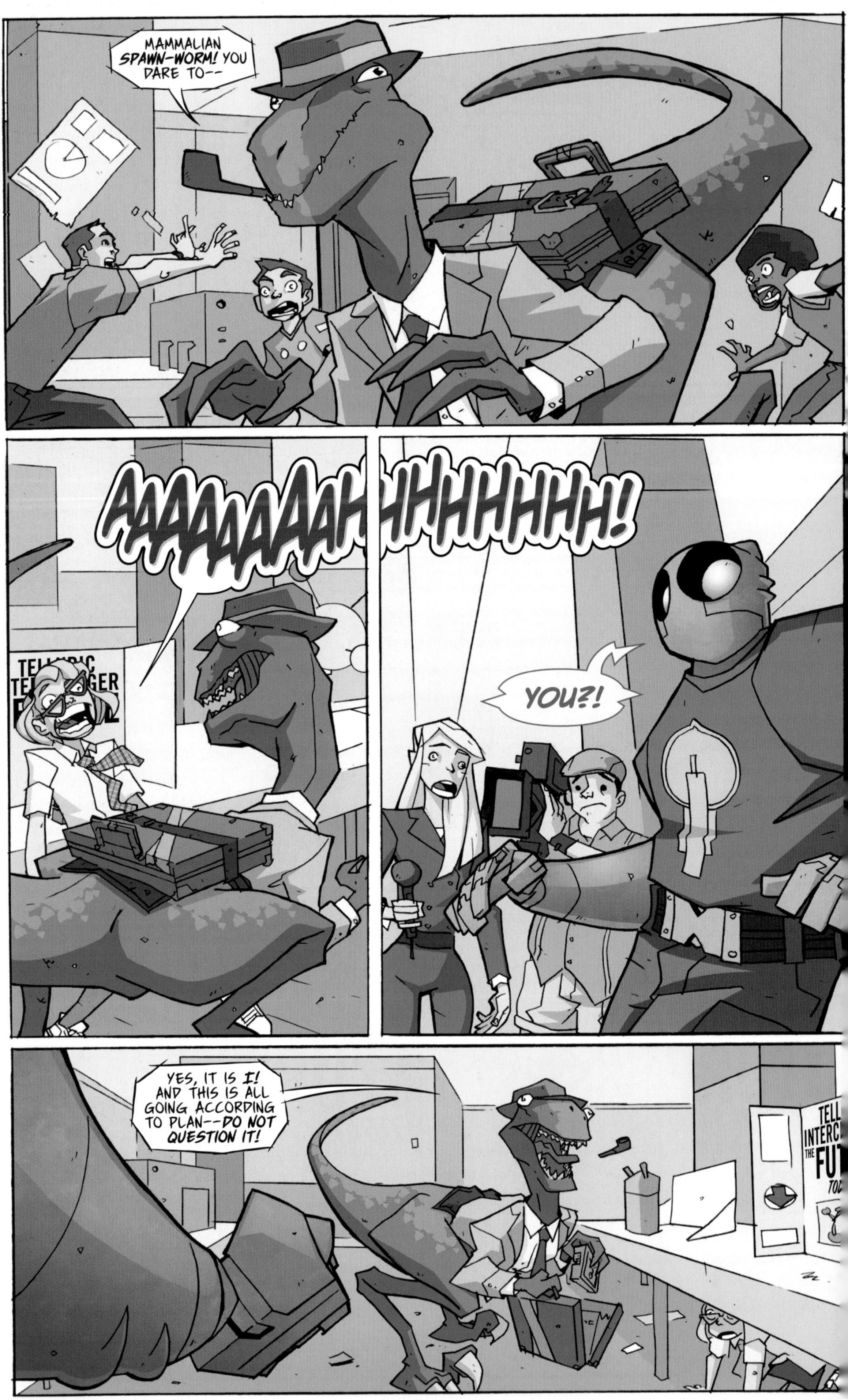
MAMMALIAN SPAWN-WORM! YOU DARE TO--
AAAAAAAAHHHHHHHH!
YOU?!
YES, IT IS I! AND THIS IS ALL GOING ACCORDING TO PLAN--DO NOT QUESTION IT!

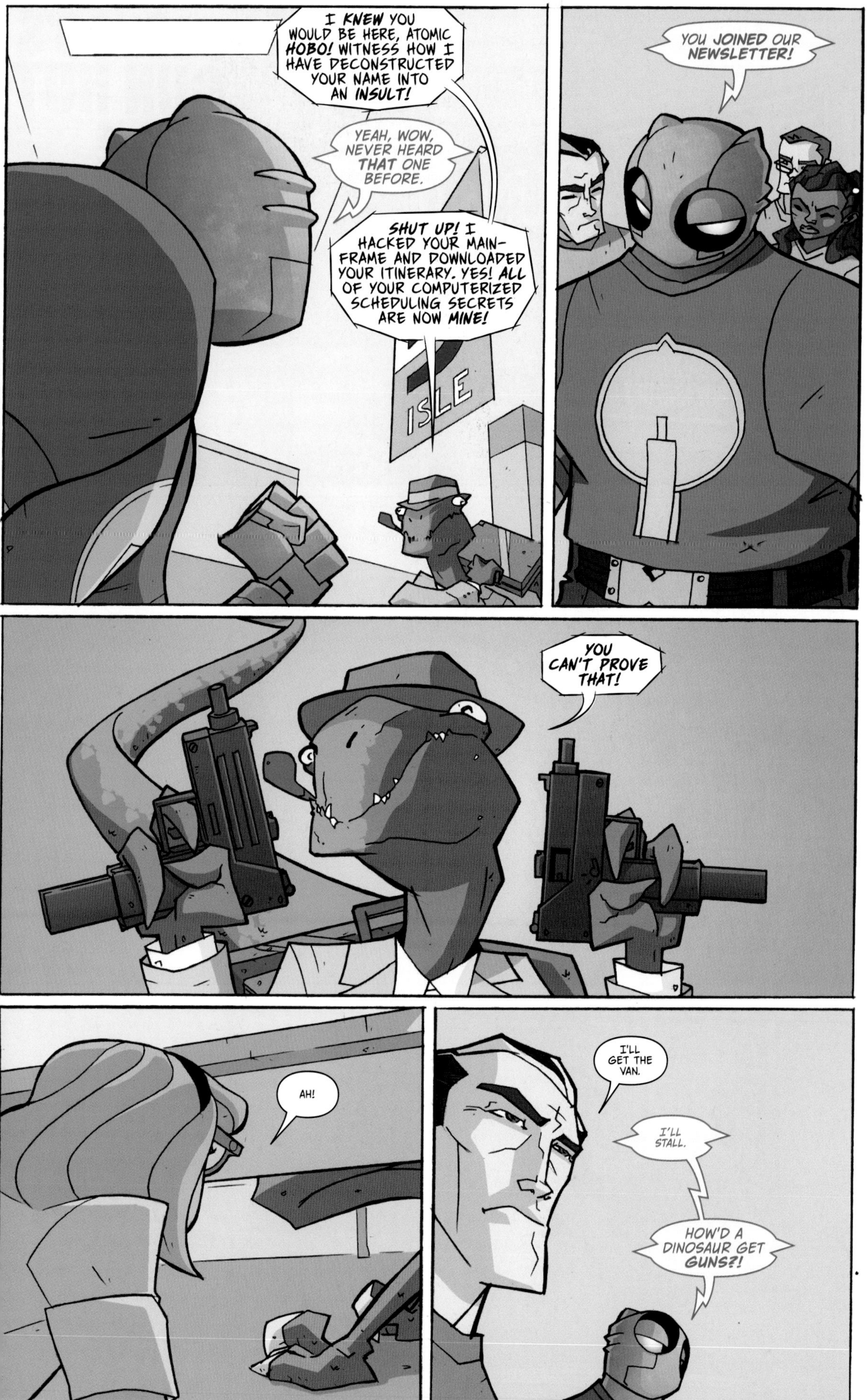
I KNEW YOU WOULD BE HERE, ATOMIC HOBO! WITNESS HOW I HAVE DECONSTRUCTED YOUR NAME INTO AN INSULT!
YEAH, WOW, NEVER HEARD THAT ONE BEFORE.
SHUT UP! I HACKED YOUR MAIN-FRAME AND DOWNLOADED YOUR ITINERARY. YES! ALL OF YOUR COMPUTERIZED SCHEDULING SECRETS ARE NOW MINE!
ISLE
YOU JOINED OUR NEWSLETTER!
YOU CAN'T PROVE THAT!
AH!
I'LL GET THE VAN.
I'LL STALL.
HOW'D A DINOSAUR GET GUNS?!

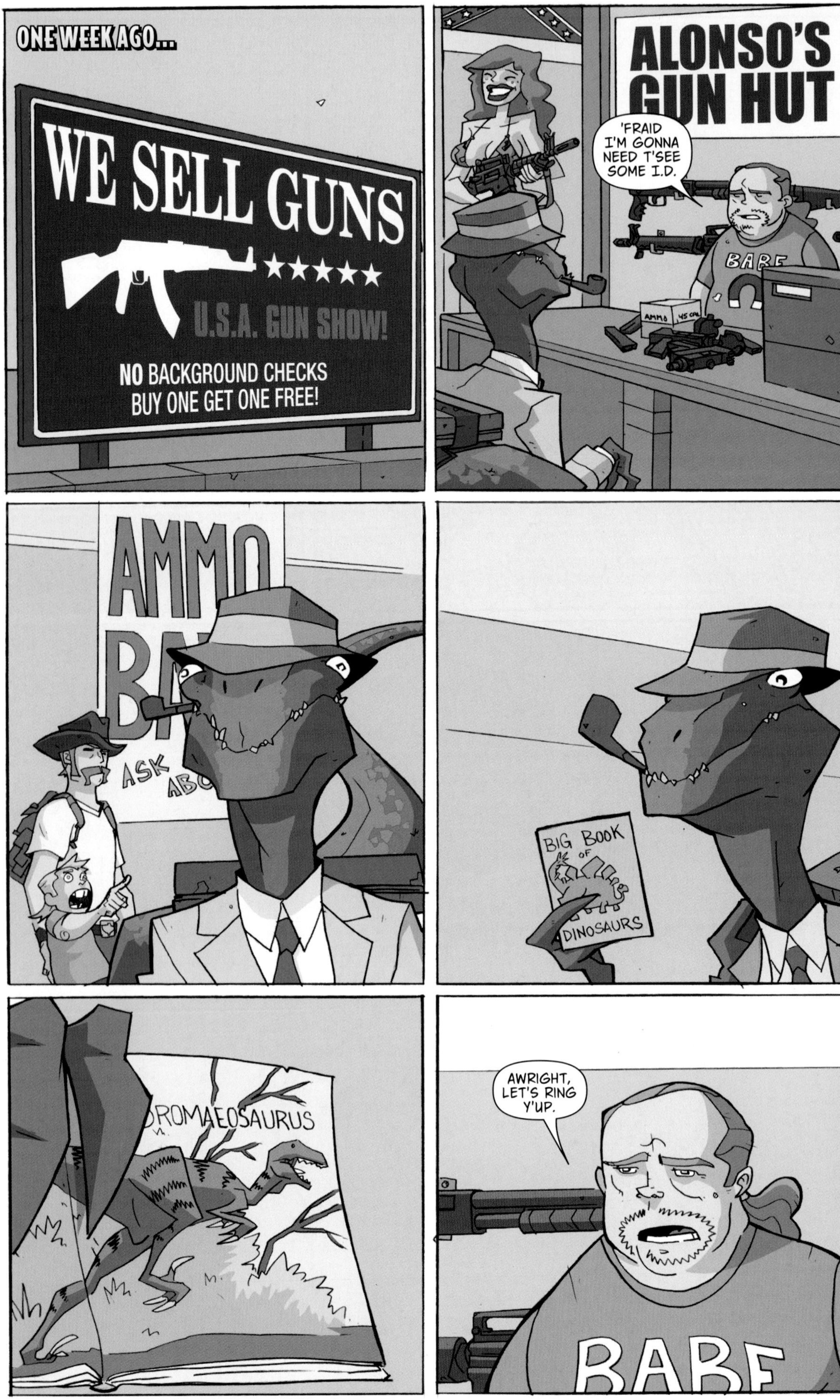
ONE WEEK AGO...
WE SELL GUNS
U.S.A. GUN SHOW!
NO BACKGROUND CHECKS
BUY ONE GET ONE FREE!
ALONSO'S GUN HUT
'FRAID I'M GONNA NEED T'SEE SOME I.D.
AMMO
.45 CAL
AMMO
ASK
BIG BOOK OF DINOSAURS
ROMAEOSAURUS
AWRIGHT, LET'S RING Y'UP.

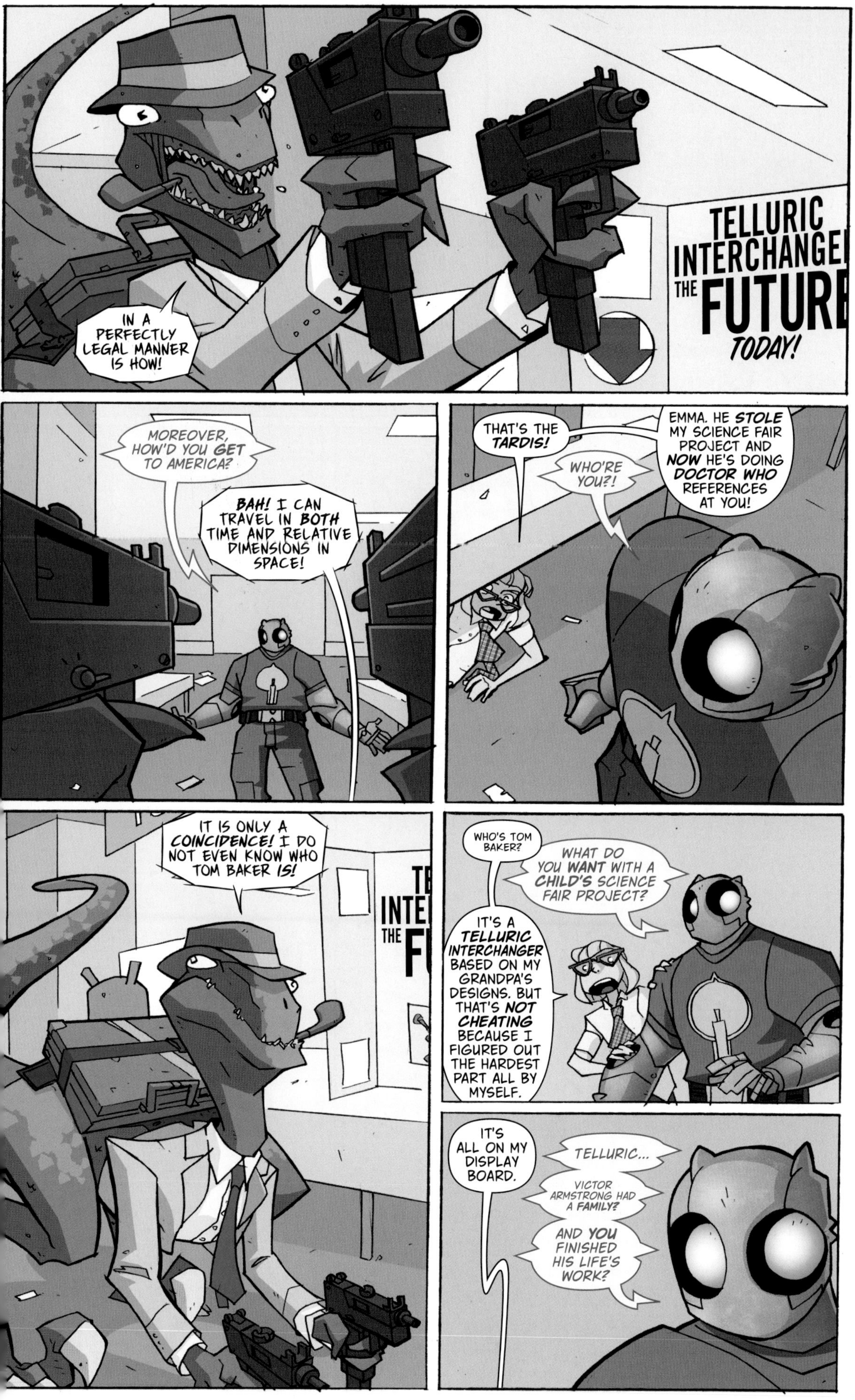
TELLURIC INTERCHANGER THE FUTURE TODAY!
IN A PERFECTLY LEGAL MANNER IS HOW!
MOREOVER, HOW'D YOU GET TO AMERICA?
BAH! I CAN TRAVEL IN BOTH TIME AND RELATIVE DIMENSIONS IN SPACE!
THAT'S THE TARDIS!
WHO'RE YOU?!
EMMA. HE STOLE MY SCIENCE FAIR PROJECT AND NOW HE'S DOING DOCTOR WHO REFERENCES AT YOU!
IT IS ONLY A COINCIDENCE! I DO NOT EVEN KNOW WHO TOM BAKER IS!
WHO'S TOM BAKER?
WHAT DO YOU WANT WITH A CHILD'S SCIENCE FAIR PROJECT?
IT'S A TELLURIC INTERCHANGER BASED ON MY GRANDPA'S DESIGNS. BUT THAT'S NOT CHEATING BECAUSE I FIGURED OUT THE HARDEST PART ALL BY MYSELF.
IT'S ALL ON MY DISPLAY BOARD.
TELLURIC...
VICTOR ARMSTRONG HAD A FAMILY?
AND YOU FINISHED HIS LIFE'S WORK?

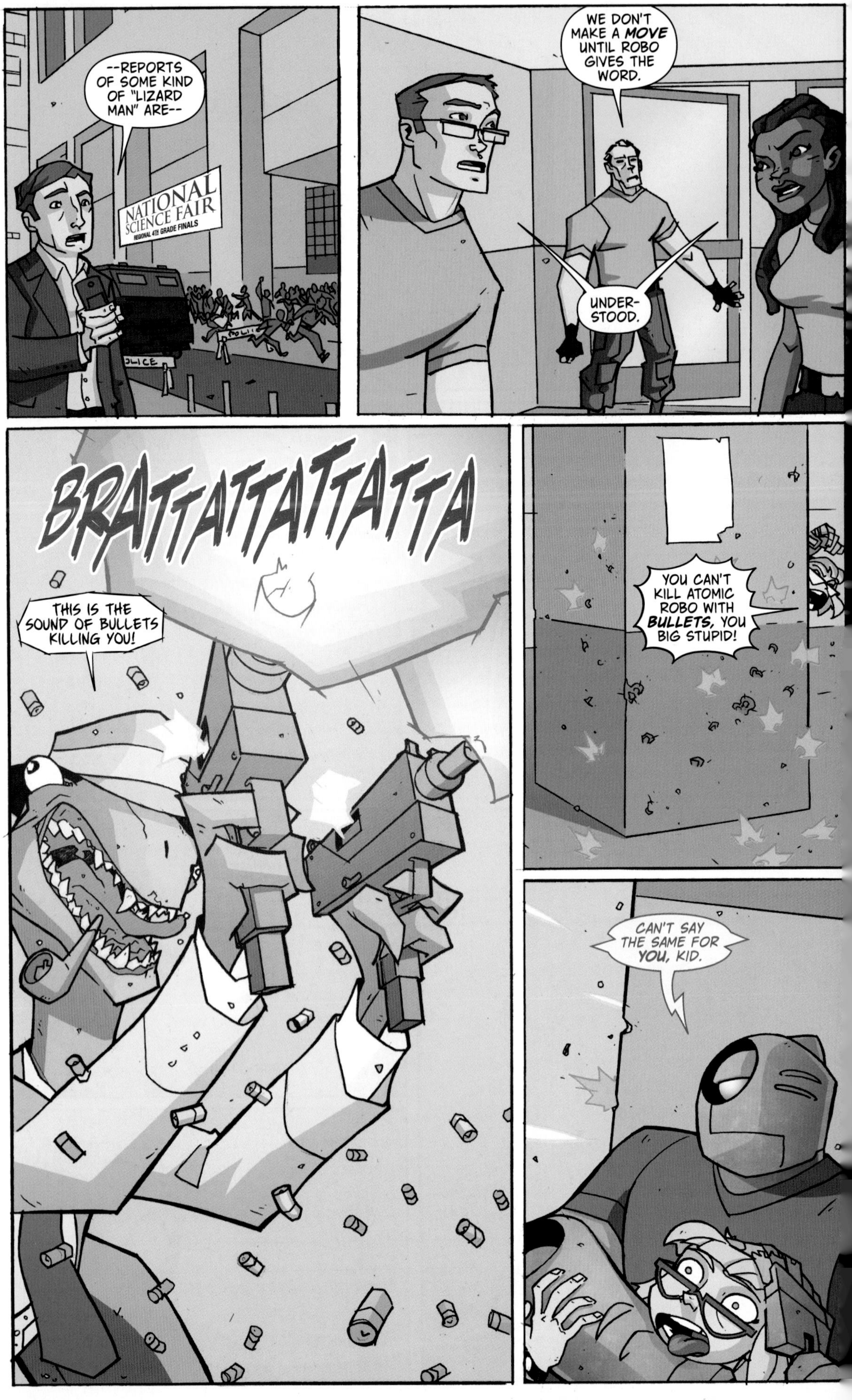
--REPORTS OF SOME KIND OF "LIZARD MAN" ARE--
NATIONAL SCIENCE FAIR
REGIONAL 4TH GRADE FINALS
WE DON'T MAKE A MOVE UNTIL ROBO GIVES THE WORD.
UNDER-STOOD.
BRATTATTATTATTA
THIS IS THE SOUND OF BULLETS KILLING YOU!
YOU CAN'T KILL ATOMIC ROBO WITH BULLETS, YOU BIG STUPID!
CAN'T SAY THE SAME FOR YOU, KID.

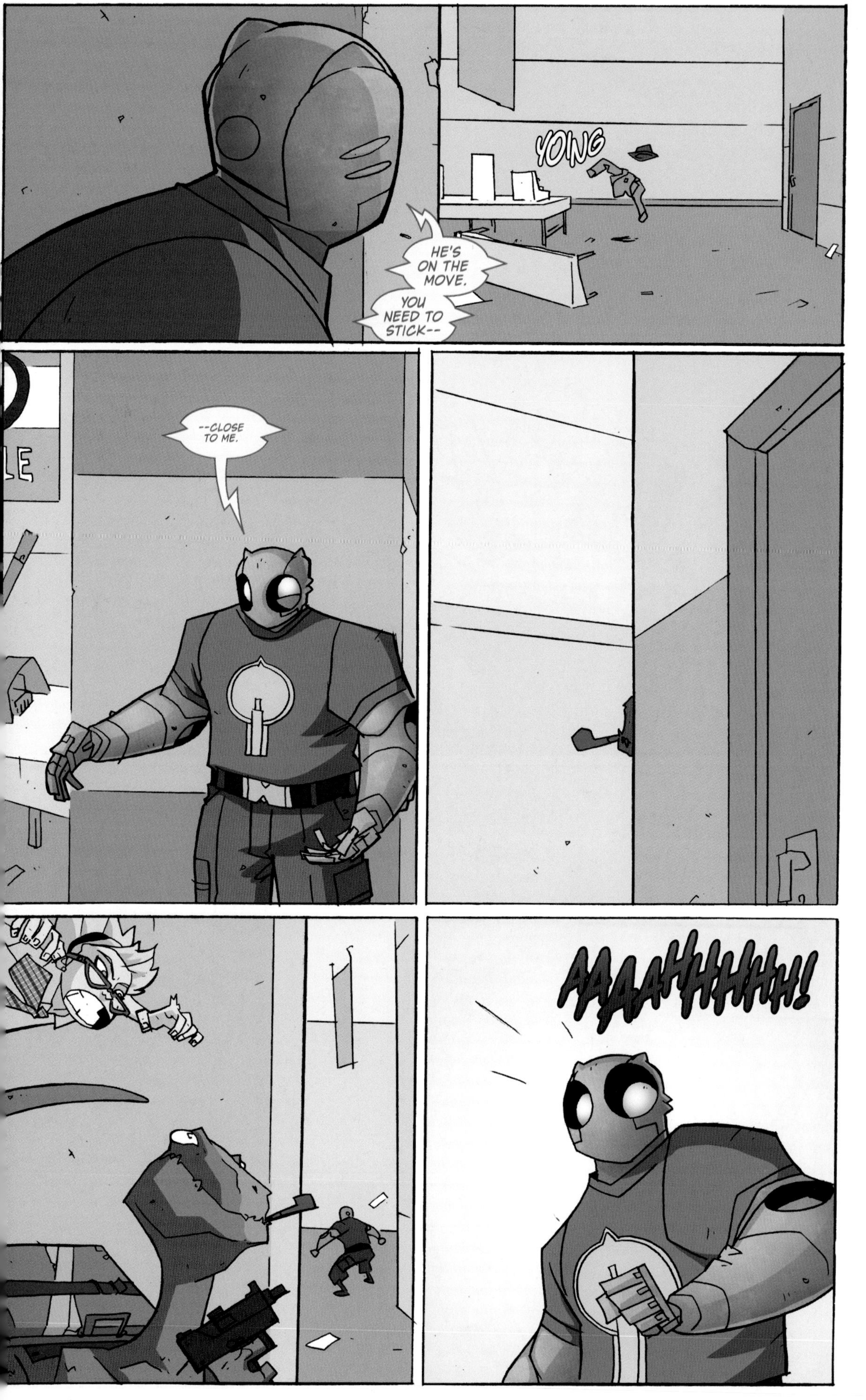
YOING
HE'S ON THE MOVE.
YOU NEED TO STICK--
--CLOSE TO ME.
AAAAHHHHH!

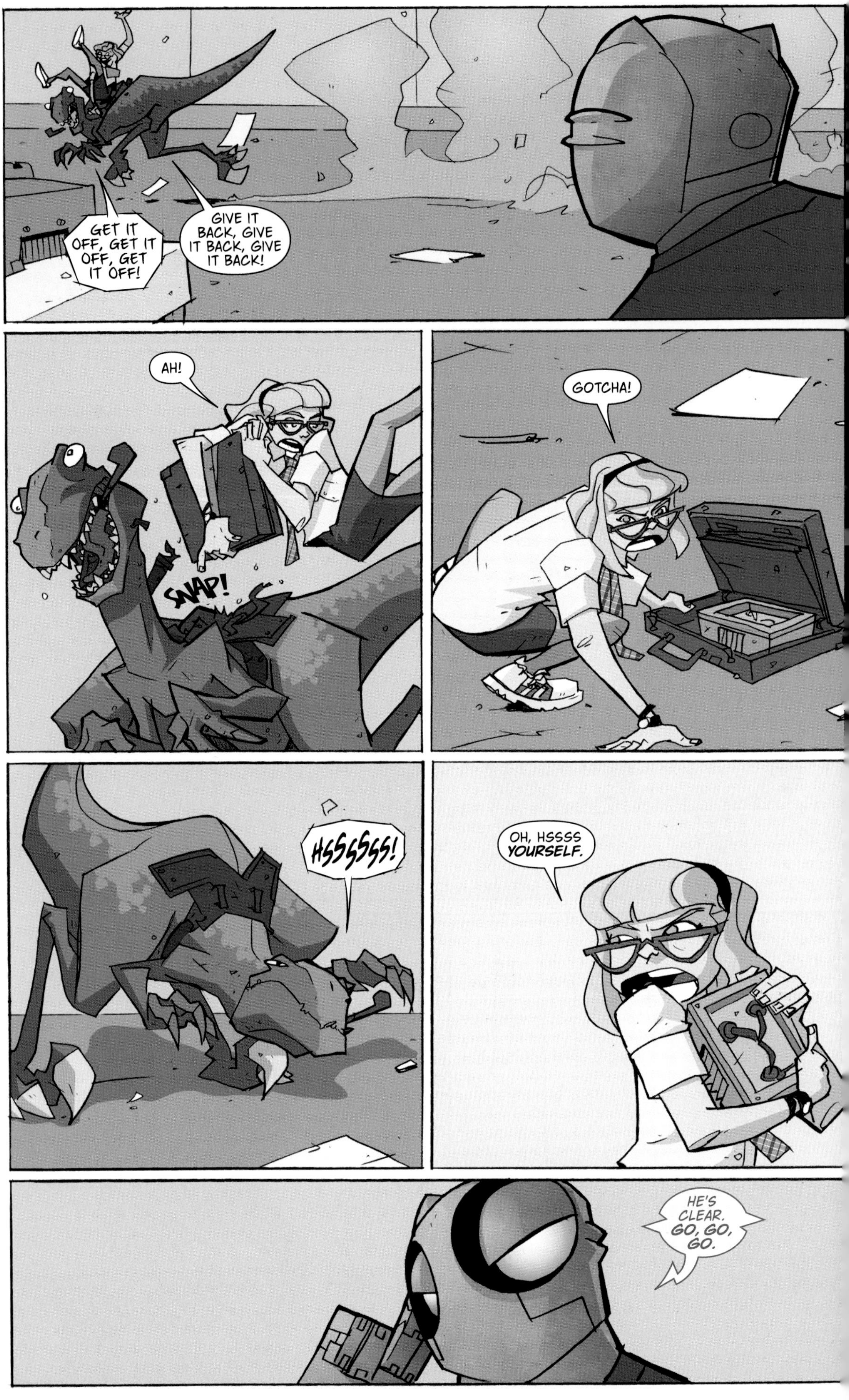

GET IT OFF, GET IT OFF, GET IT OFF!
GIVE IT BACK, GIVE IT BACK, GIVE IT BACK!
AH!
SNAP!
GOTCHA!
HSSSSSS!
OH, HSSSS YOURSELF.
HE'S CLEAR. GO, GO, GO.

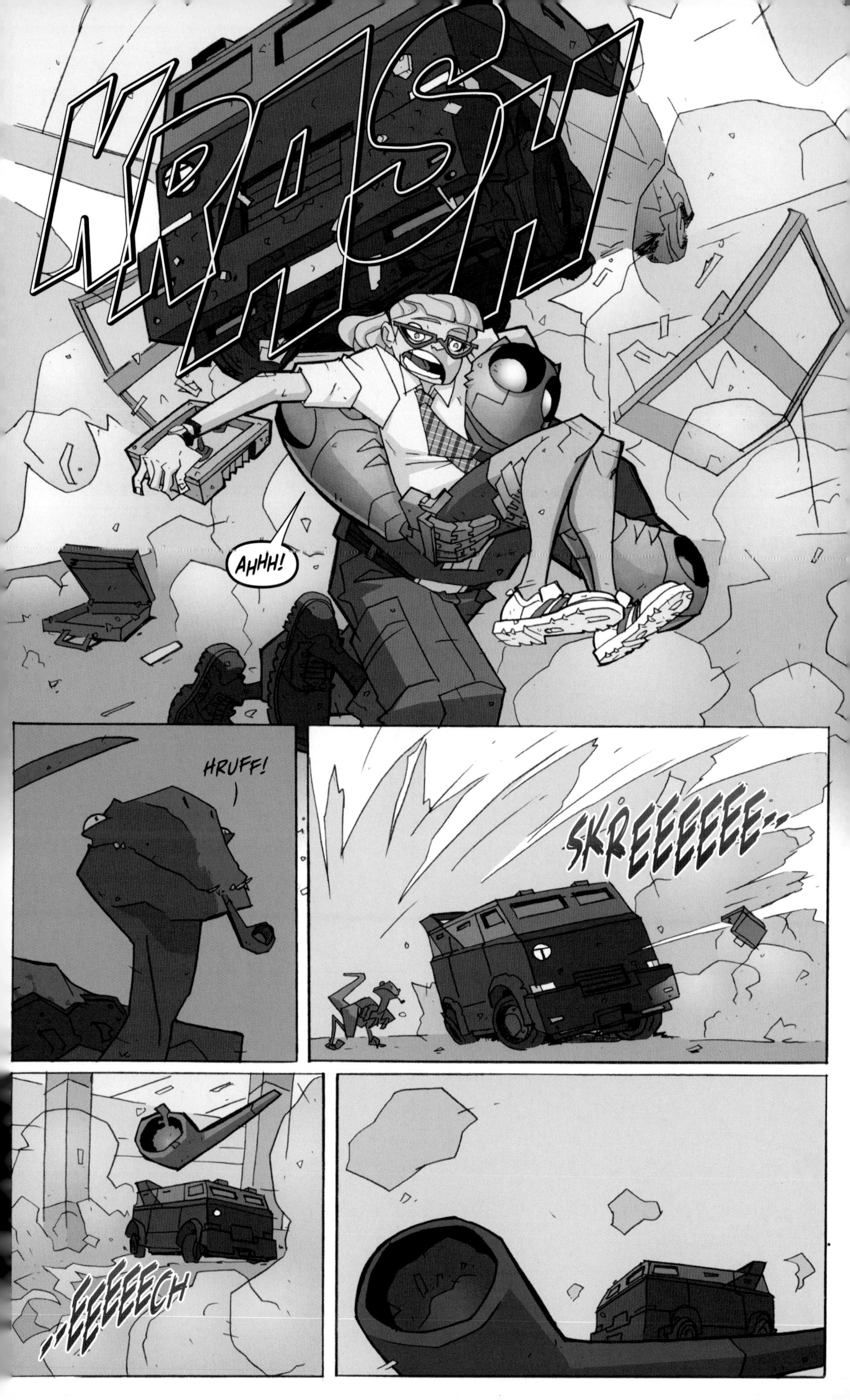
KRASH
AHHH!
HRUFF!
SKREEEEEE--
--EEEEECH

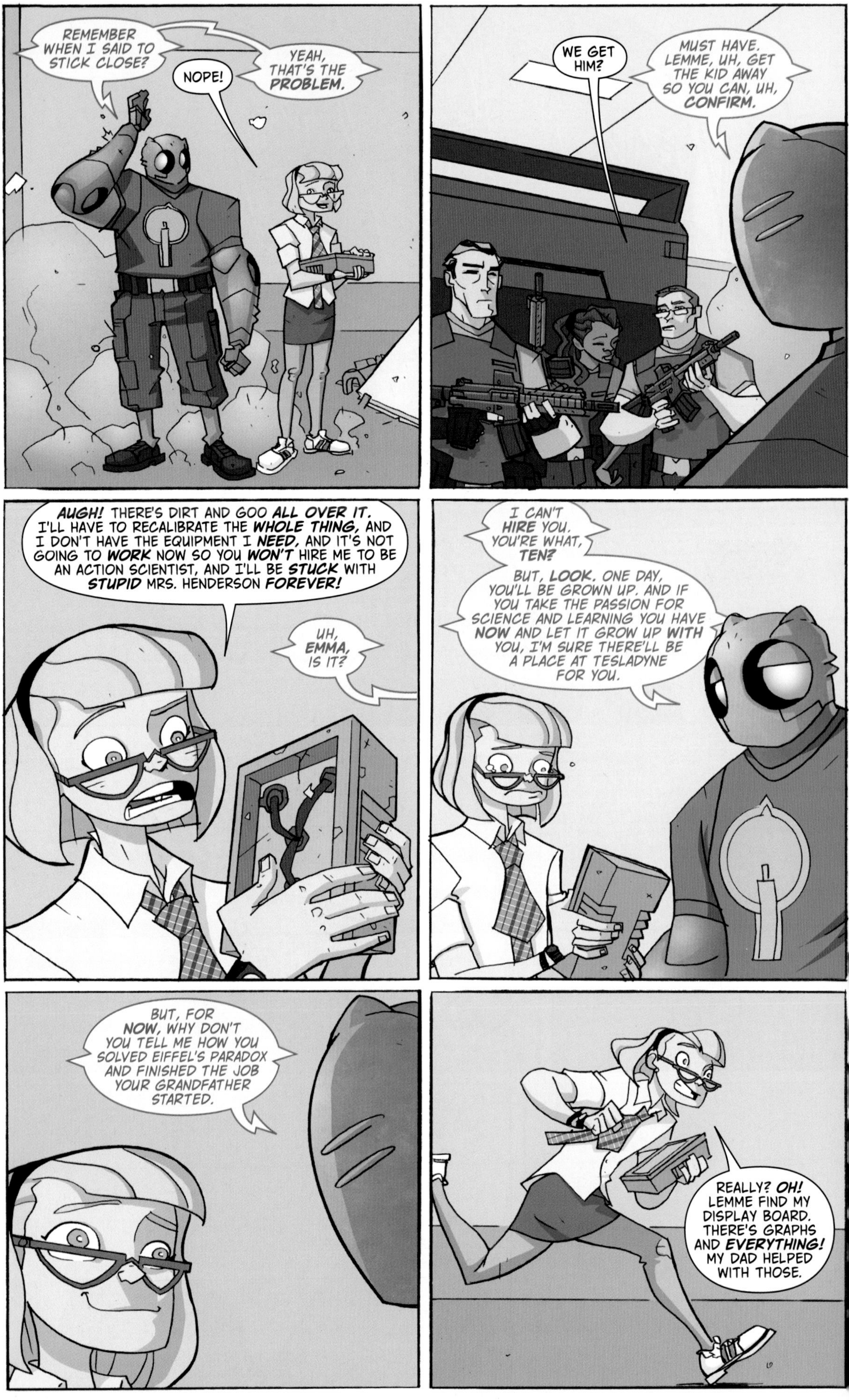
REMEMBER WHEN I SAID TO STICK CLOSE?
NOPE!
YEAH, THAT'S THE PROBLEM.
WE GET HIM?
MUST HAVE. LEMME, UH, GET THE KID AWAY SO YOU CAN, UH, CONFIRM.
AUGH! THERE'S DIRT AND GOO ALL OVER IT. I'LL HAVE TO RECALIBRATE THE WHOLE THING, AND I DON'T HAVE THE EQUIPMENT I NEED, AND IT'S NOT GOING TO WORK NOW SO YOU WON'T HIRE ME TO BE AN ACTION SCIENTIST, AND I'LL BE STUCK WITH STUPID MRS. HENDERSON FOREVER!
UH, EMMA, IS IT?
I CAN'T HIRE YOU. YOU'RE WHAT, TEN?
BUT, LOOK. ONE DAY, YOU'LL BE GROWN UP. AND IF YOU TAKE THE PASSION FOR SCIENCE AND LEARNING YOU HAVE NOW AND LET IT GROW UP WITH YOU, I'M SURE THERE'LL BE A PLACE AT TESLADYNE FOR YOU.
BUT, FOR NOW, WHY DON'T YOU TELL ME HOW YOU SOLVED EIFFEL'S PARADOX AND FINISHED THE JOB YOUR GRANDFATHER STARTED.
REALLY? OH! LEMME FIND MY DISPLAY BOARD. THERE'S GRAPHS AND EVERYTHING! MY DAD HELPED WITH THOSE.

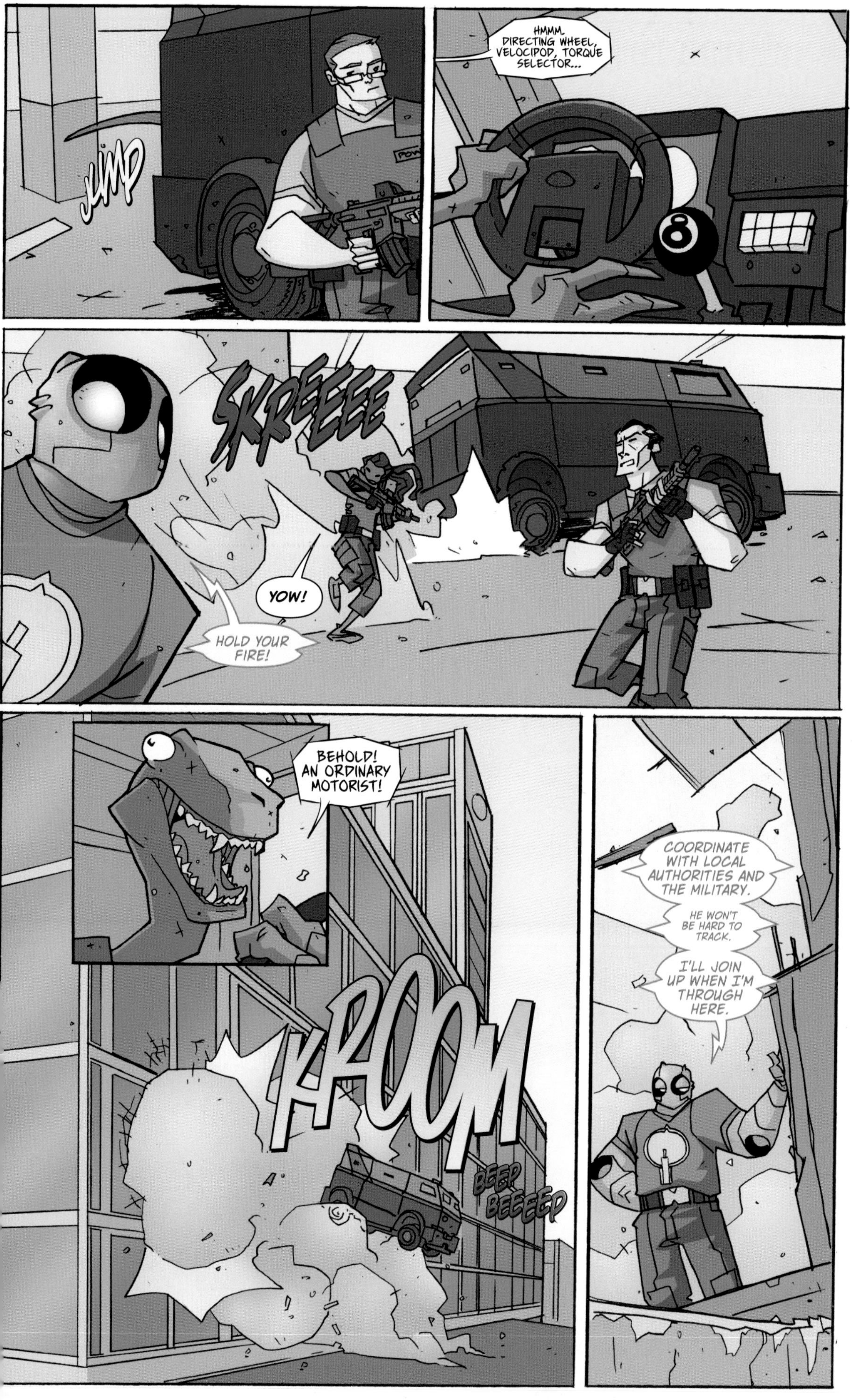
JUMP
HMMM. DIRECTING WHEEL, VELOCIPOD, TORQUE SELECTOR...
SKREEEE
YOW!
HOLD YOUR FIRE!
BEHOLD! AN ORDINARY MOTORIST!
KROOM
BEEP BEEEEP
COORDINATE WITH LOCAL AUTHORITIES AND THE MILITARY.
HE WON'T BE HARD TO TRACK.
I'LL JOIN UP WHEN I'M THROUGH HERE.

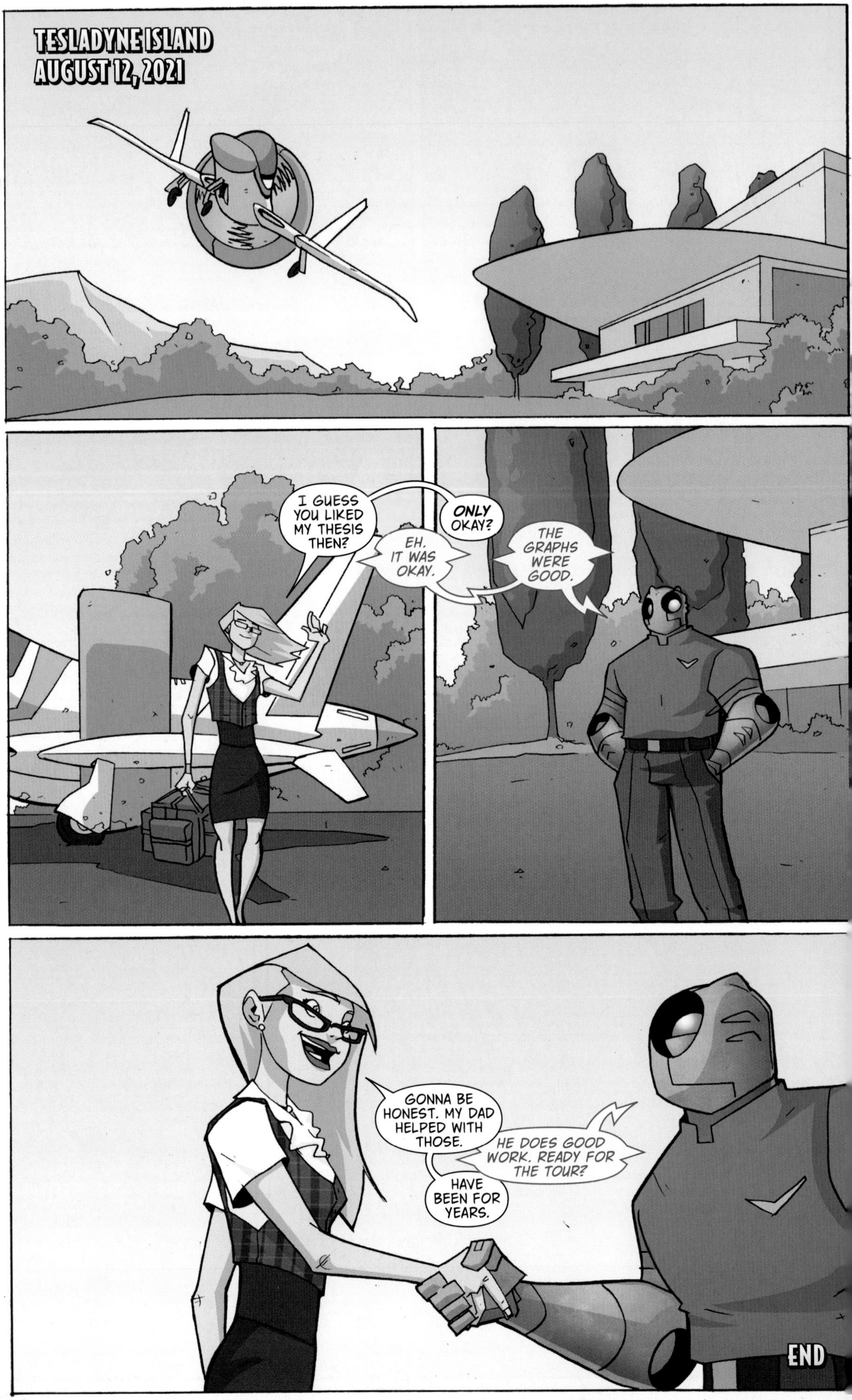
TESLADYNE ISLAND
AUGUST 12, 2021
I GUESS YOU LIKED MY THESIS THEN?
EH. IT WAS OKAY.
ONLY OKAY?
THE GRAPHS WERE GOOD.
GONNA BE HONEST. MY DAD HELPED WITH THOSE.
HE DOES GOOD WORK. READY FOR THE TOUR?
HAVE BEEN FOR YEARS.
END

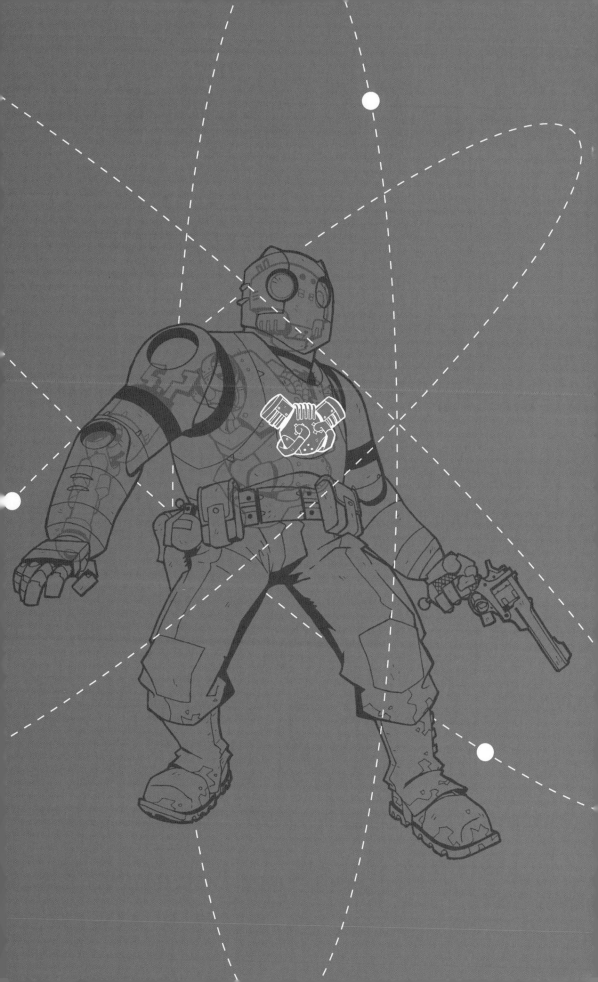

SCOTT WEGENER

SKETCHBOOK

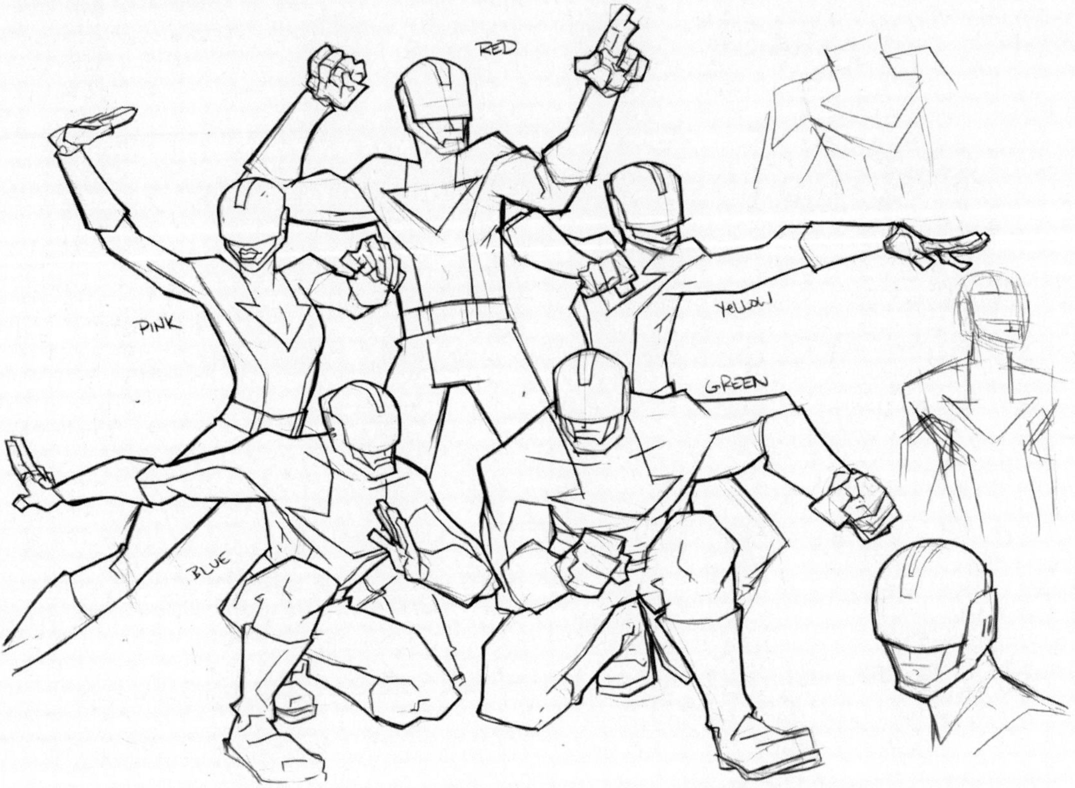
RED
PINK
YELLOW
GREEN
BLUE

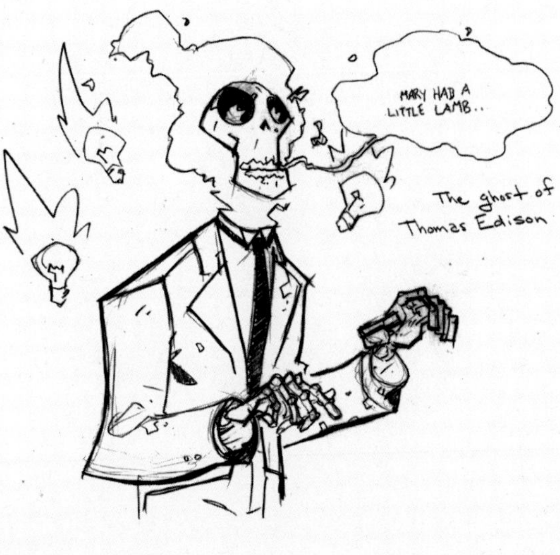
MARY HAD A LITTLE LAMB..
The ghost of Thomas Edison

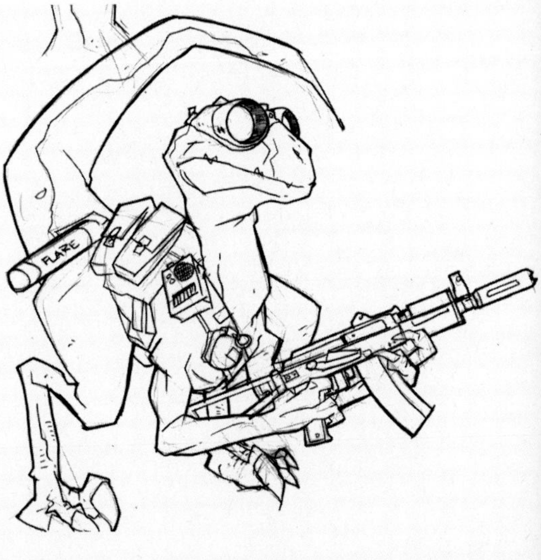
FLARE

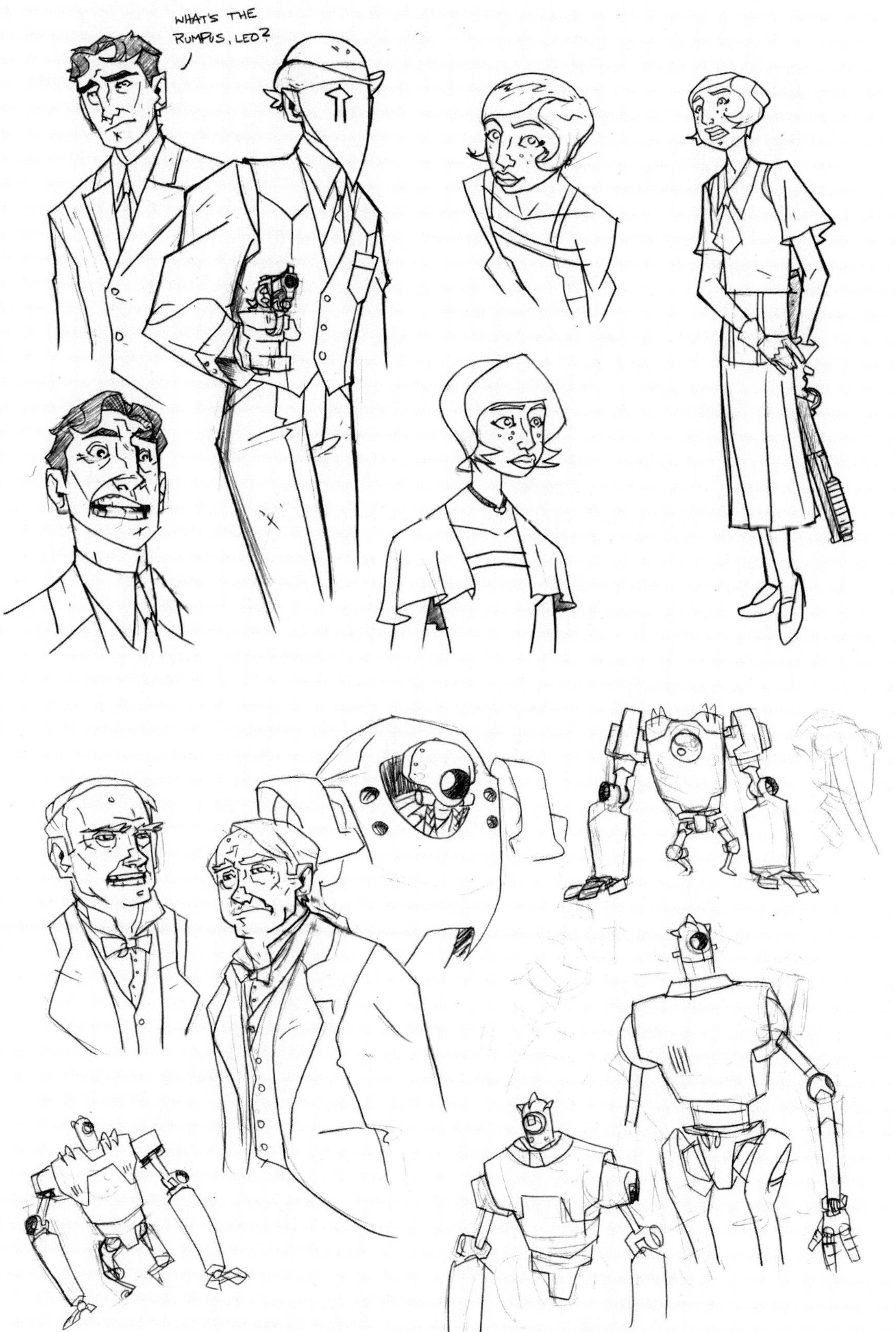
WHAT'S THE RUMPUS, LEO?

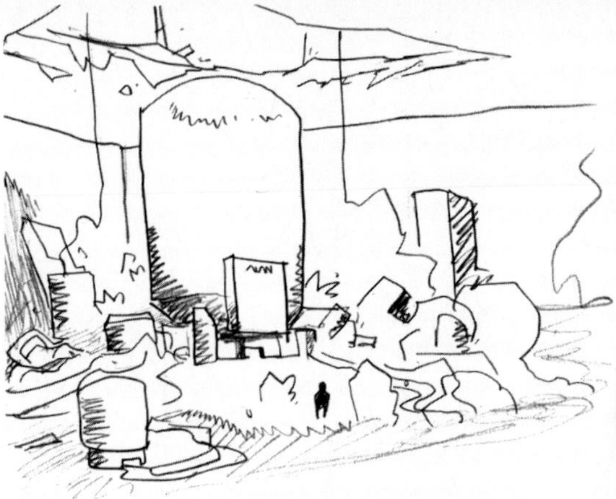

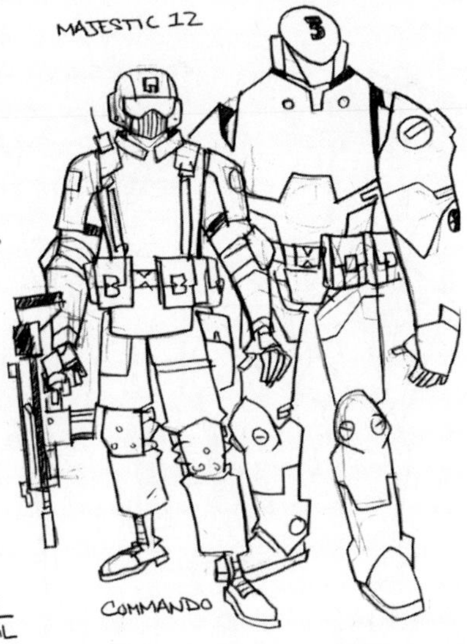
MAJESTIC 12
COMMANDO

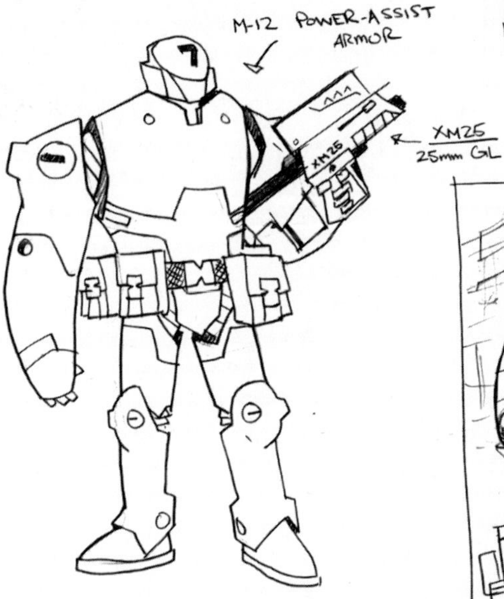
M-12 POWER-ASSIST ARMOR
XM25
25mm GL

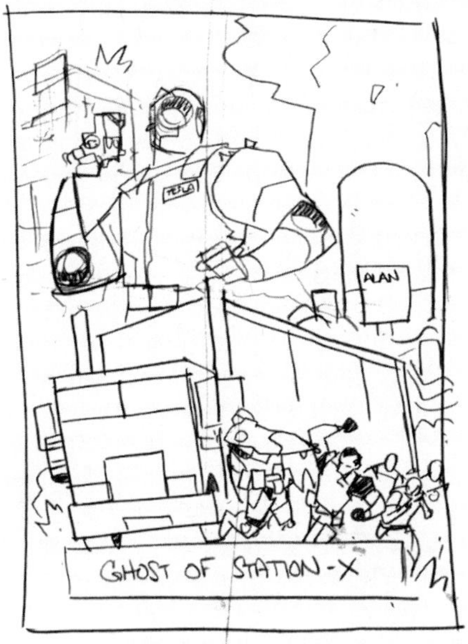
ALAN
GHOST OF STATION-X

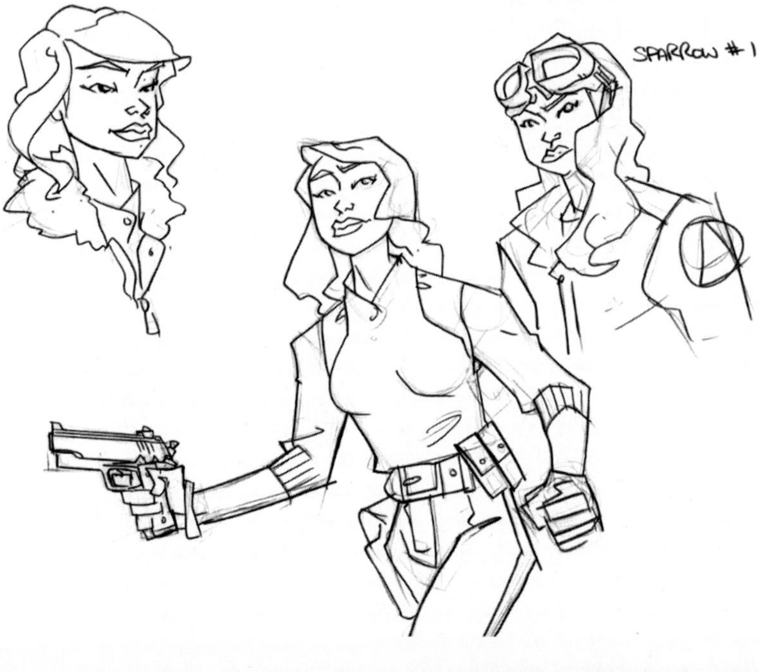
SPARROW #1

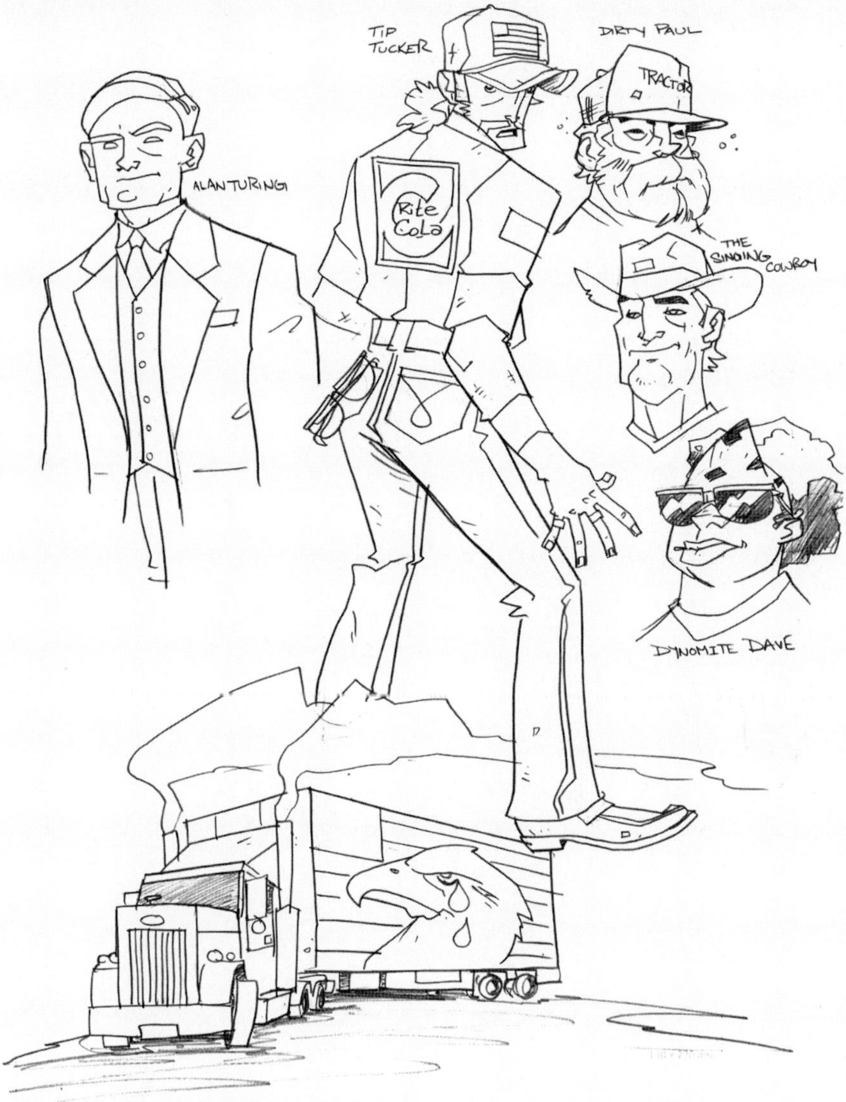
TIP TUCKER
DIRTY PAUL
TRACTOR
ALAN TURING
Rite CoLa
THE SINGING COWBOY
DYNOMITE DAVE

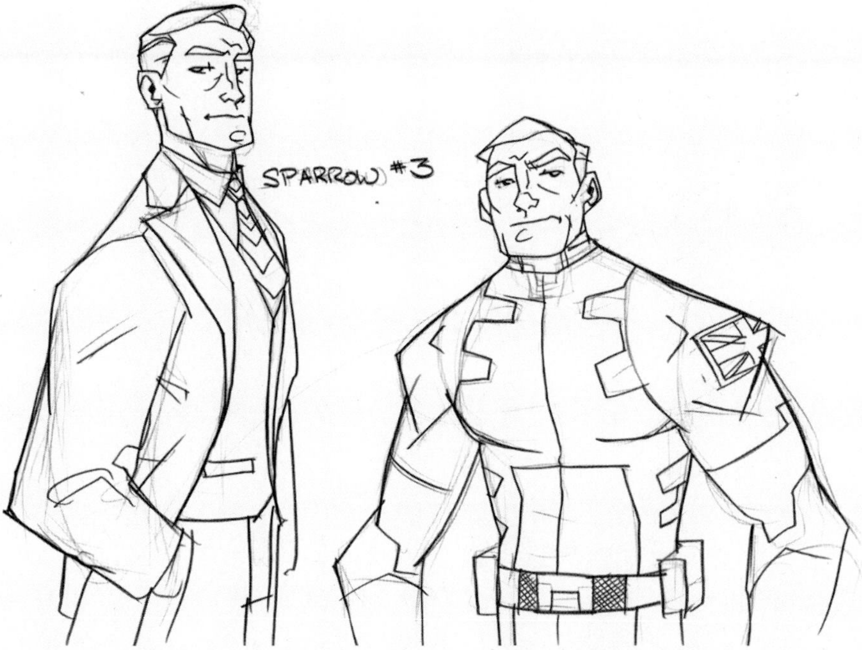
SPARROW #3

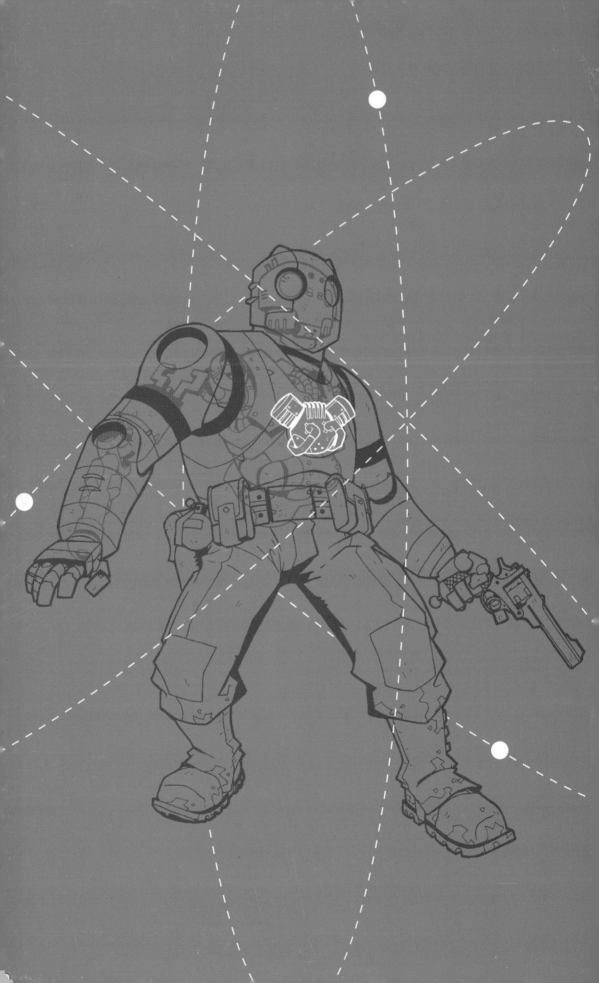